THE SAFEGUARDED HEART COMPLETE SERIES

ALL FIVE BOOKS PLUS EXCLUSIVE BONUS NOVELETTE

MELANIE A. SMITH

WICKED DREAMS PUBLISHING

Copyright © 2020 by Melanie A. Smith
All Rights Reserved
Published by Wicked Dreams Publishing
Boise, ID
info@wickeddreamspublishing.com

This is a work of fiction. Names, characters, businesses, places, events, locales, and incidents are either the products of the author's imagination or used in a fictitious manner. Any resemblance to actual persons, living or dead, or actual events is purely coincidental.

Kindle eBook ISBN: 978-1-7330748-4-1
eBook ISBN: 978-1-7330748-5-8
Paperback ISBN (v1): 978-1-7330748-6-5
Paperback ISBN (v2): 978-1-952121-48-7
Hardback ISBN: 978-1-952121-22-7

Cover design © Wicked Dreams Publishing

BOOKS BY MELANIE A. SMITH

The Safeguarded Heart Series

The Safeguarded Heart

All of Me

Never Forget

Her Dirty Secret

Recipes from the Heart: A Companion to the Safeguarded Heart Series

The Safeguarded Heart Complete Series: All Five Books and Exclusive Bonus Material

Life Lessons: A series that can be read as standalones

Never Date a Doctor

Bad Boys Don't Make Good Boyfriends

You Can't Buy Love

The Heart of Rutherford: Life Lessons Novels 1 – 3

Standalone Romance Novels

Everybody Lies

Last Kiss Under the Mistletoe

Tough Love

Finding His Redemption

Short Stories

Cruising for Love

Hot for Santa

Anthologies

Heroes With Heat and Heart 2: A Charity Anthology

CONTENTS

THE SAFEGUARDED HEART

ALL OF ME

NEVER FORGET

PART I

PART II

HER DIRTY SECRET

BONUS NOVELETTE

RECIPES FROM THE HEART: A COMPANION TO THE SAFEGUARDED HEART SERIES

THE SAFEGUARDED HEART

PROLOGUE

The threat of imminent death fills my senses, my brain clouded with pain and terror. I can't help but wonder if, knowing where it would lead, I would do anything differently. Knowing myself, likely not. My stubbornness knows no bounds, and my natural ability to persevere is what got me here in the first place.

In any case I know it's pointless to speculate, and this journey has been ten years in the making. And just as it seems like it will end in suffering and horror, so did it start, when I was only nineteen years old and broken to my core. My mind tears through memories, struggling to make sense of it all, taking me back to the time when, the pain of loss fresh once again, I turned to my grandparents. Remembering how they took me in and gave me comfort, wisdom, and direction as I climbed out of my pit of despair to finish my business degree.

My grandfather, especially, gave me so much more. His cheerful, round, and wrinkled face flashes across my memory, and warmth spreads through me, my emotions mixing in a confusing swirl. A wealthy real estate tycoon since well before I was born, Grandpa was also a patient teacher. At his side I learned about the power of cash flow, how to negotiate from a position of strength with the simple ability to say "no" and mean it, and how to build a team that would start me down the same path he had walked more than four decades ago.

I made my fair share of mistakes in those early years, and he was there to see me through them all. Those small defeats had pushed me to grow, to adapt, and at the time had seemed like natural discomforts that I needed to endure to find my way. But looking back at the costs, I lament my thick skin, my acceptance of what "came with the territory."

Because, as the moment of my demise approaches, I realize with startling clarity that the real estate business, with its many facets and complexities, is ultimately about people. It's so easy to forget, amid the drive to succeed, that people's lives are in your hands.

My strength has always been in facts and figures, the bones on which the industry operates and grows. Learning how to handle people was always the most difficult part for me. So I used the same tactic I'd applied to everything else. I compartmentalized, quantified, and planned for it. Emotion and empathy were enemies to reason and logic.

And I realize only now that approach was an illusion. A coping mechanism for my ruined ability to care deeply. To trust. To love. Perhaps the lack of those abilities is what led me here.

But that wasn't something my grandfather could teach me, and I had to learn this lesson myself.

And while my grandfather lived to proudly see me start my own business at twenty-five, I'm suddenly thankful he wasn't here to see me learn this lesson too late.

My gut wrenches at the thought of his disappointment. And at the thought of disappointing my nearly four dozen employees, who helped me build a full-service real estate investing support company. It was a niche I'd long hoped to carve, and it had just begun to bear real fruit.

As if it were a sign, in early February on nearly the anniversary of my grandfather's passing, we acquired two new major clients: The first, a large company looking for centralized property management. The second, another young but rising company that had moved into the Seattle area from San Francisco only a couple of months prior.

But nothing could have prepared me for what came next. For meeting Alessandro Giordano, the company's owner. Unspeakably handsome, with a thick Italian accent and a disarmingly charming demeanor. At least, at first.

As past events continue to spin through my frantic brain, I can't help but try to cling to the memories of those early months. The countless meetings, site visits, and rejected proposals that often brought us head-to-head in heated exchanges about almost everything. He is one of the most challenging people I've ever met. As stubborn and intelligent as he is handsome.

I remember, also, shutting down his flirtations from the start, noticing the appreciative glances from nearly every female in the office, and how frequently he returned them. It was clear from the beginning that he was a man who lusted voraciously after what he wanted and was used to getting it. I overestimated my ability to keep that part of me shut down. Or perhaps I merely underestimated his persistence.

Tears fill my eyes, and I wonder if I'll have another chance to tell him how I feel one last time. And that I forgive him.

ONE

As I ride the elevator up to my company's suite on the 30th floor, I breathe deeply, steeling myself for another challenging day. Another day of arguing with Buone Case, with Alessandro Giordano. I can't decide if I'm exhausted or thrilled by the prospect. Probably a bit of both. But, as it's Friday, there is a light at the end of the tunnel.

The elevator doors open, and I get the same small thrill I do every morning to see my company's name, Evans Realty Services, over the entryway of our reception area.

Though it's well before her usual start time, our receptionist, Lucy Drummond, has already arrived. Just, from the looks of it, as she removes her coat and starts her computer.

"Good morning, Lucy," I offer as I enter.

She looks up, momentarily surprised, her dark eyes jumping to meet mine. "Oh, Ms. Evans," she responds, "good morning. I didn't hear the elevator."

I smile warmly. "Sorry if I startled you," I apologize. "Why are you in so early?"

"I have to leave after lunch for a doctor's appointment," she explains, then adds in a dry tone, "Don't worry, there will be someone else in this afternoon to cover the phones."

Lucy has always been a bit mouthy for the year or so she's worked here, but I frankly find it kind of refreshing. And far preferable to the fake deference so many people show me.

"I have no doubt you have everything under control, as usual, Lucy," I reassure her. "I'll be in my office." Secretly, I do doubt it, as I doubt everything, but as the company grows I've had to learn to let go of micromanaging every dimension.

As usual, I don't see anyone else as I head to my office. Besides my general feeling that as the boss I should be here first, I like to be in before everyone else to have some quiet time to get ready for the day. I set my bag on my desk and hang my coat on the back of my office door, glancing at the dull, misty Seattle skyline out the window before taking a seat.

After sending a few emails, I review the latest briefing I've assembled for our weekly tag-up meeting with Buone Case. It's a summary of the relevant regulations governing build size based on property zoning. I'm hoping to use it to convince Mr. Giordano to scale back his plans or increase his budget. But the real trick will be convincing him he can't have both.

At first, I chalked up his insistence on waiting for perfection to a cultural difference — perhaps Italian real estate development is easier, more adaptable to the developer. But with several years of developing in the San Francisco Bay Area under his belt, and his clear shrewdness and business acumen, it's become clear that it's merely stubbornness. In a way I admire his tenacity, but it's bordering on being a nuisance, and in any case is impeding our ability to move forward.

A few minutes before the meeting I hear a small knock on my door. I look up, expecting to find my assistant, Maggie, checking in to remind me of the meeting, but instead am startled to see Mr. Giordano.

His dark brown hair carefully mussed, he looks more like a male model than a real estate developer leaning casually against my door frame. His fitted, tan slacks and black buttoned shirt open at the neck would be fitting for a casual Friday if they weren't clearly designer and impeccably tailored to his tall, slim frame.

"*Buongiorno*," he greets me, and as usual I must suppress a shiver of enjoyment at his deep, lilting accent. "Do you have a minute?"

"*Buongiorno*," I respond, glancing at the clock. "Of course. We have a few minutes before the meeting. Let's head to the conference room and we can talk."

I rise, bringing my laptop and folio. His appraising glance at my white button-front shirtdress belted over navy leggings reminds me why I never let him get me alone in my office.

"As you wish," he responds, hesitating in the doorway for a moment as I approach. I slow and stop a respectable distance away. "You look lovely today."

"Thank you," I respond evenly, maintaining stern eye contact. "Shall we?"

He cocks a half-smile, one he's used to disarm me before, and stays put. But I'm practiced at ignoring his flirtations by now, so I simply stand my ground, waiting impassively for him to move.

For a moment we remain motionless, staring at each other, the tension in the room palpable. His smirk deepens, and he sighs lightly, stepping aside to end the standoff and let me pass. Most days I think he just enjoys the sport of it.

I breathe an inward sigh of relief, ignoring the tingling down my spine as he walks next to me, our hands swinging closely, threatening to brush against each other in the tight hallway. I hug my things to my chest, wrapping both of my hands around the warm laptop.

Before we can get very far, Jackson Williams, my assistant for the Buone Case project, spots us on his way to the conference room and joins us.

Relieved not to be alone with Mr. Giordano, I pull Jackson into a discussion that continues into our meeting.

But by the end of the hour we've made little progress, and both Jackson and I are struggling to find new ways to explain the contradictions at hand.

"Marco and I will review the legal descriptions this afternoon," Mr. Giordano finally promises as we wrap up the meeting. "But I'd still like to find a way to stick with our original scale."

I can see Jackson ready to beat his head against the desk.

"Again, the regulations simply don't support that," I insist. "You would need a significantly larger parcel."

"We're pushing our investors to their limit as it is," replies Maria Greco, Buone Case's finance lead. "We have no room there."

Mr. Giordano narrows his eyes at the report in front of him, as if challenging it to a staring contest will change what's on the page.

"Mr. Giordano, please," I say pleadingly, "review the data objectively. We'll get back together on Monday afternoon and try to find a path forward."

He leans back in his chair, his jaw twitching. He clearly has issues conceding defeat. I'd find it endearing if it wasn't so infuriating.

"It's time for lunch anyway," he finally says dismissively. "I'm sure we could all use a break."

There is a noticeable sigh of relief from everyone in the room, and I can't help but chuckle to myself. As everyone files out, Mr. Giordano stays fixed in his chair, running a finger slowly under his chin in thought.

"Ms. Evans, please stay," he asks quietly as I'm about to leave.

The last person files out in front of me and I glance back at him apprehensively. "All right," I concede slowly, leaving the door open and setting my things back on the table.

He rises, circling the table to close the door, then drops into the chair next to me. I attempt to control the pounding of my heart as he crosses his legs thoughtfully, leaning back in his chair.

"Serafina," he starts, and I'm jolted by his use of my first name. I've been very careful to keep things as formal as possible, so I'm wary of what he'll say next. "You are obviously an incredibly capable and knowledgeable businesswoman. Otherwise, I wouldn't be using your services. But surely you didn't get where you are by settling?"

I consider my response for a moment. I know he's trying, under the guise of flattery, to trap me into letting him persist with chasing his ideal.

"Mr. Giordano," I reply pointedly, and a smirk settles across his luscious pout, "I got where I am by working within the established system. What you're holding out for isn't going to work. I strongly urge you to review the data I've provided before we continue to discuss this further."

"Are you telling me what I want is impossible?" he asks shrewdly, with a look of such intensity on his face, I wonder for a moment if we're only talking about business.

"No," I admit, "but I am telling you what you want is going to cost you more than you have to spend."

He laughs suddenly, jarring me. "Despite what Maria says, there is always a way to find more money," he replies dismissively.

I shake my head. "You misunderstand me, *signore*," I persist. "The biggest cost here is *time*. You've already spent more than two months pursuing your ideal, to no avail. It's April. If you want to build in the Seattle area, you're going to need to start. Soon."

His eyes darken a shade as he weighs my words, and he shakes his head lightly. He leans forward, placing his elbows on his knees.

"I appreciate your conservative approach," he allows, speaking into his lap at first. "It's a useful counterpoint to my methods, I see that. But what you must understand about me is, once I study a market, I have instincts about where and how to enter. I've found ignoring those instincts to be very dangerous." He looks up into my eyes for a long moment. "I'll review the data," he finally says. "But I'm not one to give up easily."

I regard him quietly. From everything I've heard of his success in San Francisco, one of the toughest markets on the planet, I can't argue that he must have good instincts. And his words make me realize my usual tenacity may have been replaced with reservations as a counterbalance to his dogged pursuit of what would amount to one of the best deals I've ever seen. But I'm hard-pressed to encourage him, as I know how often that kind of deal comes along and what the cost is of waiting for it.

"I'm sure you'll do what you feel is best," I reply reservedly, switching the cross of my legs as I fidget under his heated stare.

"I know I'm a difficult bastard," he admits, smirking again. "I can't help that I'm used to getting what I want." He leans back in his chair, tilts his head, and cocks an eyebrow suggestively.

I bite back a snappy retort by reminding myself that it's his deal. His decision. And there's no way in hell I'm giving him the satisfaction of rising to his coy taunt.

As I remain silent, he purses his lips, and for a moment I think he looks disappointed.

"I'm sure we could do this all day," he says, abruptly changing the subject, "but you must be hungry. Can I take you to lunch?"

It's not his first invitation, and I'm sure it won't be his last. But my answer is always the same, and I'm sure he expects it.

"*Grazie*, but no," I reply lightly, rising from my chair. *Thanks, but no thanks. On all counts.* "I have work to do."

I can feel his eyes on me as I leave the room. Not for the first time I consider that his interest might purely be the simple intrigue of there being a female who spurns his advances. While he's not my usual type when I do bother dating, I'd have to be blind not to find him attractive. I'm just not sure why he's so interested in me. I'm pretty, in an average sense I suppose, with long, wavy brown hair, hazel eyes, and strong features, but I'm also thicker through my arms, chest, and thighs. Despite regular exercise and a decent diet, I'll never be the thin, gorgeous model type I imagine him with.

As I enter my office, I glance back to see him heading toward the elevator. His confidence radiates off him, his charm obvious even from the small greetings and interactions he has as he goes. If I know anything, it's that giving in to him would only bring trouble.

❧

That evening I drift toward sleep on the couch while watching an old movie. Between the tensions of the day, and my half-asleep mind, my thoughts drift back to Alessandro. I roll the name over my tongue and giggle.

Two months of working together, and he still continues testing my resolve on every front. The business side I can handle. The flirtation, though, unseats me more than I'd like to admit. He drops his hints shamelessly, though never publicly, and I wonder again if he's merely seeking the thrill of victory.

But in my drifting state I don't stop the thoughts like I usually would. Instead I dangerously start to wonder what might happen if I allowed it. The surprise on his face might just be worth it.

But then, things would get complicated. And I don't like complicated. Though it has been far too long since I've done, well, someone. I giggle again sleepily and push him and any thoughts of unleashing those desires back into their cage in my mind.

TWO

Monday afternoon we're at it again, late into the day. Jackson and I have spent the afternoon discussing the report with Buone Case's team. Marco Rossi and Giovanni Bianchi, Buone Case's architect and lead engineer, respectively, seem to understand the impediments. But ultimately it is Mr. Giordano's decision. And nothing we can say will convince him to back down.

The last hour has been spent formulating alternative possibilities to meet the project specs. Everything from looking outside the target area to contacting properties not for sale but ripe for an offer. All usual avenues, but none terribly likely to put us any closer to locking something down.

It's nearly seven when everyone else decides to go home. I'm so distracted by our conversation that before I realize it, Mr. Giordano and I are alone in the conference room, and he has soundly rejected yet another of my proposed workarounds.

Completely exhausted and over the discussion, I seethe in silent fury and stand abruptly, stepping away from the table. "You can't dismiss me like that." His brown eyes flame with the same anger I feel.

"You work for me, yes?" he taunts.

It takes a lot to get under my skin, and he's done it. He's arrogant, demanding, and stubborn. He's been obstinate since day one, and I've hit my limit. And I'm done catering to him.

"No," I retort, "Evans Realty Services has contracted with your company on this project. We are not your servants, me least of all. And if you constantly refuse to see sense, I'm afraid we will be unable to meet your needs, *signore*."

He closes his mouth, runs a finger along his chin, and narrows his eyes. In one swift movement he stands and takes a step toward me. I step back, and my palms touch the wall behind me. He hovers over me and leans his head toward me with a wicked smile on his full lips. His dark eyes now dance with amusement, causing my stomach to tie into knots and my heartbeat to thunder in my ears.

"*Bravissima*. Finally. Not many people are willing to stand up to me," he says softly. He puts his lips at my ear and murmurs, "I like it."

I briefly register in surprise that he's been *waiting* for me to challenge him. But he's never been this close to me, and the sensation overwhelms me quickly. He smells of wine and spice, and it's making my head spin and my breathing accelerate. I shake my head, struggling to think clearly. He regards me for a moment and steps back.

"I apologize ... I..." and for once this man seems at a loss for words. He clears his throat. "I have never ... it won't happen again." He seems to realize he's crossed the line past his usual flirtation. But he looks disappointed.

"It's late. We're both tired. I think we should stop for the evening," I offer. But the tone in the room has changed. I am no longer angry, or exhausted. Against my better judgment, I'm intrigued.

He turns his palms out. "As you wish," he replies. But, perhaps sensing my weakness, he doesn't move. I examine the hard lines of his face, his thick, dark hair, his strong shoulders, and well-sculpted arms and chest in his designer button-up shirt. My eyes meet his, and I can tell he sees my thoughts. "If that's what you really want?"

I close my eyes briefly and take a deep breath, struggling to control the desire welling in me. But when I reopen my eyes, he is standing over me. He raises his hand and runs a finger along my cheek as if asking for permission. My inner desires spring free of their cage, and my resolve melts. And I know what my answer is.

Dear God, yes. I tip my head back and part my lips. A small smile of triumph flits across his face and he grasps me firmly by the chin.

Softly, he touches his lips to mine, his mouth warm and yielding, waiting for any sign of protest. It's been so long since I've so much as kissed anyone, and my whole body responds, shutting down any logic, any objections. A small sigh escapes me, and I kiss him back, gently moving my lips with his. My encouragement is enough. He wraps his arms around me and his kiss deepens, his tongue searching for mine.

My inhibitions melt away, and I run my hands through his hair, over his shoulders, down his arms as he presses me into the wall, his hands roving my body. His mouth moves along my jaw, neck, and shoulders, kissing and nipping a blazing trail before returning to mine.

With one hand he pulls my body to his, the other runs down my breast and circles my hardening nipple over my clothes. His warm, firm touch on my skin causes me to gasp with pleasure. He smiles and kisses my ear.

"You feel even more amazing than I'd imagined, *bella*," he murmurs into my ear, his voice like warm honey.

"Maybe if you'd spent a little less time thinking about that and focused on work," I tease him.

He puts both of his hands on my face and looks intently into my eyes, and my body tenses with anticipation.

"Yes," he admits, "but you've been a very pleasant distraction. And I'd very much like to do all manner of sinful things to you right here on this table." He kisses me softly.

"Mmmmmm," I moan. "This doesn't seem like the best place."

But even I know we are the only people in the office. Though as I've found him as frustrating as he is fascinating for the months we've worked on this project together, I feel like I shouldn't let him persuade me so easily.

"It's just you and me," he assures me, and reading my hesitation, he trails warm kisses down my neck once more. I press my palms to his strong, broad chest and gently push him away. I look up into his deep, dark eyes. He sighs. "I see."

I shake my head. "Not here," I plead softly. He raises an eyebrow. "We meet here every day. It would be very difficult for me to pretend that it didn't happen when we're all in here tomorrow," I add. He laughs, and the full, deep noise echoes around the room.

"Yes," he concedes. "Though it won't matter where for me; I already have a hard time pretending around you." He folds his hand over mine and kisses each of my fingers in turn. "And it's getting harder by the minute."

Everything logical in me protests, distrusting his motives, his sincerity. But the part of me that's responded to him all that time has been let out of her cage, and she's taken over the driver's seat. His eyes sparkle as if he knows.

"Bring your things, we're going to my place," he commands.

And the proof that his kisses and caresses have clouded my judgment and obliterated my self-control comes in the form of a giggled response to his direction, "Yes, sir."

〜

A SHORT RIDE LATER, ALESSANDRO LEADS ME INTO HIS LARGE, HIGH-CEILINGED penthouse apartment. Placing his things on a small table, he pulls my bag out of my arms and lets it drop gently to the floor before restarting his sensual assault. He wraps his hands in my hair and pulls my face greedily to his. His kisses are hard and insistent, his tongue fighting with mine as he pulls me into his bedroom. I'm past resisting now, absorbed fully in the moment, as desperate for this to happen as he seems to be.

As he backs me to the bed, his hands fly down his shirt buttons. When he's done, I eagerly push the fabric away from his body. Running my hands down his sculpted chest and stomach, I marvel at their definition, the softness of his skin over his firm muscles.

"I've wanted you since the moment I saw you," he says huskily between feverish kisses.

My pulse races as I stare lustfully at him. "I find that hard to believe," I murmur.

He shakes his head and "tsks" at me. "Then perhaps I need to convince you," he grins lasciviously at me, grasps the hem of my dress, and pulls it abruptly over my head. His eyes rove hungrily over my soft curves and my white cotton bra.

I stare back, conscious of how my tall, fleshy body must compare to the tiny, athletic Italian women he must surely be used to bedding. Goodness knows I've seen that one who works for him — Francesca, his assistant — flirt with him shamelessly.

His thick fingers tug gently at my long, brown hair. They drop to caress the top of my breast, running down my stomach, lingering over the cloth below my navel. His touch is rough and warm, and each caress sends shivers of pleasure through my whole body. In a smooth, practiced motion he's worked my leggings and panties around my hips. They fall to the floor as he deftly unclasps my bra, freeing my breasts from the binding material. I gasp at the suddenness of my nudity and he chuckles pleasurably. I step out of the pile of cloth at my feet and kick it giddily away from me.

And suddenly I'm on my back, his tongue working its way into my mouth, his hands at my breast and between my thighs. His thumbs make mirror motions, both gently circling my sensitive flesh. I cry out in pleasure, over-whelmed by his touch. My cry clearly pleases him as he sighs into my mouth and presses the stiff outline under his trousers into my thigh.

"Hmmmm, I think you just enjoy torturing me," I breathe. I sit up and grab his belt, pulling him to stand in front of me. I maintain eye contact as I deftly unhook his buckle and lower his zipper.

His dark eyes lock on mine, and his breath quickens as my thumbs pull the rest of his clothing off, unfurling his erection. Breaking away from the heat of his gaze, I look on him. "Maybe it's time to return the favor," I say softly.

I lay my hands gently on his hips and bring my open mouth a hair's breadth from his waiting erection. His sharp intake of breath brings a mischievous smile to my face. Slowly, I ease the glistening tip between my lips, swirling my tongue from bottom to top and over again, slowly, relishing his obvious pleasure.

"Ohhhh, *mio Dio*," Alessandro moans and he reaches for me.

I weave my fingers with his to keep control. And for one breath more I maintain my slow rhythm before plunging him deep into my throat, sheathing him tightly with my lips, then sucking him as I pull him back out, and over again.

His breathing accelerates, his hands squeezing mine hard. "Serafina…" my name is a plea from his lips.

I relent and replace my mouth with my hand as I stand to meet his lips with mine. His kiss is fervent as I stroke him, and I can feel the hot moisture between my legs.

He guides me back onto the bed and kneels between my legs, quickly rolling on a condom. As I watch him, my whole body aches in anticipation, the wet heat between my legs practically unbearable. He presses his forehead to mine as he slips himself inside of me. The glorious, full sensation of him is like a wake-up call, and I bite back a cry of pleasure as his own rings through the room. He pauses, kissing me, running his teeth along my lip as he pulls back. My hips twitch under him, but he presses his hands against me, pinning me under him.

"Don't stop," I beg him.

He smiles sultrily, then draws himself back further only to quickly plunge deeply into me again, holding me in place to take his pleasure. His need is obvious in his rough, full thrusts, and my body responds. I wriggle free, wrapping my legs around him, using it to rise to meet his thrusts, my breath quick and gasping. I bite my lip hard, holding back a moan.

His chest lowers over me as he falls to his rest on his arms. "Let go," he says into my ear, his tone as rough as the sex. And it pushes me over the edge. I lock my mouth onto his, our tongues greedily consuming each other. He thrusts into me and I explode, grabbing the sheets under me, my back arching off the bed, a loud cry escaping me. He buries his smile of satisfaction in my hair, his lips pressed to my neck as he moves.

As my breathing recovers, I weave my fingers into his hair and whisper in his ear, "My turn." Resting on his arms once more to meet my gaze, he looks at me questioningly. "On top," I clarify.

He lets out a small, eager moan. "If you insist," he replies.

I wiggle out from under him and he rolls onto his back, propping himself up on his elbows and watching me curiously. Lying next to him, I meet his lips with mine, stroking him with my hand. As he wraps his arms around me, I slide my leg astride his hips, hovering over him. I push myself into a fully upright position, hands on his chest, allowing my thumbs to catch his nipples as I run my fingers down him.

Swinging my hips downward, I capture him between my legs and slide him inside me, eliciting a synchronized moan of pleasure from us both. My body quivers with the excitement of having missed this for so long.

I grasp his arms tightly, gently rocking back and forth. He goes still and moans in pleasure. I gingerly rise and fall, burying him deep in me before slowly easing him out again. His hands find my hips and follow my motions, his head flung back, groan after groan escaping his lips as I ride him, my own cries of pleasure mounting. I'm nearing orgasm again when his grip on my hips tightens, slowing my pace.

"Not yet," he growls, and he pushes me off him, climbing up onto his knees while flipping me on my stomach in front of him. He pulls my ass into the air. "Spread your legs," he commands.

I push myself up on my elbows and comply. A moment later I feel him slide into me, harder than ever. His hands grasp my hips and he lunges, burying himself so he's completely sheathed in me. I suppress a scream of pleasure. He leans forward, teasing my nipple with his hand.

"Don't hold back," he rasps, slowly easing in and out. "I want to hear you."

I groan in agreement, and he gradually picks up his rhythm and depth until he is slowly, steadily pumping deeply. I want to explode under the sweet torture, but it's just out of reach. I don't withhold my moans of pleasure and protest, and I'm aching for the frenzied pace that unlocked my body's long-dormant ability to send waves of pleasure crashing through me in climax. As he goes to ease into me once more, I buck my hips impatiently, driving him in deep and hard.

He gasps. "No, Sera," he cautions, taking himself out of me. I growl in frustration and I can almost hear the smile in his voice when he says, "What do you want?"

"Fuck me, Alessandro," I breathe. He moans.

"Ah, *dolcezza*, I love hearing you say that," he sighs.

And with that he's pounding into me, taking me so roughly that it's simultaneously painful and mind-blowingly delicious. Screams rip from my throat, and I've lost the ability to tense my own body when I come, so there's no escaping the pleasure when I shatter into a million pieces. I scream his name and tighten around him, making him cry out as his orgasm meets the last throes of my own.

We both fall, panting and sweaty, to the bed. I roll over and put my hand on his heart, and he lays a leg between mine. It is minutes before either of us can speak.

"Well, that was pretty okay," I deadpan.

He laughs, clearly exhausted. "If that was just okay, I can't wait to see what you think good sex is like."

After a few minutes of catching our breath, he props himself up on an elbow and peers down at me but says nothing.

"At a loss for words, Mr. Giordano? How uncharacteristic of you," I murmur jokingly.

He smirks at me and runs his hand down my chest. "Oh, I have words, Ms. Evans. Many words. Where do I start?" he muses. He drops a kiss on my neck. "Angel." Another on my clavicle. "Goddess." Another on my chin. "Siren." Another on my forehead. "Temptress." His mouth finds mine and when he pulls away, I'm breathless. "At a loss for words, Ms. Evans?"

His chocolate eyes are twinkling, and a sideways smile hangs on his full lips. I can only manage a small smile in return before he pulls away and heads to the bathroom. And the sight of him walking away is a new joy, his backside as tight and well-muscled as his torso. His designer clothing did not do justice to the Adonis underneath.

He returns in a few minutes with a glass of water, offering it to me. I sit up slowly and take a sip. As he lays down, I slide next to him and we lay next to each other comfortably and quietly for a long while. I'm almost sure he's gone to sleep when he pulls away and sits up, leaning against the pillow to take another sip of water. Rolling onto my stomach to watch him, I can't help but stare.

"See something you like?" he teases.

I narrow my eyes and smirk at him before sliding up and reaching over him to sip from the glass he's put back on the nightstand, letting my breasts graze his arm and his chest, my hair tickling his shoulder.

His cock twitches. "Temptressss," he purrs and pulls me to him, cradling me in his lap and kissing me deeply.

Our play continues long into the night, until we are both sated and too exhausted to continue.

～

I WAKE SUDDENLY, MY HEART RACING, A GARBLED CRY DYING ON MY LIPS. I place my head in my palms and struggle to recall the feverish dream that disturbed my sleep, but it's fading away like a brief snow before the rain. Taking a deep breath, I steady myself and stretch my limbs.

Alessandro stirs next to me and the events of the previous evening rush back into my consciousness.

I've had sex with a man I'm in business with. Fuck. I ease gingerly out of bed and quietly walk to the wide windows across from the bed. The lights of Seattle twinkle around us, and the sky purples on the horizon. I look back at the clock on the bedside — five thirty-seven a.m. There's time enough for me to locate my clothing, sneak out, and get back to my condo to clean up before work.

How could I allow myself to capitulate to his advances? I look back at the bed, at Alessandro, and the answer is obvious — because I thought it merely a game to him. I never thought I'd actually end up in bed with the most stubborn, fiery, intelligent, and attractive man I'd ever met.

The exhaustion of our debates, the heat of the moment, it all made me throw my usually cautious nature to the wind. The very nature that's gotten me this far, that's made me so successful. How could I risk my company like this? My reputation? I close my eyes for a moment.

When I reopen them, my resolve is hardened. As stealthily as I can, I gather my things strewn around the floor. Thanking my lucky stars that the door is ajar, I slip into the living room and dress quickly. I don't worry whether the sound of the front door will wake him. Because once it does, it's too late anyway.

THREE

"Would you like me to call Mr. Giordano's cellphone again?" Maggie, my admin, inquires nervously.

My eyes find the clock again — nine nineteen a.m. "No, Maggie, thank you. Please have everyone meet in the conference room in five minutes. We'll proceed without him," I instruct her as confidently as I can.

But as soon as she leaves my office, I chew my lip anxiously. *Did he wake up regretting this as much as I did? Have I jeopardized our contract?* The thought makes me feel as if my heart has been plunged into ice. Our firm has just started attracting clients like Buone Case. To derail that now would be catastrophic.

Get it together, Evans, I admonish myself. I chant a mantra silently to myself — *no amount of regretting can change the past, and no amount of worrying can change the future.* I let out a breath. Gathering my things, I head for the conference room.

∽

"So, you'll see on page fifteen that we've identified four new potential sites with the zoning, acreage, and most other parameters the project requires." Jackson is giving the part of our presentation we never made it to yesterday, but he may as well be talking to himself. The Buone Case team is in the room, but without Alessandro they are distracted and, frankly, useless. Jackson glances at me, and I nod encouragingly. My eyes flit yet again to the clock on the wall. It's nine forty-eight a.m., and still no Alessandro.

Mercifully, Jackson's presentation concludes a few minutes later. He thanks everyone for their attention. I control the impulse to roll my eyes. Closing my laptop, I clear my throat to gather everyone's attention.

"Thanks very much, Jackson." I pause. "Okay, ladies and gentlemen. Now that we've all got the latest, I think we should take some time to digest this and regroup. Obviously, Mr. Giordano will need to be informed upon his arrival and I'm sure his team will need some time…" I trail off mid-sentence as Alessandro appears in the doorway, leaning casually against the frame.

He's dressed completely in black — fitted pants, button-up shirt, and well-cut jacket. He looks every inch the sexy devil, with his dark hair mussed just so as usual, his angular face in a relaxed, almost bored expression. Our eyes meet, and I can feel myself turning a myriad of shades of red. Everyone in the room turns their eyes to the door.

"Please, go on," Alessandro offers.

I clear my throat again. "Yes. Well. As I was saying, I think it best at this time that the Buone Case team meet to go over the latest and prepare for the upcoming site visits. Thank you everyone for your time. We'll leave the conference room to the Buone Case team," I say, trying to keep emotion out of my tone.

Alessandro steps into the room and places his bag on the table, letting my team pass.

Gathering my things, I steel myself, trying to shut down memories of the night before. I smooth a crease from my cream silk blouse with my free hand and step forward. "Mr. Giordano, *buongiorno*," I offer. "Extra copies of the latest site reports are here on the table. I'll be in my office. Please do let me know if you have any questions." And with that I brush past him before he can respond.

Keeping my pace even and casual, I smile shakily at Maggie on my way into my office. But as soon as I have collapsed in my chair, there is a small knock on the door.

"Yes?" I call, pulling myself up in my chair. I begin to reorder the things I've just dumped on my desk as Maggie's blond bob peeks around the door. I sigh in relief and smile brightly at her. "What is it, Maggie?"

"Ms. Evans, I wanted to remind you that you have a phone call at ten fifteen with Mr. Phillips about the meeting with the city for the Stone Way project."

I nod curtly. "Yes, thank you, Maggie. Is that all?"

"Yes, Ms. Evans." And with that she goes back to her desk.

I turn my chair to look out the window. Through the mist there looks to be a rainbow in the distance over the Smith Tower. I stand and approach the window when there is another small knock on the door.

"What is it, Maggie?" I ask impatiently, leaning toward the glass trying to see how far the rainbow stretches. When she doesn't answer, I turn, and Alessandro is standing behind me. Much too close. And a quick glance tells me that he's closed the door.

"*Buongiorno*, hmm?" he asks in a low voice. "*Sì, bella*, it is a good day." He reaches for me and before I can protest his hands are on my back, pulling me into a heated, fervent kiss.

And it's so good that I kiss him back, the dull ache between my legs flaring into a distracting yearning — until I remember myself. I pull away sharply, stepping behind my chair, putting it between us as I catch my breath.

"Mr. Giordano, please. I'm glad to see that you aren't upset by recent events, but I must insist that we try to keep this professional going forward." I'm putting on my best boss voice.

He looks confused. "Upset? Why would I be upset? Last night was incredible. Something I'd like to repeat with you here and now, in fact," he says, eyeing my fitted, navy pencil skirt. "But if you would like to be professional while we are at work, I can respect that." He steps back to the front of my desk.

I give my head a small shake. "Thank you, but I think you mistake me, *signore*," I persist. "I would appreciate if we could return to keeping this *strictly* professional."

Alessandro's mouth opens in surprise as he takes in my meaning. Me, rejecting him after the insanely amazing sex we had. It's shocking to me too, but oh so necessary, and not just for my business.

"Surely you don't mean that? I can't say I've been with many American women, but your enthusiasm seemed to suggest you enjoyed the *unprofessional* nature of the evening," he counters, his tone amused.

"I'm sorry, but this is really not the place to have this kind of discussion," I say firmly.

His dark eyes fill with lust and fire, his full lips parting slightly. "Then over dinner tonight, perhaps?"

"It's not a discussion I wish to have anywhere," I insist.

He runs his finger under his chin in that way of his, and I know he's disturbed. "If that's what you want," he finally says.

"It is," I assert as steadily as I can.

"Then I must apologize for my lapse in professionalism," he says brusquely. "My team and I will see you at our meeting this afternoon." He turns to leave but pauses at the door. He opens his mouth but closes it again and looks at me searchingly for a moment before disappearing out the door.

As soon as I'm sure he must be back in the conference room, I call Maggie into my office.

"I need you to reschedule the call with Mr. Phillips. Tell him I'm free this afternoon. And please send Jackson Williams in to me."

She nods and quickly leaves the room.

Time to give Jackson a promotion to project management lead. It's long overdue, and I'm fairly confident he can handle it. And I can't handle being in the same room as Alessandro Giordano.

∽

"I have full faith in you, Jackson," I reaffirm, shaking his hand warmly.

It's hard not to like Jackson, with his boyish looks — a young face, curly blond hair, and a tall, awkward frame. He radiates excitement and vulnerability, like now, as he's beaming from ear-to-ear, his pale blue eyes alight with enthusiasm.

"Thank you so much, Ms. Evans — I won't let you down. Will you be announcing it at the meeting this afternoon?"

"Yes, but I have other matters to attend to, so I will make the announcement first thing and then leave you to it," I respond. "But my door is always open if you need me."

Jackson nods eagerly. "Of course, thank you again so much."

∽

"And so, going forward, Mr. Williams will be your project lead. It's a formalization of the role he has been doing thus far, so I have no doubt you will be more than pleased with his efforts. I will, of course, stay abreast of things and be involved as necessary. And with that, I will leave you in his capable hands," I conclude. I've scarce dared to look at Alessandro, but I must now, and I extend my hand to him.

He shakes my hand with both of his, and he has something of the look of a wounded animal about him for a moment, but it's gone almost before I can register it.

"Thank you, Ms. Evans," he says simply.

I leave without looking back, my heart racing, and head to my private bathroom to compose myself.

∽

The week moves by in a blur of real and imagined tasks designed to keep me away from the Buone Case team. But Alessandro appears to have accepted my pushback in a way he never had before. Perhaps now that he's proven he can have me, he's no longer interested.

Though as much as I'm able to avoid more than glimpsing him during the day, the impact of what he's woken in me ripples through my conscious and unconscious mind, invading my dreams at night, beckoning me to him, touching me, wanting me. And every night I wake in a cold sweat with tears streaming down my face. By Friday I'm taciturn and withdrawn, and I'm not looking forward to the weekly tag-up meeting with Buone Case that I must attend.

❧

As our Friday meeting ends and everyone files out of the room to head home, I feel like I've been punched in the gut. Alessandro didn't so much as look at me the entire hour unless I was speaking. I'm unsettled as to why his finally respecting my boundaries bothers me, again ultimately chalking up his ability to cease his previously relentless campaign of flirting to having achieved his goal.

In any case at least the project is moving forward, finally. I sigh heavily and drag my laptop and folio back to my office. I pack my bag slowly and carefully, giving everyone plenty of time to leave. At nearly seven o'clock the office is quiet and dark, and I figure it's safe.

But on my way to the elevator I hear keys tapping. Following the noise, I find Jackson still at his desk.

"Jackson!" I say in surprise.

He jumps about a foot out of his chair in surprise.

"Oh my gosh, I'm so sorry, I didn't mean to scare you," I apologize.

He clutches his chest. "No worries, I startle easily. I thought everyone had gone home," he explains.

"I was just about to," I say, and then after a pause, "Hey, do you want to go to the pub next door for a drink? On me. As congratulations for the promotion, and the great work you've been doing."

He looks very surprised. Understandably, as I'm not exactly known for being social with my employees. Or at all.

"Oh! Uh, sure, yes, that would be great!" he exclaims. "Let me just close up here."

"Sure thing, I'll meet you at the elevator," I nod, and step away.

❧

The pub is packed with end-of-the-work-week employees downing two-dollar pints for happy hour. We manage to snag a table crammed into a corner.

"What'll it be?" I ask Jackson, dropping my blazer over the chair and putting my bag on the seat.

"I'll take a house pale ale," he responds.

Nodding, I head to the bar.

I return shortly with his beer, and a gin and tonic for me. This week has been rough, and hard alcohol is in order.

"So, Jackson, remind me how long you've been with the firm?" I ask.

Jackson replies almost instantly, "Three years, four months, and two weeks."

I laugh. "Wow, do you normally keep count?" I joke.

"Yes," he replies very seriously.

The smile drops off my face and I clear my throat. I start to realize this may not have been the wisest move when I see Maggie and Lucy enter the bar. I wave enthusiastically as Maggie stands on her tiptoes to make herself tall enough to scan the room for seats and, mercifully, she spots us and comes our way, with a very astonished look on her face.

"Maggie! Lucy! Please join us. We were just celebrating Jackson's promotion," I explain.

They both look at me skeptically but sit down. Jackson glances anxiously at Lucy and she tosses her long, dark hair over her shoulder nervously. Hmmm, an office crush maybe? Interesting.

"Actually, we were just discussing how long I've worked for ERS," Jackson says matter-of-factly.

Maggie and Lucy exchange a look.

"Oh? How long *have* you worked for Ms. Evans?" Maggie asks kindly, putting down the menu she'd started looking at.

"Three years. Four months. Two weeks," he replies stoically.

"Well, that's very nice," Maggie responds. "I've been with the company just over two years now, myself. Lucy?"

Lucy's eyes, which were scanning the room uninterestedly, snap back to Maggie. "A year next month," she replies dully, returning to looking around the room.

"Four years, five months, and ... I don't know how many weeks," I insert jokingly.

Jackson blushes, and I feel stupid for mocking him. Maggie presses her lips together and looks in her lap, while Lucy finally looks amused.

"So, what's everyone up to this weekend?" I ask.

Thankfully, they rise to the bait and we all share our plans for the weekend. Lucy even manages to engage, especially once we order food and she's eaten. The change is startling, actually, as she goes from annoyed and aloof to engaged and animated. Maggie is, as always, her sweet and kind self. And Jackson is, also as always, adorably socially awkward, especially with his constant, furtive admiration of Lucy.

My own social anxieties usually get the best of me, but with the three of them chatting I manage to relax into the rhythm, answering the occasional question or offering a nod and encouragement at appropriate points in the conversation. Social situations have never been my forte — I'm good at numbers, deals, real estate. So, I'm surprised when I'm happily engrossed in their banter for more than two hours, until drinks and food have all been consumed and they start to make their goodbyes. I finish the last of my latest gin and tonic and set the glass down on the table. It goes in and out of focus for a moment and I groan, realizing I'm more than a little intoxicated.

What. The. Actual. Fuck. I haven't been drunk since college. How many did I have? I try to remember but can't. Yep, definitely drunk.

Maggie asks me if I'm okay to get home and I assure her I am, in as composed a manner as I can. Jackson and Lucy exchange a look, clearly surprised and amused to see their boss inebriated. As soon as I'm sure they're all gone, I pop outside to let the cool evening air sober me a little and hail a cab.

SITTING IN THE BACK OF THE CAB, I REALIZE I AM ACTUALLY WAY MORE intoxicated than I thought. I should've eaten some of the food we'd ordered. I don't think I'm going to be sick, but I'm definitely woozy.

"Hey, you okay back there?" the driver checks.

I open my eyes to him eying me warily in the rearview mirror. *When did I close my eyes? Hmm.*

"Yessir," I slur, and I giggle at how drunk I sound.

Minutes later he stops the cab in front of a building that is not mine.

"Where are we?" I ask stupidly.

He gives me an address. "That's what you said right?" he asks suspiciously.

And it hits me. This is Alessandro's building. I gave him Alessandro's address. My subconscious smirks as I do my best deer-in-headlights impression and the alcohol inside me takes the driver's seat.

"Yes, yes, that's right," Alcohol says, shoving money in the cab driver's hand. So apparently Alcohol also controls my body now, I acknowledge as I slide out of the cab and strut into the building.

ALESSANDRO OPENS THE DOOR, WEARING GREY SWEATS AND A DARK T-SHIRT, looking confused. As his eyes light up with recognition, his mouth hardens into a thin line.

"What can I do for you, Ms. Evans?" he asks tightly.

"Uh oh, I'm in trouble, aren't I?" I giggle.

He steps toward me and Alcohol throws my arms around his neck. He stiffens, sniffing me, then pushes me away to arm's length, examining my face.

"You're drunk," he chastises me, then pulls me into his apartment. "Get in here before you throw up all over the hallway."

I shake my head and wobble to the couch. "Not gonna throw up. And not drunk. Just tipsy," Alcohol says sinking into the warm leather. He must have been sitting here because it smells like him too.

He sits further down the couch and shakes his head at me.

"You're more than tipsy," he accuses me. "Did you drive here?"

"Pfffff, 'course not!" I say, waving my hand dismissively.

"Well, that's a start," he says, grimacing. "Why are you here?"

I frown and Alcohol slides toward him and runs my hand up his leg. "Isn't it obvious?" Alcohol tells me to climb into his lap. "Aren't you happy to see me?" Alcohol tells me to kiss him. *Mmm*. His mouth is warm, and he tastes like wine.

He disentangles my arms from around his neck and pulls his face away, holding me in front of him. "I wish I could say that I was, but after what happened earlier this week…"

Alcohol pouts and runs my hands down his chest, to his pants. "Let's just pretend that didn't happen for tonight," Alcohol leans into his ear and whispers, slipping my tongue along his lobe. I feel him hardening under his trousers.

"*Porca miseria*! Serafina, that's not fair," he grumbles. He stands suddenly, and I tumble back onto the couch. "And I'm not going to take advantage of you in this state." He goes into the kitchen and comes back with a plate of bread and oil with herbs, and a glass of water. "Eat. Drink."

Alcohol likes when Alessandro is commanding, and it makes me eat the bread as kinkily as I can. He stares at me impassively.

After a few minutes the food and drink do their work, and I'm able to push Alcohol back into the passenger seat, though my head is still foggy and my reflexes slow. Tears of rejection well in my eyes.

"Okay, then. Well, thanks for the food. I guess I'll go now," I say in a soft voice. I stand and put the dishes in the kitchen, gripping the edge of the counter and breathing deeply. I can feel him watching me.

"You'll do no such thing," he snaps. "There is a guest room just there." He gestures to a door. "I don't trust you to get yourself home, and I'm too tired to take you. It's been a trying week, and I'm going to bed." He fumes all the way out of the room down the hall to his bedroom.

I hear his door click shut. I sit back on the couch to steady myself and contemplate leaving anyway. But he's probably right. The tears sting at my eyes again as the effects of the alcohol wear off and the humiliation sets in. What am I doing? Why the hell *did* I come here?

Because he makes you feel, my subconscious whispers. I shake my head. No. He can't make me feel anything I don't want to feel. I head angrily to the guest room, determined to escape after I've slept off the booze.

∾

My eyes fly open in the dark, my body shaking. Tears are streaming down my face. Warm arms pull me up.

"Shhh, *bella*, I'm here," Alessandro's husky voice whispers to me in the dark as he wraps his arms around me. "It's okay. You're okay." He kisses my hair.

I choke back a sob and bury my face in his naked chest, trying to will my body to stop convulsing. After a moment I'm able to stop the tears but not quite the shaking. I pull away, wiping my face with my hand.

"What are you doing in here?" I ask him weakly.

He brushes my hair out of my face. "You were screaming," he says, holding my chin and tilting my face up so I must look in his eyes. They are full of worry. "Is it just the alcohol?"

I laugh drily. "No," I reply shortly. "It's not the alcohol."

"I see," he says. "This happens often?"

I shake my head. "Not usually, no. Just lately." *Since the night I gave in to you.*

He raises an eyebrow, but mercifully doesn't inquire further. His eyes examine my face, my shaking shoulders. He places his warm palms on them and the shaking stops. I look up into his eyes again and his expression is soft and full of concern. I curse under my breath and pull away from him. "I'm fine," I scoff. "You can go back to bed." I fully intend to dress and leave as soon as he's gone, silently angry at myself for putting myself in this position.

He shakes his head, his mouth a thin line again. "Just when I think I'm starting to understand you," he murmurs angrily and starts to slide off the bed.

Without thinking, I circle my hand around his wrist, stopping him. "Alessandro, please," and my voice is thick with the tears that start flowing pitilessly down my cheeks.

He yanks his arm out of my grasp. "Please what? Make up your mind — do you want me to stay or do you want me to go?" he demands.

I shrink back from his understandable anger and confusion. I'm thinking one thing and feeling another, and it's making me behave in a manner even I find appalling.

"Please just don't be angry with me. I'm not doing it on purpose," I explain.

He sinks onto the bed and strokes his chin with his finger. "I know," he finally says, his frustration obvious in his tone. "But that doesn't make it any less infuriating to be toyed with."

I narrow my eyes. "I'm *toying* with you? How did you get there? As you may recall, *you* were the one who pursued *me*, who seduced *me*," I fume. "I wasn't confused about anything until you started this."

Anger flashes in his eyes and he rests his hands on the bed in front of me, leaning forward so his face is inches from mine. "Maybe you could do with a little confusion, Serafina," he breathes. "Maybe it's exactly what you need." And he lunges forward, his lips grabbing mine, his weight toppling me onto the pillows behind me. He pins me to the bed with his mouth and his naked torso, his hands holding my hips.

I can only resist angrily for a moment before my resolve crumbles and I'm kissing him back passionately, my hands pulling him completely onto me.

He pushes up abruptly, yanking his sweatpants to his knees and roughly sheathing himself with a condom from his pocket. He shoves my underwear aside with one hand and puts himself in me with the other. His weight falls on me again, pinning me under him as he thrusts angrily into me. I scream gutturally in pleasure, wrap my legs around him, and pull his mouth to mine. Our mouths battle, hard and hot, while we meet each other hard on each push.

His mouth drops to my ear, his hand gripping the hair on the back of my head hard, and he roughly speaks into my ear between carnal grunts of plea-sure, "Damnit, you drive me crazy." His pace quickens, he bites my shoulder and licks up my neck only to reclaim my mouth with his. As his thumb starts working one of my nipples, I pull back and bite my lip hard.

"Let go," he commands.

I stop holding back and let him hear me cry out. He greedily kisses me as I climax, my screams dissolving in his mouth.

He pulls out of me, still hard, and yanks my panties off. He kicks off his sweats and sits back on his haunches, stroking himself with one hand. "I want you on top of me," he demands.

I nod, flushed with pleasure, and take him in my hand as he lays down. Quickly climbing on him, I guide him into me.

I lean over him, my breasts grazing his chest as I rise and fall hungrily, slamming into him. He bucks his pelvis each time I fall, driving deep and hard into me. Our pace is frenzied, and it's not long before I climax again, squeezing him tightly and tipping him into orgasm with me. We both let out our last cries. I sink onto the bed next to him and I know no more.

FOUR

I'm woken by Alessandro squeezing my nipple, rolling it between his moistened thumb and finger. Seeing my eyes open, he plants a kiss on it, flicking it with his tongue. It grows hard and long, and he sinks his mouth onto it, pulling it with his teeth. A moan escapes me.

"You are an amazing alarm clock," I manage.

He laughs and strokes my face. "Imagine, if you'd just make up your mind, all the many wonderful ways I could wake you each morning," he says, smiling.

My face falls and his smile falters.

I sit up and gather my knees to my chest. "Pretty sure it was you who seduced me again," I point out. "You can't begrudge a girl a little confusion when an impossible and gorgeous man tries to lure her into a questionably ethical arrangement."

"I'm impossible?" he pouts.

I chuckle. "Come off it, we both know you're insufferable," I say, pinching his jutting bottom lip. His full, beautiful lip. I shake my head. I'm well rested, and I'm not drunk or terrorized now, so it's time to take back control of this situation. "You can't take 'no' for an answer."

"'No' is a word I don't recall actually passing your lips," he counters. "And your actions this week have unmistakably said, 'yes.'"

I sit, weighing his words, dumbfounded. And I realize he's right. He corners me in a conference room, and I end up spending the night with him. And then I stumble drunkenly into his apartment, enabling another steamy encounter.

Alessandro nods knowingly and stretches on the bed next to me. The sheets shift revealing his erection, and I'm distracted out of my forming protests.

⁓

Basking in the postcoital glow, I explore Alessandro's chest and arms with my fingers while he strokes my arm tenderly.

"A man could get used to this," he sighs.

I start to tell him not to, but he puts a finger over my lips.

"Breakfast?" he asks.

I look at the clock over his shoulder. It's almost eleven a.m. We've spent all morning in bed together.

"It's nearly lunchtime," I reply, "and I need to go." I sit up and start to dress.

He strokes my back and I swat playfully at his hand.

"Stay," he pleads. "*Per favore, bella.*"

I sigh and turn to him. "Alessandro, I have things to do," I reply. I hesitate a moment and turn to hold his hands in mine. "I've enjoyed this. It's more than I thought to look for right now. But I have responsibilities. My company, my employees." *My heart.* "I don't have room for breakfast. Or lunch." I see the familiar persistent gleam in his eye. "*Or* dinner, Alessandro." He chuckles, and I sigh. "You know what I mean."

He shakes his head. "No, I don't," he states.

"The sex is amazing. But that's all this can be. We have a professional contract. If emotions were to get involved, that could put our working relationship in jeopardy, which in turn could put my company in jeopardy. I can't allow that," I clarify.

"So just sex."

I let his words sink in. Just sex. Yes, I think I can do Just Sex. I've done Just Sex before. Sometimes ending amicably, sometimes not, but always manageably. Then again, it's never been with a client.

"Can you do that?" I ask him. And I realize I hope his answer is yes.

His thoughtful stare goes on and I start to get nervous. Somewhere in the apartment a phone rings.

"*Cazzo!*" he swears, rising from the bed. "Don't go," he commands, pulling his sweatpants on and scrambling to the phone.

I finish getting myself together, use the bathroom, and head into the living room where I hear him speaking rapidly in Italian.

He finishes his call abruptly and turns to me. "I'm sorry, I forgot I had a phone appointment. I will have to call them back shortly," he says apologetically.

"It's okay, as I said, I need to go anyway," I say, leaning my head toward the door. "Goodbye, Alessandro."

He sweeps me into his arms and kisses me deeply. *"Ciao, bella,"* he murmurs, picking up his handset. As I reach the door he calls me, "Serafina?" I pause by the door. He looks appraisingly at my rumpled clothes, his dark eyes once more filled with lust and fire. He raises an eyebrow suggestively as his eyes meet mine. "Yes. Just sex." He winks and starts to dial.

Smiling, I let myself out.

∽

DESPITE MY BEST EFFORTS TO KEEP BUSY ON SUNDAY, BY EARLY AFTERNOON I find myself back in his bed, recovering from our latest antics.

"So, what are the rules?" he asks me, trailing his fingers over my naked breasts.

I purse my lips in thought. "Hmmm. Well, I'd say, for starters, we only have sex here or at my place," I begin. "Never in the office. And we don't tell anyone."

"I can live with that," he responds, running his tongue along my nipple.

I push him away playfully. "I can't think while you're doing that," I admonish him.

He wiggles his eyebrows and I laugh. "What about other men?" he asks.

I stare at him in mock shock. "I don't know what you're into, but threesomes aren't really my style," I say, doing my best to sound horrified. His eyes widen, and he freezes. I shove him gently. "I'm *joking*."

He lets his breath out in relief. "I don't mind a little kink, but no, no threesomes," he agrees. "I meant do you still plan to see other men?"

I snort. "I don't see *any* men," I reply honestly. "I go on the occasional first date here and there, but nothing ever goes very far. So, there are no 'other men' to worry about."

"Wow," he replies.

Unsure of the nature of his astonishment, I shrug self-consciously. "It's just not on my radar," I say simply, hoping to bypass the discussion. "What about you? Surely there are other women?" I look at him expectantly, having seen his flirting both directed at myself and nearly every other woman in the office at one point or another. And I employ a lot of women.

"From time to time, but nobody serious for a very long while," he says. I look at him skeptically. "Really. In any event, there will be nobody else while I am with you. And I'd appreciate the same in return."

I weigh the possibility that he's just a huge flirt but am still dubious. "That's fair," I concede. "But if you decide you want to be with someone else, physically or otherwise, please just tell me. And I'll do the same." And I'll just have to hope he actually does.

"Fair enough. Is that all?"

I think for a moment. "I think so. You?"

"Do I get to take you on dates?" he asks.

I sit up abruptly. "No, no dates. I don't want anyone we work with seeing us together. And we only spend time alone together if it's between sexcapades. We are together for sex only, as our schedules allow. I'm okay with sleepovers if it's the most obviously convenient option."

"Sexcapades?" he laughs. I smile. "You drive a hard bargain, but I'll take what I can get."

His words worry me. "Alessandro, if you're hoping for more, this won't work." He regards me thoughtfully.

"*Bella*, I'm always hoping for more from life," he explains. "But if you're worried about me falling in love with you, don't." He kisses my fingertips. "Now, I think we've done enough talking."

～

RETURNING TO WORK ON MONDAY MORNING CARRIES NONE OF THE STRESS OF the previous week. And with the project management handed over to Jackson, I don't have to worry about being caught staring lustfully at Alessandro or having an argument with him that boils over into a passionate liaison behind closed doors. Now that I've unleashed that long-suppressed part of me, I just don't trust myself around him anymore.

As the elevator climbs to my floor, I do my best to suppress the memories of the weekend enough to wipe the humongous grin from my face. But I'm still positively chipper when I greet Maggie on my way into the office. She looks at me questioningly as I float past her into my office. I laugh as I get settled in for my first call of the morning.

～

AFTER LUNCH I SETTLE BACK AT MY DESK TO REVIEW A NEW PURCHASE AND sale agreement for one of our client's acquisitions when I'm interrupted by Nick Conrad, my finance lead, poking his head around my door.

"Got a minute, Ms. Evans?" he inquires.

"For you Nick? I have five."

He takes a seat in front of my desk. "Did you by any chance take any petty cash out on Friday afternoon?" he asks.

I frown. "No. How much is missing?"

Nick sighs. "Four hundred."

My eyebrows shoot up. "Well, *that's* a little obvious," I remark.

He nods in agreement. "Yes, usually thefts are smaller amounts over longer periods of time."

"So, you think it *is* theft, then?" I prompt.

"I've checked with the last few people on the ledger and the bookkeeper, and nothing. So yes, unfortunately, likely it's theft," he says.

"Email me the ledger, and please let me know what additional security measures you'd like to take while this is being investigated. Once I have that, I'll contact an independent investigator and get back to you as soon as we find something," I promise. "Thanks for bringing this to my attention."

Nick leaves and I push back from my desk, turning to the view of the city behind me. I take measures to make sure we attract the best employees and treat them well, so I'm especially disturbed by the theft. The amount is a pittance, it's more the principle of the matter.

My email pings, grabbing my attention — it's the ledger from Nick. I forward it and pick up the phone to talk to my PI.

It's Wednesday and I haven't heard from Alessandro, besides catching a glimpse of him here and there coming and going from meetings, so I decide to text him.

Busy tonight?

I chew my lip and wait impatiently. Thankfully, his reply comes quickly. *I am now. 20:00, my place. No underwear.*

So bossy. I grin widely.

His door opens, and I toy with the straps trailing from the belt of my long, red trench coat. Alessandro's eyebrows jump when he sees me.

"Are you going to make me stand here all night, or can I come in?" I tease.

He steps aside. "*Per favore*, come in," he offers. "Is it raining?" he inquires, trying to sound casual, but I can hear a note of excitement in his voice.

I laugh shortly. "No." As I turn I open my coat and let it fall to the floor, revealing that I'm wearing nothing but heels. His jaw drops, and he is speechless. Exactly the effect I was looking for. "You said no underwear," I say, fixing a confused look on my face. "Should I put it back on?" I reach for the trench and he pounces, pushing me onto the couch.

"Not unless you want me to rip it back off you," he growls.

LATE THAT EVENING WE LIE IN HIS BED AS HE ABSENTMINDEDLY STROKES MY hair.

"I can't believe how much sex we've managed in one evening," I say, giggling like a teenager.

He smiles down at me. "That's what happens when I'm made to wait three days for you," he admonishes me, kissing my neck gently, running his fingers lightly over my body.

"You could've asked anytime," I remind him, lazily running my fingers through his thick hair.

"I wanted to see how long it would take you to ask me," he replies.

I catch his eye. "Seriously? Why?"

He muses for a moment. "Just curious," he says finally.

I frown, unsatisfied by his answer, but unwilling to push the issue. "Well, you're going to have to wait again, because my mother is coming into town tomorrow and I don't think I'll be able to get away until she leaves on Sunday," I inform him.

He grimaces. "I take it then that I won't be meeting her?"

"We're not telling anyone else, remember? And it might be a tad hard to explain why I'm running off to meet a client at all hours of the night," I chide.

Alessandro shrugs. "So, don't explain. Wait until she's asleep, come have fun with me, and then return to your own bed," he suggests.

"She's a light sleeper. She'd hear me leave," I protest. "It's only four days, Alessandro."

He rolls toward me and hitches my leg over him. He kisses my neck and lightly skims my sex with his palm. "*Bella*," he pleads, "that's an eternity. It's like asking me to go four days without air. Or light. I'll go mad."

"Don't be so dramatic," I say, pushing away from him playfully.

"I'll just have to break down your door at night then. Take what is mine," he emphasizes the last word in a way that effectively ends the discussion.

⌒

LATER, AS I'M DRIFTING TOWARD SLEEP IN HIS DARK BEDROOM, ALESSANDRO tugs my chin gently and I look up into his eyes.

"Are you ashamed of being with me?" he asks, his voice vulnerable.

I snap awake. "No," I protest. "Why would you ask that?"

"Surely your mother would understand if you see me while she is here. But if the thought of even suggesting I exist is so awful for you, I thought," he pauses, "that you might be worried about more than our colleagues finding out. That you might be embarrassed by me, by our arrangement."

"No," I insist again. "I don't tell my mother anything. It's like handing her weapons," I explain.

He looks at me, bemused. "Your mother hurts you with what you tell her?" he asks. Afraid to speak, I swallow hard and hesitate a moment before nodding, afraid of this getting too real. "Why doesn't your father step in?"

And the fear crashes in. *Oh, Alessandro.* I shake my head vehemently. *No, no, no. I cannot have this conversation.* I go to leave the bed and he wraps his arms around my waist, pulling me back in.

"Serafina, no, don't run from me," he insists, pulling me in to his lap facing him in the dark. "You can tell me. I'm not here to judge you, I just want to understand." His soft words and warm flesh against mine work their magic.

I melt into him, burying my face in his neck so he can't read my face. "My father left my mother and I when I was twelve. I was her only outlet for all of her fear, anger, and hatred for seven years," I say thickly as a few tears escape. I brush them away immediately. "I left as soon as I could, and I try not to tell her anything about my life that you couldn't learn about me on the internet."

He smooths my hair and strokes my back. "Then why do you see her?" he asks.

I snort. Good question. "She's my mother." It's the best response I have. "Even if she's awful, she's all I've got. It's why she doesn't visit often, or for very long." *And I couldn't stand to have her rip this to shreds, to destroy the small comfort I find here in your bed.*

I slide back to the other side of the bed, and he watches me silently as I compose myself.

"*Mi dispiace,*" he murmurs. "I didn't mean to upset you."

I smile wanly. "It's okay," I say. "But really, I should go home tonight. I just realized I have some things I need there." Lies and more lies.

FIVE

"**S**erafina, darling, I don't know why you refuse to cut your hair. It's far too long and unruly," my mother says, pulling at a stray, wavy lock.

I blanche at the contact and focus on driving. We haven't even made it back to my condo and she's already lobbing insults at me.

"It's good to see you too, Mom," I reply.

She huffs a little and smooths her own shoulder-length perfectly coifed brown hair. "Do you have to work tomorrow, or do I actually get to spend time with my daughter?"

"I have to go in for a few hours in the morning, but after that I'm all yours." A few hours of peace. And getting to see Alessandro, if only briefly, and not exactly in the way I'd prefer.

"Why don't I go with you? I've never been to my big-shot daughter's company. I would just love to see you in your element," she simpers sweetly.

I cock an eyebrow at her. "Mom, you've never been interested in my work. What gives?"

"Well, you work all the time and you never mention anything about getting out socially. So, you must have friends at work. Maybe even a boyfriend?" she suggests.

I can't help it; my mouth drops open in shock. I close it quickly, hoping she didn't notice. It's like she has a sixth sense about how to go for my vulnerable spots.

"They're my employees, and I certainly have never dated anyone that works for me." Well, that much is true.

"All the same, I'd love to see it," she insists.

I sigh internally and resign myself to adjusting my morning. "Fine, Mom. I need to make a brief appearance for a meeting, but I can give you the tour," I concede. *And I'll watch you like a hawk, so you don't have a chance to humiliate me any more than absolutely necessary.*

"Oh goody," she enthuses, clapping her hands together.

∾

AFTER MY MOTHER HAS GOTTEN SETTLED IN THE GUEST ROOM, I CALL MAGGIE to let her know to cancel my morning calls and let Jackson know I'll be in for the last fifteen minutes of the tag-up meeting with Buone Case. I don't tell her my mother will be with me. I know what a gossip Maggie can be, and I don't want to spark anyone's interest ahead of time. Especially not Alessandro's.

∾

THE ELEVATOR DOORS SLIDE OPEN, AND I EXIT INTO OUR RECEPTION AREA WITH my mother in tow. I can practically feel her vibrating into another plane of existence with excitement. I'd like to think maybe she's just proud of me, but years of experience have me wondering what she's really hoping to get out of this.

"Good morning, Ms. Evans," Lucy greets us as we pass.

"Good morning, Lucy," I reply, smiling warmly at her.

"Oooh, is that your secretary?" my mother asks loudly as we pass.

I face-palm internally. "That's our receptionist," I reply tensely. I lead her through the outer office, pointing out the various departments as we go. "All our support functions are on the south side of the office," I gesture, "human resources, finance, IT, marketing, and sales. All of our direct functions are on the north side of the office," I gesture again, "project managers, land use and zoning specialists, property managers, leasing agents, and so on," I explain.

Her eyes are wide as she takes it all in. "Where are the other real estate agents? Are you the only one then?" she asks.

"Mom, legally many of our functions can only be performed by a real estate agent so more than half of our direct staff are real estate agents," I explain.

"Wow, Sera, everyone here must be so smart," she says in awe. I feel like I'm in the Twilight Zone. Is my mother impressed? She catches me staring funnily at her. "What? I'm just glad you're not trying to do this all on your own. At least you have smart people doing all the work."

And she's back.

"My office is over here. I need to pick up a few things and check in with my assistant before catching the end of a meeting," I say, moving on.

Maggie looks puzzled as I approach her desk.

"Good morning, Maggie, this is Christine Evans." I pause. "My mother."

My mother's eyes take in Maggie's plain face and short, chubby frame with disdain.

"It's a pleasure to meet you, Mrs. Evans," Maggie exclaims, extending her hand eagerly.

My mother deigns to shake it briefly. "Thank you, but it's *Ms.* Evans," she says coolly. "I'm not married. Sera's father left years ago."

The smile slips off Maggie's face.

"Well, Maggie, if you have the papers I requested, I'll be heading to the Buone Case meeting," I interject swiftly.

Maggie stares at my mother in bewilderment for a moment longer before tearing her eyes away. "Yes, of course, here they are," she replies, handing me a stack from her desk.

I work them into my bag and thank her, then lead my mother by the elbow down the hall to the conference room.

Before we go in, I pause. "Mother, please remember these are my employees. I typically don't share details of my personal life with them and I'd appreciate if you didn't either," I implore her.

She looks totally taken aback by my words. "Oh, Sera, I would never! That thing about your father was about me, not you," she rationalizes. "She called me 'Mrs.'!"

I rub my temples in frustration. "Okay, whatever, fine. You can either wait in the reception area or come in with me, as long as you sit by the door and don't say a word," I warn.

"Oh, of course I'd love to come in and see you in action!" she exclaims.

I put my hand on the doorknob and pause a moment wondering why I'm doing this. I must be a glutton for punishment.

As I go to turn the knob, the door swings open and I jump back as people start filing out. I glance in panic at my watch, wondering if I'm late, but it's only ten forty-seven. Apparently, the meeting is over early for once. When the exodus stops I look in the conference room and see Jackson and Alessandro still in discussion, standing in front of the projection screen. My mother follows me in as Jackson is animatedly talking to Alessandro about going forward on the site he's selected.

"Looks like I missed the party," I joke, interrupting their tête-à-tête. Both of their heads turn to me, and then to my mother. I look at her and she is staring at Alessandro. Hard. "Gentlemen, this is Ms. Christine Evans." I try to keep the sarcasm out of my voice at the "Ms."

Jackson hurries excitedly over to us, pumping my mother's hand. "A pleasure to meet you," he gushes to her. "I had no idea our Ms. Evans had a sister!" From his tone it's obvious he knows she is not my sister. Alessandro and I share a smirk.

My mother titters, flattered, though she hasn't more than glanced at Jackson. "How *sweet* of you! But heavens, no, I'm her *mother*," she coos, her eyes on Alessandro. "Though I was *very* young when I had her." And she *bats her eyelashes* at Alessandro.

He looks at me in astonishment and I laugh soundlessly, mouthing *I'm sorry!*

"Yes, well," I say, composing myself and moving on swiftly. "This is Jackson Williams, one of my top project managers." She finally looks at him and smiles. "And this is Mr. Giordano. We've contracted with his company to assist in expanding their development into the Puget Sound Area."

Alessandro extends his hand, which my mother grasps tightly with both of hers.

"Mr. Giordano," she says breathily, "it's so nice to meet you. I hope my daughter is taking good care of you."

I cover my mouth with my hand and cough, suppressing another laugh. *Oh, Mother, if you only knew.*

"*Piacere*," Alessandro replies, his lips twitching. "And *per favore*, call me Alessandro. Your daughter is a fine businesswoman, we are very pleased with our progress."

I'm reminded what a good first impression he makes with his ability to turn on the charm, his melodic Italian accent, and his intense good looks.

"Oh! Of course, *Alessandro.* And where are you expanding from?" my mother inquires, all but turning into a puddle of goo on the floor.

He senses the effect and lays it on thick. "Our original development was in the Campania region of Italia," he replies in a tone far more accented than usual. "We have been developing in the United States for more than five years now, mostly in California until our recent business here."

"Well, I do hope you'll decide to stay in the area," my mother replies breathily.

"I'm definitely warming to it," he says, looking at me suggestively over her shoulder.

I notice Jackson shifting uncomfortably at the charged atmosphere, and I flush with embarrassment.

"Now that we've all been introduced, Jackson, Mr. Giordano, it sounds like things are going well. I take it there was nothing you needed me for if you've already adjourned?"

Jackson straightens to attention. "No, ma'am, I think we're set. Everything is moving along nicely. We've all agreed on a site and the buyer's agent has all but said his client will take the offer. Hopefully, we'll have acceptance by early next week," he assures me.

"Excellent, Jackson, that's really excellent," I reply. *Finally.* "Thank you."

Jackson nods to Alessandro and offers a small wave to my mother, "It was nice meeting you."

"Yes, you as well, dear," she replies, barely glancing away from Alessandro long enough to acknowledge him, and Jackson disappears.

"Mr. Giordano, we don't need to take up any more of your time," I reassure him.

"Yes, I'm sure you have so many *important* things to do, Alessandro," my mother says, putting her hand on his arm. "We wouldn't want to keep you."

"Not at all, ladies, I'll just be counting the minutes until the end of my day from here," he laments.

My mother's eyes light up. "Well, we can't leave you to such misery! Come, Sera has taken the rest of the day off. We were going to have lunch and go shopping. You should join us for lunch," she proposes. I freeze and my heart drops into my shoes.

"I couldn't impose, really, and I'm sure Ms. Evans wouldn't want to be unprofessional," he says, hiding his grin.

"Yes, Mother, please, I'm not sure it's appropriate for us to intrude upon Mr. Giordano's time," I quickly agree.

But my mother isn't having it. "Don't be silly, he's just being polite. Of course, you'll come, won't you? You can tell us all about Italy, and I can tell you all about Western Washington. I've lived here all of my life, and there is so much you should see."

I look at him pleadingly, but I already know what he's going to say.

"An offer I cannot refuse," he replies, gathering his things.

"Wonderful," my mother chirps gleefully. "I just need to use the powder room. Sera?"

"First door on your left," I instruct her, pointing down the hall. And as soon as she's gone I close the door and turn to face Alessandro, shaking with anger.

"Now, before you explode," he cautions, "look how happy it's made your mother. And you'll have some help managing her for a bit of her visit."

I clench my fists and breathe deeply through my nose. "How is it going to look if we're seen leaving together for lunch with my mother?" I spit at him.

He fingers his chin. "We'll leave separately then. I'll say I forgot something and I'll meet you there. And we'll go someplace on the Eastside," he suggests.

I mash my lips together to keep from saying what's on my mind. *She'll tell you things I don't want you to know.* He steps forward and draws me into his arms, holding my chin and looking deeply into my eyes.

"What was I to do?" he asks in his softest, most winning voice. "If I had said no, do you think that would have improved your afternoon with her?" He has a point.

"You're right," I say resignedly. "Please, just try to keep her on neutral topics."

"I have a feeling there's no keeping that woman from wherever her mouth wants to wander," he laughs. "Or her eyes." His mouth droops into a frown and now I laugh.

"She's totally into you," I tease him. "Maybe it's *her* that will be sneaking out to meet you after *I'm* asleep."

He makes a disgusted face and I laugh again. I stop as I hear footsteps approach, and we spring apart. Moments later the door opens, and my mother enters.

"Let's go!" she says jubilantly.

 ~

MY MOTHER DOES NOT SHUT UP ABOUT ALESSANDRO THE WHOLE WAY TO THE restaurant. She asks questions about him, but immediately launches into her own speculations without waiting for a response.

Once we're finally all seated together I immediately order a glass of wine. Alessandro raises an eyebrow at me, but I ignore him, sipping it gratefully.

Thankfully, my mother starts to bombard Alessandro with all the questions she couldn't wait for me to answer, though frankly I didn't know the answer to most of them anyway. Through three glasses of wine and an amazing ribeye, he tells her that he is thirty-seven, has four siblings — an older brother and two younger sisters, is from Bologna, and that he wanted to be a vintner when he was a child. The last fact cracks me up — only an Italian child would want to grow up to make wine.

He's painted a vivid picture of his home country and shared several of his California exploits, and my mother has lapped up every minute of it. But after my mother orders dessert, her expression turns serious.

"Tell me, Alessandro, are you seeing anyone?" she asks baldly.

He is, understandably, surprised at the abrupt change in conversation, his eyebrows shooting up. Classic Christine Evans. Lull them into a false sense of security, then go for the jugular.

He sets down his fork and considers his response carefully. "Not as such," he hedges.

"A handsome man like you? I'm sure you are dating several women but are too chivalrous to say," she purrs. "I'll take that to mean there's no one woman in particular." She winks at him.

"I'm afraid I don't understand the purpose of your question," Alessandro says tentatively.

"Oh, dear boy," she laughs, "I don't mean to frighten you. *I'm* not after you. Unless you like cougars." She winks at him again and he *blushes*. And now I'm kind of enjoying the spectacle, my urge to rescue him waylaid by the shock on his face.

"I … that is to say, I'm sure you're very … but I'm not…" he stutters uncomfortably.

"I was *joking*," she assures him. *Sure, you were, Mom,* I think to myself, *unless he'd said yes.*

"No, no. Don't mistake me. I just wondered, since single men tend to pay more attention to single women. Now, I know my daughter keeps herself very busy at that company. But you seem to spend a lot of time with her." I don't like where this is going. "Have you seen her with anyone special?"

Oh, dear lord. "Mother, if I was seeing someone do you think I'd wave it under a client's nose?" I ask with exasperation.

"Well, you never know, and it doesn't hurt to ask. I just wish someone would catch your eye," she says pointedly, glancing at Alessandro.

Alessandro gives me a look that plainly says, *See? Even your mother wants you to date me.*

"This is not exactly a conversation I want to have with someone I'm doing business with. In public no less," I say tightly.

"You worry too much," she says dismissively. "We're all friends here! Besides," she says to Alessandro, "a mother worries. I knew that good-for-nothing ex-fiancé of hers was just going to break her heart. I mean, she was only nineteen and he was twelve years older than her! It was bound to end badly, but I didn't know it would set her off men for a full ten years."

"*Mom!*" I am livid. "I can't *believe* you!" I'm torn between anger and horror, the mixture causing my stomach to begin roiling uncomfortably.

"Oh, Serafina, calm down," my mother says sharply. "Everybody has a past. I have a past too — your father left me, just like Tom left you. And I had an almost teenaged daughter to take care of! I'm sure it's nothing as salacious as all that to your friend here."

"That's not the point! You can't go around telling my personal business to people I work with." I can't even with her right now. "Alessandro, I am *so* sorry, this is not anything you needed to hear, and I'm sure you do not want to be dragged into our family drama. Thank you very much for a mostly enjoyable lunch. I think it's best if we leave now."

I leave the table as quickly as I can without running, avoiding his reaction and hoping I can keep my lunch down long enough to escape.

"I'm sorry my daughter is so dramatic. Thank you very much for lunch," I hear my mother say behind me.

I don't speak to her on the ride home, or once we're in my condo. My stomach has settled, but my head aches and I need to be alone. Without a word, I go to my room, shut the door, and let the angry tears flow into my pillow. I cry for what feels like hours before I'm able to regain control. Two of my most painful, private histories laid out at the feet of a man who makes me feel something. It's a fool's hope that he won't use the knowledge against me.

But even my mother doesn't know everything about my relationship with Tom. How he charmed me into my first sexual experiences, which due to my naivety naturally resulted in my falling completely and hopelessly in love with him. And how he then became controlling and abusive every way but physically. Until one day when I dared to suggest we might get married someday, only to have him laugh at me, insult me, and then leave me.

And even my mother doesn't know that, to my utmost shame to this day, I begged him to take me back. For months I pursued him, until I was practically stalking him. Only to have him cruelly tell me he'd found someone else. That he was marrying someone else. So quickly. And it wasn't until years later that I realized he'd probably been cheating on me all along. Or that maybe *I* was the side piece. In any case, I also never, *never* told my mother that Tom's parting words were so close to my dad's: "Who could ever love *you*?"

SIX

Darkness had fallen when I finally emerged into the living room. My mother was sitting on the couch reading a book, which she quietly set aside.

"I made you some dinner," she says softly. "Mac and cheese casserole — your favorite. It's in the fridge."

"Thanks," I mumble, and I realize I'm ravenous. I retrieve a dish from the refrigerator and numbly watch it turn in the microwave.

After I've eaten what little I can manage, I put the rest away. I turn, and my mother is seated at the kitchen bar.

"Sera, if I'd know you were in love with him, I never would have said anything," she says.

I laugh mirthlessly. "I'm not in love with Alessandro, Mother," I retort. "I'm just fucking him."

Her eyebrows shoot up. "I see," she says rigidly. "Well, still, I had no idea, and I *am* sorry."

"It's a recent development," I allow. "You couldn't have known."

"Well, I would have if you talked to me more," she says, hurt in her voice.

"I would talk to you more if you didn't violate my trust constantly," I retort, leaving the kitchen. "I can't have this conversation with you again, Mom, we just go in circles. And the damage is done. I'm sure Alessandro will stay far away from me from now on."

"No, Sera," she pleads, following me into the living room. "You should go to him and give him a chance to prove you wrong."

I whirl in place to face her. "Why? You're my mother, and every time I give you a chance to prove me wrong you just hurt me! Why do you think I don't date? How can I trust anyone if I can't trust my own mother? Or my father, who obviously wanted away from our drama too? Not that I blame him," I add. "I can't do this, Mom. Please just leave me alone."

"You're overreacting," she says angrily. It's the mention of my father, I'm sure. It sets her off every time. Maybe I wanted to set her off. Push *her* buttons for once. "When you're done acting like a child, let me know." And with that she closes herself in the guest room.

And for reasons unbeknownst to me I start laughing manically. Sinking to my knees, I wrap my arms around my torso as I laugh, tears streaming down my face. *Boy, I'm really losing it.*

I focus on taking a few slow, deep breaths to steady myself and rise sluggishly. I need to go somewhere I can get a break. Take back control. I grab my keys and my bag and head to my office.

❧

At nearly midnight I turn away from my desk and sink into my chair, putting my feet on the credenza by the window. The lights of Seattle twinkle in the mist, and the sky is as dark as my mood. I don't know how long I've been sitting there when I hear footsteps. I tense up and look wildly around the room for something to use as a weapon.

"Serafina?" Alessandro's voice calls from the hall. I breathe a sigh of relief knowing there is no danger. Well, not the physical kind at least. My door swings open and he's there. "Thank God you're here, we were so worried."

"Alessandro, what are you doing here? Who is we?"

As if in answer, he pushes a button on his cellphone and stares at me until the other person answers. "Christine? I've found her, she's at work." He pauses. "Yes, thank you. Have a good trip, *arrivaderci*." He ends the call, tucking his phone in his pocket and striding toward me.

He drops to his knees in front of my chair. He looks a mess, his dark hair disheveled, his top two shirt buttons opened, and his clothes crumpled. He wraps his hands around mine and kisses them, looking up at me with wild eyes and a worried expression.

"I've been trying to reach you all day," he says. His voice is strained and tired. "I figured you didn't want to talk to me until your mother called me this evening to say you'd vanished."

I shake my head. "She said I *vanished*? That's a little melodramatic," I reply, rolling my eyes. "We had a fight, she went to her room. I left. And how the hell did she get your phone number?"

"I'm in the phone book," he says, waving his hand dismissively. "Why didn't you tell her you were leaving? She was in a panic. You haven't been answering your phone, and the office line goes straight to the answering service."

"You're in the phone book?" I laugh. "How terribly old fashioned of you."

"Well, it worked out pretty well in this case," he retorts, glowering at me.

"I didn't know you were such a worrywart," I fume. "I haven't been gone that long, Alessandro. I turned off my phone because I didn't want to talk. To either of you. You both knew I was upset. Can't I just be alone for a while?" I pull my hands out of his and he stands.

"I was just concerned for your well-being. I didn't know if you'd go out and get drunk again or do something else equally stupid."

"I'm a grown woman, I don't need a babysitter."

He narrows his eyes. "Yes, you've made it perfectly clear that you don't need anyone," he says flatly. "I'm sorry I came." He throws his hands in the air, but rather than leave, he sinks into one of the chairs opposite my desk.

We sit in tense silence for a few minutes.

"I'm not going to stay away from you," he says softly, breaking the stalemate. Clearly, my mother is incapable of keeping any sort of confidence. No big surprise there. "Your mother shouldn't have told me those things, of course, but it explains a great deal. I'm not going to leave you."

A great lump forms in my throat and my eyes sting. "Spare me your pity, please," I manage to choke out. "I don't want you to stick to our arrangement merely because you feel sorry for the hurt little girl who always gets left."

He steeples his fingers under his chin and shakes his head gently. "I would have said the same before I knew those things, had you cared to ask. I will not be the one to end this," he promises.

I want to believe him, but it doesn't make any sense. "I don't understand."

"I started this, as you said," he begins. "I pursued you. You told me your terms, and I accepted them. And only on your terms will this be over."

"You say that," I whisper, "But you didn't like my terms. I can tell you wanted more. You'll get frustrated and find someone who is willing to give you that." I shudder at the thought. I may be confining our tryst to a small sliver of what he wants, but it's all I can give. Even so, now that I have it, the thought of losing it is intolerable. Nothing has cleared my mind of doubt and worry like the moments of pure bliss spent with him.

"I accepted your terms, and I'm a man of my word," he assures me. He rises from the chair and walks around my desk. He offers his hand and I take it without hesitation, as if my body has a mind of its own. He pulls me up to him and grasps my chin, forcing me to look up into his eyes. "In any relationship, even one such as this, there needs to be trust. I need you to trust me." His dark eyes burn fiercely into mine, his breath hot on my face. "Do you trust me, Serafina?"

Conflicting emotions rage inside me. But trust is not something I know how to give easily. "I want to," I admit breathlessly.

He regards me for a moment. "That will have to do for now, then." And slowly he lowers his mouth to mine, circling my cheek with his thumb. His tongue invades my mouth, melting my thoughts and emotions until they drain away completely.

I return his kiss fervently, running my hands up his strong arms. This is what I need — to touch him, be touched by him, and let everything else fade into the background.

He pulls back and grabs my hand, leading me out of the room and down the hallway.

"Where are we going?" I inquire.

He turns back to me with a mischievous grin but doesn't answer. A moment later he opens the door to the conference room and pulls me in.

His hands pull at my blouse, working it out of my skirt and over my head. "I told you I wanted to have you on this table," he explains.

He unhooks my skirt and tugs it with my panties over my hips and to the floor while backing me to the table. In one swift motion he places his hands under my behind and lifts me onto the smooth surface. As he removes his clothing I unhook my bra and we're both completely naked. In the conference room. The inviolable nature of it is thrilling.

He climbs up with me and places a condom beside us. He trails kisses up my legs and then stomach, stopping to lick and tease each nipple. I moan and arch my back into the pleasurable sensation. His hand disappears between my legs, testing my readiness. He flicks me down there with a finger and I moan again. Laughing and smiling he brings his mouth to mine briefly, then drops his head between my legs, plunging his tongue into me while continue to work the area with his hand.

I'm dizzy with desire as he pleasures me, but it's just making me want him more. I call out his name in a desperate plea. It has the desired effect, and he brings his mouth back to mine. I reach between his legs to stroke him until he's moaning in my mouth.

"Condom," I whisper yearningly into his ear.

He rears back, slipping it on, and eases into me torturously slow. My back arches off the table, and I grit my teeth.

"Let go, Serafina," he urges me.

Oh yes, he likes it when I don't hold back the screams. I let my breath out in a groan and he rewards me with a hard thrust. I cry out and grip his back.

"You like it rough, don't you?" he asks.

"Oh God, yes," I moan, "please!" My plea spurs him on and he's pounding into me, his strong body heavily pinning me into the table causing me to feel the full effect of each thrust, my cries echoing through the room.

He rears back and hitches one of my legs over his shoulder, dragging me into his lap. Bracing himself with one arm, he uses his kneeling position to circle his hips, dipping in and out of me slowly and deeply, suspending my ascent to climax. I'd be frustrated at the delay, but it feels. So. Good. Finally, I've had all I can take.

I pull away from him and climb to my knees. "Lie down," I command him.

He grabs me and plunges his tongue into my mouth, his desire evident in every move, every noise he makes. I push his chest until he's lying under me, then squatting over him I sink him deep into me. We both groan in satisfaction. He offers his hands and I hold them, using them to balance as I work my hips over him. As I feel myself getting closer to climaxing, I drop my legs under me. Our flesh meets fully, and the new angle takes me closer to release. His hands are now free to rove my breasts and stomach. He licks his thumb and uses the moisture to work one nipple hard. The combination of sensations upends me into orgasm, and my muscles tighten over him. He cries out at last as we both finish.

He sits up, holding me in his lap, still inside me. We kiss softly, breathing heavily from our antics.

"I hope that lived up to your expectations, Mr. Giordano," I tease.

His teeth graze my ear and he runs his hands over my shoulders, down my arms, then brings my fingers to his lips.

"You always exceed my expectations, Ms. Evans," he agrees, brushing my hair behind my shoulders and kissing my neck.

As I'm studying his face I suddenly remember something. "Alessandro, why did you tell my mother to have a nice trip?"

He laughs loudly. "Took you long enough!" he chuckles. "She went home. She seemed to think you were in the wrong for not taking her apology gracefully, but she said she figured it was best if she removed herself from the situation nonetheless." He pauses thoughtfully. "You really weren't kidding about her."

I smile blandly. "Nope. I wish I were."

<h1 style="text-align:center">SEVEN</h1>

The weekend passes quickly in a blur of flesh, gratification, and relaxed pillow talk in between our exploits. It's an unexpected and most welcome departure from my usual workout, errand, and reality television–packed weekends. But Monday morning is the inevitability that puts a pause on our stolen moments.

Now, it's back to business. And the first thing I do is get my private investigator on the phone.

"Peter, I need an update on the petty cash theft," I dive right in, skipping the pleasantries.

"Yes, Ms. Evans, of course. I was going to call you soon," he responds. Peter Jeffries and I get along well because he's as direct as I am. "We couldn't find any deposits, but one of your employees, a Megan Stanwood, has been struggling financially recently. Lots of payday loans, that sort of thing. Her rent check payments have been most irregular so, with the open background check consent form your employees are required to sign, I was able to get her landlord's cooperation in confirming that she made a cash payment of four hundred dollars the day after the money went missing."

Bingo. "Good work, Pete. Can you please send what you've got over now? We'll need a full official report for our records, but I want to get moving on this ASAP," I request.

"Sure thing, Ms. Evans. I'll do that now and have the report to you within the week."

"Thanks."

Megan Stanwood. I purse my lips, trying to remember her. With almost fifty employees, though, I'm hard-pressed to keep track of them all. In any event, it's time to talk to HR.

⌒∾

I knock on Alison Kramer's door.

"Come in," a muffled voice calls.

I swing the door open to see a strawberry blond head buried in a filing cabinet drawer. With a mighty pull she emerges triumphantly holding a torn and bent folder.

"Sera, dear!" she shouts, tossing the folder on her desk. She rushes over and hugs me tightly. "If it isn't my favorite boss!"

I laugh. "I'm your *only* boss, Allie," I remind her.

"And one I haven't seen for a while! You haven't been hiding from me, have you?" She winks at me slyly and I blush. Her green eyes miss nothing and narrow curiously at my reaction. I have, in fact, been avoiding her.

I've been friends with Allie since college, where I got to see her brilliance with both reading people and business. It's the reason I recruited her when I started my own company, and she's been my most trusted confidant and ally.

As a friend, I've been dying to tell her about Alessandro. As the head of my human resources department, not so much.

"Just busy, as usual," I reply innocently. "How are you and David? Is the honeymoon over yet?"

"We're super," she replies dreamily. "And funny that you mention it, but we were just talking about taking another honeymoon to celebrate our first anniversary."

I roll my eyes jokingly. "Why am I not surprised?" I tease her.

She scrunches her nose up and sticks her tongue out at me. "Anyway, *boss*, what can I do for you today?"

I stick my tongue out at her too and chuckle. "Did Nick talk to you about the petty cash theft?"

"He mentioned it." She nods, gesturing to the chair in front of her desk and taking a seat herself. "Was Peter able to find anything out?"

"Yes," I say and fill her in on what he told me. "I'm sorry to say the name Megan Stanwood doesn't ring any bells with me."

"Don't be, she's a relatively recent hire and she only works part time," Allie says kindly. "She shares reception duties with Lucy Drummond. She mostly answers phones."

I look at her blankly, unwilling to admit I didn't remember that we'd hired another receptionist until she just reminded me, much less know her name or what she looks like.

"Mousy brown hair, brown eyes, average height, and generally unremarkable," she summarizes. "Easy to miss."

"Ah. How recently was she hired?" I ask.

Allie wakes up her laptop and taps a few keys. "Four months ago," she confirms.

"Why is she only part time?"

Allie skims her file. "She's twenty-six, but she's still a student. It looks like she changed schedules and reduced her hours about a month ago to accommodate her new classes."

"Well, that would certainly explain why she was suddenly short on cash," I reply drily.

"I don't know her well, but I've spoken to her several times outside of her hire process. She's quiet, reserved. She doesn't seem to be socializing with any of the other employees out of work hours that I can tell."

"How on earth do you keep track of what everyone is doing outside of work hours?" I ask her, aghast.

She cackles cheekily. "It's my *job* to know what people are up to around here. And I rather enjoy it," she explains with a twinkle in her eye.

I shake my head in amazement at Allie's commitment. "So, what's the procedure now?" I probe.

"Now, I bring her in and talk to her. Present her with the evidence, and see what she says," Allie says simply.

"Should I be in that meeting?" I ask.

"I think it would be better if you weren't," Allie says pointedly. "You can be a little intimidating. And she's likely to talk more freely when her boss isn't glowering at her." She smiles sweetly at me.

"Fine, but I'd like this dealt with swiftly, please. Call her in immediately. Then have Lucy keep an eye on her and come talk to me. I want this handled by the end of the day," I insist.

"Sure thing, boss." I stand up to leave. "Was there anything else you needed to tell me?" She gives me a probing look.

"Nope, not a thing." I avoid her stare.

"Mhm. Well, I'm here if you want to talk," she says meaningfully.

"Thanks, Allie," I say, turning before she can see how red my face is. "Talk soon."

❧

My only meeting that morning is with Shawn Phillips, for whom we are working with the city on rezoning a portion of his property. It's been a slow and tough process, and going over the latest round of proposed easements and legal descriptions with him, while necessary, is boring me to tears.

As the assigned project manager, Ben Fuller, talks Mr. Phillips through the easement diagrams, my mind wanders to Alessandro. His perfectly muscled body still amazes me no matter how many times I see it, touch it, and revel in it. His commanding tone when he demands a kiss, a position, or to hear me scream his name echoes in my thoughts, and I wonder how I'll react when he inevitably uses that same insistent cadence in the office again. I shudder lightly and struggle to bring my attention back to the meeting.

Thankfully, Alessandro won't be back in our office until Friday. He's sent most of his team back to their offices in San Francisco until further notice, and he and his assistant are working out of their temporary offices south of the city on some peripheral development tasks in preparation for closing on their new property. So, there's nothing but my own imagination to distract me from the doldrums of rezoning, property management, and the other myriad day-to-day needs of the business.

Ben asks me a question, snapping me out of my reverie, and I dig deep to find the will to re-engage in the meeting.

❧

As soon as I'm back at my desk I text Alessandro. *Buongiorno. I can't concentrate this morning thanks to you. Hope your morning is good. x*

And almost instantly he responds: *Ciao bella. Prego. Busy day, talk soon.*

I frown. Too busy for banter. Time to be a little less clingy and put my head back into work.

❧

As I'm reviewing a rather promising bid request for sourcing a large parcel to create a combo commercial retail and residential development, Allie pops her head around my half-open door.

"Good time?" she asks.

I gesture to a chair. "Please," I offer.

She sits, adjusting her skirt nervously.

"I take it your talk with Ms. Stanwood didn't go well?"

Allie grimaces. "Unfortunately, no. She was extremely guarded from the start but went completely silent after I presented the evidence."

"Did you accuse her directly?" I ask, itching for details.

Allie sighs, knowing I won't be satisfied with anything less than a blow-by-blow. "I told her we'd noticed money missing from petty cash. I didn't tell her how much. I asked her if she'd ever taken anything out of petty cash. She said no. I told her that we investigated further and had strong evidence to suggest she'd come into possession of the exact amount missing immediately after it

51

went missing. She didn't respond. So, I asked her where she got the money from," Allie describes.

"And?" I prompt, literally on the edge of my seat.

"She said she got it from a friend." Allie rolls her eyes. "So, I called her bluff with one of my own. I told her if that's true then she'll be cleared when we recover those bills from her landlord and the serial numbers don't match those of the missing petty cash."

"Holy shit. Did she take the bait?"

"She turned as white as a sheet! Then she told me I can't make her admit to anything and to tell you to go fuck yourself."

"Seriously? That's a bizarre response," I muse. And a disturbing one. "What did I ever do to her? I don't think I've ever even met her."

"I don't know, Sera," Allie sighs. "But she wouldn't say any more."

"Can we fire her based on circumstantial evidence?"

"Sera, we can fire her for any reason we want. Washington is an at-will employment state. I fired her on the spot and had security escort her out," she says blandly. "I didn't want to give her the chance to steal anything else or spread her vitriol amongst the troops before getting your approval."

I nod my head. "You absolutely made the right call. And you don't need my approval — you're the head of HR."

"I figured you'd say as much. Still, I was sorry to have to do it. And I wish I knew what her story was. She definitely made me nervous," Allie admits.

"Yes, I'm pretty alarmed by the whole situation," I agree. "Let's call together a meeting with Nick and Will tomorrow. I'd like to brief them on the situation and revise some procedures."

∽

BY THE END OF THE DAY I'M UTTERLY SPENT, AND ALL I WANT TO DO IS GO home, drink wine, and let my cares melt into a hot bath. I'd rather they melted under Alessandro's skilled caresses, but wine and bubbles will have to do as I haven't heard a peep from him since his brusque text this morning.

When I get home, the first thing I do is dig through the cupboards only to find I'm out of wine. I lean my head against the cold steel refrigerator door and groan. Just a bath then, I guess.

Stripping quickly in the bathroom, I'm pleased to find that there is still bubble bath. I run the bath and drop a generous amount in. As I tie my long brown locks up into a bun, I hear my cellphone ring in the kitchen. I contemplate letting it go to voicemail, but knowing it'll just bother me if I don't answer, I turn off the tap, wrap a towel around myself, and retrieve my phone begrudgingly.

"Hello," I say moodily.

"You don't sound happy to hear from me," Alessandro's warm voice says.

"I didn't have time to look at the caller ID," I reply, suddenly grinning like an idiot. "You know I'm always happy to hear from you. Not that I expected to since you were so *busy* today."

"Awww, don't be mad at me," he pouts. "I think I know what will make you feel better."

"Unless it's you, naked and holding a bottle of wine, I'm not particularly interested," I reply dismissively.

There's a knock on the door. "Not bad — two out of three," Alessandro says. "And if you open the door I can make that three out of three."

I drop my phone on the counter and open the door a crack to see Alessandro, wine bottle in hand as promised, smiling broadly on my doorstep. He is dressed casually in a grey cable-knit sweater and dark wash jeans, and has a very rugged five o'clock shadow on his jaw. It may be the first time I've ever seen him out while anything but perfectly coifed in a designer suit.

"Aren't you full of surprises?" I say, hiding behind the door as I open it wider in invitation.

He slips in and, grabbing me, pushes me against the back of the door. As it slides closed he runs his nose up my neck to my ear.

"*Ciao*," he murmurs, nibbling my earlobe and running his hand up my naked thigh. "Do you greet all of your guests dressed in a tiny towel that barely covers you?"

"Mmmm," I moan. "Only the good-looking ones that bring me wine." I slide under his arm and flit into the kitchen, grabbing two wine glasses from the cupboard and a corkscrew from a drawer. "Follow me."

"I'm intrigued," he answers, trailing closely behind me.

I lead him into the steamy bathroom and set the glasses and corkscrew on the wide counter before I restart the flow of hot water. "Now, are we going for three out of three or not?" I demand.

He laughs heartily and sets the wine bottle next to the glasses. Staring licentiously at me, he slowly pulls his sweater off, dropping it to the floor. He makes quite a show of removing his shoes, and then his pants, turning away and bending pointedly to move his things into a pile. Now gloriously naked, he picks up the wine and raises an eyebrow. "Is this better?" he asks.

I pretend to consider for a moment and he gives me an exasperated look. "Yes," I grant him. "Perfect."

"Now that we have that settled," he replies, uncorking the wine and pouring a generous amount in both glasses. "A toast."

He hands me a glass and touches his glass gently to mine. "To beautiful women, who can make you forget even the most frustrating of days with one tiny towel."

"To accommodating gentlemen with magnificent bottoms who rescue you from a dearth of wine and a lonely bath," I reply.

His eyes shine playfully as we both take a sip. I place my glass on the wide ledge around the sunken tub and step in, beckoning him with a finger to join me.

As I settle into his arms, I use my foot to turn off the tap and breathe a sigh of relief.

"Why was your day so frustrating?" I ask, skimming my hands over his thighs.

He sighs heavily. "I've spent all day chasing contractors and materials and all manner of details that should be in place by now. But I'm finding it ridiculously difficult to rely on anyone," he fumes.

He continues in detail about all the supplies that have been sub-par or missing, contractors who don't seem to understand what permits are required, and the like for quite a while. I find it strangely relaxing to listen to him rant at length about his troubles, as he occasionally slips out of English and into Italian when he is particularly frustrated.

Thankfully, I've worked with him long enough to understand most of it, and my ability to care about the rest has mostly been wiped away by the wine, the bath, and the gorgeous man with his legs wrapped around me.

Finally, he halts his diatribe and looks down at me apologetically. "*Mi dispiace, dolcezza,*" he murmurs, kissing my forehead. "How was your day?"

"We had to fire someone today," I grimace. "Not something I enjoy doing, but I'm particularly unsettled about this one. Something is just not right." I proceed to explain everything, and Alessandro listens intently.

When I'm finished Alessandro runs a finger along his chin. A gesture that is starting to seriously turn me on.

"I can see why you're so upset." He pauses. "Have you reported it to the police?"

"Not yet," I reply. "I was waiting until we'd confronted her, but we'll probably discuss all that tomorrow."

He frowns. "Are you at least going to have someone keep an eye on her?"

I look at him in surprise. "I hadn't even thought of that. Obviously, she has it in for me or my company, I don't know, but what can she do now?"

He shrugs. "As they say, keep your friends close and your enemies closer. Or keep a closer eye on your enemies? I don't know. I think it would be a good idea in any case," he suggests.

I take a sip of wine and weigh his words. He's probably right. I'll add that to my list for tomorrow as well. I finish my wine and place the glass on the ledge. Turning slowly so as not to slosh water on the floor, I climb into Alessandro's lap.

"You know, you are incredibly smart," I whisper into his ear. "Which is incredibly sexy." I run my tongue down his ear, along his neck.

He pulls my face to his and kisses me softly. "Says the naked, wet goddess straddling me," he purrs, and starts to work his magic on my body.

I realize quickly that I no longer care about the water cascading over the edge onto the floor as our bodies entwine, our need for each other sudden and pressing.

∽

WHILE I DRY OFF, ALESSANDRO PUTS HIS CLOTHES BACK ON. I LOOK AT HIM inquisitively in the mirror.

"You're not staying?"

"Not tonight," he states, "I didn't realize how late it is, and I have matters to attend to before the day is done."

"Okay," I say begrudgingly. "I'll see you later then."

"Yes, you will," he reassures me. He kisses me sweetly. "*Buona notte, mio tesoro.*"

And he's gone.

I walk, naked, to my bed and slip between the sheets. Eventually I fall into a fitful sleep and, for the first night in more than a week, the nightmares return.

EIGHT

"Okay, recap, team," I say. "Go." I point at Nick first.

"I will personally keep petty cash under lock and key in the safe," Nick states. "Any withdrawals will require company ID and a signature with weekly audits. And I'll do a check of our books and, with Will's help, our client accounts to make sure there was no skimming anywhere else."

I point at Will Baxter, my IT guy. "I'll do a check of all of our systems and software to support Nick's needs and to make sure she didn't tinker with anything else she wasn't supposed to."

"Why would you do that?" Allie asks, confused.

"She was a computer science major," Will replies. "She asked me for help with her homework from time to time. She was bright too. Better safe than sorry." He shrugs.

"Agreed," I say.

"And while our background checks are sound, I'll add a few psychological profiling questions to our hiring process to attempt to identify any undesirable tendencies in the future," Allie says. "I'll need you to run them by our attorney, Sera."

I nod. "Good thinking. And I'll talk to Mr. Jeffries about reporting this to the police and instituting ongoing surveillance of Ms. Stanwood until we're satisfied she will not continue to be a threat," I conclude. "Let's reconvene Thursday morning. Thank you for your time."

Nick and Will leave the conference room already in deep discussion about financial reports. Allie closes the door behind them then retakes her seat opposite me.

"You okay, Sera? This is heavy stuff," she asks tentatively.

I rub the back of my neck and nod. "It does take more out of me than I thought it would, but I'm fine," I assure her. "What about you?"

"Oh, you know me. Five by five," she says, grinning. "So, are you going to tell me why we haven't done lunch and shopping in weeks? I didn't think you could stay away from retail therapy for that long," she jokes.

"Hardy har," I reply wryly. "I've just been busy. We've got a couple major accounts and a new one possibly coming down the pipeline. It's a crucial time for the business. We're just starting to get good word-of-mouth business, and I don't want to slack off and waste that momentum."

"You know what the funny thing about that answer is? It sounds good — but it's complete bullshit. Cut the crap, Sera. I've known you for ten years. Who is he?" she asks shrewdly.

And I can't stop the dumb ear-to-ear grin from breaking across my face in time.

"I knew it!" she exclaims, slamming her hand on the table. "Details!"

"It's not what you think," I hedge. "We're just sleeping together. You know, fuck buddies."

"There's your fear of commitment again," she admonishes me. "Why can't you ever admit you're dating someone? Then you might actually have a relationship that lasts more than a month."

"Because maybe I don't want a relationship? It's working for me," I reply, a little testily.

"You only *think* it's working for you, Sera," she says, shaking her head.

"Allie, please, don't," I plead. "I'm happier this way. We've built this amazing business, I'm having incredible sex, and my mother only managed to last a little more than twenty-four hours on this last visit." I grimace slightly at the memory. "Life is pretty good."

"A day? That's all? What happened?" she presses, and I'm immediately sorry I mentioned it.

"We had a fight. Or three," I reply cautiously. "Her usual crap. I'm surprised you didn't hear about some of it. She told Maggie my father left us. Oh, *and* she told Alessandro about Tom!" I blurt the last part out before I can stop myself.

Allie's eyes widen, and she covers her mouth. "I shouldn't be surprised," she says. Then a funny look crosses her face. "Alessandro? You mean Alessandro Giordano of Buone Case?"

Shit.

"Yes," I reply, trying to breathe normally — and not turn red. And failing miserably.

"I've never heard you call him anything but Mr. Giordano," she says slowly. "When did you guys get so … oh oh oh!" She starts flapping her hands frantically.

"Allie, shhhh!" I chastise her.

"You're *sleeping* with a client?" she hisses. "That is *so* not like you!"

"Allie, I never said I was sleeping with him," I joke clumsily. She shakes a finger at me.

"Oh no you don't, Serafina Evans," she says gleefully. "Holy shit!"

I cover my eyes like a child, hoping it will make her disappear. "Allie, you're killing me," I mutter. The lack of response is worrying, and I realize she's gone silent. I drop my hands to find her frowning. "What, Allie, what is it? Am I violating some sort of contract clause? Oh, god."

"No, no," she says hastily. "It's not that."

"Then what?"

"Well, you know I keep my ears open for juicy gossip, especially when we start with a new client?" she starts.

"Go on," I say tightly. I don't know if I want to hear this.

"He's kind of a womanizer, Sera," she cringes.

I shrug. This isn't news to me. "I don't really care. Fuck buddies, remember?"

She clears her throat. Oh god, there's more. "You know Francesca, his assistant?

"Of course," I reply. "Short, ridiculously gorgeous with long, dark hair and big lips?"

"That's her. Big lips *and* a big mouth. She told me a couple months ago that they had something going. You know, 'something' with heavy undertones of 'I'm doing my boss.'"

My fears during our first sexual encounter of him bedding perfect-bodied tiny Italian women come rushing back. Ugh. "Well, that was a couple of months ago," I say, trying to sound blasé.

"Maybe," she says thoughtfully. "I hope so. But still, even through other channels he's got quite a reputation. Just be careful."

"You know me," I counter.

"Yes, you're usually the epitome of prudence," she allows. "But if he hurts you I *will* have David break both of his legs."

"As any true friend would," I joke. "I appreciate the concern. Can I go back to work now?"

"You're the boss," she replies.

∽

THE DAY WHIPS BY IN A HAZE OF ODDS AND ENDS, DISTRACTING ME FROM reviewing the contracts for our, hopefully, new client. It's a big deal not just because of the size of the project, but because of the company we'd be contracting with, Sutton Developments. They have a very large chunk of the commercial real estate market right now, and I somewhat suspect they're testing my services for a buyout. But I'm happy to play that game as, in the meantime, it will bring us quite a lot of business and, potentially, prestige.

Having promised them preliminary contracts for review by midweek, though, I really need to crack down and review the documents Keith, our contracts point man, has provided ahead of our internal review tomorrow.

I pick up my phone to check the time and notice two missed texts and a missed call with voicemail. The first text, from Alessandro, was from late this morning — *Busy tonight?* The second, also from Alessandro, was from late afternoon — *Everything okay?* The missed call and voicemail are from my mother. Knowing I won't call her back anyway, I listen to the voicemail first.

"Serafina, it's your mother. Just calling to see how you are. Hope everything is okay. I love you." That's all. She's probably just testing the waters after our fight to see if I'm still mad. No need to call her back right away, or possibly at all.

I quickly type a message to Alessandro. *Sorry, busy day. Hope yours was better than yesterday. Unfortunately, I have a hot date with some paperwork. Tomorrow night?*

I check the time once more and pay attention this time — it's almost six. I should probably eat something before attempting to read legalese. Standing up and stretching, I make for the break room to scrounge in the fridge for something to eat.

∽

AT ELEVEN I CLOSE MY LAPTOP AND REST MY HEAD ON ITS WARM SURFACE. Good enough for now. Time to go home and sleep. I look at my phone for the hundredth time, and still nothing back from Alessandro. I try not to think too much about it and head home.

∽

ON THE DRIVE MY PHONE PINGS ANNOUNCING THE ARRIVAL OF A TEXT MESSAGE, but I'm thankfully able to resist the urge to look until a few blocks later when I'm home. It's from Alessandro, of course. *Can't. Leaving for San Francisco tomorrow. Back Friday. Don't miss me too much while I'm gone.*

I scrunch my face into a frown. San Francisco. With Francesca, no doubt. Allie's warnings echo in my brain. Can I trust him to be sexually exclusive? I don't really know him that well. I'm sure *she* knows him much better. She's certainly known him a lot longer.

Gah, get ahold of yourself, Evans. You don't *want* to know him that well, right? Friends with benefits. Exclusive friends with benefits. That's not like dating, right? We don't ever go anywhere. Just sex.

Except he did want to take you on dates. And with so much sex, the pillow talk has been frequent and, occasionally, surprisingly deep. And he has met your mother.

No. No, no, no, no, no. We are not dating. And even if he is sleeping with Francesca, what do I really care? We're not in love. We use protection. It's not like we signed a contract with the terms we agreed on. *Move, Evans, and leave your thoughts behind.*

❧

THURSDAY MORNING FINDS ME NERVOUS AND OUT OF SORTS. WE'VE PROVIDED contracts to Sutton Developments, and while I'm certain we won't hear back until early the following week, I have a very good feeling about it.

Refocusing, I go over my calendar for the day. My follow-on meeting with Nick, Will, and Allie is in twenty minutes, so I give Peter Jeffries a call to check in.

"Ms. Evans, good morning. I presume you'd like a status report?"

"You presume correctly, Mr. Jeffries."

"Our research deeper into Ms. Stanwood's history hasn't provided any additional connection or incidents that would raise any flags. We've also established the subject's schedule and haven't noticed any abnormal behavior during our surveillance. Everything's pretty quiet here," he summarizes.

"*Beware of the danger signals that flag problems: silence, secretiveness, or sudden outbursts,*" I murmur. "I'm afraid we now have all three, Mr. Jeffries."

"Yes, ma'am," he replies, his tone bemused.

"Thanks, Pete, I'll check in again soon."

❧

As SOON AS I ENTER THE CONFERENCE ROOM I CAN FEEL THE PANIC ROLLING off Will and Nick. Allie sits silently, a deeply concerned expression on her face.

"They wouldn't tell me, they wanted to wait until you got here," Allie greets me.

I've never been one for beating around the bush, and I'm especially impatient given the situation. "Out with it then," I direct.

Nick speaks first. "So, first, our books are fine. Nothing additional skimmed out of our various accounts and direct dealings," he assures me.

"Am I to take it, then, that's she's stolen from our clients?" I reply, trying to stay calm.

"Not exactly," Will chimes in hesitantly.

"Mr. Baxter, please be as direct as possible before I have a heart attack at twenty-nine years old," I insist.

"Okay. Someone has rigged our property management software to ignore maintenance requests. Some have been extremely serious, but most were nuisances. Unfortunately, it has steeply increased turnover in some properties, included our largest account — Evergreen Homes," he explains. "There were two particular cases that caused large dollar figure damage, both in that company's properties."

Questions swirl in my brain.

"For how long? Is anything else in the system affected? How did this go unnoticed with both us and Evergreen?" I demand.

"Three months. The tampering also changed the daily, weekly, and monthly reports printed for both maintenance data and turnover data. Those were the only functions and parameters affected. I think if it was more widespread we would have noticed, so it was a smart attack," he explains. "I talked to our point property manager, Rachel Harris. She was made aware of both costly maintenance incidents by phone calls directly from the tenants when they didn't get a response through our automated system. Unfortunately, in both cases the tenants had to be let out of their leases due to the extent of the damage once professionals arrived on the scene. Both Rachel and Evergreen Homes agreed at the time it was the tenant's faults for either not using the maintenance reporting system correctly or not calling the emergency numbers soon enough. While not untrue, this new information definitely brings that back into question."

"What about all the other stacked maintenance requests? How many resulted in turnover?" I ask, rubbing my temples.

"Almost ten percent so far, ma'am."

I look at Will in shock. In this business, ten percent is an astronomical figure in such a short time. Evergreen Homes is going to be furious, and rightly so.

"Has the software been fixed?" I ask.

"Not yet, ma'am, I'm working on it," Will replies shakily.

"What do you need to get it done quickly?"

"It's not a matter of staffing, ma'am. It needs one set of eyes comparing previous coding to current coding and looking for hidden traps. Whoever did this was quite sophisticated," he laments.

"Can't we just reset it to the last clean data point?" Allie asks.

We all shake our heads. "That would mean losing months of cost and revenue data," I grimly respond. "I need to speak with our attorneys before I inform Evergreen Homes and anyone else affected about the issue." I pause. "You said 'whoever did this' — you don't think it was Ms. Stanwood?"

"Not alone, no," Will responds.

"She has an accomplice," Allie infers, and Will nods. "Anything from Pete yet?"

"No, but I'll let him know what's happened," I respond. "Will, keep working and let me know if you need anything. If you can, find a way to funnel out the maintenance requests so we can see them and get someone manually calculating the turnover data and editing the reports accordingly before they're filed. If you'll all excuse me, I have a good number of phone calls to make."

BY THE END OF THE DAY MY ATTORNEY HAS WORKED WITH ME ON AN OPENING statement and what I should and should not say to the affected clients. Will's team has provided me with a numerical accounting of the extent of the errors and the estimated monetary damages associated with them, both in repairs and turnover.

Three smaller companies have a minor enough hit to where we can pay the sum outright. Evergreen Homes, however, has, conservatively, overall long-term damages in the hundreds of thousands due to the high number of units we manage for them. Paying such a high amount at once would be a huge hit to the company, or to our ability to keep affordable — or any — insurance.

But most damaging will be the hit to our reputation and continued success. We will weather the current predicament financially, certainly, but that gives me little comfort knowing what this will do to our prospects.

I trudge home reluctantly, knowing I probably won't sleep anyway.

FRIDAY MORNING FINDS ME BLEARY-EYED AND IN DESPERATE NEED OF CAFFEINE. After a healthy dose of coffee, I call all four companies affected. Predictably, the smaller three, while unhappy, were placated with the promise of recompense and correction of the issue going forward, but the relationship will be tenuous at best for a long time, I know. Evergreen Homes, on the other hand, fired us on the spot.

I've called an afternoon meeting with the property management team to deliver the news, and another meeting right after for Nick and me to talk with our insurance agent. It's going to be a long and discouraging afternoon.

AT SIX O'CLOCK I DECIDE TO THROW IN THE TOWEL FOR THE DAY, AS MY MIND is just not up to slogging through the forms that need to be filled out for our insurance claims. As I'm heading for the elevator, Allie appears.

"Maggie told me you'd headed out for the day," she explains. "Dinner and drinks. Now. On me."

"No argument here," I promise.

"Pub next door?" she asks.

"No, let's go someplace closer to my place so I can drop off my car," I request.

Allie raises an eyebrow. "Planning on getting stinking drunk, are we?"

"Just being smart." *And yes.*

"Okay. Not that I would blame you in any case after the day we've had," she says.

Twenty minutes later we're happily settled in a booth and I'm nursing a gin and tonic. Allie is working on the plate of fries in the middle of the table. While I know it's probably a good idea to eat something, food is the last thing on my mind.

"How did the meeting go this afternoon?" Allie inquires.

I groan. "Do we really have to talk more about work? I'm so spent," I complain.

She looks at me apologetically but doesn't retract her question.

"Fine. People were pretty upset. I'm sure they're afraid for their jobs. I tried to reassure them we aren't planning to get rid of anyone, we still manage hundreds of units, and that we'll turn that frown upside down, there are sunshine and rainbows just beyond the yellow brick road, blah, blah, blah," I grouse.

"Well, I'm sure you were very convincing," Allie says sardonically.

And we both burst out laughing.

"I believe it, I do, it just feels like we've worked so hard to get where we are … were," I correct myself with a grimace. "You know me. I'll do it again no matter how hard it is. But that doesn't mean the thought isn't utterly exhausting."

"Sounds like you need a nice, relaxing weekend," she offers suggestively.

"Ugh, don't get me started on that either. I think he's supposed to be back today. But honestly, I'm not really in the mood to see him right now," I admit.

"Trouble in paradise?" she feigns surprise. "Almost right on time."

"What the hell does that mean?"

"It means you've been … seeing him? Is that the right word? Doing him? I don't know, whatever you guys call it, for what, almost three weeks now? I've never seen anyone last more than a month," she reminds me.

I scowl. "Not really the pep talk I need right now," I snap.

She shrugs. "Sorry." And after a pause, "Is it what I told you about him? I didn't mean to cause trouble."

I take a long sip of my drink. "I think it might be," I confess. "I know I brushed it off at first. But the more I think about it, the more it bothers me. I mean, I know this isn't a real relationship, but I'm not ok with him sleeping with other women."

"Does he know that?"

"Yes. Decidedly," I pause. "Though, admittedly, while I did ask him to tell me if he wants to be with another woman while we are together, I didn't exactly specify that he should do it *before* he sleeps with someone else."

"You're worried he's been sexing it up in San Francisco," she deduces.

I nod weakly.

"Only one way to find out," says Allie. "That is, of course, assuming you trust him to tell you the truth?"

I ruminate on that for a moment. "I do, actually," I decide. "But I don't know if I'm up for hearing that kind of truth right now."

"You'd rather be in the dark?" she asks, confused.

"Lord, no. I just don't have the energy to deal with it at the moment," I reply. "It's been one of the worst weeks on record. And that's including my Third Deal Disaster."

"You mean the 'remodeled' place you bought where the previous owner had hidden more than a hundred thousand in damages, so he could unload it?" she asks. "That was a legal battle for the books, for sure. You pretty much ruined that dude's retirement with that judgment."

I shake my head. "First of all, he ruined his own damn retirement. But that was my Second Deal Calamity. My Third Deal Disaster was the chick who trashed my car and tried to set fire to the apartment building I was evicting her from because I also inadvertently outed to her deployed boyfriend that she was living with someone else." I pause. "Why the hell did I keep going? Much less start my own real estate company?"

"Uhhh, because you've made a shit-ton of money doing it?" Allie reminds me. "And, let's be honest, you love it. Catastrophes and all."

"Not today, Allie," I sigh.

Allie considers me with a knit brow. "I don't understand how you can persevere through so much professionally, but you're not willing to take the same chances for a much greater reward."

"You mean *love*?" I tease her.

"Yes, Sera, *love*. Not all guys are like Tom," says Allie. "When you find a good one, it's all worth it."

"I really don't think that's Alessandro," I laugh. Good sex? Absolutely. Soul mate? I shake my head at the thought.

"How do you know for sure if you don't give him a real shot?"

"Allie, you are Captain Mixed Message Pants," I tell her. "Didn't you recently warn me off him?"

Allie grabs my drink and sets in on the far side of the table, shoving the plate of fries under my nose. "Okay, first, no more booze for you. 'Captain Mixed Message Pants'? Honestly, Sera," she laughs. "Secondly, I don't dislike him, per se. I will always want you to be careful. I just want you to give someone a shot. Because even if it doesn't work out, I can almost guarantee you it will never be as bad as that first time."

"I definitely need to slow down on the alcohol because that almost made sense," I grouse.

"Good. Fries!" she commands. Grumpily, I comply.

∾

"Thanks, Allie, tonight was really what I needed. But you didn't have to walk me back to my building. I'm fine now," I say.

Allie hugs me tightly. "That's what friends are for," she replies. "There's David!"

A dark blue sedan pulls up and the passenger window rolls down to reveal David leaning over the passenger seat.

"Well, hello there, lovely ladies," he waggles his eyebrows. "Can I convince one of you beautiful gals to come home with me tonight?"

I point with both hands at Allie and she giggles, climbing into the car.

"Nice to see you, David," I call.

"You too, Sera, have a good night," he replies.

"Goodnight, Sera. Call me if you need to talk," Allie offers.

"Thanks, babe, see you Monday." I quickly turn so I don't have to witness their reunion and head up to my condo.

∾

Once inside, I notice I've missed a text from Alessandro. *Tonight?*

It's after ten and I just want to cocoon myself in bed and sleep off my buzz. *Can't. Hope you had a good trip.*

His response is immediate. *No kisses?*

He's in a playful mood. Great. *Rough week. Not in the mood. Ttyl.*

I turn my phone off before he can respond and head to bed.

NINE

On Saturday I do everything I can think of to keep myself busy and my mind off work — and Alessandro. By early afternoon I've run on the treadmill, showered, had breakfast, cleaned the condo, caught up on bills and emails, had lunch, and gone grocery shopping. I'm just about to start purging my closet when the phone rings.

I glance at the screen. It's Alessandro. Knowing it will only delay the inevitable not to answer, I answer.

"*Ciao*," I greet him.

"*Ciao*," he replies. "Apparently you haven't missed me as much as I missed you."

"I did miss you," I reply honestly. "It really has just been a bad week."

"How about I come over and you can tell me about it. I'll bring wine," he promises.

I hesitate. It would be nice to work through my thoughts on everything with him. He understands the issues at stake, he's smart, and logical. But I'm vulnerable right now, and not just about the issues at work.

I suddenly feel like I'm standing on a precipice. I can either pull myself back from the edge or I can fall into a dark, unknown space.

I remember Allie's advice. "Okay," I agree.

∾

When he knocks on the door I grab the handle, take a long breath, and open the door. Dressed in dark slacks, a white button up shirt, and sporting a new, close-cropped beard, he looks even more handsome than I remember. He smiles brightly as he holds both hands behind his back.

"*Ciao,*" I greet him. "Whatcha hiding back there?"

"*Ciao,*" he replies. "I said I would come bearing wine, didn't I?" And with a flourish he extends his right arm, holding not one but two bottles of wine.

I laugh appreciatively. "You sure know how to brighten up a girl's day," I joke, gesturing for him to come in.

"Ah ah ah," he protests, and with another display of fanfare, he rolls out his other hand, which is holding a dozen long-stemmed red roses swaddled in baby's breath. His expression is guarded as he measures my reaction.

I grab the front of his shirt and pull him inside, pressing my lips firmly to his. "Thank you," I say as sincerely as I can, taking the bouquet. "They are gorgeous."

"As are you," he replies, obviously pleased with my response. He follows me to the kitchen and uncorks one of the bottles while I put the flowers in a vase.

Accepting a glass gratefully, I settle onto the couch.

"How was San Francisco?" I ask warily.

He raises an eyebrow. "Unremarkable. Why don't you tell me what's going on?"

I take a long sip of wine and pull my knees to my chest.

He shakes his head lightly, slides next to me, and pulls my legs over his lap. "Much better," he murmurs. "Now, come, talk to me, Serafina. You're worrying me."

The concern that fills his soft, insistent tone unravels my nerves, and I begin to tell him everything that's happened at work.

I go slowly, making sure I'm remembering everything, describing my concerns, my devastation, my uncertainty for the future. He listens quietly and intently without interrupting, for which I'm grateful as it lets me release everything and meander freely through what has mostly been inner dialogue until now.

By the time I'm done, a few tears have found their way languidly down my face and his expression is dark. When I have no more to say, I drain my wine glass and set it on the coffee table, waiting expectantly for his response. Alessandro is silent for several more minutes.

Finally, he asks, "Your private investigator — do you trust him?"

I look at him, bemused at his choice of question. "Yes, I've worked with him for years. He came extremely highly recommended and has never given me reason to doubt him."

"That's a start," he says thoughtfully. "But this sabotage, this *betrayal,* is unacceptable." He frowns deeply. "And you've really decided not to report this woman to the authorities? Even with your most recent findings?"

"No," I reply firmly. "I agree with Peter. Everything we have is circumstantial. She didn't admit to anything, and we don't have anything to concretely tie the theft or sabotage to her."

"So, nobody is going after this woman and her consorts?" He curls his fingers into fists menacingly and a few of his knuckles crack.

"Alessandro, please, I agree it's troubling, but don't do anything foolish," I caution him.

He laughs deprecatingly. "The joy of having ridiculous amounts of money is I don't ever personally need to do anything foolish. I have people that keep me safe. That can keep you safe."

"You're not suggesting," I can barely say it, "that you have mob ties that can take care of this?"

Alessandro laughs so hard he has to put his wine glass down. "No, *bella*," he gasps when he's able to catch his breath long enough to speak. "I'm talking about private security guards." He finally calms and wipes away the tears of laughter that had leaked from his eyes. "Truly, that was the funniest thing I've heard in a long time."

My cheeks redden, and I pull my legs back to my chest. "Sorry," I mutter, ashamed at my assumption. "Okay, so private security guards. Do you really think this is as serious as all that?"

His smile slips, and he takes my hands in his. "Serafina, when it comes to you, it's as serious as all that if there's even a chance that this person wants to harm you," he insists.

I stare into his dark, troubled eyes, alarmed at the force of his conviction.

"Alessandro, I need to ask you something."

He kisses my fingers each in turn. "Anything," he responds.

"Francesca Del Vecchio. Are you sleeping with her?"

His head snaps up in surprise. He stares at me, open mouthed for a solid minute.

"My assistant?" he hisses finally. "No. I'm not sleeping with, fucking, or doing anything else with her." His eyes are like ice and he picks up our empty wine glasses, taking them into the kitchen.

"Then why has she told people at work that you two have something going?" I press, seating myself at the counter.

He closes his eyes and shakes his head. "I don't know."

"Why would she make that up?"

His eyes fly open, and they are angry and cold, and I can tell he's on the verge of losing his temper. "Who knows? I am not interested in Francesca. She has expressed interest in me in the past, which was never returned. I. Am. Not. Fucking. Her. Nor will I *ever* fuck her," he says, quiet rage echoing in each word. He pins me with a steely stare. "I've given you my word and kept it. I am yours. I have not strayed, and I will not leave until you tell me to. I think the better question is, will you ever trust me, or are we doomed to repeat these conversations ad nauseum?"

"Okay, so you haven't fucked her," I concede, ignoring his question. "But apparently she's not the only one painting the picture of you as a Lothario."

His knuckles turn white as he grips the counter. "I really don't give a fuck what people think of me," he snaps. "They should mind their own damn business."

"So, it's true?"

"Have I asked you how many men you've been with? No. Because it doesn't matter. This," he gestures between us, "is what matters. Do you really want a number? Will it make you feel better?"

He is angrier than I've ever seen him, and its sent my pulse racing. Tears sting my eyes.

"You're right, it's none of my business." My voice is barely above a whisper, the stress of the conversation, the week, crushing my ability to speak up.

"I didn't say that," he sighs, frustrated. "My sexual past is your business. But you don't *need* to know more than that I'm healthy. And in any case, we're careful. What I'm trying to say is that the rest was before. But if you really *want* to know more, if you want to know me, I'm an open book to you. Just be careful that you want me to answer the questions."

I stare morosely at the refrigerator as I process his words. "Part of me wants to know," I admit. "But not today. I can't handle any more today." My eyes fill with tears of exhaustion. I rise slowly and walk to the bathroom, where I close the door behind me and melt to the floor, silent sobs racking my body.

A few moments later the door opens softly, and Alessandro gets to his knees in front of me, pulling me into his arms. "Serafina, I'm sorry, darling, please don't cry," he begs. "I forget. You act so strong, I forget."

"Forget what?" I ask between sobs.

He raises my chin so I'm looking into his eyes.

"That you have such a tough outer shell, but you're made of glass inside," he breathes.

I sniff deeply and brusquely wipe the tears away. "I'm not so breakable as all that," I insist, slightly insulted.

"I didn't mean to offend you," he hedges. "You have a heart. A big, beautiful heart. And you carry so much on your shoulders. That's all." He cradles my face in his hands and looks deeply into my eyes.

I don't see a trace of judgment or pity. It's like he just sees right into me. And I should be scared, but somehow, here in this moment, I'm not.

I wrap my arms around his neck and allow him to sink back onto the floor, pulling me into his lap. I rest my head on his chest and I feel him wrap his arms around me.

An indeterminate amount of time later, it could be minutes, or even hours, I hear a great rumble tear through his midsection and I laugh, breaking the spell of our embrace. I stand up gently, pulling his hands until he rises too.

"Come on," I prompt. "I'm going to make you dinner."

∾

AFTER WE HAVE CLEANED THE LAST BITES FROM OUR PLATES, ALESSANDRO leans back, rubbing his stomach appreciatively.

"You're a damn fine cook, woman," he grunts.

I smirk at him. "High praise coming from you," I reply archly.

He grins widely and ferries the dishes into the kitchen. "How about we watch a movie?" he suggests. I gape at him for a moment and he laughs. "What? I need to digest," he explains.

I shrug. "Suits me."

He settles onto the end of the couch and I climb between his legs, resting my head on his chest.

I hand him the remote and bring up my digital movie library. "Pick whatever you'd like."

He starts scrolling through the list, and I wrap my arms around his torso, snuggling into him.

∾

WARM BREATH AND SOFT TONES FLUTTER ACROSS MY EYELIDS. A LOW, MELODIC hummed tune reaches my ears as I'm rocked gently. The rocking stops and something cool touches my skin briefly before the warmth and familiar scent of wine and spice wrap around me, lulling me back into nothingness.

∾

I'M WOKEN GENTLY BY THE SOFT LIGHT OF EARLY MORNING. I'VE BEEN stripped to my underwear and I'm in my bed. I roll onto my side to see Alessandro sleeping soundly next to me, naked from the looks of it. I watch him sleep for a few minutes, noting fine wrinkles from the laugh lines he gets at the corners of his eyes and mouth, and a faint line on his forehead. Without the myriad of unpredictable expressions that constantly flit across his face, he looks stern and distinguished, his thick eyebrows set in a hard line over his dark lashes, and his full mouth in a slight natural downturn. Unconsciously, I run a finger over the corner of his mouth and across his firm, square chin in the same way he habitually strokes it himself.

His fingers wrap around mine, bringing my hand to his lips for a kiss as he opens his eyes. "*Buongiorno dolcezza*," he murmurs sleepily, wrapping his arms around me and pulling me closer. "I like sleeping with you. Why don't we sleep here more often? Your bed is better than mine, I think."

I nuzzle into his chest and consider whether to tell him it was my way of keeping him in a box. Last night ended so comfortably, and he looks so happy that I decide against it. "I hadn't thought much about it," I lie.

"Well, I like it," he declares. "And not just because we actually just slept together."

"What does that mean?" I ask, amused.

He grins down at me. "It means you're starting to trust me," he replies.

I consider for a moment and decide there's probably some truth to that. And strangely I'm still not freaking out.

"Maybe," I reply slyly. "Or maybe I'm just lulling you into a false sense of security, so I can take advantage of you." I roll him abruptly onto his back and straddle him, running my hands up his chest and leaning in to kiss him deeply.

He wraps his arms around me and sighs contentedly. "I can live with that," he says, tracing my lips with his fingers, then running his hands down my back. I can feel him hardening beneath me, and he tugs at the hem of my panties. "Off," he demands. "Condoms?"

I climb over him, off the bed and point to the nightstand on my side of the bed. As he retrieves his quarry, I remove my panties and slide into bed behind him, capturing him with my hand as he turns to me. Stroking him evenly, I trace the lines of his torso with my tongue, dropping the occasional kiss as I work my way downward. Replacing my hand with my mouth, I take him in all at once, eliciting a deep groan of pleasure.

With him fully in my mouth, I work my tongue on the underside of him, lengthening and hardening him. I watch as each pull makes his breath come harder, his moans louder. When I sense he is close, I retreat, sitting back and taking him in for a moment. His breathing slows, and he gazes at me imploringly.

He goes to reach for me, and I lazily roll my hand up the length of him and back down. He falls back onto his elbows, throwing his head back in pleasure. I stroke him harder until he's panting again. And then I stop.

He goes to move for me again, and I descend upon him using both mouth and hands in a frenzy of motion, torturing him to the edge before stopping once more. He groans in frustration.

"What do you want?" I prompt him.

He stares at me hungrily, recognition in his eyes. "Fuck me, Serafina," he begs.

"Oh, I love hearing you say that," I grin, quickly retrieving the condom and slipping it onto him. Swinging my leg over him, I descend roughly and begin to ride him. I draw his hands to my breasts and he strokes my nipples, causing my cries to meld with his.

I grind on top of him, thrusting him deeply until I'm on the brink. As I topple over the edge, I lean forward, screaming his name loudly as waves of orgasm crash through my body. Utterly spent by the rapid ascent into passion, I slide onto the bed beside him.

He doesn't move, either, and I breathlessly manage, "Did you…?"

He nods. "Screaming too loud to notice?" he smiles.

Now I nod, and he laughs his deep, throaty laugh.

When we've caught our breath and cleaned up, I pull on a T-shirt and panties and head into the kitchen to make breakfast.

As I'm grilling French toast, Alessandro emerges in his undershirt and boxer briefs, looking just-sexed rumpled and ridiculously hot. He grabs me from behind and runs his hands over my breasts. "You're all kinds of distracting," he murmurs into my ear, pressing his hips into my backside. "I have half a mind to take you on the counter."

I turn and hand him a plate of French toast. "Then you better eat something to keep your strength up," I tease him. Glaring facetiously, he takes the plate and sits at the bar. I join him shortly, and we both tuck into our food like we haven't eaten in weeks.

I look over at him with a full mouth to see his cheeks bulging and we both laugh, bits of French toast and syrup spraying over the bar, which only makes us laugh harder. I manage to swallow my mouthful, and I use my napkin to wipe bits off his chin and shirt. He playfully kisses my neck with his mouth still half full.

I beam serenely and go about finishing my breakfast.

While Alessandro cleans up from breakfast, I pop into the shower. As I'm rinsing the soap from my body, he enters the bathroom and strips.

"Mind if I join you?" he inquires.

I gaze keenly at his gorgeous body. "Not at all," I respond.

He jumps in beside me, and I run my wet hands over his chest, leaving a lingering kiss on his lips. "I was just finishing up."

"Good, now I can get you all dirty again," he replies, running his fingers between my breasts, over my stomach, and along my sex before sliding them into me.

I'm extra sensitive from our exploits first thing this morning, and I groan pleasurably and wrap my arm around his neck, sinking into him for support. My other hand finds his stiff cock under the hot water, and I work him to the same rhythm he's working me.

He pushes me against the wall of the shower, leaning his head on the cool tile behind me and groaning into my ear. The sounds of his enjoyment spur me on, and I stroke him harder and faster. He responds in kind, and we continue to urge each other on with our hands and voices until I'm screaming in ecstasy, barely managing to stay upright as he also finishes in my hand.

His mouth finds mine under the steaming stream of water and I'm lost to the feel of his hard, wet body against mine.

❧

UNSURPRISINGLY, THE DAY FINDS US ABED FOR THE MOST PART.

"I think it's time to decide which nickname I'm going to call you," Alessandro declares as he runs his fingers up and down my arm.

I scrunch my brow, confused. "You already call me Sera sometimes," I respond. "That is my nickname."

He laughs. "True," he allows. "But I was thinking more of a nickname only I call you."

"You mean a *pet name?*" I ask, aghast.

"I don't know why the suggestion offends you so. I've already given you several, if you hadn't noticed," he replies. "You can pick which you like best."

"I think you called me 'darling' once or twice," I reply, "but I don't remember any others."

He smiles. "In English, yes. Perhaps you don't speak as much Italian as I thought," he muses. "There's also been *bella, dolcezza,* and *mio tesoro.*" He ticks each off on his fingers. I stare at him blankly. "Beautiful, sweetheart, and my darling."

He regards me carefully. "I was only testing them out to see how they sounded. If you don't like any of those, you can pick a different one," he offers.

"No," I say, blushing. "I had no idea. I like those. You pick."

"Hmmm," he muses. "*Bella* is good, but so common. Everyone Italian and American with the '*Ciao, bella!*' all day long."

"So, no," I laugh, resisting the urge to point out that he, too, frequently uses the expression.

"No," he replies. "*Dolcezza* is a nice word, but a little too sappy for general use, I think. But *mio tesoro* I like."

"Why?"

"Because I get to say you're mine," he says softly, his eyes warm and inviting.

I find myself both touched and, finally, scared by his sentiment. Attempting to lighten the mood, I offer, "I can live with that, but I get to give you a nickname too. How about I call you 'buttercup'?"

He laughs heartily. "No. Decidedly not," he responds.

I turn my head to look up at him ponderously, searching for something a little less intimate. "How about Alex? Isn't 'Alessandro' the Italian version of 'Alexander'? Seems like that would work."

His brow furrows. "Yes," he replies shortly. "But it's not a pet name." A dark look passes over his face. He disentangles himself and rises from the bed.

"Have I offended you?" I ask, bemused.

"No," he sighs, pulling on his pants. "It's just not a name I want to be called from your lips."

"Sorry," I mutter self-consciously, pulling on my own clothing. "Let's just drop it." I push past him to leave, but he grabs my arm.

"No, I'm sorry," he apologizes, wrapping me in his arms. He sighs resignedly. "I told you once I was an open book to you. And I meant that. When I was younger, I did go by 'Alex.' But at some point, I decided there were too many bad memories associated with it. So, I started going by my full name."

"Ah," I say. "I see."

"Call me anything else you like. I just don't want to be 'Alex' again," he says pleadingly.

I stand on my toes and kiss him lightly. "Okay, buttercup," I whisper.

◡

ALESSANDRO RETURNS HOME FOR THE EVENING AND I'M LEFT TO CRAWL INTO bed alone. But the memory of his warmth, of our deepening connection, and the amazing moments in his arms help me drift peacefully to sleep, ready to face whatever comes next.

TEN

id-Monday morning I'm at my desk poring over monthly reports when Maggie buzzes me.

"Ms. Evans? I have Charles Sutton on the line for you."

My heart races in anticipation. "Thanks Maggie, I'll take his call now."

I slowly draw in a couple of long, deep breaths to steady myself before picking up the phone.

"Mr. Sutton, I'm so glad to hear from you," I greet him.

"Ms. Evans," he replies brusquely. "Perhaps you should wait to hear what I have to say before you get too excited."

My heart beats harder and faster, and my breath catches in my throat. "Of course, sir, what can I do for you?" I reply as steadily as I can.

"We heard a rumor last week that you had some sort of software issue that created some costly issues for your clients," he puts forth baldly. "Now, we were ready to sign on the dotted line, but naturally this has given us pause for concern."

Fuck. How on God's green earth did he hear that so quickly?

"Completely understandable," I reply smoothly. "And I hope I can allay any hesitations on your part."

"I certainly hope so too," he responds. "Are you able to tell me what happened?"

"Yes, sir. It was, unfortunately, due to tampering by an employee who has been discovered and let go. We've done a full security scan and isolated the issue to two property management report parameters which did, unfortunately, create performance and cost issues for several clients, all of which we took full and immediate responsibility for, both professionally and financially," I assure him. "It's given us the opportunity to review our position and procedures, and strengthen our systems and processes going forward. I can give you my full assurances that this was an entirely isolated incident that I have never experienced in nearly five successful years of running this business, and that I am taking every measure possible to ensure nothing like this ever happens again."

My words are met with silence and I count ten of my own frantic heartbeats before he responds.

"I'm glad to hear you've taken responsibility and are taking the appropriate measures," and I can hear the "but" coming, "but with such a large financial hit, will your company have the resources it needs to fulfill the terms of this contract?"

"Without a doubt," I say without hesitation. "I am a woman of my word, Mr. Sutton, as evidenced by our instantly bringing this to our client's attentions, owning the issue, and seeing that action was taken as soon as possible to make our clients whole again. I've been in this business long enough to have dealt with my fair share of trials, and I've got a track record that proves my ability to take them in stride and come out on top. The real estate business isn't for people who can't handle problems like this and turn it for their betterment."

"I like your attitude," he says. "Nonetheless, I propose we add a quick exit clause in case the remaining fallout renders you unable to perform any of the duties under the contract. One that doesn't require litigation to terminate the contract."

"As in, you can walk away anytime with no repercussions, no strings attached?" I ask.

"More or less, yes."

I ponder that for a moment. I'm not sure I have much of a choice, and I think he knows that.

"I can agree to the spirit of that, but I need the clause to stipulate that all expenses for work completed to date will be paid in full," I counter.

It's a minute before he responds. "I'll want detailed invoices twice a week."

Twice a week? Bit of a control freak, are we? Then again, if I were in his shoes, I'd probably ask for the same thing. Maybe more, even.

"That sounds perfectly reasonable, sir," I respond.

"Then we have a deal, Ms. Evans. I'll have my attorneys revise the paperwork for signatures this afternoon. Can you be at our offices at two?" he inquires.

"Absolutely, Mr. Sutton," I say, relieved. "I'll see you this afternoon."

After we've hung up, I consider my predicament. Alessandro's concerns rattle around my brain. I decide that there's more than a chance of harm coming from this situation, and not just for me personally, but for the dozens of employees relying on me. I call Maggie in.

"Yes, Ms. Evans?"

"Maggie, I want you to find a highly recommended corporate security firm. I want to schedule an in-house consultation and full review of our current situation, with an eye to implement new procedures across the board as necessary to secure our office, systems, records, and anything else they see fit to recommend," I direct her.

"Yes, Ms. Evans," Maggie says, quickly making notes.

"I'll be meeting with Mr. Sutton this afternoon at two p.m., otherwise you have my current schedule. I'd like a meeting as soon as possible." She nods. "Oh, and Maggie?" She pauses at the door and looks back inquiringly. "If they also cover personal security, so much the better."

"I'll see what I can find, ma'am."

⁓

CHARLES SUTTON IS A FORMIDABLE MAN IN HIS LATE FIFTIES. HIS SHORT, DARK hair is peppered with silver, and he wears a no-nonsense dark grey suit that looks like it easily costs as much as my first car did. He also wears a no-nonsense demeanor.

But it's not for nothing I've successfully grown my company in a field filled with men like him. A mix of frankness, a thick skin, and being difficult to intimidate have gotten me far in this business.

As the notary hands each of us our copies of the documents that have now been signed, he rises from his seat at the head of the table and shakes my hand firmly. I return in kind, keeping eye contact while smiling agreeably.

"I look forward to working with you, Mr. Sutton."

He inclines his head to me. "And I look forward to seeing if you live up to the hype," he replies shrewdly. "Recent unpleasant events aside, of course."

I laugh genuinely. "You're not a bullshitter, sir," I say. "I think this will work out well for everyone."

He chuckles and releases my hand, gesturing for me to precede him out of the conference room.

⁓

BACK IN MY OFFICE, I ALLOW MYSELF A SMALL HAPPY DANCE AROUND MY chair. I'm so gleefully enjoying my return to success after recent events that I don't hear Maggie come in. As I round my chair, I notice her watching me, a very surprised expression on her face.

"Maggie!" I exclaim, blushing a little. "Just celebrating our new contract. What can I do for you?"

She laughs nervously. "Congratulations, Ms. Evans," she says. "I just wanted to catch you before your project management tag-up. I've scheduled you with Hoyt Corporate Services for one p.m. tomorrow afternoon. They were highly recommended by multiple sources for corporate security."

"Wonderful! Is that all?" She seems very unnerved by my uncharacteristically chipper demeanor.

"That's all," she replies, backing uncertainly out of the room.

"Okay, off to my meeting then," I grab my laptop and breeze past her, chuckling to myself at her bemused expression.

IN THE MEETING WITH MY PROPERTY MANAGEMENT TEAM, I INSTRUCT THE LEAD project manager, Ana Englund, to oversee redistribution of the approximately two hundred remaining units among the other nine team members and to focus on researching area properties ripe for a property management switch. The team continues to seem understandably uncertain about the drastic reduction in workload, and I do my best to reassure them of my commitment to their positions and our recovery as a company. Leaving the conference room, I wonder to myself if it will be enough.

THE NEXT MORNING, I HAVE MY ANSWER IN THE FORM OF THE FIRST PROPERTY manager resignation — Sam Nichols, who has served one of our smaller clients exclusively for almost three years. He is apologetic but is concerned for his growing family and admitted to having been looking for a larger, more stable company for some time. I'm not surprised, though I am still disappointed. As I watch him leave for Allie's office, I wonder how many more there will be before all is said and done.

THAT AFTERNOON, SHORTLY BEFORE ONE P.M., MAGGIE BUZZES ME TO LET ME know that Bryce Hoyt of Hoyt Corporate Services has arrived.

"See him to the conference room and let him know that I'll be there shortly," I instruct her. I finish the email I was writing and gather my things.

On the short walk to the conference room I observe the usual hustle and bustle of the office on a weekday afternoon. Everything seems so normal, despite the fallout from the recent sabotage. But I sigh inwardly, knowing it all hangs on a thread.

As I enter the conference room, Mr. Hoyt stands to greet me. I'm taken aback instantly by his rugged good looks. He's probably in his early thirties, easily six-foot-four, with a broad, strong frame, chestnut brown hair, and bright blue eyes. He wears a well-tailored navy suit and smiles warmly as he extends his hand, which I take.

"Ms. Evans," he says in a deep baritone. "So nice to meet you." His handshake is firm and warm, and he exudes a calm strength.

"Mr. Hoyt," I reply, "I appreciate your taking a meeting with me so quickly." I release his hand and gesture for him to have a seat.

Once he returns to his chair, I seat myself across the table from him and set my things beside me.

"Call me Bryce, please. It worked out well, as we had a cancellation this afternoon," he explains.

"Their loss, my gain, then, Bryce," I reply. "And please, call me Sera. I've done some preliminary research on your company and was most impressed. Your company has a long history of happy and, most importantly, secure customers."

"When my grandfather started the company over forty years ago after leaving the FBI, he felt very strongly about avoiding red tape, jargon, and any other barriers to the everyday Joe or Josephine," he smiles, "being able to protect the businesses they'd built."

"I'm glad to hear it. Unfortunately, I'm in need of a little more protection than I'd like to be. I'm afraid I didn't think to engage your services soon enough," I say.

"That's not a problem, I'm here to help," he says, leaning toward me. "Why don't we start, then, with you telling me what's going on."

"The short version?" I sigh.

He smiles indulgently. "Whichever version you'd prefer."

I huff a small laugh and gather my thoughts. "A little more than two weeks ago we discovered a theft from our petty cash of four hundred dollars. I engaged a private investigator and through him was able to discover that one of our employees had made a cash rent payment in that exact amount the day after the money went missing. We confronted the employee. While she wouldn't admit to it, her reaction was troubling." I grimace. "She was immediately terminated."

"What troubled you about her reaction?" he presses curiously.

"She told my HR director that we couldn't make her admit to anything," I pause. "And to tell me to go fuck myself."

He laughs. "That seems like a pretty normal reaction, if you ask me," he replies.

"Except I've never met the woman that I can recall," I explain. "She was a part-time receptionist for whom we made allowances in changing her schedule to accommodate her education. Even for part-time employees we cover a portion of health insurance and offer a myriad of other benefits. We go out of our way to source good employees and treat them well."

"I see. Well, that does make her reaction somewhat odd," he allows. "Go on."

"After her dismissal we discovered that someone had tampered with our property management software," I say. "There were business and financial damages to four of our clients, one of whom represented more than half of the units we managed."

"Managed? Past tense?"

I nod. "They terminated our services as soon as they were told. Some of the issues required us to go through our insurance to ensure each client received full restitution for their damages. It also put a pending deal in jeopardy, though I was fortunately able to save that."

He gives me an assessing glance, clearly impressed, and I can't help but blush a little. "Your assistant mentioned on the phone that you are also interested in personal security. Do you have reason to believe this woman is dangerous?" he asks.

"I don't know," I admit. "The people closest to me are concerned. Will, our IT person, says he was aware of her programming skills and doesn't think she would have been able to accomplish the software damage on her own. I guess I'm concerned, too."

"I'd say you have reason to be," he agrees. "Have you filed a police report?"

"No. My PI suggested there isn't much that would accomplish," I explain. "That all of the evidence is circumstantial."

"At this point there isn't much they would do, that's true," he allows. "However, if there are issues in the future it would help establish a pattern of behavior."

I blink hard. "I hadn't thought of that."

"That's why I'm here, Sera," he replies kindly. "I suggest we meet with the rest of your team as soon as possible and start going over the various parts of your business to refine your security measures."

"Absolutely," I respond.

"Okay, you may want to write this part down, so you can bring what's needed to discuss the various aspects of protecting your business," he pauses so I can bring up the notepad on my laptop. "Human resources will want to bring their hiring documents and procedures, copies of all background checks and re-checks for employees and clients."

"We haven't done any background checks on clients," I interrupt.

"Then we'll want to do those right away," he replies, making a note. "We'll also want to review badging systems and employee training procedures. That should get us started from the people side of things."

I finish my notes and nod for him to continue. "I'll need to know from your IT person the firewall details, what kind of encryptions are used on your hard disks, if any, and the names of all software you use."

"What about in-house solutions?" I ask.

"You've created your own software?" he replies, obviously stunned.

"Mainly to connect outputs of various systems for our own reporting needs," I explain.

"Then I'll need the details on all that code and, eventually, access," he replies. "But in all honesty, in almost all cases having ad-hoc software solutions is extremely unsafe."

Will is not going to like this guy.

"Are your phones landline or VoIP?"

"Landlines," I respond. "Less secure?"

"No, actually, you're better off keeping your landlines," he replies. "I also didn't see any security cameras?"

"Correct," I confirm.

"That's an easy change. I'll bring some information on systems sized for the office, so I'll need a tour when we're done here. They range in price and obviousness, which I'll be prepared to go over with you," he explains. "And just to make sure we're on the same page, you do understand that this will be an ongoing process and partnership? We will, of course, let you know what our recommendations are and the cost for those services after our initial consultation, but maintenance of your security plan as your business grows is just as crucial."

"Absolutely," I agree emphatically. "I'm honestly a little embarrassed I hadn't thought about it sooner."

He shrugs. "I think most people want to trust their employees and their clients," he replies. "It's understandable."

I can't help but laugh and he cocks an eyebrow, clearly confused.

"The irony there being I'm not a particularly trusting person," I explain.

He considers me for a moment. "Do you have issues delegating?" he asks.

I laugh again. "You could say that," I reply. "I have to out of necessity, I suppose, but it's very difficult for me."

He examines my face carefully for a moment. "That's a lot for one person, Sera," he says softly. "Let's talk about a full delegation plan, too." He makes another note.

"Is that a security issue?" I tease.

He smiles indulgently. "It may not seem like one, but concentration of power is actually a problem," he explains. "When a lot of people rely on you, being the only one who knows how to run everything, who makes all the decisions — that can cause some serious business-flow problems. You need to be able to take a sick day, take a vacation, or otherwise just step away and have the business continue to run in your absence."

"That's a good point," I admit. "I can't remember the last time I was sick and didn't just work through it." He makes another note. "Uh, you didn't need to write that part down." I blush, and he laughs.

"So, the last thing to discuss today — personal security. I'd like to do a home review as soon as possible and discuss your usual routine."

"That sounds reasonable," I respond. "I'm usually in the office until around six or seven each evening. I'm free any night this week."

"How about tomorrow then? Say eight p.m.?"

I make a note. "Sounds good. If that's all, I can give you the office tour now."

"That's all," he agrees, rising. "After you, Sera."

❧

As I conduct his tour, nearly every woman in the place follows Bryce's progress over the floor, and some of the men too, for that matter. He makes a sketch and covers it with notes as we loop around the office. As we approach reception, Lucy eyes him appraisingly, tossing her long, black hair over her shoulder coyly.

He shakes my hand firmly, holding eye contact. "It's been great meeting you, Sera," he says genuinely. "I sincerely believe we'll be able to help you safeguard your business." He pulls my hand gently so that we both are leaning in slightly, "And, more importantly, you."

For a heartbeat the chemistry is palpable in the air. He gives me a dazzling smile and lets my hand go.

I smile back giddily. "I look forward to it," I reply. I watch him climb into the elevator, and he gives me a little wave as the doors close. I do my best to ignore Lucy's knowing smirk as I pass by.

As I enter my office, I'm surprised to find Alessandro sitting in one of the chairs opposite my desk.

"Alessandro!" I exclaim. "You startled me. What can I do for you?"

He rises and closes the office door. "Who's your new boyfriend?" His tone is dangerous.

And I'm zero to mad in three seconds flat. "You can't seriously think that was anything but business," I retort.

"You looked pretty friendly," he says in a flat voice.

"Yes, we were," I say firmly, "because he's from the corporate security company. He was here to discuss our *security* needs."

He has the good grace to look surprised and ashamed. "I didn't know."

"Well you could've asked before accusing me of openly cheating in front of you and everyone else in the office," I respond, pouting.

"That would require everyone else in the office to know you have someone to cheat *on*," he points out.

I throw my hands up. "You want me to go around and tell everyone I'm fucking you? Fine." I make for the door and he grabs my arm.

"Don't be a child," he snaps. "And I'd say we graduated past 'fucking' this weekend, wouldn't you?"

"Not really, no," I reply obstinately.

His mouth tightens into a hard line. "Have it your way, then," he replies, and leaves.

I don't hear from him the rest of the day. As I'm drifting to sleep, his angry words echo in my head and weave into my nightmares.

ELEVEN

The next evening, I meet Bryce in the lobby of my building to start the home security assessment. He arrives right on time, this time in a pair of faded jeans and fitted white T-shirt. In his casual clothes his large muscles are unmistakably on full display. I smooth my hands nervously over my black, knee-length shirtdress that is hopelessly wrinkled from the day.

"Hey, Sera," he greets me, grasping my hand firmly.

"Hey, Bryce," I return.

He smiles brightly and I'm a bit giddy again — his pleasant nature is ridiculously infectious. "I'm going to start with your concierge, if that's okay? I just want to ask him a few questions about the building's security features," he explains.

My phone pings. "Sounds good, I'll just see what this is while you do that."

He heads off, and I watch him hand his business card to the older gentleman at the desk before I look down at my phone.

It's a text from Alessandro. *I think we should talk.* I'm angered that he thinks that's a good way to start a conversation after he stormed out and didn't talk to me for more than a day.

Can't, busy. Having a security assessment of my place. I hit "send" a little more furiously than I intend to and take a deep breath to calm myself.

His response comes quickly. *By the giant?*

I roll my eyes. *His name is Bryce Hoyt.* Looking up, I see Bryce heading back toward me, so I put my phone to silent and drop it back in my pocket.

"Okay, got what I needed," he says. "Shall we go up?"

❦

I'M STANDING IN THE KITCHEN MAKING TEA AND ANSWERING BRYCE'S questions about my routine as he examines the doors, windows, and fire escape when someone knocks on the door.

Bryce stops what he's doing and gives me a look. "Expecting someone?" he asks.

"No, but it's okay, keep going," I gesture to him as I go to answer the door.

He shrugs and heads to climb out the window onto the fire escape. I swing the door open to reveal a clearly piqued Alessandro.

"Darling," he says exuberantly, "I missed you." He strides in and makes a show of kissing me passionately.

I push him away firmly, frowning. "Are you out of your mind?" I demand in a hushed tone.

His eyes narrow and his voice drops to a whisper. "Yes," he hisses. "I tend to get that way when the woman I'm with doesn't tell me a handsome, young stranger will be in her apartment at night."

"So, you came to mark your territory?" I retort quietly. "Would you like to piss all over the apartment, or perhaps you could just challenge him to a duel?"

He glowers at me as Bryce climbs back in the window, looking at me questioningly.

I clear my throat and try to wipe the angry expression from my face.

"Bryce, this is…"

Alessandro throws his arm around me and extends his hand. "I'm Alessandro Giordano, Sera's boyfriend," he offers.

My head whips toward Alessandro, my nostrils flaring, mashing my lips into a hard line to contain my outraged response.

"I'm Bryce Hoyt, doing a personal security evaluation for Ms. Evans," Bryce replies formally, giving me a concerned side glance. "It's nice to meet you, Mr. Giordano."

"I'm glad you're here Bryce, I want my girl well take care of," Alessandro says, squeezing my shoulder.

I shrug his arm off me and return to the kitchen in disgust, trying to suppress the shaking rage that's rippling through me.

"Understandably," Bryce replies. "Though I wouldn't discount how well she's done for herself up until now. She seems like a very smart woman." He smiles at me reassuringly and it melts my anger for a moment. I give him a grateful smile in return.

Alessandro stares at him icily.

"Who wants tea?" I interrupt, hoping to dissipate the tension in the room.

"I'm actually done here, I think," Bryce replies, giving Alessandro a nervous glance. "I'll be in touch soon."

"Thanks, Bryce, I really appreciate it," I reply, showing him out the door.

"Talk to you soon, Sera," he says, giving me one last small smile before he goes.

I close the door behind him and count to three. I turn slowly and stare at Alessandro, who has settled himself on the couch.

"Ready to talk?" he asks pointedly.

"No," I reply angrily, marching into the kitchen.

He approaches the bar. "Don't be like that," he urges.

I slam the teapot back onto the stove and turn the burner off. "No, *you* don't be like that," I retort. "How dare you come over here unannounced to claim me like I'm your property? And to refer to yourself as my boyfriend — without even talking to me about how I'd feel about that — un-fucking-believable. That's what you are." I can practically feel the steam coming out of my ears, and my hands are shaking.

He rounds the counter, putting only the kitchen island between us. "What was I supposed to do? Don't you see the way he looks at you?" he demands. "You invited someone who is practically a stranger into your home. One who was willing to undress you with his eyes in front of everyone. God only knows what he'd do in private." He seems perfectly composed except for his tone, which radiates fury and wrath.

Privately, I'm pleased that he's upset, given how much he's upset me. Outwardly, I scoff. "Don't be ridiculous. I thoroughly investigated his company. I would never have agreed to him being here if I thought he or his company was in any way questionable. Don't treat me like I'm stupid."

"Do you want to fuck him? Is that it?"

Every word he utters stokes the fire of my fury. I despise being treated like a child. Like my word means nothing. And his petty accusation is both untrue and unfair. He can flirt with every woman in sight, but I so much as speak to another man and this is what I get? I have to suppress the urge to throw things, to scream at him. Instead, I close my eyes, hoping when I open them I will stop seeing red.

"No, Alessandro. I didn't want to fuck him," I say carefully, as calmly as I can manage. I open my eyes and stare at him, still fuming. "The only person I want to fuck is you."

In a flash, he rounds the island and pulls me to him, claiming my lips with his, my body with his hands. The turmoil inside me responds to his hot, rough touch, and my body screams to release its anger and tension in carnal conquest. I kiss him back ferociously, my hands tearing his shirt buttons open, then quickly opening his belt and zipper.

He lifts me onto the counter, sliding my shirtdress up over my hips, and rips my panties off viciously, sheathing himself quickly with a condom. Then, throwing my legs over each of his shoulders, he pulls me to him and violently takes me. He's leaned over me, gripping my thighs tightly, eye shut firmly as we set a frantic rhythm. Every powerful lunge mixes my anger with my desire until I'm screaming in furious pleasure, egging on the enraged pounding of flesh on flesh. I climax quickly, my body arching off the counter. My muscles clench around him, and he growls gutturally in orgasm.

After a moment, he pulls away and falls back against the refrigerator, panting heavily. As he discards the used condom in the kitchen bin, I climb down from the countertop and retrieve my panties while he rights his clothing. He watches me silently, his eyes narrow and dark.

"Now get the fuck out," I demand. I go to my bedroom and slam the door behind me.

A moment later I hear the front door close sharply.

⌘

ALLIE COMES OVER IN RECORD TIME, RESPONDING TO THE ANGUISH IN MY voice, even though it's late on a work night. We sit under a blanket on the couch, passing a pint of chocolate caramel chunk ice cream back and forth.

"So, he just left?" she asks in awe.

I nod glumly. "And I know I told him to, but..."

"You wanted him to stay?"

"No. I just wish I hadn't been so *angry* at him," I admit.

Allie hands me the last of the pint and doesn't say a word.

"What?" I prompt her.

"You're not gonna like it," she promises.

I shrug. "I pretty much feel like shit right now anyway, Allie, just spit it out."

"You have feelings for him," she says.

I savor the last spoonful of caramelly, chocolatey comfort as I weigh her words.

"Anger is a feeling, yes," I hedge, and she rolls her eyes.

"You know what I mean, Sera," she insists.

I sigh and put the empty carton and spoon on the coffee table. "I don't know what I feel. I've spent so long trying to avoid doing exactly that." I pause. "I thought I could contain my relationship with him to only the things I wanted to feel."

She shakes her head vehemently. "You know that's not how it works."

"I know," I say, and I feel small and overwhelmed. And foolish.

"Tell me what he's made you feel. Besides angry," she says wryly.

"The good stuff or the bad stuff?"

She hesitates. "Start with the bad stuff."

"Besides angry? Scared, confused, and jealous, just off the top of my head," I list.

"And the good?" she prompts.

I think about this one for a moment. "Sexy. Desired. But he also listens to me. More than that, he understands me," I admit. "And I've felt more alive since this started. Before him I was so engrossed in my routine. I didn't realize how lifeless I was." I pause. "He has pet names for me," I admit sheepishly.

"And how does that make you feel?" she asks.

"Well, doctor," I joke, leaning back on the couch pillows.

"Seriously, Sera," she insists.

"At first it made me feel…" I grasp for the right word. "Cherished? Then it just scared the shit out of me."

"It sounds like he wants to be with you, Sera. Like really be with you. And it sounds like you want that too, until your fear kicks in."

"Obviously, if he's going around telling perfect strangers that he's my boyfriend," I gripe.

"He was *jealous*," she says, exasperated. "I'm not excusing his behavior, but that's a pretty normal reaction. What did he say when you got jealous of Francesca?"

"He was angry at first. But when he calmed down he told me he wanted me to know that I can come to him with anything, ask him anything." As complicated as Alessandro is at times, she's right — he obviously wants to try.

Allie presses her fingers to her temples. "I'm going to cut to the chase here, because it's late and we have work tomorrow. Think about how he makes you feel, good and bad. Picture his face," she directs me. "Do you want to end it with him? Or is there enough good for you to fight your fears and frustrations and give this guy a real shot?"

I sigh heavily and rise to clean up.

Standing in the kitchen, I place my hands on the kitchen island, remembering our exploits from earlier in the evening.

"I want to give it a real shot," I admit. "I just don't know how. And after tonight, he may not want to anymore anyway."

Allie approaches the kitchen bar. "Tell him, Sera," she pushes. "Give him the chance to tell you what *he* wants."

I glance at the clock. It's almost eleven. "Not tonight," I reply. I approach Allie and embrace her tightly. "Thanks for talking me off the ledge, Allie."

"Anytime," she offers, squeezing me back. "Goodnight, babe, love you."

I let her go and walk her to the door. "Love you too."

When she's gone, I fall fully clothed onto my bed. I let the small well of exhausted tears fall and close my eyes, surrendering to my fatigue.

∾

I throw myself into the Sutton Developments project the next day, pounding through piles of preliminary research to build a base for one of our project managers to start from. It feels good to turn myself over to the Serafina that used to shut off the world and lose herself in the details of a project, emerging only for caffeine and bathroom breaks.

My staff seems to sense my reclusiveness, as the few times I emerge throughout the day their conversations cease and they scatter back to their desks, pretending to be working diligently. It would make me laugh if I wasn't still so out of sorts.

Just as I'm about to head home at six, an email hits my inbox from Hoyt Corporate Services with their proposal. I open it eagerly and skim the contents. It's lengthy, but the bottom line seems more than reasonable. I save a copy to my desktop for perusal after dinner and pack up to head home.

Sitting at the kitchen bar, I've finished my lonely dinner and am sipping a glass of wine while reading the rest of the contract when my eyes wander to the kitchen island. I stare at it for a moment and a wave of shame washes over me at the way I treated Alessandro. I eye my computer for a moment, then snap it closed, decided that I'll finish my review in the morning. I grab my keys and purse and head out the door.

I knock softly, my stomach in knots. Part of me is hopeful and excited. But when the door opens that evaporates when I see Francesca standing in the doorway. All long, dark hair and big, red lips. She is clothed, thankfully, but barefoot. I'm too shocked to speak.

"Alessandro, *qualcuno a vederti*," she purrs toward the living room.

Alessandro appears behind her, sexily clad in black sweatpants and a black T-shirt, and he's also barefoot. When he sees me he stops cold and glances guiltily at Francesca. His shamefaced expression rips my heart out of my chest and I back away from the door.

I try to form an excuse, but the words won't come, and I turn to flee.

"Serafina, stop!" he calls commandingly. He catches up to me easily before I can get anywhere near the elevator.

I try frantically to hold back the tears a moment longer, but it's a dicey proposition. "I shouldn't have shown up unannounced," I say thickly. He shakes his head and his expression is heartbreakingly sad, but he doesn't reach for me.

"I didn't expect you," he says awkwardly.

I laugh drily. "That much is obvious."

"It's not what you think," he says, predictably.

"I very highly doubt you know what I'm thinking right now," I say sharply.

"Fine, it's not what it looks like," he clarifies. "I wanted to give you some space. We're just working." He finally touches me, tentatively sliding his hand in mine. When he realizes I won't pull away, he guides me back to the apartment, and I follow reluctantly.

He releases me and pushes the door open to reveal Francesca deep in conversation with Marco, who is similarly casually dressed in jeans and a sweater. Chinese food takeout containers litter the coffee table, and there are stacks of documents and blueprints everywhere.

"Oh," I say meekly, ashamed.

"We're almost finished," he promises. "You can stay, if you want. Or I can come over when we're done."

"I'm already here," I say timidly. "I'll just stay out of the way until everyone's gone."

"Come," he prompts, leading me down the hallway. He opens the door to a room I've never been in before. Overflowing bookshelves line the walls, and a large desk occupies the far corner of the room. "You can wait here," he points to an overstuffed chair. "Be back soon."

I set my bag on the chair and peruse the shelves. Many of the books are in Italian, so I can only make out a few titles here and there. The books in English cover a wide variety of subjects, from car maintenance to classic literature.

As I flip through a beautifully illustrated book on Da Vinci, Alessandro reappears. He leans against the doorframe and regards me sternly. I slip the book back into its place on the shelf and face him.

He continues to watch me silently for a few moments, then turns and walks out of the room. Assuming he wants me to, I follow him into the living room. I look around, noting that everyone has gone. He gestures for me to take a seat on the couch. I sit and wait nervously for him to break the silence.

He runs a finger along his chin and my heart jumps. I want to reach out and touch him, to fix what is broken, but I remain still.

Finally, he speaks. "Before I say anything else," he begins, "I owe you an apology for my behavior last night. You were right, I had no business showing up unannounced and declaring us as something we'd explicitly agreed not to be."

"Apology accepted," I say quietly. He offers a grim smile that doesn't reach his eyes. "But?" I prompt.

"But," he agrees, "whether you're willing to admit it or not, we've progressed past a casual relationship. Neither of us is treating this like just sex. And you were right — I want you to be mine, to be with me completely. But not if you're going to treat me the way you did last night."

"Alessandro, I'm sorry for the way I treated you last night too," I allow. "But you started it. And I don't want to be treated the way you treated me last night, either." I breathe slowly, trying to move past the anger.

"Fair point," he concedes. "And while I am not one to make excuses, I would like to offer you an explanation. I've never had to pursue a woman for this long before, never had a woman push me away and pull me in within the course of the same conversation for weeks on end. It's driven me a bit out of my usual sensibilities. I'd like it to stop."

My face falls. "Are you breaking up with me?" I ask fearfully.

"*Porca miseria,* woman, I just told you I want to be with you," he replies testily. "And as much as I'm used to being in the driver's seat, it would seem it's up to you. However, the one thing I can do is ask you to choose. To either be with me completely, or not at all."

"Hmmm," I feign ponderously. "Those are my only options?"

He gives me a bewildered look. "Yes," he replies slowly.

I slide toward him on the couch and look up into his eyes. I tilt my head and drop my hand on his leg. "Then I guess completely it is."

He stares coolly into my eyes for a moment longer, and I wonder if he's heard me. A smile creeps slowly onto his face. "Good," he says. "Now get the fuck out."

I slap his arm and he bursts out laughing.

"Joking! Of course, I'm joking, *bella,*" he yelps as I repeatedly smack him.

I cease my attack and cross my arms over my chest, with an affected pout. He pulls me onto his lap and strokes my hair, my cheek, my chin. He drops light kisses on my nose, cheeks, and, lastly, lips. His kiss deepens, and I sink into his arms, breathing in his special wine-and-spice aroma.

He slides his arms under me and carries me to his bedroom, setting me down gently on my feet next to the bed. Pulling his T-shirt over his head, he lets it fall to the floor. I lay my palms lightly on his chest, his heart beating strongly under my hand. He hooks his thumbs into his sweats and eases them around his hips, and they drop to the floor with his shirt. He steps out of the mound of clothing, now completely naked. I shudder in anticipation, eliciting a smile from him.

I drop my hands to the large belt cinching my shirtdress at my waist and unhook it, adding it to the pile at our feet.

"I love that you wear these dresses," he murmurs, running his hand up my thigh, then along my backside. "So easy to remove."

His other hand joins in and he slowly slides my dress up. I raise my arms compliantly to let him strip the fabric off my body, then swiftly unhook my bra and shimmy so it falls away from my body.

He lets out an appreciative sigh, dropping to a knee to allow his tongue to explore my nipples. I run my hands through his thick hair and gasp in pleasure as he teases me. His mouth continues to trace kisses downward, to my hip. He slides my underwear off to make room for his roving tongue.

His mouth returns to mine and he lifts me onto the bed, lying next to me, running his hands over me. I wrap my leg around him and shift my body against his, enjoying the feeling of his skin on mine.

"You're on birth control?" he asks. I nod. "Good. Do you trust me, Serafina?"

He rubs against me and I choke back a tortured moan. And I know I've already surrendered.

"I trust you," I breathe, and my heart expands at the truth behind the words.

He cups my cheek with one hand and covers my mouth with his, sliding his tongue along my lip. Dizzy and breathless, I feel him shift himself on top of me, into me, and the feeling of just him inside me is unbelievably incredible and overwhelming.

"Go slow," I plead.

He nods softly. I pull my legs back to receive him fully and settle my heels on his behind as he carefully tests the effects of the new sensation. He holds me gently in his arms, keeping his mouth on mine, and tilts himself slowly out, leaving me void. Just as slowly, he reenters me, and I gasp loudly into his mouth.

He shifts his head to bury his face in my hair, his mouth at my ear, "*Mio tesoro*, you feel amazing."

Even just his words are enough to pleasure me, and I moan in response. "Don't stop," I plead.

He draws up, resting himself on his forearms over me and stares into my eyes as he begins to move. He keeps a slow rhythm, but the lack of barrier makes me feel everything intensely, and I know when I climax it's going to be something to behold. For now, I focus on the building sensation and his eyes on mine.

His pace increases, and I grab him in encouragement, moving to meet him. He sits up further, now resting on his palms, and the change in position brings new waves of pleasure. I grasp the sheets beneath me and work my hips with his, moaning in abandon as he stimulates me in ways he never could before. Suddenly, I want to know what it feels like to be on top of him this way, and I tell him so.

His eyes go wide, and he leans into me, wraps his arms around my back, and flips our positions in one swift movement. A giggle bursts from my lips and he smiles up at me beatifically.

Adjusting to being on top, I bring myself up to a sitting position and the fullness of feeling deep within me causes me to cry out in pleasure. He shows his approval and enjoyment at the change and moans with me. Going slowly, I work myself over him. Once I master the sensation, I move faster, my orgasm building inside of me. He plays with my nipples, his thumbs circling and pressing my sensitive flesh, while he watches me closely, grunting appreciatively every time I slide him deep into me. As I feel myself starting to climax, I lean back, and my world explodes. It's so powerful that I can only moan lowly, even moving is difficult and my body slows.

Alessandro grabs my hips and braces me as he works himself beneath me, prolonging the pleasure. I cry out unreservedly as the orgasm continues to rip through me, and I can feel the subtle shift when he hardens further, causing a black-out level surge of pleasure. But I hang on, wanting to watch him come beneath me, his cries signaling the depth of his gratification.

My whole body tingles distractingly, and I fall on his chest, his mouth finding mine. Finally, we part breathlessly, and lie facing each other with our legs still partially entwined.

He grasps my hand and brings it to his lips, kissing each of my fingers. I gaze at him adoringly and he grins transcendently.

"Now you're really and truly mine," he declares. He props himself up on his elbow and kisses me. "Are you happy?"

"Blissfully," I reply with a sigh.

TWELVE

On Friday morning it takes me a while to get my head out of the clouds and refocus on work, but I finally manage to finish reading Bryce's proposal. It looks phenomenal, and I'm eager to start making the changes, but realize I should probably check with Nick first so he can prioritize it in our upcoming expenses. I mark the forwarded email urgent and send.

Standing a stretching widely, I go looking for Nick to ensure he reviews it as soon as possible.

∾

Entering his office, I find Nick seated on the floor surrounded by paper.

I laugh. "Wasn't the digital age supposed to put an end to this kind of thing?" I tease.

Nick looks up in surprise.

"You'd think," he chuckles, "but they didn't account for fuddy-duddies like me who need to see everything on paper, sometimes all at once, to start putting things together. Technology may advance, but it's hard to unlearn your own processes."

"Speaking of processes, I've forwarded you the Hoyt Corporate Services security proposal. I'd like to accept today and get on their schedule ASAP," I say pointedly.

"I hear you, boss," he agrees, shuffling a couple pages. "I'll wrap up here and get back to you early this afternoon."

"Thanks, Nick," I reply. I frown thoughtfully. "Is Helen enough help, or could you use another bookkeeper?"

"What?" he asks looking up, confused and distracted.

I gesture around his office. Aside from the floor around him, the whole desk and both of his extra chairs are covered in papers, and the wall behind his desk in sticky notes and ledgers.

"Oh, that." He sighs heavily. "Maybe temporarily? I've been paranoid since our discovery, so I've been redoing all of our reports by hand based on hard copy receipts, bills, and so on, and comparing them to the software reports."

"Is that really necessary?" I ask skeptically. "I thought Will didn't find any other issues besides the property management software?"

"He didn't," Nick admits. "I just can't shake the feeling."

I shiver. "I understand, Nick," I assure him. "Believe me. Of all people, I get it. But maybe you can focus your concern into reviewing the security proposal? They're going to re-review all of our systems, and hopefully be able to reassure us on that front."

"Really?" he asks hopefully.

"Yep, that's kind of the idea," I point out.

"Okay," he concedes. "I'll give it a rest for today. Thanks, Sera."

"No problem. Talk to you this afternoon," I reply.

He turns back to the stacks on the floor and I watch him for a moment longer to see if he'll keep going or not. Thankfully, he starts to pile the papers together, adding the small stacks to the teetering piles on his cabinets. I smile tolerantly and meander back to my office.

"Ms. Evans," Maggie says as I approach. "Mr. Giordano came by. He wanted to speak with you before the weekly tag-up."

"Oh?" I ask in surprise. "Where is he now?"

"I think he went to the break room for coffee," she replies. "In any case, he said he'd stop by again shortly."

"I see. Well, I'll just be doing some research, so please send him in when he returns," I instruct her.

When I get in my office I duck into my private bathroom to check myself in the mirror. I'm pleased to find my long, brown hair is still soft and wavy after the lengths I went to this morning to tame it. I also note there are flecks of green in my usually brown eyes. I smile shyly at myself, knowing that only happens when I'm really excited about something.

I return to my desk and do my best to focus on research. I haven't been working long when Maggie pokes her head in to announce Alessandro's arrival. He thanks her, and she closes the door behind him.

We stare at each other across the room for a moment.

"Are you here for business or pleasure?" I ask teasingly, rising to meet him in front of my desk.

He wraps me in his arms and kisses me gently. "I thought you had a 'no sex in the office' rule?" he jokes back.

I run my hands over his back, grabbing his behind. "Old rule," I say silkily, pulling his face to mine.

He kisses me briefly and pulls away laughing. "My, you are feisty today," he comments. "We should've ditched the condoms sooner. But I don't think I can properly pleasure you in six minutes."

I jut my lip out in a pout. "Wanna bet?" I challenge him.

He hesitates for just a moment before smirking suggestively and pushing me into the bathroom, closing the door behind us.

He presses me against the back of the door, his breath hot against my ear. "No screaming now, *mio tesoro*," he says huskily. He kisses me passionately, sliding his hand under my skirt.

I bite my lip as his thumb finds its target, revolving tantalizingly. He pulls my blouse away from my neckline, caressing my neck and shoulder with his lips, then returning his mouth to mine to work his tongue with mine. As his fingers brush along my sex, I release his mouth, gasping softly. I press my face into his chest to stifle a moan.

"Tsk, tsk, tsk," he whispers, "how are you every going to come quietly if you can't even take a little teasing?"

"Why don't you stop teasing me and find out?" I urge him.

He smiles wickedly and plunges his fingers into me suddenly, taking me as roughly as he would if he were inside me. I grip his shoulders and choke back a scream. I can feel him hardening against my leg as he watches me respond to his rapid assault.

As my breathing becomes frantic and my grip tight, he loosens his last onslaught and circles hard with his thumb and forefinger inside and out while pumping hard with the other fingers. It pushes me over the edge and I come, squeezing my eyes shut and letting out a low moan into his shoulder.

"Shhhhh, *bella*," he murmurs, pulling my face up. He covers my mouth with his and lets the last of my moans dissolve in his kiss. He gently removes his hand from between my legs and checks the watch on his other wrist. "Two minutes to spare."

I laugh softly, resting my head against his neck. "See? We may even have enough time to get to the meeting without looking like you just fingerfucked me in a bathroom."

We both dissolve into quiet, conspiratorial laughter. He gives me one last brief kiss and we prepare ourselves to head to the meeting.

Putting his hand on my office door handle, he winks at me roguishly. "I'll go first."

I blow him a kiss and he leaves me to gather my things for the meeting. As I exit my office and head to the conference room, I realize another perk of him leaving first. I get to watch him walking in front of me, his fitted trousers accentuating his gorgeous backside. I suppress a giggle, realizing he's right — I am feisty today.

As I take a seat across from him at the table, I feel my insides ache tantalizingly from our brief encounter, and I gingerly adjust myself, enjoying the sensation. He raises an eyebrow distractedly at me as Jackson calls the meeting to order.

"Great! Now that everyone is here," Jackson begins. "There's not a lot to cover, as the deal closes in two weeks. I'll give the floor to Marco and Giovanni to discuss build readiness and any remaining issues at hand."

Alessandro's architect and engineer take the floor, running through the build process open items. I start to notice midway through the meeting that every time Alessandro goes to engage, he glances sidelong at me first. It starts to make me blush, and I hope nobody else in the room notices our reactions to each other.

As the meeting wraps up, Jackson approaches me for a word. Alessandro lingers momentarily, but I shake my head faintly in a sign for him not to wait. He takes the hint and leaves reluctantly, and I'm left to wonder for a moment if he intended to make me return the favor in the conference room once everyone had left.

Shaking myself out of my hedonistic musings, I turn my attention to Jackson. "What's up?"

"I was wondering," he begins, "if you've decided who will be lead on the Sutton Developments project."

"I'd given it some thought, yes," I admit. "And while I know the Buone Case project is wrapping up and heading into a development phase that we won't be terribly involved in, the Sutton Developments project is an entirely different beast."

"I know," he agrees enthusiastically. "That's exactly why I wanted to express my interest. I know I don't have as much commercial leasing real estate experience as Ellie, but I think that with my extensive commercial residential experience and my outstanding research skills I'd be more than capable."

"Jackson, I appreciate that, but this is a very important project for us," I say gently. "And Ellie has more experience than both of us combined, on both sides. I need her pinch-hitting for us here. We have to nail this to regain our momentum."

Jackson nods despondently, and I consider the situation silently for a moment. "But," I hedge. "Since it *will* be such a large project, and you have obviously shown talent and initiative, it might be a good experience for you to assist Ellie."

His eyes brighten. "That would be awesome! Thank you so much, Ms. Evans," he gushes happily.

I smile warmly at him. "No, thank you, for carrying so much of the Buone Case project lately, Jackson," I reply. "It's been a challenging time for me, and I couldn't have managed without you."

I excuse myself for lunch, and Jackson practically skips out of the room behind me. Chuckling quietly, I return to my desk to find Nick prowling around Maggie's empty desk.

"Sera! There you are!" He sounds excited.

"Hi Nick," I reply, looking at him warily. "Had a few cups of coffee since I saw you last?"

"No!" he exclaims, waving his hands comically, and I suppress a dubious chuckle. "I read the security proposal and I wanted to tell you as soon as possible that we can absolutely make that happen from a financial end."

"That's great, Nick, but weren't we supposed to meet after lunch?"

"I couldn't wait," he admits. "I had no idea how many ways there were to deal with this. Better software, better data protection, better training — I feel like a huge weight has been lifted off my shoulders."

His clear relief radiates in his tone and mannerisms and something clicks in my brain. "Oh Nick, you didn't think any of this was *your* fault, did you?"

He stops pacing frantically and a gloomy shadow passes over his face. "I know it's silly," he admits. "But I feel like I should've known better. Done better. But this," — he waves a printout of what I can only assume is the security proposal — "I would've never thought of half of this."

I lay a hand on his shoulder reassuringly. "Nick, it wasn't your job to think of all that. This is all on me. I should've thought to seek this kind of help before it became necessary," I say. "I'm sorry." My heart breaks for the hours he must have lost worried about this.

"Thanks," he says slowly. "I know this is your company, Sera, but I've been with you almost the whole time. I see how hard you work. I just felt like I let you down. Like I let everyone down making it so easy for someone to steal from us."

"I get it, but shit happens," I say blandly. "You know how good a judge of character Allie is, how thorough she is with the hiring process, and even she was duped."

"I hadn't thought of that," he acknowledges.

"We all could have done better," I allow. "But all that matters now is what we do next."

Nick smiles and holds up the security proposal.

I nod and laugh. "I'll call Bryce Hoyt."

～

"Sera, I'm so pleased you've decided to work with us," Bryce's warm, deep voice says through the speaker phone.

"Me too," I respond. "We'll see you first thing Monday morning then?"

"Bright and early," he confirms. "We're going to hit the ground running on this one, Sera. I'll have someone start on your client background checks and I need you to tell me when you have a block of time next week to file a police report on your saboteur."

"I'll have my assistant send my schedule over," I assure him. "Have a great weekend, Bryce."

"You too, Sera," he says huskily.

After I've hung up, I can't figure out what about the exchange has left me unsettled until I remember Alessandro's accusations regarding Bryce's intentions toward me. I make a mental note to observe his interactions to see if he's the same with everyone, or if I really am getting special treatment before turning back to organizing the preliminary Sutton Developments research.

❧

Just before six, as I'm wrapping up transferring my organized research to a shared directory, Alessandro appears in my open doorway.

"*Ciao*," he greets me, grinning like a schoolboy. "Almost finished?"

I give him a fake stink eye. "Yes, but if you keep coming in here everyone's going to know what's going on," I grouse.

He saunters in, plopping happily in a chair. "I thought the rules had changed?" he asks, a twinkle in his eye.

I raise an eyebrow at him delicately, pursing my lips. "Yes, I suppose they have, Mr. Giordano," I concede.

He rises from the chair and stands next to me, leaning against the desk.

"But that doesn't mean we need to broadcast it," I warn.

He leans his face close to mine. "Maybe I want to broadcast it," he replies seductively, then takes my lips with his, pulls me to a standing position and wraps himself around me.

I break my lips away from his, gasping for air. "Alessandro, please."

His hand holds my chin, thrusting it upward so he can kiss my neck. I let out an involuntary sigh of pleasure. His lips move to my ear, his tongue wreaking havoc with my brain.

"Don't worry, *mio tesoro*, almost everyone is gone anyway," he murmurs, returning his mouth to mine.

I give in and wrap my arms around his neck, returning his heated kisses.

Suddenly I hear a small "Oh!" of surprise, and I jump out of Alessandro's embrace to see Maggie standing in the doorway.

"Everyone except Maggie," he says innocently, flashing a devilish smile.

"I'm so sorry, Ms. Evans," Maggie says, scurrying away and turning bright red.

"Wait here," I instruct Alessandro tersely.

He suppresses a smile and slides into my chair, putting his feet up on my desk. I shake my head, half annoyed, half amused, and leave the room to catch Maggie hurriedly packing her things.

"Maggie," I say, and she looks up, abashed. "I'm terribly sorry to have put you in that position. Mr. Giordano and I should have shown more discretion. Please, tell me what you needed."

"These just arrived for you," she says, still beet red, gesturing to a vase overflowing with gorgeous purple irises.

"Oh?" I ask, curious. I pluck the card nestled amongst the flowers and open it.

Thank you again. I look forward to helping you safeguard what matters most to you. —Bryce

Maggie looks at me expectantly.

"They're from Bryce Hoyt," I explain, "thanking us for accepting the security proposal." I pause. "What do purple irises mean?"

"Admiration," Alessandro offers from behind me.

I turn to see him leaning against my door frame, glaring at the flowers.

THIRTEEN

On Saturday morning, after we've finished breakfast, Alessandro leans back in his chair, quiet and contemplative.

"You're not still mad about the flowers, are you?" I ask warily.

I'm not a fan of moody, pouting Alessandro. The sex with him is decidedly not as good, and I'm on the verge of kicking him out for the day if he insists on continuing to sulk around my apartment.

He glances sidelong at me. "What if I am?" he asks.

I pick up our plates and put them in the kitchen. I contemplate trying to seduce him out of his funk again, but it didn't work last night, so I brush the idea off.

"I thought you *wanted* me to consult a security expert?" I remind him.

"Yes," he allows grumpily, "but an old, fat one."

I laugh unreservedly.

"Okay, that's not helping my hurt ego over here," he points out, and I'm startled out of my amusement.

I approach him and settle into his lap, wrapping my arms around his neck. "You have nothing to worry about from Bryce Hoyt," I promise. "I'm yours, dummy, in case you hadn't noticed." I look seriously into his eyes, letting my words sink in.

He strokes my cheek with his thumb. "Okay," he says.

I blanch in shock. "Okay?" I echo. "That's all it took?"

He laughs and shrugs. "What can I say? I believe you," he replies.

I pout a little and run my hands down his chest. "But I didn't even get to use my feminine wiles to convince you of my affections."

"Well, you know I'll never say no to that," he teases. His lips brush my jaw and he nuzzles into my neck. "But I have other plans for the day. Rain check?"

"That's not how feminine wiles work," I sigh, feigning exasperation, and he laughs.

"You'll have to show me tonight," he murmurs, kissing my neck.

"Mmmm," I respond. "Are you coming back here, or should I meet you at your place?"

"I'll pick you up at seven," he replies, still pecking at my neck.

"Why are you picking me up? That seems inefficient." I frown, confused.

"Well, my little efficiency monitor," he laughs, "I'm picking you up because I'm taking you out tonight. And before you ask, no, you don't get to know where."

And I don't know whether to pout or to protest, so I go for Option C and kiss him goodbye.

A FEW MINUTES AFTER SEVEN THERE IS A KNOCK ON THE DOOR. I GIVE MYSELF a last glance in the bathroom mirror, and I can't help but feel nervously excited. My hair is pulled back into an elegant chignon and I'm wearing my favorite red, silk halter dress. Its sweetheart neckline both compliments and contains my full chest, and it floats away from hugging my torso at the waist, falling in graceful waves to my knees. The floaty material is every little girl's dream — it's a dress that simply begs to be twirled in. Grinning playfully, I allow myself one small spin before answering the door.

I open the door to find Alessandro looking especially dashing in a dark blue suit with a buttoned vest over a crisp, white shirt open at the neck. He's been keeping the beard lately, which I approve of, especially as well-manicured as it is this evening. His dark brown hair is just long enough to really run your fingers through, though it is a bit too well-coifed now to invite such treatment. *Later, perhaps,* I think to myself, smiling coyly.

"*Ciao*," I greet him. "Would you like to come in?"

His full lips settle into my favorite sideways smile that suggests all manner of naughty things that may be going through his mind.

"Thank you, but I think it best that I don't. You look *magnifico*," he says, eyeing my dress appreciatively.

"*Grazie*. Okay then," I concede, grabbing my clutch. "Let's go."

We arrive at a restaurant hidden behind one of downtown Seattle's towering skyscrapers. It doesn't look like much from the outside and has a faded sign that says "Rossi's."

"What is this place?" I ask reticently.

Alessandro takes my hand and squeezes it gently. "It's an Italian restaurant."

I laugh. "An Italian restaurant that meets the standards of an actual Italian?"

He smirks. "Marco's family owns it," he explains. "They've been here about twenty years now. Best and most authentic Italian in Seattle."

"Will Marco be here?" I ask, my eyes widening.

"And Giovanni, and Francesca, and Maria," he replies. "And a good many other people."

I pull his hand, stopping him just outside the door. "Do they know about us already?"

Alessandro laughs. "Well, if they didn't before the other night when you showed up and I kicked them out, they do now," he smirks, and I cover my face, embarrassed. "It's fine. You worry too much."

"Comes with the package," I remind him.

He laughs and kisses me briefly before holding the door open for me. Stepping in, we are greeted by a raucous chorus of "*Ciao!*" Taking it all in, I count no fewer than thirty people, all seated around a series of tables pushed together in the center of the dining room.

Marco approaches us with a woman I presume is his wife, and they each embrace Alessandro in turn, exchanging quick pleasantries in rapid Italian.

Marco smiles brightly and folds me into an unexpected hug. "Serafina, I'm so glad you're joining us," he says warmly. "This is my wife, Angela." She shakes my hand kindly.

"*Piacere,*" I say.

She looks pleasantly surprised. "*Tu parli Italiano,*" she replies, smiling.

"*Solo un po,*" I respond. "I fear I'll get lost quickly tonight, though." I smile disarmingly.

Marco laughs. "Yes, it's a full house! Hey!" he calls to the room, approaching the table. "Everyone, you know Alessandro. This is Serafina Evans. Serafina, you know Giovanni, Francesca, and Maria" — they each give me a "ciao" as he points them out — "that's Maria's husband, Raffaele; my father, Pietro; my mama, Gianna; and more uncles, aunts, and cousins than you can probably remember," he says waving his hand vaguely at the rest, and everyone laughs.

"*Benvenuto,* Serafina," Gianna says warmly, offering Alessandro and I seats. "*Per favore,* sit, sit."

"*Grazie mille,*" I say shyly. As Alessandro has noticed before, my Italian is only so-so and, while I understand a good deal more than I can speak, even that is limited.

Maria sits next to me and she leans in close, so I can hear her. "I'm glad to see you out of work for once," she says, smiling. "It looks good on you." She laughs, and I join in.

"What can I say, Alessandro has been a good influence on me," I reply.

She smiles knowingly and gives me a wink. "And you on him."

Alessandro touches my elbow and I turn my attention to him. "If you're hungry there's some *antipasti* still on the table," he offers, gesturing to the remaining *insalata caprese*. "But the next course will be served soon."

"Where are all the other customers?" I ask, glancing around the restaurant.

Alessandro waves his hand dismissively. "It's just family tonight. One of Marco's cousins, Maria, just got married," he points to a young woman with sable hair and a pink dress. "They've had the wedding all day, and this is the family dinner after. It'll be great fun, you'll see."

I flush with embarrassment. "I wish you'd told me," I hiss. "I would've brought a present."

He laughs. "No need," he assures me.

I regard him skeptically. "Did you go to the wedding? Is that where you disappeared to today?"

He frowns at my accusation. "No, Serafina," he says crossly. "I had to work. You think I wouldn't have jumped at the chance to show you off? Besides, I wasn't invited."

I don't know which surprises me more — his annoyance or the fact that he's that proud to be with me, but it softens my attitude considerably.

"I'm sorry," I apologize, kissing him softly.

His lips melt into mine, and he prolongs the kiss for a moment before letting me pull away.

"*Va bene, bella,*" he assures me. "Just relax and enjoy the food. It's going to be amazing, if Gianna has anything to do with it."

And he's not wrong. The first course — *primo* — is served shortly. "*Fiori di zucchini farcito,*" Gianna declares triumphantly as Marco's cousins distribute plates.

I know I'm going to need to pace myself, so I sample a small bite of the cheese-stuffed zucchini flowers laid out beautifully on the plate and practically melt into my chair. I contemplate the rest of the portion warily.

"How authentic of a meal are we talking here?" I ask Alessandro.

He covers his laugh as he swallows the food in his mouth. "Fully," he replies. "You're still in for *secondo, contorno, dolce, caffe, e digestivo.*" I'm sure I look alarmed because he wraps his hand around mine and kisses my fingers. "Don't worry, Serafina. Eat. Enjoy. Don't think so much. Live like an Italian for a night."

Eyeing the rest of my plate, I decide he's right and tuck in until the plate is clean. Between each course, the alcohol and conversation flow freely. Thankfully, Marco's cousins mostly speak English, so it's only the older generation that sticks to Italian, and I'm delighted to find I'm able to participate fully.

Well, when I'm not distracted by the parade of succulent dishes, that is. The *fiori di zucchini farcito* is followed by a melt-in-your-mouth *pappardelle e sugo di carne*. For good measure I circle back to the *insalata caprese* that still sits on the table. It is light and amazing with over-the-top flavorful heirloom tomatoes, freshly made *mozzarella di bufala*, and fragrant just-picked basil.

Alessandro was not kidding about the food. Not that Italians kid about food, as I'm learning. As the *dolce* is served — a delicate *panna cotta* with berries — I decide that this procession can't possibly be called a meal by any standards I've ever known. It's more like a food orgy where each course is a new lover seducing you with its unique wiles. That is, until the next comes along to pleasure you in a whole new, exciting way.

After the *panna cotta* I am sated and sleepy. I watch in awe as another hour or two passes and they all continue to consume espressos and small shots of *limoncello*.

"How do you drink caffeine this late?" I ask Maria in awe.

"Lots of practice," she jokes, tossing back another. "Besides, we don't do this every night."

"I should think not," I reply. "I'm going to need the rest of the weekend to recover."

She laughs a laugh that I'm coming to learn from all of them translates roughly as "silly Americans."

I chuckle softly. They may have a point. I look around at the camaraderie and laughter and decide I could get used to this.

As the drinks run out, the crowd begins to thin and soon we are saying our thank yous and goodbyes. As we emerge into the cool night air, I feel the effect of the food and drink weighing on my senses.

"Ready to go home?" Alessandro asks, opening the car door for me.

I nod sleepily. "Your home?"

"If that's what you want," he replies, smiling tenderly at me.

"Yes, please," I say sleepily, settling in to the passenger seat.

∾

I MUST HAVE DRIFTED OFF AS SOON AS WE DROVE AWAY, BECAUSE THE NEXT thing I know Alessandro's strong arms are lifting me out of the car and carrying me into the elevator. When he sees that I'm awake, he allows my legs to fall gently to the floor but holds me up with an arm around my waist.

I'm able to manage getting into his apartment, though by the time we enter the bedroom I'm barely conscious. Alessandro undresses me tenderly and helps me into bed. I watch him start to remove his own clothing and something stirs in me briefly before I'm lost to sleep once again.

WHEN I WAKE IT'S STILL DARK OUT. I GLANCE AT THE CLOCK, AND ITS GLOWING numbers tell me it's just after four a.m. I reach for Alessandro and find his side of the bed empty but warm. I sit up and see him standing by the window. Slipping out of bed, I approach him from behind and wrap my arms around him. He turns and envelops me in his arms, kissing the top of my head.

"I didn't mean to wake you," he apologizes.

"It's okay," I reply. "Have you been up this whole time?"

"No, I just woke up a few minutes ago," he murmurs.

I look up into his eyes. His expression is serious but veiled.

"Is everything okay?"

"Very," he assures me, kissing me lightly. I shiver, and I'm not sure if it's being out of bed or his kiss. "Come, let's go back to bed."

I crawl in beside him, nestling myself in his arms. "What were you thinking about?" I ask.

He brushes my hair from my face and his fingers linger on my cheek. He takes a moment to respond, as if he's struggling to express himself.

"How much I want to make love to you," he breathes finally.

And his warm mouth locks on mine, his strong hands pulling me tightly against his body. I sink into him, warmth spreading through me as my body wakes under his touch.

I roll onto my back and he slides on top of me, his mouth and hands working me into a frenzy. I eagerly part my legs, allowing him to slip into me. Our mouths break apart as we both sigh in pleasure at the sensation. He places my arms around his neck. "Don't let go," he urges me, staring into my eyes as he begins to move.

The intensity of his gaze, the full length of our bodies touching, and his firm yet gentle thrusts send waves of bliss rolling through me. The pleasure is connected to a deep joy I feel in his arms, our bodies connected on a level deeper than I can describe.

I feel a tear slip from my eye and he holds me tighter, dropping his lips to my ear.

"Don't hold back," he urges softly.

And I know this isn't commanding Alessandro who is fucking me for pleasure. This is something different.

"Not anymore," I reply, drawing my knees up to urge him deeper into me, to allow him to lean in closer.

His breath quickens and his pupils dilate. His mouth descends hungrily once more upon mine, and I thread my fingers through his hair, pulling him into me in every way. His pelvis rocks rhythmically with mine as we join, and instead of the tightening I usually feel heading toward climax, my body relaxes and tears start to flow freely from my eyes.

Alessandro kisses them, kisses me. He holds my face in his hands and looks deeps into my eyes as his pace quickens.

"I love you, Serafina," he breathes softly, urgently.

I half sob and half laugh in relief. "I love you, too, Alessandro," I confess.

And my relaxed muscles spring back together to concentrate all the emotions he's made me feel in these last weeks into the center of my body, and they explode out of me as I climax in his arms. I grip him tightly, my eyes locked on his at the moment the orgasm floods through me. As he watches my climax, he spills himself into me, pressing his forehead against mine and calling out my name.

With one last, deep thrust, he settles into me and stills. I hold him, loosely wrapped in my arms and legs, as he breathes heavily, resting his head on my shoulder. It's a long while before either of us moves.

When we finally extricate our entangled bodies, he stretches himself out next to me, laying inches away, and it's as if we are staring at each other with new eyes.

"I meant it," he says softly. "It wasn't just one of those things that accidentally happened in a moment of pleasure. I mean, it was pleasurable…"

I put a finger to his lips and laugh. "I know," I assure him.

"I haven't said that to anybody in a very long time," he admits. "I didn't expect to say it tonight."

"Neither did I," I agree. "When was the last time?"

He ponders the question for a moment. "I can't say for certain. Years. Maybe two?" He shakes his head slightly as if trying to dislodge a memory. "What about you?"

"I've only said it to one other person, more than ten years ago," I reply, and fresh tears spring to my eyes.

"Shhh, *bella*," he whispers, wiping the tears away. "We don't need to say any more tonight. Let's just rest now." He folds me in his arms again and pulls the sheet over us. His mouth finds mine one last time, wiping away any memories and thoughts of past hurts that were lingering.

With a hand on his chest, I feel his breathing settle into a rhythm, and I drift off to the steady tempo created by its combination with the beat of his heart.

∾

After a long, peaceful sleep I wake alone to early afternoon sunlight streaming through the window. I stretch my limbs out, feeling the looseness in my body, unable to remember the last time I was this relaxed. My stomach rumbles, and I suppress a laugh. I didn't think I'd be hungry again for days.

I slip out of bed and look around the room for something to wear. I chance a look through Alessandro's dresser and manage to find a white T-shirt and a pair of boxers. The loose shorts hang off my hips, but at least they stay on.

I venture out of the room, into the living room, but Alessandro isn't there, nor is he in the kitchen. I find him in his office, drinking a cup of coffee and reading the newspaper at his desk, wearing only a pair of old sweats.

"Well, don't you look ridiculously sexy," I say from the doorway.

He looks up in surprise and smiles widely. "*Buon pomeriggio*, sleepyhead," he greets me, beckoning me to him.

I cross the room and settle into his lap, placing a gentle kiss on his lips.

He nuzzles my neck and his hands slide up my thighs and begin exploring. "Aren't you a nice distraction?" he murmurs appreciatively.

"I hope I'm not keeping you from anything important," I tease. "What's on the agenda today?"

He rubs my nipple with one thumb over my shirt absentmindedly as he considers the question. "Well, I need to pick up a few things, go grocery shopping, and other various errands," he replies. "Or I could spend the rest of the day making love to you." He slips his hand under the shirt and holds my breast in his hand while kissing my neck.

I groan in pleasure and protest. "As wonderful as that sounds, I'm actually starving," I admit. "After last night I didn't think I'd eat for the rest of the weekend, but there it is."

"A quick fuck then?" he asks huskily.

Before I can respond, he stands, laying me on the desk, pulling at my shorts. I lift my backside off the desk, helping him slide them down, and kicking them away from me as he pulls down his sweats just enough to take me roughly and urgently on the desk.

FOURTEEN

On Monday morning I wake before Alessandro's alarm. I shift quietly in bed so that I can turn myself to face him. His arms are flung over his head, his long legs splayed out over the large bed. He looks extremely content, and I momentarily check the urge to run my hands over his naked body. Until I remember the nipple alarm clock incident.

Grinning idiotically, I lick my finger and run it over his nipple. As it hardens, I roll it between my fingers and feel him start to shift. He opens one eye slightly and regards me sleepily. I blow on the nipple lightly, then sink my mouth onto it, sucking hard. Both of his eyes fully open and he moans deeply.

"I see what you did there," he rumbles.

I let go slowly, running his nipple through my teeth one last time, and then pull away laughing. "Good morning, sunshine," I tease him.

"I'll show you a good morning," he replies, and rolls on top of me, his erection pressing into me.

I give a small gasp of surprise before he covers my mouth with his and we proceed to wake each other up in every way possible.

∾

EARLY MORNING EXPLOITS ASIDE, I STILL MAKE IT INTO WORK BEFORE MY normal arrival time. It gives me a few minutes to collect my thoughts and prepare for the slew of meetings that will consume my day. Between meetings with Bryce, Eleanor Roberts, my senior lead project manager, and Jackson to hand over the reins on the Sutton Developments project, I won't have much time for preparation, and I'm glad for the quiet.

I'm set up in the conference room for the morning, and eventually Allie pokes her head in about fifteen minutes prior to our meeting time.

"Sera! You must be as eager to get this show on the road as I am," she remarks, settling into the chair next to me.

"I am," I admit. "Good weekend?"

"Wonderful," she gushes. "David and I hiked to Heather Lake. It was a bit cold, but stunning."

"That sounds like a lot of work," I remark drily.

"It's totally worth it," she assures me. "I'd ask how your weekend was, but judging by the gossip tearing around the office this morning, I can guess it was pretty good and likely involved a lot of time with our favorite Italian client."

I roll my eyes. "Well, that took about five minutes," I lament.

She raises an eyebrow.

"Maggie caught us kissing in my office on Friday afternoon," I explain.

"Well, aren't we throwing caution to the wind these days?"

"We are," I reply, grinning stupidly. "He told me he loves me."

Allie's jaw drops in shock. "Holy shit, Sera, that's huge! What did you say?"

I smile shyly. "I told him I loved him too," I admit.

She leans over and gives me a bone-crunching hug. "Really? Oh, Sera, dear, I'm so happy for you," she says ardently.

"Really? Because you seemed pretty worried before," I ask skeptically.

"If you're not worried, I'm not worried," she responds. "You're a big girl. And if anyone knows how much those three words mean to you, it's me. I can't imagine you jumping in without all the facts."

Her words give me pause, but my thoughts are interrupted by Maggie at the door.

"Mr. Hoyt is here for your meeting," she says. "Are you ready for him?"

"Yes, send him in please, Maggie, thank you," I reply.

Allie and I both rise as Bryce strides into the room, handsome as ever in dark slacks and a sky-blue button-up shirt that matches his eyes. I can feel Allie's eyes bugging out of her head next to me, and I realize I forgot to warn her.

"Bryce," I greet him warmly, "so good to see you." He grasps my hand genially. "This is Alison Kramer, my head of human resources."

"Ladies, good morning," he responds. Turning his dazzling smile on Allie, he shakes her hand as well, and they exchange pleasant greetings.

As he takes a seat Allie goes to sit next to me and whispers in my ear on the way, "Holy hot security advisor, Batman!" I press my lips together to suppress a smile and shoot her an exasperated look. She shrugs and beams at me beatifically.

Thankfully, Bryce is all business and before long the table is covered in papers, the whiteboard a scrawl of procedural editing. We go over all the topics Bryce had us prepare for and then some. Within a couple of hours, Allie has a large document of changes and actions.

"So, from now on you can implement your own background checks on new clients if you'd prefer," Bryce recaps, "but my assistant is already pulling together the two sets of files for your current major accounts with Buone Case and Sutton Developments to give you an idea of the kind of depth of check we can provide you, and to help minimize surprises going forward. Knowledge is power, and given your recent power struggle with Sutton, especially, you should learn everything you can about his company before moving forward on anything."

"Makes sense," I agree. "But why Buone Case? Their deal is done end of next week."

"Yes," he replies. "So, you still have time to throw up a red flag if you find anything that will affect your participation in this deal, or at the very least inform you further if you consider continuing your business with them."

"Fair enough, I suppose," I concede reluctantly.

"These are big accounts for your company," he reiterates. "I'm here to make sure I do everything in my power to help things go smoothly for you from now on. You won't need to do the level of background check we'll be providing on every client, but even for the smaller accounts you'll want to know who you're getting into bed with."

Allie coughs quietly next to me and I kick her under the table. "If that's all for me, I'll take my leave now," Allie interjects.

"Absolutely, it was a pleasure to meet you, Mrs. Kramer," Bryce responds, shaking her hand again across the table.

Allie leaves the conference room, and I can hear her chuckling to herself on her way down the hall.

"I've arranged for a separate meeting with finance and IT after lunch," I say, pressing on. "Perhaps we can go over some of the other matters at hand?"

"Absolutely," Bryce agrees.

He proceeds to walk me through selecting security cameras, and, finally, going over my personal security needs.

"I'm fairly satisfied with the access control here and at your condo. And based on our preliminary research on Ms. Stanwood, we have no reason to believe she poses any kind of physical threat to you. But as we don't know who else she's working with, or the 'why,' I would be most comfortable with your checking in with me each morning," he requests. "Otherwise, we have armed security personnel standing by at all times. If you encounter anything that concerns you, contact this number," he hands me a card, "and someone will be at your side in minutes. Program it into all your devices. Even a blank text or missed call will bring someone running. If you need to arrange for personal security for a meeting, event, or outing, or decide you would be more comfortable having it on an ongoing basis, just let me know."

"Boy, you really take your job seriously," I murmur, turning the thick card over in my fingers.

He catches my eyes and holds me pinned with an intense expression. "And I need you to take this seriously, Sera," he says, his voice a soft contrast to the heat of his gaze. "All of this," he gestures at the papers and whiteboard, "is to protect you. All the plans, all the care, is for naught if you won't help me safeguard the most important thing in this whole company — you."

I smile wryly at the fatefulness of his warning. Little does he know I've spent most of my life safeguarding myself from everyone, everything. And now, just when I'm learning to let that go, I'm being asked to re-embrace it. The irony is delicious.

"You have my full cooperation in this process."

My assurances help relax his stance, and he sighs, relieved.

"I'm glad to hear it," he replies. "Now, what's good to eat around here?"

∽

After lunch we start on IT security. As I expected, Will takes immediate umbrage with Bryce's homebrewed software security concerns. Bryce, sensing his reaction, steps lightly, but does not back down. It's quite a dance to watch. Thankfully, we're able to press through and make an action plan for Will to work with Hoyt Corporate Services' network security division on evaluating all our systems and software fully.

Nick, on the other hand, almost immediately starts worshipping the ground Bryce walks on. He eagerly documents every suggestion and bounces out of the conference already eagerly anticipating implementing the various training and compliance programs and starting his risk management matrix. Even Bryce laughs in amusement — after he's sure that Nick is gone, of course.

"Well, that was a mixed bag," I laugh.

"That's normal," Bryce replies easily. "Some people take this stuff very personally." He shrugs. "Doesn't bother me."

"Good," I reply teasingly. "You'll need a thick skin to survive us."

He smiles timidly at me. "I don't know, I'm rather enjoying myself," he replies. I blush, and he clears his throat, rising and gathering his things. "I know you have another meeting coming up. I'll see you tomorrow first thing to file that police report. And my assistant should be sending the two client background packages by courier by the end of the day."

I extend my hand to him, and his shake is reassuringly firm. "Thank you," I say sincerely. "I can't tell you how grateful I am for everything."

He winks slyly. "You're most welcome, but we're just getting started." And with a small wave, he's gone.

I slowly stack the papers in the conference room to return them to my office before the next meeting.

∾

RETURNING TO THE CONFERENCE ROOM I AM, ONCE AGAIN, SLIGHTLY EARLY. I check my phone and see a text from Alessandro.

Morning sex makes me miss you more. Hope your day is good, amore.

I smile blissfully, remembering his embraces. *Miss you too. See you tonight? <3*

His response is immediate. *Working late again. I can come sleep at your place when we're done?*

I'm glad he's not here so I don't have to hide my disappointment. After a pause I reply. *Boo. Maybe tomorrow night then. I doubt there would be much sleeping, and I have an early meeting tomorrow.*

When Ellie and Jackson enter, Alessandro still hasn't responded, and I flip my phone back to silent. I take in Ellie's tall, thin frame and note that her already tan skin seems even more deeply browned, providing quite a shocking contrast to her pale blond hair.

"Ellie!" I greet her, hugging her tightly. "We've missed you! You look like you had a nice, sunny vacation!"

"It was fabulous," she trills. "I'll show you the pictures later. But more importantly, I hear you've got something big for us to sink our teeth into!"

I laugh appreciatively. Ellie has been with me from the start, and her eagerness never fails to impress. "Absolutely. I hope you guys like big piles of research, because if you do, it's your lucky day!" Everyone chuckles appreciatively.

It takes us several hours to work through the framework of my research and go over a plan for our meeting with Sutton Developments on Wednesday morning, but by the end I'm confident that not only will we be prepared, but that Ellie and Jackson will be able to work together productively. As I wish them a good evening and head back to my office, I'm feeling pretty good about our turnaround.

Heading into my office, I catch Maggie packing up for the evening. "Goodnight, Maggie," I greet her. "Thanks for everything."

She smiles warmly. "My pleasure, Ms. Evans," she replies. "The delivery from Hoyt Corporate Services is on your desk."

"I'd completely forgotten about that, thanks," I reply. "It'll make good after-dinner reading, I'm sure."

She laughs and waves as she heads home for the night. I gather my things and head home on time, for once.

∾

AFTER DINNER, I DECIDE TO LOOK THROUGH THE SUTTON DEVELOPMENTS BRIEF first in case there are any major showstoppers. The format of the report is helpful — a summary page at the beginning lists a table of contents and status of each report, color-coded green for completed reports, red if they contain any potential flags.

There is a red flag on their past litigation, so I jump ahead. Skimming the text, it turns out to be an issue between Sutton Developments and the City of Seattle for a building code violation. Sutton refused to acknowledge the code violation, as the laws had changed over the course of the project. Foreseeably, fighting the City of Seattle in a City of Seattle court, they lost, incurring a hefty fine and, highly likely, a matching hefty bill to bring the issue up to the new code.

Everything else looks clean as a whistle, and that's saying something given the exhaustive pile of research with five-year histories on the company's financials, personal background checks on all its executive officers, Better Business Bureau files, the works. I set the thick file aside for further examination another time.

The Buone Case file looks slim in comparison, which is unsurprising as, with not quite five years incorporated and only twenty or so employees total, they have less than a quarter of Sutton Development's staff and only one executive officer — Alessandro.

As I expect, there are no red flags in Buone Case's report. While he hasn't always heeded my advice, I've never seen Alessandro be anything but completely forthright in his business dealings. And in this business, that's saying something.

A quick glance over his background check doesn't bring any surprises. No criminal record, not even so much as a speeding ticket, no lawsuits, no litigation.

I yawn widely and glance at the clock on my phone — its only just after nine. My weekend exploits must be catching up with me.

As I go to close Buone Case's file, something on Alessandro's background check catches my eye. Under the address history section there are four addresses — two in San Francisco, with dates indicating that he moved from one to the other, and two in Seattle, both for the full six months he's lived here. One I recognize, his apartment. The other I don't.

With a furrowed brow I plug the address into the maps app on my phone. University District. A rental maybe? I go to the King County Assessor's webpage and call up the property detail. The owner name is listed as GIORDANO ALESSANDRO VITTORIO. He's the sole owner, so that lends weight to the rental theory.

Still perturbed, I pull up the home's stats through my real estate agent portal. Three bedrooms, two baths, almost two thousand square feet. It's a hot neighborhood, and the home value estimate has increased a small amount even from such a recent purchase date. I check all the usual property listing sites but can't find any rental listings for the property since Alessandro purchased it.

I run a search on the address and one of the names jumps off the page. Peyton Giordano, 26, female. Previous residences include several cities in California, including San Francisco, current residence Seattle. Previous names used include Peyton Chadwick. My throat constricts as the logical conclusion forms in my mind.

I frantically search social media and find only one site with an account for a Peyton Giordano. Her profile picture is a snapshot of two people kissing, with the Space Needle looming in the background. I click to expand the photo for a closer look. The woman in the picture, presumably her, is short, athletic, and blond. The other is, unmistakably, Alessandro.

My dinner rises in my throat, and I drop my phone and run to the bathroom.

FIFTEEN

When I'm sure I won't be sick again anytime soon, I clamber back to my phone to explore Peyton's profile, but it's locked down. There are only two other public pictures of her, both alone, and lots of pictures of woods and mountains and the like. Her profile lists her as married. The profile picture is dated three months ago.

I already know Alessandro doesn't do social media, but I search for his name again and come up empty. My head spins, attempting to craft theories that explain what I've found.

I'm briefly tempted to create a profile and send her a friend request, but just as quickly dismiss the thought. It would be incredibly difficult to get any real answers online.

I poke around the internet a bit more to see if she has any other public accounts, but there is nothing else for her in either her married name or what I presume her to be her maiden name.

I realize I'm chewing my fingernails to the quick when I yelp in pain on biting flesh. I bury my face in my hands and try not to cry.

I could just ask him. Couldn't I? I laugh out loud as I imagine my opening salvo. *Hey, Alessandro, I know I just told you I love you, but I realized I may not actually know you as well as I thought I did. You aren't, by any chance, married, are you?*

How would he even respond? There are only two answers to that question. Yes and no. If the former, certainly there could be a million explanations — or excuses. But the evidence is staring at me from my phone screen. How could he possibly deny it? Does it even matter why?

I can't decide, but regardless I need to know if it's true. And if it is, I need to know how I could go so wrong, again.

A banner notification appears over Peyton's profile page — a text message. From Alessandro.

Buona notte, amore. Dream of me.

My gut wrenches and my phone falls to the floor. Burying my face in one of the couch pillows, I finally release the sobs and let the tears go.

I WAKE SCREAMING AND GASPING FOR AIR IN THE PREDAWN HOURS. I LOOK around the dark living room and realize I must have passed out on the couch in my hysteria. The nightmares that woke me flood back — a small, blond Peyton chasing me out of their home, yelling loudly that he belongs to her.

Their home. A dangerous idea possesses me. I have to see their house. I have to see her.

I'M NOT ABLE TO GET BACK TO SLEEP, SO I EMAIL ALLIE AND MAGGIE THAT I'M taking a sick day. I text Bryce the same excuse, asking to reschedule our police department trip.

As I stare morosely at the dark outside, I must fall asleep again eventually as when I wake abruptly once more it is fully light outside. I have emails from Allie and Maggie wishing me good health and telling me not to worry, everything at the office will be taken care of. I can sense the concern in both of their messages.

Bryce has similarly sent his best, asking that I let him know when I'm back on my feet. I get the sense he thinks I took his advice to try taking a step back occasionally. I'm slightly uncomfortable with the deception, but if that's one less person worried about me today, so much the better.

I head to the bathroom to ready myself for my excursion. Upon seeing my disheveled and ghastly state in the mirror, I decide to shower before leaving.

Clean and presentable once more, I dress carefully in plain khaki slacks, and a black tunic top that suits my black mood. I tie back my long, wet hair into a braid, not wanting to bother about styling it.

I ignore the kitchen, unable to even contemplate eating, and pick up my keys and bag and head to the car to make the short trip.

IN NOT QUITE TWENTY MINUTES I'M PARKED ACROSS THE STREET FROM THE two-story, modern home of the Giordanos. Glancing at the dashboard I see that it's almost ten. There are no cars in the driveway and nothing else to indicate anyone is home.

I watch the comings and goings of the neighborhood for a while, occasionally checking my email on my phone. I can't remember ever taking a sick day, and it's making me incredibly nervous on top of my already-shot nerves. I lean down to stick my phone in my bag in an attempt to let it go.

As I'm sitting back up, a car pulls into the driveway. It's a gorgeous, sleek black coupe. German. Definitely very expensive. A short, slim, and stunning blond woman exits, clad in workout gear.

Before I can stop myself, I'm climbing out of my car and calling to her. "Mrs. Giordano?"

She stops on the doorstep and eyes me suspiciously. "Yes?"

My heart sinks as she responds to the name. She stares at me expectantly, and I call on all my powers of improvisation.

"I'm sorry if I scared you," I smile disarmingly. "I'm Claire Adams." I extend my hand.

She shifts her gym bag and takes my hand. Her perfectly manicured fingers squeeze mine limply. "Are you from immigration?" she asks warily.

I seize upon the opportunity. "Yes!" I exclaim a little too enthusiastically. "I apologize, I was told you'd been informed of my visit. Is Mr. Giordano at home?"

She looks relieved, probably because now at least she knows I'm not an axe murderer or something. "No, he's not, but you're welcome to come in. I hope you haven't been waiting long," she says kindly. "Nobody told us you were coming."

"It's okay, it happens all the time," I reply. I realize suddenly that I've left everything in the car, and I imagine I look suspicious without anything in my hands. "Oh, I'm so sorry, I forgot my papers. Let me go grab those from my car."

She nods, and I dash back to my car, grab the folio and pen out of my bag, and slip my phone in my pocket after putting it on silent. Returning quickly, I find Peyton waiting for me on the doorstep, her gym bag inside the entry way.

"Please come in," she invites me. "I'll just go throw on a sweater. You can look around if you like, or have a seat, whatever you prefer. I'll be back shortly."

She disappears up the stairs and I step down into the living room and take a deep breath.

If she assumed I was from immigration, that must mean they've either been here before, or they were possibly expecting a visit at some point. I knew that Alessandro had a conditional green card, but I realize now that I didn't even think about why that was. Perhaps part of the process is a visit verifying the authenticity of their marriage? I'm guessing, but I'm no citizenship expert. In any case, I'm confident I can steer clear of outing myself.

Thankfully, if I were an immigration agent here to check on them, she wouldn't expect me to feed her the answers to the questions I'm meant to verify their responses to. I smile, grimly realizing I have the license I need to ask her for all the information I'm looking for.

Getting into the role, I stroll the living room, examining the furnishings and photographs. There are dozens of framed pictures, mostly of the two of them. I turn slowly, looking around the room for a specific picture, and spot it over the larger of two couches. Their wedding photo.

Alessandro looks younger, his hair is short, and he's clean shaven. But he's every inch the man I know, handsome as ever in a black tuxedo. Peyton glows in the photo, beaming up at her man, a vision in her pure white mermaid gown. I want to retch again, but I know if I'm going to get what I came for I'm going to have to bring my acting game.

Becoming a real estate agent has given me a good start. Years as a property manager hasn't hurt, either. I've had my fair share of training in the art of bull-shitting my way through a tough situation.

Peyton suddenly reappears. "Handsome, isn't he?" she asks wistfully.

I clear my throat and take a seat on the couch, opening my folio and poising my pen. "Yes, I suppose he is," I reply. "How long have you been married?"

She sits somberly on the smaller couch next to me, crossing her slim legs and folding her perfectly manicured fingers over her knee. "Four years next month." I stare at her expectantly. "June thirtieth," she adds.

I nod and make a note. "And what is Mr. Giordano's profession?" I ask. I need a chance to react to information I know.

"He owns his own real estate development company," she says proudly. "We moved here six months ago from San Francisco because he said it was a hot market, and I was able to transfer to the University of Washington."

"I see," I reply. "And what are you studying?"

"Nursing," she responds.

"That's a great field," I respond warmly, hoping to win her over.

She takes the bait, beaming under the praise. "I think so! I really enjoy taking care of people," she replies.

"How long do you have left before you graduate?"

"I'm supposed to be done with my degree by the end of the year," she says. "It's hard to get a job as a new nurse. I'm already nervous!"

"I'm sure you'll find something fantastic," I say encouragingly. "So, you're planning on staying in the area then?"

"Oh yes, we love it here. We go hiking and boating all the time," she gushes enthusiastically. "Are you from here?"

"Yes," I reply shortly. I tilt my head and give her a tolerant look, hoping to discourage further questions about me. It seems to work, and she stares at me expectantly.

"Owning his own business must be difficult. Do you see your husband much, Mrs. Giordano?" I inquire.

For the first time she looks more than a little uncomfortable. "He's my husband, we see each other plenty," she replies testily, but pauses before admitting, "He does have an apartment downtown, though. He stays there when he has to work late or be in the office early."

"Downtown? But you're so close here," I press.

"He doesn't like traffic, and even though the distance is short, it can be a tough commute," she explains.

"That must make your marriage difficult at times," I reply.

She shrugs. "It gives me time to do my homework," she says simply. "I see him often enough."

"When was the last time you saw him?" I push. And I can't tell if I'm feigning the suspicion in my voice or if it's real.

"Last night," she says a little coldly. "As I said, I see him often enough."

Working late, my ass. I suppress my reaction, but also sense I'm wearing out my welcome.

"I'm sure you do," I reply kindly, making a fake note. "There's only one more thing I'm supposed to ask for — do you have a recent picture of the two of you?"

"Sure," she says eagerly, clearly ready for this to be over. She gestures for me to follow her and leads me to the kitchen. Plucking a photo from the front of the refrigerator, she hands it to me.

"We went to a friend's wedding in San Francisco week before last," she explains.

I look at the picture and compare the Alessandro in the picture to the Alessandro in my memory who had just returned from San Francisco. He had a newly grown beard, which you can just see budding in the picture of them beaming and embracing on the dance floor of a large ballroom, surrounding by happy partygoers. The photo is a wedding keepsake, etched with the bride and groom's names and date in one corner. The Thursday he was in San Francisco.

"I see," I say softly. "Thank you. May I keep it?"

"Sure, yes of course, I have another copy," she accedes.

I stare for a moment at the blank space on the fridge where the picture hung, somehow saddened by the emptiness. My eyes are drawn to a black and white image just below the bare spot. She follows my eyes and smiles delicately.

"Yes," she says in response to my stare. She pulls the sonogram picture from the fridge. "I'm pregnant."

My heart is frozen in my chest and I will myself to speak. "Congratulations," I manage. "You must be thrilled."

"We are," she replies. "Alex is going to be a great dad."

"Yes," I agree, "I'm sure he will be. I think I'm done here."

∾

How I manage to make it home I'll never know. All I know is that when I do, I crawl in bed and cry until I'm too exhausted to stay awake, then surrender myself gratefully to blackness.

∾

I wake midafternoon feeling like I've been hit by a truck. My eyes are puffy and swollen, my face red and streaky. My head pounds from the trauma and lack of food. I make myself a cup of tea and nurse it contemplatively at the kitchen bar, also managing to choke down half of a plain bagel. Even the small amount of sustenance makes a big difference, and my head begins to clear.

And I find my despair slowly being replaced by anger at all the lies he must have told me. The betrayal feels like a hot, iron fist in my gut. I'm angry with myself as well, for letting my guard down and falling in love with him. And at him again, for having an affair on that poor, unsuspecting young woman, who also happens to be *pregnant* with his child! I stand furiously and pace the living room.

Okay, Evans, get a grip. I stop and close my eyes, taking a series of deep breaths. Too many people are counting on me for me to go to pieces over this. And I'm not one to wallow. I'm a doer. *So, what am I going to do?*

End it, obviously. But how?

I don't want to be the insecure mess I was when Tom left me. But I'm not the one being left this time. I consider how Alessandro will react.

I can't see calling or texting him that we're through going over well. He'll want to hear it straight from my lips. And if I try to end it with no explanation I already know he won't let it go. So that's not an option. I just don't want to hear his excuses, don't want to give him an opportunity to convince me to come back to him.

So, don't give him the opportunity.

I retrieve the photograph Peyton gave me from the table next to the door. Giving it a sorrowful glance, I return it to its spot, face down, and pick up my phone. I have a few emails, none of them urgent, and three missed text messages. All from Alessandro.

At six forty-five this morning — *Buongiorno, mio tesoro. Miss you. x*

And again, at eleven this morning — *Everything okay? Busy day?*

And just about half an hour ago — *Getting worried. Call me please? I'm working from home today.*

And my next action demonstrates that, while usually a creature of logic, deep down I'm as impulsive as any woman scorned, because I grab the photo and stuff it in my purse, slamming the door behind me on my way out.

∿

I START TO QUESTION MY ABILITY TO SEE MY RASH COURSE OF ACTION THROUGH when Alessandro answers the door shirtless and out of breath, headphones dangling around his neck. He glistens sexily, his lean, muscular torso covered in a sheen of sweat.

"Sera," he greets me in surprise and relief, holding the door open. "I was worried about you. I'm glad you're here."

I step in, and he closes the door, leaning in to kiss me. I sidestep and shake my head silently. He regards me curiously as he takes in my appearance, my expression. Thankfully, my eyes aren't as puffy, but I'm sure I still look a frightful and somber mess.

"What's wrong?" he asks, slowly realizing something is amiss. "Why aren't you at work?"

I take a seat in the chair next to the couch, and he perches himself on the arm of the couch.

"I took the day off," I finally say. He furrows his brow and I can't handle shirtless, concerned Alessandro. "Will you put a shirt on, please?"

He looks at me levelly then saunters to the treadmill in the corner. Slinging his headphones over the handle, he pulls his shirt off the side table next to it and slides it on, then reseats himself on the couch. "What is going on?" he demands.

I lean forward in the chair. "I don't know how to say this, so I'm just going to say it," I preface, and a look of terror crosses his face as he realizes what I'm about to do.

"No, Sera," he starts to protest.

I put my hand up. "Please, just let me get this out," I plead.

He pushes on, clearly understanding where I'm going and horrified. "Don't do this," he says anxiously, falling to his knees in front of me. "What can I do?" He stretches his hand out, seeking mine.

I sigh heavily and pull the picture out of my purse and place it in his open palm.

"You can go back to your wife," I say simply.

SIXTEEN

Alessandro's horrified expression is enough to settle the question of his betrayal of both women he's promised his love to.

"Where did you get this?" he finally asks.

"From Peyton," I respond evenly, averting my gaze to the ceiling and blinking back the heavy tears that have started stinging the back of my eyes.

"How did she find you?" he asks, dumbstruck.

I drop my head forward again to give him a questioning look. "She didn't; I found her. And it's not like I needed the confirmation, but it's satisfying to have it," I reply gravely.

"No, Sera, please listen to me," he insists. "I don't know what Peyton's told you, but I was going to explain everything." He sits back on the couch and buries his face in his hands.

"What's to tell? You're married. This," I gesture between us, "is over."

"Please hear me out," he begs, tears filling his eyes.

And this, exactly, is what I didn't want. Excuses. Explanations. Time for him to talk his way out of responsibility for his actions. Time for him to convince me out of my convictions.

"There is no explanation you can give me that will fix this. Why would I even believe you after you lied to me? Which is just as much of a problem, by the way," I reply. He goes to open his mouth in protest. "And please don't insult me by saying you never said you weren't married."

"That's not what I was going to say," he asserts. "You're right, I lied to you. But not the way you think."

I rub my temples. "I can't do this, Alessandro," I say tiredly. "I can't argue about this, and I don't want to hear excuses. It's over. Please, just let go. Your deal closes next week, we won't ever have to do business with each other again. I'll move on, you'll go back to your wife." And it sounds so simple coming out of my mouth, though I know it will be anything but.

"I don't want to move on," he says as tears threaten to spill down his cheeks. He squeezes his eyes closed and roughly wipes the moisture from his face. "I love you. And I think if you listened to me you would understand. My marriage is a sham."

"Okay, so don't go back to her, I don't care," I interrupt, exasperated. "But I'm not going to be with a married man. Under any circumstances. But before you decide your marriage is over you might want to think about what's best for the baby."

"What?" he asks blankly.

"Cheating on your wife is one thing, but leaving her while she's pregnant? I didn't think you were capable of such selfishness," I elaborate. "But then again, I didn't see this coming either." I gesture at the photo in his hand.

He slowly sets the photo, picture side down, onto the coffee table and stares ahead, clearly utterly shocked. "Peyton is *pregnant?*"

I give him a look of disbelief. "You can't seriously expect me to believe you didn't know that."

"I didn't," he says tightly. "That does change things."

I'm dismayed by the confused expression on his face, then distracted as I remember something else he said. "You asked if she found me. Does she know about us?"

"Yes, more or less," he says.

"Which is it, more or less?"

"She doesn't know about you specifically, but she knows I'm involved with other women," he replies. "I told you, it's not what you think, we…"

I put a hand up. "Stop. Please. I've already told you it doesn't matter. I don't want to hear any more."

"Even if it changes your mind?" he asks persistently.

"Especially if it changes my mind," I concur. "Because at the end of this conversation, you're still married." *And you still lied to me. After I told you I trusted you.* And for the first time my calm, collected demeanor slips and I feel the anguish inside spilling out with the tears that fall down my cheeks.

"Yes, that is, unfortunately, true," he admits forlornly.

He reaches out to wipe away my tears, and I wave his hand away.

"Please don't make this any harder than it is."

He looks tortured and drops his hands impotently in his lap, staring down at them. "Serafina," he says softly before raising his eyes to meet mine. "I didn't want to hurt you. I thought I could wait and perhaps never have to tell you. But obviously that was selfish, and I ended up hurting you anyway. I'm sorrier than you can possibly know."

"I'm sure you are," I acknowledge, rising. "Goodbye, Alessandro." I don't wait for his reply to leave.

⌇

As soon as I'm home I snap into my old standby defense mechanism — work mode. I call Bryce and reschedule filing the police report for the following afternoon, and I settle in to answer emails and touch base with Ellie and Jackson ahead of our meeting with Sutton Developments in the morning.

Once I'm caught up, I make a quick dinner and bring it back to the coffee table, choking it down mechanically while I go through my backlog of less urgent matters I've had on the back burner. I settle into a soothing rhythm and the night passes quickly.

⌇

Wednesday flies by just as rapidly. Our initial meeting with Sutton Developments goes extremely well, and Mr. Sutton takes to Jackson particularly, validating my decision to allow him to shadow Ellie on the project. The execution now in their hands, I'm pleased to pass the project to Ellie and Jackson, so I can monitor our security plan adjustments and focus on some general, high-level business planning for once.

I meet Bryce after lunch at the police headquarters on 5th. He looks as handsome as ever but keeps his distance physically and verbally, as if he senses my inner torment.

I note with some amusement that, even in a building packed with hunky men in uniform, Bryce still turns heads. But I'm grateful for his calm presence as he walks me through the procedure and makes sure everything is fully documented.

I return to my office with a sense of relief at having put on record the events that upended my company's stability. It's given me back a measure of control, as have all the other procedures and changes Bryce recommended, of which I'm especially appreciative given recent events.

I delve back into work, blocking out everything but the spreadsheets in front of me.

⌇

When Maggie knocks on my door at the end of the day, I'm surprised at how much time has passed. I stretch widely as she enters.

"Ms. Evans," Maggie says by way of greeting. "Mr. Giordano is here to see you."

I fold back in on myself abruptly, clenching my jaw to hold back a frustrated noise. "Please tell him I'm busy," I instruct her in a tight voice.

But he's already strolling in past her. "Come now, is that any way to treat your favorite client?" he teases, his smile directed toward easing the tension on Maggie's face at my reaction. He's forcing me to play nice for our audience.

"Of course not, please have a seat, Mr. Giordano," I gesture to a chair. "Thank you, Maggie."

She closes the door behind her on her way out, and I curse internally.

"What can I do for you, Mr. Giordano?" I stare at him coolly.

"Do you want to hear what I did today?" he asks, leaning forward in his chair.

So, it's not work related. My anger flares.

"No. I thought I made myself perfectly clear," I state firmly.

"As did I," he replies, imploring me with his eyes. "I'm not giving up."

"Unfortunately, you don't have a choice in the matter," I reply.

He runs his finger under his chin and I shift uncomfortably. A smile tugs at the corners of his mouth. "Don't I?" he asks.

"No," I reply, but my tone is uncertain at best.

He regards me thoughtfully for a moment. "I'll go," he concedes. "Another time, perhaps." He pauses at the door. "Is there any hope, Sera, for you and me?"

I press my lips together to suppress a sad smile as I can't help but give the response I'm not sure he'll even understand. "There never was much hope," I answer. "Just a fool's hope."

I sit at my desk a long while after he leaves, staring into the ever-darkening void outside my window.

∾

I DECIDE TO SKIP THE WEEKLY TAG-UP WITH BUONE CASE ON FRIDAY, FOR MY own sanity. Jackson seems fine with it. He's much more confident these days, and it's reassuring. I'm comforted, at least, to know I still have employees I can trust.

I wander into Allie's office in the afternoon, as I realize I haven't talked to her since our security meeting on Monday.

She's texting on her phone when I walk into her office, and she looks up guiltily, then with relief as she realizes it's just me.

"You know, you shouldn't look relieved," I kid. "I am still your boss."

"Psshhh," she replies. "Go ahead and fire me." She smiles widely as she finishes her message and puts down her phone. As soon as she's gotten a good look at me, she stands up and closes the door. "Good lord, Sera, are you still sick?"

"No, but that's an interesting way to greet your best friend," I reply, collapsing tiredly into one of her chairs.

She sits in the chair next to me, turning it so we're face to face. "Come on, Sera, it's me," she urges.

I look up at the ceiling and blink back tears. When I think I'll be able to keep control of myself, I look at her squarely. "You know the background checks Hoyt Corporate Services provided? Well, they led me to a rather nasty discovery," I say delicately. "Alessandro is married. To a very lovely — and pregnant — young woman named Peyton."

Allie gasps in shock. "*No!*" she protests. I nod morosely. "Do you want to talk about it?"

I shake my head vehemently and she envelops me in a hug. We embrace for a good solid minute before she releases me. I wipe the dampness from my eyes and compose myself.

"I should've known better," I lament.

"Oh, Sera, don't," she admonishes me. "Don't do that to yourself. You took a risk. I'm proud of you. And I'm terribly sorry it didn't work out."

"That's a lovely way to frame it, thank you, Allie," I say sincerely. "But I still think I'm going to need quite a lot of alcohol this evening. Game?"

"I'm all yours," she replies without hesitation. "Let's blow this pop stand."

I laugh, and we pack out for an evening of booze and dancing, the only proper sendoff for crushed dreams and a broken heart.

⁓

AROUND TWO A.M. I STUMBLE OUT OF THE ELEVATOR ONTO MY FLOOR, MOSTLY just tired, though still decently buzzed. I'm so busy fumbling with my keys as I walk down the hall that I don't notice Alessandro leaning against my doorframe. He wears his favorite linen, navy trousers that skim his taught legs perfectly, with a crisp, white button up shirt, the top few buttons of which have been undone. His dark hair is mussed and sexy, his expression tired but intense.

My keys fall to the floor as our eyes lock. He silently steps forward and retrieves them, handing them to me. "I told you, I can't give up," he says in response to my perplexed expression.

I push past him and open my door. I drop my things on the table, kick off my heels angrily, and make to close the door in his face when he puts a hand out to stop me. He stands in front of me, his breath hot on my face.

"Please, Serafina," he breathes. "I need you to understand."

He reaches out and touches my face. His fingers leave a hot trail down my cheek and I let out an involuntary sigh. I realize it's been nearly five days since we last touched, and the thought lights a fire inside me, my brain taking a backseat to the heat I feel this close to him.

"It's still a no," I reply, my voice a soft sigh. But even I hear the "yes" in my "no."

He steps in and closes the door behind him, pressing me against the wall. "Then maybe less talking, more showing," he says, and his mouth descends upon mine.

My brain wants to protest, but my body shoves it in a deep, dark room inside me and locks the door. Dizzy with alcohol and lust, I respond to his touch, twisting my fingers in his thick hair, pulling myself to him.

After a few moments of feverish kissing, he scoops me up and carries me to the bedroom. It takes us mere seconds to liberate ourselves of our clothing before we're wrapped in each other once more on the bed. He pins me under him, working his way between my legs. I allow him in eagerly, my back arching off the bed as he enters me. One of his hands finds my breast and works my nipple as he starts to move in me. I'm writhing in pleasure and torment, simultaneously furious at allowing this to be but desperately wanting more.

His tormented cries join my own and his mouth finds mine once again, his tongue wreaking havoc with my senses as he drags me toward climax. He lays his arms over mine, pinning me with his whole torso as he kisses my neck and chest, pumping into me all the while. His mouth drops to my ear.

"I can't live without you, Serafina," he groans. "I need you."

I groan loudly in protest and enjoyment. His words touch me in a way I can't guard against while he's inside me, and my need for him is just as strong. I press on his chest until he pulls back so I can climb on top of him.

I ease him inside me and sink onto him so that our bodies are fully connected as I start to work my hips. He runs his hands over my back, moaning in pleasure. I snake my fingers into his hair and kiss him deeply as I move. He pulls my face up with his hands, staring deeply into my eyes. His stare is so open and vulnerable my heart can't take it.

"I love you, Alessandro," I breathe, tears of anger and confusion threatening to spill over my cheeks.

The ferocity of his response knocks me onto my back. He hovers over me, pressing his forehead to mine. "*Ti amo*," he whispers to me, our eyes locked once more, and he slides into me, thrusting furiously until we both climax loudly and collapse in each other's arms.

The bliss I used to feel after our lovemaking is notably absent. The confused tears finally leak out of the corners of my eyes, and I lay still and quiet in his arms until I'm sure he is asleep.

I shift quietly out of bed, twisting my pillow next to him hoping it helps delay his noticing my absence. I stand at the window for a long while, considering my moment of weakness as I fully sober up.

I can't shake feeling like I should tattoo a large "A" on my chest in penance for knowingly fucking another woman's husband. The deep conviction that I simply cannot do this settles over me. I can't be with him. But I can't resist him either. And he can't seem to let go.

I pack a bag slowly and quietly and, as dawn approaches, I slip into the living room to finish my preparations.

Standing as far from the bedroom as I can manage, I place a call and wait for an answer on the other end. After many rings, my mother finally picks up, sounding very sleepy.

"Hi, Mom, I'm sorry to wake you," I say quietly.

"Is everything okay, dear?" she asks, her voice filled with concern.

"No, Mom. Can I come stay with you for a while?"

Her pause is, thankfully, short. "Of course, honey. I'm always happy to see you," she responds.

"Thanks," I sigh in relief. "I'll be home in a couple hours." We say our goodbyes and I write a note for Alessandro.

I wish I could say I'm not sorry that you managed to seduce me once again, but I am. As you once promised we would, I'm ending this on my terms. I love you, Alessandro, but I can't be with you in good conscience. Unfortunately, since you won't give up so easily, I'm left with no choice but to remove myself from the situation. I hope you'll understand and respect my decision, but then you wouldn't be the man I fell in love with. Nonetheless, I am gone.

—Your Darling Serafina

Before he can wake, I place the note on the nightstand. I resist the urge to kiss him, touch him one last time. Toting my luggage as quietly as I can, I manage to slip out of the apartment with no sign of having woken him.

SEVENTEEN

Driving up I-5, I feel the best I have in days. A weight lifts from my shoulders the farther I get from Seattle, and I'm able to enjoy the rolling, green landscapes that splay out around me. On my way through Mount Vernon, I hit up a drive-through for a quick breakfast and manage to finish all of it as I drive.

I make it to my mother's house in record time, the sun still rising in the sky. My mother greets me at the door, helping me settle my luggage into my childhood bedroom. She uncharacteristically doesn't press me for information, making small talk about the changes to the neighborhood since my last visit.

When she's run out of small talk, we sit quietly at the small, round dining room table, sipping coffee.

Throwing caution to the wind, I break the silence. "You were right, Mom," I offer. "I'm in love with Alessandro." It occurs to me for the first time that I may have had feelings for him all along, and my mother simply noticed before I did.

She nods and puts her cup down. "I know, honey," she responds. "What happened?"

I smile grimly. "I found out he's married." I take another sip of coffee, hiding my expression behind the mug so I can privately enjoy her reaction.

She doesn't disappoint — she gasps loudly as her hands fly over her mouth. "That son of a bitch!" she exclaims loudly, and I have to laugh. She puts her hand on my arm. "I'm sorry, Sera."

"It'll be okay," I say, trying to convince myself as much as her. "He tried to persuade me not to leave him, but I can't be the other woman."

"No," she agrees. "You're made of better stuff than that."

I eye her speculatively. "Thanks," I reply. "He didn't exactly make it easy to stick to my guns."

"Then I'm all the prouder of you," she responds sincerely.

"Thanks, Mom."

∽

THAT AFTERNOON I SETTLE INTO MY ROOM TO COME UP WITH MY GAME PLAN. The first order of business is to call Allie. As I pick up my phone I notice a text message from Alessandro.

I'll settle for trying to be better than the man you fell in love with and hope that you change your mind. Until then I'll do my best to give you space. Ti amo.

I close my eyes briefly and push my reaction into a place in my mind where I can deal with it later. For now, I need to focus. I scroll to Allie's cell number and place the call.

"Sera, dear," she greets me. "Did you still want to go shopping tomorrow?"

"Hey Allie," I respond. "No, there's been a slight change of plans."

"Oh? Do tell," she replies curiously.

"When I got home last night Alessandro was waiting for me," I admit.

"Omigod," she gasps.

"Yeah," I agree. "I should've known he would do something along those lines, but I wasn't thinking about it. I was so taken by surprise…"

"That you fell onto his penis?" she accurately guesses.

I laugh joylessly. "Something like that," I concede. "I regretted it immediately."

"Naturally," she replies.

"So, once he was asleep, I left. I'm at my mom's."

"You *left*?" she cries. "As in, you left him sleeping there at your place, by himself? And then went to your *mother's* house? Holy shit."

"I know," I agree. "But I needed to put some distance between us, since it seems like that's what it's going to take. He says he'll give me space, but I kind of don't believe it."

"No, you absolutely did the right thing," she agrees. "I'm just surprised you went to your mom's house."

"Yeah, me too," I laugh. "But I guess sometimes you just need your mom." I pause. "I think I'm going to move and rent out my condo."

"Wow," Allie responds. "Do you feel like you need to do that to shake him off?"

"Yes," I reply honestly. "But I also think it's time for a change."

"You know, most people just get a new hairstyle when they break up with someone," she jokes.

131

"Well, I'm not most people," I reply. "I'm going to work from here at least through this week. Buone Case's deal closes on Friday. There might be some follow-up, but that's all Jackson, and it won't require them to be in the office."

"Sounds like a plan," she agrees. "I'm proud of you, Sera."

"Thanks, Allie," I reply. "Talk soon."

Once we're off the phone, I send an email to Maggie letting her know I'll be remote for personal reasons indefinitely, with instructions not to notify anyone outside of the company without my permission. I also send a very vague email to everyone in the office instructing them to call or email me with any questions, and, finally, set an out-of-office message to the same effect.

I also realize I need to call Bryce immediately and notify him of my location, as I hadn't checked in this morning.

He picks up on the first ring. "Sera, thank God, I was just about to call you," he answers, his voice filled with concern.

"I'm so sorry, Bryce. I had a rather unexpected morning and forgot to call until just now," I apologize.

"It must have been something outrageous. You're usually so punctual," he teases, obviously relieved.

"That's one word for it," I agree drily. "I'm at my mother's house now, in Bellingham."

"Oh? Finally needed a break, huh?" he asks.

"You got me," I admit. "I'll be working remotely from here through Friday at least. I was also wondering if you could recommend a secured, temporary living space for when I return?"

"Did something happen that I need to know about?" he asks sharply.

I consider the question. "Something happened, yes, but not what you're thinking," I reply slowly.

"The Italian?" he asks matter-of-factly.

I'm aghast. "How did you know that?"

"If it was business-related, you would have told me earlier this week when you'd gone all quiet," he says pointedly.

"I guess you don't work as a security consultant if you're not highly observant," I allow, and he laughs.

"Nope," he replies. "He didn't do anything to you, did he?"

"God, no, nothing like that," I reply quickly. "It's just over. And he's having a hard time accepting that."

"I see," he says. "So, you're not concerned for your safety?"

"Not at all. I think it's just best if I remove myself as an option for him," I say delicately.

"I'm with you one hundred percent," he agrees enthusiastically, and it causes me to raise an eyebrow. There's that hint of interest again.

"At any rate, I plan to buy a new place. It was time anyway. It was the first place I ever bought, years ago. I'll rent it out eventually, but in the meantime, I could use some help getting my things into storage and setting up something temporary while I secure a new living situation."

"Absolutely, I'm happy to arrange all of that," he replies. "I'd ask if you need help securely purchasing a new place, but I imagine you know how to do that, given your line of work."

"Yes, that I do," I agree. "All of my properties are each held in their own LLC. I've been operating that way for ages."

"Smart woman," he says.

On Sunday, Mom and I spend the day setting up my old room to suit me for my stay, grocery shopping, and preparing food. We chat pleasantly throughout, and it almost feels like a normal relationship. She makes the occasional snarky comment, of course, but since there's nobody here to embarrass me in front of, I'm able to brush it off and we fall into a mellow rhythm.

Come Monday morning we establish a new routine of breakfasting together, then she heads to work, where she does bookkeeping for a large accounting firm. I spend my mornings dealing with the normal ebb and flow of work issues, and as much of my free time as possible looking for a new place. After spending so much time in Alessandro's spacious apartment, I'm ready for something bigger, with a view to match.

On Tuesday afternoon I get an email from Allie. The subject line reads, *So much for that.* I open the email curiously.

I just caught Alessandro trying to wrest your whereabouts out of Maggie. Does three-and-a-half days count as "giving you space"?

I shake my head and reply.

I'm surprised it took that long. How's everything?

Her reply comes quickly.

Five by five, boss. Keep doing what you gotta. We've got this. ;)

With a chuckle I return to my hunt for a new condo.

I'm showing my mother some listings that evening when Bryce calls.

"Bryce!" I answer, surprised. "You're working awfully late."

"Comes with the territory," he replies. "I just wanted to let you know your things are in storage and I've secured you a place, ready whenever you are. How's the apartment hunt going?"

"Not bad," I respond. "There are several places I think I'd like to check out once I get back."

"Well, if you need someone to go with you, I'm happy to help," he responds. While friendly, his response takes me by surprise.

"Isn't that a little outside of your job description?" I tease him.

"For you? Nothing's out of my job description," he replies seriously, and I'm taken aback. "But really, it's not. I'm happy to check it out with you. You know, from a security perspective."

"Boy, you really go above and beyond for your clients, don't you?" I reply edgily.

"I'm sorry if I seem forward, Sera," he says, sensing the reticence in my voice. "I just feel very strongly about helping you as much as I can."

"Is that the only reason?" I probe bluntly.

"Sort of," he admits. "But it's not what you're thinking. I'm not trying to hit on you or anything, I promise. I can't even explain it. I just feel very protective of you."

I frown, weighing his words. I have an independent streak a mile wide, so I'm naturally resistant to anyone trying to treat me like I'm incapable of taking care of myself. On the other hand, there is an ex-employee with an unknown partner, unknown motives, and a knack for sabotage out there hating my guts at this very moment. So, a handsome security expert with a yen to be at my beck and call probably isn't the worst thing in the world.

"Thanks, Bryce," I capitulate. "I'll do my best not to take advantage of that."

He laughs heartily. "Hey, I'm the one who put it out there," he replies. "If you do, it's on me for offering."

"You're a good guy, Bryce."

"Thanks, Sera. I'm honored to be working with you, really. You're a special woman."

∽

On Thursday, I find it. My new home. It's a gorgeous, recently renovated, luxury four bedroom, two-and-a-half bath, sprawling condo in one of the older sections of downtown. It has gorgeous views of Elliott Bay and amenities galore, including a bevy of security features in the unit itself. At around three thousand square feet its more than twice my current square footage. Normally I'm not one for excess, but the place just calls out to me with its simple, clean lines and lack of fussiness.

I call the seller's real estate agent immediately and am pleased to discover that, having just come on the market, there aren't any offers in. Nor are there likely to be many on this level of real estate, but I know in my gut that this is where I want to live, so I offer at asking.

"You realize it's just under four *million*, don't you, dear? Not four hundred thousand."

I've been condescended to enough in my career to not take the bait. "Absolutely," I respond as sweetly as possible. "I prefer to finance my investments for tax purposes, but if the seller needs a quick close or would prefer cash I'm happy to oblige."

"Are you sure you wouldn't rather see the property first?" she presses, clearly skeptical.

"Quite," I respond. "I'll email you the offer paperwork shortly. Please let me know where to send the earnest money."

"Ohhkay," she sighs, and I can tell she still doesn't believe I'm for real.

I confirm her email address from the listing and end the call. After I've submitted the paperwork I forward the listing to Bryce. I title the email *Home, sweet home.*

~

First thing Friday morning I call Allie.

"Mrs. Kramer," I greet her. "Good morning to you."

"And to you, Ms. Evans," she responds just as formally. "What can I do for you today?"

"I checked with Jackson yesterday, and it looks like everything is still greenlit on the Buone Case deal to close today. I'd like you to get in the loop on that and revoke Buone Case's access credentials as soon as that's wrapped," I instruct her.

"You've got it, boss," she replies. "How much longer will you stay in Bellingham?"

"Not long," I reply. "I've found a place, and as soon as my offer is accepted I'm going to order an inspection. So, I'll need to be there for that."

"Oooh, exciting!" she exclaims, and suddenly I hear voices in the background. "Hey, gotta go. Talk soon!"

~

Just after noon I get an email from Jan Rogers, the condescending real estate agent, that my cash offer has been accepted with a twelve-day close. I do a little happy dance before calling my inspector.

"Hey Rich, it's Sera Evans."

"Sera! My favorite real estate mogul! How the heck are ya, kid?"

I laugh. "I could complain, but I won't," I joke. "Do you have time to inspect a downtown condo at three thousand square feet early next week?"

"For you? Without a doubt. I can get you in Monday afternoon or Tuesday afternoon," he offers.

"Monday afternoon," I respond immediately. I'm eager to get in there and see if it's everything it seems to be. I provide Rich the details and follow on with an email to Jan. And as an afterthought, I email Bryce to see if he's available to join me. What the hell, why not?

⌇

I RECEIVE TWO MORE CALLS THAT AFTERNOON, THE FIRST FROM JACKSON gleefully sharing that Buone Case is now the proud owner of their new land parcel, for which they plan to break ground the following week after a few standard preparatory checks. The second is from Allie informing me that the Buone Case team's access has been revoked. I breathe a sigh of relief all around.

⌇

THAT EVENING, MY MOM TRUDGES IN THE DOOR, COLLAPSING IN HER FAVORITE chair dramatically.

"Hey, Mom, how was work?" I ask warily.

"A disaster," she replies affectedly. "We have a new client — a mom-and-pop ice cream shop. I went in to their office to go over their books with the owners, and they had boxes upon boxes of receipts. Nothing had been organized or cataloged. I'm going to be piecing together their books for *ages*."

"Well, I have just the thing for you then," I reply, smiling. "I'm taking you out to dinner!"

"Yay!" she exclaims, brightening. I laugh at her sudden change in mood. "Where should we go?"

"Your choice, Mom," I reply. "But no Italian."

⌇

WE DECIDE ON CHINESE FOOD, OUR OLD STANDBY. IT'S NOT FANCY, BUT there's a great dumpling restaurant not far from the house. As we get seated, the waiter asks if we're celebrating anything tonight.

"Oh!" I say, remembering suddenly. "Yes! I just bought a new place."

The waiter offers his congratulations and takes our drink orders.

"Sera, you didn't tell me you'd found a place already," my mother chides after he's gone.

"Sorry, Mom, it slipped my mind. It was a busy day, and then you were all," I pull a melodramatic face, "when you got home."

She smacks me playfully on the arm. "Tell me about it," she insists.

I resist the temptation to pretend like she's asking me to describe her dramatic entrance this evening and fill her in on the specs of the new condo. When I tell her the price, her jaw drops.

"I just ... how do you even..." she's having trouble finding words.

"It's a lot of money, I know," I concede. "But it just looked like home."

"Well, crap, for that much money it better do a whole lot more than that," she grumbles.

"I can afford it, Mom," I assure her.

"Goodness, Serafina. I knew you were doing well for yourself, but I had no idea how well," she admits.

"I am, but I couldn't afford that on the salary I draw from ERS, Mom. That money comes from the investments Grandma and Grandpa Tyler left me," I say.

"You're not using up everything they left you so quickly, are you?" my mother asks in horror.

"God, no! The cashflow from the properties they left me is more than enough to cover anything I could possibly need for several lifetimes," I promise. "I know what I'm doing."

Our waiter interrupts to deliver our drinks and takes our dinner orders before whisking efficiently off.

My mother huffs quietly, and I already know she's been biting back a snappy retort based on both the subject matter and her tight expression.

"I suppose that's why my parents left the bulk of their holdings to you instead of me," she finally grumbles.

I bite back the urge to snap back with a biting agreement of her assessment. As if my knowledge magically appeared but had been denied her. She never had any interest in Grandpa's empire while he was alive. But I lived with my grandparents while I went to college and eagerly learned everything I could from Grandpa. And after I graduated, I spent years proving that I could manage his holdings before he bequeathed them to me. I roll my eyes at the reactiveness and oversimplification of her resentment, and change the subject instead of rising to the bait.

"Alessandro's deal closed today. So, our contract with them is officially complete," I offer.

"Well, that's a blessing," she replies, taking the bait. "Now he has no reason to darken your doorstep ever again."

I grimace. "Something tells me he doesn't need a reason. But with my moving and him not having access to our offices anymore, there are no more doorsteps for him, anyway."

"Good. Once a cheater, always a cheater," she says in a vicious tone.

Perhaps following the touchy subject of being passed over as heir to her father's legacy with the even touchier subject of my perfidious ex-boyfriend wasn't the smartest tactic.

"I'm sure he has his own story, Mom," I defend him. She looks sharply at me and I put my hands up. "Hey, I'm not saying what he did was okay. I was certainly not prepared to be a part of it." I pause thoughtfully. "But I've seen him in difficult ethical situations and he never disappointed me before. So, he may have his reasons here."

"There is *never* a good reason to cheat on your spouse. *Never*."

"Geez, Mom, okay, I hear you," I say, trying to defuse her feisty tone.

My mother contemplates me carefully for a moment. "I think it's time you knew why your father really left."

EIGHTEEN

I spit out the sip of soda I just took. "Excuse me?" I ask, aghast, mopping up the mess with a napkin.

"Sera, your father left because I kicked him out. For cheating on me. On us," she says matter-of-factly.

"And you're only just now telling me this? Seventeen years later?" I'm appalled at her revelation. "What do you mean he was cheating on *us*?"

My mother sighs and folds her hands in her lap. "I didn't tell you before because I thought it would hurt too much. But given recent events, I think it's time you knew. Your father had another family. He was married to another woman — not legally, obviously — and had a child with her. He would frequently disappear," she explains. "And until I found out the truth, he never had any explanation for his behavior. I put up with it for years, and I kick myself for it to this day."

I sit there dumbstruck, unable to wrap my head around what she's told me. She sips her water primly and sets it down with an exasperated look.

"I shouldn't have told you," she says. "It was too much."

"No, Mom," I say, quietly furious. "You should have told me *much* sooner."

She looks like she's about to say something nasty in return, but before she can her face crumples. "I'm sorry, darling. I thought I was protecting you. You're right, I should have told you sooner."

"So, tell me now, Mom," I prompt.

The waiter returns at just that moment with our dinners, laying the dumpling and rice steamers around the table. When he's gone, my mother quietly fills her plate, so I do the same, trying to contain the flood of emotions I'm feeling.

After she's eaten a few pork dumplings, she puts her chopsticks down.

"When you were four years old I found out I had uterine cancer," she says. My jaw drops and I start to respond, but she motions for me to let her continue. "I never told you because you were so young. And by the time you were old enough to know, well, things were hard for our family, and I had enough to worry about."

She exhales heavily and slowly consumes another dumpling. I eat hesitantly, waiting for her to continue, wondering what other bombshells she's about to drop.

"It's why we never had more children," she begins again. "I was deeply depressed for several years, and even after I sought help at your father's behest, I still struggled. It's not something you just get over as a woman." She sniffs delicately, and I reach out and cover her hand with mine.

"I'm so sorry, Mom," I say.

She flips her palm over and gives my hand a squeeze, then withdraws to pick at her rice.

"When your father started working more and going on 'trips' on the weekend, I thought he was just tired of dealing with me," she explains. "But then, one day, when you were twelve, your father was at work, and she came to me. His other wife. She begged me to free him. He'd been telling her I knew about her and their child and was refusing to let him get a divorce, so he could truly be with her."

"How old was their child?" I ask.

"He was five, at the time," she replies.

"So, what did you do?" I probe.

"I called him every name in the book. I threw things. I threatened him. And then, when nothing I said or did got a reaction from him, I told him to leave and never come back," she admits.

"So, it wasn't Dad's choice to leave us?" I ask.

"Really, Sera, after all that I've told you, *that's* your response?"

I hear my own words in my head and my eyes pop. "No, Mom, I'm sorry, I'm not saying it was your fault," I explain. "I completely understand why you did what you did. I'm just trying to wrap my head around it."

She gives me a sideways scowl. "What else was I supposed to do? Pretend like it never happened? Tell him it was okay?" she demands. "If I hadn't kicked him out, he would have left eventually."

"It doesn't matter what he would have done," I concede. "I would have done the same, in your shoes."

My mother grabs my hand and leans in earnestly. "Yes, Sera," she says urgently. "That's exactly why I'm telling you this. You'd do the same.

You've done it. Now stick with it. Men that do this to women — they're no good."

"Mom, Alessandro is nothing like Dad," I reply, pulling my hand away.

"Why are you defending him? He may be handsome, Sera, but don't let that distract you from his actions. He's showed you who he is. Don't forget that," she insists.

I shake my head. As angry as I am with Alessandro, I can't put him in the same class as my father, especially given this information.

"Everyone makes mistakes, Mom. Some mistakes are unforgivable," I agree. "And I'm sticking to my decision — I have no intention of going back to Alessandro. But despite his issues, I can't see him ever saying what Dad said to me when he left."

My mother looks at me blankly. "I don't remember your father saying anything to you that night," she responds slowly.

"Seriously? You were standing right next to me. He said," I have to reach deep to say this calmly, "nobody could ever love me. Who says that to their kid? Or to anybody, for that matter?"

I may has well have just slapped my mother. Her face turns red and splotchy and she is utterly flabbergasted. I put down my chopsticks and push my plate away.

"Your father didn't say that to you," she manages after a moment. "He said that to *me*, Sera. He was talking to *me*. All these years, you thought your father didn't love you? That you are unlovable?"

I can see in her eyes that she now understands so much more about my relationships with men, or lack thereof. And through her admission, she's shown me a good deal about why she is the way she is too.

As my brain processes her correction I want to protest, to say she's wrong, but my adult eyes look through my childish understanding of those events that unfolded at such a tender age, and I know she's right. And the tears that threaten to spill out of my eyes are for all the years that we never spoke a word of that day.

∽

I LAY IN BED THAT NIGHT, STARING AT THE GLOWING PLASTIC STARS I AFFIXED to the ceiling when I was nine. My mother and I talked late into the evening about why she kept my father away from me after that, and in turn I told her more about what happened with both Tom and Alessandro. She wouldn't back down from lumping Alessandro with Dad, though, and my continued defensiveness at the comparison has been troubling me.

Alessandro did cheat on his wife with me. And he did claim that Peyton knew about us, though from my knothole it seemed like she was clueless. So why is my gut rejecting the link? It can't just be my love for him. Even while head over heels, before I knew, I was aware of his shortcomings. His arrogance. His penchant for moodiness. His hot temper.

But having personally witnessed his adherence to his own internal, strong moral compass, I have a hard time reconciling the depth of deceit in his actions to the Alessandro I thought I knew.

Exhausted from a tumultuous day, I file the issue away under "doesn't matter anyway" and fall into a fitful sleep.

My phone pings around seven, so I stop trying to sleep in and pick it up. Even with a crappy night's sleep I don't think there's any chance I'll be able to ignore the bright morning light peeping around the blinds.

It's a text from Bryce. *I have business in Vancouver this evening, can I stop by and take you to lunch on my way up?*

I contemplate the offer for a moment. I doubt he asks all his clients to go to lunch on a Saturday, hours from home. But I'm not planning on returning to Seattle until Monday morning, and I'll need the keys for my temporary living quarters.

Okay, bring my new keys? I type quickly.

You got it. See you around noon.

I shuffle out of bed and into the kitchen where I'm greeted by the smell of freshly brewed coffee and bacon.

"Mmmm," I say, grabbing a slice of bacon that's drying on a big, yellow plate next to the stove. "Thanks, Ma."

She smirks as I steal another piece. "You're welcome, dear. What's on the agenda for today?"

"I have some work to do this morning, and then apparently I'm having lunch with my security consultant," I respond. "But I'm open this afternoon if you still need cleaning out the garage."

"Your security consultant is driving all the way up here just to have lunch with you?" she asks archly.

"No, Mom, it's not like that," I respond to her unspoken accusation. *Except it probably is like that, for him, anyway*, I think to myself. "He's got to be in Vancouver tonight, he's just passing through."

"Okay," she replies skeptically. "If you say so."

"Yeah yeah yeah," I respond. I switch to a mocking falsetto, "'When I was your age, when a young man went out of his way to take a young woman to lunch it meant something,'"

She blushes, confirming that that was *exactly* what she was just thinking. "So, he's young, hmmm?" she counters.

"Compared to you? Yes," I tease her, and flounce out of the room with a freshly poured cup of coffee.

∽

BRYCE, PUNCTUAL AS EVER, PULLS UP EXACTLY AT NOON. I ATTEMPT TO MEET him outside before my mother can get her claws in him, but I'm no match for her handsome-man-approaching radar and find her already outside watering the flowers.

Bryce unfolds his tall frame from the car and my mother eagerly appraises him as he approaches.

"Ms. Evans," he greets my mother. "It's a pleasure to meet you."

She shakes his hand warmly. "I'm afraid you have me at a disadvantage," she coos. "Sera didn't tell me your name."

"Oh, I'm terribly sorry," he says sincerely. "Bryce Hoyt, ma'am."

Her smile slips a little at the "ma'am" and I hide a grin behind my hand.

"Well, it was nice to meet you," she replies a bit stiffly and takes her leave.

"I made her feel old, didn't I?" he asks sheepishly after the front door has closed behind her.

"Yes. That was amazing," I laugh. And I smile brightly, realizing I'm genuinely happy he's here. "Hey, Bryce."

He grins widely. "Hey, Sera. Ready for lunch?"

"You betcha," I reply.

∽

WE GRAB SOME SANDWICHES, CHIPS, AND SODAS AT A LOCAL SUB SHOP AND EAT on the benches outside in the uncharacteristically sunny and dry morning.

I happily polish off my sub in record time and Bryce chuckles. "You're easy to please," he remarks.

I shrug. "I guess so," I agree.

"One of the many things I like about you," he replies, smiling.

I internally sigh and attempt to redirect the conversation. "Anything I need to know about my interim accommodations?" I ask.

"Nothing that I can't show you on Monday," he replies.

"Oh," I say in surprise. "I didn't know you'd be personally helping me get settled. Guess you didn't need to stop by to drop off the keys then."

He brushes the remnants of his sandwich from his hands. "Since I'll be going with you to see the condo after lunch anyway, I figured I might as well," he responds. "Besides, I think we both know I was going to come here today anyway."

"Bryce," I start, a caution in my voice.

"Sera," he replies calmly, grinning. I shake my head and laugh. "I don't want to make you uncomfortable. But to be completely honest…"

"You *are* trying to hit on me?" I interrupt teasingly.

He laughs. "I did say before that I wasn't trying to do that, didn't I?" he allows.

"Yep," I agree.

"Yeah, that's not really my usual style," he says. "I guess what I'm trying to say is, I feel a connection here. And I want to know if you feel it too. I know this isn't the most professional proposition or the best timing, and you have a lot going on. But being upfront about what's on my mind *is* my style. And I don't want to keep it to myself if there's a chance you feel the same way. And if you don't, all you have to do is say the word, and I'm back in my consultant box."

I consider for a moment. "I appreciate your honesty," I say slowly. "And I'm absolutely for saying what's on your mind. I just wish I knew my own a little better right now."

He smiles tolerantly. "I get it," he says. "A lot has happened in a short amount of time. You don't need to respond now. Just, maybe think about it?"

I nod. "Definitely," I agree. I stand, encouraging our departure. "Thanks for lunch, Bryce."

"Anytime, Sera," he replies, offering his arm to me on the way back to the car.

I slip my hand through the crook of his elbow and we walk comfortably side by side.

∾

I wave to Bryce as he pulls away and return to the house to face the inquisition.

"That handsome young man has a thing for you," my mother comments as soon as I sit down next to her on the couch.

"Yes," I reply matter-of-factly. "Yes, he does."

"How do you feel about him?" she asks curiously.

I sigh heavily. "He's…"

"Hot?" my mom offers, and I laugh.

"Definitely. And he makes me feel safe," I admit. "But he's a security consultant. That's kind of his job."

"Does he take such good care of all his clients?" she asks pointedly.

"I don't know," I reply, starting to get slightly aggravated.

"We don't have to talk about this anymore," she says backing off. "You've got enough on your plate."

"It's not that," I respond. "I think I could like him. Or I would. If it weren't for…" I don't even want to say his name, but my mother nods in understanding.

"I know, honey," she says kindly. "Give it time. You might be okay sooner than you think."

"I hope so," I say softly.

NINETEEN

As rush hour winds down on Monday morning, I begin my trip back to Seattle, and reality. The drive flies by, and before I know it I'm pulling into the extended stay facility. It's close to Boeing Field, which means a longer commute than I'm used to, and I note a loud airplane flying low overhead as I enter the building.

Bryce is waiting for me in the lobby. "Good morning," he says, his smile warm as sunshine.

"Hey, Bryce," I reply, smiling back. His upbeat mood is infectious.

"Ready to see your new digs?" he asks.

"Roger dodger," I respond. "Lead the way."

"There's a concierge at the front desk at all times," he tells me, pointing toward reception. "You can pick up your mail there. There's also a gym and indoor pool down that hallway," he points behind me and I turn to look. "There are complimentary newspapers and hot breakfast daily, and laundry and dry cleaning on-site, which the daily housekeeping service can tend to for you."

"Wow," I reply, impressed. "I may never leave."

"I looked at the listing for that condo. I think you will." He winks, and gestures to a nearby elevator. Once inside he hands me a parking placard and an electronic key. At the third floor, the highest, we exit, passing three doors until he gestures to door number 321. That will be easy to remember.

Looking skeptically at the drab, grey hallway, I put my key in the slot and push the heavy door open. As I enter, I'm pleased to find that it's not the same dreary color as the rest of the building. Everything is in warm earth tones.

Two big, chocolate brown microfiber couches fill the small living room. A small, square tan dining table with four medium-brown upholstered chairs sits beyond it next to a very beige, efficient kitchen.

As I walk around I notice my personal effects scattered throughout the suite. "Did you do that?" I ask, pointing to a picture of mom and I at my college graduation.

"Sort of," he admits. "I asked our relocation techs to transfer some of your things from storage, so we could make it feel homier."

"That's sweet, Bryce, thank you," I reply, somewhat relieved that he hadn't personally been rifling through my belongings.

Bryce hangs back to let me complete my inspection. I stand by the living room windows and note that the noise of the airplanes passing overhead is low and muffled. Bryce approaches and taps on the window.

"Triple-paned," he assures me.

Continuing through the suite, I find two bedrooms connected by a large bathroom off the side of the living room opposite the kitchen and dining areas. They are both decently sized, one set up as a bedroom, the other as an office. More of my things have been set up in the bedroom, including all my clothing and shoes.

Returning to the living room, I find Bryce has settled himself on one of the couches.

"This thing is comfortable," he informs me, bouncing on it a bit like a sugared-up three-year-old.

I can't help but laugh at his enthusiasm. "Good to know," I reply. "How about we go get some lunch?"

He springs up eagerly and gestures for me to lead the way.

∾

WE GO TO A BURGER JOINT MIDWAY BETWEEN MY OFFICE AND THE NEW CONDO. Being out with Bryce is somehow both familiar and comfortable. Our conversation over lunch flows easily as he fills me in on the progress to date for all the changes we've been making.

"So, you're not going into the office today, I take it?" Bryce asks, wiping the last crumbs from his plate.

"No," I reply, still picking at my fries. "I took a personal day. Tomorrow, though."

"How are you doing, Sera?" I look up in surprise at his concerned face.

"Unexpectedly good," I reply. "In a way, this break has been really great for me. I've been able to focus on some strategic planning, which isn't something I'm able to do much of amid the day-to-day needs of the business." I pause. "What made you ask me that now?"

"The thing about my business," he explains, "is that I usually get to know people at the most tumultuous times in their lives." He considers his next words for a moment. "In the past month you've learned that an employee stole from you, that that employee was also sabotaging you, and that there is likely more treachery afoot. *And* you've gotten out of what seemed like a fairly serious relationship. And now you're uprooting yourself to move to a new place. Yet, with all that, you seem so normal. Focused. Happy, even, to be using this as an opportunity to propel yourself into the next thing." He shakes his head in disbelief. "It's just hard to believe someone can be so resilient. I'm in awe of you."

I blush at the compliment. "I'm sure it'll all hit me one of these days and I'll do my share of crying alone, in the dark, under a blanket," I joke. As if there hasn't been crying already. "And don't think I'm going to let you off for using the phrase 'treachery afoot.' I'm filing that one away for later."

"You do that," he says, smiling and leaning back in his chair. "Now, are we going to visit your new palace, or what?"

"Absolutely," I respond, reminded of the task. I rise, and he follows me out of the restaurant.

We go to Bryce's car, which is parked on the street in front of the restaurant. As he opens the door for me to get inside, someone across the street catches my eye. They are stopped and gawking at Bryce and me.

It only takes me a moment to process the sexily disheveled shock of dark brown hair, the strong shoulders, and the intense gaze. It's Alessandro, with Francesca and Giovanni at his side, looking at him curiously, clearly trying to figure out why he's stopped. As our eyes lock, I stop breathing and my heart pounds ferociously against my rib cage. Bryce notices that I've gone still and follows my gaze.

Alessandro tears his forlorn gaze from mine and fixes Bryce briefly with a fierce look before abruptly turning and continuing on with his team. The whole thing happened in less than ten seconds, but it takes me much longer than that to catch my breath.

Bryce stands by me, quietly, clearly waiting to make sure I'm okay. When I've recovered enough to move, I slide into the car and Bryce shuts the door. He rounds the vehicle and drops into the driver's seat. He looks straight ahead for a stretch, gripping the steering wheel tightly. As my pulse returns to normal, I try not to think about Alessandro.

"Are you okay?" I ask Bryce tentatively.

His hands drop from the steering wheel and he turns to me, his expression veiled. "I should be asking you that," he replies evenly.

"I'm fine," I assure him. "Seeing him just took me by surprise."

"Me too," he admits. "I'm glad he was across the street or I would have…" he squeezes his fists and shakes his head. "Never mind."

"Bryce," I say with caution in my voice. "I'm not mad at him. And you shouldn't be either."

He smiles ironically. "You wouldn't be," he says. "You're too nice. But I saw you, after. And let's just say I hope for his sake that he and I never meet when you're not around." The anger in his voice surprises me.

"Did I look that bad?" I ask curiously.

"You looked fragile," he admits. "Broken. And with what you're already going through, it made me want to hurt him. I don't know what he did to you, Sera, but you deserve better." He tries to keep his face impassive, but I can see his anger in the tight corners of his mouth, the flare of his nostrils.

"I know," I concede. And I feel the need to explain. "We weren't together very long. It was just intense. I don't trust easily, but somehow, when I'd just managed to, it all blew up in my face."

He smiles wryly. "Yeah," he says softly. "Been there." He gives my hand a squeeze, starts the car, and pulls into traffic.

❧

"There are a few minor issues," Rich says, showing me the notes on his list, "but no showstoppers. The only thing I'd even bother asking them to repair is the second bedroom cracked window frame. This high up you don't want to leave it like that."

I take the report from him, skimming it skeptically. Bryce elbows me gently. "If it's too good to be true," he says in a singsong voice and I laugh.

"It would only be too good to be true if the price tag was about a million less," I joke back.

Jan the Condescending Real Estate Agent huffs quietly in her chosen corner and I turn away, rolling my eyes.

Bryce catches me and laughs quietly. I shrug, shooting him a conspiratorial smile, and slip the report in my bag.

"I'll look for your formal response to the inspection, Ms. Evans," Jan says, leading us out. "But in the meantime, please do let me know if there's anything else you need."

"Thank you, *Jan*," I reply pointedly, stepping into the hall. "Presuming your clients will agree to have the window frame repaired I don't see any further obstacles to closing."

"Oh, I'm sure they'll be happy to," she assures me, locking the door behind us. Her phone rings and she steps away to answer it, waving dismissively at us.

"Thank God that's over," I say under my breath and pull Bryce into the elevator.

He starts to laugh, but his foot catches the gap in the floor and he tumbles forward into me.

He catches himself, bracing his arms on either side of me, leaving me pressed between his tall, muscled frame and the elevator wall as the doors slide closed behind him. I look up into his sparkling blue eyes and my breath catches in my throat, the heat between us palpable as his eyes drop to my mouth.

He slowly lowers his face to mine and, unconsciously, I rise on my toes to meet him. Our lips touch, warm and soft. It's nice. A gentle, tentative kiss, and I find I don't mind it at all. Surrendering to the moment, I allow him to deepen the kiss, his lips parting, his breath hot in my mouth for a moment before he gently releases me and pushes the button for the first floor.

As the elevator begins its long descent, he wordlessly takes my hand, pulling me smoothly to his side. I slide under his arm and he holds me there, nestled in his warm, soothing embrace, and we complete the ride down in comfortable silence.

∾

As Bryce drops the last of my bags in the suite's entryway, I hand him a bottle of water.

"It's all that was in the fridge," I lament. "Thanks for your help."

He waves a hand at the bags indifferently. "You didn't have that much stuff, but you're welcome," he replies.

I smile and settle into the overstuffed couch. "Not just for that," I say. "For everything. I don't know how I would have managed without you."

He sits next to me, his arm brushing against mine. "Sera, I don't think there's anything you couldn't do if you decided to," he says confidently. He pulls away to look in my eyes. "But I'm happy to help you however I can, all the same."

I contemplate him for a moment. "I don't know what I did to impress you so much." My tone is skeptical.

He laughs and smiles his bright-as-sunshine smile that always ends up mirrored on my face, then shrugs. "I don't think it's something you did, per se," he replies. "I have a superpower." He waggles his eyebrows and I laugh.

"You can make women melt into your protective embrace using only your boyish charm?" I tease.

"No," he says, blushing. "I'm just really good at reading people."

"Oh. That makes sense too," I agree.

He smiles and rises from the couch. "I should go and let you get settled in," he replies. I see him to the door and he hesitates before leaving. "I enjoyed spending the day with you, Sera."

"Me too," I reply shyly.

"Can I take you on a real date sometime?"

"I think I'd like that, Bryce," I say honestly, and his smile is back in full force.

"How about I pick you up Friday at seven?" he offers.

"You don't waste time, do you?" I laugh. "Okay."

"Talk to you soon, then."

☙

I GO INTO THE OFFICE EXTRA EARLY THE NEXT MORNING TO AVOID ANY potential traffic. It also seems like a good idea since I've been out of the office for so long. Everything looks the same as I set myself back up at my desk. By the time everyone has arrived, I'm sipping my third cup of coffee.

"Ms. Evans!" Maggie's excited greeting causes me to look up in surprise.

She rushes toward me and I stand and hug her, because it seems like the thing to do. I'm a bit shocked by her warm greeting, and I examine her for a moment. A sudden rush of appreciation for this woman who's helped me for so long without complaint washes over me.

"Maggie, you've worked for me for two years," I tell her. "You should really call me Sera."

She smiles brightly. "I'll try," she replies. "Welcome back. Everyone has missed you."

"I've missed everyone too," I respond. "Are we set up for a full team meeting this morning?"

"Absolutely," she assures me. "I've brought in several boxes of pastries from a certain favorite bakery of yours as a special treat."

My mouth fills with saliva. "Ohhhh, Maggie, have I ever told you that you're my favorite person ever?" I say. "You didn't happen to get any coconut cream pie bites, did you?"

"No, they were fresh out," she replies, her face falling. She whips something out from behind her back and presents a clear container with a single slice of the amazing pie. "So, I got you your own piece!"

I jump up and down, clapping my hands and she laughs merrily. "Thank you, thank you, thank you."

"You're welcome, Ms. Evans," she says, then blushes. "I mean, Sera."

Realizing I haven't had anything but coffee this morning, as soon as Maggie is gone I blissfully descend upon the pie.

☙

THE TEAM MEETING IS FILLED WITH RAUCOUS LAUGHTER AND ENJOYMENT, BOTH of the incredible pastries and the stories of all that I've missed. It seems there were a lot of things forgotten or neglected that made people really miss my involvement and presence. Their clear relief at having me back is touching.

I'm also extremely pleased with the progress our property management team has made in recruiting new accounts. They've managed to garner nearly fifty new units, significantly bolstering engagement and a general feeling of optimism on the team. I make a mental note to give Ana, our property management lead, a significant raise on her next salary review.

Our project management team is chugging along, busy as usual, and the Sutton Developments project is progressing nicely. Ellie and Jackson have identified three potential sites that they're nearly ready to present to Mr. Sutton. I commend them on their speed and hope privately that we'll be able to make progress rapidly enough to impress Mr. Sutton and keep him from concluding that we lack the resources to meet his needs.

By early afternoon I've fully settled back into my usual rhythms.

But at three p.m. it all falls spectacularly apart when Jackson comes crashing into my office unannounced, pale as a sheet. Ellie tails after him, frantically calling for him to calm down.

"Jackson!" I exclaim. "What's wrong?"

But he's blubbering incoherently, and I can't make out anything from the sounds coming out of his mouth.

"I'm sorry, Ms. Evans," Ellie gasps, out of breath from chasing Jackson. "I tried to tell him that we needed to come up with a solution before we barged into your office."

"A solution for what? Did Mr. Sutton contact you?" I go cold as the blood leaves my face.

"No, it has nothing to do with that," she says. "I heard him on the phone and tried to get him to talk to me about it before he came to you."

"You're killing me here, Ellie," I say through clenched teeth.

Jackson finally finds his words. "It's Buone Case," he moans. "Their land is unbuildable."

TWENTY

"What do you mean, 'unbuildable'?" I demand.

"Giovanni was at the site yesterday as the equipment was being brought in to clear the plot," Jackson explains. "Something about the shift of the soil as the machines rolled in bothered him, so he had some samples taken to compare to the original report. They came back today. The soil composition is completely different. They'll take a full sample set tomorrow, but it appears to be completely unsuitable for their purposes."

I'm speechless as I process the ramifications of this. Buone Case is not a large company. An issue this big could sink them if their investors get wind of it before we can fix it.

At the terror of this thought, my brain finally snaps back and straight into problem-solving mode.

"What about underpinning?" I ask. "Or anchors?"

"He's talking to Marco, but that would require a fairly extensive redesign based on the existing build plan," he replies. "Which could take months."

"Can they dig down? Replace foundation soil?" I press.

Jackson shrugs. "I don't know," he says honestly. "It was Marco who called, I think they're still reacting to the situation."

"Reacting or panicking?" Ellie mutters.

"I'm so sorry, Sera, I don't know how this happened. I can go look through the paperwork and try to figure out what went wrong."

I stop Jackson by holding my hand up. "That can wait. I'm sure they're doing what they can to see if there's a way to move forward on the plot they purchased, but weren't there other options?" I ask.

"Yes, three," he replies. "We offered on one as a backup but withdrew when we put the preferred parcel under contract."

"Find out which of those, if any, are still available and get me the selling agents on the phone as soon as possible," I instruct. "In the meantime, I want both of your sets of eyes on those alternatives checking every detail. Be ready to assist their team with whatever paperwork they'll need to move forward on another site."

"Sure thing, boss," Jackson replies. "I have copies of the permits they pulled. I'll create the applications and grease the wheels for anything still available."

Jackson and Ellie start to leave.

"Oh, and Jackson?" I call after him. He pauses at the door. "When did they get the soil samples back?"

"This morning," he replies.

I nod grimly, and they scurry off to begin damage control. I take a deep breath and pick up the phone to call Alessandro.

"Serafina," he answers on the first ring. "You've heard." His warm, rough voice bears no trace of anger, just gloomy exhaustion.

Hearing him again stirs something deep inside me, but I suppress it and try to focus. "Yes," I reply, my voice cracking anyway. "I can't imagine how busy you must be right now, but I wanted to let you know that we'll do everything we can from our end to get you back on schedule. And then we'll figure out how the hell this happened."

He doesn't respond for a moment. "I appreciate that," he finally says, and I let out my breath.

I stop myself from asking all the questions that are running through my brain and ask simply, "What do you need?"

He sighs heavily. "I don't suppose 'you' is an acceptable answer?"

I want to laugh and cry in equal measure, but I stay silent, holding back tears.

"I didn't think so," he mutters. "I don't know, we're still in discovery mode. Marco and Giovanni are doing everything they can. I don't have anything to share with our investors yet, and even if I did I don't want to breathe a word of it to them until I have a plan. I feel pretty useless right now."

"I'm so sorry," I reply, blinking the moisture from my eyes. I clear my voice. "Jackson tells me there were alternative parcels. We're looking into their current statuses and starting the paperwork across the board to push forward on whatever we can lock down as soon as possible."

"I'm not sure that's necessary until we know the full situation here," he replies doubtfully.

"I'm not leaving anything to chance," I insist. "I am going to make sure you have every option available to you, to your investors. You are not going to take this hit alone while I'm here. We are going to aggressively pursue every path to get you back on track as soon as humanly possible. Or faster, if I have anything to do with it."

"*Grazie mille*," he responds. "We'll have additional members of our team here by this evening, so we should have the bandwidth to keep you better informed soon."

"We'll throw everyone we've got at this too, whatever you need, just ask," I assure him. I chew on my last question for a moment before uttering it. "Alessandro, why didn't you call me when you found out?"

He takes a while to reply. "Because nothing was worth hurting you over if you didn't want to hear from me," he responds.

The depth of his regard for my feelings slams into me like a brick wall. He'd stake *millions* of dollars and his company, his reputation, on not disturbing my emotional state? Part of me wants to shake him for his lack of consideration for his employees, for himself. But mostly it cracks the door open on the well of anguish I've locked away deep inside. And it reminds me how much he really had worked his way into my heart.

Because even though I've done everything I can to erase our time together from my mind and heart, in this moment I realize I love him more than I ever have, and I miss him so completely that I can't contain the tears any longer. They spill over my cheeks, mourning what can't be.

"Serafina?" he asks after a moment. "Are you okay?"

I laugh wryly. "I'm fine, Alessandro," I reply thickly. *And by FINE, I mean Fucked up, Insecure, Neurotic, and Emotional.* "Talk to you soon."

∽

Jackson, Ellie, and I work late into the evening filling out forms and reviewing data. At eleven p.m. I call it for the evening and thank them for their help.

Sitting at my desk, I shuffle through the stack of papers, reviewing our progress so far. Given the enormity of what's at stake, even the considerable progress we've made just doesn't feel like enough. While we have verbal acceptance on the two properties that are still available, even a fast cash close could take as much as a few weeks. And that's assuming the site inspections that we've preordered confirm our previous data with no additional surprises. And the stack of permits is all completed, but even with our usual contacts in the appropriate places, getting through bureaucracy in a hurry is a crapshoot.

I turn away from the stacks, staring into the night and trying to find peace in this storm. The challenges in front of us are not insurmountable. I'm not even all that concerned about the potential further damage to our company's reputation. I think we've demonstrated our resiliency at this point.

The pile of cash I'll be personally doling out for this doesn't even faze me. I've always known if it came down to it I'd use every penny I had to save my company. And if I can't save our relationship, it's the least I can do, I suppose.

And like a flash, I finally realize what's really bothering me most of all. Alessandro is hurting. And I can't be there for him. At least, not in the way that we both yearn for. I shake the thought from my head, fighting my natural instincts to try to save us. These are the repercussions of his choices. He's made his bed, and now he gets to lie in it alone.

⌣

First thing on Wednesday I transmit the offers and permitting paperwork, and arrange for all the necessary same-day wire transfers. I wait patiently and am rewarded with offer acceptances by lunchtime. This is where the real work begins.

For the remainder of the week I have all twelve of my project managers working on coordinating with Buone Case, the selling agents on inspections, the title company on paperwork, the city and county on permitting, and the chasing of countless other details. Everyone is bustling in a full-court press, working against the clock to help re-secure Alessandro's company's future.

After lunch on Friday I get a text from Bryce. *Can't wait to see you tonight. Hope your week is good.*

Shit. Amidst the scramble, I had completely forgotten our date, and we have so much more to do before I can even think about going home, much less anything else. My fingers fly over the keys, texting him back.

Bryce, I'm so sorry, I completely forgot. We've had a major issue this week that has occupied my full attention. Rain check?

My phone rings a moment later, and Bryce's concern is apparent in his greeting. "Hey, you okay?" he asks.

"Mostly," I reply. "I'll explain it all later. It's just a mess, and we're under a time crunch."

"Don't forget to take care of yourself, Sera," he reminds me gently. "Have you eaten anything today?"

I have to think about that for a minute, and I realize the answer is no. "I'll eat when I get home," I reply impatiently. "I really am sorry. It would've been nice to take a break from all of this."

"Hmmm. How about this? I'll come to you and make you dinner while you work. You can take a few minutes to eat, and then I'll get to see you and I'll know you at least got one square meal in this week," he offers.

I can't help but chuckle appreciatively at his persistence. "You can cook?" I ask skeptically.

"Hey, I'll have you know I make a mean bowl of spaghetti," he jokes.

"How can I say no to that?" I tease. "I'll tell you what. If you can wait until nine I'm all yours. You're right, I do need a break. And a low-key dinner at home sounds perfect."

"I can't wait," Bryce says eagerly, all sunshine and cheer once again. "See you later, Sera."

Amazingly, by eight we've done everything we can do for the day anyway, so I send everyone home. I shut everything off and wearily trudge home myself.

∽

ONCE I'M BACK IN MY SUITE, I DECIDE TO TAKE A QUICK SHOWER BEFORE Bryce arrives. As the heat soothes my tired body, I try to clear my mind of all the stress of the week. The hot water runs out before I'm able to achieve that goal, though.

I sigh resignedly and step out to dry off and dress.

As I'm sliding on a long-sleeved, red shirtdress over black leggings, the doorbell rings. I pad quickly to answer it, opening the door to Bryce and his usual sunshine-smile.

"Hey, Bryce," I greet him, grabbing one of the bags he's carrying. "Come in, let me help you."

"Thanks, Sera." He grins, and we deposit the groceries in the kitchen.

"I need to finish getting ready," I admit. "You okay here?"

"You bet," he assures me. I turn to leave, and he calls out, "Hey, Sera?" I turn, and he quickly closes the short distance between us, leaning in and kissing me briefly, sweetly. "Hi."

I smile. "Hey," I reply.

He laughs and returns to the kitchen, and I head off to dry my hair.

∽

AS WE FINISH THE REMNANTS OF OUR MEAL, I SIGH CONTENTEDLY. "THIS WAS exactly what I needed. Thanks, Bryce." I polish off my wine and push back my plate.

"I'm glad you liked it," he replies, taking the dishes to the kitchen.

"Hey," I protest, "you cooked! I'm supposed to do that."

He comes back wagging a finger at me. "Not tonight. You've had a hard week." He offers me a hand, which I take gladly, and uses it to lead me to the couch. "Why don't you tell me more about it?"

I flop down next to him, eyeing him skeptically. "You really want me to bore you with all that?"

"I couldn't be bored around you if I tried, Sera."

I shrug. "Okay," I reply.

As he rubs my shoulders, I spend the next fifteen minutes giving him more than the brief highlights I'd mentioned over dinner and answering the occasional question. He's very attentive and interested, and it does feel good to process things verbally with someone who doesn't have an emotional stake in it.

As I finish my story, he strokes my hand with his thumb thoughtfully. "You really just have had all manner of bad luck lately, haven't you?" he asks, frowning.

I laugh drily. "That's one way to put it," I reply. "But when it rains, it pours I guess, right? Tell me about your week."

"My week was pretty dull," he says. "Mostly just meetings, filing briefs, that sort of thing. I thought about you a lot."

He squeezes my hand gently and I blush. He moves his hand to my chin and turns my face toward his. I look up into his eyes nervously. They are a deep, glittering blue and fixed intently on my face, eyeing my lips hungrily. I can read the desire in his expression, feel it in the heat that has suddenly sprung up between us, and I suddenly realize I'm not ready for more. Not yet.

I pull away gently, scooting back into the couch and out of his embrace. His expression shifts quickly to embarrassed understanding.

"I'm sorry," he offers softly. "I didn't mean to…"

"No, please, don't. It's not…" I stop myself from saying, *It's not you, it's me.* I take a deep breath and start again. "You have nothing to apologize for. I appreciate that you care about me. I care about you too. It's just been a shitty time. And I'm easily overwhelmed these days." It's mostly true, anyway, and the kindest way I can think to keep him at a safe distance.

He studies my face intently, chewing on his bottom lip. "I don't want to overwhelm you," he finally says. "Why don't we call it a night?"

He starts to rise from the couch and my gut twists unpleasantly at the thought of leaving things like this. I grab his wrist, pulling him back down to sit next to me.

"Stay, please," I plead. "Let's just watch a movie or something."

His sunshine smile appears, crinkling the corners of his eyes. I smile back, relieved, and sink gratefully into the crook of his arm as we settle in to find something *else* to entertain us.

TWENTY-ONE

I'm woken by the sun filtering in the living room windows behind us and the muted sound of a jet overhead. As my eyes adjust, I realize I'm lying against Bryce, who is slumped back into the couch, legs up on the ottoman in front of him. His face is peaceful in sleep, and his long, heavy arm is draped around me. The TV plays lowly still, and I gingerly stretch my limbs, trying to shake out the sore stiffness of having fallen asleep in such an awkward position.

Contemplating how best to extricate myself, I'm somehow drawn back into thinking about my situation. Bryce was right about one thing last night — it's been a shitty time for me. I've been stolen from, sabotaged, lost a major client, gained another under shaky terms, and now I've somehow failed someone I care deeply for in a career-ending way. It's almost too much to be chance.

My heart jumps into my throat as a realization hits me. As if my brain had been working on the connection all night.

It's not a coincidence. It's more sabotage.

I shake Bryce awake. He stirs sleepily and cracks a broad smile.

"Good morning, gorgeous," he greets me, stretching widely and releasing me from being pinned next to him.

"I realized something," I say urgently, sitting up. My tone shifts his mood and he sits up beside me, alert. "It was sabotage, Bryce. Somebody tampered with that soil report."

He scratches his neck and considers me, clearly unconvinced. "That's a big leap, Sera," he replies slowly, clearly still waking up. "What makes you think that's the case?"

"A million reasons," I say, my words toppling quickly out. "It's just too much of a coincidence, this all happening in such a short time. Those reports would be easy to fake. Ms. Stanwood had full access to our systems, and her last week there was when we were pulling all the due diligence reports for Buone Case's deal. But most of all, I just know it, Bryce. I feel it."

He studies me carefully for a minute as he adjusts his rumpled shirt. "Okay," he says. "I'll investigate it."

"Thank you," I reply, grateful that he's finally taking me seriously.

He laughs and musses my hair. "You know I trust you," he says, and I cock an eyebrow skeptically. "If you think this was sabotage, you're probably right. I'll find the evidence if it's there. First thing Monday morning we'll get our digital forensic experts on it. We'll probably need your help, of course, but they should be able to determine if that was the case."

I hug him tightly. "Thanks, Bryce." Pulling back, I look hard at him, wishing I wasn't in this place. Wishing I'd met him some other time.

My cellphone rings, interrupting my thoughts. I grab it from the side table. It's Alessandro.

"*Buongiorno*," I greet him, simultaneously signaling to Bryce who my caller is.

He grimaces but takes the hint and heads to the bathroom.

"*Buongiorno*," Alessandro greets me. "I just wanted to let you know that we concluded negotiations with our second choice this morning. They're going to allow us to do all our preparatory work ahead of closing. Assuming all goes to plan, we may only start two to three weeks later than planned."

I sigh in relief. "That's great news, Alessandro," I reply. "And please assure your investors that we will cover any additional costs due to the delay."

"What's that going to do to your company, Sera?" His voice is filled with concern. "Do you have that kind of cash?"

I realize I never told Alessandro about my inherited empire. "My company does not," I admit. "But I do. Don't worry about it."

He's quiet as he processes that I'm personally paying to save him. *Yes, you jackass, that's what you screwed up.*

"You've been amazing through this, Sera," he responds, his voice full of affection and sorrow. "I don't know how I would have handled this without you."

I bite my lip, unsure of how to respond. "You wouldn't have been in this mess if it weren't for me," I finally reply.

"Don't," he protests. "It was a mistake. I'm sure we'll figure out how it happened."

"I'm pretty sure I know how it happened," I interrupt.

"What do you mean?"

"I've been so busy fixing it, it only just hit me," I tell him. "It was more sabotage, Alessandro."

He takes merely a beat to process that. "Fuck. You're right," he breathes.

His innate trust causes a wave of grief to pass through me. "We're going to prove it, and we're going to stop these bastards," I promise him. "But in the meantime, please be careful. I'm not sure what else the saboteurs may have up their sleeve and I could never forgive myself if anything happened to you."

"Sera, I…" the rest of Alessandro's words are drowned out as Bryce steps out of the bathroom.

"You don't happen to have an extra toothbrush, do you?" he asks.

I facepalm internally and gesture fiercely at the cupboard next to the bathroom door. Bryce retrieves his quarry and disappears back into the bathroom.

The line is silent.

"Are you still there?" I ask timidly.

"I'm here," Alessandro replies tightly, and I know he's heard Bryce. "I didn't know you were occupied. I'll let you go. Take care, Serafina."

I start to protest. But he's already gone.

∽

ON SUNDAY AFTERNOON ALLIE AND I STROLL THROUGH THE MALL, LUGGING our retail spoils. Between stores I've just managed to fill her in on the events from Friday night into Saturday morning.

"God, Sera, I don't know which issue to unpack first," she says, slumping down on a bench and releasing her bags.

"Yes, you do," I tease, sitting down next to her.

"You're right," she replies. "Are you sure you're ready to date this guy?"

I inhale deeply. "No?" I admit. "But I kind of am already." I groan dramatically. "What do I doooo?"

"Geez, Sera, what a conundrum," Allie mockingly ponders. "Yet *another* gorgeous guy beating down your door — one who's *not* already taken — who is willing to take it as slow as you want. What's the problem again?"

"I know, it sounds ridiculous," I allow. "I *do* like him. We get along well. I'm totally comfortable around him. But I'm just not ready. It's only been a few weeks."

"I guess," she responds. "But you and Alessandro only dated for, what? Like a month? So, a few weeks is more than half of the relationship and you know the rule." She smiles teasingly.

I smile back wryly. "You mean the 'It takes half the length of the relationship to get over it' hypothesis? Aside from that being complete, fabricated bullshit, I've never been one to pay much attention to the rules anyway," I remind her. And some people affect you more deeply than others. I sigh deeply and come to a decision. "I'm just not ready. And I don't want to string Bryce along."

"No, that wouldn't be very nice," she agrees.

We sit silently for a moment as I suppress the urge to run through the consequences of that decision. The potential for losing Bryce altogether. Thankfully, Allie interrupts my reverie before I can get too far.

"So, you really think Megan and her crew are still messing with you?"

"Well, *still* may be an overstatement. That report would have been tampered with ages ago, and it's only now playing out," I explain. "But it does make me scared of what else she might have done."

"Good thing you've got a hunky security guy ready to jump in and help you fight your battles," she remarks. "Maybe you *should* wait to break up with him."

I shove her lightly. "That wouldn't be very nice," I reply mockingly, and she laughs.

⁓

On Monday morning my first priority is investigating what happened with the original soil report for Buone Case's deal. We jump in eagerly, sending Bryce everything we have. I push from my mind when and how I will let Bryce down easily. For now, I need to focus, and I need to see if I'm right about what happened. Not that it matters much with Alessandro's next deal moving forward, but I have a foreboding sense of unease, and I need the facts.

After a brief review with my team, we decide that we'll need to request both a digital and hard copy of the original report from the engineering firm, so I have Jackson place the request immediately. The evidence now under examination, there's not much to do but wait for the results of the investigation.

⁓

On Tuesday I get a call reminding me that my condo purchase closes the next day. In all the turmoil I'd completely forgotten, and I realize I'll need to have my things delivered this weekend, so I call Bryce to arrange it, even though I still haven't decided how to break things off with him.

"Hey gorgeous," he answers. "How's the day treating you so far?"

"Not bad, you?" I ask.

"Better now that I'm talking to you."

A twinge of guilt wrings in my gut. His being adorably smitten with me is not going to make it easy to dump him.

"Hey, so, my condo closes tomorrow," I say, opting for avoidance.

"Oh? That's quick," he replies.

"Cash purchase," I remind him. "Can we arrange to have my items in storage delivered this weekend?"

"No problem," he assures me. "How about I take you out to celebrate tomorrow night?"

"Okay," I agree reluctantly. A little more than a day to find the words and work up the courage. I swallow hard.

"Great, I'll pick you up at seven?"

"Sure thing."

"Bye, gorgeous," he says brightly.

"See ya, Bryce."

∽

THE NOTARY FROM THE TITLE COMPANY LEAVES MY OFFICE AROUND FOUR P.M. on Wednesday, leaving me with a pile of papers, keys, and a yearning to leave work early to go do cartwheels in my new condo.

After attempting to press through it for another twenty minutes, I give in and pack up for the day and head to my new home.

∽

I LEAN MY HEAD ON THE WARM GLASS, WATCHING THE SUN GLITTER ON ELLIOTT Bay. Standing alone in the empty condo, I feel desolation where I expected joy. Something about its barrenness, with the gorgeous views of the city sprawled out around me, just makes me feel isolated and adrift.

The events of the last weeks finally seem to be weighing heavily on my shoulders, and I feel myself spiraling into dangerous territory, as if I'm floating into a tempest. Bryce is supposed to pick me up from my extended-stay suite in two hours, but the thought brings me no pleasure because of what I know I must do.

I pull out my phone, contemplating whether or not to rip off the bandage. I start the call before I can chicken out.

"Hey, gorgeous." Bryce's sunshine radiates through the line.

"Hi," I say softly. "Listen, I can't make dinner."

"No problem," he says smoothly. "Rain check?"

I sigh. "I'm sorry, Bryce, but I think it would be best if we didn't date," I lay it out bluntly.

"Ah."

"You're a great guy," I say, feeling like a cliché, "but I just can't right now."

"I see," he says quietly. "I'm disappointed. But I understand." Something in me senses the lie, but I'm still relieved, beyond belief. "Thanks for giving it a shot." His tone, while wry, is also laced with sadness.

"How could I not?" I muse out loud. He makes a noncommittal noise and, feeling like an ass, I decide it's best to end this conversation as quickly as possible. "See you, Bryce."

"See you, Sera."

Hanging up, I slide to the floor and wrap my arms around my legs. All the feelings I've been suppressing wash through me, and I let the tears flow freely for a few minutes without interference.

When they stop, I wander out of the building, and decide to walk aimlessly for a while. It's rush hour and the bustle of the city around me is strangely calming, my own cares and concerns a drop in the ocean of humanity around me. Cars whiz by, café patrons sip coffee at covered tables along the sidewalk, a street vendor yells loudly to draw people in.

I feel less alone observing the activity around me. I walk past a construction site and manage a fond smile as I watch the workers clean up for the day, their behemoth starting to claw its iron talons toward the sky as the materials come together, magically creating a new economy where once there was none.

After a while my feet stop, and I examine my surroundings. I am not surprised to find myself standing in front of Alessandro's building. I think I knew I was headed here all along, though to what end I cannot say. My mind hasn't changed.

As I exit the elevator I wonder what I hope to accomplish. I'm already angry with myself that I'm asking to make things worse for us both, but my subconscious overrides me and I move forward.

I knock at his door, hoping he doesn't answer. Hoping he's not home.

But the door swings open to reveal him standing there in his black sweats and a black T-shirt, his wet hair longer than it was when I last saw him, his beard thick and overgrown. We stare at each other wordlessly for a moment before he steps back in invitation.

I enter silently, and he closes the door behind me. I turn and he's there, next to me, his dark eyes sad and imploring. Being here with him, I realize it's a lost fight. I need him. He's worked his way in now, and his absence has left a gaping chasm that I've filled with work and other distractions. But ultimately never replacing my need for him. I let out a small, strangled sob and he closes the gap between us, wrapping me in his arms.

I rest my head on his chest and wrap my arms around him. "I'm sorry," I sob quietly. *For being here. For torturing you like this. For saying one thing and wanting another, and somehow expecting you to accept both truths.* And another part of me is riddled with guilt and disgust knowing I'd asked the same of Bryce, and in doing so I might have lost him too.

Alessandro seems to understand my unspoken torment, because he shushes me and holds me tighter, resting his chin on my head as I release my anguish.

After a few minutes he frees me from his arms and slips his hands in mine, pulling me to the bedroom. I resist, fear tearing a hole through my chest, and I shake my head.

"Just to rest, darling," he whispers soothingly.

Reassured, I follow. We lay down next to each other, face to face, and he holds me in his arms, singing softly in Italian. Exhaustion rolls over me and I pass out in Alessandro's arms.

∽

I'M WOKEN SOONER THAN I'D LIKE BY THE SOFT CARESS OF ALESSANDRO'S hands moving along my face.

"Time to wake, *mio tesoro*," he whispers. "If you sleep too much now you won't sleep tonight."

My eyelids flutter open to his deep eyes searching for mine. I can't help but smile sadly, and he smiles back.

"Hi," I say simply.

"*Ciao*," he offers.

And we both laugh.

"I miss you," I say.

"I can tell," he replies, stroking my face. "I miss you more than I can say. But something tells me this isn't our reunion."

"No," I say sadly. "I wish it were, but you know I…"

"Shhhh," he admonishes me. "I know." He holds my face in his hand. "I can be patient."

I shake my head sadly, and say, "I wish patience was all it took."

"You'll see, *bella*," he assures me. "I think you need me as much as I need you."

I consider denying it, but it's pointless. I'm here. My need for him is obvious.

"I didn't think you'd be happy to see me," I admit.

"Why? Because you're dating the giant?" he asks baldly.

"I'm not dating the giant," I reply crossly.

"Aren't you? I've seen you together with my own eyes," he says darkly. "And you spent the night together."

Again, his accusation is undeniable, but not in the way he thinks.

"I wanted to want to date him," I admit. "But in the end…" — I resist saying, *It's only you I want* — "moving on is more difficult than I thought it would be." He looks at me like he knew exactly what I was going to say anyway, and I pull away, sitting up abruptly. "I shouldn't have come."

"All the same, I'm glad you did," he replies, sitting up next to me. "I told you, I'm not giving up."

"Why not?" I ask, turning toward him earnestly. "You know how I feel."

"Because I know something you don't know," he admits, a smile playing around his lips. "But you've told me you don't want excuses and explanations."

"No, I don't," I agree, angry at only myself. "Believing the words of an eager lover is what got me into this situation."

He laughs at my summary of him. "An eager lover," his tongue caresses the words and he runs his finger along his chin as he considers them. "Yes, I suppose I am that. For you."

He fixes me with his intense stare, and I feel the heat rising inside me.

"Come, I think it's time you go before I can't resist you any longer," he prompts.

I give a small smile of agreement and follow him to the door.

"You know I'm here for you, whenever you need me," he promises.

"I know," I respond. I give him a last, lingering look.

He grabs my hand and pulls me into one last hug, kissing the top of my head. Goodbye too painful a word to utter, we part in silence.

TWENTY-TWO

"Show me the counteroffer," I instruct Ellie and Jackson. They hand me the stack of papers and I scan through them. A few lines catch my eye and I look up at Ellie. "This reads like they have another bidder."

Ellie shifts uncomfortably. "Yes, we think they do," she admits.

"You know that's a whole different ball game," I chide. "Why didn't you mention that up front?"

Ellie shrugs. "I wasn't sure," she replies. "And I didn't want to give more than we had to."

I rub my neck, frustrated. For all of Ellie's knowledge, she often lacks tenacity.

"Ellie, we don't have room to dick around here," I say, cutting to the chase. "I'll have a serious conversation with the seller's agent and will find out if they have another bidder and, if I can, who it is. You guys need to ask Sutton what their limits are if you don't already know." I pause, frustrated. "This is a very important account, and this is the only property that Sutton is interested in. So next time, if you need help, don't wait so long to ask."

I pick up my handset, dismissing Ellie and Jackson, and make the call.

＊

As I'm wrapping up a phone call with the real estate agent representing Sutton's competing bidder, Jackson pokes his head back into my office and I gesture for him to sit while I finish.

"Well, if that's their plan, I think I'm able to see that we both get what we want, Jake," I say.

"How's that?" he asks, curious.

I've known Jake Roberts for years and he's never one to turn down a deal.

"I have a client that recently purchased a property that meets your client's specs, but they ended up going with a different site," I reply. "I guarantee you that he will wholesale you that property if you'll withdraw your bid. Everyone wins."

"Send me the paperwork," he responds. "And if it lines up, we've got a deal."

"You got it, Jake," I reply. "Pleasure doing business with you. Talk soon."

"Bye, Sera."

I hang up the phone and yelp triumphantly.

"Did you just do what I think you just did?" Jackson asks, his eyes wide.

"If you think I just baited the competing bidder out of being interested in the same property as Sutton Developments and into buying the property Buone Case won't be able to use, I sure as fuck did," I say matter-of-factly, and Jackson laughs. "You can let Mr. Giordano know when you're done here. Now, what can I do for you, Jackson?"

"Well, I had Mr. Sutton's bottom line figures for you, but it sounds like that may be moot now," he offers.

"Indeed," I agree. "And once I've locked down Jake's client, I think we should play hardball on Mr. Sutton's offer." I grin mischievously, enjoying the mounting victories.

∾

BY THE END OF THE DAY ON FRIDAY, JAKE'S CLIENT IS LOCKED INTO A purchase and sale on Alessandro's original property with minimal loss, and the offer paperwork has been submitted for the plot that Sutton Developments is after. With things shaping up nicely, I call it a day and head out to start moving into my new condo.

∾

ON SATURDAY THE RELOCATION TECHS MOVE ALL MY OLD FURNITURE IN. Moving into twice the space, everything I have looks small and inadequate in its new setting, and I realize I'm going to have to do some major shopping to make this place feel like home. Rather cheered by the thought, I call Allie and ask if she wants to go with me to the local big-box furniture store.

"Seriously?" she asks when I make my proposal.

"Yes, Allie, I happen to appreciate fine, build-it-yourself Swedish furniture," I reply.

"Really?"

"Actually, yes. I know it's silly, but I find it extremely satisfying to put a piece of furniture together," I admit. "Plus, walking around that place is practically a workout. Two birds, one stone!"

Allie laughs. "All right," she concedes. "But I might have a hard time convincing David he can't come. He loves that place."

"The more, the merrier," I respond.

"Okay," she agrees. "Pick us up in half an hour?"

"You got it."

∾

"So what kind of look are you going for?" Allie asks, turning a blue throw pillow in her hands.

"White," I respond immediately. "Lots of white." The color of perfection.

Allie raises her eyebrows. "Clearly you aren't planning on having children," she jokes.

"Not any time soon," I reply. "Missing one key element to make that happen."

David waves a hand airily. "Aren't there places to take care of that part these days?"

I give him a funny look. "Like a bordello?"

Allie laughs. "I think he meant like a sperm bank. Do they even have bordellos here? And do bordellos even have dudes?"

David shakes his head. "Forget I said anything. I'm not touching any of that with a ten-foot pole."

"I bet they have those at bordellos too," I joke, and Allie whacks me with the pillow, rolling her eyes.

"Seriously, Sera, you should think about the future," Allie presses. "Even if you don't have kids, maybe you'll want to get a dog or a cat or something. Pets and white furniture don't mix either."

"Allie, you know I'm not prone to ostentatious displays of wealth," I reply. "But given my finances, I think I could probably afford to replace a houseful of this furniture without too much trouble."

"That's not the point," she persists. "It's about having the *option*."

I stop in front of a display of potted plants. "I suddenly get the feeling this has nothing to do with me," I say suspiciously. "What's up, Allie?"

Allie looks askance at David and he shrugs. She looks back at me and presses her lips together. "I'm pregnant, Sera," she admits, beaming.

I freeze for a moment, my eyes wide. She looks at me curiously, waiting for me to react.

I shriek loudly and throw my arms around her. She shrieks too and suddenly we're jumping up and down together, laughing.

"Congratulations, you guys!" I scream, pulling David into the huddle.

He begrudgingly joins our hug. "But I'm not jumping up and down," he protests, and Allie and I laugh.

Releasing them both, I hold her at arm's length. "You look happy," I decide.

She nods excitedly. "We're *so* happy," she gushes. She and David share a loving look and a small stab of pain radiates through my chest, causing my smile to disappear.

I turn away and start walking again to disguise my reaction. "Well, don't worry," I assure her. "Your baby can come mess up my white furniture anytime."

"Gee, thanks," Allie replies sardonically. "That won't make me feel like a jerk at all."

"So, should we be looking at baby stuff while we're here?" I ask, plastering a smile back on my lips and facing her.

"Oh no, it's way too early for that," she responds. "But if you want, we can start talking about the new paid maternity leave program I'm thinking of implementing." She winks slyly at me and loops her arm through mine as we continue our shopping.

∼

THAT EVENING I SIT AMONG PILES OF BOXES, THOUGH I'VE LONG SINCE LOST the will to unpack. I decide to give up and collapse into the lone armchair I've pointed at the wall of windows in the living room. I turn the lights off, grab a glass of wine, and sink into the chair to watch the glow of the city out the window.

As I sip my wine I recall the look that Allie and David shared, their love and connection on full display to the world. I wonder suddenly if Alessandro used to look at Peyton like that. If knowing she was pregnant has changed anything between them for the better.

And for the first time I wonder what the story is there, and why he's so convinced it would make a difference. Because if David ever did to Allie what Alessandro has done to Peyton, I'd kill him.

But the fact remains that Alessandro fills my thoughts more than I like. And that moving on from him might be nearly impossible. That I might get sucked right back in, despite my deep moral objections. It seems like an irresolvable conundrum.

I drain my wine glass and look around my spectacular new apartment, at the gorgeous view of Seattle sprawled out at my feet, realizing it's a hollow enjoyment without someone to share it with.

∾

EXHAUSTED AND DISHEARTENED, I SPEND SUNDAY IN A FOG, ALLOWING MYSELF a day of wallowing while I assemble and arrange my new furniture. But Monday morning I am determined to get back on the horse.

Thankfully, the day starts well, with the acceptance of Sutton Development's offer. I've decided to take a more hands-on approach in supervising Ellie and Jackson to ensure that Mr. Sutton is nothing less than fully satisfied with our performance.

"I want to personally deliver the earnest monies to the title company," I instruct Ellie and Jackson.

"So, are all three of us going to Sutton Developments, then?" Jackson asks, confused.

"That might be a bit much," Ellie remarks, and I have to agree.

"Just one of us is fine. I'd like to personally reassure Mr. Sutton anyway, so I can handle it," I reply.

As I leave my office I find Lucy seated at Maggie's desk, peering expectantly at me as I exit my office. She must have heard us talking.

"Lucy!" I exclaim in surprise. "Where's Maggie?"

"Hello, Ms. Evans," she replies. "Maggie's off today, remember? She put in for it a few weeks ago."

"Oh," I reply. I did not remember that, but then with everything going on, that's not surprising. "Okay, thank you for reminding me."

"Of course, Ms. Evans," she replies, smiling. "There are only a few things she asked me to look after today. I'll be in reception most of the time, so if you need any help you can find me there."

"Thanks, Lucy," I respond. "I'll be back in a bit."

"Sure thing, Ms. Evans," she responds.

∾

MR. SUTTON IS IN A FINE MOOD, AND HE'S DROPPING COMPLIMENTS LIKE candy. I hand him his copies of the completed offer paperwork.

"Ms. Evans, against the odds, you've impressed me," he admits, taking the papers and handing me the earnest money check in turn. I take it, trying not to show my disapproval — despite my trying to convince him to use electronic transfer, he's simply a creature of habit. "Your redirection of Puget Sound Realty's interest not only garnered us the parcel but also at a lower price than we'd expected to commit to."

171

I slip the check into a zippered compartment in my folio and zip my folio into my bag.

"It was my pleasure, Mr. Sutton," I respond, straightening up. "I'm glad we've exceeded your expectations and sincerely hope that we continue to do so."

"Indeed, young lady," he replies. He extends his hand, and I shake it cordially. "And it was a pleasure seeing you again."

"Thank you, sir, you as well," I respond. "We'll be in touch soon."

IT'S ALMOST NOON WHEN I ARRIVE AT THE TITLE COMPANY TO FIND THAT THEIR escrow officer has taken lunch. Unfortunately, there's nobody else to accept the deposit, so I return to my office until I'm able to come back in the afternoon, cursing Mr. Sutton's insistence on using a physical check.

Thankfully, the afternoon passes in a blur of spreadsheets and meetings, and I'm able to just escape in time to make it back to the title company before they close at five. Handing the check to the escrow officer gives me a great sense of relief and accomplishment, and I head straight home after, more exhausted than usual.

A GOOD SHOWER AND A HOT MEAL HAVE LEFT ME RELATIVELY RELAXED AND calm, so when my mother calls I find I'm actually pleased at the opportunity to catch up.

"Hi, Mom," I answer.

"Sera, dear, how are you?" she asks.

"It's been an interesting week, but I'm okay," I reply. "How are you?"

"Good, good, honey," she replies vaguely. "I just wanted to make sure you are okay. I enjoyed having you home, but you hadn't visited in so long. I'm worried about you is all. And with everything I told you, I just wanted to check in."

"Thanks, Mom, I appreciate it," I respond tiredly. "Is that all?"

"No," she says nervously. "After we talked about your dad I did a lot of thinking. About how mad you were that I didn't tell you sooner, and how I kept him and your brother away from you for so long."

My interest piqued, I scoot anxiously into a sitting position. "I'm not sure where you're going with this," I reply nervously.

"I know where they are, Sera," she finally says plainly. "And how to contact them. If you wanted to reach out."

I'm shocked into silence. With everything going on I hadn't even thought about it, and I'm not sure what to say.

"Are you still there?" my mom asks.

"Yes, I'm here," I whisper. "I just don't know what to do with that."

"It's okay, honey, I just wanted to tell you that it's okay with me if you do want to try to get in touch," she replies.

My brain starts to catch up. "How do you even know where they are?"

"After your father left, his mother, your Grandma Evans, would still call occasionally," she explains. "We never talked about your father, just you mostly. So, I called her after you left, and we finally had the chat we probably should have had years ago as well."

"Wow, Mom," I reply, stunned at the continued fount of new information. "Are you okay?"

I'm also more than a little awed that my failed relationship has somehow led my mother down this path. I've never heard her so selflessly concerned about me, and she's more than scaled back on all the nastiness that's had me keeping her at arm's length all these years. At least something good seems to be coming out of it.

"Absolutely, Sera, don't be ridiculous," she says. "This is all for you. I've made my peace with it years ago." I roll my eyes.

"Whatever you say, Mom," I respond.

"Anyway, she was happy to tell me what your dad and brother have been up to, where they are, the whole nine yards," she explains.

"And you're suddenly magically okay with me talking to Dad?" I ask skeptically.

She takes a moment to respond. "I can't say I'm thrilled about the prospect, no," she admits. "But if it's what you want, then I'll learn to be. I don't want us to go backward, Sera. I feel like we've started to mend things between us, so this is me showing you that I want to be in your life, on your terms."

My eyes fill with tears. Despite the years of difficulty getting along with my mother, she's still my mom and I've always wanted exactly this. It's another bittersweet and unexpected positive that's come of the mess that is my life right now.

"That means more to me than you know," I tell her, my voice thick and strained. "But I don't think now is the time. Maybe someday. But it's nice to know I have the option."

"Just let me know," she promises. "Love you, kiddo."

"Love you too, Mom."

TWENTY-THREE

First thing Tuesday morning I call to check in with Bryce, as usual.

"Sera," he greets me, his tone grave.

My heart sinks in my chest. "What's up, Bryce? Everything okay?"

"We need to meet with you today. At our offices," he replies cryptically. "When can you and Will make it in?"

"Will doesn't usually get in until around nine, but pretty much any time after that that you're ready for us," I respond.

"Good, we'll see you at nine thirty then?"

"Absolutely," I reply, mystified and deeply concerned.

∽

WILL IS A BUNDLE OF NERVES AS WE'RE SHOWN TO A CONFERENCE ROOM NEXT to Bryce's office. Bryce and a slight, sandy-haired man in his mid-twenties are hunched over a laptop when we enter, seemingly hooking it into the projection system.

They both rise as we approach the table.

"Hey, Sera," Bryce greets me, a shadow of his usual smile plastered on his face. "Thanks for getting here so quickly."

"Of course," I reply as calmly as I can, but my stomach is tied in knots.

Bryce gestures to the man next to him. "This is Paul Mullins, the IT specialist assigned to your account," he says.

I extend my hand and Paul takes it, his grip soft and tentative. "Nice to meet you, Ms. Evans," he says politely. "Good to see you, Will."

Will nods to Paul and we all settle around the table.

"Okay, Bryce, you know me," I state. "Let's get whatever is going on out on the table please." I'm not one to show my anxiety, but the tension is killing me, and I'm fidgeting like crazy.

Bryce gestures for Paul to go ahead, and Paul kicks on the overhead projector.

"I'll take you through our findings," Paul begins. "Will has seen some of this, but we have a good deal more to add to our briefing from last week, much of it of key concern ..."

This guy is going to put me in an early grave. I shoot Bryce a deeply impatient look.

"Paul, I'm going to give them the short version first, if you don't mind," Bryce interrupts. Paul shrugs in response and nods his head. "Our initial data seemed to confirm Will's findings, and that all of the tampering originated from one computer — the one in reception. However, that machine is clearly used by most of the staff for various purposes, so that doesn't give us much."

"Have you confirmed that the soil report was tampered with?" I ask.

"Yes," Bryce verifies. "Portions of a report from another file were pasted over the original file. The hard copy and digital copy originals confirm the results showed completely different soil properties. The report was clearly doctored to make that parcel appear as the most attractive option."

"Well, at least we know that's what happened," I reply with a sigh.

"Yes, you were right," he agrees. "But that's not the worst of it." Bryce takes a deep breath. "Last night we found monitoring software embedded in one of your in-house report processes. The process itself was one of several designed to pull data from almost every system you run, from financials to customer reports to payroll, for various metrics and reports. The monitoring software was designed to raw-dump that data through external means."

"Are you telling me that someone still has access to everything we've got?" I clarify.

"That's exactly what I'm telling you," Bryce responds. He glances sidelong at Paul. "But what I haven't told you yet is that the software was installed *after* you fired Megan Stanwood."

Will curses loudly and all the color drains from his face. I try my best not to panic.

"You have a mole, Sera," Bryce says.

"So, her partner is still working at my company?" I'm trying to wrap my head around this.

Will starts shaking his head. "Nobody else in the company could have helped her with the original software sabotage," he says, his voice unsteady. "And she couldn't have written that spyware herself either."

"She has *two* accomplices?" I gasp.

"At least," Paul says. "But this isn't all bad."

"What the hell does that mean?" I ask hotly.

Bryce raises an eyebrow and Paul shrinks back, clearly startled by my vehemence.

"I'm sorry," I apologize quickly, "this is all a lot to handle. Please, go on."

"It means that if they're monitoring you, that gives us an opening to monitor them," Paul clarifies. "It means that we can catch whoever this is red-handed."

"Well, I like that idea," I admit. "But doesn't that mean we have to keep letting them spy on us?"

"Only until they attempt their next data dump," Bryce says. "Once they initiate that, the police will be there to arrest them before it's finished."

"I can live with that," I reply. "Will?"

And nervous, shrinking Will leans forward, his face twisted in anger and responds, "Let's nail the fuckers." We all laugh despite ourselves.

"Paul, why don't you run through the particulars with Will," Bryce suggests. "Sera, I'd like a word with you in my office while they do that, if you don't mind."

"Of course," I agree, secretly pleased to not be subjected to the fine detail but a little apprehensive about being alone with Bryce.

Nonetheless, I follow him out of the conference room and into his office. He closes the door and takes a seat on the wide sofa opposite his desk, gesturing for me to join him. I sit down a careful distance away.

"Do you trust Will?" Bryce asks, getting to the point quickly.

"You think he's helping Ms. Stanwood?" I respond, surprised.

"He seems awfully nervous," Bryce points out. "Is he always like that?"

"Wouldn't you be if you were him?" I scoff. "But yes, he does have a rather nervous personality. He doesn't do particularly well under pressure."

Bryce considers that for a moment. "Has he had any unexplained absences lately?"

I frown uncertainly. "I don't think so," I reply. "What does that have to do with anything?"

"Your inside man or woman is going to be anxious," he responds. "They're going to be trying their hardest to act normally, but it's a high-stakes situation. They're going to be doing things differently than normal whether they are conscious of it or not. They'll be out of their routine."

"Maggie was gone on Monday," I reflect. "Do you think she did it too?"

"Come on, Sera," Bryce chides. "I'm trying to help."

"Okay, okay," I agree. "You're right, I'm sorry."

"I haven't seen you behave like this. Ever."

My eyebrows shoot together. "Behave like what, exactly?" I ask sharply.

He gestures to me. "Like that. Snappy. Rude."

There he goes saying exactly what's on his mind again. Normally, it's one of the things I appreciate most about him. Right now, it's just annoying. Though I suppose he has a point.

"I don't know who to trust anymore," I admit. "I guess it's getting to me a little. I'm sorry."

"It's okay, Sera, it's understandable. But you do have at least one person. Talk to Allie," Bryce urges. "You trust her beyond the shadow of a doubt, right?"

"Absolutely," I reply unequivocally.

"Good," he says. "But don't talk to anyone else about this. And make sure Will does the same. You don't want them to know you're onto them. Also, ask Allie for the attendance records for anyone who has accessed that computer since this started." He pauses. "I'll be honest, that's more than seventy-five percent of your employees, but if we can piece this together sooner rather than waiting for them to strike again, so much the better."

I take a deep breath and nod in agreement. "Okay, I can do that," I say.

"I've appended all of this to your police report as well," he adds. "Everything is documented. I've been assured that based on the evidence that the police are ready to respond when we notify them that the hacker has triggered another data dump."

"That's great, thanks," I reply, rubbing the back of my neck.

"Are you going to be okay, Sera?"

I smile sadly at him. "I'll be fine," I say softly. "Thanks, Bryce. Are you going to be okay?"

He smiles sadly back. "I don't know," he admits. "Probably."

"You know I wish…"

He cuts me off. "I know. Me too. Please, don't worry about it. You've got enough going on. I'm still in your corner, Sera."

I shake my head to fight the tears stinging the back of my eyes. "I don't deserve your loyalty, Bryce, but you have no idea how much I appreciate it."

His expression softens, and he grabs my hands, pulling me into a bear hug. "You deserve it, and more," he murmurs into my hair. He doesn't hold me long before letting me fall back into my place on the couch beside him.

"Come on," he says, standing with a menacing scowl. "I'd like to have a conversation with Will about keeping his trap shut long enough to catch these bastards. Think he'll be able to manage it?"

I laugh. "If you keep up that tough act, he'll be too afraid to cross you," I assure him.

"Me? I'm a teddy bear," he smiles his sunshine smile and winks at me.

"*I* know that," I reply. "But I promise I won't tell Will." I wink back, and we head out of his office together.

~

As soon as we're back in the ERS office, I go to Allie.

"Busy?" I ask, poking my head around her door.

"Nothing that can't wait," she replies, motioning for me to come in. I enter, closing the door behind me, sinking gratefully into a chair. "You look pooped."

"I am pooped," I reply sullenly. "But we're getting closer to sorting out this sabotage bullshit."

"Oh?" she asks. "Do tell."

I explain everything Bryce told me this morning, including describing how the attendance reports may help point us to the culprit.

She looks skeptical. "I can give you all of that by the end of the day, but I don't think it's going to help," she says.

"Why not?" I ask.

She shrugs. "I keep a pretty close eye on things around here, and I haven't noticed any strange comings or goings," she replies. "But if it'll make Bryce feel like we're being proactive, it can't hurt, I guess."

"At this point, Allie, I'll do anything," I respond. "He's right. It's best if we can resolve this before anything else happens."

"You're both right," she relents. "Like I said, it can't hurt. I'll let you know as soon as I'm able to pull the data together."

"Thanks, Allie," I respond. "Will can send you the list of employees."

I leave her to it, going back to my office to distract myself with other work.

But by midnight my eyes are dry and sore, and I'm ready to agree with Allie. There just isn't anything in the attendance reports or employee files that seems out of the ordinary. Unless there's something I'm just not careful enough to notice, we are just going to have to wait for them to make their next move.

~

On Wednesday morning I remember that we should let Alessandro know the news on the soil report. I ask Jackson to take care of it, not wanting to stir that pot.

Walking back to my office from Jackson's desk, I can't help but jump at every sound. My paranoia is off the charts, and everyone is a dangerous suspect.

Come midafternoon my nerves are completely frayed, and I wander into the breakroom looking for comfort food. Unfortunately, the usual box of donuts is completely empty at this late hour, and there's nothing in the cupboards. I'm sitting at the breakroom table, resting my forehead on its cool surface when my cellphone rings, causing me to jolt out of my reverie.

"Serafina Evans," I answer without checking the caller ID.

"Ms. Evans, this is Reagan Fuller, the escrow officer for the property purchase of your client, Sutton Developments. I'm afraid there's an issue with the earnest money check."

I sit bolt upright. "What kind of issue?"

"The check was returned by the bank," she says. "And unless we receive the earnest money by close of business at five p.m. today I'm afraid we'll have to inform the seller that they should move on to their next offer."

My frantic brain looks at the breakroom clock and registers that it's not quite three p.m. And secondly that she just said, "next offer."

"What next offer?" I demand, sprinting out of the breakroom to Jackson's desk.

"They let us know that they had another interested party after acceptance, willing to pay more," she explains. "I've emailed you a copy of the check and the return. I would highly recommend you do everything you can to rectify this in time."

Well, no shit, lady. "I'm glad this was caught before it was too late," I reply. "Thank you, Ms. Fuller, I'll be in touch shortly."

Jackson looks at me like I'm nuts as I barrel up to his desk.

"Jackson, we've got a big fucking problem. I don't have time to explain. You're driving me to Sutton Developments. Now."

We charge through reception and I mash the elevator call button. Lucy looks at us curiously and Jackson shrugs in response. Ignoring them both, I call Charles Sutton.

"Mr. Sutton," I greet him brusquely. "We've got a problem."

"I'm all ears, Ms. Evans," he replies gruffly.

The elevator arrives, and I pull Jackson in behind me. I recount my conversation with Ms. Fuller as quickly as I can while descending in the elevator. The tension on the other end of the line is almost audible when I'm finished, and Jackson looks horrorstruck beside me.

"What's your plan?" Mr. Sutton asks.

Exiting the elevator into the parking garage, I cross my fingers that the call doesn't drop. "I'm heading to meet you now. We need to get your closest bank branch and cut a cashier's check for the earnest money. They won't accept a regular check anymore and we don't have time for a wire transfer."

"5th and Weller," he directs. "I'll be there in less than ten minutes."

"We'll be there in five." I turn to Jackson. "5th and Weller."

He nods tightly and steers us out of the parking garage. The usual downtown traffic doesn't allow us to go quickly, but thankfully it's only a mile or so away, and Jackson pulls up to the curb in front of the bank in just over six minutes.

"Keep the engine running, we're going to the title company after this," I tell him.

As soon as I'm at the doors, I start scanning the area. I don't see Mr. Sutton, so I go inside and do a quick scan of the lobby for him. As soon as I realize he's not inside either, I return to the front to wait for him. I'm waiting less than thirty seconds when another car pulls up behind Jackson and Mr. Sutton emerges from the back.

"Ms. Evans," he greets me tightly. "Let's get this taken care of." He holds the bank door open for me.

"Certainly, sir," I respond as I walk through.

We accompany each other in tense silence. He speaks only to the teller, and through his unique combination of presence and intimidation tactics, we walk out of the bank less ten minutes later with a cashier's check for seventy-five thousand dollars in hand.

"Let's take my car," he barks as his driver opens the door for him.

I nod, calling Jackson as I climb in. He answers immediately.

"Jackson, I'm riding with Mr. Sutton to the title company. You can return to the office," I direct.

"Yes, ma'am," he replies, his voice shaking.

As I hang up I nervously note the time — it's three twenty-four p.m. I carefully give the address to the driver and Mr. Sutton looks at me uneasily. The address is in Shoreline, some twenty miles north. In the burgeoning rush hour traffic that can easily be an hour drive.

I call the title company next and let Ms. Fuller know that we are en route with cashier's check in hand. She wishes us luck. Hanging up, I take in Charles Sutton's sour expression and realize I'm going to need a whole lot more than luck to save this account, even if we do manage to get the check in on time.

"Mr. Sutton, may I see your checkbook, please?" I ask.

Since he used it to confirm the correct account from which to withdraw the funds, I know he has it in his briefcase. He regards me for a moment before opening his briefcase and handing it to me.

I lay it carefully on my lap and scroll through my phone, bringing up the original check image from Ms. Fuller's email. Opening the book, I hold my phone up and compare the account numbers to verify my suspicion.

"The account number doesn't match," I murmur, confirming my guess. I zoom in on the photo. "The check was doctored." *The mole.*

"Precisely how did that happen?" he asks gruffly.

"Mr. Sutton, I'm afraid your original concerns about my company were not unfounded," I admit. He raises an eyebrow and I sigh heavily. I decide to take a shot on honesty and disclose fully the nature of the situation. "I engaged a security company in our efforts to recover from our mishap. They recently discovered spyware indicating that the employee we fired was not working alone. It seems likely that their accomplice, who we have yet to identify, is still working for me and is behind this."

He considers that for a moment, his graying head leaned forward, fingers steepled under his nose.

"You knew you had a leak and you kept a check for seventy-five thousand dollars laying around?"

"No, sir," I respond vehemently. "I was only informed of the leak yesterday." I resist explaining why I had to take the check back to my office at all, unwilling to sound like I'm making excuses. And I definitely rule out an "I told you so" for using a paper check instead of a wire transfer.

"I see," he replies slowly. "Have there been any other issues I should be aware of?"

"Not with your account, no," I say. I consider whether to disclose the Buone Case issue and decide its best to lay all the cards on the table. "We did find one other report they tampered with that impacted another client. That has been taken care of. And so will this."

"How can I be sure of that if you have a traitor in your midst?" he asks shrewdly.

"My security company advised me to let them use the spyware to trace back to the culprits," I respond. "I have full confidence that will put an end to this matter in short order. But I understand if the uncertainty is too great for you, sir."

Mr. Sutton stares at the traffic zooming the opposite direction on the freeway for a while.

"I knew your grandfather well once," he says. He turns toward me, a sad look in his eyes. "I was terribly sorry to hear of his passing."

Of all the responses I expected, that wasn't even on the list. It takes me a moment to recover my wits, but I'm unsure of how to respond.

"Me too," I finally say softly.

He turns back to looking out the window and says nothing for the rest of the drive, nor when we arrive. He simply follows me in and, at four forty-two p.m., hands the check to Ms. Fuller.

TWENTY-FOUR

The silence on the drive back to Seattle is deafening. I use the time to read my email discreetly, wondering how long this freeze-out will last.

When the car stops in front of my office, he finally turns to me with a deeply contemplative look and says, "Let's let things settle for a day. I'd like to talk to you first thing Friday morning at my office."

"I'll clear my schedule," I assure him, and, exchanging farewells, I exit the vehicle.

I watch the car drive away, then slowly make the journey back to my office, not sure how to feel.

As I exit the elevator, Jackson and Lucy are deep in tense conversation at her desk. They both look up, startled by the soft ping heralding my arrival. I'm not sure if it's my slumped shoulders, clenched jaw, and dead expression or just their general worry over the situation, but they both look petrified.

"Did you make it?" Jackson asks tentatively.

"Yes," I reply. And I just manage to stop myself from saying "But we're probably fucked anyway."

"Then why do you look like your best friend just died?" Lucy asks.

Jackson shoots her an angry look.

"Sorry," she mutters, rolling her eyes.

"No, it's okay," I sigh. "I'm just not sure it did any good."

"What does that mean?" Jackson asks.

I shrug. "There's a quick exit clause in the contract. It means he's probably on the verge of exercising that at any minute," I say grumpily. "It's a problem for another day. Go home, guys, it's late. Thanks for your help today, Jackson."

I feel both sets of eyes following me as I trudge past.

∽

I BARELY SLEEP AT ALL THAT NIGHT, WHICH DOESN'T HELP MY INCREASINGLY bad mood. I shut myself in my office most of the day Thursday, and my employees obligingly avoid me the few times I venture out.

The tone in the office is morose at best, but even Allie leaves me to hide in my cave. At six o'clock I step out of my office to find everyone gone. I feel like the shittiest boss ever because I know that all the cash influx in the world won't save my company if Sutton pulls out of his contract. My carefully built reputation will be completely ruined.

Before I leave, I slowly walk the full circuit of the office, taking note of all the family pictures displayed at people's desks and the messy appointment calendars that clearly show lighter loads all around.

So many futures in my hands, including my pregnant best friend's.

I've rarely questioned my ability to keep pressing forward, but in the dark, silent office, I feel weakened by the continuous attacks seemingly from all sides. And I don't know where to find the strength to keep going.

∽

I WAKE TO A LOUD POUNDING NOISE REVERBERATING OFF THE WALLS, AND IT takes me a moment to realize it's not from my nightmares. It's someone at my front door. I scramble sleepily for my phone to see what time it is. I barely note that it's only just after five a.m. before I notice the string of missed calls and texts.

I scramble out of bed, pulling on a pair of leggings under my sleep shirt, and stumble to the door sleepily. Through the peephole I see Bryce.

"It's me, Sera," he calls. "Open up."

I open the door, letting him in, and he rushes hurriedly in past me. I close the door and turn to find him pacing.

"You weren't answering your calls or texts," he says, agitated.

"I'm fine, Bryce," I assure him. "You didn't have to try to break down the door." I move to collapse onto one of the new, fluffy white sofas, but he grabs me by the arms.

"I *know* you're fine, Sera," he says urgently, and for the first time I really look at his face. He's *excited*. "That's why I came."

My tired brain is having trouble forming sentences. "What is ... why are you ... give me a minute to wake up, please," I grumble.

He rolls his eyes and shakes me gently. "We've got them," he says eagerly. "Megan Stanwood and her computer expert. They triggered another download in the middle of the night. They've been found and arrested."

His words are like a bucket of ice water poured over my drowsy head, and suddenly I'm fully awake.

"*Holy shit*," I gasp. Bryce laughs and lifts me up, spinning me around. "That's fantastic!" He finally allows me to slump down onto the couch, astonished. "Who was her accomplice? Have they said who in ERS they were working with?"

"They don't have anything from them yet, but they've only been in custody a couple hours," he responds. "We know from checking the accomplice's ID that his name is Christopher Walker, and from his prints they were able to figure out that he works on the college campus where Megan Stanwood was attending classes."

"Then this isn't over," I say, my voice barely above a whisper.

Bryce sits down on the couch next to me and catches my gaze reassuringly. "They're just getting started, Sera," he says soothingly. "They've just barely been booked. They'll need to be given the opportunity to obtain legal counsel, and then they can be questioned. But this will be over, one way or the other."

"But what if they won't give up the name?" I press. My fears and anxieties of the previous evening begin to gnaw at my insides afresh and I bury my face in my hands.

"Hey, look at me," Bryce says, gently pulling my hands down. "I told you, I'm in your corner. I've got a plan."

"Really?" I ask hopefully. He nods and laughs.

"Really," he replies. "I'm here to help you."

"Okay, hotshot, what's the plan?" I ask.

"You're going to call an all-hands meeting first thing this morning to announce that all computers have been taken offline due to a cyberattack," he says. "Now that Ms. Stanwood and Mr. Walker are in custody, if your spy doesn't already know they soon will anyway."

"If they already know, won't they just not show up today?" I ask ponderously. "Or if they don't know, won't that just scare them off?"

"Exactly," Bryce says. "Between you and Allie, you need to record who is and isn't there. And it'll be obvious who it is if they run. And either way, well, problem solved."

"And what if they don't run?" I press. "What if they just wait it out?"

"With their accomplices in police custody, ready to be questioned at any moment? Not likely."

"So, for argument's sake, let's say they are either that stupid or that ballsy," I push.

He shrugs. "I wasn't kidding about the computers. Paul is there right now installing new features on all of your machines."

"I'm listening," I prompt.

"The computers will be equipped with a two-step login process. The first step can only be satisfied by a unique ID card that will be assigned to each employee at the meeting this morning. The second by thumbprint," he explains. "If anyone leaves their computer idle without locking it for more than a minute, they'll be required to re-log in. Your traitor isn't going to get away with anything else, even if they do stay."

I'm impressed with his plan, but I can see at least one glaring hole instantly. "Bryce, my people all have laptops. I'm sure at least some of them take them home at night," I point out.

"Already covered. Paul already had a list of all your machines and their assignees from Will. He has a list of the six that weren't in the office when he arrived this morning and Will and I are going to collect those as they arrive with their owners," he answers. "Which reminds me, I'm going to need your laptop." My favorite Bryce classic sunshine-smile appears, and I can't help but feel reassured.

"You'll be there too?" I ask in a small voice.

"Just in case," he replies. "It's all downhill from here, Sera."

And for the first time in what feels like a very long time, I feel hopeful.

"Oh!" I exclaim, remembering my promise of the day before yesterday. "I was supposed to meet Charles Sutton this morning."

"Sounds like you have a few calls to make. Why don't you get dressed and we'll go into the office?" he suggests.

⁓

BY SIX FIFTEEN PAUL, WILL, BRYCE, ALLIE AND I ARE ALL IN THE OFFICE. Paul and Will are working on modifying the computers. Allie is working on calling the leads into a nine o'clock meeting, and having the leads call their teams to pass on the summons.

"Hey, Sera," Allie says, poking her head into the conference room. "Do we need the entire property maintenance team or just Ian?"

Bryce raises an eyebrow. "Do they use the computers here?" he asks.

"No," I provide. "Just Ian. Everyone else is off-site. I don't think they've ever even been here."

"Then just Ian," Bryce replies.

Allie nods and ducks out of the room once more. I look at the two piles flanking Paul and Will. The pile of machines to be processed is slowly, but surely, dwindling.

"Think we'll be ready in time?" I ask Bryce nervously.

"Yes," Paul says shortly without looking up.

Bryce and I exchange an amused look.

"Okay, then I'm going to go call Charles Sutton," I say, and head to my office.

I start scrolling through the names on my phone and make a mental note to change Alessandro's entry, so I don't have to scroll past it every time I open my address book. Even just the passing thought of him feels like a hot, iron fist clutching my insides.

As I hover over his name, like kismet, the phone rings and it's Alessandro calling. I stand gaping at the phone for a moment before I decide to answer it.

"*Buongiorno*," I greet him. "Were your Spidey senses tingling?"

"*Che cosa?*" Alessandro replies, clearly confused.

I smile briefly. "Never mind. What's up?"

"Can we talk?" he asks.

"Now's not really a great time," I reply, wondering where this is going.

"I'm sorry, I'm all over the place," he says. "I don't mean now. I mean, can we meet and talk? Tonight, if you're available?"

"Is it something to do with your build?" I ask, my heart racing for a moment.

"No, no," he assures me quickly. "I have something I need to tell you."

"Alessandro," I sigh. Not this again. "I really can't do this right now."

"Is something going on?" he asks, perhaps finally sensing that the tension in my voice may not be solely about him.

I pause for a moment, not sure if I should say. But he was affected by this too, and I don't see any way it can interfere with our plans. "They caught Megan Stanwood and her associate hacking into our system last night. They've been arrested and we're in the middle of executing a plan to plug the internal leak. So, we're a little busy now."

"That's great news," he replies slowly. "But all the same, if you can, it's important to me that we talk."

And now, even amid my worry about my company, the anguish in his voice strikes a chord deep in me, and I can't deny him.

"Okay," I relent. "Meet me in front of my office building at six p.m."

"Thank you," he replies throatily. "I'll see you then. *In bocca al lupo*, Serafina."

I laugh quietly. "What does that mean?"

And I can hear the smile in his voice when he replies, "I think you'd need to be Italian to really understand. But I suppose what I mean to say is, I hope things go well for you today."

"*Grazie*," I reply softly. "*Ciao*, Alessandro."

"*Ciao*, Serafina."

After he is gone, I stare blankly at my phone screen for a minute before remembering that I was about to call Mr. Sutton.

Perhaps not surprisingly given the hour, when I place the call, it goes to his voicemail.

"Mr. Sutton, this is Serafina Evans," I start, my voice shaking. "Unfortunately, I'm going to need to reschedule our morning meeting. I'm terribly sorry to do this at the last minute, but we've had a development with our compromised security. I'm pleased to share with you that the hackers have been apprehended, but I need to be here this morning to work with our security company to shore up the leak. I'm happy to meet with you this afternoon, or anytime next week of your choosing. I'll be busy with our security team and preparing for a staff meeting this morning, but I'll be checking my messages and email until I go into the staff meeting at nine. I look forward to hearing from you and, again, my apologies."

I drop my phone on the desk and sink into my chair. I turn and stare out the window into the bright blue sky. *At least the weather's nice today*, I can't help but reflect. And the thought makes me laugh until tears well in my eyes. You know you're from Seattle when even amid perhaps the worst crisis you've ever faced, you can still appreciate a sunny day.

TWENTY-FIVE

|

A s the last person files into the conference room, Allie pulls the door
closed and slips through the tightly squeezed mass of bodies, dropping a piece of paper between Bryce and me.

Maggie says Mr. Sutton just called and he will see you at one p.m.

*Only two people are missing — Roberta Oliver: vacation, and Gary Peter-
son: called in sick this morning.*

Bryce points to Gary's name and gives me a questioning look. I use my pen
and write "leasing agent" next to his name. After considering for a moment, I
write "project manager" next to Roberta's for good measure.

Setting my pen down, I rise and gather everyone's attention. Several dozen
pairs of curious eyes stare at me.

"Good morning everyone," I greet them. "I'm just going to skip the bullshit, because I'm sure you all want to know what's going on."

Nervous laughter ripples through the room.

"As you all know, a little more than six weeks ago we fired our part-time
receptionist, Ms. Stanwood," I begin. "We have all been suffering from the
fallout of the tampering she did while she was employed here. What we did not
know until recently was that she has since been spying on us, attempting to
continue her sabotage."

My revelation is met with gasps and low rumbles of disbelief.

"Fortunately, Ms. Stanwood and her accomplice were apprehended last
night after attempting to extract more information from our computer systems,"
I share. I try to keep an eye out for particularly nervous glances, but there are so
many it seems futile. So, I continue. "All of our computers have been taken

offline and modified with new security features. You will receive those back after this meeting, or, for those of you who turned your laptops in upon arrival, a bit later this morning. Will is going to explain the new security features, but first I'd like to pause here and answer any questions you may have."

Karen Quinlan, one of our dedicated real estate agents, raises her hand.

"Karen?" I prompt.

"Has any of our personal data been compromised?"

"No," Allie steps in and responds. "All of our detailed personnel data is stored on a machine that stays locked down in my office and is not connected to the network. The only information that could possibly have been leaked are names and home addresses as shown on your paystubs."

"If anyone is concerned about identity theft issues, I am more than happy to provide credit monitoring and restoration service coverage," I offer.

Karen nods, seemingly satisfied. The next hand in the air is Keith Nystrom's.

"What about our client's data?" he asks.

As head of our contracts, I'm not surprised by his question.

"We've scanned every network-accessible project and property management record, and have found no evidence of any additional tampering," Will offers.

"And the police are investigating what else may have been done with the data received by the perpetrators," Bryce adds.

"It's a situation we will continue to keep an eye on," I assure Keith.

He looks unsatisfied but unfortunately, I don't have anything else to offer him. The room falls silent.

"No more questions?" I ask.

"What about the Sutton account?" Jackson calls from the back of the room.

"I'm afraid we don't know yet, Jackson," I reply. "I'll be meeting with Mr. Sutton this afternoon."

I give the ensuing silence another minute. "Okay, Will, can you please take us through the new computing security features?" I prompt, sitting back down.

Will rises and takes everyone through the procedure. There are a few questions when he's done, which are easily fielded by Will and Paul. When they've concluded, I rise once again.

"Thanks for coming, everyone. I know this was a lot to take in," I say, my voice thick with the multitude of emotions I'm feeling. "I'm deeply appreciative for the work you all do for this company every day, and I don't want these setbacks to define us. Let's go back out there and keep doing what we do best."

Bryce, Allie, and I step outside the conference room as the team lines up to collect their machines, access cards, and have their thumbprints scanned into the system.

When we are out of earshot, Bryce turns to Allie. "Gary Peterson?"

"Definitely sick. He couldn't even call in himself; his wife had to call for him. I could hear him puking in the background," she replies in disgust.

"She could be in on it," he replies. "He could have been faking."

"What do you want me to do, ask for a vomit sample?" Allie asks, practically gagging at the suggestion.

"No, I'm just playing devil's advocate. The plan still stands. If he is the mole and he was faking an illness, that means he knows."

"Okay, so now what?" I ask Bryce.

He shrugs. "Now we wait and see what happens."

"And do what?" Allie asks. "Just go about our business?"

"Pretty much," Bryce confirms. "I'll be here until Paul is satisfied everything is up and running, likely through the afternoon. So, we'll be here to see if someone bails out before the end of the day."

"And if they don't?" I ask. "What if they just suck it up and stay?" The thought of continuing to employ someone who may still yet destroy my company makes me sick to my stomach.

"One thing at a time, Sera," he says. "The police are still working on Ms. Stanwood and Mr. Walker, and now we know the mole knows that. Let that percolate, and we'll see what happens."

❧

EVERYTHING IS EERILY QUIET LEADING UP TO MY MEETING WITH CHARLES Sutton. I feel odd leaving at a time like this, but Bryce assures me he'll be my eyes and ears while I'm away. And it's not exactly a meeting I can miss. So, at one p.m. on the dot, I am at Mr. Sutton's office, waiting nervously for his assistant to let me know he's ready for me.

The spacious office still feels closed in by all the dark paneling and sable wood furniture. The air is warm and still, and I can hear his assistant's heels clacking on the dark tile floors as she flits around the office, tidying this or that, offering me a glass of water, answering phones.

My dim mood must frighten her off, because eventually her heels click away and don't return.

"Ms. Evans." I'm startled and look up to see Charles Sutton standing two feet from me, an expectant expression on his face. "I'm terribly sorry if I scared you."

I clear my throat and rise to my feet. "No need, Mr. Sutton," I respond graciously. "I was just lost in thought."

He leads me to his office. "Understandably," he allows. "You must have a lot on your mind."

We enter his office and he gestures for me to take a seat opposite his large, sable desk as he settles in his chair.

"That's putting it mildly," I reply drily.

He smiles humorlessly and leans forward in his chair. "Well, then, I don't want to keep you any longer than necessary," he responds. "Shall we get down to brass tacks?"

"Please," I respond, gesturing for him to continue. I shift in my rigid and uncomfortable chair and briefly wonder if he chose it for that reason. He certainly has me at an advantage, in many ways.

"So, then, have you identified your leak?" he inquires.

"Not yet," I admit. "But our security consultant has implemented measures that would make it impossible to hide the identity of anyone attempting to do further damage. And the police will soon be questioning their accomplices."

"That's good to know," he says contemplatively.

And I don't know if it's his measured responses or having hit my limit of uncertainty, but I suddenly just can't take it anymore. "Sir, do you plan to cancel our contract?"

Mr. Sutton eyes me levelly. "No, Ms. Evans, I do not."

I'm surprised at both getting a direct answer and having it be favorable. I'd thought for sure we'd lost his business.

"With all due respect, sir," I say tightly, "is there anything else you brought me here for today? Because if not, I think my attentions would be better served ensuring all of the hard work we've done to secure the best interests of both my company and your deal does not go to waste."

"There is, actually," he replies. "I'd very much like to hire you, Ms. Evans."

Again, he surprises me.

"Why?" I can't help but ask.

He chuckles softly. "From the moment I met you, I saw a great deal of your grandfather in you. You're hardheaded, smart, and persistent."

"But what about all the issues we've had?" I protest.

"Ms. Evans," he starts. "In this world, there is very little we can control. You don't get where I am without learning how to mitigate risks and adjust for the rest." He pauses and eyes me appraisingly. "You, young lady, show an immense amount of talent at adjusting. It's one thing to account for the day-to-day challenges of working in our field — red tape, nervous investors, cut-throat competition — the obstacles go on and on. The additional challenges you've been faced with recently are an entirely different sort. And yet, here you are."

I look at him skeptically. Yes, here I am. A complete mess personally and professionally. He smiles indulgently at my confusion.

"I imagine you're feeling rather overwhelmed by all of this," he allows. "I'm sure you've got even more going on than I care to know. I'm not asking you for an answer today. But I would very much like to take you under my wing. I think it would be incredibly beneficial for us both."

"But what would happen to my company?" I manage to ask.

He spreads his hands out. "That depends," he replies. "There are several ways to structure such a relationship. I'm open to negotiation."

I swallow hard, considering his proposal. It's just too much to take in all at once. "How long do I have to think about it?"

"May I call you Sera?" he asks, and I nod. "Sera, my intent was not to make this already difficult time tougher for you. I had hoped it would relieve some of your burden knowing that you can turn to me. So please, take all the time you need. And let me know if there's anything I can do to be of assistance in the meantime."

"I still don't understand," I say, at a loss. "Why?" His offer is too good to be true. I would have far more to gain from such an arrangement than he would.

He steeples his fingers under his nose, as I've seen him do when contemplating in the past.

"Sera, I want you to understand. I would be highly interested in you regardless, as I'm fond of mentoring smart, young people such as yourself," he explains. "But the reason I'm here today is because your grandfather did for me exactly what I am proposing to do for you. Your grandfather mentored me when I was just getting started in this business. He taught me everything he knew. I wouldn't be the man I am today if it weren't for him."

I'm dumbstruck by his admission. "I had no idea," I breathe. "He never mentioned you."

"I'm sure it never came up, as your grandfather mentored a good many young investors," he says dismissively. "And by the time you got to know your grandfather in that capacity I'd long since been running my company here, and he and I had no more than the occasional lunch. But he always spoke very fondly of you, from when you were quite young. He said you would be his finest protégé someday. Were I a less successful man I would have been insulted."

I smile wryly. "That sounds like Grandpa Tyler," I reply.

"He was right. Even apart from the advantage you had as his granddaughter, you stand out," he insists. "I'm not making you this offer because I owe your grandfather, though I do. It's on your own merits." He takes a deep breath. "But I think I've blown enough sunshine up your ass for one afternoon."

I laugh appreciatively at the break in tension. "Yes, I should get back," I agree. "Thank you for your time, Mr. Sutton. And your generous offer. I will consider it fully."

"See that you do," he murmurs speculatively, dismissing me with a nod.

⌇

When I walk back into the office, I find Jackson at Lucy's desk once again, my exit from the elevator startling them once more out of their tête-à-tête.

While there is no rule against office romances, I do find myself a little annoyed at their obviousness, and I'm sure my expression shows it based on Jackson's guilty look.

"Ms. Evans," he greets me. "How did it go with Mr. Sutton?"

I glance at Lucy and she pretends to busy herself with work. I almost laugh but decide to keep my disapproving expression fixed in place for a while longer to discourage their behavior in the future.

"Well, we haven't lost the contract," I reply, not wanting to admit exactly what happened yet.

"Oh gosh, that's such a relief," Jackson says. "So, he's not mad?"

"Not in the least," I respond. "I don't think you and Ellie will have any troubles dealing with him in the future."

"Excellent," he replies. "I'll go tell Ellie."

"I think that would be a good use of your time," I say pointedly, looking between him and Lucy.

They both look away from each other guiltily and I return to my office, where I allow myself a good chuckle at their expressions before returning to work.

∾

Around four-thirty Bryce stops by to let me know he and Paul are done and heading out for the day. He looks utterly exhausted, and a wave of gratitude washes over me for all he's done for me.

"Thank you, Bryce, for everything." I step around my desk to give him a firm hug.

"Anytime, gorgeous," he murmurs into my hair.

I pull away and grimace at him facetiously. He flashes me his sunshine-smile, and I can't help but mirror it back.

"I can't be in a bad mood around you," I tease him. "Time for you to get out."

"Okay, okay, I'm going!" he replies, and I walk with him to the elevator.

As we pass Lucy I'm pleased to see that she appears to be working, Jackson nowhere in sight. I make a mental note to ask Allie what's been going on between those two and for how long.

Bryce pushes the elevator call button. "I'll let you know if I hear anything further from the police."

"Still nothing?" I sigh.

"Hey," he says, locking eyes with me. "That doesn't mean anything. It's still early. Give them some time. Go home, try to relax this weekend."

"I'm not great at relaxing, even under the best of circumstances," I grouse. "I despise uncertainty."

"Sera, there's nothing you can do about it," he replies. "They'll either give up their partner to save their own asses, or they won't, and they'll face harsher sentencing. Odds are overwhelming that they will. And soon. Try to stay positive."

"I'm positive I won't relax this weekend," I joke.

"Fine, have it your way," he replies. The elevator arrives. "Bye, Sera."

"Bye, Bryce," I reply with a wave.

Lucy gives me a nervous smile as I pass her desk again. And on my way by Maggie's desk, I notice her wrestling with her new thumbprint scanner.

"Everything okay there, Maggie?" I ask.

She looks up in surprise. "Yes, I think I just got jam on it," she says crossly, and I can't help but laugh.

But I can hold back on my urge to joke about her "jamming" the new tech. She doesn't look like she's in the mood for humor, and frankly my heart's not really in it anyway.

"I think it's trying to tell you to go home, Maggie," I reply instead. "Really. You guys should all go home. It's been a rough day."

"Really?" she asks brightly.

"Really," I confirm. "Tell Lucy, too, and anyone else that's still here."

"Thanks, Sera," she blushes.

"Have a great weekend, Maggie," I respond.

❧

Just before six o'clock I close my laptop and lock it in my desk. I may not relax this weekend, but I've also decided not to take work home with me. Maybe it'll help. I lock up my office door for good measure, and head to the elevator through the quiet office.

As I walk by Lucy's desk, I'm surprised to find her still working.

"Hey Lucy," I greet her, and she looks up in surprise. "Didn't Maggie tell you I let everyone go earlier?"

"Oh, yeah, she did, Ms. Evans," Lucy replies. "I just got behind today and had some things I didn't want to leave until Monday morning."

"I appreciate that, but maybe In the future you could spend a little less time talking with Jackson and a little more time working so you can go home on time?" I suggest, and she blushes furiously. I make another mental note to have a similar conversation with Jackson later. "I'm not entirely comfortable with you being in the office late by yourself."

"You do it all the time," she replies, then seems to realize her impertinence and hastily adds, "but you're right, I'll go home now."

I check my watch and realize I'm due to meet Alessandro. I push the elevator button, hoping it'll hurry Lucy along.

Thankfully, it does, and as the elevator doors slide open, she rushes out to join me while still stuffing things into her bag.

She follows in behind me and as the elevator doors close, I see her push the button for the penthouse suite four floors up.

"Lucy, I need to go down," I say, confused.

I turn to look at her and realize I'm staring straight down the barrel of a gun.

TWENTY-SIX

"If you make a noise I'll blow your goddamned head off." Lucy's usual casual and irreverent tone has been replaced by a harsh, clipped timbre.

I freeze in place as my brain scrambles to catch up. "It's you," I whisper. She smirks malevolently.

"Took you fucking long enough."

The elevator doors open with a ping, admitting us to the top floor.

"Move," she demands.

As she looks over her shoulder to step carefully out of the elevator, I drop my hand into my pocket, clutching my cellphone as I slowly obey. I glance down and find the "9" and press it. A small tone sounds and her head whips back to me.

"Take your cellphone out of your pocket and drop it on the floor. Now."

I slowly slide my finger to the next position as I raise my hand.

"Don't get cute with me, *Sera*. DROP IT!"

I press down and release the phone. Its hard-shelled case prevents it from shattering on impact, but Lucy, keeping her eyes trained on me, retrieves it and looks at the screen. She holds down the power button to shut off the phone.

"Trying to dial 911?" she shakes her head slowly. "It didn't work, Sera."

That's not who I was trying to reach, but hearing that the call didn't go through makes the blood drain from my face.

"What do you want?" I demand, finding my voice. "Money? Is that what this is about? Or were you just sabotaging my company for your own sick pleasure?"

"Something like that," she responds. "Now turn around and keep moving."

As she guides me into the inner office, I'm finally able to look around. The whole floor appears to be unoccupied and under renovation. She guides me to a chair near the large windows.

"Sit," she commands.

I comply, trying to figure out how to stall her. She tosses me a roll of duct tape that was sitting on the desk beside the chair. The chilling realization that she planned this sends shivers down my spine.

"Tape your ankles to the chair legs."

I stare at her for a moment, agog.

She cocks the hammer of the revolver. "I've been trained to kill, Sera. Don't test me."

I swallow hard and secure my ankles to the chair.

"Now tape your right hand to the arm rest," she directs.

I slowly wrap the tape around my wrist, to the chair, my hands shaking with fear and adrenaline. When I'm done, she relaxes her stance and places the revolver on the desk next to her. She approaches me and snatches the roll of tape, quickly and deftly using it to secure my other wrist to the second arm rest.

"Good. Now I get to explain to you why you're going to die tonight," she rages. "Why you deserve to die."

"Where did you learn how to use a gun?" I ask shakily, hoping to divert her.

"In the military," she replies nonchalantly, stepping back and leaning on the desk.

I appraise her for a moment, realizing I don't know her all that well. I'd put her around my age, maybe a bit younger. Her long, straight black hair reaches halfway down her back, her dark eyes angry and calculating. I've always thought of her as a small person, but on closer inspection I see that she's wiry. I'm not a fighter in the least, so even though I have several inches and easily thirty or forty pounds on her, I realize she's probably a good deal stronger than me. Not that I can fight her off while I'm bound to a chair anyway.

"Yes, look closely, Sera," she says cuttingly. "Not that it matters. You clearly have no idea who I am. Just another employee. Just another face. Just another casualty of your ambition."

I work to suppress my indignant response, but I'm sure it flits across my face. "Are you going to tell me what I did to deserve this, or are you just going to bore me to death?" I ask tightly. Stupidly. My words make her eyes bulge for a moment. *Great, Sera, taunt the crazy girl with the gun.*

And then she lets out a manic laugh. "You've got balls, I'll give you that," she replies. "Okay. Let's do it your way. Does the name Gabrielle Grayson mean anything to you?"

My heart stops at the name and recognition, followed quickly by anger, wells up inside me.

"You're the crazy bitch who trashed my car and tried to burn down your apartment," I respond.

My Third Deal Disaster. In the flesh. She smiles widely and makes a show of taking a bow.

"Very good, Ms. Evans," she responds. "Though 'crazy bitch' might be a little harsh. Had you bothered to show up for the legal proceedings, I never could have gotten this far without being recognized. At the time it infuriated me, but I suppose I should thank you."

"Are you seriously telling me you've been sabotaging me this whole time, that you plan to *kill* me," I spit, "for pressing charges over your insane behavior?"

And my mouth has finally gotten me in trouble. She approaches me quickly and reels back, punching me in the face, hard. My head snaps backward and lights pop in my vision. I can feel blood flowing out of my nose as pain shoots through my head.

"*My* insane behavior?" she hisses. "You have no idea what a heartless bitch you are, do you?"

I stare at her, bewildered, and not just from the blow. My brain struggles to make sense of her words amid the pain continuing to radiate through my face.

Admittedly, in my early days of investing I was quite zealous to buy low-income properties, end the leases of the existing tenants, and renovate to put in better tenants, all for better cash flow. Exactly the circumstances that led to our involvement with each other.

But I've never considered myself *heartless*. I've always done everything by the book and worked with people when they came to me with a request that I could reasonably accommodate. I'm no slumlord, but neither can you be a bleeding heart in this business. You'd end up in financial ruin before long.

"Apparently not," I reply quietly, attempting to wipe my nose on my shoulder. "Why don't you educate me?"

I can feel my hands going numb and I hope stalling for time will bring Alessandro looking for me. Except I remember he doesn't have access to the elevator anymore. Fuck. Or maybe he won't even try. Maybe he'll think I changed my mind, and I'm avoiding him. I try to focus on my captor, hoping she takes the bait.

"Oh, gladly," she scoffs. "I think you already know the little 'lease termination' letter that you sent to me, my deployed fiancé, *and* my roommate clued them in about each other."

I suppress a smirk. "So, it's my fault you got caught cheating?"

"You have no fucking clue what was happening," she fumes, stepping forward to lean in, her face inches from mine. "You don't know me." She takes a breath and straightens up, tossing her hair over her shoulder angrily. "My fiancé was a violent asshole. I wasn't going to stay with him. But my boyfriend? I was protecting him by not telling him. Maybe if you'd bothered to talk to any of us, tell us what you were doing…"

"Seriously? Your boyfriend wasn't on the lease," I retort. "Maybe you shouldn't have shacked up with him in a place your fiancé was legally responsible for. And I sure as hell didn't force you to commit property damage and arson."

She steps forward, livid, and I'm afraid she's going to hit me again, but thankfully she doesn't.

"My life was already ruined. It didn't matter anyway," she responds quietly, leaning back against the desk again. "My fiancé was a high-ranking officer. When he found out, he told me he was going to lie to get me dishonorably discharged. He knew I was counting on going to school on the GI Bill after I left the military. I came from nothing. I had nothing. With a DD and no GI Bill I figured I may as well have a criminal record too. It's just a shame the building didn't actually burn down and ruin you. So, I had to find another way to do it."

"How the fuck did you ever get hired at my company?" I ask in disbelief.

"Seriously?" she replies condescendingly. "Identity theft is easy these days. Well, that is, until you put in your stupid fucking thumbprint scanners. And with Megan gone, there was no one to manipulate into getting around that. Plus, I'm sure she'll be giving me up any minute to the cops."

"If I were her, I'd give you up too," I reply honestly. "You used her as a scapegoat, didn't you? What did you promise her? My money?"

"Your money," she admits. "And she was in love with me. I let her believe I returned her feelings, that we were going to hold your company ransom for millions and then run away together. I tossed her a few pity fucks and had her eating right out of my hand. Until she got her stupid ass fired over a measly four hundred dollars."

"Is Jackson in on this too?" I ask tensely.

She laughs uproariously for a minute. "That idiot? Are you kidding me? God, no," she gasps, wiping tears of laughter from her eyes. "I didn't even need to sleep with him to make him my bitch. A little flirting, a little innuendo, and the desperate loser lets me go through all the Buone Case project files to 'help' him organize everything. He's so trusting, he didn't even notice when I had Megan swap in the altered file."

"And I imagine having full access to my office, the Sutton check wasn't hard to tamper with," I deduce blandly.

She smiles widely in acknowledgement and stands, picking up the revolver. She approaches me with it hanging loosely in her hand by her side.

"So, what now — you're just going to shoot me?" I ask incredulously. "And then what? Walk away?"

"If I can't ruin you like you ruined me, then yes, you deserve it and so much more," she agrees. "But there's no walking away for me. I have nothing left."

So, we're both going to die tonight. And nobody knows where I am. She raises the gun and points it between my eyes.

"Please," I beg, "I'll pay you. Whatever you want. You can go somewhere and start fresh."

Her grip tightens on the gun and I start to feel dizzy from terror.

"You think I want the money you earned fucking over people like me? Ruining people for your greed?" she fumes. "You're an unfeeling monster. You don't give a shit about anyone, just your precious career, your reputation, your *money*." She spits the last word at me. "And your money isn't going to buy you out of justice."

My heart races and I'm desperate to keep her talking. "You're right," I agree, letting my face crumple. She lowers the gun a fraction, and she looks stunned. "I'm a horrible person, I can't even…"

And suddenly there's noise and motion from the elevator, and two people move toward us. Her head whips around, and I use the distraction to try to wriggle out of my bonds, but I just knock myself over in the chair, landing hard on the ground on my left side, smacking my temple against the cold tile floor.

From my sideways vantage point, I see Bryce and Alessandro. They've separated so they're on either side of her, and she's frantically trying to decide who to point her gun at. Only Bryce is armed, and he's looking fixedly at her, gun at the ready.

"Put your weapon on the floor," Bryce commands. "*Now!*"

I look at Alessandro to find him staring back at me, desperation and horror on his face.

Gabrielle swings the gun wildly between the two men for a moment, a guttural scream of frustration ripping out of her. "No!"

Bryce advances, raising his gun to point it at her chest. His motion triggers a reflex in her, and before I can tear my eyes away, she places the revolver in her mouth and pulls the trigger. My eyes are fixed in horror as the back of her skull blows apart, and I'm showered with bits of hair, skull, blood, and brain.

The force of the shot topples her body backward, and she lands on the tiles in front of me, the blood quickly pooling around her head and seeping into my clothing, over the exposed skin of my legs. The viscous liquid is warm on my flesh, and I gag, trying to turn my head so I at least don't have to see it. But even with my eyes averted I can smell it — the heavy tang of gunpowder mixed with the sharp smell of her blood. I vomit in the back of my mouth but manage to choke it back down.

I can also hear a low, visceral sound, and I realize I'm making the tortured noise that is somewhere between grunting and crying as tears pour out, mixing with the blood that is still coming out of my nose and dripping onto the floor under my cheek.

Alessandro makes it to me, pulling the chair away from Gabrielle's body and lifting me back into a sitting position. Freed from being pinned against the ground, my shoulders heave, shaking my whole upper body.

Alessandro puts his hands on my shoulders, then moves them to cup my face, his eyes desperately seeking mine. "Shhhh, *bella*," he cries softly. "I'm here. It's over."

I nod fervently, stilling ever so slightly but continuing to sob uncontrollably. As he unwinds the tape binding my limbs to the chair, I see Bryce behind him on the phone.

As the last of my bonds are removed, Bryce ends the call and joins us.

"Sera," Bryce says, his voice strangled and tense. "The police are on the way. You're safe now." He takes my right hand in both of his, using his fingers to gently rub feeling back into my wrist as he looks me over.

Alessandro kneels next to me, gripping my other hand.

"How did you find me?" I ask weakly. My face, wrists, and ankles throb achingly, and my whole body feels heavy and tired.

"The emergency line rang from you, then cut out," he explains. "So, I traced it. When I saw your phone had connected through the top floor's Wi-Fi I came running. The Italian was standing outside the building and followed me in."

I sigh in relief that the call had, in fact, gone through despite Gabrielle's claim it hadn't. I shudder thinking about what would have happened if it didn't.

Bryce continues his examination, using his hands to lightly skim my limbs and face. "Is it just your nose?" he asks.

I shake my head faintly and touch my left temple gently with my hand. I bring it away and don't see any blood. "I bumped my head when I fell," I manage to whisper. "And she punched me." I touch my nose gingerly and wince at the pain.

"Sera, I'm so sorry," he replies vehemently. "I never should have left your side until we knew who it was."

I shake my head weakly and close my eyes, too exhausted to even respond that I don't blame him.

The elevator pings once more and police officers and medics pour out. The noise immediately makes my head pound harder, and I grab pleadingly for Alessandro's calming touch. He squeezes my hand and wraps his arm around me reassuringly as one of the medics comes to examine me.

I'm barely aware of his inspection; my eyes are fixed on Bryce as he starts to talk to one of the officers. They glance over at me repeatedly. I look away, overwhelmed, knowing I'll have to tell them my story soon.

The medic asks me a few questions, which I answer as shortly as I can, as speaking compounds the pain in my face and my head. He looks at Alessandro and they exchange words, but my hearing is fading, and so is the light. Through a haze I realize that I must be losing consciousness.

TWENTY-SEVEN

When I open my eyes, everything is white and blurry, and I feel like I'm floating. I panic for a moment, thinking I've died, until I turn my head and see through my hazy vision Alessandro, sleeping in a chair next to me. I take a few calming breaths, and my sight comes back into focus as I examine my surroundings.

It's just a hospital room. A very white, clean hospital room. A small, silver machine beeps quietly next to my bed, and a long clear line snakes into my hand. I extend my fingers, checking that I have full feeling back. My wrists are purple and tender, but I don't have any trouble moving them. When I'm satisfied, I stretch my legs, making sure they still work too.

Gingerly, I feel the stiff center of my face and trace the outline of bandaging covering my nose and part of my cheeks. I feel a little cloudy and tired, but otherwise in one piece. And I'm hungry. So hungry that upon realizing it, my stomach rumbles loudly. Loudly enough to wake Alessandro.

"Serafina," he says softly, clearly surprised and pleased to see me awake. He leans forward and takes my hand in his. His liquid, dark brown eyes are filled with love and concern, his hair and beard long and disheveled. "How are you feeling?"

As I contemplate his question, I take note that he's changed his clothes since I last saw him. I struggle to remember when that was, and suddenly a rush of memories flood me, my eyes filling with tears.

"Oh, *mio tesoro*," he murmurs, quickly moving to sit next to me on the bed.

He pulls me gently into his embrace, and I rest my head gratefully against his chest. He holds me quietly for a few minutes until a nurse walks in. She's middle-aged, with pale red hair pulled into a bun and bright pink scrubs. Her friendly smile helps me collect myself.

"Ah, I see we're awake finally," she remarks. "I'm your day nurse, Beth. How are you feeling, dear?"

"A little foggy," I admit, my voice cracking from disuse. I realize I'm hearing my voice as if someone else is speaking. "And a little floaty."

She smiles again, indulgently this time. "That'll be the pain meds," she agrees. "You were asleep a long time. We didn't know if you were hurting, so we didn't want to take the chance."

"How long was I out?" I ask, looking around for a clock.

"It's Saturday afternoon," she replies, and looks at her watch. "Almost four p.m."

I've been unconscious for more than twenty-one hours. My eyes widen, and I gape at her for a moment. I look at Alessandro, still hovering over me on the bed. "Where is Bryce?" I ask.

"I'll call him in a moment," Alessandro replies softly. "Don't worry."

Nurse Beth flits gently around me, checking my pulse, my temperature, my bandages. Alessandro slides back into his chair to allow her full access, hanging off the edge of the seat nervously.

"Well, your vitals look strong," she finally declares. "Physically, you're doing just fine. If the doctor agrees, I think you'll be able to go home tomorrow morning."

"Why not tonight?" Alessandro asks tensely.

"She's just woken up," Nurse Beth chides. "We'll need to observe her for a while longer." She turns back to me. "The police have been asking after you regularly. I think they'll want to speak to you as soon as they can, but I can hold them off if you don't think you're up for it."

I manage a small, grateful smile. Her gentleness is calming, and I take a deep breath to help steady myself further.

"I'd like to talk to Bryce before that, if I can?" I ask. "Then I think if he's here, and Alessandro is here, then, yes, I think I can manage. But I'd also like to eat first, if that's okay?"

She smiles and pats my hand reassuringly. "I'll go get the doctor, so he can clear you for food," she agrees.

Alessandro pulls his phone out of his pocket, punches in the call, then puts the phone to his ear.

I gesture for him to hand me the phone. "Please? I'd like to talk to him," I ask softly.

Alessandro gives me a guarded look, and I wonder if he's offended at my need to talk to Bryce. After a moment he hands me the phone, and before I can even put it to my ear I hear Bryce answering.

"Alessandro? Are you there? Is she okay?" he asks when I manage to get the phone to my ear.

"It's me, Bryce," I say. "I'm okay."

"Oh, thank God," he breathes. "You're awake. I'm coming to you right now, Sera. I'll be there as soon as I can. How are you feeling?"

"I'll be okay, I think," I reply. "Are you okay?"

"God, Sera, what a question." He laughs, and I can hear a car door closing, and an engine starting. "I'm fine, I've just been out of my mind worrying about you all day. I'm in the car, so I'm going to hang up and drive now, okay? I'll see you soon."

"Okay," I agree. "Thanks, Bryce, see you soon."

I hand the phone back to Alessandro. He climbs back onto the bed and holds me in his arms again, and I sink gratefully into his embrace.

"You don't have to talk the police today if you don't want to," he assures me, stroking my hair gently.

"It's okay," I murmur. "I want to. I want to put this all behind me."

As he comforts me I work hard to suppress the memories, to not think about Gabrielle's accusations, not until I must. I need to be strong enough to get through the next little while, then I can go home and hide.

While we wait the doctor examines me and agrees with Nurse Beth's assessment, asking her to bring me food while he removes my IV and a catheter I hadn't been aware of until that moment. Relieved to be freed of both, I tuck into the small plate of applesauce, crackers, cheese, and juice that is placed before me. Alessandro watches me, pleased, while I devour everything.

Bryce arrives shortly after I finish eating but apparently can't tell me anything until I've spoken to the police. When he's assured that I'm physically up to the task, and has my approval, he calls the detective in charge of the case.

Soon after a short, stern man in his late forties, with dense, curly black hair, an olive complexion, and kind, intelligent brown eyes enters the room. A uniformed officer enters behind him, hovering near the door.

"Hello, Ms. Evans," he greets me, settling himself in the chair next to my bed. "I'm Detective Stanley. How are you feeling?"

I suppress the urge to respond that I'm getting a little tired of being asked how I'm feeling.

"Just peachy," I reply with a sardonic edge to my voice.

He smiles tolerantly. "I'm glad to hear it," he responds. "I'll keep this as brief as possible, I don't want to overtax you after your ordeal." He lays a recorder on his knee next to a notepad and clicks it on. "Ms. Evans, can you please describe to me the events of yesterday evening, June 18th, 2018?"

Closing my eyes briefly, I take myself back to leaving my office, and walk him through everything as closely as I can remember it. He asks few clarifying questions, and I'm able to focus on letting it all flow out of me. I try hard not to look at the pained expressions on Alessandro's and Bryce's faces, but instead focus on getting the story out as fully and accurately as I'm able to remember it.

Before I know it I'm at the end of the tale, sharing Gabrielle's accusations, her harsh recrimination, her perception at my murder equating to justice served.

When I stop, Detective Stanley looks at me expectantly. "How did you respond?" he asks, seemingly genuinely curious.

I feel hot tears slide down my cheeks as I answer. "I agreed with her."

His eyebrows shoot up, but he says nothing.

"She didn't expect it, and it made her pause long enough for Alessandro and Bryce to arrive, distracting her from shooting me," I end simply.

He makes a few, final notes on his pad and puts his pen down.

"Thank you for your statement, Ms. Evans," he replies. He turns off his recorder. "I'd like to share a few things with you now, if you're feeling up for it."

Curious, I gingerly wipe the tears from my face and nod faintly.

"Ms. Grayson's accomplice, Ms. Stanwood, gave her up not long after she attacked you," he explains. I give him a confused look that asks how she could give her up when we already knew it was her.

"We thought it best not to share the events of yesterday evening with Ms. Stanwood right away," he clarifies, answering my unspoken question. "We told her there had been a development, and it broke her. She told us everything, completely corroborating what you've just shared with me."

I let out a heavy sigh. But where I should feel relief, I only feel sorrow. Detective Stanley looks at me sympathetically.

"You should also know that Ms. Grayson was a deeply troubled young woman," he says softly. "After serving time for her original crimes against you, she was in and out of trouble with the law and had shown suicidal tendencies at times. At one point she was even under a psychiatric hold for suicide watch. She was unbalanced, Ms. Evans. We knew she was a danger to herself. Unfortunately, there either wasn't sufficient evidence, or it was overlooked that she clearly posed a danger to others. Or, to you, more specifically."

My head dips and I let my anxious tears fall into my lap. "Maybe I did deserve it," I mumble.

"To be kidnapped? Assaulted? Murdered?" Detective Stanley asks reproachfully. "Nobody deserves that, Ms. Evans."

I look up into his kind eyes.

"Maybe not," I accede. "But if it weren't for me..."

Bryce steps forward abruptly. "That's enough for today," he says commandingly. "Sera, you're tired and disoriented. I think you should rest now."

I know Bryce hates it when others criticize me, but I feel a fresh wave of affection for him for his objecting to me criticizing myself.

Alessandro steps up next to Bryce and folds his arms over his chest, in clear solidarity with him. The sight of them both defending me is almost too much to take in my weakened state.

Detective Stanley looks between Bryce, Alessandro, and me.

"Thank you for your time, Ms. Evans," Detective Stanley responds, rising from his chair. "I would tell you to take care of yourself, but it looks like you're already being well taken care of. I'm sure we'll be speaking again soon."

He exits the room, and the uniformed officer follows silently behind him. I look apprehensively between Bryce and Alessandro, unsure of what they're thinking now that they know the whole story.

"I should be going too," Bryce offers. "You really should rest more, Sera, you've been through an awful lot." He hugs me delicately, kissing the top of my head. When he pulls back, he pauses a moment and looks me in the eye. "When you're feeling better, if you need to talk, I'm always here for you." His sunshine-smile breaks across his face and I can't help but feel better.

"Thanks, Bryce," I respond. "For everything. You saved my life." I squeeze his hand.

"Anytime, gorgeous," he replies, winking at me. "See you later."

He leaves, and Alessandro settles on the end of the bed.

"He loves you, I think," Alessandro remarks.

I consider that for a moment. "Yes, he probably does," I agree.

"Do you love him?" There is no accusation in his voice, just curiosity.

"I care about Bryce," I admit. "But I'm not in love with him."

Alessandro nods, trying — and failing — to hide his relief. I look longingly at him, wishing for his body pressed against mine, wanting the solace I used to find in his arms. Despite my exhaustion, despite everything we've been through, seeing him here for me like this makes me want him more than ever, in every way.

I look up at the ceiling, willing the tears that start stinging the back of my eyes to go away. Bryce is right, I am tired, and I'm weary of crying. Seeing my distress, Alessandro moves to my bedside and grasps my hand.

"Do you want me to go too?" he asks gently.

I'm torn by his simple question. The thought of being without him floods me with all the feelings of gloom and misery I've fought these last weeks. But wanting what can't be is its own special torment as well. In my fragile mental state, the question is more than I can handle, and the tears flow afresh. I wipe them away tiredly.

"I don't know," I admit, laughing a little at myself.

He smiles benevolently and stretches out next to me again, drawing me into his arms. I accept his embrace appreciatively.

"Then I'll stay until you're asleep," he says.

We lay quietly next to each other, and I soon feel myself drifting off.

∾

I wake again the next morning to voices outside my door.

Nurse Beth's voice floats through the crack in the door. "Yes, physically she's just fine," she says reassuringly. "She can go home whenever she likes."

"Then why is she sleeping so much?" Alessandro's voice replies.

"It's likely just a mental coping mechanism," Nurse Beth replies. "She's been through a lot. It would be best if someone saw her home, got her settled in."

"I see," Alessandro says contemplatively. "Thank you. You've been an angel."

"Oh, dear, it's just my job," she replies, the pleasure from his flattery evident in her tone.

As the door swings open quietly, I scoot up into a sitting position.

"You're up," Alessandro remarks, smiling brightly.

I take in the sight of him, noting he's trimmed his beard. And even in simple dark-wash jeans and a black T-shirt he looks ridiculously gorgeous.

"Yes," I agree. "You don't have to take me home."

He cocks an eyebrow. "You heard."

I nod. "I should call Allie anyway," I press. "Or my mom. You've done enough."

He smirks at me. "I'm taking you home, Serafina," he replies firmly. "It's no trouble at all. And Bryce has already spoken to Allie, and I to your mother."

My jaw drops. "You called my mom?" I ask a little more angrily than I intended to.

He drops a bag of clothes on the end of the bed. "No, she called your mobile phone while you were asleep yesterday. I thought it best to let her know that you were okay," he responds impatiently. "I bought you some clothes."

Flipping back the blanket, I swing my legs out of bed and grumpily grab the bag. "Thanks," I reply crossly. I look in the bag to find a blue shirtdress. I raise my eyebrows, and he smiles innocently in answer as he settles into a chair.

∾

The doctor clears me for release, instructing me to avoid any contact sports until my bruised nose has healed fully. *As if I were about to head out for a round of tennis,* I can't help but think snappily.

But I am in awe that my nose somehow wasn't broken and that the swelling has mostly receded, leaving only deep discoloration and tenderness in its place.

Alessandro takes me home, and the secret of my new residence is lost in the process. He whistles appreciatively as we enter the spacious living room.

"Nice place," he remarks. "Needed a change of view?" He walks to the windows, admiring the panorama.

"Something like that," I agree nonchalantly, settling onto the couch. "What are those?" I attempt to distract him by pointing at a vase of flowers in the kitchen.

He gives me a look and strides toward them, plucking a small card out of the arrangement. "Your mother sent them," he replies, looking at me inquisitively.

I can tell that he knows I'm hiding something. He's silent for a beat as he stares at me. Then I can almost see the realization dawn on his face.

"Did you move so I couldn't find you?" he asks pointedly.

"Maybe," I admit sheepishly.

He takes a seat next to me and examines my face carefully. "*Mi dispiace,*" he murmurs, taking my hand. "You know the last thing I want to do is cause you pain."

I squeeze his hand. "I know," I reply. "So, we never got to the part where you told me what was so urgent that you had to see me on Friday."

"We don't have to talk about that now," he replies. "You should rest. Are you hungry?" Now I sense *he's* attempting to divert *me*.

"What's going on, Alessandro?" I ask fearfully.

"We can talk about it later," he replies. "You should rest and eat some lunch. I don't think it's a good idea for you to get worked up."

My already overtaxed brain jumps to the worst possibilities, and I feel panic rising in my chest. "I think it's going to get me a lot more worked up if I don't know what's going on," I insist rigidly.

"I..." he starts, pausing to chew on his lip thoughtfully. "Well, to start, I'm not married anymore."

As I process what this means, my panic turns to excitement. And then I remember the baby.

"But ... Peyton," I stutter. "The baby?"

"I tried telling you, my marriage was a sham," he replies. "And if she actually is pregnant," his tone makes it clear that he doubts this very much, "then it's not mine."

"So, you're divorced? Since when?" I press.

"Thursday," he admits. "I'd filed the paperwork ages ago, before I ever met you. But she fought me tooth and nail. I think the pregnancy was just another of her tactics."

"So why did she finally agree to a divorce?" I ask.

"I can't go into it right now," he responds, pulling his hand away from mine and stroking his chin absentmindedly. "It's a long, complicated, and unpleasant story anyway."

"Oh," I reply in a small voice.

His reticence makes me wonder if he no longer trusts me. And if he no longer trusts me, perhaps he no longer wants to be with me? I shudder lightly at the thought.

"So, what are you going to do now?"

"I'm going to stay with you today," he says. "Make sure you're okay. I can't think about anything else after that. Let's just focus on today."

His morose tone concerns me deeply. "Alessandro, if you've changed your mind, please just say so," I urge. "But my feelings haven't changed. This past month without you has been awful. If you're not married, it doesn't have to be that way anymore. I want to be with you."

"I can't do this to you now," he says sadly, avoiding my heated gaze.

His words knock the wind out of me. He has changed his mind. My face throbs slightly as the tears well in my eyes.

"You're already doing it," I whisper. "Just get it over with. Tell me you don't love me anymore."

He lets out a strangled cry and runs his hands over his face. "I have to go back to Italy," he says softly. "I'm leaving tomorrow."

"Why?" I demand, leaning toward him, pulling at his arm so it drops away from his face. "For how long?"

"Because I must," he says miserably.

"For how long?" I press, undeterred.

He shakes his head sadly, wrapping his fingers around mine. "I won't be coming back."

TWENTY-EIGHT

"No," I protest. My whole body protests. I wrap my arms around myself as I start to shake. "Tell me why. Please."

Alessandro slides next to me and cups my face in his hands. "It's better if I don't," he sighs. "Not now."

I shake my head. "Do you still love me at all?" I ask pleadingly.

His torment is clear on his face. "Completely," he admits.

"Then talk to me," I plead. "Be with me."

He runs his thumbs down my jaw, dropping his hands to mine. "I want to," he says earnestly. "But I can't. It's better if you don't know everything right now. Trust me, Serafina."

"Does that mean you can tell me later?" I ask hopefully.

He smiles sadly. "Maybe someday," he agrees, "but by then I hope you have moved on. I want you to be happy."

"You make me happy," I insist.

"Do I?" he asks softly.

"It took me a long time to admit it to myself," I reply. "But I've never been as happy as I was when I realized I loved you. When I let myself be with you."

"But you didn't have the full story then," he reminds me. "And I can't give it to you now. I can't lead you into something not knowing — and even if I could, in this case, I wouldn't." Each admission makes his frown deepen, his voice more resolute, and it's terrifying.

"What about Buone Case?" I ask.

He shrugs and turns his palms up. "Marco has already taken it over," he replies simply. "I've walked away."

"I don't understand," I reply, frustrated.

I search his face for clues to the answers he refuses to provide. My brain scrambles for any connection, any bit of information he could have mentioned that would be causing him to cut ties and flee like this, but I come up hopelessly empty. And, for the first time, I wish I'd listened to his story all those weeks ago.

"I know, *bella*," he murmurs. "That's why you have to trust me."

He raises his hand and runs a finger along my cheek as if asking for permission, exactly the way he did the first time only a couple of short months ago. And my answer hasn't changed.

My lips meet his fervently, searching for the answers in his kiss. His mouth moves with mine gently, careful of my injuries. The familiar feeling of his warm hands skimming my body and his mouth hungrily exploring mine wakens my long-suppressed need for him. I pull impatiently at his shirt, and he allows me to remove it, as eager to be touched as I am to touch him.

I wrap an arm around his neck, pulling myself into his lap, running my other hand greedily over his taut chest as our tongues intertwine. He pulls his mouth away and sighs in pleasure, then nips a trail down my neck.

Suddenly, he lowers his mouth to my breast and pulls at my nipple through the fabric. A moan escapes me, and his hands tighten around my waist, gathering the fabric of the shirtdress and lifting it over my head. Clearly eager to finish undressing me, he pulls at my bra until my breasts topple out, then returns his mouth to my nipple, sucking it deeply, causing me to moan louder. I reach between his legs to find him ready, and I stroke him longingly through his jeans.

He pulls back abruptly to remove them, toppling me back onto the couch. I use the opportunity to shimmy out of my panties and discard them on the floor, as he returns to me, naked and as gorgeous as ever. His eyes fixed intently on my bare skin, he quickly slides into me unforgivingly.

Covering my mouth with his, he begins thrusting roughly, bracing himself with one hand, his other behind my back, pulling me to him with each push. He breathes heavily into my mouth between each passionate kiss, and I'm overwhelmed by his taste, his wine-and-spice smell that I missed so much, and the feeling of his skin against mine.

Surrendering completely to his desirous consumption of my body, I climax, shuddering under him as the gratification tears through me. My tightening muscles pull him in too, and he groans loudly, his orgasm emptying him into me.

As he lays over me catching his breath, I wrap myself around him gratefully. My need for him went so much deeper than I realized. Here, in his arms, I finally feel whole again, the despair of the last day, the last weeks, forgotten.

He looks deeply into my eyes and places a gentle kiss on each of my cheeks.

"You're beautiful," he murmurs.

"I'm yours," I respond.

He shakes his head and buries his face in my hair.

Pulling his head back up, I look deeply into his eyes. "I love you," I insist ardently. "Nothing you've said or done has changed that."

He regards me carefully, as if he's not sure how to reply. "I love you too," he finally says. "But I still have to go."

I bite back the tears and decide against pressing him further. If he won't explain, and he won't change his mind, there's no point in arguing during our last hours together.

"Then let's have some lunch," I reply, yielding for the moment. "And then we'll go upstairs and enjoy what time we have left."

His eyes search mine before he kisses me sorrowfully and withdraws. I quietly put my dress back on, skipping the undergarments. I pad into the kitchen to assemble some simple sandwiches and fruit, taking my time as I process what has transpired between us.

A bittersweet mix of desire and sorrow hangs in the air, as we eat silently, his foot nestled against mine.

After we've eaten and cleaned up, I lean against the counter, staring forlornly out the window. He leans on the other side of the counter, watching me.

"I can't stand to see you so sad, *mio tesoro*," he breathes.

I turn a rueful smile toward him. "I'm sorry," I reply. "I guess I can't help it."

"I can leave now if you'd prefer?" he says. "I'm not good with…"

"Don't," I stop him. "Not yet, please." Rounding the counter, I take his hand and lead him upstairs.

Standing next to the bed, I remove my dress.

"I think we have some catching up to do first," I breathe sensually, running my hands over his still-bare chest, down to the waistband of his jeans. "Off."

He smiles suggestively, and unzips his pants slowly, teasing me with a peek at his nakedness. Focusing all my energy on the task at hand, I bite my lip in anticipation, dropping to my knees to strip him, and then to pleasure him.

∽

THROUGH THE AFTERNOON AND INTO THE EVENING, WE REVEL IN EACH OTHER, ardently enjoying our brief reunion. As we lay on the bed, spent from our most recent explorations, the sun sets over the bay out the window and the sky is a brilliant blend of orange, pink, and purple.

"When?" I ask softly, breaking a long silence.

"First thing in the morning," he replies quietly. "I'll need to leave by seven."

I consider his response, trying to be grateful that I'll have him all night.

"I know, it doesn't seem fair," he allows, turning on his side to look at me. "But at least we had today. At least I know you'll be okay."

We've broken our unspoken pact for the day not to speak of it, and with the break the flood of emotions fills me once more.

"I wish I could say the same," I reply.

"I'll be fine," he assures me, "After a while, anyway. But never the same without you."

"Will I ever see you again?" I ask sullenly.

He kisses each of my fingers in turn before answering. "I expect we'll see each other in our dreams for a long while," he admits. "Besides that, I can't promise anything."

And it's too painful to speak any more of it. I cry silently next to him, and he holds me until I fall asleep.

～

I WAKE AGAIN, SPRINGING UP FROM MY SLUMBER TO A GORGEOUS PURPLING sky, but its beauty is lost on me as I gasp for breath, sweat beading on my forehead. More nightmares. I'd expected them, expected a looming Gabrielle threatening my life. But she was nowhere to be found. Only Alessandro was there, distantly, out of reach, fading into the dark.

I turn and find him asleep next to me, and I'm suddenly oddly thankful for the nightmares. Now that they've woken me, I'll have time to say a proper goodbye. I lean over him and lightly kiss his full lips. He stirs slowly, and I run my hands down his cool chest, continuing to press kisses to his mouth, rousing him gently from his slumber.

His eyes open, taking in my face in the dim light. His mouth finally responds, opening to me, meeting my tongue with his own. I slide my leg over his torso, so I sit astride him, deepening my kiss passionately.

His whole body begins to respond, his hands roving over my backside, his breath quickening. I lightly circle my hips over his, and he begins to harden under the stimulus.

"Mmmmm," he moans. "What a nice way to wake up." He finds the wet warmth between my legs and slides slowly and deeply in, hardening fully as he goes.

I let out a gasp of pleasure. "Imagine, if you'd just change your mind, all the many wonderful ways I could wake you like this each morning," I paraphrase him with a smile.

"It's not my mind that would need changing, *dolcezza*," he murmurs.

I kiss him softly. "Hmmm," I muse, sitting up and sinking fully onto him. He moans appreciatively. "Then I guess I'll just have to remind you what you'll be missing."

Leaning back, I rock my hips, eliciting groans of pleasure from us both. I change my pace and angle every few thrusts, enjoying the altering sensations. Drawing up on my heels, I ride him forcefully until he's loudly enjoying himself, my breasts bouncing in his hands, his thumbs teasing my nipples and driving me pleasantly to distraction.

Before I can bring him too close to the edge, he pushes up, spinning me onto my front, taking me from behind.

"Two can play at that game," he growls, starting to take me hard, and I bury muffled screams into the comforter.

He leans over me, gripping the base of my neck gently, turning my head so he can hear me. It also drives him deeper into me, and before I can hold back the tide, an orgasm floods through me.

As my body relaxes, he flips me onto my back and takes me again, his body pressed fully into mine, his arms pinning mine over my head. His mouth is at my ear, and I can hear his heavy breathing, his low moans of pleasure. I encourage him with my legs, pulling him deep on each thrust, tilting to meet him as he works over me.

I put my mouth to his ear and between moans, trace his lobe with my tongue. The stimulus quickens his pace and he finishes in a frenzy, crying out loudly.

As he relaxes into me, I whisper in his ear, "*Ti amo*, Alessandro."

He pulls up and looks in my eyes. "*Ti amo*, Serafina," he replies.

We stare at each other, perfectly happy, if only for just this moment. He kisses me softly, only releasing me when his alarm sounds a few minutes later.

～

AND BEFORE LONG HE IS DRESSED AND READY TO GO. HE SITS ON THE BED NEXT to me, tugging at my shirtdress playfully. "I'll miss these."

I smile sadly, scooting to the edge of the bed so I can walk him out.

"Stay here," he urges. "I want to remember you just like this."

I bite my lip, holding in the tears, and nod. He's right. If I follow him to the door, if I see him leaving, I won't let him go gracefully.

"I can't say it," I whisper. I can't even think the word.

He nods in agreement, mashing his lips together. "Me neither," he replies. He kisses me one last time, and then he's gone.

TWENTY-NINE

To my surprise, I don't cry at all after he leaves. All I feel is a gaping emptiness, and as I methodically make my breakfast I'm glad Allie insisted I take the whole week off. I expect I'll go through a range of emotions as I process this. Not something I want to do in the office.

But at the same time, wallowing at home all day isn't going to help, either. Considering my predicament for a moment, my fingers hover over the address book on my phone. Given recent events, I decide to just go for it.

"Sera," Allie answers, sounding surprised. "Are you okay?"

"Not really," I admit. "But probably not for the reasons you think."

"I was waiting for you to need me, whatever the reasons," she assures me. "How can I help?"

"Take the afternoon off?" I ask tentatively.

"Sure thing, boss," she replies. "Retail therapy?"

"Retail therapy," I agree.

∾

Lunch finds us at a burgers and beers establishment at the mall. Allie is surrounded by half a dozen shopping bags to my one lonely bag holding a sweater I thought my mom would like. Evidence of my lack of enthusiasm for anything right now. As we wait for our order, Allie sits silently, waiting for me to talk.

"So, Bryce told you what happened on Friday?" I put forth.

She nods. "You don't have to talk about it if you don't want to," she offers.

216

"But I'm happy to listen. I hate to see you so devastated, Sera. I'm so sorry you had to go through that."

I run my finger lightly over my nose. The deep purpling had started to turn to a sickly green yellow since the day before, with a smattering of bluish patches remaining. But while the physical trauma is already fading, the emotional trauma has been usurped by Alessandro's departure.

"I was pretty upset about it when I came to on Saturday," I admit. "But it's almost like a distant memory now." I sigh heavily, not really knowing where to start.

Allie looks at me, concerned. "Bryce told me Alessandro took you home yesterday," she admits. "You didn't sleep with him, did you?"

I don't know whether to be annoyed at Bryce for sharing that with her, or thankful that I don't have to explain why he was even there in the first place. In either case, I choose not to be annoyed by the inherent judgment in her question.

"Yes, but only because he's not married anymore," I confess and inform her all at once.

She gasps in shock. "Sera! Omigod," she gushes. "He got divorced?"

"Yep," I confirm.

"Well, that's a nice surprise?" she hazards. But then she looks confused. "So why do you look so distraught?"

The waiter delivers our salads, and I pick forlornly at mine for a minute. She eats quietly, clearly on the edge of her seat waiting for my answer but unwilling to be anything but perfectly accommodating for fear of scaring me away.

"He left," I say finally. "Went back to Italy. For good, it seems."

She drops her fork on her plate in shock. "What? How? Doesn't he own a company here?" she asks, my answer bringing her only more confusion.

I shrug. "He wouldn't explain himself, Allie," I reply gloomily. "He just gave everything up and left, just like that. I have no idea why."

"So, he tells you he's not married anymore but is leaving the country, so you have sex with him?" Allie is not normally this judgmental, so I'm surprised by the distinctly critical edge to her tone.

But I don't blame her. It was a hell of a way to torture myself. "I can't explain it," I reply tiredly. "I love him." *I'm drawn to him. I can't stay away from him. I need him.* I keep those thoughts to myself, as I know they won't help the conversation any.

She huffs lowly. "Clearly, he doesn't give two shits about you," she fumes. Her words cut through my numbness and tears spring to my eyes.

I put my fork down and push my plate away. "He loves me, Allie," I insist. "He clearly thought he was sparing me some great pain. I wanted to talk him out of it, but he's even more stubborn than I am."

"Well, that's saying something," she replies. She regards me for a moment. "I'm sorry, Sera, I just see how much you're hurting, and I hate that he did that to you. Especially after everything he's already put you through, and everything else that's been happening."

"When it rains, it pours," I respond dully. It's quickly becoming my favorite idiom.

"Well, I hate to say this, but maybe you should come back to work," Allie suggests. "I think everyone is pretty freaked out, and seeing you in one piece wouldn't hurt. I know how much you like burying your emotions in work."

I smile wryly. "True story," I admit. "Maybe tomorrow." It would be good to have a distraction, and a sense of normalcy. The only other thing I could think to do this week was to visit my mother, but I don't think I could handle the inevitable inquisition that would unleash.

"Good, then maybe you can personally tell Charles Sutton to back off and wait for you to call him when you're ready," she responds. "Because he won't listen to me."

My ears perk up. "Mr. Sutton keeps calling?" I ask.

"That's an understatement," she replies. "I have no idea what's got his knickers in a twist. I told him you wouldn't be in today, and I wasn't sure when you would. It kind of set him off and he called Ellie, Jackson, and Maggie, fishing for an explanation."

"I met with him on Friday and told him about the arrests, but mentioned we hadn't caught the mole yet," I explain. "And then he offered me a job."

"Really?" Allie's eyebrows shoot up. "What did you say?"

"Well, it was more of an open-ended invitation to hire me," I add. "I told him I'd think about it. I imagine the recent drama followed by silence has him concerned."

"What would happen to ERS?" Allie asks, worried.

"Don't worry, Allie, you're not going to lose your job," I assure her.

She looks guilty. "I'm not just worried about me. I'm worried about everyone, you included. That company is your life," she says.

Her wording stops me cold in my tracks. I'm extremely proud of my accomplishments, but hearing ERS referred to as "my life" disturbs me in a way I can't quite put my finger on right away.

We eat in silence as I attempt to name my concern. And then it hits me.

"Allie, have you ever heard that saying, 'No one ever said on their deathbed, 'I wish I'd spent more time at the office'"?" I ask.

"Of course," she replies slowly. "What are you getting at, Sera?"

I study her for a moment, contemplating Charles Sutton's offer.

"I think it's time I spent a little less time working," I reply frankly. "I need to meet with Mr. Sutton."

"Now?" Allie asks, looking wistfully at her half-finished salad.

I chuckle. "No, Allie, let's finish eating our lunch first," I reply, pulling my plate back toward myself. "And then maybe something with chocolate in it while we're at it." My mind has kicked into high gear again, finally, and it's made me ravenous.

∽

MR. SUTTON ARRIVES AT MY APARTMENT THE FOLLOWING MORNING AT TEN A.M. as agreed. I show him in and offer him a seat in the living room.

"Can I get you anything to drink, Mr. Sutton?" I ask kindly.

He waves me off. "No, I'm fine, thank you," he replies, and I settle on the couch across from him. "And I think you can start calling me Charles."

I'm a little surprised but happy that he still seems keen on forming a bond. "Of course, Charles," I reply. "I imagine you want to know what's going on."

"Direct as ever, young lady," he says approvingly. "I was highly concerned when I couldn't get ahold of you yesterday after last week's events."

"Naturally," I allow. "And I wanted to share the tale in person, as it is rather unbelievable."

"I assumed as much from the shiner on your face," he replies blandly, and I can't help but laugh. "Well, I trust all is well, since you seem to be in decent spirits."

"Indeed," I agree. "The events of the last few days have thrown a few things sharply into contrast for me."

"Oh?" he asks curiously. "Do tell."

"All right," I reply agreeably. I choose my words carefully so as not to alarm him. "As I was leaving work on Friday, the leak made herself known to me."

"Speak plainly, Sera," he encourages me. "You're not going to give me a heart attack if that's what you're worried about. I'm made of tough stuff."

I laugh appreciatively. "Okay, then," I reply. "One of my employees kidnapped me at gunpoint and tied me to a chair in the penthouse of our building, where she proceeded to explain why she has been sabotaging me, and why she was about to kill me." I pause, appreciating his shocked expression. "Thankfully, I was able to stall her long enough for the cavalry to show up and stop her, but unfortunately not before she punched me in the face for being impertinent. I spent a little more than a day in the hospital, mostly for shock. She didn't even manage to break my nose properly." I shrug nonchalantly.

Charles guffaws and slaps his knee. "You're a robust woman," he chortles. "That's quite a tale, and I'm glad to hear you are relatively unscathed. Why was she after you?"

"In one of my early deals, I bought the apartment building she lived in and terminated all the leases to renovate and re-rent at a higher price point," I explain. "The paperwork clued her deployed fiancé that she was living with another man. Apparently, they had some serious domestic issues come from it, and as a result, in her anger, she destroyed my car and set fire to her apartment attempting to stop my greedy, heartless, money-grubbing ways. When that didn't work, she came after me after she'd been dishonorably discharged from the military and served her time, orchestrating the events of the past few months to take me and my company down."

He ruminates on that for a bit, then asks thoughtfully, "The words 'greedy,' 'heartless,' and 'money-grubbing' — your word choice or hers?"

I have to think about that, and I'm not quite sure. "I can't honestly remember," I admit. "If I chose them, it's paraphrasing her accusations against me."

"Do you consider yourself to be those things?"

"I'm not the most socially aware person at times," I admit. "And her words affected me deeply at first. But other events since have made me acutely aware that I am none of those things."

He smiles, clearly satisfied with my answer. "I'm glad to hear you've once again taken a negative and found the positive in it."

"Oh, I have, sir," I agree. I begin to weigh my next words but stop myself. If I can be blunt with anyone, its Charles Sutton, and I'm about to lay all of my cards on the table, so there's no point in being coy about it. "Are you married, Charles? Do you have a family?"

"Of course," he replies, bemused. "I've been married nearly thirty-five years. My Marcia and I have three wonderful sons."

"Has your career ever gotten in the way of being a family man?" I press.

"There have been difficult times," he admits. "And goodness knows I'm something of a workaholic. But I chose wisely, and I love my wife and my children. I know where my priorities are, even if I've walked the line on occasion."

I'd asked to set up my lead-in, but his answer honestly touches me. And it makes me confident that I'm placing my trust in good hands.

"Charles, I want to work for you," I state simply. "But I'm at a crossroads, and my service would come at a fairly steep price."

He regards me attentively. "I'm listening."

"I currently have forty-three employees. Seven business support function employees, a project management team of fourteen, a property management team of nineteen, and our general brokerage of three. Are you willing to absorb those employees?"

He considers carefully for a few minutes before replying, "We can take everyone except the property management team," he says slowly. "It's not a business I've ever been interested in." He pauses. "However, we can create a subsidiary company for property management services if you have someone willing to run it. If they produce results, we'll keep them. If it's more trouble than it's worth, we'll cut them loose."

I ponder his counteroffer. "I'll check with my property management lead. If she's amenable, I think that would be better than having to drop hundreds of units and cut all those jobs," I agree. "But I want at least a ninety-day trial."

"Reasonable," he replies. "And what of you?"

I hesitate, knowing he'll like this next part less. "I need to take time off," I respond. "I'll be leaving the country for an indefinite period. When I return, I'm all yours."

As expected, his eyebrows shoot up and his jaw drops. "That's quite an ask," he admits. "Any idea exactly how indefinite we're talking?"

"A few months, maybe?" I hazard. "I wish I knew. I'm sorry. I know it's a lot to expect."

"A few months is nothing," he says, surprising me. "I thought we might be talking about years." He looks closely at me for a few minutes and smiles kindly. "He must be quite a young man."

And I must wear my heart on my sleeve more than I thought.

"I think so," I reply. "But that's what I need to find out."

"You don't trust easily, do you, Sera?" he asks shrewdly.

"No, sir," I agree. I've always kept my heart under lock and key, safeguarded from the world.

"Good," he commends me. "We have an agreement, then." He stands, offering his hand.

I scramble to my feet and shake it in disbelief. "Thank you, Charles," I respond.

✺

AS SOON AS HE'S GONE, I CALL BRYCE.

"Hey, gorgeous," he greets me, sunshine-smile in his voice.

"Hey, Bryce," I return. "I need your help."

"Anything for you, Sera," he says. "What is it?"

"It's Alessandro," I respond. "He's gone back to Italy. And I need you to help me find him."

There's silence on the other end for a beat. "Am I allowed to ask why?"

"Because I love him," I say simply. "And I'm going after him."

ALL OF ME

PROLOGUE

ALESSANDRO

I'm jolted awake by the plane beginning what surely must be its slow descent. I run my hands through my messy hair and over my beard, smoothing the chaos as well as I can. I've always been able to sleep on airplanes, though my rest this time was unfortunately short and more disturbed than usual.

I rub my chin contemplatively, knowing it will be a long time until I sleep peacefully again.

To avoid succumbing to the anxiety that is tearing my insides to shreds, I begin ordering my belongings for landing, starting with removing and coiling the headphones that were piping classical music into my ears as I slept. Partially to soothe the turmoil, partially to avoid the overly interested, middle-aged woman seated next to me.

Sure enough, as if my removing the headphones was the invitation she had been waiting for, she offers me a simpering smile and puts her hand on my bicep, running her fingers along its hard length to the edge of my short-sleeved black polo shirt. I resist the urge to recoil, my jaw tensing with the effort of smoothing my features into relaxed indifference.

"They announced that we'll be landing in half an hour," she says softly, suggestively, her dull blue eyes staring longingly into my own dark eyes. "Last chance to use the lavatories." She raises her painted-on eyebrows delicately and flips her poorly dyed ashy-blond hair over her shoulder coyly. Then she rises slowly, excusing herself past the elderly woman in the aisle seat. Pausing dramatically, she gives me a meaningful look before heading down the aisle. As if we'd had some interaction, some conversation that made her think I'd want to fuck her in a cramped, disgusting airplane bathroom. Or anywhere, for that matter.

The elderly woman huffs and rolls her eyes at the woman as she departs.

"On behalf of womankind," she croaks to me, "I'd like to apologize for that dingbat."

The humor is an unexpected shot of light in the dark, and a deep rumble of appreciative laughter rolls through me despite myself.

"Thank you," I reply sincerely. "But there's no need."

She smirks unreservedly in response, leaning her head toward me conspiratorially and says, "It's okay to not be a gentleman sometimes. Women like her," she jerks her head toward the back of the plane, "only see that as encouragement."

For that exact reason I've purposely avoided turning on the charm until now, though I've also been too broken and tired, too distracted. But this white-haired, feisty old woman has cut through my foul mood. And for that I give her a wink, and a genuine crooked smile.

"I'll keep that in mind," I assure her amiably.

And, as usual, the charm works its magic, and even this weathered, wise lady blushes and waves me away coquettishly, pretending to turn back to her knitting.

"Save it for someone your age," she admonishes me.

Her words bring a whisper on the wind to my ears — *Serafina* — and the smile drops abruptly from my lips. My chest tightens and breathing becomes difficult. I turn and stare out the window, but as the plane descends through the clouds, there is nothing to distract me. I close my eyes and try to breathe through it.

When I reopen them, I find the old lady considering me carefully, her shrewd gaze seeming to pierce straight through me.

"Sometimes we don't know just how much we love someone until we lose them," she says quietly. She returns to her knitting, her needles clacking softly.

I note the sense of sorrow within her words, and the delicate, gold band on her ring finger. I examine her for a moment. Her features are fine and soft, gently curved amongst her wrinkled skin. Her hands, however, are strong and calloused. This is a woman who has worked hard and known life, and love, and laughter. I suddenly wish I'd been seated next to her this whole flight.

"Is it worth it?" I ask her, abruptly breaking the silence.

She looks up in surprise, dropping a stitch. "Love?" she replies.

I nod. Her answering smile lights up her whole face.

But before she can respond, a flight attendant announces our final descent and requests everyone to return to their seats and buckle up. The old woman focuses on stowing her knitting, so I take the last moments of opportunity that the added space of the empty seat beside me provides to stretch my long legs. Window seats are not meant for someone who is six feet tall, and I can feel the tension in my neck and cramped limbs.

Moments later the seats creak and a heavy bottom drops into the chair next to me. Its occupant pointedly ignores me, and I suppress a smile as I prepare to land. To start the search that will hopefully yield answers. Answers that will, in turn, hopefully give me the power I need to shatter the obstacles keeping me from what I want. From the woman I love. Before I've lost her forever.

I stare blankly out the window as the ground swells to meet us, itching to get out of the plane and begin hunting.

Finally, the wheels meet the earth in a mighty jolt and the reassuring pressure of the brakes engaging pushes me forward in my seat. Another ping sounds throughout the cabin, followed by the calm, smooth female flight attendant's voice.

"Ladies and gentlemen, welcome to San Francisco International Airport. Local time is eleven twenty-seven a.m. and the temperature is a foggy sixty-two degrees."

ONE

"San Francisco? Are you sure?"

Bryce drops a file on the coffee table in answer, removes his just-from-church tan blazer and collapses into the chair across from the couch I'm seated on. The stiff, white dress shirt and brown slacks he wears underneath are rumpled, and he looks exhausted. His long, muscled legs splay out comically as he sinks his six-foot-four frame into the relatively small chair.

"I'm sure," he responds grimly, running a hand through his chestnut hair, his blue eyes dark and hard.

Ignoring his moodiness, I snatch up the file and eagerly peruse its contents. It's quick, as there's not much there.

"And you're sure he didn't catch a connecting flight out of the country?" I press.

Bryce levels a look at me, the closest to annoyed I've ever seen him get. "I'm sure, Sera," he huffs. "He was only ID'd boarding a flight to San Francisco. No scans through customs or to any other destinations."

I shake my head, confused. "It's only been six days. Maybe it's a stopover?" I flop back onto the couch.

Bryce eyes me, his gaze trailing over the last yellow remnants of the bruising that only a week ago sprawled the complete center of my face. The evidence of the attack by a mentally unbalanced woman shouldering a massive grudge against me that almost ended my life — the end of a long saga of sabotage and betrayal. I sweep my long, wavy brown hair in close around me self-consciously.

"I'll keep an eye on it," he replies, hesitating. "But my monitoring him is not exactly on the up-and-up. I've got to be careful about what I dig into and how often."

My eyes flick up to his in surprise. "I'm sorry, Bryce, I didn't realize I was putting you in that position," I respond.

A half-truth, really, as I know my request for help finding Alessandro made Bryce deeply uncomfortable. I thought they'd forged some sort of peace in rescuing me from my attacker and the aftermath, but Bryce's cautious protests have made it clear that he's as angry with Alessandro as ever, and that he's only helping because I asked. Well, insisted, really.

He leans forward in his chair, his sky-blue eyes now reserved and contemplative. He chews his lip, clearly carefully choosing his next words.

"You know I'd do anything for you, Sera," he breathes. "But this guy. He relentlessly pursed you until you fell for him while lying about being married. And then right after what you just went through, he hurt you again. And now it seems there are lies around that too." Bryce shakes his head sadly, running another hand through his hair, aggravated.

"I can tell he didn't want to," I insist. "And whatever his reason for not telling me he was married in the first place, it's moot now. He's not married anymore. What I can't understand is why he insisted he had to go back to Italy, but now he's in San Francisco?" I shake my head. "I don't get it. But there *is* an explanation. I just don't know what it is. And I *need* to know what it is, Bryce." I mash my lips together, willing him to understand.

"I guess I'd want to know why too," he admits, sighing deeply. "But I'd like to go to San Francisco with you."

My answer vehemently escapes my lips before I can stop it. "*No.*"

Alessandro made it clear before he left that he had no intention of providing me with answers, possibly even that he *couldn't*. If Bryce were there it would drastically reduce my odds of getting through to Alessandro.

Bryce smirks at me, shaking his head. "You know I could follow you. Whether you want me to or not."

I glare at him. Of course I know. It's why I hired him as a security consultant in the first place, when my attacker and her girlfriend were working together to sabotage my company, raining down chaos on my client list through various attacks, and eventually attacking me physically when their attempts to damage my business didn't work. And it was Bryce who cracked the case and saved me from being beaten and almost shot by that maniac. But while I know I should be grateful, his obvious threat still annoys me, and I can't stop my nostrils from flaring in outrage.

But I do manage to bite back my angry response. Because I know how deeply Bryce cares for me. And not just because he's clearly in love with me, as evidenced by his attempt to date me while Alessandro and I were broken up.

But because through everything we've become close. And if the tables were turned, I'd probably be protective of him too.

"But you won't," I finally reply. I try not to let my sorrow seep into my tone or my expression. I hate that this is driving a wedge between Bryce and me.

"You're right, I won't," he agrees, "not if you really don't want me to. I just wish I had a better understanding of why you're doing this."

I ruminate on that for a moment. I decide to skip the obvious "because I love him" as he's heard it before, and I know it's a sensitive subject for him.

"Because even if it doesn't work out, I'd rather regret doing something than doing nothing," I finally offer.

He considers me thoughtfully for a moment. "Well, I can't argue with that," he admits, giving me a half-hearted smile. A ghost of the bright-as-sunshine smile that usually radiates from him so easily. The smile I haven't seen since before that awful night. But once again I shut down the thought before it can go far. I know someday I'll have to process everything that happened. But not today. "When are you leaving?"

I breathe in deeply through my nose and out through my mouth. "Tomorrow," I answer.

"What about ERS? Sutton?" Bryce presses.

ERS. Evans Realty Services. The company I've slaved to build for nearly five years. The company that will be no more as Charles Sutton, my last client, agreed to absorb it into his own, larger company. In exchange for me. Well, when I'm done figuring things out with Alessandro anyway.

I can't help wondering if Charles Sutton only wants to mentor me, to shape me for his own purposes, because my grandfather did the same for him. Or if, as he says, he truly sees potential in me. Either way, it was an opportunity that came along at exactly the right time. And I'm ready to give up the burden of being in charge. At twenty-nine years old I'm already burnt out. And I'm ready to go after what really matters.

"Everything is already in motion," I reply softly. In less than a week, I've managed to arrange for the absorption of my company into Sutton Developments. It's far from over, but there's nothing that can't wait a few days. I meet his gaze. "I didn't see anything in that file on where he's staying."

A muscle twitches in Bryce's jaw. "He hasn't checked in to a hotel or made any other purchases. He must be using cash. Which may make finding him difficult."

"Where would you start?"

Bryce looks like he doesn't want to answer that question for a moment, but finally he says, "If he doesn't want to be found, if he gets wind that you're looking for him, from what you've told me, he will probably leave. I'll run a banking and credit history report, see if there are any places in the area he used to frequent. That's where you'll start."

A heavy pause ensues before he speaks again. "If that doesn't work, there's also a short list in the file of his known associates who are still in the area. He's likely staying with one or more of them. See if anyone on the list rings a bell with you. Before you approach any of them, observe first. Once *casually* during the middle of the day to get a lay of the land. Then again in the evening — find something inconspicuous to do with yourself and watch from a distance for a couple hours." He spits his instructions out tersely, and I know he's incredibly uncomfortable, for many reasons.

"And what if I need to approach someone?" I ask tensely. I hadn't even thought of needing to undertake such subterfuge, and the dawning realization of the challenge before me is sending ripples of apprehension through me.

"The safest people to approach are the ones who work at the places he's frequented," he explains. "Bring a picture. Ask if they've seen him. The less you say, the better. If you need to tell them why, have a simple, clean story ready."

"And if I have to approach someone he knows?" I press.

"Would you be comfortable pretending to be from immigration again?" he asks, cracking a smile.

In my desperation for his help, I'd ended up confessing many of the details of my relationship with Alessandro, including its downfall. He was extremely impressed with my detective work of the day I tricked Alessandro's wife into confirming that he was, in fact, married and much more. He even jokingly offered me a job. Clearly, it's something he's going to remember for a while.

"I can do something *like* that," I agree. "But he may know about that."

"Then probably not worth the risk," Bryce concedes.

I rub the back of my neck and pick up the file again, searching for the list of names. And I pause with it in my hand, a thought occurring to me.

"Do you think he'd tell me where he was if I just asked him?" I ask. "It sounds silly, but maybe it's worth a shot?"

"First," Bryce replies slowly, "you'd have to be able to get ahold of him. And his cell number and email address no longer work."

I blanch at the information. "How do you know that?" I ask stupidly.

Bryce looks around blankly for a minute, then when his eyes land on me again he jumps a little in his seat theatrically. "Oh, hi! I didn't see you there," he says leaning forward, offering me a hand. "I'm Bryce Hoyt, and I work for a *security* company. It's nice to meet you." I smack his hand away, feigning a glare. "That was the first thing I tried, Sera. This ain't my first rodeo."

He winks at me, and I stick my tongue out at him in response. He laughs honestly, and the sound unravels the tight coil in my chest just a bit. I can't help but smile back.

I mull suggesting I ask Marco Rossi, Giovanni Bianchi, Maria Greco, or Francesca Del Vecchio, Alessandro's former team here in Seattle, but immediately dismiss the thought knowing even if they were open to helping me find him that they'd also likely tell him. Especially since Marco and Alessandro are like brothers. He'd never give me information Alessandro didn't want me to have, much less go behind his back to do it. The hard way it is.

I stand, wandering to the window wall and gazing out at downtown Seattle. I feel rather than hear Bryce approach.

"Where'd you go, Sera?" Bryce asks quietly from beside me.

I snap my head up to catch his concerned gaze more than half a foot above my own eye level. I smile at the reminder of how much bigger than me he is with his towering, broad, muscled frame. Because at five-foot-nine and curvy I'm not used to feeling so small. And somehow it makes me feel safe.

He reaches out and tugs absentmindedly at a lock of my hair. I can feel the heat in my face at the affection in his gesture.

"Sorry," I reply sheepishly. "I'm already mentally preparing, I guess."

"Good. You're going to need to do a lot more of that."

∾

THE NEXT DAY, AS MY TAXI DRIVES OUT OF SOUTH SAN FRANCISCO AND INTO the city proper, my first thought is that it looks an awful lot like Seattle — there are gorgeous vistas in every direction and some stunning architecture. But it's also dirtier, more run-down, and more crowded. With the tech industry continuing to migrate north, though, I realize I may be looking into a crystal ball of Seattle's future. Both cities by a bay, both havens for not just tech giants but other professionals and urbanites. And while San Francisco is a shade more temperate, the beauty and outdoorsy lifestyle of the Puget Sound is drawing more and more people into the area. Not to mention the vastly more affordable housing. Which is, of course, exactly how I came to meet Alessandro Giordano, as his real estate investing company expanded into territory rife with opportunities for savvy investors.

I know Buone Case, the company he owned, still has offices here in San Francisco. But in my gut, I know he didn't come back here to work, so trying to find him there isn't at the top of my list. And the thought of lists reminds me to pull up the email from Bryce on my phone with the three locations that Alessandro used to frequent. All are within walking distance of the hotel I'll be staying at near the Museum of Modern Art, though San Francisco, like Seattle, seems to be just as hilly, though still very walkable.

As we arrive at the hotel, I realize just how close to the museum I'll be — literally a stone's throw. I glance longingly at the simple façade. While it's exactly the kind of place I could spend hours upon hours losing myself, not this trip. I step out of the cab into the early afternoon sunlight, and, luggage in tow, head into the hotel so I can quickly check in and get moving.

∼

REMAINING IN THE LAVISH HOTEL ROOM IS RIDICULOUSLY TEMPTING. APART from a spacious and lush living room and bedroom, my suite comes with its own personal butler and gorgeous city views on two sides of the generously sized common area. I suppose I should have expected as much, as it is a five-star hotel. But I don't travel often, so I figured what the hell. And while I'm glad I splurged, I have to resist the urge to ask my butler for help combing the city.

Smiling thinly to myself, I lean back into the plush, grey couch to plan my route for the afternoon. Plotting the three stops in my map app shows a near-linear path, not much more than a mile from the hotel. I grab my purse and slide on my sneakers, heading back out into the cool sunshine of the day.

Walking through the city, it feels like Seattle too. The mile to the bookstore isn't even very sloped, and the tall buildings and bustling traffic are a familiar and comforting backdrop for my stroll. There's even a faint whiff of salty sea air from the bay.

As I go, I try to practice what I'll say in my head, but I've never been terribly good at planning that sort of thing ahead of time, so I give up quickly. It'll just have to come in the moment, like it always does.

Before I know it, I can see the bookstore ahead on the opposite side of the street, the salmon and black building squatter than those around it. As I look left before crossing the road, I'm stopped short by the sight of the Transamerica Pyramid thrusting into the sky behind me, its iconic architecture drawing the eye of many on the street. Some, like myself, have stopped to gaze upon it in awe.

Briefly the tallest building west of Chicago, it still commands the eye and the imagination with its unique shape and sheen. I remember suddenly that it was another Italian — Amadeo Giannini — who actually founded the Transamerica Corporation. And just like that I'm slammed back to reality.

I take out my phone, pulling up the snapshot I took of the photo Peyton, Alessandro's now ex-wife, gave me the day I tricked her into confirming they were married. I zoom it in on just Alessandro and step down into the bookshop.

The shop has a funky vibe, with shelves upon shelves of tightly packed books, posters of all kinds, and signs directing its patrons to yet more books. It's neither stuffy like a library nor tidy and cold like a chain store. Rather, it's cozy and full of life, and I instantly understand why Alessandro came here often.

Unfortunately, it's also clearly a very popular stop for both locals and tourists, as the kind gentleman behind the counter is skeptical he'll recall the "friend" I'm searching for even before I've shown him the picture. And as he suspected, he doesn't.

I thank him, though I'm more than a little disappointed. But I'm also too enthralled by the store to not take a quick stroll through their fiction section, lovingly fingering some of the unique finds as I meander. When I leave, I thank him yet again and head to my next stop, a café only a few blocks away.

I have to stifle a laugh as I'm greeted by the bold colors of the Italian flag and the word "ESPRESSO" emblazoned under the shop's name like a beckoning call to the coffee-obsessed true Italian.

Entering the small shop, the aroma of coffee and pastries wraps me in a warm cocoon of happiness. The woman behind the counter greets me with a smile.

"Welcome! What can I get for you today?" she asks warmly. She looks to be a few years younger than me and has a kind face framed by a sharp, golden-brown bob.

I smile back as my eyes rove over the pastries displayed. "An espresso, please," I reply. "And," I point to a gorgeous, heart-shaped jam thumbprint cookie, "one of those too, please."

"My favorite," she replies, plating a cookie. She rings me up before making the espresso. "Anything else today?"

"Actually, there is. I'm looking for a friend," I hand her a large bill for the tab and measure her reaction carefully. Since she still seems to be eagerly listening, I continue. "He moved away about eight months ago and we lost touch, but I think he's back now. He used to come in here all the time, though, so I thought maybe you'd seen him?"

"It's certainly possible. We have a lot of regulars, and I know most of them — I've been here almost three years," she replies, and excitement unfolds in my gut. "What does he look like?"

I bring up the picture on my phone and show it to her. Her face lights up with recognition.

"Alessandro," she says in an exaggerated imitation of his accent as she heads to the espresso machine. "Doppio espresso, every day as soon as we opened."

I make an effort to laugh casually, trying not to let my excitement show. "That's him. Have you seen him lately?"

"Not in months," she responds.

And I deflate like a popped balloon. She hands me my espresso.

"Thanks anyway," I reply, dropping my considerable change in the tip jar with a smile.

"No problem," she says, her eyes widening slightly as she watches the bills settle. "Do you want to leave your name and number in case he stops by?"

"Oh gosh, no, that's okay. I'm sure I'll catch up with him sooner or later." She shrugs, and I take a seat at a nearby table.

I examine the espresso, noting the perfect crema on top. I sip it, and the rich flavor wraps around my tongue. I follow it with a bite of cookie, and I'm instantly hooked.

"Damn, that's good," I remark to myself. I can see the barista give a faint smile behind the counter. A little embarrassed, I finish my espresso and cookie quickly, giving her a smile on my way out.

"Come back soon," she calls after me, and I nod faintly as I leave.

Emerging into the fading afternoon light, it occurs to me that Alessandro may yet stop there, and I silently hope I'm able to find him before super-memory-chick back there blows my cover.

I start trekking the short walk to the last stop on the list — unsurprisingly, an Italian restaurant. Supposedly *the* best Italian restaurant in San Francisco. I arrive to a more muted display of the colors of the Italian flag at the entrance of another small, cozy establishment. Unfortunately, it's currently closed. I glance at my watch. The restaurant won't open for another hour. And after the cookie and espresso, I'm not particularly hungry.

Realizing I should have thought this through a bit better, I decide to return to the hotel and come back later for dinner. On the bright side, I get a long look at the Transamerica building once more as I make my way back.

Once in my room, I opt for a soothing shower. The hot water unknots my tense muscles, and the fluffy robe afterward feels like heaven. I sink onto the bed to rest my eyes for a minute before getting dressed once more.

∽

I WAKE IN THE DARK AND CURSE MYSELF FOR NOT SETTING AN ALARM. A glance at the clock on the nightstand tells me its two a.m. I strip off my robe and crawl between the sheets, making a mental note to make a reservation once I'm up. The bed is so luxuriously soft, and I'm still so tired from my travels, that I'm asleep again almost instantly.

∽

WHEN I WAKE FOR THE DAY, MY FIRST ACT IS TO MAKE THE RESERVATION AT the restaurant for eight p.m. that night. That done, I pull on a pair of jeans and a white T-shirt and sit down to review the list of Alessandro's known contacts in the area.

The list is only five names long, and none of them sound familiar. I decide to rent a car for the day as the addresses are scattered around the city, and my lack of results yesterday has me itching for progress.

By ten a.m. I find myself in a blue coupe headed for the Presidio. Even at this late hour, traffic is slow going. I roll my windows down and try to enjoy the warm breeze as I crawl toward my destination.

As I roll by the marina, I see signs for a Fourth of July party at Pier 39. I glance at my phone's display, surprised to see that it's Tuesday, July third. The Fourth of July is *tomorrow*.

I scrunch my brow, wondering where the time went. But I guess I've had other things on my mind these last weeks. I tap the steering wheel impatiently, knowing I better make the best of things today, as I'm unsure whether trying to run covert surveillance on a holiday is a good idea.

When traffic finally breaks up, it's smooth sailing to the address my phone is guiding me to. Until I see the guard gate at the entrance to the community. It's unmanned, only offering a mounted keypad with a speaker box. I look around apprehensively, wondering if I should hover nearby and wait for someone to open the gate, or even try to bluff my way in. But the impressive houses beyond give me pause, as I have no idea what kind of security the community might have. I decide against chancing it, opting to move on to the second stop on my list.

I head south to the Richmond neighborhood, toward Golden Gate Park, noting wryly that at least my hunt will take me on a decently comprehensive driving tour of the city.

As I approach the next address, with thankfully zero barriers, the rather average looking neighborhood has me itching, not for the first time today, to pull up my real estate agent apps to check prices in the area. I resist, trying to focus on the task at hand.

In classic San Francisco style, the buildings are packed against one another, each climbing close to their likely regulated height. I pass by the address on the list slowly, and the building's tan exterior and drawn shades give no hint as to what's inside.

Unfortunately, there is no way to "casually" observe much more than that, as there's not really anywhere to park, nor any pretense under which to approach the house. Not that I think it would do much good if I don't intend to knock anyway. I take a lap around the block and approach from the opposite direction, but a second look doesn't yield any new information. I decide to come back this evening, I'll have to park at a nearby business and walk by to get a closer look.

I spend the rest of the morning and into the afternoon visiting the other three addresses, stopping only briefly for a quick lunch. The third address was nearly identical to the second, tan house, but purple and in a slightly more run-down neighborhood. The one after that had so much junk piled in the yard that I didn't even bother with a second look; I simply crossed it off the list and continued on, unable to see Alessandro, with his immaculate attention to detail and appearance, staying in a place like that. The final address has a for sale sign out front, and a quick look at the listing clearly shows that the house is empty.

With two viable options for evening surveillance, I return to the hotel to regroup. Once back, I step into the shower, again letting the hot water work the tension from my back and limbs. It's short-lived relief, but I take what I can get.

As afternoon shifts into evening, I decide to return to the second, tan house to observe until my reservation. I opt for a comfortable, stretchy black shirt-dress over black leggings, bringing a maroon cardigan along, since I know temperatures will drop when the sun sets. I slip on a pair of black flats to complete the look, allowing both a decent appearance for the seemingly casual restaurant but enough comfort to stroll inconspicuously by the house a few times.

Due to traffic, it's nearly six p.m. when I find a playground to park near, a few blocks from the house. I note, ironically, that it's called Rossi Playground. I think of Marco and wonder how he's handling running Buone Case since taking it over so Alessandro could do whatever it is he's doing.

Willing myself to focus, I step out into the cooling evening air and start my stroll.

❧

ON MY THIRD LAP PAST THE HOUSE, I'VE RUN OUT OF CONVENIENT EXCUSES TO stop within sight distance. I have no shoelaces to tie, and I can only pretend I dropped my keys so many times. None of the passes offer up anything of further use. While I can see that there are now lights on inside, no cars are in the driveway, and I haven't been able to catch anyone going in or out, or even peeping out of the drapes. There isn't even a nosy neighbor to feign conversation with about looking to buy a house in the area. Nonetheless, I persist until it's time to return to the car to make it in time for my reservation. By the time I do I'm starving and discouraged, with sore feet.

I'm especially grumpy when I'm not able to find a parking spot close to the restaurant and am forced to walk another good distance. I slip on the maroon cardigan against the slight chill of the evening and make my way slowly past the few blocks of shops. As I approach, I take a deep breath and try to let go of my frustrations. I'm going to need to be charming and approachable to get answers without raising suspicion.

Fixing a neutral expression on my face, I enter. The hostess stand is just inside the door, and a plump, friendly looking middle-aged Italian woman greets me.

"*Benvenuto!*"

"*Grazie,*" I reply, slipping into my best impression of a warm smile despite my exhaustion. "I have a reservation for one under Evans."

As she examines a list on her podium I note that the small restaurant is absolutely packed, with every seat at the bar occupied as well, and I wonder where exactly she's going to seat me.

"Serafina?" she asks in her lovely, lilting accent.

"Yes," I agree. "Sera."

"Sera," she replies, smiling. "I'm terribly sorry, but with the upcoming holiday we've unfortunately overbooked for the evening. Would you mind sharing with another single? There's a gentleman you could join who just ordered. He's a friend of the family, and I can promise he's very well behaved." She smiles encouragingly. "Or you're welcome to wait a few minutes for a table to open up. It shouldn't be long."

I bristle slightly but considering I'm hoping to get information from her, refusing doesn't seem like the best option. And her warm smile and mannerisms tell me that she really would understand if I'd rather not. But it also occurs to me that if this person she wants to seat me with knows the owners, he may be able to help too. And agreeing would certainly put me at an advantage regardless.

"I'm happy to share a table," I respond, returning her smile.

"*Grazie mille*," she responds sincerely, clasping her hands together. "It is much appreciated, and we'll get you something good for your troubles." She lifts a menu from a pocket on the side of her stand and gestures for me to follow her.

She leads me through the dimly lit restaurant, heading for the very back corner. The back few tables are tucked behind a waiter's station, so I can't see my table companion through the packed tables between us.

"*Ciao*," she greets him. "*Ti dispiace condividere?*"

"*Nessun problema*," a deep, melodic voice replies. And I freeze before she even steps aside, gesturing to the chair across from him, as I don't need to see the shock of artfully tousled, dark brown hair nor the warm, liquid brown eyes that meet mine to know that I've just found Alessandro.

TWO

ALESSANDRO

As Sofia steps aside to reveal the young lady she's asked me to share my table with, I'm confused for a moment wondering if, having just been thinking of Serafina, my vision is playing tricks on me. But as I realize it's not, that Serafina is really standing before me, looking alarmed but as beautiful as ever, my heart skips a beat before it starts pounding madly.

Thankfully the shock renders my face blank, though I'm sure it registers in my eyes. I work to keep my expression fixed as Sofia glances nervously at Serafina's stunned look.

"Is it okay?" Sofia asks her uncertainly.

Serafina doesn't take her eyes off me as she answers. "Yes, thank you." She slides into the chair, dazed, and Sofia hands her a menu before glancing at me questioningly.

Gathering my wits, I shrug lightly and, mollified, Sofia returns to the front of the restaurant.

It takes me a moment of examining my unexpected dinner companion, of absorbing that she's really here, before I can speak. "How…?" But my words fail me before the question can even fully form.

Her face is pale and drawn, and I can tell she's still recovering from the shock of seeing me as well. Interesting. "It's my turn not to give up," she replies with a meek, apologetic smile.

I want to laugh, and cry, and kiss her, and admonish her for using my words against me, but I don't know who might be listening. And if I've learned anything this past week, it's that the danger I'm in, the suspicion of which drove me from Serafina's side in the first place, is very real. And if those pursuing me learn what she means to me, I dare not even think of the consequences.

"What I meant to say is, how, exactly, did you know I'd be here?" I ask, scanning the restaurant nervously. I'd tapped in to my cash reserves when I followed the trail here and took pains to stay out of the system as much as possible, thinking I'd be practically untraceable.

"Bryce. He told me you were in San Francisco. But I didn't know you'd be here tonight," she replies. "I mean, he told me you used to come here often." Her expression is all apologies and longing. "How else was I supposed to find you? Apparently, I can't call or email you anymore."

I frown, running a finger under my chin. The giant sent her here. That's a twist, though with his expertise it explains how she found me. Though I was fairly certain when we spoke last, while Serafina lay unconscious in the hospital, that his threat to "make sure bad things happened to me if I hurt her again" meant he didn't want her coming anywhere near me. And yet, he helped her do exactly that.

"You weren't supposed to find me at all," I respond bluntly.

"You're not glad to see me?" she asks, catching my eye. A gentle tease, and I can tell she's searching for a warmer welcome. But she has no clue the danger at hand, and I can't find a smile or cute response to give her. My only thought is to convince her to forget me, to protect her, and to get her back on a plane to Seattle as soon as possible.

I simply stare at her for a moment before shrugging noncommittally. "It's nice to see you again," I reply casually. "If you're hungry, I recommend the house special."

She arches her eyebrows at my indifferent response, but the waiter arrives, blocking any immediate reply. As suggested, she goes ahead and orders the house special. I add a bottle of wine for good measure. Something to take the edge off. When he leaves, she sweeps her long hair over one shoulder and places her shapely arms on the table, leaning forward on them.

"I need to know why," she says baldly. Her beautiful, light brown eyes are flecked with green, and I have to resist the urge to reach out and touch her.

I lean back in my chair, crossing my legs under the table and smoothing my dark gray linen trousers as I consider my response carefully. Thankfully the waiter is already back with the wine, giving me a bit longer to gather my thoughts. He uncorks the bottle, pouring a small amount in my glass. I swirl it carefully, inhaling deeply as I watch Serafina shift uncomfortably in her chair. I take a sip, barely tasting it, and nod to the waiter. He pours our glasses slowly, then leaves the bottle behind and departs once more.

I take a long drink, then set my glass back down. I mirror Serafina's posture and lean forward so our faces are close enough to speak quietly and avoid being overhead, but still a respectable enough distance away to not raise the interest of a casual observer.

"I can't offer you any more information than you already have," I reply lowly. "Especially not here. Let's just enjoy our dinner, shall we?" I lean back in my seat once more, making a point to keep my expression neutral.

"Then where?" she demands quietly but firmly. "When? When are you going to trust me enough to tell me what's going on? To let me make the decision for myself?"

"I think we can agree," I reply guardedly, "that there are some things best not shared, *especially* with people you trust."

She looks at me, clearly confused. "What is that supposed to mean?"

I smile cryptically. "How's the giant? Still in love with you?"

Her nostrils flare and she clenches her jaw. Good. My comments are hitting their mark.

"At least he's honest with me," she retorts.

I raise an eyebrow. And I hate myself before I even say my next words. "Then maybe you should go back to him," I suggest casually, draining my wine glass.

Her mouth opens and closes several times. "You don't mean that."

Her voice is low and breathy. It sends a shiver down my spine. I pour myself another glass to mask my reaction.

"Oh, but I do." I level a sharp look at her. "I thought I made it clear where things stood." *Forgive the pain I must cause you, mio tesoro, and just go,* I plead silently, *before something much worse happens to you.*

"You're not going to get rid of me that easily," she counters, her eyes narrowing.

"I don't see that you have much of a choice," I reply calmly.

"Don't I?"

This time I can't hide my smile. I wonder sometimes if she remembers everything I've ever said to her, the clever girl. Her answering smile is hopeful but sad. But before anything further can be said, our food arrives.

"*Buon appetito,*" our waiter says softly.

We each mumble our thanks as he leaves. We eat in uncomfortable silence for a bit before she sets her fork down and pushes her plate back.

"Something wrong with your food?" I ask archly. She's barely eaten anything.

"I'm not as hungry as I thought," she says quietly, taking a deep drink of wine.

"Then maybe you should slow down on the alcohol," I remark drily, glancing pointedly at her now-empty glass.

"Maybe you should mind your own business," she retorts hotly.

I can feel anger rising in me at her words, but I master it before it can get far. "I'm just trying to look out for you," I explain. *And not just about the alcohol, damnit.*

"I can take care of myself," she pouts. She shakes her head lightly. "This isn't what I came here to talk about, Alessandro. I thought…"

I set my fork down and lean over my plate, hands clasped in front of me. "You thought what? After I told you why I was leaving that it was a good idea for you to follow? That I'd want to involve you? You thought wrong."

I stare intensely at her, trying to tell her with my eyes what I can't with my lips. *The threat was more real than I thought. They've been watching me. If they don't already know about you, I can't risk them finding out.* But I know if I tell her these things it won't deter her, stubborn as she is. And the last time she underestimated a threat it nearly got her killed. I can't let that happen to her again.

From the anger in her eyes, in her demeanor, I can see that she doesn't understand what I'm trying to say. And she's furious.

"This isn't you."

As usual, she sees straight through me. I smile grimly. "Maybe you just weren't listening closely enough before," I suggest, spreading my hands in front of me.

She rises from her chair, quietly fuming. She shakes her head and turns to leave.

"Where are you going?" I ask as indifferently as I can.

"Back to my hotel," she seethes. She drops a card on the table, with the name of a nearby luxury hotel. "If you come to your senses you know where to find me. But I'm leaving before I say something I don't mean. Or worse, something I *do* mean."

I watch her silently as she walks out. And I'm angry. Not at her, but at myself, for having to be that way with her. Returning my eyes to the card, I flip it over. She's written her room number on the back. I quietly shred the card and tuck the remnants into my pocket. And then I pick up my fork and return to eating my dinner in solitude.

As the restaurant clears, I continue drinking until Sofia and her husband, Luca, are done for the evening and sit down at the table next to mine.

"Who was the girl?" Luca asks, rubbing his round belly.

"Leave him alone, Luca," Sofia chastises him. "And I told you not to eat so many cannoli."

Luca grins widely at her.

"It's okay," I reply. "She was just a friend. I told her about this restaurant, but she didn't expect to run into me here." I suppress a heavy sigh. I dislike lying, despite what others seem to think.

"Good! Tell all your friends," Luca laughs. The chef pokes his head out of the kitchen and signals Luca. "I'll be back." He rises slowly, shuffling away.

"I know it's not my business, Alessandro, but I saw her when she left," Sofia says softly. Her kind, brown eyes, so much like my own mama's, meet mine. "*Sei più gentile di così.*"

I shoot her an angry look. *I* know *I'm kinder than that. That was the point.*

"You're right," I agree, finishing yet another glass of wine. "It's not your business."

Sofia raises her hands in a gesture of surrender. "If that's how you want her to remember you."

Her words are like a punch in the gut. "That's low, Sofia."

She stands to follow Luca into the kitchen and fixes me with a stern look. "*È vero.*"

Yes, it's true. But it's still a cheap shot.

She turns and starts walking away but can't resist a parting parry. "I hope I don't see you back at the house later."

I shake my head. Sofia has always been a busybody. But when she's right, she's right. Before I can stop myself, I'm out in the cool night air.

∽

It's only a little after ten p.m. when I knock on her door, so I know she must still be awake. But she doesn't answer, and I'm suddenly afraid she's already gone. I knock again, louder, and wait a good while. And still no response.

I do the only other thing I can think of — I call the front desk. But they say she's still here and connect me to her phone. Sure enough, I can hear it ringing inside. And ringing. And ringing. Now I'm really starting to panic, wondering if she ran into trouble on the way home. But finally, she answers.

"Hello?" She sounds annoyed.

"Open your goddamn door," I order her.

A moment later, the door cracks open and she peeks out at me. I push the door open, step inside, and close it behind me. Her hair is up in a messy bun and she is dripping wet with a large, fluffy white towel wrapped around her. I breathe a sigh of relief. She's here. She's safe. She was just taking a shower.

"What the hell?" she asks angrily.

"I've been knocking for fifteen minutes," I tell her. "I thought something had happened to you."

She glares at me and turns away. "What do you care?" she scoffs, heading toward the bedroom.

She's still mad. And she has every right to be. But her dismissal roils the anger I'd suppressed earlier in the evening, and like the flip of a switch, I'm mad too. I stride quickly for her, spinning her around by her wrist.

"You damn well know that I care," I respond hotly.

She yanks her arm out of my grasp, clutching the towel to her naked body. And I'm suddenly very aware of how much of her is showing, and it's been long enough since I was with her that I'm suddenly finding it very hard to keep my wits about me.

"Are we Dr. Jekyll now? What, no more Mr. Hyde?"

I huff a short laugh, unable to stop staring at the hand clutching the edges of the towel together over her chest. "I'd say I'm usually a bit of both, honestly."

"*Honestly*," she scoffs. "Glad we're being *honest* now." She waves a hand around as she speaks, and in her fervor her towel slips from her grip slightly, exposing the top of her round, heavy breasts.

A bolt of lust shoots through me and I squeeze my eyes shut tightly. "Can you please put some clothes on?" I ask. I open my eyes to see that she is smiling, realizing suddenly that she has the upper hand.

"No, I don't think I will," she replies serenely.

"Serafina," I beg.

She takes one step toward me, letting the towel slip just a bit more. I swallow hard, and my cock twitches.

"Tell me why you had to leave," she prompts.

I shake my head dimly, my eyes on her chest. She takes another step toward me, within touching distance. She drops the towel so she's holding it in by a corner in front of her, clinging to a small scrap of the fabric that keeps her from exposing herself to me completely. Though one perfect, rosy nipple is just visible around the edge of the towel.

"Tell me," she repeats.

My breathing is heavy, and my palms are itching to grab her. "It's not safe," I say dumbly.

She cocks her head to the side. "For who?"

I open my mouth to protest and she removes the clip holding her hair up and shakes out her long, damp tresses.

"Tell me." Her sexy whisper sends a shiver down my back once again.

I'm hypnotized, and the tight rein I keep on what I want her to know has evaporated. "For either of us," I breathe. "I wouldn't have left if I had any other choice."

She steps forward, her body pressing against mine, only the towel between us. My hand has a mind of its own as it lightly wraps around her glorious, naked backside.

"There's always another choice." Her sweet, cinnamon-honey scent fills my senses and my head swims.

"No," I protest. "There's not. Not until I stop whoever is after us."

The words tumbling out surprise me, as I have no recollection of forming them. All I can think of is her hand on the towel. And her nipple, ripe for sucking. My lips part and I know I'm breathing heavily.

She raises an eyebrow. "Who threatened you? Let me help you, Alessandro," she purrs.

I shake my head, trying to clear the fog of my desire for her. "No," I whisper.

She smiles seductively up at me, with a look of triumphant lust and fire. "I think I can change your mind," she murmurs. And she drops the towel, sliding her arms around my neck.

And I have no more words, no more conscious stream of thought, only the burning need to feel her, taste her. I lean into her, my lips searching for hers. When our faces meet, I'm wrapped in her scent, my hands sliding over her soft, delicious body. My hands slip under her backside, lifting her to me. Her legs wrap around me, and I carry her through the bedroom door, laying her out on the humongous, cloudlike bed inside.

I pull my mouth from hers and slide my hands down her chest, over her hips, lightly grazing the dampness between her legs. I control myself long enough to get an eyeful of her large, firm breasts, those perfect nipples peaked with anticipation, her soft stomach and the stunning curves of her thighs an invitation for the heat roiling inside me. She pulls a leg up, exposing herself to me, her gaze fiery and taunting.

And like a summons, I drop to my knees, my mouth finding the glistening, wet mound between her thighs. My tongue probes for the small bundle at its zenith, and when she gasps loudly I know I've found the spot. I work it with increasing ardor, adding a finger, then two, then pumping them in time with my circling tongue. She writhes under me, her gasps egging me on, her fingers entwined in the bedding, her salty-peachy taste filling my mouth. One of her hands reaches for me, and I grasp it with my free hand. Her grip is as tight as she is under my provocation, and I don't think I can wait much longer to take her.

But I press through, controlling the churning heat inside, determined to see her through to climax. I switch my assault, squeezing the small bundle of nerves between my thumb and forefinger, plunging my tongue into her. She cries out and tightens around me, and I know she's on the edge. I let go of her hand and search for her nipple. I'm just able to reach it, rolling it between my fingers as I work her below. It's enough to push her over the edge, and she screams, a warm gush meeting my lips as she climaxes.

I release her as she tumbles down from her ascent, quickly pulling my black V-neck sweater off and unbuttoning the gray trousers. But before I can finish removing them, she's there, unzipping the fly and yanking my pants and black boxer-briefs over my backside, freeing my erection completely. I'm not even able to finish removing them before her mouth is on my cock, her hand working the base as she unleashes her tongue on the tip. She slides the two toward each other in concentric motions until I can barely stand through the waves of pleasure.

She stops abruptly, scooting back on the bed, beckoning me to her. I mindlessly respond instantly, crawling eagerly over the covers to her waiting hands. She firmly pushes me onto my back, sitting astride me over my thighs. She hovers just out of reach, stroking me gently with one hand, licking her lips. The sight almost makes me climax on the spot.

"Who is it?" she asks.

And in my lust fog, I stare at her, confused. She laughs softly, realizing I'm not all there.

"Who threatened you?"

Through the haze, I realize she's still working me for information. Clever, clever girl. She raises her eyebrows, squeezing me harder. I moan deeply.

"You fight dirty," I manage to reply.

She grins in agreement, releasing me, and sliding her breasts up the length of me to cover my mouth with hers. Her tongue finds mine, and our bodies meld together. I run my hands over her, itching to be inside her.

"You'll forgive me if I've had to resort to creative methods of interrogation," she whispers in my ear. She runs her tongue along its edge, breathing heavily. "Tell me, darling, who threatened you." She sits up astride my stomach, my cock tickling her backside, the slight brushing driving me mad.

"I'm not saying another woman's name while you're naked on top of me," I reply, frustrated.

Her eyes light up with understanding. She knows who I mean. My former wife. It's hard to even *think* the word in my current state.

"You're afraid of her?" she asks, running her fingernails over my nipples.

"Not at first," I admit. "But she made specific threats. And the more I learn…" I shake my head, cursing my traitor tongue and her absolute power over me.

Serafina positions herself over my waiting erection, her hand holding me, so the tip just grazes her warm wetness. "Keep going," she encourages me.

Giving in, I grit my teeth and move to buck myself into her, but she's ready for me. She slides back out of reach, shaking her head and smiling.

"That's not how we play, lover."

I sit up, but she's too fast for me. She descends upon me once again with her mouth and hands so feverishly that I fall back onto the bed, almost spilling myself into her mouth instantly. But she knows exactly how to back off to avoid that, keeping me right on the edge, begging for release.

"*Per favore*, Serafina," I plead.

"What did you learn?" she prompts, continuing to work me with her hand.

Sweet unholy torture. "She's not working alone. But I haven't..." I moan loudly, and she slackens her grip. "I haven't figured out who she's working with. But they've been watching me for a long time. That's all I know." I'm practically dizzy with anticipation and delayed pleasure, and I beg her silently with my eyes to give me what I need.

She smiles grimly, mounting me, and plunging me deep into her tight, hot sex. I ache inside her, needing more. I grip her hips tightly, pushing up, urging her on.

But she holds firm and still on top of me. "See, that wasn't so hard," she croons, smiling mischievously.

I huff a tortured laugh. It's abruptly cut off as she pulls my hands to her breasts and begins to ride me. I can tell she means it this time, and I'm practically weeping with relief as the sweet, wet thrusts cause the tension to ball quickly in me before erupting out into her in hot fire. I scream my release at the same time she does, and she tightens around me, extending the last small bit of what I had left in me.

Too tired to be angry that she managed to seduce the information out of me — well, some of it at least — I pull her toward me roughly, spending the last of the fire in me on claiming her with my tongue and hands.

When I'm completely spent, I bury my face in her hair, my hands cupping her backside. We lay together, sweaty and slick from sex, until we are both breathing normally again.

"I'm sorry," she eventually says softly.

I look down into her eyes. She doesn't look sorry. She looks fucking amazing, and like she knows it.

"Are you?"

She laughs. "No," she admits.

I smile down at her, despite myself.

"And now I know," she adds.

"Yes," I agree resignedly. "Now you know."

She considers me for a long while. "You followed her here, didn't you?"

It's not a question. And she's not wrong, but I don't confirm it. Though she clearly knows me well enough to glean the answer from my face or my body language.

"That's what you're doing. You're following her. Trying to figure out who she's working with. What they can really do to you."

Again, I stay silent. She extricates herself from me and rises from the bed, and I roll onto my side to watch her walk away. She almost makes it to the bathroom before she turns to me.

"I'd just be a liability to you on this little mission, I suppose?" The anguish on her face is heartbreaking, and the picture of her standing there — naked to me in every way, with my seed dripping down the inside of her thigh — nearly breaks me. But it also reminds me how vulnerable she is, and why I must fight like hell to keep her out of this. To keep her safe.

"You'd be a liability to yourself," I correct her. "If they don't know about you — and I have good reason to believe they don't — I don't want to give them that knowledge by keeping you close for my own, selfish reasons."

She shakes her head, turning back toward the bathroom. "I'm going to take a bath," she mumbles.

I sit up on the bed. "Didn't you just shower?" I tease her.

She shoots me a dirty look over her shoulder as she turns on the taps for the huge, raised tub. "Somebody got me all dirty again," she pouts, beckoning me with a crooked finger.

I slide off the bed, grinning madly as I take her in my arms. "Temptressssss," I purr into her ear.

I kiss her soft neck, shoulders, and breasts as the tub fills, running my tongue along her nipple as she arches into me. I take it between my teeth, and suck until she's moaning. Dropping a hand between her legs, I use the wetness that still remains from our frenzied fuck on the bed to gently work her. She clings to me, clearly devoid of strength after her assault on me. I reciprocate the torture she just enacted upon me, drawing her to the brink, then pulling back just as the tub finishes filling. Watching her pant has me hardening again.

I step into the tub, pulling her with me. I lean her over the edge facing away from me, so I can enter her from behind. She sinks against me, groaning in pleasure. I reach under her and grasp her breasts in my hands, squeezing her nipples between my fingers as I use the grip to pull her onto me. In this position, I'm fully inside her, her spent cunt tight even without orgasming. It's like a silken, gloved fist and it feels like heaven. I pump into her steadily over and over, our groans of pleasure growing louder together, until I eventually feel her tightening around me even further. Knowing she's ready to climax again, I let loose, pounding into her ferociously until we're both over the edge once more. My world explodes, and my grip on her slackens as I again cry out my release. Our moans mingle as we finish, and she goes limp in my arms, clinging to the side of the tub. I sink back into the hot water and she settles into my lap, her head lazing against my shoulder.

I wrap my hands around hers, tracing small circles with my thumbs.

"Have we ever just made love once?" she asks contemplatively. "Without almost immediately going at it again?"

I laugh appreciatively at the observation. "Probably," I reply, kissing her neck. "But I'm usually far too turned on by you to be satisfied only having you once."

She turns her face to mine and kisses me briefly. "If you don't want me to come with you, I won't," she says softly. "But does that mean we can't still be whatever it is that we are?"

"Serafina," I start, turning her face back to mine. "You have been everything to me. From the moment you agreed to be mine. It's why I need to do this." She kisses me again, sweetly this time. "Please, let me do this, on my own, my way. And if I can, then I will come back to you, knowing that there's nothing keeping us apart. That there's nothing to worry about."

"Okay," she agrees.

In shock, I twist her around in the tub so she's facing me. "*Okay?*" I ask, aghast.

She shrugs. "Okay." She smiles furtively. "I can't *make* you take me along for the ride. And honestly, I don't think I'd want to go. I mean, I would, if you wanted me to. But you don't. And while it'll be like leaving a body part behind, I'll manage, I suppose."

I look at her skeptically. "I think you could make me if you tried," I concede. "You just played me like a fiddle back there." I tip my head toward the bedroom and she laughs.

"Desperate times," she replies, grinning mischievously. "I'll try to use my powers for good, I promise."

THREE

Despite the ridiculously amazing sex and the exhaustion that followed, I find my sleep is as disturbed as it has been of late. My nightmares have been a constant companion these past months. So much so that I can feel their presence as I drift to sleep, lurking in my subconscious, waiting to torment me night after night.

They were better once, almost nonexistent even, when we were together and happy, Alessandro and me. For that brief time. Our reunion has given me a sliver of hope that we'll have that again, but it's overshadowed by the uncertainty that remains. My nightmares rip me awake once more, in the early hours of the morning.

I spring up, covered in sweat, half mad with terror as shadowy figures chase me from sleep. I press my palms into my eyes, willing the tears away. Once I'm certain of their retreat, I look around the room, now wide awake.

A shaft of moonlight glows through a crack in the drapes, casting a dim light over the room. Alessandro sleeps soundly next to me, splayed out on his back as always, looking both younger and older at once. I slip quietly from the bed and pad to the window, peeping through the drapes at the city sprawled around us.

I haven't had time for private reflection on everything I've learned since finding Alessandro last night. And while I don't have all the details, I know enough. And the way I uncovered it was surprisingly empowering. I've never used sex against a man like that, much less a man as stubborn, virile, and commanding as Alessandro is. That it worked is beyond comprehension.

But despite my reassurances to the contrary, a large part of me wants to follow him into anything if it means never being parted from him again. When he's not with me I feel less than whole. But the volatility of our relationship makes me wonder how much of that is what I want him to be, as opposed to what he actually is. If the idea of him is more fulfilling than being with him.

I shake my head in disagreement with my own doubts. Being with him, waking up with him most mornings, was the happiest period of my life. But I know even if I stay with him through this, to wherever it takes us, it won't be like it was. He'll be worried, distracted, and overbearing. Much like he was at the height of our most contentious moments, before we were together, before we were even lovers.

I certainly haven't forgotten how insufferably insistent he can be when he sets his mind to how something should happen. How laser-focused he is on details, on seeing things through to the vision he has in his mind. I have first-hand experience of the strife that comes from getting between him and what he is pursuing.

And, quite frankly, if we ever ran across Peyton again, I'd have a hard time not beating the living shit out of the two-faced bitch. Because however she kept him in that marriage, and whatever threats she made, one day, I'll make her pay.

But that thread of anger is exactly why I need to stay out of this. This is the kind of thing I won't be able to stay cool and logical about. I can't deny that Alessandro is right — I'll just put myself in harm's way and make myself into a constant worry for him in an already stressful situation.

So, as much as it kills me, having as much information as I need in order to understand, I know in my gut that I must let him go. And hope like hell he comes back to me in one piece.

I turn from my vantage point at the window and look back at the bed. Alessandro has rolled over, his arm reaching for the spot where I slept minutes ago as if his subconscious knows I've left it. For a moment I contemplate leaving right now, bypassing another cycle of rending ourselves from each other. As amazing as it's been, it's also been like tearing open a wound where the skin had just begun to knit back together. But I know I'd suffer the pain again and again, even if those were the only terms under which I could be with him.

Some visceral part of me knows it shouldn't be this way, that I shouldn't need him so much, that I'm a perfectly whole person without him, but that small sliver isn't as strong as the rest of me. And the rest of me needs him like air, water, or food. Even now, simply standing apart from him takes conscious effort. To not go to him, and wrap myself around him, losing myself in his warm embrace. Memorizing every inch of him. Refilling my lungs with his wine-and-spice smell. I'm like a druggie. And he's my drug. Can it last? Or is it, like any addiction, doomed to consume me, body and soul? All I can hope is that I get the chance to find out.

I return to the bed and, knowing that I won't get back to sleep otherwise, proceed to wake him in a way I know he won't mind being stirred.

I WAKE TO THE SMELL OF COFFEE AND TO SUNLIGHT PEEKING THROUGH THE drapes. Unsurprisingly, I'm alone. I slip out of bed and into the fluffy bathrobe, and tread into the living room area. Alessandro sits on the couch in only his boxer-briefs, sipping a cappuccino and reading a newspaper. A glance at the clock shows it's ten thirty-four a.m.

"Cutting it kind of close with that cappuccino, aren't we?" I tease him.

He glances up from his paper, then folds it onto the coffee table and sets down his cup when he sees that the front of my robe is open. "It's not eleven yet," he says defensively, staring at my chest. "And I slept late because someone," he gives me a pointed look as I stride toward him and settle in his lap, "disrupted my sleep with her sexy antics."

I press a kiss to his lips, lingering for a moment before pulling away. "Are you complaining?"

He smiles indulgently. "No," he admits, running a hand down my chest. He stoops and places a kiss on my nipple, which immediately hardens in response. He smiles beatifically up at me, and I can't help but laugh. His smile fades and his gaze intensifies. "How long do you plan to stay?"

I'd answered this question for myself after our predawn lovemaking, deciding that there was no point in dragging it out. For too long anyway. "This evening," I respond simply. "I'll book a flight shortly. But the room is paid for through tomorrow. You should stay."

He nods sullenly. "Thank you, I think I will. I hadn't planned anything for today, so it works out well," he responds. "But you'll miss the fireworks."

I laugh, turning in his lap to wrap my legs around him. "We have all day to put on our own fireworks show," I promise him, covering his lips with mine.

And by the time we're done with our first "show" the cappuccino is cold, though it's well past the time any sensible Italian would drink it anyway. We opt, instead, to order in lunch, eating it while spread out naked on the bed.

As I pop a grape into Alessandro's waiting mouth, he sighs contentedly. "Let's just stay here forever," he remarks, munching on the grape.

I laugh and pop one in my own mouth. "Okay," I agree. "But don't you think they'll find us eventually?"

Alessandro shoots me a dirty look. "Way to ruin the mood," he grumbles facetiously.

I watch him eat the rest of the grapes, content in his presence for the moment. But my brain is never silent, and, while I know *enough*, I suddenly want to know *more*.

"What are you going to do? When you figure out whoever is behind this?"

He eyes me gravely, considering the question. "I've thought a lot about that," he admits. "And I suppose there's no way to know until I'm there. But I imagine there's a debt to be paid, whatever that means to them. I can only hope the price isn't too steep."

"It just doesn't make any sense," I say persistently. "Why would Peyton be involved?"

Alessandro sits up and gives me a grim stare. "That is exactly what bothers me most," he replies, rubbing his chin. "And it means they've been planning this for a long time. And it's personal."

"But who would have that kind of grudge against you?"

"It would probably take less time to guess who it wasn't," he remarks drily. "You know how it is in our business. Everything is personal." He pauses. "I never thought about it, but you probably understand better than anyone. Going through your mental list of who could hate you so much that they'd come after you in such a way. It's maddening."

"I do understand," I agree softly. "Why didn't you tell me? We should be a team."

He smiles down at me. "I'd like that," he admits. "But I didn't tell you for the same reason it's hard for me to think of us as a team, in this matter anyway. My instincts are to protect you, not thrust you out into danger alongside me."

"When you put it that way, I'm hard-pressed to argue with you," I admit.

"We've been a team before, Sera," he says. "And we will be again. Just not on this."

He's being more reasonable than I would have expected. His defensiveness over the situation has given way almost completely to a serene but limited acceptance of my knowing just enough to go along with his decision. And in his way, even though I pushed him into it, I can tell he's now willingly trusting me with the knowledge, giving what he can while still holding on to what he needs to do.

"We're compromising," I realize suddenly, and I smile up at him.

He laughs and pushes my hair behind my shoulders. "Yes, I suppose we are," he responds, looking fondly at me. "I like it." His mouth settles into my favorite sexy, crooked smile, and a slow fire kindles deep within me.

"Someday," I say, climbing to my knees in front of him. "When there's no more danger, and we've tired of pleasuring each other all day, maybe we'll be able to live like normal people. Go out to eat. Watch movies. Take a walk in the park. I think I'd like that."

"Someday," he agrees, running his hands up my arms to cup my face in his palms. "But not today."

And the fire in me grows as it lights in his eyes, and we return to enjoying each other. Because it's just where we are. Who we are, together, in this moment. And as he takes me roughly on the bed, I happily surrender "someday" for right now.

∾

GETTING READY IN THE BATHROOM JUST BEFORE FIVE, I LAMENT HOW QUICKLY the day has passed, and that I'll need to leave shortly to catch my seven-thirty flight back to Seattle. I take a last look at myself in the mirror, realizing suddenly that the last of the bruising has faded. That I'm healed. I smile at the appropriateness of it — there's been a lot of healing happening, and I have a seed of hope for the future.

Though as I drag my mind back to why I'm leaving, there's also a seed of fear for what Alessandro must do next, and for the separation that's coming. I leave the bathroom and find him in the living room, once again perusing the paper. I lean against the bedroom doorframe and observe him, drinking in a last private look.

His dark hair is sexily disheveled as usual, his full beard well-groomed and accentuating the sharp lines of his jaw. His dark eyes are full of life and intelligence, and he consumes the newspaper the way he does everything — with rapt intensity and total focus. His broad shoulders are relaxed, his tall and slim, but well-muscled, frame stretched out languidly, legs crossed on the coffee table. I'm a little sad he's gotten dressed.

I pull my phone from my pocket. "Say cheese," I call. He glances up and gives me his best crooked, sexy smile and I take the picture. He beckons me over and pulls me into his lap. Turning the phone around, he flips the camera and takes a picture of us. Then he turns, covering my mouth with his and snaps another. He returns my phone with a smile.

"Just in case you start to forget," he says, winking.

"I'm just sad you aren't naked," I tease. "You know, so I can remember that too." I smile slyly at him and he raises an eyebrow.

"Next time, perhaps," he replies, his voice husky.

I tuck myself under his arm and snuggle next to him on the couch, resting my head on his chest. "Will I be able to reach you?"

"I've been changing disposable phones every few days," he replies, his deep voice rumbling through his chest and reverberating in my ear. "But I set up an anonymous email. You can contact me there, but only if you set up your own as well. I don't want there to be any way to trace my contact with you." He shifts away from me and uses the hotel pen and paper on the coffee table to jot down the email address. He hands me the paper, and I fold it into my pocket.

"Boy, you're really going cloak and dagger on this, aren't you?"

His brows scrunch together. "What does that mean?"

I smile indulgently at him. "You sound like a spy," I clarify.

He shrugs. "That's kind of the idea," he replies.

"Have you done this sort of thing before?" I ask suspiciously.

He smirks at me. "After a fashion," he admits. "Don't worry, Serafina, I can take care of myself. It'll be fine."

"I hope so," I murmur. I look back up at him and put a hand on his face. "I'd like to hear your voice every now and again. If that's possible."

His gaze is intense as he leans in to kiss me. His lips meet mine softly at first, but when I part mine to move with his, he slides his tongue in and wraps himself around me. Just as the heat begins to rise in me, he pulls back, leaving me wanting more.

"I'd like to hear your voice too. I'll try to call regularly, before I switch phones," he promises.

"Thank you." I kiss him softly once more before disentangling myself and rising from the couch. "I should finish packing."

He picks up his newspaper and I return to the bedroom.

When I emerge a few minutes later, luggage in tow, he is waiting to hand me my phone.

"Don't forget this," he teases me, winking, "or I won't be able to call you."

I take it from him, fighting a wave of emotion at the tone in his voice. Because I know it means goodbye. "Be careful," I reply in the same tone.

"I will," he promises, his eyes smoldering with the same intensity I feel for him right now.

I step toward him tentatively, and place a hand on his chest, over his heart. He slides one hand over mine then grasps my chin with his other hand, tilting my face up so he can look into my eyes.

My vision blurs as tears begin to swim in my eyes. I blink, then feel them spill onto my cheeks. His face full of emotion, he gently kisses the tears away, then touches his lips to mine. And the kiss is tender, sweet, and full of sorrow. When our lips part, he rests his forehead against mine.

"*Ti amo*, Serafina," he murmurs. "I love you."

I choke back the anguished cry rising in my throat. I don't want to make this harder for either of us. "I love you too, Alessandro," I reply, my voice shaking with the effort.

He releases me slowly and nods. I take the cue and leave with no goodbye. Only love.

FOUR

I realize I may have lingered too long when I barely make it to my gate before the doors close. I thought Seattle traffic was bad, but it's got *nothing* on San Francisco. On the bright side, it gives me little time to think about staying, as I'm forced to hurry to my seat so the plane can depart.

I slide into my row, the last of first class, and note that the airplane isn't more than half full. The seat next to me is empty as well, so at least it will be a comfortable and quiet ride. I turn off my cellphone and tuck it in my bag under the seat in front of me.

Once we're at altitude, I turn it back on, thinking I'll catch up on email. But as soon as I unlock it, it opens to a video. The first, frozen frame is Alessandro's face, and my breath catches in my throat. I scramble for the headphones in my bag.

As soon as I'm hooked in, I turn the volume to max and hit play. I note that the time of the video was right before I left. He must have taken it while I was packing.

"*Mio tesoro*," his deep voice rumbles through my ears. "I wish I had a video of you, so I could hear your voice and see you smile while we are apart. But, even though I can't, I figured I could leave one for you. And," he sets the phone down and there is a flurry of motion and the sound of fabric swishing until he picks the phone back up shirtless. The tight knot in my chest unravels into a burst of delighted laughter. "As requested, at least partly, a little skin for you." He winks roguishly and laughs, and the sound sends warmth through me. "I love you, Serafina Evans. And I can't wait to come back to you and show you how much. Take care of yourself, *bella*, while I'm gone. We'll talk soon. I promise." He kisses his fingers and presses them to the camera lens. Then the video stops.

And I let the tears that follow flow until there are no more. It takes a while.

❦

ON THE CAB RIDE BACK TO MY CONDO, I CALL BRYCE TO LET HIM KNOW I'M back and safe. Traffic is slow from all of the Fourth of July revelers returning home from the fireworks shows, so I have some time to kill.

"Hey, gorgeous," he answers, sounding almost like his sunshine self again.

"Hey, Bryce. I'm back," I reply.

"I know." And I can practically hear the grin in his voice. I realize he must have been tracking me and I roll my eyes, huffing a laugh.

"I should've realized you would," I chuckle.

"Are you going in to work tomorrow?" he asks.

"Maybe," I hedge. "If I can get a few things done in the morning."

"I'm sure they'll survive another day without you," he remarks drily. "Do you have time for lunch with your favorite security consultant?"

"You're not my security consultant anymore," I remind him teasingly. Not now that Sutton Developments is absorbing Evans Realty Services.

"Sera," he says, exasperated. "Just because I'm not *your* security consultant doesn't mean I can't still be your *favorite* security consultant. Though you have used my ad hoc services recently, might I remind you."

I can only assume he's referring to his detective work finding Alessandro. Even still, I laugh appreciatively. "I didn't pay you for that, so it's doesn't count," I point out.

"Touché," he responds, chuckling.

I laugh, softly this time. "Yes, let's have lunch," I agree.

"Great. The usual?" he asks.

"Sounds good," I agree.

"Then I'll see you at eleven thirty," he responds.

"See you then. Goodnight, Bryce."

"Goodnight, Sera."

I end the call, still chuckling to myself. He has to be just about the perkiest dude I've ever known. And I'm so glad he's back to his normal, annoyingly chipper self.

Given the hour, I don't try calling anyone else. I just add it to the rather long list of things to do tomorrow. And, though tired from recent events, I find I'm actually itching to get back in the swing of things — back to work. I'm going to need the distraction.

❦

THE NEXT MORNING, I'M HOME, SITTING IN THE CHAIR POINTED AT THE WINDOW wall. I silently watch the sky brighten with the rising sun, the city awakening beneath me while I sip a cappuccino slowly, drawing its warmth into me. Along with the reminder of Alessandro.

I watched his video as I tried to fall asleep the night before, wondering if he'd actually stayed in the hotel room or not. But either way, I dreamt of him in that gigantic, fluffy bed. Well, of *us* in that bed.

Once I've finished my coffee and it's a decent enough hour, I call Allie.

"Alison Kramer," she answers distractedly.

"Hey, Allie, it's me," I greet her.

"Sera!" she peals. "I don't know if I'm more excited that my best friend is back or my boss. I don't know how you keep this shit show running like you do! How was San Francisco?"

I don't know how to answer that, so I laugh. "It's a long story. I'll tell you when we're able to sit down face-to-face. But more importantly, how are *you*? How's the baby?"

"I'm great, now that I'm out of the first trimester and not vomiting at the sight of food anymore," she jokes. "I swear, I've actually *lost* weight since I got pregnant."

"Eek, well, I'm glad you're doing better anyway," I reply. "How is the Sutton Developments transition planning going?"

"Eh," she replies noncommittally. "There's still a lot to work out. Keith has been arguing with the attorneys constantly, and Sutton's son is a pain in the ass. We could really use you back in the office."

Sutton's son? I hadn't realized one of Charles Sutton's sons worked with him, and I find my interest is definitely piqued by the fact.

"Say no more, Allie, I'll be in after lunch," I promise.

"Really? Oh, Sera, I know you've had a lot going on, but that would be just fantastic," she breathes.

"I'm ready to get back on the horse," I reply. "Let's get all the leads and department heads in a meeting at two. And ask Maggie to schedule me for a call with Charles Sutton as late in the afternoon as possible."

"I'll do my best," she responds. "Thanks, Sera. I can't wait to give you a big ol' hug!"

We both laugh and say our farewells. Having decided to delay calling Charles Sutton until I've talked with my team, I call my mom next instead. When she doesn't answer I realize she's probably already at work, so I simply leave her a voicemail assuring her that I'm back safely from my trip, that everything is okay, and that I'll talk to her soon.

Caffeinated and squared away on calls, I stand, ready to tackle the mountain of mail, bills, and errands that I've neglected since pretty much before life got so complicated. I shake my head lightly, pushing down everything that's happened recently, good and bad, and shift my focus back to the two-week backlog of household chores ahead. Because I'm not going to get far without food or toilet paper. And if I'm going to sort out what promises to be an arduous tangle of paperwork and frayed nerves, I'm going to need to have my shit together.

By eleven-thirty I'm waiting outside the burger joint that, through the few lunches we've had together, has become the "usual" for Bryce and me. I'm feeling pretty good, having tackled the important stuff, showered, and dressed in my favorite summer dress — a knee-length, muted orange and yellow short-sleeved dress that flows out in soft waves from the waist. It makes me feel oh so pretty. I chuckle as I smooth it over my hips, then tap a matched-yellow-ballet-slipper-clad food impatiently. I don't do well with hungry.

By the time Bryce is almost ten minutes late, I find myself getting down-right pissy and dig my phone out of my bag to text him. As I'm typing, I see him jogging around the corner. And something about the sight of him running toward me in dark dress pants and a white button-up shirt evaporates my irritation. I try to convince myself it's because he's clearly hustling to meet me and not because I can see his muscles rippling through his shirt.

"I'm so sorry, Sera," he says breathlessly. "My dad forgot a meeting this morning and I had to pinch-hit for him. It took longer than I thought."

"It's okay, but food. Now. Please." He grins at my poor imitation of civility. "And I need to go in to the office today after all, so let's do this."

"Sure thing," he agrees as he does elevator eyes over me. I arch an eyebrow and purse my lips in disapproval. "Sorry, but you look fantastic, Sera."

"Thanks," I reply drily, ushering him into the restaurant irritably, "but save the hungry look for the food."

He chuckles but wisely doesn't respond as we get seated in a booth. Our waitress almost immediately brings water, and I don't let her leave until we've ordered. Which she doesn't seem to mind once she's had an eyeful of Bryce.

Once she's gone, I flash a mock surly look at Bryce. "Aren't you going to ask me if I found him?"

Bryce shakes his head. "Nope."

I scrunch up my face. "Why not?"

He smiles indulgently in response. "Because I know you did."

"And how exactly do you know that?"

He points his thumbs at himself and smiles. "Security consultant." Even in the face of my foul mood he still manages to stay droll. He laughs at my sour expression. "Honestly, Sera, it's not rocket science. Anything done electroni-cally can be traced. Dinner reservations, for example. Or, more specifically, when someone *doesn't* use their credit card to pay for a meal for which they had dinner reservations. Implying that perhaps someone *else* paid for that meal. Not a strong enough indicator by itself, it's true, but when coupled with the same someone returning from San Francisco without checking out of their hotel room…" He gives me a pointed look. "Shall I go on?"

"Show-off," I reply drily. "God, Bryce, I feel a little violated."

I was joking, mostly, but his answering frown is quite serious.

"I'm sorry, I didn't mean to overstep," he responds carefully.

"It's okay," I assure him. "I know you were just trying to look out for me. Was the hotel room bugged too? Or do you want me to tell you what happened?"

He shudders. "Uh, no, I don't want to hear about that part," he says, obviously revolted.

"For crying out loud, Bryce, I'm not talking about sex," I say, exasperated. "I told you I went there to get an explanation for why he left."

"Oh. And?" he prompts.

"And I got it," I say simply.

"Well, that's good." Bryce's expression is stoic, and I can't tell if he really doesn't want to know what happened, or if something else is going on. And I realize suddenly that it might be a violation of Alessandro's trust to tell Bryce the full story anyway.

Bryce sighs resignedly. "So where does that leave things?"

"I don't know," I say honestly. "I understand why he had to leave now. I wasn't there to change his mind. So now that I know, I'm back."

"That's it?" he asks in disbelief, finally looking honestly interested. "He's not coming back? You're not going to follow him anymore?"

"No and no," I reply succinctly, shifting uncomfortably.

"But it's not over," he guesses shrewdly. "Between you two."

I can see him holding his breath once he finishes his sentence-that's-really-a-question. Ah. I level a look at him as I realize we've hit the crux of Bryce's issue. He wanted to know, but he didn't want to know. We do so well as friends that sometimes I forget until that undercurrent of his feelings for me shows and I realize that they're still there.

"No," I admit. "It's not."

We sit in awkward silence for a moment. Long enough for the waitress to arrive with our food. Thankfully, Bryce changes the subject to work, launching into a story about the half-dozen things his dad has forgotten to tell him in the last week and how crazy it's made him having to run around taking care of missed meetings and messes. By the time we're done with lunch, the awkwardness has vanished and we're back to our usual comfortable banter.

As we leave he holds the door open for me, watching me closely as I exit into the hot July sun.

"I sure am glad you're back," he says, joining me on the sidewalk. "Hopefully, now you can put this all behind you and move on."

"I hope so too," I agree. "I'm excited to go to work for Sutton as well. It's going to be a whole new chapter."

"Look at you, on to the next thing again," Bryce says, smiling. "I'm parked this way," he jerks his thumb in the opposite direction I need to go, "but I'll see you soon?"

"You betcha," I respond. I step forward tentatively, and he opens his arms to me. Smiling brightly, I slide against him and give him a good squeeze. One that he returns in kind, and then some. I release him and step back, noting the sunshine smile plastered on his face once again. "Thanks for everything."

"Anytime," he assures me. And with a wink, he's off.

I text Allie to let her know I'm on my way in and set off to walk the few blocks to my office in hopes of soaking up as much sunshine as I can.

∽

As I step into the elevator and the doors close, something shifts inside me and panic rises in my throat. Having been kidnapped at gunpoint in this very elevator, I should have expected to react this way upon my return. Overwhelmed by the memory, I instinctually stop my train of thought in its tracks. *No. Deal with it.* I insist to my panicked brain. *It's over. You're fine. This is the same elevator you've taken to and from work every day for years.* I repeat the last part to myself over and over, and it works long enough to make it to my floor. But stepping out of the elevator I'm clammy and shaky. I take a moment to breathe deeply and steady myself.

Before I have a chance to recover fully, I hear shuffling and whispers. My panic almost takes back over until I hear someone whisper rather loudly, "Shhhh, she's coming!"

It's enough to snap me back to reality, and I take a moment to collect myself, since it sounds like I'm about to be on the business end of a "surprise" greeting. I try my best to suppress my amused smile and stroll nonchalantly in.

"Welcome back!" forty-plus voices cheer as I round the corner. A large banner with the same message hangs over the reception desk, and balloons and flowers adorn the desk. Allie and Maggie, my assistant, stand in the center of the crowd, beaming and applauding. I gather them both in a hug and allow the tears stinging the back of my eyes to leak out. Tears that are partly due to the warm welcome but also partly due to the lingering fear of riding in the elevator. But the former is a better excuse to be emotional and trembling.

"Thank you so much, everybody!" I cry. "I missed you guys so much." A hug-receiving line starts, and I happily embrace them all until there's nobody left.

"We missed you too," Maggie replies, lingering alongside Allie as people return to their desks.

"Apparently," I murmur, looking at the gorgeous flower arrangements appreciatively.

Allie hugs me tightly, and when she releases me I hold her at arm's length, noting that she looks softer around her midsection, fuller in the face, and extremely happy.

"You're a sight for sore eyes, Allie," I say fervently. She gives me an appraising once over in return.

"Love the dress," she remarks, "but you look like you've seen a ghost."

I press my lips together. Not much gets by Allie.

"I was just surprised," I lie.

"Mhm," she says, clearly unconvinced. "Well, in any case, you have a little more than an hour to get caught back up. Because we need the patented ass-kicking methods of Serafina Evans, Real Estate Badass, to get this thing done."

A smile splits across my face. "I'm totally putting that on my business cards," I reply.

She crosses her arms over her chest impatiently.

"Don't worry, Allie, I've already been studying up," I promise her. "But I'll get back to it, boss."

"Ugh. I'm not the boss anymore! And thank God for that," she replies, waving me away. "It was awful. Like I said, I don't know how you do it."

"What, you didn't enjoy ordering everyone around?" I joke as we head down the hall toward my office.

"It would've been more fun if they actually did what I told them to do," she replies cynically, splitting off toward her own office. "See you in a bit."

I nod a goodbye and head into my office.

Everything looks pretty much the same. Warm sunshine emanates through the windows, making the room a few degrees warmer than the hall as well as illuminating everything with the bright glow of precious sunlight. But so much of the main area and my office reminds me of that awful night. I shake my head softly, lamenting that one bad memory can ruin all the rest.

While my laptop starts up I look around the room, briefly reflecting that at least we won't be here much longer, and I try to overwrite the horrible memories of that night with all the other good ones that have happened here. As my eyes fall on the bathroom door, behind which Alessandro and I fooled around not two months ago, even the good memories catch me off guard. And I make a note to push for the physical move to Sutton Developments as soon as possible.

∼

THE MEETING GOES MUCH BETTER THAN I EXPECTED BASED ON ALLIE'S dramatic claims. The project management team, while a little reticent that they'll potentially expand their responsibilities into a side of the business we've not dealt with heavily, are still generally excited for the challenge. Our brokerage is fine to move, as Sutton Developments doesn't have their own corresponding department, so it'll effectively just be more business, and thus more job security, for them. And Keith's objections to the paperwork, while completely accurate, are minor enough to be put to bed easily.

It's the property management side of things that's beginning to worry me. I had approached our lead property manager, Ana Englund, and discussed the responsibilities of running that branch completely. She seemed enthusiastic, and I have no doubt in her skills as a property manager. But her business management skills are looking to be a problem. And I'm not the only one who thinks so — our senior leasing agent, Nancy Sherwood, was apparently so unhappy with the decision that, while I was away, she quit. Fortunately, we still have four other leasing agents, which is plenty to cover the number of units we currently manage. But I'm going to have to keep a close eye on Ana and likely spend much more time mentoring her than I'd planned. And I don't think Charles Sutton will be pleased, as that was the branch of my company he was least enthusiastic to keep.

But I'll find out shortly, as our first conversation in nearly a week is only minutes away. My eyes flick again to the bathroom door, and my thoughts drift to Alessandro. It's only been two days since I saw him, but it feels like so much longer. And I can't help but wonder where he is right now. What he's doing. And if he's okay.

My intercom buzzes, and Maggie tells me Charles Sutton is on the phone.

"Sera," he greets me when I pick up the call. "I was so glad to hear you're back so soon."

"Thanks, Charles, it's good to be back," I reply. "I'm looking forward to wrapping up the paperwork and getting started on our merger."

"Indeed?" he replies, clearly surprised. "I thought Mr. Nystrom was having kittens over the contract rider."

I can't help but chuckle at the perfect description of Keith's anxious tendencies. "I assure you sir, that while I support his concerns, I think I have some wording that will work for everyone. Mr. Nystrom has already approved, and I'll pass it by our attorney first thing tomorrow."

"Excellent," he responds, pleased. "Since we will be wrapping up the paperwork soon then, we should start having daily meetings here to do some integration planning and defining roles."

"That sounds like a good next step," I agree. "Shall we begin on Monday?"

"Absolutely."

∽

FRIDAY MORNING THE PAPERWORK IS REVISED TO THE APPROVAL OF ALL, WITH final signatures arranged for the following week. I find myself excited at the change, and I hope it's the right decision for my company. And for me.

I work a long day, diving deeply into the state of things with my teams in preparation for my discussions with Sutton the following week.

But I'm home in time to watch the sun set over Elliott Bay. Sinking deeply into my viewing chair with a large glass of wine, I watch the bright yellow fade into a mellow orange, and the mellow orange fade into a shining pink, which in turns becomes a hazy purple. As the purple begins to fade into the blue of night, and my wine glass has been emptied several times over, my phone rings.

My heart jumps, and I scramble to read the caller ID. But it's just my mom.

"Hi, Mom," I greet her.

"Serafina, darling," she trills, "I'm so sorry I didn't call you back sooner. It's been an interesting week."

Ah, the melodrama. How I didn't miss it.

"Everything okay?" I ask tentatively.

She sighs heavily. "I won't burden you with the details," she begins, and I'm already rolling my eyes because I hate when she gets like this, "but your father called."

I sit up abruptly. Now she has my attention.

"What? When?" I demand.

"Earlier this week," she responds. "I knew you were busy, so I didn't want to bother you. And then I started thinking about whether I should even tell you, but obviously I decided to. Your grandmother told him we'd spoken. So, he called me. It was less than pleasant, but that's nothing you need to worry about."

"Then why are you telling me?" I wonder out loud.

She's silent for a short stretch. Then finally she replies, "Because he wants to talk to you. And maybe even see you."

My eyebrows practically hit my hairline. "*He* called *you* because he wants to see *me*?" I'm incredulous. After all these years, why now?

"If you don't want to, you don't have to." She sounds pleased that I seem less than eager to reconcile with him. "I'll send you a text message with his phone number. It's up to you."

"Did he say anything about why he's never tried to contact me all these years?" I ask quietly.

"He knew he'd have to go through me," my mother replies carefully. "And he didn't want to make things harder for anyone. I told him that was ridiculous. If he was a real man..."

"Mom, please," I interrupt her. "No drama. At least, no *extra* drama."

"Well, then, that's everything he said that's relevant," she says. "We didn't talk long anyway."

I take a deep breath. "Are you okay?" I ask her.

"Oh please," she responds. "I'm fine. I'm perfectly capable of handling myself."

"Of that I have no doubt," I admit, chuckling.

"Anyway," she deflects, "how did things go in San Francisco?"

I sigh deeply, trying to figure out the best way to answer her and end the line of questioning quickly.

"It went as well as can be expected," I say carefully. "I found him. We talked. I found out what's going on. We agreed that he needs some time to figure out some personal things. And then maybe we can be together. But for now, I'm back. Focusing on work."

"Well, that's good, sweetheart," she says. "As long as you're happy, that's all that matters to me."

"Thanks, Mom," I reply genuinely. Then I abruptly change the subject, and we spend the rest of our conversation catching up on less gut-wrenching topics.

Even after I bid her goodnight and hang up, I spend a long time staring at the night sky, thinking about everything.

Gabrielle Grayson aka Lucy Drummond aka my saboteur and would-be murderer. A shudder of pain and terror rolls through me. Alessandro Giordano. A shudder of bittersweet pleasure. Kent Evans. A shudder of too many emotions to name. Even remembering my father's name is odd and disconcerting, not having thought nor spoken it in years.

With everything that's happened lately, I can't say I've even fully processed the fact that my father did not, as I'd thought, choose to leave us when I was twelve years old. That he did not, as I'd also thought, with his parting words tell me that I was unlovable. Not that the truth is much better — that my mother, who'd found out he'd been cheating on her for years with another woman, whom he'd "married" and had a child with no less, had kicked him out in a rage. It was to her he directed his words — telling her that nobody could ever love her.

Any relief I felt after my mother clarified that those words were directed at her was replaced with disgust and indignation. Thinking those words were directed at me messed me up for a long time. But the truth is just as bad — and just as untrue. My mother, while a difficult woman to like, is not unlovable. She's proud, fierce, and a pain in the ass. But I love her. And I'm going to look that bastard in the eye and tell him exactly that.

FIVE

I wake on Saturday morning with startling mental clarity. Especially considering that, after I talked to my mother, I needed a considerable amount of wine to handle sifting through my mental baggage.

Unfortunately, my clarity has come with a giant side helping of anger, and I wonder if I shouldn't call Allie first to try to burn some of it off by talking it out with her. But I dismiss the idea, knowing it will almost certainly get me even more worked up. I opt, instead, to pound it out on the treadmill for a good forty-five minutes.

Afterward, I realize it was decidedly the better choice. While I'm not exactly calm, I'm in a much less hostile frame of mind. I shower and eat a quick breakfast before picking up my phone.

I take a few deep breaths and place the call.

"Hello?"

Hearing my father's voice, I freeze in panic. And I'm suddenly not sure I can do this.

"Hello?" he says again.

"Hi," I say slowly. "It's Sera." I resist adding, "You know, your daughter."

"Sera," he breathes out. "I'm so glad you called."

"You wanted to talk to me?" I ask tightly.

"Yes, I understand that your mother told you her side. Of what actually happened." He sounds as tense and awkward as I feel.

"And I suppose you want to tell me *your* side?" I respond peevishly.

"If you want to hear it," he replies quietly, "yes — I'd very much like to do exactly that."

"There are a lot of things I want," I admit. "But I'm not sure that any of it matters anymore."

"It matters to me," he asserts. "And if there's anything you need to say to me, I want to hear it."

I roll my eyes. I hate it when people say shit like that. Because ninety-nine percent of the time they're simply trying to satisfy their own need to feel like they are being the bigger person. And I know from hard-earned experience that they *don't* really want to hear it, and they definitely *don't* want to take responsibility for anything that comes from hearing it.

"Please, Sera. I'll come to you. I'll meet you wherever you want. You can leave anytime. I just want a chance to explain. And to ask for your forgiveness. Beg for it, if I need to. Please."

My whole being screams at me to hang up. To not trust him. But my own words ring in my head, and I realize this is yet another of those crossroads — another time when I want to be able to look back and regret doing something rather than doing nothing, than walking away.

"Fine," I reply tersely. "Next Saturday. Noon. I'll text you the address."

"Thank you," he says, relieved. "I'll see you then, Sera."

"Goodbye, *Kent*," I reply. And then I hang up.

And I don't want to talk to my mother about it, but I feel I owe her a heads-up. So I text her. *Talked to him. He's meeting me for lunch next Saturday at noon. Stay tuned.*

My next move is to call Allie.

She answers quickly, perky as ever. "Hey, babe, what's up?"

"Hi," I reply in a deeply morose tone.

"Oh, dear lord," she responds. "Who died?"

I'm so perturbed that I'm long past witty banter. All I have left is bluntness. "I just talked to my father."

Whatever it was she expected to hear, it was clearly not that, as stunned silence follows.

After a few painful moments I continue. "And we're having lunch next Saturday. He wants to *explain*."

The sound — or lack thereof — of Allie's shocked silence is so entertaining that it almost knocks me out of my funk. Almost.

"I..." Allie starts to stutter.

But I can hear David calling for her in the background. She must put a hand over the phone because I hear a muffled "Just a minute!" before she speaks to me again.

"Can you come over for dinner? I want to make sure I have enough time to do this conversation justice. And cake. There'll have to be cake."

I laugh drily. "Well, if there's going to be cake, how can I say no?"

"Good. Five o'clock okay?" she asks.

"Five o'clock? What, are we going for the early bird special at the nearby diner, grandma?" I tease her.

"There's my girl," she teases back. "But yeah, pretty much. Sorry, Sera, that's when the baby wants to eat. Gotta do what the baby says."

She's adopted a mock-serious mommy tone, and I can't help but laugh, truly and honestly this time. "Five o'clock it is, then."

"Sorry I can't talk more now," she apologizes.

"It's okay," I respond. "Oddly enough, I already feel better. But there still better be cake."

Allie laughs lightly. "Don't worry about that. Baby heard 'cake.' Now baby *needs* cake."

"I think I'm going to get along well with this kid," I joke. "See you guys then."

"Bye, Sera."

∾

AFTER A SATISFYING DINNER, WE SIT AROUND THE KRAMERS' DINING ROOM table indulging each in our own tiny lava cake.

As I savor a spoonful, I can't help but let out an appreciative moan. "This is *so* good, you guys," I say, and gesture with a spoon at the chocolate cream topping. "I especially like that you put chocolate on top of chocolate cake that has more chocolate in it."

Allie smiles sublimely. "What can I say? Baby loves chocolate." She gobbles down her last bite and looks contemplatively at the chocolate-smeared plate.

"Do it," I tease her. She gives David a mischievous grin and licks the dish greedily.

He suppresses a laugh and pretends to scowl at her. "In front of guests? Really?" he jokingly admonishes her.

"Sera doesn't count," Allie replies matter-of-factly, wiping a bit of chocolate from her chin.

"True story," I agree, finishing my cake. Since there's still some chocolate on it, I hand my dish to Allie and wiggle my eyebrows at her suggestively.

She laughs but instead of cleaning it herself, she takes it and stands up to bring it into the kitchen. "Thanks, but I don't want to give my poor, well-mannered husband an aneurysm," she replies.

I shrug and lean back in my chair. "Suit yourself," I respond. I release a sigh of contentment. "Thanks for dinner, guys. And for listening."

I hadn't ranted at length, especially since Allie was already up to date on the situation, but just enough to burn off some of the lingering annoyance at the situation. But I tore through those feelings and quickly got back to just not wanting to think about it any more than I have to.

"Anytime," Allie replies warmly, returning to her seat.

"What about all this merger stuff?" David inserts, changing the subject. "Does it feel weird to give up working for yourself? Having your own company?"

"*David*," Allie hisses as if he's asked something atrociously inappropriate.

"It's fine," I say to Allie. I consider my response, trying to boil down the many thoughts I've had on the topic. "I think there are parts I'll miss. But I'm not the best delegator, so having my own company was difficult. It's just more than I think is good for me to take on in the long run."

David looks at me quizzically. "Isn't your company like fifty people? What does everyone else do?" Allie grimaces at him and smacks him on the arm. "I didn't mean you; I know how hard you work."

"They do plenty," I agree, smiling pointedly at Allie. "But that doesn't mean I wasn't still all over everything, checking it, rechecking it, tweaking it. It wouldn't be so bad if things hadn't picked up so much. I just suck at turning down work. And I might have figured it out, but I realized there are other important things I want out of life. Things that take time."

Allie rubs her burgeoning belly, smiling fondly in agreement.

"What about this Sutton guy?" David persists. "Do you think you'll be okay working for him? And having your people report to him now?"

I smirk, starting to see where David is going with this. "If you're worried about how he'll treat Allie, about whether she'll still have a job if she wants it after the baby," I state, "don't. First, we're still working everything out. Second, I will *always* make sure Allie is taken care of."

Allie scrunches her face up at us. "You know, Allie is pretty good at taking care of herself," she grumbles.

"We know that," David assures her, wrapping his hand over hers. "And I guess I was asking that. But we care about you too, Sera. We want to make sure this is what you really want."

I try my best not to bristle at his use of *we* because I know he means well. *They* mean well.

"Thanks," I reply grudgingly. "I appreciate that." I take a deep breath. "I have a lot of respect for Charles Sutton, and there's a lot I can learn from him. But it will be different, and it'll be a big adjustment. Honestly though? I hadn't even thought too far into the details. It just felt right. It was a door that opened at exactly the time I needed it, and it's a fantastic opportunity. But I'm just as sure that if it doesn't pan out, I'll be fine. My employees will be fine. And everything else, I'll figure out."

"I have complete faith in you, Sera," Allie says softly.

I look up into her big, green eyes, full of love and loyalty. Blinking back tears, I rise from my chair and rush around the table to hug her.

"Thanks, Allie, that means the world to me."

And as we embrace, I say a silent prayer that I don't disappoint her.

∽

I keep busy on Sunday with various odds and ends and a bit of work, but by the end of the day I'm heartsick and tired of my own negative thoughts creeping in on me. About everything. When my phone rings across the room as I'm cleaning up my dinner dishes, I hastily turn off the water and dry my hands, sprinting for it, hoping it's Alessandro.

My breath hitches in my throat when I see it's a number I don't know.

"Hello?" I answer anxiously.

"*Buona sera, mio tesoro.*" Hearing Alessandro's deep voice pulls on something deep inside me, and relieved, happy tears spring to my eyes as I sink into the couch gratefully.

"*Buona sera, amore mio,*" I respond, my voice thick with emotion.

"It's so good to hear your voice," he says huskily.

"You too," I agree. "I miss you."

"I miss you," he responds. "But I'm sure you have enough keeping you busy. How are things going?"

"Fine. The merger is moving forward," I say hastily, eager to move on to talking about what's going on with him. To know if he'll be coming back to me soon. "And it might be keeping me plenty busy, but I still think about you all the time. How are things going there?"

"There's progress," he admits warily. "I found her."

"That's good?" I reply, unsure.

"It was a start," he says. "But I didn't learn much before she left today. She took a flight. To Rome."

I pause, shocked, and suddenly understanding his lack of enthusiasm. "Rome?" I'm not even sure what to do with that. "Why would she go to Rome?"

"I don't know," he admits grimly. "I have my suspicions. I highly doubt she's taking a vacation but, in any case, I couldn't get on her flight. Which, frankly, isn't the worst thing. It's best if I make some additional arrangements before I go."

"You're going back to Italy," I whisper. "For real this time."

"Yes, for real this time. I'm sorry, I know it's not what you wanted to hear."

I contemplate that for a moment. I'm not sure exactly what I *did* want to hear. Short of, "Everything is fine now and I'm coming back to you this very moment." But I knew how unlikely that was to happen so soon.

"But if she's not in the country anymore, what is there to worry about now?" I ask.

"She's not acting alone, Serafina," he reminds me firmly. "There is everything to fear until I know what was behind her threats. *Who* else is behind them. And to do that, I must keep following her. This time the trail won't be cold at least. I have time to arrange to have her followed until I can get there."

I breathe out a deep sigh. "Okay," I concede. "I just can't believe it's only been four days since I've seen you. It feels like so much longer. And if you leave…"

"I know," he interrupts me. "I know. You don't think I wish more than anything that I was there with you right now? Holding you? Making love to you?"

His words send a sharp jolt straight through me. My heart races in my chest and my body aches with longing.

"I wish that too," I admit breathlessly.

"Do you?" he asks seductively. And I can tell he recognized the need in my voice. "What are you wearing, Serafina?"

A smile creeps across my face. "You first."

"I'm in bed, about to go to sleep since I have to get up early for my flight in the morning. I'm wearing what I always wear to sleep."

"So, nothing?" I bite my lip hard at the thought of his slim, well-muscled body. Of him, alone in bed, naked and wanting me.

"Nothing," he confirms roughly. "And if I were there with you, I'd be ripping off whatever it is you're clearly still wearing. But, as it is, I'm going to have to ask you to run your hands down your chest, over those gorgeous nipples of yours and touch yourself between your legs for me."

I hesitate for a moment, flushed with excitement but unsure, having never had phone sex before, if it's something I can manage.

"Please, Serafina. I'm getting hard just thinking about it."

Any reservations I'd had are dust in the wind at his erotic plea. I do as he asked, grazing an already-erect nipple over my T-shirt as I slide my hand under the waistband of my shorts, slipping a finger into the dampening flesh between my legs. As I hit *that* spot, the spot I know he wants me to touch, I let out a small gasp of pleasure.

"Good," he purrs. "Now tell me what you want."

"I want to hear you too," I reply, panting into the phone. "I want you to touch yourself."

"I already am," he admits. "Since the moment I heard your voice, it's been impossible to think of anything else." A moan passes his lips, and from its tenor I know exactly how he's working himself, as I've done so many times before. The visual of it causes me to work myself harder, and I moan too.

"I've never done this," I confess. "But Alessandro," I moan again, "I am *so* wet right now."

"Ohhh, Sera," he groans. "You drive me crazy. I wish I were inside you, fucking you harder and harder until…"

As he was speaking, I slipped two fingers into myself, and my gasping cry cuts him off. "I want you so bad right now," I breathe. I start pumping furiously, and from the low, wet slapping I hear accompanying his moans I know he's working himself just as hard.

"Yes," he encourages me. "Oh, God, yes."

I writhe with pleasure at the erogenous noises emanating from him. And, pretending it's him touching me, I sink another finger in, deepening my assault. I picture his gorgeous face, remember what he feels like on me, in me. And the tension builds inside me, my moans reaching a crescendo. Sensing my ascent, he calls out my name, and it pushes me over the edge.

I can feel myself tighten, the orgasm flooding through me, and I scream in release. Not a moment later I hear him cry out as well. Panting and only sated in a very basic sense, I slip my hand out from under my shorts and loose a sigh.

"That was interesting," I remark reflectively.

He lets out a low chuckle. "And only a shadow of what I want," he admits. "But it'll do for now." He pauses. "Are you all right?"

"I'm fine," I reply, slightly confused. "I mean, I agree, it wasn't as satisfying as getting to touch you. But it was stimulating."

"That's not what I meant, but I'm glad to hear it all the same," he replies. "I meant, how are you, really?"

Ah. He means deep down, how am I doing? Though I'm still not sure which specific issue he's referring to. Does he want to know if being back has forced me to deal with the issues from my ordeal? Or perhaps if I'm struggling with dissolving my company? Or simply with being away from him and worrying about the threats he's facing? In any case, the only option I have is to reassure him that all is well. Because he has enough to worry about.

"I'm *fine*," I reiterate. "But if you don't figure this out soon, I'm going to be forced to follow you to Rome, so I can fuck you properly."

"Hmmm, phone sex makes you feisty," he notes, clearly pleased.

"You make me feisty," I respond throatily.

He laughs a deep, melodic laugh. "I'll take that as a compliment," he replies. "I'll call again soon, okay?"

"Okay. I love you, Alessandro."

"I love you, Serafina."

SIX

On Monday afternoon, I'm on my way into Sutton Developments for our first planning meeting when my phone rings. The caller ID tells me its Bryce. I pause outside the entrance and answer.

"Hey, everything okay?" I ask abruptly.

"Hi, yeah, bad time?" he probes tentatively.

"I'm heading into a meeting. What's up?" I reply.

"It's not quick. Are you free for dinner tomorrow?" he asks grimly.

His tone worries me. "Sure, but I can do tonight too," I offer.

"It's not urgent," he responds, but continues to sound troubled nonetheless.

"What, do you have a hot date or something?" I joke wryly, half hoping it's true. For whose sake I'm not sure.

He snorts. "Yeah, with some surveillance reports. It's going to be *sexy*."

I laugh drily. "Okay, tomorrow then," I respond, bemused. "Bye, Bryce."

"Bye, Sera."

I hang up frowning. His voice was all rain clouds and gloom, no sunshine in sight. Glancing at the clock on my phone, I realize that I don't have time to wonder if has to do with me or not and enter the building.

∽

SUTTON'S ASSISTANT ANABELLE HAS SHOWN ME INTO OUR USUAL CONFERENCE room, where I await his arrival. It's just me today, so he can break down his organizational structure and explain how he envisions folding in my employees. And myself.

I set out my folio and pen, and nervously tap the pen against the page. Finally, the door opens, and three men file in.

Charles Sutton enters first, cutting a daunting figure in a well-tailored black suit. With his dark, silvering hair and serious expression, he looks more like a well-dressed funeral director than the president and CEO of one of the most successful real estate development companies in the Seattle area.

I rise to greet him, extending my hand. As he takes it, a small smile forms on his face, softening the harshness of his expression.

"Sera," he greets me warmly. "So good to see you." He presses my hand with both of his and turns to the men behind him.

Charles gestures to the first man, who is around my height. His shoulders are broad and his form substantial, but he nonetheless is a lean, vigorous looking man in his early forties with dark brown hair, kind dark eyes, and a wide nose and mouth.

"Serafina Evans, I'd like you to meet Suraj Singh," he says formally. "Suraj heads our research and acquisitions department."

Suraj dips his head politely as he shakes my hand. His grip is firm but not aggressively so.

"It's a pleasure to meet you, Ms. Evans," he says, smiling kindly. His voice, also, is soft and kind.

"The pleasure is all mine, Mr. Singh," I reply, dipping my head and smiling in return.

He releases my hand and steps around the table to take a seat as Charles gestures to the other gentleman, who is leaning in the doorway giving me an appraising look.

"And this is my son, Daniel," Charles continues. "He heads our development and build management department."

I extend my hand and take a step toward Daniel Sutton. He is the physical opposite of his father — barely taller than me, with dark blond hair and watery blue eyes. While clearly in his early-to-mid thirties, he has none of his father's aura of vitality and authority; rather, he has a considerably world-weary look about him. One that his sour expression isn't helping. He regards me for a moment longer before accepting my handshake. His grip nearly crushes my hand, but I don't flinch as I maintain eye contact and do my best to return in kind.

"Welcome," he says in a tone that implies anything but the word's meaning.

"Thank you," I reply sweetly. "I'm *so* glad to be here."

He finally breaks the handshake and I resist the urge to nurse my crushed digits. I watch Suraj's eyes follow Daniel until he's seated. Charles and I follow suit and take our seats.

"We will have much to cover this week," Charles starts. "What I'd like to do today is share my initial vision with you."

"I'm all ears," I reply.

Charles opens the file he brought with him and hands me a simple organization chart. I scan it briefly and flick my eyes back to his when I'm done.

"It's rather straightforward, really," he says. "Your business functions — human resources, finance, IT, contracts — fold directly into our existing structure," he indicates the leftmost column, "then you oversee our new real estate consulting services division, heading your twelve project managers," he gestures to a highlighted column on the right. "And your realty services and land use and zoning specialists will serve both your division and the land acquisitions function of Suraj's division." He points at two boxes at the bottom dotted-lined to both mentioned divisions.

Straightforward, yes. But, at the very least, it's missing a rather key piece.

"I presume," I begin slowly, "that I'll still be permitted to oversee the subsidiary property management company that will be formed from that division of my company?"

Charles steeples his fingers under his chin. "The idea was to see if it could survive on its own," he responds.

"Actually, the idea was, if I recall your wording correctly, to see if it could produce results. Without a business backbone, I don't see how that's possible," I say honestly.

"Most property management companies function that way," Daniel pipes up.

I raise an eyebrow at him. His know-it-all tone rubs me the wrong way, and his statement makes it obvious that he knows next to nothing about the topic.

"And likewise, many of them fail for that exact reason," I say sharply. "It's why we weren't strictly a property management company."

"Then why did you agree to separate it?" Charles asks pointedly, though not unkindly.

"Because you said you weren't interested in running a property management company," I respond. "And you won't be. Ana Englund is perfectly capable of running the subsidiary company *from a property management perspective*. But she needs management oversight. Your proposal was to have it be a wholly owned subsidiary. Which means we have operational and strategic responsibility for it."

"A poor choice of words, then, perhaps," Charles insists. "But my intent was never to split your focus."

"It will take very little of my time," I assure him. "And it's a veritable cash cow when managed properly, which Ana *will* eventually be able to do on her own. Besides, based on your proposal, you only have me directly managing a quarter of my previous total staff. I didn't sign on to be that underutilized."

Suraj's eyebrows shoot up and a hint of a smile plays around his mouth.

Daniel, unsurprisingly, looks like he's smelled something foul. But my focus is on Charles. Waiting for his reaction.

"Direct as ever, young lady," Charles replies. "My *proposal* was simply the tip of the iceberg and was merely an explanation of how I foresee the departments aligning. Yes, you will be solely responsible for overseeing and expanding the real estate consulting services department as we deem fit." He pauses and his eyes flick to his son. "However, you will also learn *every other aspect* of this business. I want you to be hands-on in each area from the get-go. And while I want you to learn, I also want your input. There is no substitute for fresh eyes. I'm going to be asking a lot of you right out of the gate. You'll have large adjustments to make transitioning your own people and learning the ropes, but I fully expect much more from you on identifying issues and helping to reshape this business."

Daniel opens his mouth in protest, but Charles puts a hand up, looking at me expectantly. Suraj looks on in polite interest. I work to keep my features calm, masking the excitement at his words.

Reshaping this business. While I knew he was interested in mentoring me while using my talents to his benefit, this was more than I could have hoped for. A small sliver of me thinks it's too much, but mostly I'm thrilled by the challenge. Especially given the shock and indignation on Daniel's face. And I don't know why I dislike him so much already, having not exchanged but ten words with him, but his reaction makes it all the sweeter.

I nod coolly. "In that case," I respond, looking each of them in the eye in turn. "We'd best get started."

We spend the afternoon reviewing the structure and operations of Sutton Developments and discussing strengths and opportunities. Suraj appears to be a kind, patient teacher, and his calm demeanor is a welcome counterbalance to Daniel's harsh and abrupt manner. But I quickly learn that both are extremely shrewd and intelligent, though in very different ways. And while my initial dislike of Daniel doesn't fade, I can tell he could be either a formidable enemy or an invaluable ally, depending on how things unfold. And despite my visceral animosity toward him, I decide to do everything in my power to purse the latter.

~

Tuesday finds me splitting my time again between ERS in the morning and Sutton Developments in the afternoon. This time I'm meeting with Sutton and his two office managers to discuss more practical matters as, with an initial understanding of Sutton's structure, I'm confident in pushing forward on integrating the companies sooner rather than later.

"How soon can we make this happen?" I begin, smiling pleasantly.

"You were right about her," Kelly Donaldson, the senior office manager, says drolly to Charles. Her round, grandmotherly appearance makes her seem inviting and warm, but she's as blunt as I am and, I suspect, all business — not someone to bullshit or trifle with. Charles gives her a small smile. She looks back to me. "We currently occupy the bottom two floors of the building. The top floor was storage that we rented out. We've arranged with the occupant to have the floor cleared by midweek."

"But," Tammy Lin, the other office manager, interjects, "it will really depend on what you're bringing with you."

I spread my hands in front of me. "We can bring it all, or I can arrange to leave any or all of it behind," I offer agreeably. "Whatever works best."

Tammy nods, her dark bob bouncing on her shoulders, and makes a note. "Good. Then we can move everything over the weekend and be ready for your team to join us on Monday."

"Just like that?" I ask, a little shocked at how easy it sounds.

"Pretty much," Kelly laughs. "We'll have to iron out the details this week, but I think it's doable."

"You ladies are miracle workers," I reply. "I'll put you in touch with my admin, Maggie, so we can get started."

I look at Charles and he raises his eyebrows and smirks at me.

"I'm sorry. Too fast?" I ask self-consciously. "It is, of course, up to you."

He waves me off mid-sentence. "Not at all," he replies. "I'm just a little surprised. We don't sign the contracts until tomorrow, yet here you are, ready to go."

I offer a small smile and a shrug. "No point in wasting time."

"As usual, we're on the same page," he agrees. And he gives me a *real* smile. A warm, genuine, fatherly smile.

And as much as I've been trying to play it cool, composed, and businesslike, I can't help but smile back in kind. And for the first time in a long time, I feel optimistic. It feels good.

❧

THE FEELING CARRIES ME THROUGH THE DAY, AND WHEN I GO TO MEET BRYCE for dinner at someplace a little more upscale than our usual, I'm still riding the high on the promise of good things to come.

But seeing Bryce enter the lobby looking like a train wreck abruptly brings me back to earth. He's still his usual towering, ruggedly handsome self, albeit in a slightly-more-wrinkled-than-usual navy button-up shirt and tan khakis. But his disheveled shock of thick, chestnut hair gives away that he's been running his hands through it constantly. And his face is more serious than I've ever seen it, with absolutely no trace of his usual upbeat manner. He looks somber and tired, and I'm immediately worried again.

"Hey," he greets me with a sigh.

"Hey," I reply unsteadily. "You okay?"

His mouth tightens in a thin line and his nostrils flare as he releases another huffed sigh through his nose. "Nope."

I lay my hand on his arm and look up warily into his eyes. "We can skip this," I gesture to the restaurant. "Go someplace quieter. Or rain check. Whatever you want."

He gives me a small, joyless smile. "Thanks, Sera, but I'm starving," he replies. "Let's just eat."

"Okay," I reply skeptically. "But let's sit at the bar. You'll get food faster that way."

He nods and follows me into the bar. Since it's a Tuesday night, it's pretty empty and there are several options. Bryce heads for a small booth opposite the bar. I pull menus out of the caddy on the table and hand him one.

A waitress comes to take our order quickly. I order a chicken salad. Bryce orders steak and whiskey. As the waitress leaves I raise an eyebrow at him.

"Rough day, huh?" I tease him. Bryce runs his hands over his face and nods. "Dish, Hoyt. Get it off your chest."

He drops his hands and looks me squarely in the eye.

"Your boyfriend went back to Italy," he responds dully.

I pull a confused face. "I know," I reply slowly. "But that can't possibly be what you're upset about."

"You know?" he asks incredulously.

"He called me on Sunday night. To tell me he was going to Rome," I respond.

"Oh," he replies quietly, leaning back. "I thought for sure it'd spook you."

"Nope, not spooked," I assure him. But he doesn't look reassured. "You're starting to freak me out over here. What's going on?"

The waitress drops our drinks on the table, and Bryce downs half his glass before he responds.

"My mom insisted that my dad get checked out by a doctor. She's noticed him forgetting things too," he finally says contemplatively, swirling the remaining contents of his glass. "They think it's stress, but they're running more tests. He's been told not to work until they can figure out what's causing his memory issues."

"Ah," I say softly. "You're worried about your dad."

He shrugs. "Of course," he agrees, "But he also left a huge fucking mess." I blink hard. I can't recall ever hearing Bryce curse. It's weird. "Whatever is going on with him, it's been going on for a long time. And shit is hitting the fan constantly now, and I'm having to clean it all up." He pauses, silently fuming. "I'm *angry*. Angry at him for covering this up for so long. For doing this to me. And my mom, and my sister." He shakes his head and drains the rest of his whiskey.

I stare blankly at Bryce, unsure of how to respond. Not because I don't want to reassure him, but because it's like I'm staring at a completely different person. The absence of joy on his face has changed his appearance enough. But I just don't know what to do with the foul mouth, hard drinking, and anger coming from him.

And for once, even after a prolonged, awkward silence, he doesn't apologize for his outburst like he normally would. He simply goes to the bar to refill his whiskey.

Not that I think he needs to apologize, but it bothers me because the Bryce I know would feel like he needed to. Like he'd somehow inconvenienced or scared me with his vitriol. Finally, something slowly clunks into place in my brain as he sits back down, sipping his whiskey once more.

"You thought I was going to run after Alessandro," I realize. "That I'd leave. One more pile of shit hitting the fan."

He looks up at me grimly, and the answer is apparent in his appraising look.

"Bryce," I say sadly, catching his eye. "I wouldn't leave you at a time like this."

He sets his glass down firmly, the amber liquid sloshing dangerously close to the lip of the glass, and gives me a hard stare back.

"Wouldn't you?" he demands.

His tone is so accusatory that all I can do is look at him in shock as our food is delivered. Not that I'm hungry any longer. But he dives right into his steak, stabbing at it angrily.

"No, I wouldn't," I reiterate firmly.

He snorts. "Sure you would, Sera. If *he* asked you to, you'd go running," he states, popping a bite of steak and mashed potatoes into his mouth.

And I feel like I've been slapped. My gut instinct is to protest, but I have to stop and ask myself if that's true. If Bryce needed me but Alessandro wanted me, would I abandon Bryce for Alessandro? *Yes, probably,* says a little voice in my head.

But, no. NO. After all that Bryce has done for me, I wouldn't. He saved my *life*, for fuck's sake. I have to think I wouldn't be so weak, so awful a friend as that. And it occurs to me, ultimately, that I'm *not* being asked to choose. I'm not making a wrong decision. Bryce is shit-stirring because he's angry. He's *trying* to pick a fight with me.

"Well, he's not asking, so do you want me here or not?" I snap. I realize as soon as the words are out of my mouth that it was the wrong thing to say to him while he's in this mood. Not that I'm sure there was a right thing to say. In any case, the harsh look in his eyes already tells me what he's going to do. He's going to keep pushing until I leave. My heart drops in my chest before he even speaks his next words.

"Do whatever you want," he says dismissively, finishing his second whiskey. "I don't care." He leaves the table briefly for another refill.

When he returns, I clench my jaw and prepare to take the high road. "I'm sorry you're upset, Bryce," I say, carefully controlling my anger, "but I'm not your enemy. And I don't appreciate being treated like one."

Bryce downs his whiskey in one go and slams the empty glass down hard enough on the table that I flinch. Even the bartender looks up in surprise. "You want to talk about treating people poorly, Sera?" he hisses. "Let's talk about it. I'm just a fucking joke to you. You know how I feel and you let me fawn all over you, so you can feel good about yourself when your boyfriend's not around. And occasionally you mix it up by using me so you can find him and get back to fucking him. Who is treating who like shit here?"

"You're drunk," I whisper, my face bloodless, tears pooling in my eyes. "And you're upset. I've never been anything but completely honest with you. And I've never, *never* treated you the way you're treating me right now."

He leans back in his seat, pushing his half-eaten food away. "You can't be honest with me, Sera. You can't even be honest with yourself."

"What the fuck does that mean?" I ask with deadly calm.

He laughs mirthlessly. "It means you ignore shit you don't want to deal with. Like the fact that you don't seem to give a flying rat's ass about what it does to me to be friend-zoned so I'm always second to an asshole that lies to you constantly. Or that you have feelings for me too, but you're too preoccupied with abandoning your dreams so you can be ready for whenever the asshole decides to waltz back into your life to notice. Or maybe, that you were just fucking held at gunpoint two-and-a-half weeks ago, but you like to pretend like it didn't happen. Like ignoring it will mean you don't have to deal with the fact that you're *terrified*."

A look of realization dawns on his face, causing him to pause his rant, but not for long. "Well, there's an epiphany! That's probably why you chase after that prick. Because he'll never really be there for you like I am. So you don't ever have to really be in a real relationship that requires real trust and intimacy. Because God knows *that's* terrified you for *years*."

When he's done, he crosses his arms over his chest smugly, staring me down as if daring me to respond. But I'm beyond words at this point, my jaw on the floor. Even the bartender is openly staring, a half-dried pint glass and rag frozen in his hands. I look from Bryce to the bartender and back.

And with the heat of the moment passed, the smile starts to slip off Bryce's face. And in this moment, he's no longer the charismatic, gorgeous man that unfortunately still couldn't distract me from the man I was already falling in love with. As if I'd had a choice. Because if I did, I have no doubt that I would have chosen Bryce. Until now.

I stand, shaking, and pull a twenty-dollar bill from my purse, placing it on the table.

"I don't know who you are," I manage to say, my voice husky and full of rage and tears. "But if my friend Bryce ever shows back up, tell him to give me a call."

And then I walk away without looking back. I don't get far before the tears begin to fall.

SEVEN

I only manage a few, fitful hours of sleep that night. I can't help but lie awake, weighing Bryce's words. Wondering how much merit there is in them, or if they were just the tired, drunken ramblings of a man going through something awful.

In either case, I still can't stop thinking about it. Have I really treated him so poorly? He's right, we've always walked that line between friends and more. But even when we dated, ever so briefly, while Alessandro and I were apart, I have to admit I've never thought I could feel for Bryce what he feels for me. Not because he isn't worthy, but because I was already in love with someone else when I met him, even if I didn't want to admit it to myself yet. But was continuing to be his friend anyway so awful? I'd always thought of it as his decision. Because while I do care for him, I've made sure he knows where he stands with me.

Yes, I decide, it was his choice to be my friend. To help me when I asked for it. Even if I needed more from him than I was able to give back. But I *was* already falling in love with Alessandro when I met Bryce. There just wasn't room for both in my torn and tattered heart. But as I learned to trust Alessandro, I think it healed me. And paved the way so I could start trusting others again too. I can't regret falling in love with Alessandro over Bryce, however problematic it has been. Because of it, I was able to be whatever I am with Bryce. But our once-easy friendship is now a complicated mess.

I also can't help but wonder, would it have been different if I'd met Bryce first? I shake the thought out of my head. There's no point in speculating.

That's not how it happened. And no amount of wishing it were some other way will change what is.

Even after the awful things he said, though, I don't want to abandon Bryce to whatever he's going through. But I can't help but be terrified by that person in the bar. It really was like the man I knew was gone. Utterly and completely. I never even dreamed Bryce capable of saying those kinds of things to me. Possibly even of *thinking* those things. It's like his super-ego had an arm wrestling match with his id and lost horribly, allowing his id to run his mouth *and* his brain. But then, most men are often controlled by the primitive reactions and desires on the id's level. I just hope it doesn't keep running the show for long. Because I miss *my* Bryce already.

∽

AS I ANNOUNCE OUR MOVE DATE IN A TEAM MEETING ON WEDNESDAY, I TRY TO inject the enthusiasm I felt yesterday into my voice to cover the exhaustion and disappointment that replaced it after id-Bryce's appearance at dinner. Not that it matters much anyway, as most everyone is wrapped up in their own reactions. Allie, not surprisingly, corners me after the meeting.

After everyone has filed back to their desks, she closes the conference room door. She takes a seat next to me and leans forward on the table.

"What happened?" she asks tolerantly.

I shake my head sullenly. "God, am I that bad an actress?" I grumble. "Did I just totally freak everyone out?"

"Not at all," Allie reassures me. "None of them know you like I do." She pauses. "Is it Alessandro? Did something happen to him?"

"No, he's fine, as far as I know," I breathe. "It's Bryce."

Allie raises an eyebrow. "Did you two…?" She looks at me suggestively.

"No!" I protest vehemently. "We had a fight. At dinner last night. Or, rather, he said some awful things to me and I left."

"Bryce?" Allie asks in disbelief. "What did he say?"

Once I've rehashed the conversation and told her everything, her look of disbelief has devolved into abject shock and horror.

"Yeah," I affirm. "That's pretty much where I'm at. It took me most of the night to pick my jaw up off the floor."

"Wow, Sera," she finally says. "I'm so sorry."

I wave a hand in the air dismissively. "This, too, shall pass."

"You know none of that is true, right?" she asks, looking at me inquisitively. "It's his problem if he expects more. You've done nothing but tell him exactly how it is the whole time. I don't know where he gets off blaming you for his following you around like a puppy."

I bark a short, cynical laugh. "I don't blame myself, either," I agree. "But I still don't like having contributed to where he's at right now."

"I get that," she allows. And then, after a pause. "Do *you* think you only fell for Alessandro because you knew it couldn't go anywhere?"

I sigh heavily. "How could I possibly have known that?" I ask, irritated. Not at Allie, just at the continued emotional toll it's taking on me. "Sure, he had a reputation. But I didn't fall for him because he's gorgeous, or because he's fantastic in bed. I fell for *him*, for who he is. *Despite* everything else."

"I know," she replies confidently, and I look over at her in shock. She smirks. "I just wanted to make sure you knew that too." She rises from the table and gestures for me to follow her. "Come on, we have work to do."

I look at her questioningly. "What, exactly, are you referring to?" I ask suspiciously.

"We're going to plan a party," she replies. "A farewell party for the office. Because I think we can both agree that everyone around here," she looks pointedly at me, "could really use to let loose for a while."

I follow her, grimacing as I try to think of how I can explain to her that that's part of the reason I'm even doing this. Because as the boss, it's almost always completely unacceptable for me to let loose.

"Then you better be scheduling an after-party," I reply as we reach her office. "Because I'm not going full drunk-girl-dancing-on-a-bar in front of everyone here."

"Eh, we're a little too old for that anyway," she replies, smiling and rubbing her pregnant belly.

"If you say so," I reply. "Then what did you have in mind?"

She smiles mischievously and closes her office door behind us.

✺

I ARRIVE EARLY ON FRIDAY MORNING TO HELP ALLIE ENACT HER FAREWELL party vision. As a catering company sets up a lavish breakfast spread in the conference room, Allie and I work together to assemble a photo booth, swag bags, and several "awards" selected from submissions the previous day. She won't show me what they're for until it's time to give them out, and my curiosity is piqued. But she shoos me off to "whip up a speech," as if that's how I operate. I give her a wide berth nonetheless, snagging a pastry from the conference room and retreating to my office for a few quiet minutes before everyone arrives.

As I enjoy my breakfast, I sit in my big, comfy chair and kick my heels up on the credenza under the window to stare one last time at the view of Seattle and the bay. Even at this early hour, I can see boats cruising the water and throngs of tourists swarming the streets. It's the first time I've felt comfortable in my office again, like the shadow of past events — good and bad — no longer holds sway on the cusp of our departure.

I remember, suddenly, that I'm supposed to meet my father for lunch tomorrow, and my mellow mood sours. I consider calling my mom for a moment before I realize she's at work. My circle of support has drastically dwindled between Alessandro being gone, Allie being preoccupied growing a human being, and id-Bryce's appearance. I'm mostly on my own to deal with everything. I polish off the bear claw I was eating and suck the sticky sugar off my fingers. At least the food is good. And, with a smirk, I step out of my office to join the festivities.

As I stroll through the office, I note that during my short break everyone has arrived, and the party is already in full swing — people are snacking, socializing, and snapping goofy pictures with the wide variety of photo booth props. I lurk around the small clusters of those saying their goodbyes to each other or discussing what the new company might be like. I engage little, mostly just absorbing the upbeat excitement floating in the air, happy that everyone seems to be mostly ready for this change.

Before I know it, Allie pulls me up on a makeshift podium in reception to say a few words. As I watch everyone gather, I can't help but get a little emotional at the finality of the moment. When everyone is present, I take a deep breath and gather my thoughts.

"Thanks for tearing yourself away from the pastries," I greet the crowd. A small ripple of laughter flows through the room. "I started Evans Realty Services more than four-and-a-half years ago in the hopes of finding the best and brightest to bring my vision of a full-service real estate company to life." And I can't help it, my voice is thick with emotion. I clear my throat a bit and steady myself. "Thanks to you all, I've surpassed even my wildest hopes and dreams for this company. And together we've done *amazing* things. So even though things are changing, it's because I know we're ready for the next big thing. Through Sutton Development's established channels, we will get to work on bigger, more exciting projects than ever before. You'll *all* be exposed to new parts of the industry and get opportunities we wouldn't have had access to otherwise. This is truly going to be the opportunity of a lifetime — for all of us." I hold each of their gazes in turn as I speak. My eyes finally land on Allie next to me.

She steps up next to me lightly, as if sensing the wave of emotion that's about to overtake me. "And while we have exciting things on the horizon," she interjects, "We also wanted to take a few minutes to look behind us." She holds up a stack of certificates. "I reviewed your submissions yesterday and selected three in particular to receive awards." She hands the first one to me. "Sera, will you please do the honors?"

I look down at the certificate in my hands and bite back a laugh. "The first award goes to Melissa Thomas," I announce, grinning. "For the funniest property management moment — 'tenant submits application citing occupation as *sperm donor.*'" The crowd bursts into appreciative laughter as Melissa steps up and takes a bow, accepting her certificate, along with a larger swag bag that Allie hands to her.

Allie hands me a second certificate and, once again, I have to suppress my reaction. "The second award goes to Mark Hamilton," I announce. "For the most awkward leasing agent moment — 'having to show a unit to a friend's wife, who showed up hoping to rent the place with the boyfriend neither of us knew about.'" On cue, the whole team groans sympathetically. Mark bounds up with a grin to accept his goodies.

As I read the third certificate, I give Allie a look. "You're killing me here, Allie," I gripe.

She laughs and motions for me to read it out loud.

I sigh dramatically. "And finally, to our one and only head broker, Frank Ignacio," I continue. "For the *grossest* real estate agent moment — oh god, Allie, do I really have to read this?" Frank laughs in the back of the room. "'That time a very famous, wealthy client wouldn't be deterred from taking a shit in a nonworking toilet.'"

And everyone, including me, absolutely loses it as Frank accepts his award. Finally, when the noise subsides, Allie announces that she's pinned the rest of the submissions to the conference room wall. Everyone eagerly heads to peruse those that didn't land awards, and I manage to snag another bear claw before they've all been claimed by the crowd taking one last pass at the breakfast bar while they chuckle over the other crazy stories.

As the party dies down, Allie announces that everyone is welcome to stay and polish off the food, but that they're also free to leave early. Cheers erupt all around, and people start heading out, taking a smaller swag bag each. I hover in reception, assuring them each that I'll see them soon.

Once they're all gone, including Allie, I return to my office. Everyone else already packed yesterday, but I left it for today. I wanted to be alone, knowing I'd need room and time to come to terms with the end of an era.

∿

Late that evening at home, I lean against the glass wall in the living room, the coolness against my forehead soothing the dull aching in my skull. Watching the cars below is surreal, their tiny lights snaking through the streets like glowing ants in a black maze. I nearly jump out of my skin when my phone rings in my pocket.

"Hello?" I answer nervously.

"*Ciao*." I release my breath. Alessandro. He's okay. I hadn't had much time to worry this week, but he's never been far from my thoughts.

"I'm so glad it's you," I say. "How are you?"

"I don't know, Sera. It's strange, being here. Seeing her here."

"Have you learned anything?" I ask.

He sighs. "Where she's staying. What she does each day. But nothing of use yet," he admits. "There is someone else in the house with her, but I haven't laid eyes on them, much less figured out why she's here. I'm tempted to just go knock on the damn door and ask her."

"I doubt she'd tell you," I respond, "and from what you've implied, I don't think that's the best idea."

"I know, Sera, I wasn't being serious." He's frustrated.

I try to change tactics. "Why is it strange, being there?" I ask curiously.

"I left almost six years ago now," he replies thoughtfully. "And I didn't leave under the best of circumstances. I didn't think I'd ever come back."

"Why did you leave?" I ask, suddenly realizing that, oddly, we've never discussed it before.

"There wasn't one reason," he replies carefully. "The company I was working for was a dead end. I was one of the few who knew what they were doing. And I had a mentor. At first, he was amazing. But he quickly became very strange and limiting. There were family problems too…" he stops himself as if he didn't mean to say it. "It was just a mess. It was time for me to move on."

I'm suddenly suspicious that we'd never discussed it because clearly there are parts of the story he doesn't want me to know. "And you had to leave your country, your home, to do that?" I ask skeptically. The more I think about it, the more I realize something about his explanation is definitely lacking.

"It's complicated," he replies cryptically, sounded exhausted even though I know it's morning where he is. "I'm sorry, I really can't go into it right now. Suffice it to say I burned a good number of bridges when I left. So, there are a several people that I can think of that she could be working with. But I can't find *any* connection she would have had to any of them, so I'm just going to have to keep at it. I'm tapping my contacts as minimally as possible. I don't want it widely known that I'm here. And that's not making it easy."

I mash my lips together tightly, unwilling to press him on the issue, but also unsure of how to help. And I certainly don't want to push him into action when I have no idea what he would even do or the cost of trying to force answers. I wish I was on better terms with Bryce right now or that Alessandro and Bryce were somehow closer. Because he's the only person I can think of that could help. The distance from both men I care for most stings sharply in my gut.

"I'm sorry," Alessandro murmurs. "I'm not in the best of moods. And I'm sure you want to go to bed."

I slump to the floor, pressing my head against the glass wall once again, staring up at the stars this time.

"All I want is you back, safe," I reply, feeling every inch of the distance between us. Physical and otherwise.

"Then I'd best get back to it."

A single tear slides down my cheek. "Okay. Thanks for calling," I murmur.

"*Ti amo*, Serafina."

"I love you too, Alessandro."

After he hangs up, I realize I still haven't told him about anything that's been going on with me. And that this time he didn't ask.

∼

I'M STILL NOT IN THE BEST OF MOODS AS I GET READY TO MEET MY FATHER FOR lunch. As if he weren't already starting out at a disadvantage. I've chosen a rather nice bistro, mostly since it's on the north end of downtown, where I rarely venture for any reason because it's much more touristy.

I choose a simple, light blue shirtdress and flat, braided leather sandals, as the mid-July heat is in full effect. I quickly pull my hair into a messy bun, not bothering to apply any makeup. I'm not exactly trying to impress him.

On the drive, I stick within sight of the water as it's always had a calming effect on me. Something about imagining what lurks beneath its surface, in depths that can't be seen, puts everything in perspective. It reminds me that we are all just small fish in a very big pond.

I arrive early, so that I can be seated and ready to order when he appears. And when he does, I almost don't recognize him. I'm more surprised than I should be, considering I haven't seen him in more than fifteen years. And much as I misunderstood things I heard through my childish ears, my childish eyes remember a much different man. He's less than my memory of him. Not short, at around six feet, but he no longer inspires any of the fear or awe I had of him as a child. His thinning brown hair, once so close to the same shade as mine, is muted and dull with age. Even his still-sturdy frame seems less large and imposing, though the air about him remains austere and daunting. I'm not sure if time has simply worn him down, or if my memories of him made him more. Probably a bit of both.

I make no move of welcome once he spots me through the crowded restaurant and begins moving toward me. How he recognizes me, I'm not even sure as he hasn't seen me since I was an awkward, overweight, pimply teenager.

He stops politely beside the table. "Hello, Sera," he greets me seriously.

I nod in greeting. "Kent," I say, my tongue crisp on my teeth as I say his name. I gesture for him to sit and he does, slowly and carefully as one would around an animal that might claw their eyes out as soon as they make one wrong move.

"Thank you for meeting me," he says. "I half expected you not to come."

I try not to register the tinge of insult I take from his likely innocuous supposition as he picks up a menu, scanning it while keeping measure of my expression.

"I said I would," I reply, bristling slightly despite my determination to remain impassive. "And *I* don't break *my* promises." It's a cheap shot, I know. But I just can't help it.

He folds his menu onto the table and sighs. "I guess I deserved that," he allows.

A waiter appears and takes our orders, whisking our menus away with him as he departs.

"Why don't you say what you came here to say," I suggest, folding my hands in my lap, "and we can decide what you deserve later."

A smile tugs at the corners of his mouth and he leans back in his chair, crossing his legs.

"Very well then," he agrees. "I'm sorry, Sera. I wish I'd been more involved in your life after I left. I never wanted to abandon you, and I let my issues with your mother get in the way of having a relationship with you. I've regretted that for years. But once you were an adult, I didn't know whether you'd even want to hear from me anymore."

"So you just didn't bother checking?" I ask bitingly.

"I was a coward," he admits. "And I didn't know what your mother had or had not told you."

"I see. You're sorry you didn't try harder to see me, but you're not sorry you had another family. Another child. One that, clearly, you did see."

He leans forward, putting his arms on the table so he can wring his fingers together while he formulates his response.

"No," he finally says. "I'm not sorry I had another family. I *am* sorry for the pain it caused you and your mother. But I don't owe you an explanation for what happened between your mother and me. As your parent, however, I *do* owe you an apology for not being there for you. I wish I had a better excuse for it, but I don't. All I can do is try to show you how terribly sorry I am."

"Say I believed you," I humor him. "What then? What do you want from me?"

"I just want to know you," he replies, dropping his eyes to his hands. And his tone, his look, his countenance, are all consistently sincere. He flicks his eyes up to meet mine. "Can you forgive me?"

I sigh deeply. I've never been one to hold grudges. But forgiveness and trust are two very different things, not that I'm inclined to hand over either. With everything that's happened lately, I find myself running short on both. I'm quiet for a long while before I answer his question. He fidgets under the long silence but doesn't dare to break it.

"I don't know," I finally reply honestly. "Probably. But I don't have much bandwidth for, well, anything right now. I've got a lot going on." And while it's the truth, it's also a shield. I don't know if I *want* him to know me.

He shifts uncomfortably in his chair. "I understand," he replies. "I didn't mean to barge into your life and demand anything." He pauses thoughtfully for a moment. "Let's just have lunch."

Since we're already doing exactly that, I simply nod in response. An awkward silence ensues as we wait for our meals. But another benefit of having run my own company is that I'm fairly used to awkward business lunches, so using those skills we manage to make it through the meal fairly well. I offer little, and he spends most of the time telling me about what he does and asking about mundane things like our old house, how my mother is, and so on.

He mercifully doesn't try to tell me "his side of the story" or ask me anything terribly personal. And at the end, he even pays for lunch.

"I'm glad I got to see you," he says as we stroll through the door into the bright day.

I consider him thoughtfully for a moment. "You know what? Me too," I admit.

He beams at my response. I realize I do feel relieved, and even like there might be some part of me that needs to deal with this part of my past. Maybe, going slowly, I could do this.

"Would you..." he hesitates, clearly nervous. "Would you want to do it again sometime? You could even meet your brother. If you want."

I chew on my lip for a moment before responding. "I'll think about it."

"That's fair," he replies slowly. "But I'll be out of the state on a business trip for most of August. How about we plan to do lunch again in two weeks, before I go? And if you decide you want me to, I'll bring him along."

Despite his attempt at nonchalance I can sense that, for whatever reason, it's important to him that his children meet. And, admittedly, I am curious. But I'm still not even sure I want to see my father again so soon, much less the brother I only recently learned exists.

"I'll think about it," I repeat, and I can't help but smile a little at my own stubbornness.

My father laughs. "Some things never change," he says, smiling. "I never could make you do anything you didn't want to do."

I offer a small shrug in response and he laughs again.

"I'll give you a call that week. Take care, Sera."

"Thanks for lunch," I respond. And with a small wave, we part.

As I walk back to my car, I call my mom, knowing she's likely been on edge and waiting for a report. I keep it brief, as I just don't have the mental energy for much more than summarizing everything that happened. She's quiet and doesn't offer much resistance to my ending the call quickly. Thankful, I start the short drive home, so I can collapse into my favorite chair with a bottle of wine.

EIGHT

T he rest of the weekend and the following week pass in a blur. The former of sullen drinking, the latter of moving, reorganizing, and settling in to our new home at Sutton Developments, though I spend a good portion of the week going back and forth to the ERS offices, coaching Ana and helping her find a new office space more suited to the reduced team size. But overall, I'm happy with her progress up the learning curve, and I'm confident that I won't need to coddle her much longer.

At Sutton Developments, Charles has arranged for us to have everything we need to settle in, and almost every member of his staff welcomes us with open, helpful arms. Except Daniel, of course. But thankfully, aside from seeing him in the bevy of meetings I've started attending to get up to speed, he mostly just avoids me. Even with my own steep learning curve to tackle, I'm still able to focus on balancing the relocation and meeting our regular weekly commitments to our current clients. Charles has helped there too, mostly by agreeing not to add any new work to our plates until things calm down. It's no small blessing, as between those few main tasks I'm swamped.

I'm so fully occupied, in fact, that it's not until the end of the week that I realize I still haven't heard anything from Bryce. While I can't help worrying, I'm not exactly clamoring for another encounter with id-Bryce and decide it's still best to let him come to me.

And yet, on Saturday as I take care of all my usual errands, I almost call him. That one spectacularly awful dinner aside, I miss him. More than I want to think about.

As I finish dinner, with all my errands done I don't have much else to do besides sinking back into my favorite chair with more wine. As I cradle the empty glass in my lap, I realize who else I miss. *What* else I miss. Though it's only been two-and-a-half weeks since we parted, and little more than a week since I've heard Alessandro's voice, I want *more*. As I stare sullenly out the window, a deep longing washes over me. The physicality of the week hasn't helped. My muscles are tense, aching to be soothed.

I refill my wine glass and wander upstairs to the raised tub, filling it with piping hot water and bubbles. Stripping my clothes, I sink gratefully into the comforting heat. It calms the worst of the restlessness, and I sip my wine in hopes that it will help with everything else. Never having been one much for self-pleasure, I'm considering it briefly nonetheless when my phone rings.

Setting my wine glass down, I reach for the phone on the counter. My breath hitches in my throat seeing the international number.

"Hi," I answer, my voice low and breathy.

"*Ciao.*" His voice alone is enough to make me ache, but its low, rough tone is off somehow.

"How are you?" I ask delicately.

"I've had better days," he responds morosely. "How are you?"

"Missing you," I admit. "Naked. In the tub."

"Is that so?" He sounds wary but intrigued, so I push a little more.

"Yes, and as a matter of fact, I was just wishing you were here with me. I miss you in *so* many ways," I purr.

"I miss you too," he replies, but his tone is still odd — guarded. "You have no idea."

"I think I do," I say, remembering how he initiated our first telephonic encounter. "What are you wearing Alessandro?" I start skimming my free hand down my chest, the heat between my legs rising.

But he doesn't respond for long enough that I self-consciously stop as my hand comes to rest between my legs. Though even the light touch of my fingertips has me biting my lip, eager for his response, and a small sigh escapes my lips.

"Please," he finally begs, and for a moment I think he's ready to play. "Don't." His response is a bucket of ice water over my libido, and I shrink back into myself, mumbling an apology.

He lets out a low growl that surprises me.

"What's wrong?" I ask meekly.

"I'm sorry, Serafina. I'm just too distracted. There's too much at stake," he says, his frustration clear in the hardness of his voice. "I don't have anything concrete to tell you. Just suspicions."

"Of what?" I press.

"I can't, not yet," he replies.

And now my own frustration is no longer just physical. "How are we right back to this place?" I ask testily. His unresponsiveness is so like when he left me that I can't help but be reactive.

"Because we're right back to it not being safe," he responds just as testily.

"Then why did you call?" I snap.

"Because I said I would," he sighs. "And because I wanted to hear your voice."

"Well, you've heard it," I retort.

"Yes," he agrees. "I'll go now. I'm sorry, Serafina."

"Goodbye, Alessandro." And I hang up before I can say what I'm really thinking.

THE WORKWEEK BEGINS ONCE MORE, AND I'M HAPPY FOR THE DISTRACTION. I barely slept after I spoke to Alessandro, and I was in a foul mood all Sunday. I do my best to lose myself in re-establishing a rhythm and try not to take out my continued personal frustrations on my team, or on anyone else at Sutton Developments, for that matter.

When Allie calls me into her new office on Tuesday afternoon, I'm bracing myself for a lecture, assuming the unpleasantness stewing beneath the surface unknowingly spilled over when I wasn't paying attention and somehow triggered her finely tuned Sera-needs-a-talking-to radar.

But when I arrive, I find her and one of my project managers, Heather Irving, sitting quietly in wait. Sensing the tension, I close the door behind me.

"Hey guys, what's up?" Allie looks up at me from under a furrowed brow. Heather shifts nervously in her chair. As I sit down in the chair next to Heather, I note her anxiously fidgeting with her long, black braids, her full, dark lips set in a firm frown.

When it's clear that Heather isn't going to speak, Allie does. "Ms. Irving is submitting her resignation," Allie explains from her seat behind her desk. "I asked that she tell you personally."

I raise an eyebrow and turn to Heather, a slight, dark-skinned girl in her mid-twenties, though she has the air of someone much younger. She's always been on the quiet side but is sharp and has already been a valued contributor to our team in the six months or so that she's worked for me.

"I'm so sorry to hear that," I tell her honestly. "Is there anything we can do to change your mind?" She shakes her head so violently that I'm a bit taken aback.

"I mean, no, thank you," she amends in her quiet, girlish voice. "I just want to pursue other opportunities."

I glance at Allie and she shrugs imperceptibly.

"If you've been offered another position, I'm happy to see what we can do to match the pay or job description," I offer, feeling her out.

"It's not that," she replies reluctantly.

I consider her for a moment. She looks, quite frankly, rather terrified.

"Heather, did something happen that we should know about?" I ask gently.

The slight widening of her eyes tells me that my instincts are right. Something happened here. But she doesn't want to say what.

"If so, I'd like to know. Anything that is enough to drive away a valuable employee is something I need to know about. And if it's something to do with our new situation, it's especially important that I have that information. Because we still have time to call this off if there's a serious issue."

"No," she offers quickly. She clears her throat. "Nothing happened that you need to be concerned with. I just think it's time for me to move on."

I don't need to look at Allie to silently agree that we've just been lied to — the mistruth hangs thick in the air. Even Heather looks ashamed of it. But I know pressing her won't help, either.

"Okay," I respond. "But please, if you decide there's anything we should know, please don't hesitate to call Allie or myself."

Heather swallows hard and nods. "Thank you, Ms. Evans."

I rise and round the desk, grabbing a pen and sticky note from the corner of Allie's desk. I scribble a note to her. *Standard severance. Let's talk when you're done.* I slide the note to Allie and she looks at me questioningly, and I know it's because we've never given severance to an employee who quit. I give her a hard look in return that clearly says, *Just do it.* With a last, concerned look at Heather, I say goodbye and return to my office to wait for Allie.

⸙

NOT TWENTY MINUTES LATER, ALLIE STEPS INTO MY OFFICE AND CLOSES THE door behind her. She shifts a box out of her way and drags a chair in front of my desk, plopping down tiredly.

"I hate this part of the job," she says.

"You didn't fire her," I point out. "She quit."

"I know," Allie muses, "but it's still awkward as ass."

I shrug. "Comes with the territory. Did she give you any other hints as to what might have driven her to quit so suddenly? Obviously, it has to do with all this." I gesture to the office and boxes around me.

Allie rubs her belly thoughtfully. "No, not really. She just seemed *scared*," she admits.

I press my lips together grimly. "I had no idea," I admit. "I've been so busy this past week. Everyone seemed to be doing rather well, I thought."

"I thought so too," Allie agrees. "And I've been keeping my eyes and ears wide open."

"Well, keep it up," I encourage her.

We're interrupted by a knock on the door, followed by Maggie's head popping in. "Mr. Sutton wants a quick word on a potential new client for our team," she says.

My eyebrows jump in surprise. "Tell him I'll be right there," I instruct her.

Allie gives me a look. "And so, it begins," she murmurs.

WITH CHARLES SUTTON'S GRACE PERIOD SEEMINGLY OVER, SEVERAL NEW requests for proposals hit the team at once, and we untiringly dive into the new work. So far, it's nothing out of our wheelhouse, but it keeps me at work late on Tuesday and Wednesday. When I drag myself home on Wednesday night, I'm not pleased to hear my phone ring just as I'm about to pass out on the bed.

I glance at the phone and note that it's just past nine p.m. And it's my father calling. Begrudgingly, I answer.

"Sera, I'm not calling you too late, am I?"

"It's fine, I'm still up," I reply, trying to sound perkier than I feel. "I assume you're calling to confirm for Saturday?"

"Yes," he responds. "And to see if you wanted me to bring Hunter."

Hunter? I guess I hadn't heard my half-brother's name before. Interesting.

"Sure, yeah, that's fine," I hear myself say through a tired fog.

"Oh! Okay, well, then I guess we'll see you Saturday at noon. Same place?"

"Sounds good." I'm barely awake.

"Goodnight, Sera."

"Goodnight, Kent." I end the call and turn off the light, surrendering to exhaustion.

IT'S NOT UNTIL THE NEXT MORNING, AS I DRINK MY FIRST CUP OF COFFEE AT MY desk, that I realize what I'd agreed to. I shake my head at my own stupidity for answering the phone when I should've ignored it and gone to sleep. Oh, well. That ship has sailed, and I had to meet him sometime. Maybe his presence will even make things slightly less awkward.

I shake my head, trying to refocus on the notepad in front of me. I have a meeting with Charles, Suraj, and Daniel to prepare for. They want to hear my first impressions and concerns, so I settle in to organize my meeting notes.

THAT AFTERNOON I ENTER THE CONFERENCE ROOM TO FIND EVERYONE ALREADY seated and in the middle of a discussion. They all look up as I enter, and I can feel the heat on my cheeks. Charles is at the head of the table, as usual, with Daniel on his right and Suraj on his left.

"Am I late?" I ask tentatively, taking a seat next to Suraj. Suraj smiles at me warmly and shakes his head.

"Not at all," Charles assures me. "We were in a meeting before this that ended early. We've just been discussing our performance metrics as we approach the end of the month."

"Don't stop on my account," I reply, quietly opening my notes and pretending to absorb myself in reviewing them. But I'm laser-focused on their discussion as they continue to debate the cause of disappointing operational indicators.

"There's no one root cause," Daniel insists. "Each project's numbers are solid. We're just not growing our revenue streams quickly enough."

"I agree," Suraj says. "We're running more or less to estimates, except on a couple larger add-ons. It's just the market. Things aren't as hot as they have been the past couple of years."

I snort involuntarily, then freeze. I slowly look up to see all three men staring at me.

"You disagree?" Daniel asks archly.

I close my notepad. "No," I reply carefully. "I agree that the market is stagnating. But you're also picking your projects poorly."

Daniel bristles visibly. As head of development, he's typically the one to identify potential projects, so I'm not surprised that he takes it as a direct insult.

"Elaborate," Charles requests succinctly, steepling his fingers under his nose.

I take a deep breath and press my lips together. "Okay," I agree. "I've reviewed your performance metrics. They're an amalgamation of the metrics of each individual project with aggressive short-term goals for each. And most of your projects fall under one of three categories — large luxury townhouse and condo developments, large luxury retail development with luxury condos built over them, or standard to luxury retail spaces."

"And your point?" Daniel asks in a curt tone.

I eye him evenly. "My point is you're too niche," I reply. "Too entrenched in high-end spaces, large builds. It takes too long to sell out those kinds of spaces, so you don't see great results in your shorter-term metrics. You need to diversify into other areas that sell faster to balance out your revenue. Hot areas. Ecologically sustainable builds. Efficiency housing. That sort of thing."

"We've looked into ecologically sustainable builds," Daniel says, waving a hand dismissively. "Sourcing the materials is too difficult and costly."

"Then you haven't accurately balanced against market prices, reduced maintenance costs, and long-term ROI," I insist. "Not to mention economies of scale. Have you done a full analysis based on a specific project proposal? Or series of projects? There is always a sweet spot. It's a whole untapped market."

Charles turns to Daniel, waiting for his response. Daniel shifts uncomfortably in his chair and fights to keep a scowl off his face.

"Not exactly," he begrudgingly admits. "My suppliers said—"

"Only what is in their own interest," I interject. "Surely you know better than to take their word as law?"

"I'm not accustomed to being interrupted," Daniel retorts sharply.

"She has a point," Suraj says softly. "Perhaps it's time to revisit the issue more fully."

"Be my guest," Daniel replies, rising from the table. "I'm afraid I need to get back to work. I wouldn't want to leave things alone too long. My suppliers might start walking all over me, after all."

We all stare at him as he goes.

"Don't worry about him," Charles assures me gruffly after the door has closed behind Daniel. "He's not used to being put in his place, especially by a woman."

I raise an eyebrow. While I can absolutely see Daniel being a sexist pig, Charles didn't so much strike me as the type. But perhaps the two are more alike than I thought? Regardless, Charles' words concern me.

"What Charles means to say," Suraj offers, "is that we are very glad to have a fresh voice. Especially one that isn't easily intimidated into silence."

I turn my head slowly toward Suraj and consider him carefully for a moment. I initially took his calm manner and genial smile as comforting traits. But I do wonder what he *really* thinks. If he's simply projecting what he wants me to see, but underneath is just as bad as Daniel. I mean, why would he put up with it otherwise?

I shake myself a little, mildly ashamed of the unfounded negativity. Suraj has been nothing but kind to me. And only time will tell what I've really gotten myself into.

"I'm glad to hear it," I finally reply. "Shall we discuss efficiency housing then?"

Charles and Suraj exchange a look and both men uncharacteristically burst out laughing. I press my lips together to suppress my embarrassed smile, but I'm also secretly pleased that they seem delighted by someone standing up to Daniel. It means, at least, that they're not fond of his antics, either, and I try to take heart from that.

"Yes," Charles says after he calms down. "Let's."

NINE

I start the weekend with extremely mixed feelings. I'm thankful to get a break from the dagger-stare and silent treatment Daniel bestowed upon me for the rest of the week, but the impending lunch with my father and half-brother isn't exactly a thrilling prospect, either.

I know next to nothing about Hunter. My father was extremely careful to avoid talking about him at our first lunch, for which I was grateful at the time. But now I'm not sure what I'll say to him.

I stick to my usual coping tactic — distraction — by spending the morning thoroughly cleaning the condo. Just as I'm about to hop in the shower, my father calls.

"Sera, I'm so sorry to do this, but we're not going to make it," he greets me.

"Um, sure, okay," I reply, confused. "Thanks for letting me know. Is everything all right?"

He lets out a foreboding sigh. "I'm afraid I was overly optimistic about Hunter's feelings toward meeting you."

My eyebrows shoot toward my hairline. "And you waited until now to tell me that?" I ask incredulously.

"I made the mistake of not checking with him first," he replies carefully.

And in the background I hear someone grumble, "It's called an ambush, Dad."

I mash my lips together in a hard line, suppressing annoyance and anger. Annoyance at being cancelled on at the last minute, and anger because, well, who the hell is *he* to not want to meet *me*? I mean, seriously, how was he the wronged party in this whole mess?

"I see," I finally reply tightly. "Some other time, perhaps."

"Yes," he agrees. "Take care, Sera. I hope to talk to you soon."

"Have a good business trip," I respond. "Bye."

"Goodbye, Sera."

I chuck my phone onto my bed and storm angrily into the shower.

As the hot water courses over me, yet fails to soothe the tension in my limbs, I wonder why I'm so bothered. I wasn't exactly looking forward to lunch anyway, so shouldn't I be happy that it was called off? Except I realize it feels like yet another thing going wrong in my life. Another rejection. And I just wish everything didn't have to be such an uphill battle.

BUT ON SUNDAY AFTERNOON, I GET A CALL THAT WIPES MY PETTY COMPLAINTS off the map. The moment I see David's name flash on my phone, as if a sixth sense kicks in, I know something is horribly wrong.

"David," I answer, tense. "What's up?"

"Sera," his voice is thick and hoarse. "It's Allie. She's lost the baby."

I feel like someone has punched a dagger through my chest as pain radiates through me. Tears stream from my eyes, and I want to beg him to tell me it's not true. But as I struggle to master myself and respond, I realize if I feel this way, I can't even imagine how David is feeling. How *Allie* is feeling.

"Where are you?" I finally manage to ask.

"Harborview Medical emergency room," he replies throatily. "But, Sera—"

"I'll be there as soon as I can," I interrupt him, choking back a strangled sob.

"Sera, she doesn't want to see anyone," he continues. "She's out of her mind."

A fresh wave of tears spills across my cheeks, and my heart breaks open for my best friend, for the agony she must be going through.

"I'm coming anyway," I insist.

He sniffs loudly. "I knew you'd say that. But don't say I didn't warn you."

"Can I bring you anything? Do you need anything from home? Or food?" I ask.

"No," he replies. "Maybe later. I can't even think about anything else right now."

I stop myself from saying, "I understand," because I know I really can't, but instead settle for, "I'll see you soon."

As I enter the emergency room, I do my best to compose myself. My own devastation can wait. It's time to be here for Allie and David. I text David a short message — *I'm in the waiting room.*

A few minutes later, he emerges through the double doors behind the check-in station. His wavy dark blond hair is all over the place, and his usually clear blue eyes are stormy and rimmed with red. He embraces me somberly, and I wrap my arms around his shaking torso. He lets out one, sharp sob and gives me a squeeze before releasing me.

"I'm glad you're here," he says. "They want to take her in for a D&C, but she's refusing. They've given her a few minutes to calm down, but they need to do it. She's bleeding too badly."

The hurt in my heart spears through my body once more. "Can I try talking to her?"

He looks at me warily for a moment. "Since I can't seem to calm her down enough to convince her, it's worth a shot," he finally agrees. "She won't be happy that I called you. But at this point I'll try anything. I'd rather avoid them having to sedate her while she's like this."

I nod, understanding. If Allie didn't want something to happen, she'd fight it with every fiber of her being.

I don't ask if he's called Allie's mother. I know she's in Nebraska, so it wouldn't do much good in any case. And outside of family, I've known Allie the longest anyway. I put on my brave face and let him lead me to her room. I can hear the hysterical sobs before he even opens the door.

"Al?" he asks tentatively, poking his head around the door.

"Go away," I hear her shaking voice respond from inside before it devolves back into the heartrending bawling I'd heard as we approached.

"Let me try," I whisper to him.

He shrugs and steps back from the door, sinking despondently into a chair on the wall opposite her room. I enter quietly and close the door behind me. In the dim light I see Allie's shaking form under a thin hospital blanket, her back to the door.

I lick my dry lips and approach the bed, clearing my throat to announce myself. Allie's head swings wildly toward me.

The utter desolation etched into her fine features almost cracks my careful mask, but my presence surprises her enough that her cries subside to low, tortured gasps as I round the wide bed and settle on the edge facing her, one leg propped up on the side so I'm sitting next to her. She stares at me, eyes wild, as if barely recognizing me.

Without a word, I open my arms to her. She shifts her head onto my lap and clings to my leg, sobbing. I silently lean in to her, resting my head on hers and wrapping my arms around her back. And I let her cry as my tears slip silently into her hair.

After a time, I hear her sobs subside and her breathing even out, and I know she's fallen asleep, overtaken by the exhaustion of her despair. I continue to hold her until sometime later, when David quietly enters, a nurse at his back.

The nurse steps around him. "They're ready for her in surgery," she says apologetically.

"Give us just one more minute, please," I ask quietly. The nurse nods and steps outside, where I can see her hovering in the hallway.

I look down at Allie and sigh, stroking her hair back from her face. "Allie?" I prod gently, rubbing her back. Her eyes open slowly, and she sniffs loudly. "Allie, the doctors need to take care of you. Please," I plead, "please let them."

She starts sobbing quietly, but after a moment she nods. I nod in turn to David, who steps out to fetch the nurse. And, with David and I on either side of her, holding her hands, she finally allows them to prepare her. We promise to be there when she wakes, and they sedate her. Mercifully, she quickly dissolves back into the oblivion of unconsciousness, and David and I numbly shuffle to the waiting room.

As we settle tensely into seats facing the doors, David takes my hand. A single tear rolls down his cheek as he squeezes it tightly. "Thank you," he whispers.

I nod, unable to form words through my sorrow, and squeeze back. And we wait quietly, our hands clinging to each other for the small sliver of comfort it lends.

Not more than fifteen minutes later, the surgeon steps into the waiting room. David releases my hand and rises to meet him.

"Mr. Kramer?" he asks, and David nods. "Your wife's procedure went just fine. Given her level of distress, we've decided it's best to keep her sedated so that she can rest and recover overnight. You'll be able to take her home tomorrow, but she should still take it easy for another day or two after."

"Thank you, doctor," he responds.

And with a curt nod and sympathetic look, the surgeon returns through the doors. David slumps back into the chair next to me.

"Tell me how I can help," I say to him. "I can stay here if you need to go home. Or I can bring you anything you need. Or I can just stay with you and keep you company. Whatever you need."

David gives me a thin, forced smile. "Thanks, Sera, but Allie won't be awake until tomorrow, and I think I just need some time to process all of this. I can get some food in the cafeteria, and I'll sleep on the bench in her room. You can go home."

I fight the urge to insist on helping, and simply nod. "Okay," I breathe. "But call me if you change your mind. I'll take care of things at work. Just let me know if she needs me. I'll call after work tomorrow."

He gives my hand one last squeeze, and I know it's a dismissal. I take the cue and rise, but I have to force my feet to move. Leaving feels wrong, but I know there's nothing that's going to feel right.

TEN

Monday dawns after a sleepless night, and I relay Allie's excuses to her new department head. I resolve to go see her after work rather than simply calling, but the visit is more troubling than reassuring. Allie barely speaks and, while she thanks me for being there for her, asks me to give her some space while she deals with things. I return home that evening, disturbed and more than a little concerned for my friend.

It's not until I'm heading to bed that I realize I hadn't heard from Alessandro over the weekend, per his usual routine. I'd be concerned, but after our last conversation, I imagine he's going to avoid calling again until he has something he can share to avoid another fight about his withholding things from me. And I still haven't heard from Bryce. Trying not to feel friendless and alone, I surrender to my exhaustion.

∽

THE REST OF THE WEEK BRINGS FURTHER STRUGGLES AS I START TO NOTICE Daniel undermining me subtly. It starts in little ways — a thinly disguised put down in a staff meeting. Interrupting me on a phone call with Charles and a potential new client, which I wouldn't have even noticed had he not made such a big deal the week before about how rude it is to interrupt someone.

It doesn't take long before he starts accelerating his campaign of interference and nasty comments, and by Friday I'm pretty fed up. When I learn he's bumped my team meeting out of our conference room, citing a pressing meeting with a client, I'm more than a little irked. Still, I suppress the urge to confront him, knowing it will do no good. But the immaturity of it all grates on me. And as I head home, driving much more angrily than usual, I'm once again faced with the feeling that everything is just so much harder than it should be right now.

I eat a light dinner at home but have little appetite. For food, anyway. Wine, however, I've definitely been drinking more than my fair share of these days. I can't help but wonder if everything that has happened is a sign. That I'm pursuing all the wrong things: Alessandro, this merger, a relationship with my father. Maybe those are all the wrong choices for me. I feel like I'm losing everyone I care for and making enemies of everyone else.

I sigh, finishing yet another glass of wine, and admit to myself that I'm probably being a tad overdramatic. I'm not a great mental processor. I'm used to working things out verbally, preferably with someone who knows me well. But the only person that's an option with at the moment is my mother and, while our relationship is vastly better than it once was, we're not yet quite to the heavy, soul-deep stuff that I currently find myself mired in.

As darkness falls over the city, I slow my drinking and stare out the window wall at the few visible stars in the sky, feeling small and alone in the universe. I palm my phone, pulling up my address book, contemplating. My mental math tells me it has been more than three weeks since I saw Bryce.

Fuck it. I place the call. And immediately panic. I end the call as quickly as I can, hoping it didn't have time to ring through. I'd resolved not to call him. To let him call me, just as I'd spat at him as I walked out that night. I'm just tipsy, and weak, and shaken up from everything. I take a deep breath and push myself out of the chair, determined to put my slightly drunk self to bed immediately when my phone rings. It's Bryce, calling me back.

"Bryce," I answer, careful not to let the alcohol affect my voice. "Hi. I'm sorry, but I called you by mistake."

"Did you?" His voice has a sharp, alluring edge to it. I don't respond. "Well, either way, I think it's about time we talked."

"Is it?" I ask, attempting nonchalance.

"Or I can talk, you listen," he allows. "But it's more fun if you talk too." His deep voice is notably missing its former sunshine and ease, but the edgy playfulness that has replaced it is bewitching.

"I'm not sure I have anything to say," I counter. "But then, I guess that all depends on what you want to talk about."

He chuckles, and even his laugh is different. It's hollow. "I've been meaning to call you," he says. "But I wasn't sure you'd answer after what happened."

"Mmmm," I reply noncommittally.

"Exactly," he responds. Then I hear him take a deep breath. "I want to apologize. I shouldn't have said those things to you."

I cock an eyebrow, reading between the lines. "But you meant them," I assert.

"Yes, I meant them," he agrees. "But that doesn't excuse the way I behaved."

"No, it doesn't," I concur.

"I'm sorry, Sera. Can you forgive me?" He sounds sincere, and just hearing his voice reminds me how very much I miss him.

"Yes," I admit readily. "I accept your apology."

"Seriously? That's it?" he asks incredulously.

I laugh. "Yes, that's it," I confirm. "You're lucky I happen to be badly in need of a friend right now."

"Excuse me?" he responds indignantly. "Are you serious right now?"

I bite my lip, realizing that I implied I only forgave him because I was desperate for someone to listen to me whine.

"I'm sorry," I say hurriedly. "Fuck. It's been a shit few weeks, Bryce. And I've missed you. That's all."

"Sera," he says tensely, "I don't want to be an asshole again, but I need you to realize I'm not a consolation prize. I'm not the guy you're going to turn to anymore when you can't be with whoever else it is you'd rather be with at the moment."

"That's completely fair. But for what it's worth, you've never been a consolation prize to me. But I understand if you feel that way," I admit, chagrined. "Does this mean we can't be friends?"

He sighs impatiently. "I don't know," he replies. "I'd like to be your friend, but I'm not sure I can."

"Wow," I respond softly. "Okay, well, thanks for the apology anyway. Take care, I guess?"

"This isn't happening the way I wanted it to," he groans, clearly frustrated. "I mean I'm not sure I can *just* be your friend. I want to. But the dynamic we had is not going to work for me anymore."

"I don't know what that means," I admit.

"Me neither," he agrees, laughing. "But we'll figure it out. I miss you too, Sera."

Relief washes through me, followed by exhaustion.

"Let's leave it there for now then," I say. "And hopefully we'll talk again soon."

"Okay," he agrees. "Goodnight, Sera."

"Goodnight, Bryce."

That night, for the first time in a long time, I sleep soundly.

∽

Over the weekend I attempt to contact Allie, but she ignores my calls and texts. Taking the hint, I leave her be and bury myself in work and errands.

The following week, things continue to be a low level of nasty between Daniel and me. Well, mostly from him, and I spend my time reminding myself not to rise to the bait.

But on Wednesday, I learn through procurement that Daniel cancelled a software order I'd placed. Mystified and fed up, I storm into his office.

He looks up disinterestedly as I close the door loudly behind me and approach his desk, fuming.

"What?" he asks sharply, barely glancing at me as he types at his laptop.

I toss the procurement form at him. "Why did you cancel this order?"

He glances at the paper and adds it to the trash bin besides his desk.

"You don't need it," he replies, continuing to ignore me.

"Actually, I do," I retort. "And who gave you the authority to cancel my orders?"

Daniel sighs dramatically and looks up from his screen.

"You already have project management software, and so does my project management team. We don't need a third set," he explains condescendingly, ignoring my question.

I squeeze my hands into fists, my nails digging into my palms. "Our software is out of date. We needed to upgrade. And your system is even worse."

He shrugs nonchalantly. "I think it works fine."

"Thankfully, your opinion in this matter is irrelevant," I insist. "I am ordering the software. And if you have an issue with something I order, or with anything else, for that matter, please discuss it with me *first*."

Daniel leans back in his chair, eyeing me speculatively. "That's exactly your problem," he drawls. "You think you have authority here."

The cold glint in his eye is, frankly, rather terrifying. I suppress my anger and fear and respond as dispassionately as I can.

"I don't work for you," I remind him coolly. "And if you're unclear as to what powers I'm allowed, perhaps we should discuss it with Charles."

Daniel rises from his chair and walks around me to the door, blocking my exit and glowering at me. I freeze, unsure of his intentions.

"Listen carefully," he hisses ominously. "If you think some know-it-all cunt is going to waltz in here and take over my family's business — *my* business — you must be even stupider than I thought you were. If you don't do exactly as I tell you, and stay the fuck out of my way, you're going to regret it."

My jaw drops open in shock before I can stop it. "I'm going to do my job," I insist tightly, my voice quavering with anger. "If you have a problem with that, I suggest you take it up with *our* boss. And if you threaten me again, *you're* going to regret it." I push past him and grab the door handle, but he's too fast for me.

He slams against the door violently with one hand, his other hand rising and curling into a fist. Wide-eyed with shock and fear, I instinctively recoil. My reaction stops him in his tracks and he drops both arms to his sides.

"You've got a big mouth, you know that?" he says softly, menacingly, as he advances on me. I stand my ground, though terror rips through me as he stops inches from me, looking into my eyes threateningly. "I don't put up with stupid bitches who don't know their place. And if you say anything about this to anyone," he looks me up and down, leering, "I'll have to find another way to show you who's the *real* boss around here."

My terror melts once again into anger. "How *dare* you speak to me like that?" I seethe. I make to move around him and he blocks my path. "Get the fuck out of my way right now, or I'm going to scream."

He shakes his head and laughs, then leans dangerously close so our faces are almost touching. His watery blue eyes are ice cold as they lock on mine. "I don't think you will. Because then it will be my word against yours. And do you really think my father is going to believe you or his own son when I tell him that his new protégé came on to me in my office and threatened to lie about me if I refused her advances? After fucking that Italian client of yours, everyone knows you're just a horny little—"

Even I'm surprised as my hand flies out of nowhere and strikes him across the face, hard. He runs his fingers over the red mark spreading across his cheek and chuckles.

"Lucky for you, I like it rough." He pauses. "Say a word about this to anyone and I will ruin you," he promises. "Your career, your employees. And then I'll return that little smack a hundred times over." He steps back and opens the door.

I can see his assistant peering around the corner from her desk. Not knowing what else to do, I leave without a word, pale as a sheet. I return to my office, closing the door behind me. Leaning against the back of the door, tears of shock, rage, and horror start streaming down my face. I wrap my arms around myself to stop the shaking. It's minutes before I'm able to breathe through the initial trauma and calm myself.

As I sink into my chair, it occurs to me that this merger may have been one of the worst mistakes of my career. Because even if I go straight to Charles and he believes me, the fallout would be awful for everyone.

I sit in my office motionless and overtaken with indecision for the rest of the afternoon. By the end of the day I still can't decide whether to say something. Or whether to stay or call off the merger. I realize I don't have to choose now. But, for good measure, I document my full conversation with Daniel in an email and send it to myself before I go home. In case I need the proof later.

I opt to ignore Daniel for the rest of the week and, for once, he seems happy to do the same. On Friday I get a text from Bryce. *Lunch tomorrow?*

Relief courses through me, and not just because Bryce is talking to me again and wants to see me, but because I realize he's the perfect person to talk to about Daniel. I pause at the thought, wondering if that's crossing the line of leaning on him too hard. I decide it's worth broaching the subject, at least.

Love to. When and where? I respond. His return text comes swiftly. He chooses a Japanese restaurant over our former usual. And not our usual time either. My gut twinges a little at the clear message — it's a new era, no more "usual" Bryce and Sera.

∾

Bryce is even at the restaurant already when I arrive, waiting at a table. Also, not the usual. He stands to greet me, and I'm taken aback by the changes to his appearance. His hair used to be long enough to run his fingers through, curling gently around his collar, but now it's closely cropped and styled, highlighting the sharp angles of his cheekbones. The cheekbones are new too, or at least I'm certain they didn't used to be that well defined. He's clearly lost weight. Not that he was in any way heavy before, but he's obviously lost body fat and possibly gained even more muscle mass. The sinews and veins of his huge biceps pop against the cuffs of his white polo shirt, and his thick thigh muscles strain his fitted khakis. He looks *hot*. He smirks at my open-mouthed shock. I snap my jaw shut and lean in for a brief hug. He even *smells* hot. Like summer sky, wind, and evergreen.

I clear my throat as I take a seat. "It's good to see you," I say. I'm having a hard time tearing my eyes away, in fact.

His blue eyes sparkle knowingly as he returns my gaze. "You too," he replies, clearly amused.

"You look good," I say, attempting nonchalance and failing miserably.

He smirks again and shrugs, opening his menu. "I've started lifting more seriously, watching what I eat. It helps with the stress," he explains simply.

I flip my menu open too, and we both peruse in silence for a few moments. I choose quickly and close my menu, considering him as he makes his selection. "How's your dad?" I ask softly.

His eyes flick up to mine and hold my gaze for a moment before returning to his menu. He finishes choosing and closes it, tossing it away from him toward the edge of the table.

"Not great," he admits. "He won't eat unless someone feeds him, and he barely talks anymore. He has around-the-clock care now." He leans back in his chair, running his hands over his head. I try not to notice his arm muscles flexing as he does so, or the tightening in my body in response.

"What's the prognosis?" I press.

He shakes his head. "They don't really know. It's progressing faster than typical dementia." He looks like he really doesn't want to talk about it.

"I'm so sorry, Bryce."

"Don't be. It is what it is."

I close my eyes and take a short breath before I reopen them. "But I imagine that's been hard on your family," I say obviously, unsure of what else to offer.

"My mom most of all," he agrees. And after a pause, "It hasn't been a picnic at work, either." He doesn't say any more.

I fidget in my chair, deciding whether to try to draw more out of him. He's certainly less verbose than he once was.

"I can imagine," I reply vaguely. I tear my eyes from his and try to forget my own struggles at work, but a small sigh escapes me.

"Sounds like I'm not the only one with work troubles," he observes.

I huff a small laugh as the waiter approaches to take our order.

When he leaves, Bryce leans forward on his arms, knitting his fingers together nervously.

"Tell me about it," he prompts quietly.

His cool manner is a little disconcerting. It has none of the serenity and calming power it once had. In fact, if anything, it's unnerving. Like he's subtly interrogating me or something. I can't quite put my finger on it.

"Okay," I agree, leaning away from his intensity. "Charles Sutton has a son — Daniel — that works for him. Turns out Daniel doesn't like me very much. It has made things uncomfortable."

Bryce cocks his head to the side. "That's unfortunate," he replies. "But I've never known you to be cowed by anyone. Not even when you should be."

"No," I agree with a smirk. "And while he does scare me a little, I'm not going to let him intimidate me. I'm just not sure how to handle him."

"He scares you?" Bryce's sharp tone, while so unlike the sweet protective one he used to use, still has the same tenor of concern.

And I realize I'll need to be careful not to give away exactly how disturbing my conversation with Daniel was. Because the Bryce I knew would be ready to tear Daniel limb from limb if he knew exactly what went down.

And while I suspect Bryce is now trying to be less involved in my life, I'm not interested in unleashing him on an unsuspecting Daniel. So I couch our encounter in carefully chosen truths.

"You know how men can be," I say flippantly, waving my hand. "They don't realize being physically bigger can be a little daunting to a woman during a heated conversation. He's just threatened by me. He thinks I'm trying to steal the legacy he intends to inherit from his father."

"Are you?" Bryce asks with a hint of amusement.

I look up at him sharply. "No," I reply firmly.

Bryce runs a hand over his hair again, as if he enjoys the feel of the short, fuzzy cut. "What about Charles Sutton?" he asks.

"What about him?" I respond drily.

"Well," Bryce starts, "it did sound like he wanted to groom you to help run his company."

"*Help* being the operative word," I point out.

Bryce looks me in the eye, and it's like his gaze pierces straight through me. "Is this guy threatened *by* you, or did he threaten *you*?"

"How did you know that?" I gasp.

Bryce chuckles and leans back in his chair. "I know the type," he replies. "And I'm guessing you're telling me all this because you want my help."

I frown but can't keep the guilty look off my face. "I'd happily take any advice you have," I concede.

His response is quick, automatic. "Dig up some dirt on him. Threaten him back. Or hold onto it and, if he really pisses you off, use it against him."

I'm surprised at both the glib tone and the calculating malice of his advice. "Do you always fight this dirty?" I ask. I'd meant it teasingly, but as the words come out of my mouth, they hang in the air with a meaning I hadn't meant to imbue them with.

Bryce raises an eyebrow at me and considers me carefully. He rolls his bottom lip through his teeth and I can't tear my eyes from it.

"Yes," he finally replies. "Welcome to my dirty side, Sera. I'd gotten a little tired of playing nice all the time." His low voice is laden with suggestive tension. He takes a sip of his water, breaking the spellbinding eye contact, but I still find myself unable to speak. Or breathe properly.

And this time when the food is delivered, I've lost my appetite for entirely different reasons.

⌒

LYING IN BED THAT NIGHT, I REPLAY THE LUNCH IN MY HEAD. WHILE THERE was a shadow of my Bryce in there, so much about him was changed, the events of the last weeks hardening him, body and soul. I should mourn the loss of my cheery friend, but the cool, sure manner that has replaced it is equal parts enticing and terrifying. And I find I don't mind the combination.

I drift off to sleep, remembering our parting. The way he looked down seriously into my eyes before stepping forward, his scent and the heat rolling off him wrapping around me, to place what should have been a chaste kiss on my cheek before leaving. Except that it was all I could do to stay still, to not turn my face and capture his lips with mine. And I know he was just as aware of the tension between us as I was. I want to chalk it up to it having been nearly six weeks since I've had sex, but I can't help worrying that it's something more.

But my tense flesh and the heat between my legs betrays me. I dream of him. Of us. Naked, my own soft curves entangled with his long, muscular frame. Of his head between my legs, his tongue working with his fingers to pleasure me. And while I'm somehow aware that it's a dream, that it's not actually happening, the orgasm that rips through me, pulling me from sleep, is absolutely real.

ELEVEN

The dream was so lifelike, and the release that followed so undeniably real, that I find myself preoccupied on Sunday morning with wondering whether I'd just cheated on Alessandro. But I know it's silly, because it wasn't real. And even if it *had* been real, would it be cheating? Not that I have any plans to live out that fantasy, but it does make me realize that we hadn't exactly made any promises to each other.

But deep down I know Alessandro wouldn't be with anyone else. And the thought makes me feel even guiltier. Both for having those thoughts about Bryce and for giving Alessandro such a hard time on the phone when we last spoke. And in trying to remember exactly what I'd said, I realize it has been more than three weeks since I've heard from him. I've been so preoccupied with things here, I hadn't realized that it had been quite so long.

Unease starts to unfurl in my stomach. I pace the living room for a while, considering the reasons he might not have called. But none of them calm my increasing anxiety. And some of them lead me into downright panic. I'm on the verge of booking a flight to Rome when I remember the email address. The one he gave me to contact him if I needed to.

I scramble desperately for the scrap of paper I'd tucked in the inner flap of my folio. I sigh with relief when I find it, and type out a short email on my phone, too rushed to wait for my laptop to start up.

Haven't heard from you. Getting worried. Call me or at least let me know you're okay. Ti amo. I stare at the blank subject line for a minute and, unable to come up with anything, send it anyway. Rather than feeling better, I feel a new tension as I realize I'm going to be on edge constantly while I wait for a response.

And while I wait, I figure it's time to check on Allie. The phone rings and rings, and I think she's not going to answer when, finally, I hear her voice.

"Hi," she greets me simply, her voice sounding tired and morose.

"Allie," I breathe, relieved she answered. "How are you doing?"

She's been out of work for two full weeks, so I know clearly she's not doing great. And I feel stupid for even asking, but I'm not sure what else to say.

"I'm all healed up," she replies in the same dead, even tone. "But I still can't—"

"I know," I say quickly to spare her having to explain. "I'm glad you're better physically, at least. Are you ready for a visit? Can I bring you anything?"

"I appreciate that, Sera, but I just still need to be alone. I'm sorry."

"Oh, Allie," I reply, tears welling up in my eyes. "You don't have to apologize to me, babe. You just take all the time you need."

There's a long pause before Allie finally replies. "I am. I don't think I'm coming back to work, Sera."

"You mean this week?" I ask

"I mean ever," she clarifies.

My heart sinks in my chest.

"I don't understand," I whisper. And my brain really has stopped in its tracks, unable to process her statement.

"I just can't. I can't face any of it right now," she replies. I can hear her sobbing quietly. "I'm sorry, Sera." Over the phone I hear fumbling and receding sobs.

"Allie?" Thuds. More fumbling.

"Sera," David's voice comes on the line. "I'm sorry. Allie is having difficulty dealing with things."

"That's an understatement," I reply heatedly.

"I know," he agrees. "I've never seen her like this. I've asked her to get help, but she's just not ready."

"I don't care if she's ready," I say angrily. "You need to get her back to the doctor. *Now*. Don't let this fester, David. Something is wrong."

"She lost a child, Sera, of course something is wrong," he snaps. "You think I don't know that?"

I instantly regret not being more tactful. Because clearly David is still struggling too.

"I know you do," I reply, taking my tone down. "I know this is hard for both of you. What I'm trying to say is that there is still something *physically* wrong with Allie. It's normal to be upset. But this is way beyond that. Depression isn't just mental, David. She's not just going to snap out of this. She needs help. Whether she wants it or not."

A loud sniff tells me that David is in tears. I made David cry. *Could I be any bigger of a shit?*

"You're right," he finally replies thickly. "You're right. I'll take her to the doctor first thing tomorrow."

I breathe a huge sigh of relief. "Thank you. Let me know if you need anything, okay?"

"Okay. Thanks, Sera," he replies.

"Anytime, David. I love you both so much. Hang in there. Get help. I'll talk to you soon," I promise.

∽

BUT I'M SPARED CHECKING BACK IN AS BARELY A DAY PASSES WHEN I HEAR from David on Monday afternoon. He tells me Allie is napping after reluctantly seeing the doctor, but he is reassured as her symptoms were, in fact, diagnosed as depression. Because with a diagnosis comes the promise of help — a dim light at the end of the tunnel. But it will be a tough battle and, after much discussion, Allie and David have still agreed that it's best if Allie takes a leave of absence from work.

While I'm sad at still being without my closest friend and confidant by my side, especially given my ongoing struggles with Daniel's attitude toward me, I'm more relieved that she's getting the help she needs to heal. And I know even without Allie to confide in, I'll navigate these issues, but I still selfishly wish that she were here. It's just not the same without her.

Daniel continues to treat me with cold indifference, but others are starting to pick up on the tension. But nobody, not even Charles, breathes a word about it. And without anyone to talk to, I'm afraid it's becoming my new norm. And that thought scares me almost as much as facing it alone.

∽

I'M DISTRACTED ENOUGH BY MY CONCERNS ABOUT ALLIE AND WORK THAT I don't even think of Bryce until midday Tuesday when my phone rings and his name flashes across the display. I gladly accept the call, pleased with anything that will interrupt the tension of my day.

"Hey, Bryce, what's up?"

"Sera," he breathes my name, and I instantly suspect something is wrong. "Are you busy?"

"Never too busy for you," I assure him. "Are you okay?"

He sniffs loudly, confirming my suspicions. "My dad passed away this morning." His every word is laced with sorrow, and my heart crumbles for him.

"Oh, Bryce," I reply, tearing up. "I'm so sorry. What can I do?"

"There isn't much to do at the moment," he replies thickly. "My mom wanted to be alone with him until…" He chokes back a sob, unable to finish his sentence.

The thought of Bryce crying throws me because despite everything we've been through, I've rarely ever seen him more than a little upset about *anything*. My heart aches for him, and the sadness that's lurked under the surface lately hits me full force.

"Where are you?" I ask softly.

"Home. Just processing. I don't know what else to do right now. I just thought you should know," he replies, clearly struggling to keep it together.

I decide instantly that this is one person in my life I'm not going to leave to their own despair. And I might need the comfort of his presence as much as he needs mine.

"I'm coming over," I reply in a firm tone. "Stay put."

There's a long pause on the other end of the line.

"You don't have to do that," he responds. But I can tell he wants me to.

"I know. I'll be there as soon as I can," I assure him.

"Thanks, Sera." His relief is palpable.

As soon as I hang up I gather my things and poke my head in Charles' office. He's chatting idly with Daniel, whom I do my best to ignore. Charles stops speaking and looks at me inquiringly.

"Sorry to interrupt. I need to take the afternoon off," I inform him. "So I won't be able to make our meeting. I'll catch up with you first thing tomorrow?"

"Everything okay?" Charles asks, subtly probing for a reason.

"I'm fine," I assure him. I debate how much to reveal. Somehow, I don't think "a close friend's father died" will go over well. But I can't think of the distress in Bryce's voice without wanting to run to him. And if I'm being honest, I'm not exactly sorry to be leaving. But I shove the latter observation deep down. "It's just an emergent one-off personal issue that needs to be dealt with right away."

Charles considers for a moment, but as I've been nose to the grindstone for a full month, he's not exactly in a position to begrudge me an afternoon.

"Well, thanks for letting me know," he finally replies. "We'll see you tomorrow."

I smile joylessly and take my leave.

⁓

WITHIN A HALF HOUR I'M AT BRYCE'S DOOR WITH A BOTTLE OF WHISKEY IN one hand and a bouquet of white roses in the other. I ring the doorbell and hide the bottle behind my back.

He opens the door, his eyes rimmed with red and his face stained with tears. Before I can utter a word, his arms wrap around my waist and he pulls me into him, burying his face in my hair. I can feel his anguish in the tight grip he has on me and the cool moisture on his cheek where it touches my neck. We stand for a moment, half in his apartment, half out, as he takes what solace he needs from the warmth of our bodies pressed together. When he finally releases me, he wordlessly plants a kiss on my forehead and steps back to allow me in.

I offer the roses as he closes the door behind me. "It's not much, but I had to bring something," I explain.

He nods grimly as he takes them. "Thanks." He brings them into the kitchen. While he rummages in the cupboards, presumably looking for a vase, I glance around, realizing I've never actually been inside his apartment before.

It's a typical bachelor pad — sparse, with dark utilitarian furniture and little decoration. But it's tidy and clean, and it smells like him. As I turn back toward the kitchen, I realize he's putting the flowers into a large plastic mug.

"No vase, huh?" I tease gently.

His answering smile is dull and lifeless. "No, but this'll do."

"You look like you could use a drink," I reply, setting the bottle of whiskey on the counter next to the flowers.

He gives a dry laugh and nods. "You read my mind," he responds. "Want one?" I nod, and he retrieves two glasses and pours a generous amount for each of us.

He saunters into the living room, dropping defeatedly onto the large, leather couch. I perch in the matched chair adjacent to him, but he shakes his head and beckons me to sit next to him with his free hand. I comply silently, still unnerved by his overall quieter manner.

I slide into the corner of the couch, facing him, with one knee touching the side of his leg. I touch his arm gently as he sips his whiskey. "You can talk to me," I say softly, encouragingly.

He gives me a speculative side-eye glance and sets his glass down on the coffee table. I follow suit, my drink untouched. He slides his arm onto the couch behind me and crooks his knee up as he turns to face me.

"I don't feel like talking," he replies. His eyes rove over my face, and I look down, tugging my dusty pink shirtdress over my knees self-consciously. When I find the courage to meet his gaze again, his eyes are a stormy grey-blue and aren't so much focused on me as they just happen to be fixed in my direction. I can tell he's retreated deeply into his own thoughts.

His gaze is so lost and forlorn that, before I can stop myself, I reach a hand out to touch his cheek and bring him back to the present moment. But before my fingertips can make contact with his face, his head snaps back and his fist closes around my hand. He sits up, his eyes wide.

"I'm sorry," I apologize, blushing to the roots of my hair. I make to pull my hand from his grip, but he tugs it gently toward him.

"It's okay," he assures me. "You just startled me." He lowers his hand into his lap, taking mine with it, and gently strokes his thumb over my palm. The touch sends tingles up my arm, and I can feel my cheeks still flushed with heat.

I swallow hard and lick my lips, willing myself to find words again. "Clearly. You've obviously got a lot to deal with right now. I can go if you want. I just wanted to see you and to let you know I'm here if you need me. But I don't want to make this harder for you."

He continues absentmindedly stroking my hand and it takes all my effort to focus my eyes on his face. "I said I don't feel like talking," he responds, his voice low and tired, "not that I didn't want you here. I'm glad you're here."

When his eyes meet mine this time, I see the conflict. The old Bryce, filled with longing for what could have been between us, warring with this new, harder Bryce. And I don't know under what terms he had hoped to restart our friendship, but I can see his struggle with his grief for his father, and his desire to be comforted.

And I know suddenly without a doubt that I'm more than capable of being whatever he needs me to be right now without crossing any lines, if that's what must be done. And not just because he's been there for me more times than I care to think about. But because I care for him deeply, and it's what he needs.

I open my arms to him, and he doesn't even hesitate before falling into me, tucking his head against my heart and wrapping his long arms around my torso. As I feel his body shake with tears and sobs of grief, I slide down into his embrace, resting my cheek on the top of his head. With one hand, I stroke the back of his head, the other I wrap around his quivering shoulder. I tuck my knees into his midsection and he sinks deeper into my chest, his warm tears rolling over our entwined arms.

As I hold him through his anguish, I banish all my own heartache, focusing on rubbing slow circles on his back, and on honoring his unspoken need for someone strong enough to unconditionally console him through this ordeal.

At some point we must have drifted off, tangled together, because I open my eyes and note several hours have passed. I can't see Bryce's face, but his body is still, his breathing even and heavy. I loathe waking him, but my biological needs are pressing, and I don't think I can disentangle myself while he's unconscious, as his torso has me completely pinned to the couch.

"Bryce," I prompt softly, my voice cracking from disuse. I tug gently on his arm.

He stirs finally and sits up languidly. "What time is it?" he asks hoarsely, rubbing his eyes.

"Almost five," I reply. "Where's your bathroom?"

He gestures vaguely down a hall I hadn't noticed, and I shoot off the couch.

When I return to the living room, our glasses have been cleaned up and Bryce is standing near the door, keys in hand.

"I need to pick my mom up from the hospital," he explains.

I gather my purse and meet him at the door, frowning. "Are you okay to drive?"

He gives me a deeply impatient look. "Sera, I had half a drink, hours ago. I'm fine."

I push his shoulder lightly. "I wasn't talking about the alcohol," I retort. I stop short of reminding him of the leaky, blubbering mess he was earlier this afternoon, but clearly the look on my face says enough. I can tell I'm annoying him, as he mashes his lips together and his nostrils flare.

"I'm fine," he repeats.

"All right," I relent. "I'm just concerned about you. You'll let me know if there's anything I can do to help?"

He takes a deep breath and runs a hand over his head. "Of course," he replies finally, opening the door.

I move toward it and he grabs me by the hand, pulling me into a gruff hug. I breathe in his scent, my fingers trailing over the taut muscles of his chest, and press out of his embrace after a moment. He releases me, and I know from the closed look on his face that we're back once more to our new tightrope walk, the comfort of our closeness this afternoon at an end.

But as I walk away, I can feel his eyes follow me down the hallway. And I'm bothered by how much that pleases me.

TWELVE

On Wednesday morning I step out of Charles' office and head downstairs to meet my team. As I round the corner into the open cubicle area that holds not only my team but most of the other project-management-related functions, I run into Daniel.

"I see you decided we were worth your time today," he remarks snidely, blocking my path. I make to go around him, but he shifts, making that impossible. "What, you can't even be bothered to speak to any of us anymore?"

I see a few heads peering over the low cubicle walls at his purposely loud, attention-grabbing comments.

"Hello, Daniel," I reply shortly. "It's so nice to see you too. Now if you don't mind, I need to meet with my team."

He folds his arms over his chest. "I do mind, actually. Care to share what exactly was more important than your job yesterday afternoon?"

"I do mind, actually," I reply mockingly. "As it's none of your business."

He is distracted by my response, so I take the opportunity to push past him.

"Having to pick up your slack *is* my business," he replies loudly to my back.

I stop and whirl around. "Oh, *please*," I say hotly, not bothering to keep my voice down. "As if I left anything that required your immediate and precious attention. And if there was anything so urgent, you could have called me. But I can see instead of using common sense, you'd rather be a passive-aggressive asshole to try to make me look bad in front of the entire office." More heads pop up over cubicle walls. "Next time, I'll make sure my loved ones know that all deaths and other family emergencies should be after business hours, so you aren't inconvenienced."

A low "ooooh" erupts amongst the crowd of onlookers. If my words weren't enough, their response leaves Daniel completely at a loss. His face turns beet red, his eyes shifting nervously between me and the spectators, realizing his attempt at humiliating me has backfired spectacularly.

"That's not … I didn't…" he sputters. His confusion quickly turns to rage. "Everyone back to work!" he barks.

All heads duck back down, and Daniel storms off before anything more can be said.

I can't help but give a small, satisfied smirk as I head to my meeting.

∽

THE REST OF THE DAY IS GLORIOUSLY FREE OF DANIEL-RELATED DRAMA, AS HIS mortification keeps him from being near me unless absolutely necessary. And even then, while he's unable to contain his furious glares, he doesn't speak a word to me or interfere in any of my affairs. In the absence of his usual campaign of taunts and undermining me at every turn, I manage to have an exceptionally productive day.

Early that evening I'm feeling especially motivated. Or perhaps I'm antsy, having checked my email for the millionth time with still no response from Alessandro. I've resolved not to worry, as there's literally nothing I can do. Even if I wanted to go after him, I wouldn't know where to begin. And there's no way in hell I'm broaching that subject with Bryce.

At that thought, I realize I need to check in with him. He answers on the first ring.

"Hey, gorgeous," he answers distractedly. I'm taken aback at his former usual greeting, and my heart melts a little at the emergence of that small sliver of what we were.

"Hey," I reply, controlling the emotion in my voice. "Bad time?"

"No," he assures me. "No. I'm at my mom's, but I can talk for a few minutes."

"How is she doing?" I ask.

Bryce sighs deeply. "She's devastated. My sister, my aunt, and I are all trying to help her plan the funeral, but it's rough. Practically every decision sends her into hysterics. And there's so much other shit to take care of. It's rough going all around."

"Your father's estate plan didn't cover final arrangements?" I ask the question before I even consider that it might be insulting. Surely, they'd have already thought of that.

322

"I don't know," he replies. "I hadn't looked into it. We're still kind of in react mode."

"I get it," I say. "This is unimaginably huge, for all of you. When is the funeral?"

"Sunday," he responds distractedly.

"As in this Sunday?" I'm incredulous. They clearly haven't even looked into Bryce's father's final wishes and they're planning to hold a funeral in not quite four days?

"Yes," he replies. "Mom wants it over with."

"Bryce, text me the address," I demand. "I'm coming over to help. Now."

"Sera…"

"Don't start that 'Sera' shit with me, Bryce. This is what I do. I organize things. I make things happen. Now, I'm coming over there to get as much of this taken care of as I possibly can, so you either give me the address or I'm going to use my real estate agent powers to find your parent's house, so help me God."

Bryce's answering chuckle brings me back to earth a bit. I didn't realize how angry I'd gotten all of a sudden.

"Okay. I'll send it to you as soon as I hang up," he agrees.

"Damn straight. See you soon." I hang up before he can respond and whip into action, gathering everything I'll need.

As promised, my phone pings with Bryce's text before I'm even done. And within minutes, I'm on my way to their house in West Seattle.

∾

"Hey," Bryce greets me at the door, looking rumpled and weary in jeans and a T-shirt. He gives me a quick side hug and escorts me into the huge, ornate foyer.

"Hey," I reply softly, looking up at him. I don't have time to say anything else as a woman my age pops into the room looking a little more enthusiastic than I'd expect under the circumstances. I look back up at Bryce expectantly, and he releases me from his side.

"Sera, this is my sister, Emily," he says. "Emily, this is Serafina Evans."

Emily's blue eyes, so like her brother's, sparkle at the introduction. She is around my height but slender and wild-looking, with the same thick, wavy chestnut hair as Bryce cascading down her back. She rushes forward and embraces me tightly.

"It's so nice to finally meet you," she says. "Bryce won't shut up about you. I'm just sorry we didn't get to meet sooner, under better circumstances." She steps back and smiles sadly at me, and I realize she's excited because of *me*.

I shoot Bryce a surprised and pointed look.

"Em, don't embarrass me," Bryce mutters, blushing furiously.

"It's okay," I assure him. "It's nice to meet you too, Emily. I'm so sorry for your loss."

"Thank you," she replies sincerely, grabbing my hand. "Come on, you should meet my mom too."

I look at Bryce again, checking to make sure he's okay with her pulling me into the living room. He shrugs and follows.

I barely have time to register the lavish décor of the living room — with its light grey walls, thick grey-and-white damask curtains, finely carved upholstered wood furniture, and arrangement upon arrangement of white flowers of all kinds displayed on every surface — before Emily has pulled me to a stop in front of the largest greyish-blue settee where two older women sit.

Both women have the same hair and eye color as Bryce and his sister. But Bryce unmistakably looks like the older of the two. Bryce seats himself next to her and folds his large hand over hers.

"Mom, this is my friend Sera," he says to her gently. "She's here to help with the funeral arrangements."

The tenderness in his voice and countenance bring tears to my eyes. I can practically feel his love and concern for her radiating off him. She places her other hand over his, squeezing his palm.

"Mrs. Hoyt," I say, my voice catching. I clear my throat. "I've been thinking about you ever since I heard. I'm so sorry for your loss. This must be so hard for you."

"Rebecca, please," she replies, gesturing for me to sit on the smaller couch opposite her. "And thank you. It has been much more difficult than I thought it would be. Even when you know it's coming." She presses a handkerchief to her eyes.

"I didn't know your husband, Rebecca, and I want to hear more about him sometime. But for now, I'm here to take as much of this off your shoulders as I can," I offer.

Bryce's eyes meet mine, and they are filled with love and sorrow. My breath catches in my throat, surrounded as I am by all the emotion in the room.

Rebecca nods thankfully as the tears slip down her cheeks, clearly unable to speak. The other older woman offers her hand.

"I'm Rebecca's sister, Charlotte," she offers. "Thank you for coming."

I lean forward and gently squeeze her hand in greeting. "I'm glad to be able to help," I admit.

"Well, we need lots of it," Emily chimes in. "We've been trying to get things together, but there's just so much to do."

I rise from my chair, slinging my bag over my shoulder. "I'll need to know what you've done so far, where your father's important papers are, and the contact information for his attorney. Leave the rest to me."

Emily arches an eyebrow at Bryce. "You weren't kidding about her," she says. Bryce huffs a small, dry laugh and shrugs. "This way."

With a brief farewell, I take my leave and follow Emily down a long hallway into what is unmistakably a man's study.

"Where can I set up?" I ask tentatively.

Emily points to the large desk that was clearly her father's. "It's the best place," she replies, noting my hesitation. "Really, it's okay. I'll pull up a chair and get you what you need."

Reluctantly, I settle into the giant black leather seat behind the desk. It smells of aftershave and cigars. The desk is neat and tidy, with no personal effects other than a framed picture of the family. Bryce's father was nearly as tall as he was. I can see that Emily looks more like him though, with her sharp features and willowy frame.

"What was his name?" I ask softly, embarrassed that I'd never asked, as Emily pulls her chair next to mine.

Emily looks longingly at the photograph for a moment before responding. "Landon. Landon Jeffrey Hoyt."

∽

EMILY IMPARTS EVERYTHING THAT'S BEEN DONE SO FAR WHICH, AS IT HAPPENS, is actually not very much, and I ask her a few questions before getting the contact information I need and dismissing her. What I don't share with her, nor had I with Bryce, was that I've handled exactly this situation not once, but twice in the last five years when both of my mother's parents passed away. It's a struggle to suppress those memories as I work through the list I've drafted, but for Bryce's sake, and his family's, I do.

By the end of the evening I've spoken to the family lawyer, located the estate documents in a filing cabinet, and have a good handle on what needs to be done to pull everything off by Sunday. Thankfully, there are precious few details that Landon Jeffrey Hoyt didn't leave instructions for.

When I emerge around ten p.m., Rebecca has already gone to bed and Bryce, Emily, and Charlotte are sitting in the living room talking in hushed tones. As I approach, I swear I hear my name, but their conversation ceases and their heads whip toward me as I enter the room.

"I have good news," I start. They all look at me expectantly as I take a seat next to Bryce on the large sofa. "I've located the estate documents and spoken with the family attorney, in a general sense of course, as he couldn't discuss any of the details with me."

"And?" Bryce prompts expectantly.

"And your father has already paid for a family-only private funeral at a nearby funeral home. One of you needs to contact them first thing tomorrow to set up a time slot for Sunday. Everything has already been selected — casket, flowers, music — it's all done."

Bryce sinks back into the sofa, clearly relieved.

"I can do that," Emily offers. "I have the rest of the week off."

I hand her the sheet with the funeral home information and summary of arrangements.

Bryce nods. "Me too," he adds. "What can I do?"

"While the funeral will be small, his final arrangements also stipulated for a large wake after, here at the house." I hand Bryce the relevant pages. "He was pretty specific about the guest list, décor, music, food, you name it."

Bryce skims the list, a sad, wry smile appearing on his face. "That's Dad. He was almost as organized as you are," he says fondly. He glances up at me. "I can take care of this."

"I can help too," I assure him. "I still have to work the rest of the week, but I'm all yours this weekend." I think I see Emily and Charlotte share a look, but I ignore it and press on. "The attorney needs to speak with you, Bryce. About the company. He says you haven't returned his calls."

Bryce frowns, folding the paper in his hand nervously. "I know. I just can't deal with it right now."

I suppress a sigh. "Unfortunately, there are a few pressing matters that need your attention now," I insist. He looks at me defiantly, and I can read his unspoken message. "And you can't send someone else. It has to be you. There are things you need to sign. It won't take long, Bryce, and you'll feel better once it's done."

He twirls the page in his hands a few more times. "Fine. I'll do it first thing tomorrow," he concedes.

"Good," I breathe, relieved. "Your mother will need to talk to him eventually too, but that can wait. For now," I produce the final sheet, "I think she's the best person to proof his obituary. He wrote it a couple of years ago, so it shouldn't be too much work. But it'll probably be very difficult for her to do alone."

Charlotte plucks it from my hand. "I'll help her," she responds.

"Then that's it for this week. But if your mother needs help with any of the estate paperwork afterward, I'm happy to help," I offer. "I've been through it more than once, and most lawyers suck at making sure you really understand what you're signing and everything that needs to be done."

Charlotte looks at me sadly. "Who did you lose, dear?" she asks kindly.

I blush softly and blink back tears. "My grandparents," I admit.

Bryce gives me a strange look, then pulls me under his arm and kisses the top of my head. The look between Emily and Charlotte is unmistakable this time.

"I'm sorry to hear that," Charlotte murmurs. I brush away the tears and disentangle myself from Bryce's embrace.

"Thank you," I respond. "I should really be going now. But I'll check in with you, Bryce, after work tomorrow."

"I'll walk you out," he agrees.

I say goodnight to Emily and Charlotte and let Bryce lead me to the door. He steps out onto the front porch into the warm August night. I let him wrap me in another of his warm hugs and try not to think about how much I enjoy it — how good he smells, or the feel of his tall, muscled frame against me, or the tenderness in his embrace.

As I drive home, I tell myself it's just loneliness and sorrow and empathy that are stirring whatever emotions that I'm feeling for Bryce. I also try to suppress the guilt when I realize I hadn't thought of Alessandro nor checked my email all evening. And when I get home I'm too tired and overwhelmed to do so, and opt instead to fall asleep fully clothed on top of the covers.

∽

AT BRYCE'S INVITATION, I REJOIN HIS FAMILY ON SATURDAY AFTERNOON TO SET up for the wake the following day and to stay over so I'm on hand to help with final preparations in the morning. Even between the five of us — well, four mostly, as Rebecca is still too distraught to do much — it still takes all afternoon and into the evening before we're able to settle in for a late dinner.

We eat in relative silence, the impending activities too somber for words. When we're done, Bryce leads me out into the back yard, to a small swing on the patio. It's barely big enough for us both, and I'm forced to sit up against Bryce, his long arm slung behind my shoulders. We sit quietly for a few minutes, staring up at the stars.

I formulate several sentences and chicken out, unsure of what to say. While Bryce has clearly needed the physical comfort, he's still so much quieter than he once was. But given the weight of all that he's been dealing with, it's understandable. Still, I don't want to unbalance whatever tenuous equilibrium we've achieved.

"I'm glad you're here," he finally says, breaking the silence. "I didn't want this to be confusing, but I also didn't realize until just now how much I needed someone to lean on this week."

"I did," I admit. "And I'm glad I could be here for you. You've been…"

Bryce shakes his head in a silent plea to not go there. I stop immediately, looking down into my entangled hands, blushing. No talking about feelings. Message received.

A rough finger pulls at my chin, breaking the spell of my self-flagellation. Bryce tilts my head to look up at him. His eyes glitter in the darkness of the night, searching mine for something. His finger stays on my chin, holding me so I'm unable to break his gaze. Not that I could if I wanted to. Whatever passes between us in this moment is something I can't even put into words. It's beyond attraction, beyond sorrow. It's a tug on my heart that I can't deny.

I lift my head up further toward him and part my lips. He sucks in his breath sharply and runs a rough thumb over my bottom lip, leaning in slowly until he's merely inches away.

"If I didn't know better, I'd think you wanted me to kiss you," he murmurs, his breath warm on my face.

My heart thunders in my chest. "Maybe I do," I whisper, unable to lie to him.

His lips settle into an amused smirk, and I can't tear my gaze from them. He leans in, touching his nose gently to mine. If I moved forward even a little, my lips would be pressed against his. My stomach tumbles at the thought, but I remain perfectly still, waiting to see what he does.

"Well, maybe I will sometime," he murmurs.

He releases me and returns his gaze to the stars. The butterflies in my stomach turn to lead, and I don't know how to react. Or what I really feel for him. And whether I should be feeling it at all.

But for now, maybe I'm just relieved. Because that part of me that still belongs to Alessandro squirms uncomfortably at whatever just almost happened between Bryce and me. Though admittedly, that part is undernourished and unsure. It's been four weeks since I've so much as heard from the man who claims to love me but still left me. And the more time passes, the harder it is to remember why that was for the best. Because on top of not having made any promises to each other, it's starting to look more and more like I may never hear from him again. In fact, I have to work to pull the memory of his face, his voice, to mind.

But I also know I can't overwrite the ache and uncertainty of Alessandro's absence with something I may only be feeling because of the unfortunate passing of Bryce's father and the tumultuous events in my own life. And I know Bryce once had feelings for me, but his need for me now is clearly mostly based in his grief. To start something now would, at best, be a small comfort to us both. At worst, it could obliterate any hope of keeping him in my life. My gut twists painfully, and that thought stops whatever yen had started to grow in me this past week, hardening my resolve to put anything I feel aside and focus only on being there for Bryce, and trusting that once it's all behind us things will be clearer. Easier.

My resolve is tested again sooner than I'd thought when Bryce walks me to my guest room.

"If you need anything, I'm two doors down," he says, leaning against the doorframe and looking down at me. "The bathroom is the first door."

Looking up into his face, I nod, not trusting myself to speak. Because despite the war in my heart, the sight of him towering over me — tortured, sad, and exquisitely handsome — I realize I'm only human. And I want to touch him, to make love to him, to wipe away his worries with flesh on flesh.

I'm suddenly thankful we're having this conversation by the light of the moon filtering into the room, because if the lights were on I'm sure he'd see the flush in my face. As it is, I'm having trouble keeping my breathing even from the desire welling in me.

It's just the situation, I tell myself, willing my body into submission.

"Thanks," I finally manage. "I'll see you in the morning."

He regards me stoically for a few more moments before turning to leave. "Goodnight, Sera."

"Goodnight, Bryce."

Once he's gone, I check my phone. I have a missed call from Allie. Another sharp pain tugs at my heart. Knowing it's too late, I vow to call her back tomorrow and make my way to bed, overwhelmed by the emotion of the day.

THIRTEEN

BRYCE

I'm lying awake in bed when my alarm goes off at five. I shut it off absentmindedly, still brooding on the events of the previous evening. Kicking myself, really, for not giving in to the come-hither looks Sera was throwing me last night. But being close to her this week, needing to be close to someone, has thrown everything into chaos as it is.

Ignoring the tension in my groin, I roll out of bed and throw on running clothes to work off the strain by pounding the pavement instead. Even though I almost never run on Sundays. But that's how worked up I am.

An hour later, I'm dripping with sweat but still tense as ever. I down a protein shake in the kitchen as the first light of day creeps over the horizon. The house is quiet, everyone still clearly abed. Though I'm sure, like me, nobody slept all that well.

Stripping off my sweat-soaked shirt, I head to the bathroom to shower. The heat of the shower wraps around me like an old friend, but just the thought of Sera sleeping in the next room has me hard again. I grit my teeth as I work myself, imagining my hand is her hand, her mouth, her sex. I explode quietly under the stream of water, both momentarily sated and frustrated that she's still forefront in my mind at moments like this, despite my determination to stop thinking about her like that.

Done with the shower, I wrap a towel around my waist and head to my room. As I'm opening the door, Sera's door snicks open and she slips into the hallway. She's so preoccupied with being quiet that she doesn't notice me at first and I'm able to get a full look at her. And I'm reminded why it's so hard to stop being attracted to her. Her long, wavy brown hair is in complete, sexy disarray, and she's wearing an oversized shirt that clearly shows her full breasts are free of a bra. The shirt hangs just below her crotch, putting her shapely legs on display. I can't help but gawk a little and be thankful that I just abated my erection in the shower. Because it would be hard to hide in this towel.

After a few steps she looks up and her eyes meet mine. She freezes. I give her a small smirk as I watch her eyes travel to my lips, then chest, then down.

"Good morning, gorgeous," I say before I can help the words. I curse internally at my second slip. I swore to myself I'd stop calling her that. But I'm not exactly as in control of myself as I'd like to be these days.

"Hi," she squeaks, clearly unnerved. "I'm just going to…" she points to the bathroom and slips inside quickly. I step into my own room to dress for the day, the black clothes I'd laid out on the bed a reminder of what's to come that sobers me considerably.

⁓

I'm standing in the kitchen drinking coffee when Em joins me. She looks like hell, but I don't say anything.

"Why do you look so much better than I feel?" she grouses at me.

"If it helps, I feel like you look," I counter. She glares at me as she pours a cup of coffee for herself.

"It most certainly does not," she replies haughtily.

Aunt Charlotte appears and catches us feigning stink eye at each other as she starts preparing breakfast. "Your mother will be down shortly," she warns us. "Behave, please." As if we're still children to be scolded.

Mom and Sera enter the kitchen together shortly after, engaged in quiet conversation. The sight of them together makes me nervous in a way I can't quite explain, and I clear my throat. Their heads snap up.

Their tête-à-tête broken, my mother moves to help Aunt Char with breakfast and Sera takes a seat at the dining room table, eyeing me nervously.

In true Sera form, she's wearing a black shirtdress, cinched at the waist with a black belt. I realize everyone is already dressed in their finest blacks, myself included, and the thought adds to the somber tone of the day.

"Coffee?" I ask Sera.

"Yes, please," she responds.

I pour her a cup and drop in cream but no sugar.

She looks at me inquisitively as I set it down in front of her and plop into the chair next to her. "I didn't realize you knew how I take my coffee."

I wave my hand, brushing it off. Like hell I'm going to confess that I've catalogued her every preference. I'd explain it's years of training in observing people, but I know if I say it out loud it will probably sound like something more than it is.

"We have to leave in an hour for the funeral," I remind her. "It'd be a squeeze in Aunt Char's car, so we can drive separately if you want."

She looks up at me like a deer frozen in headlights. "I hadn't assumed I was invited to the funeral," she admits. "Since it's family only. I thought I'd stay here and make sure everything is ready for the wake."

Em and Aunt Char share another of their looks that they think nobody notices. I ignore it as usual, but I can tell Sera sees it too.

Mom pauses flipping the bacon. "Sera, dear, you're more than welcome. In fact, I insist," she says warmly. "I don't know what we would have done without you this week."

For the first time since it happened, my mother sounds strong again. And I have no doubt that it's, as she says, in no small part due to Sera's efforts and her authoritative presence that leaves you confident that everything is going to be taken care of. I look down into my coffee, tears burning in my eyes. For so many reasons. When I've mastered myself, I look up to find Sera staring at me. Silently asking for confirmation.

"I want you there," I admit, in a quiet tone that will reach only her ears.

She gives a small nod of understanding and, when nobody is looking, reaches out to give my hand a gentle squeeze.

<hr>

When we file out of the funeral home two hours later, everyone is in tears. The ceremony was short and simple, but exactly what we needed. No frills, no fanfare. Just enough time to see him, remember him, and say goodbye. Aunt Char and Em hold each other as they walk ahead, and my mother is tucked under my left arm, sobbing quietly into my chest as we exit. Sera walks on my right at a respectful distance.

My father's still form flashes through my mind again, and more tears silently find their way down my face. In the presence of others, I suppress the lifetime of memories threatening to reduce me to the mess I was earlier in the week. I can only hope I'm strong enough to save that for later, when I'm alone once more.

Just when I feel like I'm going to lose that battle, Sera's warm hand slips into mine and she gives me a strong squeeze. I look over at her, her hazel eyes brimming with the tears and anguish I'm sure is reflected in my face. I squeeze her hand back, grateful not to be the sole pillar of strength in our miserable party.

❧

We make it back to the house well ahead of the start of the wake. Sera heads to start preparing, but I pull her aside into the living room. Without a word, she opens her arms to me, and I gratefully fold myself around her. Her quiet strength calms me, which is exactly what I needed, and I release her once I'm sure I'll be able to manage on my own for a while. I watch her walk away, concentrating on making my mind blank and numb.

As people start to arrive, I position myself at the front of the house to act as a buffer so that my mother has time to prepare herself for the steady stream of well-wishers that are arriving.

And arrive they do — well more than a hundred of them over the course of two hours. I barely see any of my family members as I let the wave of mourners flow through and over me, their kind and well-meant words drops in a tumultuous ocean of grief. I both hear them and don't as I surrender to the experience.

By the time people have stopped arriving, I feel like a broken shell and seek out the solitude of the patio. I'm not there long when a hand holding a plate of food drops in front of me. I look up to see Sera's face, full of concern. I accept the food gratefully, and she hands me a generous glass of whiskey to go with it. I don't realize my hands are shaking until I take it from her.

"I should bring some food to your mom," she says softly. "I'll be back as soon as I can, okay?"

I nod mutely, unable to even voice my thanks. I feel as though talking will unleash the dam holding back the pain of it all. But she disappears, not needing me to say anything. Grateful, I concentrate on eating.

Once I've finished my food I realize I should go in and check on my mom as well, so I rise reluctantly, dropping my dishes in the kitchen. Feeling ever so slightly stronger for the food and alcohol, I find my mother in the living room leaning on Aunt Char and listening blankly to one of dad's golf buddies extend his condolences. Sera sits next to her with a plate of untouched food.

I touch Sera's arm to get her attention. "I've got this," I assure her, taking the plate and her place.

She rests her hand on my shoulder and squeezes it reassuringly. "Let me know if you need anything," she responds, and retreats to the kitchen.

It doesn't take but a look at my mom to realize she's about to pass out, so I manage to convince her to have a few bites of food between conversations. Once she's looking less peaked, I take the empty plate back to the kitchen to find Sera leaning against the counter, looking uncomfortable.

"You okay?" I ask her as I get myself more whiskey.

She gives me an incredulous look. "I'm fine," she replies impatiently. "How are you holding up?"

"Trying not to think about any of it. Failing miserably," I admit.

She bites her lip and visibly restrains herself from reaching for me. I lean back into the counter behind me, encouraging the distance between us.

"What's bothering you the most?" she asks.

Her question catches me off guard. And it's an interesting one.

"I'm now the president of Hoyt Corporate Services," I admit.

She looks confused. "That's a bad thing?" she asks.

I sigh heavily. "No. Yes. I don't know," I reply, frustrated. I regroup to come up with the shortest possible explanation. "I knew it would happen someday. I just didn't think it would be so soon."

"You're worried you're not ready?" she guesses.

I stare down as I swirl the whiskey in my glass. "I know I'm not ready," I admit. I look up at her. She bites her lip again, and I look away.

"The Bryce I know can handle anything," she says softly but confidently. I huff a snort of disagreement and down the rest of the amber liquid. "You may doubt yourself, but anyone who knows you can see how capable you are."

I meet her gaze. "I know I'm capable. But there was so much I wanted to do before I took on that kind of responsibility," I clarify. The alcohol warms me and enhances the relaxing effect of the first glass.

"Like what?" she asks.

"Fall in love. Travel. Get married. Have kids. I don't know, take your pick," I reply, watching her closely.

She looks deeply conflicted, and I hope it's because she's having doubts. About the Italian prick. Her feelings for me. All of the above. And I'm just out of my mind enough to want to encourage those doubts, against my recent determination to keep her at a distance, as a friend. But she hasn't been making that easy. As usual.

I set my glass down and slowly push myself to a standing position.

"Can't you restructure? Distribute the responsibility?" she suggests, warily watching me as I slowly advance on her.

"I suppose I could," I agree. "But like I said, I've been trying not to think about it. I've got enough on my mind right now." I stop inches from her, looking down into her face. It's all I can do to let the heat between us simmer, to see how she responds, to see if she asks for it again this time.

She's no longer casually leaning against the counter but is tensely gripping its edge with her hands. "I can imagine," she murmurs, looking up at me like she's hypnotized. Her lips part slightly and my gaze drops, watching them expand and contract slightly with her labored breathing. My mouth dips slightly toward hers like it has a mind of its own.

She straightens up and presses a hand on my chest. "We shouldn't," she says softly. But the desire in her eyes betrays her.

I slide my hands around her hips and pull her gently toward me. I run a hand lightly up her back. "That's not what you said last night," I murmur.

Her eyes widen in surprise, and I can't help giving her a devilish smirk as I lower my face to hers, the wide chasm of pain in my gut overriding my good sense and resolve. I can feel her melt into me as I reach for her lips with mine.

"Shit," a voice exclaims from the doorway. Glass shatters.

Startled, we jump apart, breaking the spell. I look over and Em is standing in the doorway, a broken tumbler of dark liquid at her feet. Sera rushes to grab towels to help clean up the mess.

Emily makes a hasty retreat once things are put to rights, and Sera glances nervously at me.

"We should probably get back to your mom," she says. And I know the moment has passed. I nod and follow her into the living room.

And I'm not sure if I'm more annoyed at myself for knowing better, or relieved that she seems as confused as I am.

∽

We spend time in the living room with the remaining smattering of guests, Aunt Char surreptitiously continuing to feed mom.

As the wake winds down, I'm surprised to hear the doorbell ring again. Em leaves the room to answer it. But even I'm not prepared for who she returns with. Holding a bouquet of flowers, Madison Connolly stands before the assembly. All eyes turn to her, and not just because she's a late arrival.

Madison has always been stunning. The perfect five-and-a-half-foot-tall beauty queen that she is, her long blond hair perfectly styled, her bright blue eyes expertly outlined to stand out in her heart-shaped face, she wears a black minidress that can only be described as outrageously sexy. The halter cut pulls her small, firm breasts into pleasing cleavage, and the clingy fabric outlines her tiny waist and narrow hips.

She looks the same as she did a year ago when we painfully decided to end our relationship of three years. I'd only just managed to get over her when I met Sera. Or maybe because I met Sera. My heart thuds uncomfortably in my chest.

"Madison. What are you doing here?" I ask sharply. It's not much of a greeting, I know, but she wasn't exactly invited, and I'm completely thrown off.

"I saw the obituary in the paper today," she replies in her breathy, feminine voice. "I had to come pay my respects." She approaches my mother and offers the flowers. My mother accepts them, but almost immediately hands them off to Aunt Char. "I'm sorry for your loss."

"Thank you, Madison," my mom replies formally. "Do sit down."

Madison takes a seat beside me on the sofa opposite my mother. I shift toward Sera, almost unconsciously. Madison takes clear note and leans forward, extending her hand to Sera.

"I'm Madison Connolly," she introduces herself.

Sera glances at me nervously and takes her hand. "Serafina Evans," she responds. While everyone else in the room has gone back to their conversations, my family is tensely watching the exchange between the two women. "How do you know the Hoyts?" Sera's tone is polite, but clearly as mystified as I am at Madison's sudden appearance.

"Bryce and I were together for years," Madison replies, dropping a hand on my knee. I'm too stunned to react. "I adored his father. I was so sad to hear the news."

"I see," Sera replies, eyeing Madison's hand as it subtly strokes my knee.

"And you?" Madison asks, eyeing Sera.

"I'm a friend of Bryce's," Sera replies hesitantly.

Em huffs quietly in her corner. I throw her a pleading look, but she avoids my gaze, clearly unwilling to interfere.

"How nice," Madison replies, then turns her attention back to me. "Bryce, darling, does this mean you'll be taking over the family business now?"

"I…" before I can even formulate a full response, Sera excuses herself and ducks into the kitchen. I try to go after her, but Madison squeezes my knee gently, drawing my attention back to her, looking at me expectantly for a response. "Yes, I already have actually."

She engages me sympathetically on how difficult that must be, and by the time there's a polite break in the conversation, Sera has rejoined the crowd in the living room, chatting with Em in the corner. So I continue to talk to Madison as the afternoon wears on, becoming more absorbed in the conversation.

And after a while, I actually find it a relief to talk to someone I've known for so long, who knows me. I don't have to explain my fears to Madison. She remembers them all and is a good listener. And while our breakup was devastating and necessary, I can tell she still cares for me. I'm not sure how I feel about her, but it's an unexpected comfort. It feels nice to just talk to a woman I'm not interested in.

It's nearly dinner time when Sera gently interrupts. I look around, surprised to see that besides us three only Aunt Char is still in the room.

"Can I talk to you for a sec?" she asks, eyeing Madison guardedly.

"Sure," I reply. "Please excuse me, Madison." Madison nods understandingly, and I step into the kitchen with Sera.

"Everything's all cleaned up. I'm going to head home," she says, fidgeting with her belt.

I realize I've been ignoring her for the better part of the afternoon, and I suddenly feel like a world-class ass.

"I'm so sorry, Sera. I hadn't seen Madison in so long, I just got absorbed in catching up with her. If you stay we can—"

"No," she interrupts. "Don't apologize. You looked happy talking to her. You should go back in there."

I'm silent as I try to figure out if she's sincere. Because I know I didn't misinterpret what almost happened in this very room earlier today.

"It's surprisingly nice to see her, but she's my past, Sera," I explain.

Sera contemplates me for a moment before responding. "There are things you need right now that I can't give you." The unspoken implication that Madison can give those things to me is simple but powerful.

"You've given me more than enough," I correct her. "Thank you. For being here for me. And my family. You're a good friend." I open my arms to her and let her come to me. I breathe a sigh of relief when she does. "It's going to be a crazy week, but I want to see you next weekend, okay?"

She nods into my chest. I kiss the top of her head.

"Walk me out?" she asks, pulling away from my chest and smiling up at me.

"Of course," I reply.

A few minutes later as I wave her off from the porch, Madison appears by my side.

"Do you love her?" Madison asks.

I turn and give her an impatient look. "What do you want, Madison?" I ask tiredly. I can't help but wonder why she reappeared now. Because I know it's not just to pay her respects to my father, whom she barely acknowledged when we were together.

"She loves you, you know," Madison asserts.

I glance over at her. Her expression is open and sympathetic.

"Not like that," I reply. I walk back into the house and Madison follows. Everyone else has gone, and it's only us in the foyer.

"You're wrong," she replies nonchalantly.

I shake my head and run a hand over my hair. "She's in love with someone else," I mumble.

"It's possible to be in love with two people at the same time. Besides, what could the other guy possibly have that you don't?" she asks coyly.

I smile wryly at her. "She was with him first," I reply.

"Was? She's not now?" Madison asks.

"It's complicated," I respond.

Madison rolls her eyes. "If they're not married, you still have a shot," she encourages me.

"It doesn't matter anymore," I say with a note of finality. I'm over talking about this with the woman who wouldn't commit to marrying me. "What are you doing here?"

"I thought you might need a friend," she says suggestively. I eye her speculatively. "You look good, Bryce. A little too good, considering."

"Don't be fooled. I'm a fucking mess," I reply angrily.

Madison steps closer. Close enough that the smell of her perfume wraps around me. She runs a finger down my chest. "Need a distraction?" she asks softly, peering up at me from under her eyelashes.

I look down at her stoically, unsure of how to respond. She takes the opportunity to unhook the fabric behind her neck. And with a shimmy, her dress falls to the floor, revealing her naked body underneath.

Despite myself, I feel my cock harden as I take in her lithe form. "Goddammit, Madison, my mother could come downstairs any minute." She always was an exhibitionist.

"Then you'd better take me to your bedroom," she whispers invitingly.

My chest aches, my heart unable to expand enough to contain all the emotions I've felt this week. I close my eyes to block it all out. Madison takes the opportunity to lift my hand to her breast. My eyes fly open in surprise as she strokes her pink nipple with my thumb and moans softly.

My control slips and my baser needs take over. "Fuck." I grab her dress from the floor and shove it in her arms, lifting her by the waist.

She wraps her legs around me as her lips find mine and I stride purposefully down the hall. Our tongues wrestle in a practiced dance as I close the door behind us and drop her onto the bed.

All the angst, all the tension coils like a spring inside me as I relieve myself of my clothes and pounce on the naked beauty in front of me. Sensing my acute need, Madison opens her legs to me, guiding me into her. It's been so long and the sensation is so overwhelming that it takes all of my strength to adjust to the tight, wet grip of her around me.

She lifts my head in her hands and stares into my eyes. "Stay with me, big boy," she breathes.

I nod and bury my face in her hair once more, moving slowly and deliberately. There was a time that I enjoyed nothing more than looking into her eyes as we fucked, watching every look of pleasure pass over her face, but now, after everything, I just need to imagine she's someone else.

But even that is too much, and I'm overwhelmed with emotion and sensation. I pull back, needing to regroup. Before she can question me, I drop between her legs. If I can't keep my shit together, I can at least pleasure her until I can.

I spread her wide open, and run a finger down her seam, parting her for my mouth. I gently flick with my tongue, and she tightens under the assault, writhing and moaning. With a smirk, I slide a finger deep in her, causing her to arch off the bed. It pleases me to watch — I've always enjoyed the controlled response of this act. As I work my tongue over her with increasing intensity, I add another finger, curling them toward me inside her. Her hips buck off the bed and I suck her sensitive flesh into my mouth to keep locked onto her.

Her moans escalate, and I unlatch my mouth, sliding my teeth gently over her most sensitive part as I pull away.

"Shhhh," I admonish her. "They'll hear you."

She nods and bites her lip hard, her fingers gripping the sheets, so I renew my assault in full force, pumping and curling my fingers furiously as I suck her back in with my lips, flicking my tongue rapidly. A stream of curse words whispers through her teeth as she tightens around my hand and finishes as quietly as she can.

I relent, using the moisture on my hand to stroke myself as I climb back onto the bed between her legs. Feeling more in control, I lift her to me and slide in slowly. She's still tight from her climax, and I focus on keeping it together. When she's expanded to accommodate me, I hold her legs astride my chest and pump slowly, fully in, fully out, and over again.

I close my eyes, surrendering to the sensation. Her hips rise to meet me as I increase my pace. I feel her fingertips graze my cock as she works her clit to our rhythm. I rest one of her legs against me and reach a hand down to grasp the tip of her breast. She arches into my touch and my hips as all her most sensitive spots are stimulated simultaneously.

I lean forward into her, deepening my assault, increasing the pounding to a frenzy, our hips slamming into each other. She's controlling her moans like a good girl, and the only noise in the room is our labored breathing and the arousing sound of skin slapping on skin.

Her breathing accelerates again, and she whimpers, and I know she's close. Falling on her completely, I rock myself into her madly, the tension coiling in a crescendo. It's not long before we both shatter under the pleasure. I let out the low groan I've been holding back as the last hot lick of gratification ripples through me and come to a rest, quivering over her small frame, her legs wrapped tightly around me.

My face buried in the bed beside her head, I relish the feeling of release and the sticky, sweaty, realness of our entwined bodies. And I realize it's probably for the best that Sera and I didn't end up here. I wasn't lying to Madison. I'm a fucking mess. And I needed this, even though I didn't realize how much. But I think Sera might have. And while part of her might have wanted to give it to me, it's just better for everyone if we didn't go there. Because, at the end of the day, I feel like I just don't have anything real to give right now.

Madison pushes a small hand against my sweaty shoulder, bringing me back to myself, and I roll off her obligingly. We lay quietly as our breathing returns to normal. I'm not sure what to say, or what she expects.

"Thanks," I finally say, awkwardly. She gives me an incredulous look and bursts out laughing. And to my immense surprise, I join in until tears are leaking out of my eyes.

When the fit of laughter has passed, she rolls onto her side to face me. I put an arm under my neck to prop my head up, so I can meet her gaze.

"You're welcome," she replies. She traces a finger down the center of my chest. "You really do look amazing. Why'd you wait until we'd broken up to get this ripped?" I give her a disbelieving smirk.

"I've always been this ripped. I just padded it over with a solid layer of burgers and beers," I respond drolly.

She groans. "Men. I swear. You cut out a few burgers, eat a few vegetables and you get the V," she says, running her fingertips along my hip.

I shrug nonchalantly. "If I knew that's what did it for you, I would've cut them out a long time ago," I tease. It was a joke, but suddenly I realize it sounded way more serious than I meant it.

Thankfully, she doesn't seem to take it all that seriously. She simply shrugs back and smiles. "I don't know a woman alive who could resist this," she replies, running her palm over my six-pack.

It feels nice, but I'm so spent it gets zero reaction. "I know one," I murmur.

Madison raises an eyebrow. "Has she seen it?" she asks disbelievingly.

I chuckle. "This morning, actually, after I showered," I reply.

"Well, make sure she sees it a few more times, and I promise it'll work its magic," she says confidently.

"Heh. Well, I'm not above fighting dirty these days," I admit, "but I'm not exactly in a magical place right now."

Madison gives me an appraising look. "Are you sure about that?" she asks shrewdly. I sit up and pull my pants back on.

"I don't really want to talk about it," I deflect. Madison shrugs and rises from the bed, slipping into her dress.

"Suit yourself. It was good seeing you, Bryce."

I eye her speculatively as she heads to the door. "That's it?" I ask skeptically. She flips her hair over her shoulder and smiles at me as she opens the door.

"That's it," she replies. And with that, she's gone. And I'm alone with my grief once again.

FOURTEEN

I t's not until lunchtime on Monday that I realize I'd forgotten to call Allie back. But calling her only dumps me into her voicemail. I hang up without leaving a message, making a note so I remember to try again after work. And then I return to the same fog I've been in since I left the Hoyts' house yesterday.

For what feels like the millionth time, the mental image of Bryce in that towel distracts me from everything but breathing. And even that is difficult. The smooth curve of his massive pecs flowing into the tight muscles of his abs and the defined, dark trail of hair leading down the perfectly taut plane of his lower abdomen were so head-spinningly distracting that I still don't know how I managed to look him in the face for the rest of the day. Knowing he was built was one thing. Seeing it was another.

Almost as distracting is remembering Funeral Barbie showing up and capturing Bryce's attention for the bulk of the day. On top of her being exactly the kind of woman I imagined he'd be interested in, it was more disturbing to watch him pour his heart out to her for hours while I took care of, well, pretty much everything. It just reinforced the feeling his unnerving silence had given me all week — that he's not interested in being anything more than friends. Despite our almost-kisses. And even those, I know, were likely just borne of the confusion of the grieving process.

But I'm carefully refusing to acknowledge the hot boil of jealousy in my gut and the implications of it. Because I know torturing myself wondering whether Bryce grief-fucked Madison isn't going to help anything, so I bury myself back in work.

∼

THE REST OF THE DAY PASSES MORE SLOWLY THAN I EVER THOUGHT POSSIBLE, but I battle my way through. Finally home, I sink gratefully into my favorite chair and call Allie.

"Hello?" she answers.

I'm beyond relieved to hear her voice. "Allie, I'm sorry," I breathe. "I had a rough weekend. I meant to call you back yesterday and I completely spaced. I'm so, so, so sorry."

The line is silent for so long that I'm starting to think she's not there anymore when she finally responds. "It's fine." Her words are tight, and it's obvious she doesn't really mean them.

"It's not fine," I admit. "You've been going through so much, and I haven't checked in in a week. I feel just awful."

A heavy sigh issues across the line. "You should."

I can't help but chuckle. "You're right. What can I do? Bring you chocolate? Booze? Do you need to shop? Mani-pedi?"

"Yes, to all of those. Eventually. I'm still working on things."

"Tell me about it," I prompt.

Reluctantly, Allie explains her therapy and the side effects of the antidepressants they've put her on, and that she's still struggling with the basics — eating, showering, talking. But the more she talks, the lighter her voice sounds. It's difficult, but I simply listen. At so many points I want to interject, reassure her, or even be there with her to hug her. But having been through depression myself, I hang back, allowing her to set the pace and level of conversation.

I don't mention Daniel, Alessandro, or Bryce, or my mixed-up feelings. But when she's done, I do ask her when I can see her again. We make a lunch date for Sunday, and I hang up, near tears. I can't decide if they are happy tears for my recovering best friend, or simply tears from all the emotions that have raged in me lately. In either case, I take care of a few things and retire early, exhausted in every way possible.

∼

ON TUESDAY, I STOP BY THE GROCERY STORE ON MY WAY HOME. IN THE BREAD aisle I spot a familiar set of long, black braids. As I approach, I realize it is, in fact, Heather Irving. My project manager who abruptly quit under dubious circumstances.

"Heather?" I place myself a respectable distance away so as not to startle her.

She looks up from reading a cracker box in surprise. "Ms. Evans," she replies. "How are you?"

"Heather, you don't work for me anymore, call me Sera, please," I insist. "I'm okay. We've missed you. How are you doing?"

She puts the cracker box back on the shelf and chews on her lip. "Making do," she replies. "I got a job at a broker's office in Fremont. It's not the same, but it's okay."

"Well, I'm glad to hear you were able to find something so soon," I respond. "Maybe put in a good word for me." I meant it as a joke, but her eyes widen seriously. "I'm kidding. It's just a little more difficult at the new office than I thought it would be."

"It's not…" she trails off, looking like she wants to say something. I prompt her with silence and open body language. "It's not Daniel, is it?" She practically whispers the question.

My heart drops. "Well, yes, actually," I admit. "He's…" I pause, searching for the word until I notice the tears in Heather's eyes. "Maybe you know what he is."

Heather glances around nervously, licks her lips and nods. My throat constricts, and I try to think of a way to get Heather alone without scaring her in hopes of getting the full story.

Taking a gamble, I step toward her and lean in a little, so I can speak quietly.

"Why don't we get some sandwiches and go sit in Pioneer Square and talk about it," I suggest. Heather looks terrified and unsure. "Please, Heather. If he's treated anyone else like this, I need to know."

"Okay," she says, barely above a whisper.

I step back and nod, leading her out into the warm evening air.

∽

A short while later, we've managed to snag a bench with our food, and I'm quietly munching while Heather's food sits beside her, untouched. I let the silence prompt her once more, and I'm not disappointed.

"The afternoon of the day before I quit, Daniel invited me into his office," she starts, picking at a piece of shredded lettuce. "We'd flirted a little during the move, and he said he wanted to get to know me better. To see how my skill set might be used more widely in the company." She pauses, twirling a braid absentmindedly as she sips her soda. "We talked shop for a while, and then he got up and closed the door. It made me a little nervous, but he sat back down, and we talked about our personal lives for a bit, so I relaxed, figuring he thought it was a conversation best had privately. We were talking about books we'd read recently, and he asked if I'd ever read those popular ones — the ones with BDSM." She blushes furiously, and I drop my food, my stomach already roiling at what I suspect is to come.

"What did you say?" I manage to choke out.

"I told him I had," she admits. "He asked if I enjoyed them. I told him I liked the idea that love could give you the strength to change who you are. But the other stuff is not really my scene."

"He was disappointed," I guess.

She throws me an uncharacteristically sharp look. "He was angry," she corrects me. "All of a sudden. Like he was a different person. He got in my face and demanded that I admit that I was just..." she chokes on the words and tears well in her eyes again, "a dirty little whore that needed to be punished."

"Oh, Heather," I gasp, grabbing her hand and squeezing.

She squeezes back and wipes the tears away with her other hand, and signals that she wants to continue.

"I tried to push him away, but he hit me. Told me to shut up. That if anyone heard me, he'd destroy me." Her voice is barely above a whisper as she angrily wipes tears from her eyes. I dig a tissue out of my bag and hand it to her, giving her a moment to collect herself. "It was late by then, and I was pretty sure everyone had gone home. I told him I wasn't going to fight him. To just do what he wanted. I just wanted to get it over with. To get out of there. I didn't know what else to do. It was my fault. I should have said no. I should have fought."

The fury that unfurls in me at her words is like nothing I've ever felt before. And it takes every ounce of my not inconsiderable self-control to say my next words in a measured enough tone not to scare Heather, not to make her feel as if my anger is in any way directed at her.

"It was *not* your fault," I hiss. I want to grab her face and make her look at me. "Heather." Her eyes slowly slide to mine. "It was not. Your. Fault."

She shakes her head. "I shouldn't have gone in there alone, and I..." I close my eyes and hold up a hand for her to stop, reining in my rage again. I take a deep breath and open my eyes.

"He told you it was your fault, didn't he?" I seethe.

She nods miserably. "He said I wouldn't have come into his office if I didn't want it. And if I told anyone what happened they'd never believe me anyway. And if I did that he'd make sure everyone knew what a slut I was. That they'd never believe he did anything wrong. It was my word against his."

"You should know that he said similar things to me. But our conversation happened in the middle of the day, and I was lucky enough to get out before he could touch me," I say. My admission sends Heather over the edge, and she starts sobbing uncontrollably. I offer my arms to her and she collapses against me gratefully. I run my hand over her hair, murmuring to her over and over, "It's not your fault."

Eventually her sobs subside, and she uses the last of my tissues to wipe away her tears.

"Thank you for telling me all this, Heather," I tell her. There's an ache in my chest that's suddenly grown exponentially. I can't even begin to imagine how she must feel. And why so many bad things are happening to the people I care about.

"I'm sorry I didn't tell you before. I could've stopped him from..." she starts, until I shush her.

"It doesn't matter. What matters is what we do next. Can I tell you what I think we should do?" I ask carefully. Heather nods meekly. "Good. I want to take you to the police station. Right now. I think you should report this."

Heather looks terrified. "But when he finds out he'll come after me," she whispers.

I shake my head vehemently. "I will *not* let that bastard hurt you again," I promise her. "If it's okay with you, I'm going to call a friend and ask him to come with us. Do you remember Bryce Hoyt?"

Heather nods. "Your security consultant," she says.

"That's him. He's got friends at the police department. I'd like to ask for his help, if that's okay with you," I reply.

Heather stares into the distance for a bit, sniffing loudly.

"Okay," she finally agrees.

I let out a sigh of relief and pull out my phone. Bryce answers immediately.

"Hey, Sera, what's up?" he asks curtly.

"Hey," I reply, steadying my voice. "I need you to meet me at the police station. How soon can you do that?" I can almost hear the deadly calm on the other end of the line.

"Give me fifteen minutes," he replies. "Are you okay?"

"I'm fine," I promise. "I'll explain when I see you."

He hangs up before I can say goodbye, but I'm not offended, only thankful he's understood the urgency.

I offer a hand to Heather as I rise. "I'm going to be with you as long as you need me," I promise.

She takes my hand and rises. "Let's go."

∿

HEATHER AND I AREN'T WAITING AT THE POLICE STATION LONG WHEN BRYCE strides through the doors, obviously straight from work, in tailored black pants and a black short-sleeved button-front shirt, a gun holstered under his left arm and looking admittedly rather angry and terrifying. Heather shrinks into me a little, and I give Bryce a wary look. His body language immediately softens, sensing the fear of the quaking girl half-hidden behind me.

"Thanks for coming," I greet him, gripping Heather's hand. "This is Heather Irving. She used to work for me. And she needs our help."

"Hi, Heather," he says in a soft voice. "I don't know what happened, but I'll do whatever I can, okay?"

Heather slinks out from behind me and nods. "Thank you," she whispers.

"Who do we need to see?" he asks me.

"Do they have a special officer who deals with sexual assault?" I ask carefully.

Bryce's mouth hardens into a thin line. "They do," he responds tightly. He leads us to the information desk and checks in with the officer on duty. The officer retreats down a long hall and Bryce turns back to us. "It'll just be a minute."

As promised, little time passes and a slender Latina officer emerges with the desk officer. She approaches us.

"Natalie," Bryce greets her. She nods in acknowledgement. "Heather, this is Officer Natalie Ramirez. She's going to take your statement. Do you want Sera or I to come with you?"

Officer Ramirez gives Heather a warm smile. Heather glances sidelong at me. "I'd like to go by myself, please," she replies, just above a whisper.

I give her hand one last squeeze and let her go. "We'll be right here waiting, okay?" I assure her.

She nods and lets Officer Ramirez lead her away. And I'm left wondering what she left out of her story that she didn't want me hearing when she gave her statement.

As soon as I'm sure she's gone, I collapse into the reception room chair behind me, burying my face in my hands. Bryce sits next to me and rubs my back soothingly for a minute while I collect myself.

"Heather quit a month ago. Right after we moved to Sutton Developments. Wouldn't say why," I explain.

"Let me guess. Daniel Sutton?" he asks. I shoot Bryce a shocked look. He shakes his head and leans back in his chair. "You told me he threatened you. You must have known I'd investigate the guy."

I understand the implication immediately. "He's done this before?" I ask incredulously. I'm so shocked that my voice is barely audible.

"He's been accused of sexual harassment before, yes," Bryce admits. "But the case was ultimately dropped. If you think for one second that I'd let you keep working with someone who was convicted of sexual misconduct, you obviously don't know me very well."

I'm so overwhelmed, I don't even bother scolding him for thinking he could "let" me do anything.

"I need to share something with Officer Ramirez when they're done," I say.

Bryce is so silent I have to glance up at him to see if he's heard me. And when I do I can tell he absolutely has. His gorgeous face is contorted into an unrecognizable mask of cold fury.

"Explain, please," he hisses.

"He didn't touch me," I assure him, resting my hand on his arm. "The things he said to Heather were very similar to things he said to me. Threats he made. If it could help them establish a pattern or lend weight to her story, I want to go on record."

Bryce's hand clamps over mine, almost to the point of pain. "Tell me what he said," he demands.

I'm torn. If I tell him, I know he'll be furious. Both at what Daniel said and for my downplaying it in the first place. But if I go on record, he'll probably find out anyway.

"He told me to stay out of his way or I'd regret it. And then he said if I told anyone he threatened me, he'd tell them I came on to him and he rejected me, so it's just sour grapes. And then it would be my word against his," I pause, trying to remember what other venom he'd spewed to make me slap him. "And he knew about me and Alessandro. He said everyone knew that we were fucking, so nobody would believe I wasn't trying to fuck him too. I slapped him for that."

Bryce gives a small laugh. "That's my girl," he murmurs.

Heat flushes my cheeks, and I try to ignore it. "He promised to ruin me. And to beat me if I told on him," I conclude.

Bryce runs a hand over his hair, but his fury has abated, and he's not reacting as poorly as I thought he would. "We'll get Heather somewhere safe until they're able to press charges," Bryce assures me. "If Heather's story has those same elements, along with your statement and the original charges, I think they'll have what they need."

I consider that for a moment. "What if Heather doesn't want to press charges? What if Daniel won't admit to anything? It's been a month, I'm sure there's no physical evidence left," I protest.

"The state will probably do it anyway. Anyone who sees how scared that girl is will know the truth," he points out.

I find a small relief in that, until something else occurs to me. "What about me, Bryce? Is it safe for me to go back to work tomorrow? I'm not even sure I can, knowing what I know," I say, shuddering.

"He won't have any idea you're involved," Bryce replies. "But I, for one, am not really thrilled about the prospect of you being near that guy. Though I don't think you're in any immediate danger. And I'm always a phone call away."

I look at Bryce as the truth of his words sink deep into me. Bryce *is* always a phone call away. Even when we weren't talking, I think I knew that. That he'd always be there for me. We've been through so much together, it's hard to imagine it any other way now. It pains me in a way I can't quite name, until it clicks. *If only I could say the same for Alessandro.*

Bryce's eyebrows shoot up, and I realize I must have actually said the words. I can feel my face flush again. "I didn't mean to say that out loud."

"He's not answering your calls?" Bryce asks resignedly.

I shake my head. "I don't even have a phone number for him. I tried to email him, but he didn't respond. I thought about trying to find him," I admit.

"As in, going to Italy?" he asks. I nod, embarrassed by how stupid it must sound to him. "I don't think that's a good idea."

"Me, neither," I sigh. "But it's been a month and I'm beyond worried. I know it would be pointless at best, dangerous at worst. But what else am I supposed to do? Maybe it'd be a good excuse to take off work, so I don't have to deal with Daniel."

Bryce runs a hand jerkily over his hair. "I'll make a call," he finally says. "I'll see if I can get a bead on him." The sorrow and gratitude that washes over me causes a lump to form in my throat. Sorrow for putting Bryce through this. Gratitude for answers. Or the hope of answers. Finally.

"Thank you," I breathe. "I feel like I've been hanging over a precipice this whole time."

He gives me a look that tells me it explains a lot. "You're welcome," he replies. "Besides, you don't want to leave in case Heather needs you. And you might want to clue Charles Sutton in on what his son has been getting into."

I realize he's right. And I wonder whether Charles will be surprised. There's only one way to find out.

FIFTEEN

I insist on seeing Charles first thing on Wednesday morning. Perplexed, he cancels a call and sees me into his office, shutting the door behind us. I have a brief moment of pause at the act but am almost immediately embarrassed at the thought. Charles has been nothing but good to me. It's Daniel who's the monster.

"What can I do for you this morning?" Charles opens, looking at me kindly and with concern from behind his desk. His large hands are folded loosely over his dark grey suit jacket in a gesture of complete comfort and trust.

I feel bad for the hell I'm about to unleash. "I need to tell you something," I start. "And it needs to be kept in complete confidence."

Charles frowns and leans forward. "I would hope by now you know you can trust me," he says sternly.

"I do, but this is different. I considered asking someone from HR to join us as well, but I wanted to give you this news first," I explain.

His eyebrows shoot up. "You have my word," he agrees solemnly.

I take a deep breath and prepare to just say it. Like me, I know Charles isn't one for suspense or beating around the bush. "Do you remember the young woman who used to work for me who quit right after we moved?" Charles nods, acknowledging that he recalls. "Last night she filed sexual assault charges against Daniel. It's the reason she quit."

Whatever he was expecting, it clearly wasn't that.

"She claims my son sexually assaulted her?" He is incredulous.

"He groomed her, after a fashion. Then raped her in his office. Then threatened her."

Charles steeples his fingers under his nose, shaking his head and clearly deeply troubled. "And I take it that you believe her?" he asks.

"Without a doubt," I reply emphatically. "He made similar threats to me."

Charles looks up, very surprised now. "And what exactly is it that you would like me to do, Sera?" he asks, stone-faced.

"I…" I stutter and stop. I'm at a loss. It's almost a nonresponse, though I'm not sure what I expected. "I just thought you should know. The police will likely be questioning him shortly. And I intend to go to HR after this to provide them with the same information. But I wanted to tell you first."

Charles leans back in his chair, grim faced. "If you had come to me right away, I would have told you to do exactly that. This is not the first time something like this has happened. But the other times there were always questions. Uncertainties. And it was nothing quite as serious as this."

I don't miss that he said *times*. As in more than once. But that's not my biggest issue with his response.

"You won't take the word of my employee that he raped her, but you'll trust mine that he threatened me?" I ask heatedly. I don't know if I should be flattered or disgusted, but I'm leaning heavily toward the latter.

"I didn't mean that at all," he responds. "This young woman's allegation is an escalation from past events. And a very serious one. But since I don't know her at all, yes, your experience and assessment of the situation lends a great deal of weight to her claim. But I would have believed your story with or without hers." Charles pauses for a moment, looking seriously conflicted about whatever he plans to say next.

"I didn't intend to put you in a position to explain or defend his actions," I offer. "And, ultimately, the police will take it from here. There is truly nothing more you need to say."

Charles dips his head in acknowledgement. "Nonetheless, I want you to know that I love my son. But as his father, I am aware of his shortcomings. Perhaps more acutely than anyone. Part of what has made him so successful is his aggressive tendencies. But throughout his life that same quality has also gotten him into a great deal of trouble. It is up to him to deal with the consequences of his actions and choices. I think he has known and resented that I have no tolerance for his inadequacies for some time. So I believe it will come as no surprise to him when I make no move to shield him from whatever is to come."

"Meaning?" I press.

"I have long since decided that Daniel will not be my successor," Charles replies matter-of-factly. "It's in large part why I decided to take you on. I see that potential in you. I haven't openly shared that decision with anyone until now. And I trust that you will keep *that* in confidence." He looks at me pointedly over his steepled fingertips.

"Yes, sir," I agree. I had suspected something along those lines, but nothing of the magnitude to which he just admitted.

Bryce was right: Charles has been grooming me to take over his empire. And I'm sure even though he didn't know for sure, Daniel sensed the threat. His actions toward me certainly speak to that.

"Thank you," Charles replies softly. "Then, if we're done here, I believe you have something to discuss with Mrs. Harris in human resources. I'd prefer that she was prepared before law enforcement arrives."

I nod, rising. "I appreciate your response to all of this. Truly," I tell him sincerely.

Charles smiles pensively, and I turn and leave before my emotions get the better of me.

∽

By lunchtime Daniel has been suspended pending internal investigation and sent home. It's an obvious move to get him out of the building so nobody sees the cops bringing him in for questioning. But, through Bryce, I know that that's exactly what happens on Wednesday afternoon. Thankfully, Heather was also able to relocate to stay with family for her safety, and Officer Ramirez and Bryce helped her get a restraining order started for added protection. It leaves me nervous and wondering where my added protection is.

I know I can call Bryce if I need to, but between helping me with Heather and managing the transition to full responsibility for Hoyt Corporate Services, not to mention still mourning the loss of his father, I can hear in his voice how stretched thin he is. So I swallow my fears, pretend everything is fine, and return to work on Thursday like nothing has happened.

But the atmosphere at work is no better than before Daniel was suspended. The flurry of office gossip is all off-mark, as the only three people still at the company who know the true story — Charles, Brooklyn Harris, and myself — sure as hell aren't going to share what's really going on. To evade conversation about it, I must isolate myself all day, and by quitting time I'm ready for some hard alcohol from the strain of it all.

But with Allie out of commission, Bryce overtaxed, and Alessandro still far away and unreachable, I can't think of anyone to call. And drinking alone just seems too sad. I'm scrolling through my address book when I'm reminded that Emily had programmed her number in at the wake and told me to call her sometime to get together. And it actually seems like a pretty perfect solution.

∽

"I'm so glad you were available," I say to Emily, sipping my margarita.

She smiles fondly at me from across the table. "I'm glad you called," she admits. "I was going to check on you soon anyway."

"That seems a little backward. I should be the one checking on you, considering," I reply.

Emily shrugs. "Thanks, but I'll be all right," she assures me. I give her a disbelieving look. "Really. I think at some point it might hit me hard, but I'm strangely okay right now."

"Well, that's good?" I hazard. She chuckles. "So what made you think you needed to check in on me?"

Emily gives me a pointed look. "Oh, you know, the short, blond bitch who stomped all over my brother's heart back to torture him by scaring off the best thing that's ever happened to him?" she replies glibly.

As someone who doesn't usually embarrass easily, I find myself blushing an awful lot these days. And I wonder how much Emily knows about the complicated situation with Alessandro, Bryce, and me. And how much she has guessed about my feelings for her brother. But mostly I can't even process her referring to me as the best thing that's ever happened to Bryce. Because how things have unfolded between us has been one of the most challenging situations of my life. And that's saying something.

"Bryce can take care of himself," I mumble. "And I'm going to need empirical proof that I've done anything but take advantage of his giving nature."

"Well, I'll give him that now," Emily admits. "But he used to be a huge doormat. Especially where Madison was concerned. Lately, though, not so much. Not even for you. But meeting you brought him out of the epic funk he was in for months. He was back to his normal, chipper self for a while there."

"And now he's not, also thanks to me," I sigh. I take a big gulp of my drink and find Emily looking sympathetically at me. "But I'm kind of relieved to hear his mood swings are an established pattern. I thought I broke him."

Emily laughs loudly. "Oh, honey, no," she chortles. "I think he's finally exactly where he needs to be."

"You think? It's not too much? His taking over your dad's company? He's still so young," I respond, concerned.

"He'll manage," she assures me. "I meant he's finally in the right headspace. Neither doormat nor asshole. I know you guys weren't talking for a while, but when he went full asshole on you it took him a couple weeks to realize what a jerk he was being. To everyone, by the way, not just you."

"Yeesh. I'm so sorry for unleashing that," I reply, cringing.

She waves a hand dismissively. "In case you hadn't figured it out, that was *not* your fault. A lot of things pushed him to that point. But he needed to get there, and then get through it. And he'll get through this too, but I'm finally seeing signs that he's on the right path," she says.

"Good. I want him to be happy," I respond. I stare down into my drink, blinking back tears.

"You make him happy," she informs me gently. I snort derisively. "Think what you want. But why else can't he stay away from you?"

"I don't think he wants that kind of relationship with me anymore," I reply. Voicing it, I realize that I feel disappointed. "But it's better that way. Things are complicated for me right now too."

Emily cocks her head to the side. "Tell me about it," she replies, taking a sip of her Long Island iced tea.

So I do. We talk for hours, and it feels good to get it all off my chest. And through it I manage to learn a bit about her too. When I head home around ten, while it may be my decently drunk state, I feel lighter. And like I have a new friend.

❧

I WAKE, STILL MILDLY BUZZED, IN THE DEEPEST DARK OF NIGHT TO A cacophony of sound. I have trouble functioning for a moment, unsure of what hell has broken loose in my condo. When I finally come to enough to connect that my security system is alerting me of an intruder, I bolt upright in bed, instantly terrified. I reach under the bed for the baseball bat I keep there and clutch its grip tightly with both hands as I slither out from under the covers.

My eyes flit to the nightstand and note the absence of my phone. *Shit.* I left it on the kitchen counter when I got home last night, tipsy as I was. The closest security panel is in the hall at the top of the stairs. It will tell me where the breach was. But the alarm also automatically alerts building security and the police, so after a moment of frantic thought I opt to stay where I am.

Crouched behind the bed with my back to the wall, my brain chaotically races through the possibilities. But the only viable explanation I can dredge up is Daniel. My heart hammers loudly in my chest as the minutes crawl by and the alarm continues to blare. But nothing else.

Finally, the alarm stops, and I hear feet pounding up the stairs.

A voice shouts from the hallway. "Ms. Evans, building security!"

I chew my lip for a moment. If they managed to turn off the alarm, they must be legitimate, I reason. I creep to the door and peek out. The man is indeed wearing the building's security officer uniform, and his gun is drawn and pointed at the floor. I open the door wider.

"I'm here," I call. "Is it safe?"

His head swings toward me and he holsters his gun. "Yes, ma'am," he affirms.

I step out of the bedroom, still clinging to the bat. His eyes drop to it and he instinctively rests a hand on his gun. I quickly drop the bat to my feet. A uniformed police officer appears at the top of the stairs.

"Downstairs is clear," he relays to the security guard. He notices me in my oversized shirt. "Ma'am, if you'd like to get dressed and come downstairs, we can talk."

I nod meekly and duck back into my room to change as the security guard checks the other bedrooms.

When I descend the stairs a few minutes later, the two men are standing in the entryway talking. I approach carefully, waiting for a break in their conversation, but they stop talking when the security guard notices me.

"Ms. Evans, I'm Security Officer Bridges. I'm sorry to inform you that someone did break in through your front door tonight. We still aren't sure how they escaped, but we're checking the security footage now," he assures me.

"Were they gone when you got here?" I ask, wrapping my grey shawl tightly around me.

"Affirmative," Officer Bridges replies. "You will need to meet with our security chief tomorrow to review the situation."

I nod in understanding. With the adrenaline finally wearing off, fear starts to settle in. And I'm putting all my effort into controlling the shaking that is starting to rip through my body.

"Ma'am, your door will need to be replaced," the police officer notes. "It's probably best if you stay somewhere else tonight, or until you can get it fixed. Is there anyone you can stay with? Or can we escort you to a hotel?"

"She can stay with me," a deep voice says from the door.

I whirl around to see Bryce towering in the doorway, in sweats and a T-shirt, looking like he just fought a bear. He's out of breath, with a crazed look in his eye, and his hair and clothes are disheveled. The second he lays eyes on me, he strides into the room and pulls me into his arms. I gratefully embrace him, burying my face in his broad chest, inhaling his familiar, comforting scent.

Bryce extends a hand to the police officer, and it's clear that they know each other. "Jack," he says to the man. "Good to see you."

Officer Jack shakes Bryce's hand. "You too, Bryce." Officer Jack looks at me. "Looks like you're in good hands."

I nod gratefully. "Thank you for your help, officer," I reply.

"We'll be in touch tomorrow," Security Officer Bridges assures me. "I'm terribly sorry about this, ma'am."

"Thank you," I respond. "It could have ended much worse if it wasn't for you."

He gives me a small smile. "Just doing my job." He looks up at Bryce. "Take care of her."

Bryce squeezes me tighter. "I will. Thank you," Bryce responds.

The officers leave, closing the door. And I can see the broken frame and lock rendering it useless. I bury my face back in Bryce's chest and choke back a sob. He rubs my back gently.

"You have no idea how relieved I am that you're okay," he murmurs into my hair. I look up into his face. He looks exhausted and scared, and it pushes me closer to falling apart to see him upset.

"How did you even know?" I ask, confused. He strokes my cheek with his thumb and smiles.

"The alarm company notified me when you didn't respond. I'm still listed as your emergency contact," he explains.

"Well, thank god for that," I reply.

As his expression softens and my immediate terror recedes, I become painfully aware that we're still locked in a tight embrace, staring ardently into each other's eyes. And that I'm still tipsy enough that I don't have full control over my thoughts. And they're definitely headed down a path that ends in rejection. I make to push away from Bryce and he frowns, pulling me closer and dropping his face closer to mine, inhaling deeply.

"Have you been drinking?" he asks.

"What time is it?" I respond. He gives me a funny look.

"Almost two a.m."

"Not today, I haven't." I smile innocently up at him. "I take it you haven't talked to your sister recently."

Now he really looks confused. "Not since yesterday afternoon. What does that have to do with anything?"

I smile cryptically in response. Something tells me he wouldn't appreciate our talking about him.

"I'm going to go pack a few things," I say, dodging the question. "I'll be right back."

I make a quick exit before he can press any further. And once I'm upstairs I chug the water next to my bed. Time to finish sobering up fast. I don't want to push this night from awful to the worst night of my life by following up a breaking-and-entering situation with drunkenly pursuing and being rejected by a man who is likely back with his ridiculously gorgeous ex-girlfriend.

I sigh heavily as I stuff clothes into a bag. When Bryce appeared and put me under his protection, I was so relieved. But as the reality of the situation sets in, I realize how awkward this is going to be. Because just as I'm sure he's fallen out of love with me, I think I may be doing exactly the opposite.

SIXTEEN

I put on my game face as I descend the stairs, my small pack slung over one shoulder. I find Bryce crouched, examining the door. He runs a finger over the doorjamb and shakes his head.

"This is pretty amateur stuff," he mumbles. "Looks like they just used a crowbar to open it."

"So much for high-tech security," I grumble.

He stands, wiping his hands on his sweatpants. "Hey, that high-tech security saved your ass," he reminds me. He looks me up and down and gently tugs the pack off my shoulder. "Come on, let's get you back to bed." He tucks me under his arm and together we make our way to his place.

I'm quiet the whole way, half trying to make my tired brain absorb the events of the evening, half trying to stay awake. But when we get to Bryce's place, I fail epically at the latter. The last thing I remember is slumping against Bryce in the hallway before everything goes dark.

⌇

I'M WOKEN AROUND SEVEN BY BRYCE'S WEIGHT SETTLING ONTO THE BED. I open one eye slowly, blinking against the daylight.

"Good morning, sunshine," he teases me. "I have to go in a minute."

He's still dressing in all black and looks about as rested as I feel. In other words, hardly at all. I instantly feel horrible for adding to his already full plate.

I sit up groggily and take in my surroundings. It's clearly a guest bedroom and, thankfully, I appear to still be fully dressed in my leggings and shawl, with just my shoes removed and set on the floor beside the bed.

I look back to Bryce, who is regarding me tolerantly as I regain functionality.

"Thanks for letting me stay," I say. "I'll get out of your hair as soon as I can."

He smiles dimly. "Stay as long as you'd like," he assures me. "There's coffee in the kitchen. Just lock up on your way out."

I nod in understanding, biting back all the things I really want to say to him as the reality of what almost happened hit me. And how sharply it's thrown into contrast what's important to me. Who is important. But Bryce rises from the bed before I can even put it all to words.

"Bryce?" I call after him.

He stops in the doorway and looks back at me questioningly. I scramble off the bed and hurry to wrap my arms around him before he leaves. I try to throw all my unspeakable emotions into the gesture, not trusting myself to give a proper voice to them now. He hesitates before squeezing me back, and I let go more quickly than I'd planned, suddenly very self-conscious.

"See ya, Sera."

"See ya, Bryce."

I slump back onto the bed as soon as I hear the front door close. Tears start to flow unreservedly down my face. It's all too much. Again.

When I've collected myself, I call in to take a personal day. I explain the break-in to Brooklyn, downplaying the danger. But I want her to know, both so my absence isn't unexplained and in case it's relevant later. In case it was Daniel, or someone acting on his behalf. I shudder lightly at the thought and gather my things to head home. It's time to find out what happened.

∽

"There," the day security officer, Katlyn Ferris, points at the screen. "That's where our external feed first picks them up."

I watch the hatted, gloved figure deftly keep their face hidden from the camera as they enter the building. Officer Ferris taps a few keys and the lobby feed picks up, following their progress. The intruder shoots across the lobby suddenly, yanking the stairwell door open and disappearing. A few more taps. "And fifteen minutes later." A third camera feed picks up, in the hall on my floor. My door is farthest from the camera, but you can see the figure step close to the door and, with quick movements and minimal noise, slip a crowbar from inside their garments and expertly pop the door open in seconds.

The chief guard, a stern, fit Englishman in his sixties named Bernard Shaw, looks on grimly as the figure dashes back to the stairwell the moment the alarm sounds.

"That will do," he instructs Officer Ferris, who kills the feed. Bernard turns to me primly. "The perpetrator then waited at the bottom of the stairs until the coast was clear and walked right out the front door. Not a single camera captured their face."

I slump into the uncomfortable metal chair in the security office. "So we have nothing?" I ask dully.

Officer Ferris looks nervously at her boss. "Not exactly," she hedges. "There are several things the feeds tell us. This person knew where the cameras were. They also knew the parts of the lobby that were more visible from the front desk. So they'd been observing the building or were given insider knowledge. And, finally, they were unaware that there would be additional security once they entered your unit. Which leads me to believe that it is unlikely that they had inside help. Because any of our security officers would have known that."

"Why did they take the stairs?" I ask.

Mr. Shaw peers at me over his spectacles. "To get to the elevators you must pass the reception desk and security office. The stairs are closer to the door and, while visible from both of those vantage points, they are less obvious and easier to navigate to," he explains. "We will continue to review our past feeds to see if there is any unusual activity. But for now, we will question anyone who might have seen this person and review the security tapes. It is highly unlikely that they will attempt to gain access to your condominium again."

It should make me feel better, but somehow I'm still uneasy. I rub my eyes, the exhaustion catching up with me. "When will the door be fixed?"

"It's being done as we speak. You are free to reenter at any time," Mr. Shaw offers. I nod dully and switch to rubbing the back of my neck.

"Thank you," I murmur, rising from the chair. "Please keep me informed."

"Of course, madam," he responds. "And if there is anything else we can do, please let me know."

I shoulder my pack and head home. As the elevator carries me back to the scene of the crime, the familiar terror of feeling unsafe creeps through me. But this time the danger happened in my own home. That's a little harder to run from.

I announce myself to the workman at the door and he lets me pass. I walk to the window wall and perch on the edge of my favorite chair, not comfortable enough to sink into its depths quite yet. In fact, having my back to the door is so nerve-racking that I switch to sitting on the floor, leaning against the windows. The view is spectacular, but my slight fear of heights kicks in if I dare to look down for too long. Instead, I stare at the horizon, trying to suppress the overwhelming panic and appreciate the beauty of the late-summer day.

But I feel baseless. Like home is no longer home. This condo was a symbol of my achievement, a well-earned indulgence so that I could enjoy and appreciate the fruits of my labor. And despite the tumultuous months past, including the events of the previous evening, I don't want to leave it. But I don't want to be alone, either.

For a moment I let myself imagine being a normal girl. In love with a normal boy. With normal lives. We could live together. Make each other breakfast. Make love on every surface of this spacious abode. Just be. Happy and safe. It seems like too much to ask. But what scares me the most is that, a few months ago I would have wanted all that with Alessandro. But now, even if he'd stayed, I know that there was only a fleeting time with him that things were simple and easy. Most of the time it has just been so *hard*. And this, well, whatever we are now, is the most difficult of all. Because I don't know if we're even still anything to each other. Or where he is. If he's okay. And if he is, why he hasn't contacted me in more than a month.

And I realize I've spent more of our short relationship wondering where we stand than not. When all I need is someone here, now, ready to comfort me in my time of need. And I know the one person who has been there for me through all of this, who I'm just starting to realize is everything I need, everything I want .... I shake my head, willing myself out of my pity party. It's too late. I realized it too late.

My phone rings, breaking the silence around me. Bryce's name flashes on my phone's screen.

"I was just thinking about you," I say after I answer the call. I bite my lip, wishing the words back into my mouth.

"Oh? Good things, I hope," Bryce's deep voice responds. He sounds amused.

"The best. Thank you again for letting me stay last night," I say softly.

"Anytime. What's the sitrep on our perp?" Bryce asks.

I chuckle and resist the urge to tease him about his language, instead relaying what I know. He chews on it thoughtfully.

"It definitely doesn't sound random. And with the timing..." he begins contemplatively.

"I know," I agree. "Daniel. It was my first thought too."

"Well, maybe. But it sounds like this person did quite a bit of recon prior to the fact. And while you weren't on the best terms with Daniel, it doesn't sound like there was anything serious enough to warrant that kind of behavior from him. Besides, if Daniel wanted to attack you, he seems like the kind of guy who would do it himself. And on his own turf."

"Huh," I respond. "I hadn't thought about that. Then who?"

"Didn't you say your half-brother didn't seem happy about your being back in your father's and his life?" he asks.

"Hunter? I seriously doubt—"

"You don't know him at all, Sera," Bryce interjects. "The kid has anger issues." The implication of his statement sinks in instantly.

"Damnit, Bryce, do you investigate everyone even remotely connected to me?" I demand.

His low chuckle sounds over the line. "I can't help it," he replies winningly. "Force of habit."

"Isn't that like an abuse of your position or something?" I pout.

"I promise I only use my powers for good," he teases back. "Speaking of which. Tomorrow. I'm picking you up at eight."

"In the morning?" I ask.

"Yes. Is that a problem?" he replies archly.

"I've been traumatized. I think I need to sleep in," I whine. I meant it to sound serious and pitiful, but it's hard to hide the smile in my voice.

"That is letting you sleep in," he says.

"What the hell time do you get up on a Saturday?" I demand jokingly.

"I'm up at five every day, Sera. I work out. I have breakfast. Take a shower. By eight my morning is practically half over," he explains patiently.

The words *take a shower* ring through my head, and the memory of Bryce in a towel drifts through my mind again.

"Fine," I concede. "I'll see you at eight."

"Good." I can hear the triumphant smile in his voice. "Wear something you can move in."

∾

"When you said I should wear something I can move in, this isn't what I thought you had in mind," I tell Bryce nervously as we walk through the gym.

While I would normally enjoy the eye candy, the bevy of tall, insanely muscled men covered in tattoos surrounding us is a little intimidating. Not to mention their open ogling that is definitely making me regret my choice of cute blue-and-green fitted capri yoga pants with a matched tank bra.

I wrap my arms self-consciously around the sliver of soft midsection showing, wishing I'd thought to throw a T-shirt or light hoodie on over the tank. Bryce smirks at me and continues to lead me through the machines to one of a few small rooms in the back of the gym.

The room we enter is bare but for the mirrors covering the longest wall opposite the door and the thick, black mats on the floor. I stop in the middle of the room, anxiously awaiting whatever Bryce has planned. He squares off opposite me, hands on his hips. I size him up in his black basketball shorts and black oversized sleeveless shirt. He's more distractingly gorgeous than any man here, which is saying something.

"What is this place?" I ask. "Why do all these guys look like ridiculously good-looking gang members?"

Bryce laughs, and his smile lights up a small, forgotten part of my heart. It's been a long time since I've seen him smile like that. It's almost his patented sunshine smile. I like it more than I care to admit to myself.

"If by 'gang' you mean 'military,' then yes, they're gang members," he replies. "I guess the Navy can be a *little* like a gang." He's still grinning inanely at me, and I can't help but laugh. He looks like a little kid.

"Geez, Bryce, I didn't take you for the type to fall in with such a rough crowd," I tease. Bryce raises an eyebrow and gives me a look of disbelief. "What? What did I say?"

"Nothing, I just thought you knew," he replies. "But then, maybe I never specifically told you."

"Told me what?" I ask, confused.

"I was a SEAL. Did you seriously not know that? It's on my bio on the company website, and there are pictures and stuff all over my apartment," he says. Then after a moment, he teasingly continues, "Geez, Evans, for a smart chick you're not very observant."

I blush furiously. I did *not* know that. But it explains a lot.

"Why don't you talk about it more?" I deflect.

He shrugs. "It was a long time ago."

"You're only thirty-four, Bryce — it couldn't have been that long ago."

"It feels like a long time ago," he amends. He levels a look at me that says this part of the conversation is over. "In any case, I brought you here to teach you the basics of self-defense."

Oh. OH. "That sounds like a really good idea," I admit. "Considering the only self-defense I've learned is from movies."

He nods, clearly unsurprised by the information. "The biggest thing they get wrong is *why* you react," he says. "You're not trying to be a hero here and lay the bad guy out on his ass so you can fire witty remarks at him until the police magically show up. Be aware of your surroundings, try not to get in a place where there isn't someone around. But if you do, and you're attacked, assume help isn't coming — so your objective should always be to get away. You may not be a small woman, but most men are going to have the advantage over you. Even if they're shorter or skinnier or much older, they're likely stronger. So don't get cocky and think you can take someone on. Do what you need to do to run. And whenever you see that opening, take it."

I nod. "So are you going to attack me a bunch now?" I ask hesitantly. I must look scared because Bryce laughs.

"Yes, Sera, that's exactly what I'm going to do." He grins maniacally at me. The bastard is going to enjoy this. "But I'm going to teach you a few things first."

"Thank god," I breathe. "All right, Yoda, let's do this."

He shows me how to hold my arms up in front of me when threatened so I can use them to strike or deflect. Then he shows me how to kick effectively, standing or from the ground. I'm feeling pretty confident until he starts the next part.

"This time you can only learn by doing. I'm going to teach you how to use the momentum of someone pushing or pulling you against them."

"Do I get to flip you over?" I ask excitedly.

He rolls his eyes. "Lord, no," he scoffs. "Don't ever try that. You're likely to seriously hurt yourself. Think simpler — move *with* your attacker to land a punch or kick that will help you break free." I give him a completely confused look. "I know. I just have to show you."

"And how exactly are you going to do that?" I ask meekly. I'm not frail by any stretch, but at around a hundred and sixty pounds I'm guessing Bryce easily has eighty or more pounds on me. Of pure muscle. Not to mention a good seven inches of height.

Bryce loosens his posture and stands in front of me. "Don't worry, I'll tell you what I'm going to do before I do it. And I'll go easy at first until you get the hang of it, okay?"

"Okay," I squeak nervously.

But he dives in anyway despite my obvious hesitation. "Now, if I go to grab you with one hand," Bryce reaches his left arm up slowly and grabs my right shoulder gently, "you lean into the motion on that side." I roll my shoulder back. "And lash out with the heel of your other hand like I showed you before." I swing my left palm up to meet his nose. "Good. Again."

We repeat the motion several times, faster each time. Then we switch to the other side and do the same. Bryce takes me through a full series of face-to-face grabs with various combinations. And by the end, I'm feeling much less vulnerable than the break-in of a couple nights ago had left me.

"Good, you're really getting it," he says. "You're just going to have to practice. A lot. Until it's instinct."

I give him a wary look. "You're not going to randomly start grabbing me, are you?" I ask.

A shit-eating grin breaks across his face. "Not unless you want me to," he replies huskily, and I blush. He clears his throat and reverts to teacher mode. "Let's try grabs from behind."

He turns me around gently and tucks me against his body, wrapping his arms around my front. He starts demonstrating the various ways someone could pull my body, but his mouth is at my ear, his breath hot on my neck and, pressed up against him this way I'm suddenly finding it very hard to concentrate. The feeling of his hard body against my back reminds me of the almost-kisses. And how long it's been since I've had so much contact with someone.

"So you want to lean to one side, hook your leg around to pull theirs out from under them." He nudges my right leg with his until I wrap my foot behind his knee. "Then strike backward with the opposite arm."

It takes all my effort to pull myself back to the present moment and nudge my elbow into his stomach. "Like this?" I ask.

"No. With your arms pinned you don't have any distance to put force into swinging your elbow," he explains. He releases his left arm and straightens mine out, flattening my hand so the heel of my palm is pointed backward, and slowly swings my arm to his crotch until it's a hair from touching his shorts. "Like that. Hit them in the groin."

And I don't know who shifts — him or me, but my hand grazes him through the fabric. His sharp intake of breath tells me that I touched exactly what I thought I did. The thought sends a flush of heat through me, and I can't help myself — I turn my head to look back up at him. His eyes meet mine and my breath catches in my throat. I slowly turn myself in his arms until I'm facing him.

"They're definitely going to be holding you too tightly to do that," he murmurs hoarsely, staring down into my eyes.

Looking up into his dancing blue eyes, I'm suddenly not sure I can make a move. I tentatively place a hand on his chest, feeling the hard muscle through his thin shirt. The arm that had been holding me in front of him is now wrapped around my waist. But Bryce's expression closes abruptly, and he folds his hand over mine and gently removes it from his chest while stepping back.

"I think that's enough for today," he declares huskily. He looks uncomfortable and turns away.

A cold tide of rejection washes any remaining heat from my body. "Bryce, I'm sorry, I didn't mean to…" I start, but he turns back around, raising a hand to stop me.

"Don't," he commands.

I bite my lip to hold back a small, strangled cry that is trying to break free. Tears sting the back of my eyes. Bryce, seeing my distress, crosses the short distance he'd put between us. He grasps my chin, titling my head up to look into my eyes.

"Stop. Whatever it is you're beating yourself up for right now," he insists. He draws a deep breath before he continues, his voice softened considerably. "You've been through a lot lately. And you're vulnerable right now." He pauses, and I can tell he's struggling with how to say what he wants to say next. Finally, his eyes looking searchingly into mine, he continues, "It seems like ever since we met you've been torn in pieces. If you choose me, I want it to be with all of you. I won't settle for anything less."

His words tug at the edge of my reason. In this moment, I want all of him. I want him to hold me until all my fears, uncertainties, and insecurities fall away and all that's left is us. But he's right. Until I can give him all of me, it's just not a fair thing to ask of him. I nod softly, and he drops his hand from my chin. He suppresses a sigh as I follow him quietly out of the room, more confused and defenseless than ever.

SEVENTEEN

I meet Allie as planned on Sunday at our favorite brunch spot. And the sight of her is so familiar and comforting it makes me want to cry. She stands outside the restaurant, nervously smoothing her peach tulle skirt and tugging at the hem of her white eyelet-lace sleeveless top. Her long, strawberry-blond hair has been carefully braided over one shoulder. The only trace of the ordeal she's been through is her green eyes — they have a dull look and are rimmed in red. But as soon as she sees me, they warm as her face breaks into a smile.

"Sera," she breathes, embracing me tightly. "It's so good to see you."

"I missed you," I reply, squeezing her back. I let her go, holding her at arm's length. "You look fantastic."

She blushes and waves a hand at me. "This old thing?" she jokes. We both laugh, and the sound warms me. "Let's do this. I'm starving."

If I didn't know better, I wouldn't think there was anything different about her. Pleased, I hold the door open and follow her in.

We make small talk about things like the weather and traffic. Once we're seated and have ordered ridiculous amounts of breakfast foods, I smile patiently at her, waiting for her cue to talk about anything more serious.

"If you're waiting for me to spill my guts, it's not gonna happen," she says quietly into her mimosa.

I huff a small laugh. "Whatever you want to talk about, Allie," I offer. "I'm just so fucking happy to see you, you don't even know."

She snorts. "Been boring without me?" she teases. The smile slides off my face and she raises an eyebrow. "You just went completely pale."

"A lot has happened," I admit. "But I'm sure you have enough on your plate."

"Please," she replies, rolling her eyes. "I promise I won't break. I could use the distraction from my own problems."

I eye her skeptically. "Are you sure? Because some of it's pretty serious," I say. "Well, most of it, actually."

She presses her lips together and sighs heavily. "I'm sure. I promise. We can talk about my issues when I'm ready. But for now, I would really like to not be treated like I'm made of glass," she insists.

I'm silent for a few moments, unsure of how to begin. "I can't even remember when to start," I admit.

Allie taps her fingers on the table while she thinks about that. "We'd finished moving to Sutton Developments." She pauses. "And Heather quit." Another pause. "And I think you were supposed to meet your brother?"

I blanch, realizing how long it's been since we've talked. Really talked. "Alessandro was in Italy, and I wasn't talking to Bryce," I recall. Allie nods. "God, that seems like a lifetime ago."

She eyes me quizzically as our food arrives. "It was just about a month, Sera," she replies flippantly. She dives into a stack of pancakes, talking through a mouthful. "What could you possibly have gotten into in that short a time?"

Suddenly, I'm not so hungry. So I talk instead. Slowly and carefully filling Allie in on everything that's happened. Carefully because I want to watch her reactions, to make sure I'm not overwhelming her, and taking small bites of food when I feel like she needs time to process.

As I relay it all, I realize how much it is, and I start to understand the tightness I didn't even notice in my chest until now. I start with the lunch that didn't happen and the brother who seemingly isn't ready to have anything to do with me. I'd almost forgotten that particular sting. Then I tell her how I stopped hearing from Alessandro and started talking to Bryce again, and how different he's been. Only to be followed by the passing of his father, and our growing closeness. I'm especially careful with those parts, though, telling her what happened but reserving how I feel about it all. But there's no fooling Allie.

"If this Madison chick hadn't showed up, do you think you two would've..." she stabs at the air with her fork and I can't help but laugh.

"No," I reply firmly. "That was not the time to go starting anything. We were still figuring out how to be around each other when his dad passed. I didn't want to make it worse."

"Were?" she asks shrewdly.

Damn. I forgot how sharp she is. I shrug, feigning nonchalance as I shove my last piece of bacon in my mouth.

"That was a week ago. A lot has happened," I reply after swallowing.

She stares at me incredulously. "You keep saying that. Out with it then," she prompts.

I chew on my lip anxiously, not sure how much to tell her about Heather.

"Come on, Sera, it's me. I know I've been struggling, but you're not going to damage me."

"You keep saying that," I joke. "But I'm not so sure."

She sighs heavily in response and sets down her fork. "Look," she starts seriously. "I get that what I went through, what I'm going through, is scary for the people who care about me. It's been *super* hard for David, and I'm trying to be patient with his doting on me constantly like I'm a fragile creature that needs shielding from this cruel world." Despite her claim, even I can hear the obvious impatience in her tone. "But I need to get back to life again. Real life. And I thought I could count on you, of all people, not to treat me like I need to be sheltered. It's my own problems I'm struggling with, not other people's. I *want* to hear that I'm not the only one who is going through things. That my problems aren't the end-all-be-all. Really."

I can't help but smirk. "Be careful what you wish for," I reply.

She levels an impatient look at me, and I laugh.

"Okay." So I tell her. All of it. About what really made Heather quit. About our time at the police station, and my conversation with Charles the next day. And about the middle-of-the-night break-in after a night of drinking that left me terrified and led to the ridiculously confusing self-defense training with Bryce.

Allie's frown deepens throughout, and when I'm done we both fall silent for a while. I take the opportunity to finish the last of my food.

"Who'd you go drinking with?" she finally asks. I'm taken aback by her question, and not just because it wasn't the part of my story I expected her to hone in on.

"Bryce's sister, Emily," I reply. Her brows knit together in a scowl. And I realize she's *jealous*. "I needed someone to talk to. Who *didn't* know me well. I just needed to get things off my chest. Loosen up a little." And while Allie looks a little reassured, she is still pouting a bit.

"So I haven't been replaced?" she asks.

I suppress a laugh, knowing that won't help. But I can't hide my smile, and it loosens her frown a bit. "Of *course* not," I reassure her. "Nobody could ever replace you."

"Good," she concedes. "Now, about you and Bryce."

I press my lips into a thin line and huff a breath out through my nose. "I'm just not sure how to feel right now," I admit. "I think there's too much going on. With the break-in. With not knowing what the hell is happening with Alessandro. Bryce is right. I'm in no place to trust my feelings right now."

Allie squints at me uncertainly. "You don't have to trust them, but don't pretend like you're not having them," she replies. "Don't go backward, Sera."

"I'm not going backward," I promise. "But I feel like I can't go forward, either. How can I possibly decide when everything is still so up in the air?"

"Nobody is asking you to," she points out. "You've never been one to fully commit to something without *knowing* it's the right thing. But that time will come, and then you'll know exactly what to do."

"You think?" I ask skeptically.

"Yes," she replies confidently. "Deciding to really be with someone with everything you've got is not exactly a fact-based decision. Which, let's face it, is more in your wheelhouse. But you've got good instincts, Sera. Pay attention. See things for what they are. Then listen to your heart. I don't think it's going to lead you astray."

"I hope not," I reply, unsure.

"Well, you can talk to me," she says. Then a grimace flashes across her face. "Or Emily."

I feign an unamused glare at her. "I think you'd like her," I respond. "No need to be catty."

She smiles innocently. "Who's being catty?" she asks.

I can't help but laugh. "It's good to have you back, Allie."

"It's good to be back, Sera."

And as we smile at each other across the table, a small ray of hope shines on my leaden heart.

∽

I CAN'T HELP BUT STILL BE ON EDGE THE FOLLOWING DAYS — AND NIGHTS — as being in my own home is no longer the refuge it once was, and I know it's going to be a long while before I feel safe again. I'm trying my hardest not to think about Alessandro, or Bryce, or Daniel. It's all just too much. So I trudge through, sinking into the monotony of work.

It's not until Wednesday morning when I enter my office that the routine is disturbed. As soon as I walk in, I know something is different. It takes me a few minutes of carefully scanning my desk, the cabinets, and the furniture to put my finger on it. And once I do, I realize it's because it's extremely subtle. Something I wouldn't have even noticed if I wasn't so anally retentive.

It's only a few small things — files that were perfectly aligned on the cabinet now askew, pencils and pens shuffled in their holder where they were separated, objects on my desk in slightly different positions. Someone has been rifling through my things. I carefully back out of my office and check in with Maggie.

"Hey, Mags," I greet her as she sets up for the morning.

She looks up, startled. "Everything all right, Sera?" she asks.

I smile, pleased that she's finally comfortable calling me by my first name. "I think so," I reply. "Did anyone go in my office after I left yesterday?"

She looks at me quizzically. "Not that I know of," she responds slowly. "Is anything missing?"

"I'm not sure, actually, I just had a funny feeling," I reply, brushing it off. "Never mind. Thanks, Maggie."

"Of course," she murmurs as I go back to my office.

I close the door behind me and settle carefully in to conduct a more thorough search to see if anything is, in fact, missing. But a few minutes later I come up empty handed. Nothing gone, everything just slightly off. I frown, unable to shake off the violated feeling.

I realize I'm probably just being overly sensitive. With the break-in last week, my radar is just on extra-high. It's almost certainly nothing. Maybe Charles looking for a client file or something similarly innocuous. I shake myself out of my reverie and hunker back down into my routine.

§

At home that night I find it hard to stay out of my own head, so I decide to make a few phone calls. First, I check in with Bryce, then Emily, then Allie. I leave my mother for last, knowing it will be a long call since we haven't spoken in some time. She is understandably angry that I didn't share everything sooner and concerned for my safety. I do my best to reassure her, but it sounds hollow even in my ears as, if I'm being honest, I'm still terrified myself.

By the time I'm done, I'm drained. But I still can't turn my brain off. I sit in my favorite chair, staring out into the summer night. Could my mystery prowler really be Hunter? While I tend to side with Bryce, that it just doesn't seem like Daniel's style, I find it hard to believe the brother I've never met would have such an extreme reaction toward me. But then, I never would have guessed Gabrielle Grayson would hatch an elaborate plan to destroy me and, ultimately, try to kill me. There's just no accounting for crazy sometimes.

And while I'm thankful for Bryce's involvement, it occurs to me that he has to deal with this sort of shit all. The. Time. And while I blindly didn't realize he had a military background, I should've realized it had taken extensive training to give him the skillset to do what he does. But the roll-with-it attitude is all Bryce. He's just the right combination of laid-back and assertive. And, as usually happens when I think about him for too long, I eventually am revisited by the mental image of him in that towel. I wonder briefly if my feelings for him aren't simply borne of sexual frustration. But then, that totally ignores the feelings I've always had for him and suppressed for other reasons. Or one sexy and charming Italian reason named Alessandro Giordano.

I sigh deeply and decide it's time to break out the wine. But before I can open a bottle, I'm suddenly reminded of the last time I indulged and was caught still tipsy in a dangerous situation. My stomach lurches and I decide against it. Instead, I head to bed where I rest fitfully, plagued by nightmares once more.

EIGHTEEN

On Thursday morning, Heather calls me. She wants to update me on the case but is reluctant to discuss it on the phone, so we arrange to meet after work at her parent's house in Mountlake Terrace.

I arrive at six as planned and find Heather waiting just inside the door — she manages to open it before I even knock. She ushers me in and nearly knocks me over with a tight hug.

"Nice to see you too, Heather," I tease her. She pulls back, swinging her long braids over her shoulder and smiling self-consciously.

"Thanks for coming," she replies. "My mom made dinner. I hope you're hungry." She leads me toward the dining room where an array of amazing aromas drift toward me.

"I'm suddenly ravenous," I reply appreciatively.

"Good, because my parents can't wait to meet you," she admits. She smiles mischievously. "And nothing makes my mom happier than feeding people. Just be warned — we're all huggers."

I laugh and shrug, following her into the dining room where a tall, athletic man in his fifties is setting the table. Heather introduces him as her father, Ronald. As warned, he uses my proffered hand to pull me into a tight hug.

"Thank you so much, for everything you've done for my daughter," he says fervently as he releases me.

I blush hotly, unsure of what he knows. "Heather is an amazing young woman. I wish I could do more for her," I hedge with a small smile.

"Nonsense," he replies as a curvy, ebony-skinned woman enters from the kitchen. If it weren't for the grey streaks in her hair I'd swear she was the same age as Heather. "Catherine, this is Serafina Evans." Catherine sets the roasting pan she was carrying on the table and hurries around to deliver my third hug in as many minutes. I can't help but laugh.

"Welcome, welcome," Catherine says excitedly.

"I certainly feel welcomed," I say, laughing still. Once I'm released and her parents are busy bringing food in, I catch Heather's eye and quietly ask to speak to her. She slips around the table and we turn away from her mother and father. "How much do they know?" I ask softly.

"It's okay," she assures me. "They know pretty much everything. The big stuff, anyway."

I nod, relieved. "And how are you doing?" I ask.

She pushes out a deep breath and shrugs. "I'm nervous, but…"

We are interrupted by Ronald declaring it's time to eat. We all slide into our chairs and the talk veers into more neutral areas. They want to know all about how I came to do what I do, and it comes out that Heather has apparently built me up to them as some sort of paragon of real estate success. It's very flattering but also fairly embarrassing. I play up Heather's strengths as much as I can to divert the conversation from myself. Thankfully, it mostly works, but by the end of the meal I can tell Heather is ready to take a break from the spotlight.

Ronald and Catherine assure us that everything is taken care of and encourage us to adjourn to the living room. We settle into a well-worn tan microfiber sofa, full and comfortable after the delicious meal.

"Your mom is a fantastic cook," I tell her, reiterating the compliment I'd just given Catherine.

"She is," Heather says absently.

"So are you going to tell me what's on your mind or what?" I tease her.

She smiles vaguely. "They've just issued an arrest warrant. They're bringing charges against Daniel," she says succinctly.

I gasp, my hands flying to my mouth. "Really? That's fantastic," I breathe. "Why don't you look happier?"

She shrugs lightly. "I guess I just feel like I've been looking over my shoulder ever since it happened. But even more so since last week," she admits. "And until they actually have him in custody, I'll just feel like every shadow is him, waiting to get me." She shakes her head.

"Hey," I say, catching her eye. "I completely understand. Believe me. Have you talked to anyone about this? A counselor maybe?" Heather nods that she has, and I release a breath.

"Yes, Officer Ramirez set me up with someone first thing," Heather replies. "And I don't want to keep being the victim of what he did, but it's going to take some time. And going to trial isn't going to be easy." She twists her fingers nervously in her braids.

"Do they need you to testify?" I ask, hoping there's some way to not make her face this all over again for the coming weeks.

"Need? I don't know. But I'm going to," she replies. "Moreover, I want to be there. I want to see justice done. I need to see it. But that doesn't mean it's going to be simple. They're preparing me, though, so I know what kind of questions I'll be asked. So I won't feel blindsided, at least."

I rest a reassuring hand on her knee. "I'll be there with you, if you need me," I respond.

Her answering smile is so bittersweet that my heart breaks for her. "Thank you," she says, brushing away a tear.

She changes the subject, and we talk about her new job for a while before I head home for the night. Of course, not before I receive a final round of hugs from every Irving. I'm a little jealous of the love in their house as I climb into my car, my heart warmed from having experienced it.

It's not until I'm merging onto the freeway that it occurs to me the same car has been behind me since shortly after I left their house. I try to shake off the feeling. Surely the freeway is a common enough destination that it's a coincidence. Though some of Heather's paranoia may have heightened my own, I can't help but remain concerned as it continues to stay a comfortable distance behind me for miles.

I switch lanes as a test, and it follows shortly after. The nervous feeling in my gut grows, and a few minutes later I switch lanes again, this time traversing two lanes. And it follows. My throat constricts, and I'm just about to use my car's Bluetooth to place a call when the car exits the freeway one exit before my own. I release the air in my lungs, my shoulders slumping in relief. Though I'm left feeling something like a suspicious nutjob as I finish the drive home.

∾

It's not until Friday morning, when Bryce calls to tell me that Daniel has been taken into custody, that I realize I forgot to call him and tell him about my dinner with Heather. After I explain that I've just been distracted, I can tell he's not mad, but the concern in his voice is unmistakable. And I silently wonder how many times this man is going to have to watch me come undone before he decides it's just not worth the drama. I reassure him that I'm fine and we make plans for the next day.

The tone in the office is somber as word spreads of Daniel's arrest. I decide to check on Charles that afternoon after some very tense and unusually short meetings. I knock on his door and wait for his response to enter.

"Yes?" he calls. I pop the door open. When he sees it's me, he gestures for me to come in. I close the door behind me and perch in one of the chairs opposite his desk.

"Hi," I say feebly. Charles huffs and gives me the smallest of smiles. "I'm so sorry, Charles. I can't imagine how hard this must be on you."

"It's no picnic," he agrees. "But I'm hard-pressed to feel put out. I'm still struggling to come to terms with my son's behavior."

"Has he admitted to anything?" I ask, curious.

"Not that I know of," Charles replies, peering at me shrewdly. "He never was one to take responsibility quickly. And certainly not when it could come with jail time and the ruin of everything he holds dear."

"But you think he's guilty," I reply. It's not really a question. I can tell by his words and his tone that he thinks Daniel did it.

"The opinion of an old man is neither here nor there," he responds vaguely. "At the very least, I must now accept that Daniel's suspension is more than temporary. Suraj has been managing Daniel's department, but I'd like to split it between the both of you starting next week. If that's okay with you."

"Of course," I reply. "Anything I can do, just let me know."

"You'll be heading both project management teams now," he responds. "That will more or less even out the numbers between you." He heaves a deep sigh. "I've also engaged services to help manage the legal and external aspects of this development."

I scrunch my brows together. "External aspects?" I ask, confused. And then it hits me. "You mean, like PR? You're afraid of the bad press?" I'm a little aghast that *that's* one of his concerns right now.

"In a sense," he admits. "I simply want to make sure nobody here says or does anything to interfere with Daniel's trial."

Oh. Not the angle I was expecting. "You're not worried we'll lose clients?" I persist.

"Of course I am," he responds. "I'd be a fool not to. And if there's anything to be done to that end, we will. Within the bounds of my discretion."

I eye him warily for a moment but realize I'm going to need to trust his judgment. The path ahead is going to be rocky enough without more internal drama.

"I trust you," I assure him. "As I said, if there's anything I can do, let me know."

Charles rubs his chin in a way that reminds me of Alessandro, and a pain totally unrelated to the situation shoots through my chest.

"Thank you, Sera, I appreciate that more than you know," he admits wearily.

I leave him to his thoughts and lose myself in work once more.

When I next think to look at the clock it's after seven and everyone has clearly gone home. I start my own journey home, exhausted from the day, the week, these past few months. It's hard to say what exactly.

But almost as soon as I'm on a main road, I'm once again plagued by the suspicion that I'm being followed. The car behind me is the exact make and model of the one I swore was following me the night before. I decide to make a complete loop of right turns, all on main roads, to test the theory. The dark sedan follows me from a few cars back this time, until I'm done with the loop, and I can tell they must realize what I've done, that I'm onto them, because they don't hide behind other cars anymore, moving up to stay right on my tail.

Panic starts to flutter in my chest, but I suppress it, trying to think of who to call. I rule out Bryce, not wanting to drag him into my web of crazy again. And as tough as Allie seems, I can't lay this at her doorstep right now. The only other person I can think to call is Emily.

As her phone rings, I pray hard that she answers. And quickly. And she does.

"Hey, Sera, how's it going?" She sounds so cheerful I almost feel bad.

"Emily, I hate to do this to you, but I think I'm being followed. Can I meet you somewhere? Right now?" I ask, struggling to contain the terror in my voice.

"Holy shit, Sera, why didn't you call Bryce?" Emily demands.

"Please, Emily, can we talk about that later?" I beg.

"Fuck. Yes, of course. I'm just at home. Fire Station 25 is a block from my house. I'll meet you there," she directs. I plug the destination into my navigation system.

"I'll be there in less than ten minutes," I reply. "Thanks, Emily."

"Be safe, Sera, see you soon," she responds.

I hang up and accelerate through the next turn, hoping to lose my tail. But they stick on me like glue. I glance in my rearview mirror, trying to get a look at the driver, but it's too difficult to make anything out without stopping to draw them in closer. I scrap any hope of getting the license plate number safely and focus on getting to the fire station.

It's not long before I arrive to see Emily and a firefighter in a plain, navy uniform standing on the main steps. She waves me down and points at the driveway spot next to the walkway they're on. I pull in tentatively and swivel my head around in time to see the dark sedan continuing to accelerate down the street. I breathe a sigh of relief and hop out, hugging Emily tightly.

"It was the black car behind me." The words topple out of my mouth and are barely understandable. The firefighter nods.

"I got the plates," he replies, and I want to cry with relief. "There's a police station just a couple blocks from here. I'll go with you to make a report."

"Can I hug you?" I ask, holding back tears.

He laughs and nods. "Sure thing, ma'am," he replies. And I can't help but embrace him gratefully. "I'm Brad, by the way. Brad Hanson."

"Well, Brad, today you're my knight in shining armor," I reply, releasing him. "Shall we?" I climb back into the car and Brad folds his long frame into the passenger seat, while Emily pops into the backseat.

The police station is, in fact, literally just a couple of blocks away, and there is no sign of the black sedan on our short journey. There is ample parking on the street in front of it, and we park quickly and enter the building together.

Firefighter Brad enlists the officer at the desk and together they take down the details quickly. The officer pulls up the information on the vehicle. We are all disappointed to find the plates are old, no longer registered, and the last vehicle they were registered to does not match the description of the one that was following me. The officer offers to take the report anyway. Emily insists that we do, and Firefighter Brad takes his leave.

"Too bad he had to go," Emily whispers to me as the desk officer continues to type into her computer. "He was cute!"

I glance back at his retreating form, noting that I suppose she was right. "I hadn't really noticed," I admit. "Do you really think we need to finish the report?"

Emily eyes me levelly. "You've already excluded my brother from this. He'll kill me if I don't make you," she replies.

And I know she's right. Thankfully, it doesn't take long, and within a half hour an officer escorts us to my car and we make the short journey to Emily's place without incident, parking in the underground, gated garage for her building.

Emily leads me up to her apartment, which is small, cozy, and covered in crazy posters, fabrics, and musical instruments.

I point at a mandolin. "Do you really play all these?" I ask, in awe.

Emily grins and plops in a crocheted-blanket-covered armchair. "Yep!" She pulls the instrument into her lap and plucks a short tune with a smile. "Now, are you going to tell me why you didn't want to call my brother?"

I sink into the small, patchwork couch next to her and bury my face in my hands. "You're going to think it's stupid," I grouse. I hear her put the instrument down and feel her tug at one of my arms.

"Come on," she prompts. "I'll let you stay overnight! It'll be like a slumber party. But I can't harbor a fugitive from Bryce Hoyt. I know better. Spill."

"You're going to call him, aren't you?" I reply miserably, catching her implication.

She shrugs. "He has a way of finding these things out on his own," she reminds me. "I'm not going to tell him."

I eye her skeptically. "You want *me* to call him," I respond.

She smiles beatifically. "I would if I were you," she replies in a singsong voice.

It's enough to crack my mood, and I laugh appreciatively. "Fine, I'll call him. It's not like I wanted to *hide* it from him. I just feel like I interrupt a lot of his days with my drama. I'm like a magnet lately."

"I don't think he minds," she replies drily, picking up the mandolin again and strumming it softly.

"I'm not sure why you think that," I reply. "But even if he doesn't, I do. I hate relying on other people. And I feel like I rely on him *a lot*."

"But he can rely on you too," she points out. "That's what having a relationship is all about."

I can't help the dirty look I shoot her. "Except we don't. Have a relationship, that is. Not like that," I correct her.

Emily shrugs. "If you say so," she replies, again in her singsong voice.

I sigh resignedly. "I'd have to tell him anyway. I'm supposed to see him in the morning for another training session of some sort. He won't tell me what, so he was going to pick me up."

"Good. The less time I have to hide this from him the better. You can use the balcony if you'd like," she replies. She points at a small door next to the kitchen.

"Thanks." I grab my phone and head out onto the slip of a balcony and place the call. I stare at the setting sun as I wait for him to answer. It takes a while, and I can't stop my mouth from settling into a concerned frown.

"Sera," he finally answers, out of breath. "What's up?"

"I didn't interrupt anything, did I?" I ask nervously.

There's a beat of silence on the other end.

"It's okay, I have a sec," he replies.

"I won't keep you, then. I just wanted to let you know you can pick me up at your sister's place tomorrow morning," I say quietly.

"You're at Emily's?" he asks, confused.

"Yes," I reply simply.

Another beat of silence.

"You can tell me more tomorrow. I have to go," he says abruptly.

"Okay, sorry to have bothered you. See you tomorrow," I mumble.

He ends the call without responding, and I can't help but wonder — *what the hell?* And then an explanation pops into my head. A blond one.

I go back inside and the expression on my face betrays me.

"He was mad, wasn't he?" Emily squeaks.

I shake my head, disturbed. "He was busy," I say softly, my eyes wide. "And out of breath. He wouldn't answer the phone while he was…" I trail off, shaking my head and looking back out at the descending twilight.

Emily pales a little and her nostrils flare. "He could just be working out," she suggests feebly. I roll my eyes. "Not *that* kind of workout. I meant…"

"Save it, Emily, it's his business. And we both know he works out in the morning." I pause, suppressing a disgusted shudder. "You know what? I actually really don't want to know who or what he was doing."

Emily grimaces and slinks into the kitchen, emerging moments later as I sink into the couch.

"Booze?" She holds an icy bottle of vodka and two shot glasses aloft with a conciliatory smile.

I laugh drily. "I don't think vodka is the answer to my problems. But it's worth a shot," I joke.

Emily groans as she settles into the couch next to me. "That will be funnier once I've had a few of these," she replies, pouring the shots.

"Do you always drink this much?" I tease her after her first couple of rounds.

"Pretty much," she replies, expertly slinging back another shot. "Just remember, Sera — nobody ever told an epic story that started with, 'Dude, this one time I ate so much salad.'"

I know I shouldn't encourage her, but I laugh anyway. "So what's new with you? Seeing anyone?" I press her, setting down my shot glass.

Emily pulls a face and shakes her head while pouring another shot. "I'm on my fourth shot of vodka and it's not even nine p.m. on a Friday night. What do you think?" She downs the shot and sets her glass next to mine.

"Okay, then," I concede. "Ever fallen stupid in love with the wrong person?"

Emily gives me some serious side-eye. "Of course. Who hasn't? But that wasn't a loaded question at all." She pauses. "So are we talking about the Italian guy right now? Or someone else?"

I contemplate the ceiling for a moment, the vodka pleasantly warming and numbing me.

"Yes," I respond. I look over at Emily, and we both burst out laughing. After the laughter subsides we sit in companionable silence for a bit.

"Sera," Emily says softly.

My head snaps up and I realize I must have started drifting off. The living room lights are off now and the light over the stove casts a dim glow that allows me to still see most of what's around me.

"Lay down right here, okay?"

I lean into the couch as she slides a blanket over me. And I'm out before I can even thank her.

NINETEEN

Despite my early bedtime, I manage to sleep until almost seven a.m. Emily isn't up yet, so I scrounge the supplies to make coffee and hope the smell doesn't wake her. I take my cup onto the balcony and sit in the small metal chair there, holding the hot cup close in the cool of the early morning.

I don't realize how long I've been out here until Bryce appears through the small door, his large frame even more pronounced in the tiny space. I barely glance at him as I continue to survey the buildings around me, watching them come to life with activity.

"You sleep in that?" he finally asks.

I look down at my cranberry shirtdress. It's rumpled but perfectly serviceable. "Yes. But I'm sure I can borrow clothes from Emily if I'm violating dress code," I reply drily, still avoiding his gaze. I realize I'm more bothered by what I suspect he was up to last night than I thought I was.

"Wear what you want," he replies dismissively, folding his arms over his broad chest. I try not to stare at his rippling biceps as he eyes me speculatively. "You care to tell me why you were at the East Precinct last night?"

I shoot him an angry glare. "I'll show you mine if you show me yours," I reply snarkily. And after a moment's pause, "You know what? I take it back. No, I don't care to tell you. And I don't really care to have all of my movements monitored."

His expression remains stoic, his gaze fixed on me. "I was going to teach you to shoot today," he says offhandedly. "But I think that's off the table."

"Oh? Why's that?" I can barely contain my annoyance.

"I don't think I want to put a gun in your hand when you're this angry with me," he replies evenly. "Why *are* you so angry, Sera?"

I clench my jaw, realizing he's right. I'm unreasonably angry, and he's free to spend the night with whomever he wants. Maybe I'm just mad at myself for thinking he was still waiting for me. For hoping, even though I knew better, that I still had a shot with him.

"Why do you even need me to tell you what happened?" I grumble, diverting the conversation. "Can't you just read the police report?"

A muscle twitches in his jaw and he shifts his weight to his other foot. "I did, actually. But I'd still like to hear it from you," he replies.

He looks so concerned that my anger melts until only sadness remains. And I realize that that's what the anger was protecting me from. I set my coffee mug down on the small table next to me.

"I'm just tired of all this drama," I reply, digging the heels of my hands into my eyes. "I just want it all to go away. The more I talk about it, the longer it lives." I move to running my hands through my hair, frustrated.

Bryce crosses the short distance between us and squats down next to me so he's looking up into my face.

"We'll get through this," he promises. "But to help you, I need to know what's going on."

My eyes rove over his short, thick chestnut hair. I note that it's grown out a little, and it makes me want to run my fingers through it. His sky-blue eyes sparkle with intensity as he stares at me. I have to bite my lip hard to hold back the tears threatening to form.

"It's all in the report," I sigh. "Someone was following me when I left work yesterday. I called Em and she met me at the fire station. They escorted us to the police station to make the report." I pause. "Though I can't remember if I told them that the same car had followed me the night before. But it took off when I was still deciding whether I was being paranoid."

"You did," he replies softly. "You really didn't get a look at the driver?" I shake my head. He sighs and sinks onto the concrete, his back against the balcony railing. "I have other news."

I look at him expectantly. "Well? Are you going to tell me, or should I go get more coffee?" I ask, irritated.

Bryce's eyes flick up to mine. He has a wary look about him that makes my heart sink in my chest.

"You're killing me here."

"Daniel posted bail this morning," he replies hesitantly. He shifts against the rails.

I frown. "How is that possible? Are violent criminals really given that option?" I ask.

"The judge must have thought he was low enough risk not to re-offend or run. Though his bail was quite high," Bryce amends.

"Okay," I say slowly. "So that's not good. But I guess honestly I'm not that surprised, either." Bryce looks away guiltily. "There's more, isn't there?"

His eyes return to mine. "There's more," he agrees. He clears his throat and leans forward, draping his long arms over his knees. "My sources located your boyfriend. They spotted him walking into a bank in Rome with another man two days ago. He was unharmed and didn't seem under duress."

I'm struck dumb by the information. It takes my brain what feels like an eternity to even make full sense of the words.

"He's alive? He's okay?" I finally manage. Bryce nods. "Do they know where he is? Where he's staying?"

Bryce's expression clouds over. "Damnit, Sera, you're not going after him," he snaps.

I open my mouth to protest, but I know he's right, so I close it. And as the information truly sinks in, my composure begins to crumble. I can see in Bryce's eyes that he expects it. I summon every bit of willpower left in my tired, ravaged heart and force down my reaction until I can fully experience it privately. I return to staring numbly at the horizon. Bryce is still looking at me apprehensively.

I meet his gaze and shrug. "If you don't want to tell me, don't," I say evenly.

"I couldn't even if I wanted to," he admits. "They weren't able to track him back to wherever he's holed up. But…"

"What?" I ask sharply.

Bryce looks at me imploringly. "The bastard doesn't deserve you if he can't even be bothered to man up and break things off instead of leaving you in this purgatory." His every word is filled with venom.

I close my eyes and shake my head. I refuse to discuss this with Bryce when I haven't even had a chance to process it. "Why does it matter to you what he does? Or what I do about it?" I ask, not really expecting or looking for an answer. I sigh heavily.

"Because you matter to me," he replies. I bite back a retort, but he sees it. "Spit it out."

"If I matter so much, then answer one question," I respond. He looks at me anxiously, waiting. "What were you doing last night that you could barely talk to me?"

His expression closes so fast that I don't even need him to confirm it. Not really.

"I answered the phone, didn't I?" he responds tightly. "But I'm not at your beck and call. I can't be everything, everywhere you want always. I'm your friend, Sera, not your personal security guard."

"I know," I agree. "But that wasn't my question." I rise from the chair and step over him to get to the door. I stop with the door open and turn back to him. "If we're friends, there's no reason for you not to tell me. And if we're friends, then whoever I choose to love is not really your decision." *Even if it's you.*

I slip back into the apartment, still numb, to find Emily hovering in the kitchen. Clearly, she's heard every word.

"You okay?" she asks softly.

I huff out a breath and set my coffee cup in the sink. "No. Thanks for the place to crash, Em," I reply.

And with that, I take my leave of both Hoyt siblings. But I can feel their eyes on my back as the door closes behind me.

BACK IN MY FAVORITE CHAIR WITH A BOTTLE OF WINE AT MY FEET AND A GLASS in hand, I finally feel the pressure of other's expectations lifted enough to start handling what I learned this morning.

Alessandro. Alive. Unharmed. Casually strolling into a bank with a friend. Yet not a word or whisper for six weeks to reassure me or at least let me know where things stand. I can't help but think his silence speaks louder than anything he would have to say on the matter. Because if he truly cared for me, even if he couldn't be with me anymore, wouldn't he find a way to tell me that? Surely, he must know how worried I've been.

My mind races with a thousand explanations that excuse his lack of contact. I shake them out of my head, frustrated. There's no point in guessing. All I have to go on is what I know. So I decide to switch tactics. If someone I cared about was in this position, what would I think?

I sink into the frame of mind and, trying to put myself outside of the situation emotionally, spin through the events. Say Emily started dating a man who'd pursued her for months, only to find out a month later — after falling in love with him — that he was married. Then another month later, something horrible happens to her after which she finds out he's gotten divorced, but he still can't be with her because he's got to run off to figure out why his crazy ex-wife is making serious threats against him that could affect her own safety. And then he's gone for a month when she stops hearing from him. And another six weeks later, realizing she's falling for the one man who's actually been there for her through all of this, she's sitting around wondering what to do about it when she learns her paramour has been just fine and dandy this whole time.

Even I realize how ridiculous it sounds. But the missing piece, and what there is no accounting for, is love. The force I've resisted all these years due to its destructive nature, its ability to make even the smartest among us do some truly unwise things.

I think back to Bryce's demand — that he won't settle for anything less than all of me. And the truth of that condition is undeniable by either logic or love. How can you be with only part of someone? Painfully, is the answer, I realize. Because that's what it's always been with Alessandro, and what he protested against from my side at the beginning of our relationship. But even before I gave all of myself to him, I only ever had part of him. Even when I let myself fall in love with him, I didn't know he still technically belonged to someone else. Even after it tore us apart I still loved him, but we couldn't be together. And we haven't been able to be together since, for this reason and then that.

But the hardest part is not knowing. Is Alessandro still working on clearing the obstacles in the way of our being together without mortal peril hanging over our heads? Or has he simply changed his mind and hasn't been able to bring himself to tell me? Neither explains his complete lack of contact. And I know he'd be furious with me if our roles were reversed. But would he give up on me without knowing?

I stand, pacing nervously in front of the glass wall, the heat of the waning summer radiating off its smooth face. I feel like a caged, wounded animal. It's no wonder I lashed out at Bryce this morning. I contemplate going for a walk to clear my head, but I know that's a bad idea when Daniel has made bail and I've had someone following me the last two nights. Not to mention the break-in. And I still can't shake the feeling that it's all connected.

I'm torn from my reverie by a soft knock on the door. Warily, I approach soundlessly and peer through the peephole. I breathe a sigh of relief when I see Emily's familiar chestnut waves. I open the door to find her chewing her lip, looking completely contrite and cheerless.

"Why am I not surprised?" I greet her. "Are all you Hoyts just big, fat meddlers?" I give her a small smile to let her know I'm not serious and step aside, gesturing for her to enter.

She steps past me into the condo and I close the door behind her. Before she says anything, she gives me a brief, tender hug. "I can't help it," she finally replies. "If you saw your face when you left, you'd be here too." She pauses. "That made a lot more sense in my head."

I can't help laughing. "I get what you meant," I assure her. "Come, sit down. There might be some wine left." I grab another wine glass and a second bottle from the kitchen as she settles into the overstuffed white couch next to my chair.

When we're both seated with full glasses, she looks contemplatively into hers as she swirls the dark liquid in circles. "I just didn't want you to be alone," she finally says.

I throw her a grateful smile, blinking away tears. "Thanks, Em," I reply softly.

She beams at me. "I noticed you've started calling me that," she says.

"Is it okay?" I ask tentatively. I've heard Bryce call her that so many times that it's clearly rubbed off. But it was so subconscious that I didn't even register it and consider that it might be too personal.

"More than okay," she assures me, leaning over to squeeze my free hand. "Now. Talk."

I can't help but grimace. "Really? I feel like such a drain," I admit. "I swear I'm not always this much drama."

Emily shakes her head and smirks. "We all go through phases where it seems like everything is going wrong," she replies. "And even aside from that, we're all going through something pretty much all the time anyway. It's okay to need someone to listen. Or be a sanity check. Or whatever it is you need."

I take a deep breath and let it out in a sigh. "You're right," I agree. "I guess I'm still learning to let people in." Emily sips her wine tolerantly as she waits for me to continue. "I know I've told you about Alessandro before, so I'm guessing you pretty much understood what you heard this morning?"

"Pretty much," she confirms. "So you haven't heard from this guy in weeks and now you find out he's been on a Roman holiday. Must sting a bit."

"Six weeks," I clarify. "And yes, it stings. A lot."

"It's the people we love the most who have the greatest capacity to cause us pain," she responds.

"Preach," I reply with a sigh. "It feels like falling in love is part choice, part fate. But how do you decide when to *stop* loving someone?"

Emily fingers the stem of her wine glass as she considers her response. "I don't think you ever stop," she finally offers. "I think all you can do is decide when it's not worth beating your head against a wall anymore."

"Easier said than done," I grumble.

Emily laughs. "Touché." She pauses. "Do you want my opinion?"

"Can't hurt," I reply drily.

She catches and holds my gaze. "This dude is selfish. You don't want to be with someone selfish. You're a giver, Sera. You want to be with a giver," she says plainly.

I'm not surprised by her take on the matter. But it still feels contrary to what I know about Alessandro. "I don't think he's selfish. He has his reasons. I just don't know what they are right now," I reply with a sigh.

"Yes, because he's not sharing, because there's nothing in it for him. Look," she says, staring at me squarely, "I get that you love this guy. But he's lied to you, hidden things from you, and still isn't being forthcoming. Whatever his story is, it doesn't matter. He's quite obviously doing things in a way that works for *him*. I'm not saying he doesn't love you. I'm saying he can't love you the way you deserve to be loved."

"Now you just sound like your brother," I reply sullenly.

Emily throws a hand up. "Thank god one of us does," she replies. "Bryce may let people walk all over him sometimes — okay not people, women — but he's been through a lot and has seen even more. And he has a gift for cutting through the façade people put on and seeing them for who they are."

"You mean researching them and finding every sordid detail of their past," I grumble.

Emily raises an eyebrow. "Who has he done that to?" she asks.

I roll my eyes. "Um, everyone remotely connected to me? It's obnoxious. I don't know how you stand it," I grumble.

She looks at me, confused. "He's never done that to me," she replies slowly. She's silent for a moment. "But he *can* be very protective."

I snort. "That's an understatement," I scoff, burying my face in my free hand.

"What are you waiting for?" Emily asks softly.

"What do you mean?" I ask, dropping my hand back into my lap.

"What has to happen for you to move on from this guy? How long are you going to wait for him?" she presses.

"I don't know," I reply honestly.

Emily taps the side of her glass in thought. "I don't blame you. I can't say I'd find the decision easy if it were me. But there's an opportunity cost," she eventually says. "To waiting."

Her words jog something in my memory. "I'd rather regret doing something than doing nothing," I murmur.

Emily snaps her head up. "Then do something," she urges me.

I look back at her sadly. "I think I've done everything I can," I reply despondently. "I can't reach Alessandro. There's nowhere for me to call. He either didn't get or is choosing to not reply to my email. And not even Bryce could find where he's staying in Rome. And despite your brother's low opinion of me, I'm not stupid enough to go there and wander around looking for him."

"I wasn't suggesting that," Emily responds. "I agree completely — you've done everything you can do. Except move on."

Her words sink deeply into my consciousness. And I realize she's beyond right. The only thing I can do now is choose to keep waiting for him to decide to contact me, or I can decide to go forward with my life. And waiting isn't doing anything at all.

"You're absolutely right," I breathe. "I'm done waiting." The immense sorrow I feel at the decision is only matched by the feeling of freedom that follows. Tears flow out of my eyes at the release, and I set my wine glass down before it can tumble out of my shaking hand.

Emily sets aside her own and opens her arms to me. I crawl onto the couch next to her, gratefully accepting the offered embrace. She holds me for a good while until the tears finally stop.

"So are you going to go after my brother now or what?" Emily murmurs into my hair once I've settled.

I pull away, facing her on the couch. "I'm not sure I can even be friends with him anymore," I admit. "I thought for a while there he might still…" I sniff deeply, reigning back my emotions in the aftermath of the tears. "But if last night is any indication, I think he really has finally moved on. I don't want to keep making things harder for him."

Emily scowls and eyes me sternly. "That's not doing something, Evans," she reprimands me. "You don't know anything for sure. Would you rather guess or know? Because this is one case where you *can* know. You just have to be brave enough to ask."

I huff a small laugh and shove her shoulder playfully. "You're really smart, you know that?" I tease her.

She smiles widely. "Yes, I am," she agrees imperiously.

I laugh. "And so humble," I tease.

"One of my many virtues," she jokes back. "But seriously, no matter what happens, let's still be friends. Pinky swear on it?" She holds up her little finger.

I chuckle and hook mine with hers. "Pinky swear," I agree.

TWENTY

I t takes me hours after Emily leaves to work up the courage to go see Bryce. Knocking on his door is the hardest part. Because until I do that, I can always turn back. Before I can chicken out, I give three hard raps on the door. And my stomach immediately goes from a ball of butterflies to a clenched knot. I count to distract myself. When I'm to fifteen I realize expecting him to be home on a Saturday night might have been ridiculous. At thirty I stop, and I'm debating whether to knock again or give up when the door swings open.

Bryce's eyes travel over my face for several heartbeats. But we're both silent. I take in his casual attire — navy basketball shorts and a plain, white T-shirt and am thankful that at least I don't appear to have interrupted anything.

"Can we talk?" I ask, breaking first.

Bryce shrugs and steps back. I enter, hovering near the door, unsure whether he really wants me here. He seats himself on the couch and gestures for me to sit. When I'm perched reluctantly on the other end, I find myself needing to work up my courage once again. He sighs impatiently.

"What is it you wanted to talk about?" he prompts. He's not going to make this easy.

"You said something this morning," I start, my voice cracking with the strain of trying to keep my tone even. "You called him my boyfriend." I look up to meet his steely gaze. "He's not. He hasn't been for months. And no matter what you think, I have no intention of going after him."

Bryce's expression softens ever so slightly. "You still love him, though," he replies.

I nod, biting back a wave of tears. "I do. But I'm done waiting. I'm done chasing the wrong guy. Because you were right. What he's doing," I pause for breath, "it doesn't matter why. It's not okay. And I'm tired. Of waiting for answers. Of wasting my energy worrying about someone who..." I shake my head.

"Who what?" Bryce leans forward, clearly eager to hear the end of the sentence.

"Who is selfish," I say simply. "But I'm not here to bad-mouth Alessandro. I'm just over it. And I..." My rambling train of thought is interrupted by a soft knock on the door. Bryce looks at me, clearly confused. "Go ahead and get it."

He rises from the couch, and I take the opportunity to wipe away the tears that had formed at the corners of my eyes and to collect myself as he answers the door.

"Hey, soldier, you lonesome tonight?"

My head whips around at the high, feminine voice. And just around Bryce's side I see her. All blond hair, short dress, and tall heels. The Funeral Barbie disguise dropped, she's clearly gone full seductress. And every fear I had about what Bryce was doing and who he was doing it with comes to life in front of my eyes.

"Now's not a good time," Bryce responds tightly, but she pushes past him anyway.

I rise frantically from the couch, a lump in my throat. Madison catches sight of me and freezes.

"Oh, I didn't know you had company," she purrs in my direction.

Bryce continues to hold the door open behind her. "Madison. Not. Now," he says commandingly.

She glances back at him coquettishly. "Ask nicely, Bryce, darling," she prompts him.

"Please," he replies through gritted teeth.

She casts a simpering smile at me, flaunting her control of him over me. "Okay," she agrees, slinking back to his side and planting a kiss on his cheek. "I'll just come back later."

"I think it would be best if you didn't," he says tightly.

She cocks an eyebrow at him. "Some other time then," she suggests as she exits. She blows him one last kiss over her shoulder as he closes the door.

The silence hangs heavy in the air for several heartbeats.

"Since the funeral?" I ask.

He turns back to me slowly. "It's not what you think," he says.

I keep a tight rein on my expression. "I just want to hear it from you, Bryce," I reply pleadingly. "Same as you wanted to hear about the police report from me."

"Yes, since the funeral," he confirms.

I nod, choking back the emotion threatening to overtake me. "The rest is a two-way street too. We're just friends. I have no business telling you who to love," I say. My voice sounds far surer than I feel. Inside, I'm falling apart.

"Sera, I don't…" he starts.

I hold a hand up to stop him. "You don't owe me an explanation. I think I'm done here. You should call Madison and tell her to come back. Maybe you can still salvage your evening," I manage to get out. I push past him and head for the door.

"I may not owe you an explanation, but I'd like to give you one," he growls.

I take my hand off the doorknob and spin to face him. "I'm not stupid, Bryce, there's nothing to explain. You're back with your ex. I get it. Message received loud and clear. I just…" I bite back the nasty comment I'd been about to make. "I need to stop. Now. Before I say something I can't take back." I turn and leave, not giving him a chance to draw me into another fight.

Furious, I burst out of the building into the cool night air. I make for where I thought I'd parked around the corner, but don't find my car. Remembering I'd parked somewhere different this time, I whirl around, angry at Bryce for distracting me so badly that I can't even properly recall where I put my vehicle, when someone grabs me hard from behind. It takes me only a fraction of a second to realize whoever it is isn't tall enough to be Bryce. And they sure as hell don't smell good enough to be Madison.

I throw my head back and my feet fly out from under me as my assailant lifts me up.

"Let me go *now*!" I screech, writhing in his vice grip.

"You're a bossy little bitch," a low voice growls in my ear. I feel myself being hauled backward toward a dark clump of bushes. "Shut your fucking mouth, or I'll show you who's the *real* boss."

My blood turns to ice, but I don't give myself time to think about why the words bother me beyond the obvious threat.

With an intensity I didn't think myself capable of, I focus on remembering Bryce's lesson. I throw myself to the right, hooking my foot around the thick leg behind mine. Pulling as hard as I can with my foot, I simultaneously leverage as much distance as possible and slam the heel of my left hand back hard. Both efforts bear fruit and my attacker cries out in pain, falling to the ground. His arms spring open, and I barely manage not to spill onto the concrete in front of me as I break free. I don't waste time looking back, breaking into a sprint to get back to the building's entrance. As I round the corner, I see Bryce standing on the walkway ahead of me and I bolt toward him. His head whips in my direction and his eyes go wide as saucers as I slam into him.

"Someone," my breath comes in sharp pants, making talking difficult, "grabbed me."

"*Fuck*. Get inside. Now," he barks. He drags me wordlessly back into the building and up to his apartment. He doesn't let go of me as he finds his phone and calls the police. When he hangs up, he pulls away, leveling his face with mine. "Stay here. Don't open the door for anyone but me." He leaps back into action, disappearing into the back of the apartment and returning with a pistol in his hands and an ID case strapped to his waistband.

I want to beg him not to leave, but I can't even form the words. And once he's slipped out the door, locking it behind him, I'm glad I couldn't. Because it gives me time to break down in private. And to remember where I'd heard those words before. My frantic brain pulls the memory out. Of Daniel. Warning me not to tell anyone about his threats against me. It's hard to remember, but his exact words were something like, *If you say anything about this, I'll have to find another way to show you who's the real boss around here.* Terrifyingly similar. A deep shudder rolls through my body. I try not to think more about it, but as the minutes tick by it gets harder.

Finally, I hear sirens. And a few minutes later a knock.

"It's me," Bryce's voice calls through the door.

I scramble to open it and find him there with a uniformed officer at his side, a portly man a bit older than Bryce with straw-colored hair and a mustache. "Sera, this is Officer Abbott."

"Ma'am," Officer Abbott offers with a tip of his hat. "I'm sorry to hear about what happened tonight."

Bryce leads us to the living room, leaving the door partially open and setting his holstered gun on the kitchen counter. I glance at the door nervously and Bryce catches my look.

"His partner is still checking outside," he explains. "He'll be in shortly." I nod and fold myself into the corner of the couch facing the door, ready to get this over with. Again.

Officer Abbott gives me a sympathetic look. "I know this is probably the last thing you want to do right now. But it's important that I take a statement while events are still fresh in your mind."

"It's okay," I reply. "I'm unfortunately getting kind of used to it."

Bryce grimaces from the armchair next to me but stays silent. I sigh and give them the facts in as fine a detail as I can. I must do a good job of it, because there are no questions from the peanut gallery, and Officer Abbott is heading out the door before his partner even has a chance to join us. His radio crackles briefly and he exchanges words with someone.

"Nothing outside. I trust you'll be in to the station tomorrow, Bryce?" Officer Abbott asks.

I look at Bryce, who nods in reply.

"Thanks, Al," Bryce replies.

With a last tip of his hat, Officer Al is gone. Bryce turns to me, looking wearier than I've seen him since his father's funeral.

"I can take you home if you want, but I'd prefer if you stayed here," he says.

"I'll stay," I reply meekly. "There's something I didn't tell Officer Al."

Bryce raises an eyebrow and presses his lips together. "And why not?" he asks through gritted teeth.

"Because I'm not sure. It didn't sound like Daniel. I mean, I think they were trying not to use their real voice, but…" I feel like a stuttering mess, so I stop and take a breath. "What he said, about showing me who the real boss is? Daniel said those *exact* words to me in his office the day he threatened me."

"Ah." That's all Bryce says. But he looks as troubled as I feel. He looks back down into my eyes. "I'll talk to the detective in charge of his case tomorrow. Try to get some sleep. You're safe here." And without so much as a reassuring glance, he retreats to his room.

TWENTY-ONE

BRYCE

As soon as I'm alone, I take a swing at the punching bag in the corner of my bedroom. Bare-fisted, I pummel it until I'm breathing hard and have burned off a good amount of rage. Rage at Madison for her unannounced appearance. At the bastard stalking Sera. At myself. I could go on, but I finally give in to my exhaustion and flop onto the bed.

The dull ache in my knuckles and arms keeps me awake. But not as much as remembering the look of terror on Sera's face. Eventually, I slip into a restless sleep.

❧

I wake at my usual time, though it's the one day I don't bother with alarms. Not that I usually need one anyway. I trudge toward the kitchen set on making coffee when I spot Sera asleep on the couch.

"For Pete's sake," I grumble. I turn around and open the guest bedroom door before scooping her up gently. She stirs against my chest as I move her, but I manage to get her onto the bed without waking her fully. Closing the door behind me, I head back to the kitchen.

More than an hour later I've managed to get through two cups of coffee and most of the newspaper when Sera emerges.

"I was fine on the couch," she grouses, pouring herself a cup of coffee.

I raise an eyebrow but remain silent.

She plops into a dining chair across from me. "I didn't know anyone still read the paper."

"Well, I have since I was ten. Not about to stop now," I say shortly.

"You read the newspaper when you were ten?" she asks doubtfully.

I glance up at her. "Okay, fine, I used to just read the comics," I concede. I can see her trying not to smile and for a moment I'm hopeful that we can get through all of this.

"Can I go home now?" she asks testily.

I fold the last section that I was reading onto the table. "If you want," I allow. "And I know you had a rough night, but first I'd like it if we could talk about what happened before that."

She sets her mug down and pushes it away. "I'd rather not, if it's all the same," she grumbles.

I grimace and loose a sigh. "I don't want there to be bad blood between us," I explain.

She levels an angry glare at me. "Then maybe you should've been honest with me in the first place," she retorts.

I clench my jaw at the accusation in her words and tone and choose my response carefully. "Exactly how was I dishonest?" I ask.

"'If you choose me, I want it to be with all of you. I won't settle for anything less,'" she mimics. She's throwing my words back at me with spite. "But you weren't exactly in a position to offer that yourself, were you?" Her fury morphs quickly into something far more devastating as tears fill her eyes.

"Madison means nothing to me," I reply evenly.

She scoffs. "Bullshit," she fumes. "You're just like him. You say you want me under your terms, like I'm not living up to your exacting criteria, then I find out it's a complete double standard. You want all of me without having to give up your little side pieces. I'm so fucking sick of it."

"It's not like that," I protest.

"Which part? You wanting me? Or her being your side piece?" she demands. But she quickly rises from the table, not waiting for an answer. "I'm leaving. It's daytime. I remember where my car is now. Thanks for everything." She turns on her heel to go.

"So that's it? You just leave every time the conversation gets a little diffi-cult?" I call after her.

"Yep," she responds flippantly without turning around. "And you don't need to bother trying to follow me this time. I'm sure you have to report to your girlfriend to give her a good fuck before church, soldier." The door clicks shut behind her.

Well, shit. That didn't go as planned.

I clean up and throw on a pair of khakis and a blue polo. And then I head to the police department. Because, despite what Sera thinks, the tradition of going to church every Sunday died with my father. He's the only reason I went anyway. Hell, he's the only reason I did a lot of things.

∽

Abbott left a note that he hadn't found anything yet to add on the assault file, so I head to talk to Detective Jacobs, lead on Daniel Sutton's case. And though it's Sunday, I know he'll be here. Even without the high-profile case the guy's a workaholic. Always has been.

And sure enough, I see his full head of messy brown hair bowed over his desk, examining something with a magnifying glass. I rap my knuckles on his door to get his attention.

"Hey, Tim," I call out. He pops up from scrutinizing the paper in front of him and gives me a wide grin.

"Hoyt!" he exclaims, jumping up to clap his hand in mine and throw his other arm around me. He gives me a one-shoulder hug and releases, shoving me jokingly. "They keep letting your ass in here? Gotta tell them to up the security in this place."

"You're just pissed I didn't let them seduce me into this gig," I joke back. "I mean, I know SEALs gotta stick together, but this is all you, man."

He laughs and settles into his chair. "Yep. You know how much I love this shit," he replies, offering me a seat with a gesture. I slide into a chair. "But I'm guessing you're not here to catch up."

"Not today, Timmy," I lament. "I'm here because Serafina Evans was attacked last night."

Tim's eyebrows shoot up. "The chick that works with Sutton?" he asks. I can tell I have his full attention now. "They catch the guy?"

I shake my head. "She didn't even get a look at him. But he said something to her. Threatened her, actually. With the exact wording Daniel Sutton threatened her almost a month ago. And she was followed home from your vic's house on Thursday night." Tim's eyebrows climb so high this time, they're threatening to merge with his hairline.

"Is that so?" he murmurs. But other than surprise, his expression gives nothing away.

"It is. Any way it could've been your guy?" I watch his face carefully, but he wipes any expression from his face and levels a blank stare back at me.

"You know I can't tell you anything," he replies evenly. I hold his gaze. "But I'll look into it. Who took the report?"

"Al. At almost ten last night."

I purposely don't mention her being followed on Friday night, since Sutton was in jail at the time. An accomplice wouldn't be out of the question, and he's still my number one suspect. But I know Tim. If he had that information he wouldn't pursue Sutton with the same gusto. Especially since nothing much came of the stalking or the assault. A bloodhound, this one, but not terribly excited when there's no blood, so to speak.

"I appreciate it, Tim." I let silence hang in the air a bit, seeing if he'll offer anything else. But he doesn't.

"Anything for you, Hoyt," he replies when he's done sizing me up. I huff a laugh, doubtful. But I'll take what I can get. And I know I'm not going to get anything else out of Tim Jacobs today. I toy momentarily with the idea of going directly to the DA. But I both don't have the kind of connections with that office that I do with the Seattle PD, and I don't dare go around Tim. I've got to think about the long game and not piss off some of my best allies.

"I'll let you get back to it," I respond. "Nice seeing you, Timmy."

"You too, Hoyt."

I leave, still relatively unsatisfied and fairly certain Tim will take his dear sweet time looking into it. Time in which I'm not willing to gamble with Sera's safety. I silently thank my father for insisting I not join the force after being discharged. Because if I were a police officer I wouldn't be able to do what I'm about to do. It's time to ask the bastard himself. Once I'm back in the car, it doesn't take long to find Daniel Sutton's address.

∽

I PULL UP AND AM IMMEDIATELY DISGUSTED BY THE OBNOXIOUSLY MODERN, overly lavish residence in the exclusive Medina neighborhood. Looking around the front of the house, I don't see a garage or any vehicles. The driveway must be on another side of the house. Deciding to look later, I pull a pistol from the glove compartment and hang it from my belt, adding my ID holder next to it. As I approach the front door, I note the security cameras and realize I'm going to have to play this one more conservatively than I'd like.

I take a deep breath and ring the bell. An older Hispanic woman answers almost immediately. "Yes?" Her expression is stern, her voice full of suspicion as she glances at the gun on my hip. "You police?" Despite her small stature, I can immediately tell she's not someone to mess with.

"No, ma'am. My name is Bryce Hoyt. I'm a private security consultant. I'm here to talk to Mr. Sutton," I respond.

"You have an appointment?" she asks sharply.

I can't help but smile. Sutton doesn't deserve such a faithful helper.

"I'm afraid I don't. But it's in Mr. Sutton's best interest to speak with me," I reply calmly. She eyes me a bit longer before nodding her head.

"You wait here." She closes the door.

I'm guessing by her guarded nature and failure to admit me to the house that I'm not the first stranger to come looking for answers from Daniel Sutton.

When the door reopens a few minutes later, the most average looking man I've ever laid eyes on stands before me. I'm not sure what I expected. Someone as vicious or ugly outside as he is inside, perhaps, even though I know that's not how it goes. But even his expression and his body language are unremarkable. Though he looks as exhausted as I feel.

"Can I help you?" he asks sharply in a likewise ordinary voice.

I hand him the business card I'd pulled from my ID holder, hoping it will help put him at ease.

"Mr. Sutton, I'm Bryce Hoyt. I run a private security company. I'd like to speak with you about some information I have related to your case," I explain carefully. I stay loose, fixing a casual expression on my face. I just need to get in the door. If he lets me in, I may have a shot at getting something useful out of him. But there's no overcoming the disadvantage of standing on a threshold.

He throws me a skeptical glance. "I've never heard of you. What could you possibly know?"

I cautiously select the truths to present. "I know Heather Irving. I met her when I did security work for Evans Realty Services. And I was at the police department the day she filed a report against you."

Daniel glances nervously toward the street, clearly afraid of who might have heard. He steps back, swinging the door open. I internally breathe a sigh of relief.

"Come in, Mr. Hoyt," he offers. "It seems we may have things to discuss after all."

He leads me through the vast foyer and into a formal living room stuffed with overwrought furniture and antiques. The place looks like it was decorated by a seventy-year-old woman.

"Nice place you've got here," I murmur. One lie won't hurt.

He offers me a seat on a stuffy, hard-backed tufted leather divan and settles into a matched armchair across from it.

"Thank you," he replies stiffly, then turns toward the back of the room. "Estella!" The Hispanic woman who answered the front door appears through an archway. "I'd like coffee, please." He turns to me expectantly.

"Nothing for me, thank you," I say. He nods curtly, and the older woman disappears.

"So who exactly are you working for, Mr. Hoyt?" Daniel asks, turning his weak blue eyes on me questioningly.

I get the sense immediately that he's not as smart as he thinks he is. "I'm afraid that's confidential," I reply apologetically.

"You said you did some work for Serafina Evans," he points out shrewdly. "She wouldn't happen to be who you're working for now, would she?"

Maybe he's not as stupid as he looks. But I seize the opportunity to turn it to my advantage.

"Lord, no. I haven't worked for Ms. Evans since her company was absorbed by yours," I reply, feigning disgust. The revulsion is meant to draw him in, but technically the rest is true. I don't work for Sera.

Daniel smirks at me. "You're lucky you don't *have* to work with her," he responds. "If it was my choice, I wouldn't, either."

"Oh? What did she do to *you*?" I ask with practiced indifference and the subtle insinuation that I'm a fellow "victim" of hers.

"Nothing much," he says. But his wrathful tone betrays him. "Just poison my own father against me. Attempt to steal my hard-earned place in the company I helped him build into what it is today. And I'm fairly certain that she also had something to do with Ms. Irving's fabrications."

"Fuck," I respond, snorting. "It sounds like you have more of a beef against her than I do."

"You don't know the half of it," he seethes. He starts to say something else and then stops.

"It's okay," I reply, sensing his struggle. "I know you probably can't say anything with everything that's going on." Daniel sighs, relieved.

"Exactly," he agrees. "But let's just say, since this whole thing started I've steered clear of anyone and everyone, even my own family, but I hope I'm around when someone takes her down. I'm just sad it won't be me."

"Right. If I were you, I'd want to see her in a world of hurt," I agree zealously.

Estella enters with a tray and sets it on the table next to Daniel before exiting once more. Daniel picks up the coffee and sips it thoughtfully.

"You know, as long as she's professionally destroyed, it's all the same to me," Daniel finally replies.

I keenly note his purposeful use of the word *professionally.* Not exactly the singular focus I'd expect of a deranged stalker. Which makes me think that, while he's deranged, it's unlikely he'd go after Sera in the ways she's been pursued these past weeks. He just wants her to keep her paws off his perceived birthright.

"But enough about Ms. Evans. You said you have information?"

I clear my throat. Having already learned most of what I needed to know, I need to wrap this up in a way that seems plausible and possibly even confirms my conclusion further.

"Given that the investigation is still ongoing," I hedge carefully, "I can't divulge everything. But I'm trying to prove, on someone else's behalf, where you were this past Thursday evening. Or where you *weren't* to be exact."

"If this investigation has to do with my case, this is the first I've heard of it.

To what end are you trying to prove my whereabouts?" Daniel asks distrustfully.

"I didn't say it was your case," I reply, smiling politely. "But it is related. If I can establish where you were, I may be able to head off any future issues for you."

And this is really the moment of truth. Have I established enough of a rapport for him to trust me? If not, I'll settle for him being gullible enough to answer anyway. I try not to hold my breath as I wait for his answer.

"As I said, I haven't been to see anyone. In fact, I haven't left the house since…" he pauses to think about it, "Since I stopped working last Wednesday."

I nod, focusing on not letting out a sigh of relief. "I presume your house-keeper and security cameras will corroborate that?" I ask.

"Of course," he replies unflinchingly.

"Good," I respond, stopping short of warning him to be prepared to provide that evidence when the police come asking. I'm already toeing the line of obstruction of justice. "I appreciate your cooperation, Mr. Sutton."

Daniel looks at me incredulously. "That's all?" he asks suspiciously.

"That's all," I assure him. "I'm sorry I'm not able to tell you more. But you've been extremely helpful." I rise and offer my hand, which he also rises to take. His handshake is uncomfortably firm, and I smile, unsurprised. This guy obviously has a *lot* to compensate for. He smiles back, thinking the gesture friendly, and I suppress a laugh. "Best of luck to you." *You're gonna need it.*

"Thank you, Mr. Hoyt," he replies, seeing me to the door. As I descend the steps of his front walkway, he calls after me. "I trust you'd rather I didn't mention this visit to anyone from the police department?"

I turn around and spread my arms open, offering a final smile. "By all means, tell whomever you wish," I encourage him.

He nods curtly and closes the door. This guy really is a pompous asshole if he thinks that kind of test is going to work. But I'm fairly confident his even asking, and then accepting my response, means he's highly unlikely to say anything anyway, since he obviously thinks there's a shot I'm trying to help him.

I finally let out that sigh of relief. And on my way out, I drive around the corner and eye the cars in the driveway leading to the back of the house. Flashy red sports car. Tan SUV. Green coupe, probably the housekeeper's as it's the only practical vehicle. Nothing matching Sera's stalker's vehicle. I'd gone in expecting to find him linked in some way. But I'm leaving fairly convinced he's not. It's a relief on one hand, but a troubling mystery on the other.

My stomach rumbles, and I decide to stop for lunch before heading to my next destination. I'm going to need all the strength I can get to deal with Madison.

∽

By the time I knock on her door, I'm sweating and cranky from struggling to find a parking spot in the hilly Green Lake neighborhood on a hot and sunny late summer afternoon. So much for being at the top of my game.

She finally answers, fanning herself lazily with a folded piece of paper and looking ridiculously racy in pink barely-more-than-underwear shorts and a tiny white sports bra.

"Bryce, darling," she greets me. "I'm glad to see you." She pulls me into the apartment, standing on her toes with her hands around my neck, trying to land a kiss. I firmly disentangle her arms and step back.

"I'm not here for that," I reply.

She settles onto a spot on the couch with a fan pointing at it. I sit on the opposite end, facing her with my knee crooked up to discourage her from getting too close.

"What *are* you here for then?" she asks, pulling her blond locks off her sweaty neck. She's continuing to lay the sexy act on thick, unaware that I've resolved not to fall for it anymore.

"You had no right to show up like that last night," I reply.

She eyes me speculatively. "I just thought you might be up for a little fun," she pouts. "Haven't we been having a good time, darling?"

"Please don't call me that," I snap. "And I wouldn't exactly call it a good time. Momentary weakness, perhaps."

"You and I have different definitions of momentary," she replies, smirking. "Three times is a pattern, dearie."

"It's over is what it is," I correct her.

She arches an eyebrow and purses her lips. "Your little girlfriend wasn't happy to see me, I take it?" she asks shrewdly. "To be honest, I was surprised to see her there after you came running to me last Saturday with a case of blue balls."

"Don't be so crass, Madison, it's unbecoming," I snap.

She grins at my choice of words. "Yes, there's been lots of coming. But I guess no more," she sighs. "Oh, well, it was fun while it lasted."

"Can you be serious for a minute?" I growl, frustrated. "Look. I'm sorry. I'm not trying to blame you. I just haven't been myself. But I can't do this anymore. I won't. So please, just don't call me, don't come to see me, and I'll do the same. Everything will go back to how it was."

Madison's expression softens and the pity in her eyes is almost worse than the attempted seduction. "It's not something you can take back," she replies. "But if that's what you want, then okay."

I look at her skeptically.

"Really. Cross my heart." She runs a finger in an X over her left breast.

I snap my eyes back to hers, so I don't stare.

"Thank you," I breathe, relieved. I rise from the couch. "Take care, Madison. I'm sorry for everything."

She opens the door for me and gives me a sad look. "And here I thought your coming to me that one time meant you were giving in. Can't lie, I'm a little disappointed. But I'll get over it," she says, leaning on the door.

I suppress an eye roll. I'm sure she'll be over it by being under someone else in no time flat. She certainly didn't waste any time doing exactly that as soon as our relationship ended the first time.

"I have no doubt," I reply wryly. "Bye, Maddie."

I don't even wait until I'm back at the car to call Sera. It rings once and goes to voicemail.

"Son of a bitch," I mutter, trying to suppress my annoyance. I place the call again. And again, after one ring it goes to voicemail. Now I'm *really* annoyed. I call her one final time, ready to leave a voicemail if that's how she wants to play it. But this time, she actually answers.

"Boy, you just can't take a hint, can you?" She sounds as angry as I am annoyed.

I don't even bother with apologies or small talk, as I know my window to keep her listening is short.

"I saw Daniel." My words are met with silence, and I know I have her attention.

"*Excuse me?*" Now she sounds furious. "What did you do, Bryce?"

"Don't worry, I used all my best super-secret security guy tricks. He's none the wiser. But I'm also fairly certain he had nothing to do with following or attacking you," I reply.

"And exactly how do you know that?" she asks, her voice echoing on the other end of the line.

"Where are you?" I ask suspiciously.

"I'm in the garage in my building," she replies impatiently.

"Coming or going?" I demand.

"Relax. I just went through a drive-through coffee stand. I ran out," she responds snippily. I hear the noises of an elevator.

"You think someone won't follow you again just because it's daytime?" I press.

She heaves a dramatic sigh. "Fine, next time I'll call you and make you get my coffee. If you're not my personal security guard, you can be my errand boy," she responds, her voice dripping with sarcasm. Man, she's really pissed.

"I'm just worried. If Daniel isn't the one after you…" I pause. There's a soft ping on her end and I hear her moving. "I'm not sure how to figure out who is." Sera suddenly sucks in a sharp breath. There are a few beats of silence, and I'm wondering why that was so shocking when she finally responds.

"I think I might have an idea," she replies, her voice quavering.

My hackles rise. "Are you okay?" I ask, fighting a sudden tightness in my chest.

"I'm fine. We'll talk about it later. I have to go," she replies vaguely. And the line goes dead.

TWENTY-TWO

I concentrate on not dropping my phone or my coffee as I approach the door, my heart pounding in my chest, eyes locked on Alessandro. I slide my phone blindly into my back pocket as I stop a few paces away.

Alessandro stares back. Now that I'm close enough, my eyes can't drink him in quickly enough. His thick, dark brown hair is disheveled, his chocolate brown eyes filled with love and longing. His dark jeans and black T-shirt are loose — he looks like he's lost weight from his already lean frame. In fact, he looks gaunt. Haunted. And he's just as at a loss for words as I am.

"Are you really here?" I finally manage.

"I'm here," he affirms, his voice tired and more lilting than I recall. He steps forward and wraps his arms around me. I sink into his warm embrace, fighting back tears as I inhale deeply of his familiar wine and spice scent. When he pulls away, he stays close, brushing the hair from my face, running his fingers down my jaw. I look up into his eyes, still unable to believe what I'm seeing. "Did you miss me?" His thumb drops to my lip and traces a line that sends fire shooting through my core. I almost forget to be angry. Almost.

I slowly wrap my free hand around his and draw his thumb away from my mouth, vigilantly working to control the myriad of emotions roiling inside me.

"Let's go inside," I reply. I unlock the door and he follows me in.

Once I've put my coffee down, we settle onto the couch. Well, perch on the edge of our seats is more like it. The tension in the room is palpable, and I know he's confused as to why I stopped him from touching me.

"I'm glad to see you're okay," he finally says, breaking the awkward silence. "But I'm a little surprised you don't seem completely happy to see me."

I stare at him, shocked and bemused, unsure which part of that to unpack first. "Why wouldn't I be okay?" I ask.

He frowns and leans back into the couch, crossing his legs and clearly agitated. "That's a long story," he hedges.

"It would be shorter if you'd bothered talking to me these past weeks." I don't even try to keep the annoyance and rage out of my tone.

A look of understanding crosses his face and he leans forward, earnestly folding his hands around mine. "For that, I am truly sorry," he says solemnly. "You must understand it was necessary."

"Well, I don't. Care to explain it to me?" I scoff. Even I feel like I should be more relieved to see him. But I'm not. Now that the initial wave of relief has passed, I really am just mad.

"Serafina, please don't be so angry with me," he pleads.

I want to throw my hands up in frustration. He and Bryce really are more alike than I'd realized. Both completely unaware of the impact of their actions and words.

"I *am* angry. Wouldn't you be?" I ask, turning it back on him.

He runs a finger under his chin thoughtfully and the memory of all the things that gesture used to make me feel makes me want to cry.

"Yes," he concedes. "I'd be infuriated." He looks so forlorn, so defeated, that my anger collapses in on itself. "*Mi dispiace, mio tesoro.*"

The apology is my final undoing, and hot tears spill down my cheeks, a wretched sob tearing itself from my throat. He's holding me in an instant, his warm, rough hands tracing my jaw, his legs pressed against mine. I wrap my hands around his forearms, but only to hang on as the sobs rip out of me. His forehead meets mine, and I can feel him desperately trying to calm me with his touch.

Finally, his lips crash into mine, hot and wet. My overwhelmed body responds, my lips parting to receive his tongue. Our mouths work together fervently, as if their dance can erase the pain and confusion of our separation and subsequent reunion. Long-suppressed need awakens in me, and I nearly swoon with desire for him. It's so overwhelming, it takes a conscious effort to rein it in.

As my control returns, I break away, panting. My gut twists, and I have to search myself to name the feeling that is rising to the top of the ocean of emotions churning inside me. It's disloyalty. As if I'm betraying Bryce.

My anger turns inward at the thought. At how foolish I've been to feel so deeply for two such different men with the same disastrous results. Because now, even though I've consciously chosen Bryce, he hasn't chosen me. He's chosen someone else.

But touching Alessandro still feels wrong. Like an insult to myself, to the decision I'd made. Because his reappearance makes it no less valid. No less likely for there to be an explanation that changes things.

I collect myself completely, the flow of tears stopping, before I dare to speak again. I look up into Alessandro's patient eyes, the same sorrow I feel etched on his face.

"Why are you here?" I ask quietly, calmly.

"Because you are in danger," he replies. "And it's my fault."

I stare into his devastated face for what feels like minutes before it clicks. "The break-in, being followed, the *attack*," I whisper. "It was all because of you?"

Reluctantly, Alessandro nods.

"Explain. Now." My words hiss between my teeth.

Alessandro looks up at the ceiling, blinking back his own tears. When he looks at me again, I try to smooth the anger from my features, knowing it won't help now.

"It was exactly what I feared," he begins. "After we last spoke all those weeks ago, I gave in. I couldn't find the answers on my own. So I contacted a friend who I knew could help. And what we found was much, much worse than I even dreamed. That is why you didn't hear from me. Because I didn't want it to lead them to you. But yesterday we learned they'd found you anyway. Through an email you sent. It didn't take long from there to learn that they were going after you, to drag you to Rome to use against me. I came immediately. I can't even tell you the panic I've been in. How happy I am that you're okay. But now you must come with me. So I can keep you safe from them. If they know I'm here…"

I throw up a hand, having heard enough. "Please," I breathe. "Stop. It's all too much."

He nods understandingly. "I realize how it must have seemed to you," he agrees. "Everything you must have felt, how serious this all is—"

"No," I interrupt quietly. He stops, staring at me, confusion written all over his face. "It's too much of the same. The same vague non-answers. The same excuses for keeping me in the dark. The same threats looming in the background keeping us from just being together and living our lives free of the worry of what *might* happen."

"I assure you, these are very dangerous people and the threat against my life, and now yours, is very real," he replies somberly. I search his eyes and find no exaggeration. He's truly terrified.

"I'm sorry you're going through this," I say slowly. "But I don't see how uprooting my life to hide with you in Italy is going to be any better."

"We'd be together," he says earnestly. "I have the contacts there. It wouldn't be a prison, Serafina. You would be protected. You wouldn't have to fear for your safety any longer."

I laugh humorlessly. "At what cost?" I ask. "Giving up everything and everyone else I care about? And what about your safety? If what you say is true, you'll be in danger regardless."

"For now," he admits. "But not forever."

"Can't you protect me here? Can't you just stay here with me, where we met? Where we fell in love? Where our lives are?" I beg. "I just want to go back to that. Is there any way?" I have to ask. But I already know the answer even before his face falls.

"I wish there were, *amore mio*," he murmurs. "But no. My life is no longer here. There are things I must go back and do. And I can't leave you here, where I can't protect you."

"Alessandro, I'm not yours to protect," I reply. I may as well have slapped him in the face. He starts to rise, but I pull him back down. "Please. I need to say this." He sits back down, a solitary tear falling down his cheek. "I love you. I do. But it's not enough. You left. And then I stopped hearing from you. I was out of my mind until I realized that it was pointless. Whatever your reasons, you've kept me out of it. And in doing that you separated yourself from me, and made decisions on your own that affected me, without so much as checking in."

"I had to, I couldn't..."

"Even before you left, Alessandro. You were doing this. You asked me to be with you completely or not at all once while keeping from me that you weren't mine completely. Then even after you were free to be with me and all *this* started, you still kept it from me. I had to hunt you down and seduce it out of you, for fuck's sake." I shake my head, staring down into my hands. "I've hung on because I love you. But it's only gotten harder. You've only pushed me farther away. And now you're asking me to give up everything after shutting me out completely for *six weeks*. While I sat here, not knowing if you were dead or alive. Not knowing if you still loved me, or if you'd changed your mind. And not knowing the true nature of the danger I was facing." I stop to take a deep breath.

Alessandro is still, silent, and pale. I stare at him sorrowfully. None of this is what I wanted for us.

"You're right," he admits. "I'm selfish. To ask this of you after everything."

"Thank you," I reply simply.

He shakes his head and runs his hands over his face. "I understand if it's too much to ask," he says. "But please think about it?"

I huff an incredulous laugh and shake my head. "I can't go with you," I reply firmly. "It's too late."

His lower lip starts trembling and he grabs my hands. "Don't say that," he insists. "I know this is hard. It's hard for me too. To ask this of you. To ask more of you than you've already given. But everything I've done—"

"Please, please, please, do not say you've done it for me," I object vehemently, withdrawing my hands from his. The ashamed look on his face confirms that's exactly what he was going to say. "If that were really true, you would've asked what *I* wanted. What *I* thought *we* should do. You've done all of this for *you,* Alessandro."

And with those words, the last glimmer of hope for us inside me dies. Because their truth rings through the room. And even he doesn't have the balls to deny it.

My heart softens, watching him grapple with the knowledge that it's over. I fold my hand back over his and squeeze. He looks at me, a perfect picture of misery.

"I wish I could go back and do things differently," he says sorrowfully.

I smile sadly back at him. "But then you wouldn't be the man I fell in love with," I reply.

"I don't know how I can leave not knowing whether or not you'll be safe," he admits. "I'll do what I can from my end. But even if they know we're through, it won't take away how much you mean to me. That's why they're after you."

"Staying won't help that," I point out.

I contemplate telling him how I escaped my attacker. About the security features of the building. And that I still have Bryce. Until a sharp pain in my chest reminds me that I don't. And remembering that renders me unable to speak. I try to control my breathing as panic threatens the edges of my composure.

"I could ask Marco to look out for you," he offers.

I laugh. "Marco has enough to worry about right now, I'm sure," I reply. "Besides, I'll be fine. I promise. You were the one who once extolled the virtues of hiring personal security guards. Lord knows I have the money to hire the best protection."

Alessandro considers that for a moment. "You're not going to hire the giant, are you?" he asks reticently.

I want to laugh, but pain shoots through my chest again. "No," I reply softly. "That's not an option." I look up into Alessandro's soft, sad eyes once more. "I'll make some calls as soon as I can. I'll be protected around the clock. You needn't worry."

"Nonetheless, I will," he says softly.

He smiles my favorite sideways smile and I can't help it, I pull him to me and wrap my arms around him fiercely. He embraces me readily, stroking my hair and holding me tightly until I let go. I rise, taking his hand in mine one final time, and walk him to the door.

"Be careful," I plead.

He nods and gives my hand one last squeeze. Then he leans in, touching his lips gently to mine.

"Goodbye, Serafina Evans."

"*Arrivederci*, Alessandro Giordano."

TWENTY-THREE

True to my word, I spend the rest of the day researching private security online. It keeps me focused enough so the last shattered piece of my heart that belonged to Alessandro doesn't completely incapacitate me. It wouldn't be so bad if that part wasn't right next to the crushed piece that belongs to Bryce. But I'm proud of myself for finally sticking to my guns and not settling for being treated like shit. Even if, in the end, I'm alone. Funny how that's exactly what I used to prefer. Now, who knows? Allie would probably call that growth. I call it exhausting. My whole world has been upended more times than I can count lately.

I shake away the depressing train of thought and refocus on the screen in front of me. Resigned to my task for the following day, I email work to let everyone know I'll be taking the day off. I save the list of companies and shut down my computer, ready to drink myself numb to ride out the rest of the evening.

❦

I'M REGRETTING MY ALCOHOL-RELATED DECISION THE NEXT MORNING WHEN I wake with a pounding headache. But somehow it occurs to me, while I wait for the ibuprofen to kick in, to ask Maggie which of the private security companies on my list had the best recommendations, and if there are any others she'd discovered when she did her search several months ago. Besides Hoyt Corporate Services, of course.

It turns out to be a huge time saver as only two of the companies I'd sourced were well recommended *and* do personal armed security. And only one has availability to start immediately. I schedule an in-home meeting for the afternoon to get set up.

And then I spend the rest of the morning cleaning out the downstairs bedroom to ready it for its new occupants.

⁓

At several minutes past the hour of the meeting, I sit in the dining room, cradling a cup of tea and tapping my foot impatiently. Finally, the doorbell rings.

I open the door to a put-together blond woman with a sleek bun and a no-nonsense plum-colored bespoke suit and a tall, stern man with salt-and-pepper hair who appears to be in his forties.

"Ms. Evans?" the blond asks, extending a hand.

"Yes, you must be Ms. Pruitt," I respond, shaking her hand. "Please, come in."

"Please, call me Lisa," she responds as she enters, scanning the room appraisingly. "And this is Mr. Wallace." She gestures to the stern man. He dips his head briefly and firmly shakes my hand.

I lead them both to the living room and they take a seat on the couch as I settle into my armchair.

"Thank you for seeing me on such short notice," I say. "As I explained on the phone, having been attacked the night before last, I'm ready for some peace of mind."

She leans forward eagerly. "I can imagine. Any of the incidents you described would be cause for concern. In any case, I'm confident we can help you," she agrees.

"I'm glad to hear it. I've reviewed the contracts you emailed, and everything seems fine. Why don't you tell me a little more about the practical aspects of the arrangement?" I prompt.

"Certainly," she responds. "Your contract includes one guard, to be present at all times. Actually, it will be three guards, each working an eight-hour shift. As each guard will be present for a different portion of your day, each may have recommendations on security precautions, schedule modifications, or other adjustments to ensure your continued safety. It is, of course, up to you which recommendations to follow. We will always do our best to protect you in a way that suits *your* needs, as long as there is no immediate danger."

"Sounds reasonable," I agree.

She nods curtly and continues. "We have received your deposit, so I simply need to verify your identification and witness your signing of the contracts. As a reminder, you can cancel your contract at any time, for any reason, with seventy-two hours' notice. If for any reason there is a particular security guard you feel isn't a good fit, please let us know and we will remove them from your rotation, no questions asked. Do you have any additional questions?" Her speech done, she looks at me expectantly.

"The contract was fairly thorough," I allow. "I understand that I will be responsible for all costs including food, travel, and incidentals, but am I understanding correctly that the guards will not actually be living here?"

"That's correct," she agrees. "They'll simply need to use the room requested as a base, especially for the night shift. But they will only utilize it as necessary for the eight hours they are each assigned to your security detail."

"What are the shift times?" I ask.

"There is some flexibility, and we recommend adjusting them to your schedule," she explains. "What time do you usually start and finish work?"

"I start between seven and eight a.m. and usually finish between six and seven p.m."

"Then I think shifts starting each at six a.m., two p.m., and ten p.m. would be best. Does that work for you?" she asks. She's all business as she primly folds her hands in her lap, awaiting my response.

"Well, I'll let you know if it doesn't," I reply with a small smile.

Her perfect mask doesn't crack. "Certainly," she agrees.

I want to chuckle. This woman is like a robot. But I suppress it and focus on the paperwork she's laying out on the coffee table.

"Please initial here to acknowledge that your guard, and therefore you, are GPS-tracked at all times," she points, and I obligingly scribble my initials. "And here to accept use of the provided driver service as your primary method of transportation." Another scribble. "And sign and date here to accept the full contract terms." A bigger scribble. "And that's it. Oh, and as stipulated in the contract, each guard has signed nondisclosure agreements as part of their general employment requirements not to share any personal information regarding their clients for both the duration of your utilizing our services and after termination."

"Naturally," I reply drily, glancing at Mr. Wallace.

He's barely moved a muscle this whole time. Maybe they're all robots. I almost giggle.

Lisa rises, extending a hand once more. "It's been a pleasure meeting you," she says mechanically. "I'll leave you and Mr. Wallace to get acquainted."

I see her to the door, and immediately notice my new, Mr. Wallace-shaped shadow tailing me. I glance over my shoulder at him. This is going to take some getting used to.

Once we are alone, I size Mr. Wallace up a bit more thoroughly. His impeccable black suit and tie and white shirt look starchy and uncomfortable. Or maybe that's just his stiff demeanor.

"Mr. Wallace," I say. "Do you have a first name?"

His stern façade cracks just a bit as the corner of his mouth lifts. "Yes, ma'am," he replies. His first words. His voice is commanding and just as severe as his demeanor. "Ross, ma'am."

I let out a small cough to cover a laugh. "I see," I reply. "May I call you Ross? Or would you prefer Mr. Wallace?"

"Ross is fine, ma'am," he responds.

"Call me, Sera, please. No need for 'ma'am,'" I encourage him. He nods. "Thank you. Now, is there anything we need to cover before I give you a tour?"

"We can cover most things as we go. But most important," he says, holding up a cellphone. "This is the cellphone assigned to only you that your guard or driver will carry at all times. You should program this number into your phone. It is how you will let whoever is on duty know when you are ready to be picked up from a location. It is your connection to us."

I nod and pull out my cellphone and he helps me program the number in.

"Okay," I say when it's done. "Let me show you around."

As we stroll the rooms he asks questions about my habits, my work, my visitors, that sort of thing. It's clear he'll be filling out some sort of report, and I can't help but mess with him a little here and there. Through that, I'm pleased to find he clearly does have a sense of humor, it's just carefully controlled as part of the whole serious bodyguard schtick. Most important, though, I find I'm more comfortable with him than I thought I'd be. Which is huge. Because the last thing I need right now is more difficult shit to deal with.

❧

AT THE TEN P.M. SHIFT CHANGE, HOWEVER, A NEW KIND OF CHALLENGE presents itself in the form of Bodyguard Number Two. From the moment Ross lets him in, I know I'm in trouble. Because he's one of the most attractive people I've ever seen. At just over six feet, with blond hair, green eyes, full lips, and a swimmer's body under his well-tailored black suit, I'm immediately mesmerized. He extends a broad hand and flashes a dazzling smile full of bright white teeth.

"Tristan Thomas," he introduces himself. His honeyed voice matches his Midwest good looks perfectly. I'd put him in his late twenties. I clear my throat.

"I'm Sera," my voice comes out a squeak. I inwardly roll my eyes at myself. I'm sure he gets this reaction a lot, but I somewhat despise myself for letting him have this effect on me.

His smile widens, and my hand lingers on his for what feels like a fraction of a second too long. "I'll just be a few minutes. Ross and I should sync up before he leaves," Tristan excuses himself.

I retire to the kitchen to finish the dinner dishes and watch them talk as Ross gives Tristan the tour. And in less than ten minutes, Ross is wishing me a good night and heading out the door. Tristan stands at the window wall, gazing out at the city sparkling in the velvety blue night.

"Nice view," he remarks.

I set down the dishtowel and approach, stopping a few paces behind him. "It is," I agree.

He turns to note that I've come closer.

"I should be getting to bed soon."

Tristan nods. "I'll be in the guest room, then," he replies. "Does the security system have multiple modes?"

I take him to the panel in the living room and flip through the settings. He chooses a door and window monitoring setting, leaving him free to roam without setting off any alarms.

"Help yourself to anything in the kitchen or whatever you need," I say. "Is there anything else I can get for you before I go to bed?" I keep my eyes locked on his, refusing to let them travel down his gloriously attractive body. I do not need to leave him thinking that I'm on that list of things he can have before bed, despite how hard my heart is pounding in my chest being close to him. *God, what is wrong with me?*

Tristan smiles knowingly. "No," he replies. "I'm just going to go call my boyfriend before he goes to bed."

I'm sure the shock passes over my face, but all I can think is, *Oh, thank god.* "Sounds good," I respond, trying not to sound as relieved as I feel. "Goodnight."

As I fall asleep, I briefly wonder if Tristan really is gay, or if he realized that an icy shock is the fastest way to douse an inferno.

∽

Being driven to work with yet another bodyguard beside me is a trip, to say the least. Thankfully, this one I like the best so far. Aiden Green is a slim, dark-haired man in his fifties. He's incredibly laid-back and very friendly, and with his Irish accent, subtle deference, and impeccable manners, he makes me feel like royalty. Or someone very important, anyway. It's hard to describe. But for the first time I'm not self-conscious at all for needing to be under the watchful eye of an armed guard. Though the thought of getting comfortable with it is strangely disconcerting too.

Work is a welcome reprieve from the drama of the past few days, and I happily surrender to the familiar ebb and flow of meetings, deadlines, and decision making. I allow myself to sink deeply into a new routine, my only companions out of work being Ross, Tristan, and Aiden. But I know it can't last forever. Especially if the mounting log of missed calls and text messages is any indication.

My mother, father, Allie, and Emily have all contacted me. And I've ignored them all in turn, unable or unwilling to remove myself from the careful bubble where I don't think about the one person I haven't heard from — Bryce. He's the one person I want to talk to the most. The one person whose silence pains me more than I allow myself to think about. But every time I start to wonder if I'm truly so easy to forget, I force my emotions back down.

Dodging my own thoughts and the attempts at communication of my friends and family gets easier when Tristan is switched to swing shift on Wednesday. I still find him ridiculously attractive, but with the pressure of any possible sexual tension removed, I find he's actually the best companion of my three protectors. It makes sense since he's the closest to my age. But it turns out he's also a sweet, intelligent guy. And he's very interested in what I do, so we have plenty to discuss to keep my mind off other things.

But on Thursday evening, ignoring everything I can't deal with finally catches up with me when someone furiously pounds on the door. Tristan jumps up from the couch beside me, hand on his gun.

"Serafina Evans, I know you're in there," Emily's voice calls through the door. I heave a sigh and climb out of my armchair, signaling Tristan to stand down. "You pinky swore! You'd better open the door this instant, or I swear to god I'm going to force my brother to come down here and…"

I swing the door open and level an annoyed glare at Emily. "And what?" I demand with a smirk.

Emily pushes past me into the condo. "Moot. Why have you been ignoring me?" she demands. She stops dead as she spots Tristan. "Oh."

"Tristan, this is my friend, Emily. Emily, Tristan."

Emily looks Tristan up and down. He's removed his jacket, but he still looks like hot, sexy business in his crisp, fitted white shirt, skinny black tie, and slim-fit black slacks.

"And Tristan is?" Emily's face is filled with questions and something bordering on anger.

"A bodyguard," I reply simply. "Tristan, can you please give us some privacy?"

Tristan nods curtly, clearly alarmed at the sudden, demanding intruder.

"You know where I am if you need me," he assures me. He ducks into the guest room off the entryway, and I turn back to Emily, who has settled herself on the couch.

"Did I just step into a movie? Because that dude is unnaturally hot," Emily says.

I huff a laugh. "Yes, he is. And so, so gay," I reply.

"Damnit," Emily jokes. "Oh well. Probably out of my league regardless. A bodyguard, huh?"

I sigh heavily as I sink into my armchair. "A bodyguard," I confirm. "I'm not sure if you'd heard…"

"About the attack?" She nods. "I'm so sorry, Sera. I wanted to give you some space, with everything, but when you didn't message or call me back, I kinda freaked out."

"And then came barging over here?" I say sweetly.

"Ehhh, sort of. I tried to get my brother to come, but he refused. Something about you promising to call him back and then not. So he figures if you want to talk to him you will."

Oh, shit. With everything that happened, my mind glitched out on promising to talk to him later about whoever was following me.

"Fuuuuuck," I respond. "I'd completely forgotten about that. What else did he tell you?"

"That you got the wrong idea," she replies.

I snort. "That's rich. I think I got exactly the right idea," I grumble.

"Meaning what?" she asks sharply.

"Meaning he's a double-standard-setting, unavailable, demanding jackass, just like Alessandro," I snap.

"Wow, tell me how you really feel," she responds.

"Seriously, Emily. He's fucking Madison. And he had the balls to make me think *I* was what was holding us back from being together," I retort.

"*Was* fucking Madison," she replies.

I wave a hand. "Whatever. It's doesn't matter anymore. He made his bed, and he clearly didn't really want me in it," I say, starting to shake with suppressed emotion.

"Why would you say that?" Emily asks sadly. She is sincerely confused, and I wonder how much he told her.

I sigh heavily, unsure of where to even begin. I start by telling her my version of what happened after she last visited me here. I explain that I tried to tell Bryce about my decision, and what I felt for him, but only got to the former before Madison showed up. And then after I was attacked, the next morning was so difficult. Because his actions and his words were so mismatched, it was unbearable. And how I lost hope that day. Only to fortuitously be tested about the decision that started it all when Alessandro reappeared.

When I tell her about our conversation and how I stood my ground, a proud look settles over her. And when I tell her that all the danger I've been facing is tied to him, she looks as grim as I feel. But she lets me finish, lets me explain how, even in the face of all that, I still stayed strong. And I feel better for having relived those painful moments.

"It made me realize something," I explain, finishing my story. "They both wanted something from me that they weren't prepared to give themselves. So you were right about Alessandro. I saw his selfishness in every word he said to me. But you were wrong about Bryce. Maybe he hasn't moved on, but what he did was just as selfish."

"Maybe," Emily concedes thoughtfully. "But I've been there for him through everything you guys have gone through. You're not perfect either, Sera. And I say that now, knowing you, and knowing that you aren't a selfish person. But that's the thing. Everyone can be selfish sometimes. Especially when they're hurting."

Her words break the bubble I've wrapped myself in, and my carefully stoic demeanor collapses. Because she's right. I know how much I've hurt Bryce throughout all of this. And how much he's been going through. How much we've both been going through. It abruptly all rushes back, and it's too much. I can't catch my breath, and panic overtakes me as the tears I've suppressed all week finally come all at once. Emily looks at me, a heartbreakingly sad expression on her face, and it makes it so much worse.

"I can't..." my sobs stop me from finishing. I shake my head as the tears pour out. I breathe in deeply, fighting to control myself until I've regained the ability to speak. "I have nothing left. Even if I could make it right. I wouldn't begin to know how anymore. And I swear to you, Emily, I know how good Bryce is. I can forgive his selfishness, because you're right. I've done the same to him. Probably worse. But if he really wanted me, why was I the one chasing him?"

"Does it matter who chases who?" she asks, fighting her own tears. "I just want to see you both happy."

I shake my head. "Twice now I've decided to be done with Alessandro. I told Bryce I was. And I guess I didn't believe it myself until I had to say it to Alessandro himself. But I am. I wasn't lying, and I've proven that. But all Bryce said was that Madison doesn't mean anything to him. Not that he was done. Not that he wanted me. He hasn't said that..." I can't think since when. I shake my head again. "I can't even remember the last time. Too long. I've made a fool of myself."

"Sera, please, just try," she pleads.

I snap my head up, angrily wiping away fresh tears. "Has he told you that he loves me? That he's not seeing Madison anymore because he wants to be with me?" I demand. Her blank stare is all the answer I need. "Exactly. So you, Emily, please, just stop. If you want us both to be happy, let us move on. There's nothing else I can do now."

"You're not wrong," Emily's voice quavers with emotion. "He hasn't said any of that to me. But he doesn't need to. I know him. He's in love with you, Sera."

I laugh a tired, tearful laugh. And I don't want to be cruel to Emily, but she's crossed the line into meddling. And I'm so, so tired of it all.

"If that were true, wouldn't he be here telling me that instead of you? It's not exactly an epic journey. He lives about ten minutes away. I'm the one who's been repeatedly stalked and assaulted. And now I'm basically a prisoner to my circumstances until this all blows over. I've got enough on my plate, for fuck's sake. I've told him where I stand. If he has something to say about it, maybe he should try not sending his sister to do it for him." I expect Emily to be offended at the very least.

But she's not. She just looks sad. "You're right," she murmurs.

I catch her eye, trying to apologize silently, trying to communicate the affection I have for her. That I know she just wants to help. I'm not sure if I manage it, but we both sit in contemplative silence for a bit.

"I should go." Emily rises from the couch and I follow, with no intention of stopping her.

She stops at the door and turns to embrace me. I squeeze her tightly, putting my frustration aside. When she releases me, I hold it together long enough for her to leave.

I'm on the floor, slumped against the door for who knows how long when I feel Tristan's strong body slide down next to me, his solid, warm arm wrapping around me from the side. I lean into him and let go, my hot, salty tears staining his crisp, cool white shirt. And since I'm pretty sure this is outside his job description, I'm especially grateful that he makes no move to stop the wanton destruction of his uniform as I let all my grief out. Finally.

TWENTY-FOUR

Friday is miserable. Tired from a night of little sleep and plenty of tears, I struggle to make it through the day even with large doses of caffeine. But it's not so much the exhaustion as it is that I've embraced the reality of everything that's happened. And it's a lot, but I know I'll be okay. I've survived worse, after all.

Tristan meets me after work in front of the building, escorting me into the back of a black sedan. And I just want to go home and bury myself under blankets and booze for the weekend. As we start our drive, I stare out the window at the gathering rain clouds. Summer has finally started to melt into the first vestiges of fall. While it's still warm, a humid darkness threatens the sky, coordinating well with the darkness of my mood.

When we get home I silently grab a bottle of whiskey from the kitchen and settle into my chair with a fuzzy brown blanket wrapped around me, intent on watching the rain and getting stinking drunk. But before I can bring the bottle to my lips, Tristan kneels in front of me, his green eyes clouded with worry.

"Sera," he says softly. "I hate to do this to you, but I need you to not drink yet. My boss is coming by."

I stare at him quizzically. "Your boss?" I ask dully. "Why?"

"He wants to check on things here. If he sees you drinking like this, he might think I'm not taking very good care of you," he explains.

I snort. "I didn't know keeping your charges from drowning their sorrows was part of your job," I reply.

Tristan frowns, and I'm immediately sorry.

"Tristan. Forgive me. Of course, I won't drink until he's gone."

Tristan nods solemnly. "Thank you," he replies, clearly relieved.

I sigh and heave myself from the chair to return the bottle to the cupboard. "Will I need to speak to him?" I ask dully.

"Yes. I'm sorry for the short notice, but I only heard this afternoon," he replies.

I sigh resignedly. "It's okay. I'll go get cleaned up then. How long do I have?" I ask.

"He'll be here soon," Tristan replies apologetically.

I suppress my irritation and nod, heading up the stairs. My dress is crumpled, and I could use a long, hot shower, but I'll have to settle for a quick rinse and an even quicker change of clothes.

Ten minutes later I'm headed back downstairs in black yoga pants and grey T-shirt when I hear a voice downstairs. Tristan is filling someone in on the week's events, which is to say, basically explaining my going back and forth to work. I pause for a moment to see if he'll mention Emily's visit and my subsequent breakdown, but when I halt on the stair it creaks and Tristan stops speaking. My cover blown, I continue down the stairs. As I round the corner into the main living space, I'm stopped short. Standing next to Tristan in the dining area is the last person I expected to see.

Bryce's clear blue eyes meet mine, and my heart drops into my stomach. It's so pronounced that I physically grab my midsection in surprise, tears springing to my eyes. He looks the same as he always does. Heartbreakingly handsome in khakis and a white polo, his chestnut hair freshly cut, though he's perhaps a tad leaner than the last time I saw him only five days ago.

Tristan glances nervously between us as I approach. I didn't even realize my legs were carrying me forward until I stop next to Tristan, my eyes breaking from Bryce's to stare accusingly at my should-be protector.

"I thought you said your boss was coming by," I say accusingly. "What the hell is this?"

Tristan looks deeply uncomfortable, but it's Bryce who answers.

"I *am* his boss," he asserts. "The company you contracted is the private security company we acquired in order to offer those services to our clients."

I glance between the two, Tristan continuing to remain awkwardly silent. And I realize what a difficult position this must put him in.

"You can go, Tristan," I assure him.

Tristan looks at Bryce, who nods in agreement. And I've never seen anyone move so fast. When the guest room door closes behind him moments later, I look back up at Bryce.

"Why are you here?" I ask, my heart heavy with pain and longing. Even now, amid the anguish and sorrow of the past week, I just want to reach out to him, to feel his arms around me. It's a special kind of torture having to be this close to him.

"I talked to Emily last night," he replies, as if that explains everything. I shrug and crumple into a dining room chair. "God, Sera, you look like hell." He pulls out the chair next to me and sits down facing me.

"Gee, thanks," I reply sarcastically, picking at my fingernails. "You look like you're doing just fine."

"I'm not. I've been worried sick about you this week," he replies.

I look at him skeptically. "Did you know? When Alessandro came back? Did you get one of your notification thingies?" I demand.

A smile tugs at the corners of his mouth. "No," he admits. "I stopped monitoring the situation after he was located."

"Oh," I say softly. "How much did Emily tell you?"

"I made her tell me everything. She wasn't happy about it. Said she was betraying your confidence," he replies.

"Then why did she do it?" I asked, annoyed.

"Because she's worried about you too. About us," he responds softly.

"There is no 'us,'" I remind him.

His lips press into a thin line and his nostrils flare. "I think it's time to set a few things straight," he responds slowly. "But I want you to promise me that you'll finish this conversation and not run in the middle of it. I want you to have all the information before you decide to hate me."

I stare at him, somewhere between sad, angry, and confused. I don't bother correcting him by explaining that I could never hate him. "Fine," I whisper. "I promise."

Bryce nods, leaning back in his chair and running a hand over his hair. "When we had that fight the week after you came back from San Francisco, I was at the start of one of the most difficult periods of my life," he admits. "You know I was in love with you." The past tense and his averted gaze are like a knife to my heart, but I only nod and stay silent. "And we knew something was wrong with my father. Nobody talked about it, but we all knew. And it was making work, well, you remember." I nod again, and he takes a deep breath.

It's a minute before he continues again. "I decided after our fight that I wasn't going to go after you. If you wanted to talk to me, that was on you. And if you did, I was determined to keep you at a distance until I didn't have those kinds of feelings anymore. And then my father died, and I was a fucking mess. Much worse than before."

I can see his agitation as he runs his hands over his hair repeatedly, hard and fast. It makes me want to hold his hands in mine to steady him. Because even knowing what comes next, I can't stop what I feel for him. Even if he can.

"Everything was jumbled. And you were such a pillar of strength for me that week. The day of the funeral, lines were blurred. It was harder for me to wish away my feelings. When you left that day, I was weak again. And I admit it, I let Madison seduce me, even though I knew better."

I raise an eyebrow. I'd like to tell him it's cheap to blame her, but I also acutely remember the pain and confusion grief can cause.

"And after that?" I point out.

He grimaces. "The next time was after the day in the gym," he admits. "I was frustrated. I didn't intend for it to happen again. And I meant what I said to you that day. But I didn't think for a minute that I was what you really wanted. I just didn't want you to think you could try it out without being serious about it. I didn't want to start things up again just to have them stop like they had before."

I realize it's time to tell him what I couldn't get to when Madison showed up the night I came to confess everything to him. Because even though it may do no good, he's being honest with me. And he deserves the same in return.

"You were," I reply, but he looks confused. "What I wanted," I clarify. "That's what I was trying to tell you before the attack. But even before Madison showed up, I was pretty sure you'd been with her the night before."

He looks surprised at that bit of information. "Then why didn't you tell me that after she was gone?" he asks incredulously.

I shrug, twisting my fingers together in my lap. "Suspecting it was one thing. But seeing her there, the way she talked to you, I knew I didn't have a shot once I was sure you two were together," I say, my voice barely above a whisper.

He shakes his head miserably. "That last night with her was another huge mistake. And not one I sought out. I should have put a stop to it then, but I hoped I could just avoid it happening again. I never meant for you to be hurt by it. And I meant it when I said she means nothing to me. Madison did some awful things that caused me to end our relationship in the first place. I would have never, in my right mind, gone anywhere near her like that ever again."

His explanation makes sense but brings me no peace. I close my eyes and inhale deeply through my nose. His evergreen summer scent flows through me, causing another sharp pain in my chest. When I open my eyes, Bryce is staring at me. The compassion in his expression is almost too much, and I shift uncomfortably in my chair.

"I believe you," I respond, sensing he was waiting for me to say something. I'm not sure what else to say. But it seems to satisfy him anyway.

"I ended it on Sunday. It's not what I wanted in the first place. If I could go back, I wouldn't make that mistake again. And I never meant for it to hurt or confuse you," he explains.

I pull a leg up to my chest and wrap my arms around it. "Well. Now I know. Thank you for setting the record straight," I reply tiredly.

"I'm not done," he persists.

Tears sting the back of my eyes. I'm not sure how much more he can expect me to take. But I promised. "Go on," I allow.

He laughs and shakes his head. "You don't get it, do you?"

I look up at him, annoyed. "I don't get what's funny about this," I agree.

He smiles and shakes his head, leaning forward intently. "It's funny because I'm an idiot. From the moment I met you, Serafina Evans, I've been crazy, ridiculously, madly in love with you. I'm an idiot for thinking I could snap out of that. An idiot for letting Madison worm her way between us. But mostly, I'm an idiot for not accepting you on whatever terms you wanted me. Because, all of you or not, any of you is better than none."

My heart stops as I gape up at him.

He drops to his knees in front of me, pulling my leg down and taking my hands in his. He looks earnestly into my eyes, his handsome face awash with worry. "Can you forgive me?"

I continue to stare at him, bewildered, a thousand emotions running through me at once. "I guess Emily didn't tell you *everything*, then," I murmur.

His expression falters, giving way to confusion.

"I've hurt you too, Bryce. I've been selfish. I've jerked you around. I never meant to, same as you, but sometimes the path our hearts take isn't straight or easy. But I know in my heart that you are good. So good. Maybe too good for me. So yes, I forgive you. Do you forgive me?"

Bryce laughs, full and hearty, and it's hard not to smile in response. "Considering I just told you you've had my undying love from day one, yes, I think I can forgive you," he replies, his eyes sparkling. "But I'm not. Too good for you, that is." His expression is suddenly serious again. "And I'm not going to pressure you. I just want you to be happy. And if you're really happier without me…"

I pull a hand free and press it over his mouth. "You really *are* an idiot," I say, laughing. "You don't get it, do you?" I can feel the grin break across his face under my hand as he realizes what I'm about to say. "I'm crazy, ridiculously, madly in love with you too, Bryce Hoyt." I drop my hand from his face. And there it is. My sunshine smile. My heart leaps in my chest, a different and wholly welcome pang of emotion.

Through a mist of happy tears, I watch his hands rise to my face. Then I feel them, warm and rough, holding me gently as he brings his mouth to mine. Our lips meet softly, wet with the tears streaming down my face. Warmth spreads through me as his mouth presses into mine more insistently. His tongue parts my lips, meeting my own fervently as I slide my hands over his shoulders and down the firm muscles of his back. He moves a hand to my lower back, and pulling me with him, he settles on the floor between our chairs, forcing me to sit astride him as he plants kisses down my jaw and neck. It's bliss, being in his arms finally.

And when his lips find mine again I'm dizzy and flushed, and a small noise escapes me as his hands rove over me. But I'm also suddenly very aware that we're groping each other in the middle of the dining room floor. I push him away gently, so we can slow down, and I take the opportunity to look deeply into his eyes.

"This isn't anything like the first time I kissed you," I remark.

He laughs easily, pulling me up from the floor. Now standing, he holds me against his body, leaning in to whisper huskily in my ear. "No, it's not," he agrees, running his nose along my earlobe and sending jolts of electricity shooting through me. "But you were a bit distracted then." He continues to softly kiss my neck.

With my cheek resting against his taut chest, I'm finding it difficult to do anything but breathe through the pleasure of his touch. "I'd say I'm pretty well distracted now," I huff.

He pulls away, laughing once more and flashing his sunshine smile.

I touch it with the tips of my fingers, a reflecting smile on my face. "I missed this."

His eyes sparkle as he runs his fingertips down my jaw.

"It's getting late," he murmurs, suddenly distracted. "Shift change is in an hour."

Reminded of Tristan in the other room, I disentangle myself from Bryce and sigh. He looks disappointed for a fraction of a second, so I lay my hand reassuringly on his arm.

"Stay," I say.

A sexy smirk settles on his face and his eyes dance with desire, sending warmth shooting through my core. Bryce turns toward the guest room.

"Tristan," he calls.

I slide back into my dining room chair, attempting to breathe normally and push back the rosy flush I feel on my cheeks. Tristan pops out of his room and rejoins us.

"Shifts are suspended until further notice."

Tristan eyes my red face and disheveled clothes and is unable to suppress a smile. "Yes, sir," he agrees happily. He gives me a friendly smile and wave. "Bye, Sera." I can almost hear the unspoken, "Have fun."

I laugh. "Bye, Tristan," I respond.

Bryce and I are both still as Tristan takes his leave. When the door has quietly closed behind him, Bryce's large, warm hand tugs at mine, pulling me back into a standing position.

A sudden bout of shyness overtakes me as I realize we are alone together, for the first time in a long time, with the expectation of more. But this time is so very different. Because I want him more than I've ever wanted anyone or anything. He's been my protector, my best friend, and my rock. And I know I can trust him with all of me. That he sees me, warts and all, and still chooses me. I've never been so vulnerable. Or so happy.

He stares down at me patiently, his hands lightly skimming my arms.

"What are you thinking?" I ask him.

He smiles furtively. "That I'm the luckiest bastard alive," he replies. His eyes darken, his hands wrapping firmly around my waist. "And that it's about damn time I took you to bed."

A pleasurable shudder shoots through me, and I wrap my arms around his neck, pulling his face to mine. I expect the intensity of his kiss, but I don't expect the slow, sensual exploration as our bodies meld together. When I'm nearly breathless with desire, he pulls back for a moment, stroking my face gently. He slides his finger down to my chin, then pulls my lips back to his. This time his mouth is unrelenting, taking mine in greedily, his tongue still slowly stoking the fire in me.

And suddenly he's lifted me up, wrapping my legs around his torso. He supports my weight with his hands under me as his lips continue to work with mine. He carries me upstairs, and I feel my back hit the bedroom door.

He uses the flat surface to pause, pressing me against it and grinding his hips into me. A low groan rumbles through his chest, and I break my mouth from his, sighing with pleasure. But he doesn't stop, and his mouth continues greedily kissing and sucking down my neck. Finally, his hand reaches for the doorknob and we spill into the bedroom.

He lays me gently on the bed, hovering over me, staring into my eyes as if he could derive all his pleasure from the simple act of seeing my love for him there. Abruptly, he rears back and hooks his thumbs in his collar, pulling his shirt forward over his head and removing it. A small noise escapes me as I'm face to face with the mental image that's been haunting me for weeks. But now I can use my hands to explore the perfect planes of his chest and stomach. My fingers are icy on his warm skin, but he leans into my touch nonetheless. I bite my lip, concentrating, as I drop my hands to his belt.

Bryce pulls back, smiling and shaking his head. "Tit for…" he trails off. "Well, you know." He winks, and I have to laugh.

I wriggle into a sitting position and let him remove my shirt. As he tosses it over the side of the bed, I deftly reach behind my back and unhook my bra, tossing it after the discarded shirt. When he sees me topless, his lips part and his tongue slides across his bottom lip. But his control is flawless as he leisurely leans down and blows a hot breath across the tip of my breast.

It tickles slightly, and I bite my lip to suppress a giggle. He smiles up at me before running his nose over the sensitive flesh. It responds, the peak lengthening, the skin around it tightening. He groans appreciatively and sinks his warm mouth over it, gently working it with his tongue. He sucks away as he pulls up, and I groan involuntarily at the sensation. He languidly trails more warm kisses down my stomach, stopping at the top fold of my pants. His fingers travel along the thick seam, teasing my sensitive flesh as he drops occasional kisses along the way. My hips are twitching in anticipation.

"So impatient," he laughs. He crawls up the length of my torso to plant a firm kiss on my lips.

For a moment, I savor his weight on me, the feeling of his tight muscles against my soft chest, and the warmth of his lips. Then, with a stroke of his nose on mine, he drops away again, and before I'm even aware of what he's doing, his capable hands have pulled my bottoms off completely, leaving me naked. With another decisive lunge, his strong hands separate and lift my legs, exposing me to his waiting mouth. He gives me a final, sexy smirk as his head disappears between my thighs.

The first slow, gentle touch of his tongue sends a jolt through me. I work to still myself, eager for more. He masterfully increases his pace and pressure so that I'm not overwhelmed, but the intense ache that begins to build almost immediately is borderline unbearable. So when he adds a finger to the mix I can't control the arch of my hips. But he hangs on, his skillful tongue and hand following my movements as I work myself involuntarily with his motions. When he inserts another finger, though, I nearly fly off the bed. The now-rapid pressure inside and out is driving me insane as the ache builds to an intense explosion. I cry out, the ascent to my climax more slow and intense than I've ever experienced. And just when I think it's about to end, he flexes his fingers inside me and redoubles the weighty caress of his wicked tongue. Pleasure so deep and powerful carries me over the edge, and my body shakes with the immensity of my orgasm. As I crash back to earth, he slowly withdraws, leaving one last gentle, hot kiss on my inner thigh before sliding up next to me.

I turn toward him as his mouth finds mine, and the taste of me on his lips is another level of eroticism I was unprepared for.

It takes me a moment to stop panting, to regain control of my jelly-like limbs, and to find my voice again.

"That was insane," I admit.

He laughs and kisses my neck. I weave my fingers through the short, thick, chestnut hair on top of his head as his tongue plays along the tender skin of my clavicle.

"Good insane?" he asks.

"Mind-blowing, life-altering insane," I assure him. "Let's-call-off-the-shifts-for-the-rest-of-the-weekend insane."

"Wow, and I thought *I* enjoyed that," he teases.

I look at him in disbelief. "You really are a giver, aren't you?" I ask incredulously.

He kisses me deeply, pulling back and sliding his teeth across my lip along the way.

"I suppose. I certainly enjoyed giving you that orgasm. You have no idea how sexy you are when you're coming in my mouth," he responds.

And I didn't think it possible again so soon, but I feel myself grow wet at his words. "Bryce Hoyt," I say in mock shock. "I had no idea you were so dirty." I push him onto his back. "I like it."

And intent on returning the favor, I remove his pants, only to discover the largest, most beautiful cock I've ever seen. He smiles down at me proudly as I take it in, running my hands over it to convince myself it's real. It's a little daunting for what I had planned, but I accept the challenge happily.

As Bryce did, I take my time pleasuring him, using my lips, tongue, hands, and anything else that occurs to me to slowly build his pleasure. He's so huge that taking the entire length of him into my mouth isn't possible, but it's a fun challenge nonetheless. And the next pleasant surprise is the amazing noises he makes, affirming his pleasure the whole way with low moans, pleased gasps, and guttural groans. It's almost enough to make me come all over again. And I can tell I've brought him close when his breathing takes a sharp turn toward sustained, wailing gasps.

"Ohhhh, baby," he pleads. "If you don't stop, I'm going to come in your mouth."

I don't answer, simply catching his eye as I bear down on him, sliding him all the way back in my throat as I twist my grip around the wide base of him. His lets out another groan and throws his head back as he finds his release. His every cry, the taste of him, watching his long, muscled frame contract with pleasure under my touch almost overwhelms me with ecstasy. And I realize fully Emily's point about being with a giver. Because the bliss found by two people who would do anything to please each other is staggering.

And when I return to his arms, there's no need to say anything. He simply folds himself around me as we both drift into a deep, satisfying sleep.

TWENTY-FIVE

For once Bryce sleeps past five. I actually wake up before him, the first vestiges of daylight peeking around the shades. His heavy frame is draped all around me, making escape impossible. Not that I mind terribly. Even though the places our bodies touch are warm and slightly tacky with the sweat that's dried between us, it's intensely gratifying to be so close to him. To be his at last.

After a few minutes of laying naked underneath his gorgeous body, I'm unable to keep from touching him. I trace the bulging muscles in his arms lightly with my fingers, marveling at their definition. With my hand resting in the crook of his elbow, my thumb hovers close to one of his nipples. And I can't resist rubbing it in a firm circle over the dark flesh, watching it pucker and snap to attention. It finally stirs him, a low groan rumbling through his chest as his hips reflexively press into me.

He starts to harden before his eyes even open, and I can't help slinging a leg over him, pulling in to him so I can feel him stiffen against me. His baby blues peek out from under his eyelids and a smile curls his lips.

"Best. Wake-up. Ever," he mumbles, finding my lips with his. He abruptly rolls on top of me, sliding himself fully between my thighs.

I gasp in surprise, but his mouth tugs at mine, cutting me off with his kiss. When he pulls away to give attention to my neck, I wrap my legs around him.

"You haven't seen anything yet," I reply, tilting my pelvis up to capture him. And it's a good thing that he wasn't fully hard yet, because even at half mast, he fills me completely. My gasp isn't hampered this time as he's buried his face in my neck, his own groan of pleasure escaping his lips. "Don't stop." My plea stirs him, and I can feel him harden fully as I expand around him.

Ever so gently, he rocks into me, sending shockwaves of intense pleasure crashing through me.

He rears up over me, resting on his forearms, so he can watch my face as he picks up his pace. I can tell he's making sure he's not hurting me, and the tenderness makes me want to cry. I urge him on with my moans, and soon we're hurtling toward ecstasy together.

He pulls back onto his haunches, and it pulls him out enough so the pressure isn't as intense. But it also allows him to use his thumb to start circling the sensitive nub above where he's thrusting. The unexpected move upends my control.

"Ohmyfuckinggod," I gasp. Bryce looks at me questioningly and eases off. I shake my head violently. "Don't. Stop."

He smiles and leans in to kiss me. His lips are soft and sensual as he continues to gently slide in and out. He runs his nose along my cheek and drops his mouth to my ear. "Love you, baby," he whispers.

I whimper from the pleasure of it all, unable to respond. He seems to understand as he rears back once more, renewing his patient thrusts and dexterous stroking, adeptly increasing his speed until we're both moaning loudly.

"Holy…" I gasp. "I'm going to…"

Bryce nods, pressing into me with his thumb and speeding the tilting of his hips into a bed-shaking frenzy. The added sight of his muscles tensed and the sweat sheening on his chest from his concentrated efforts drive me straight into orgasm. And if past orgasms shattered me into a million pieces, this one sends me into ten million. And over again as he continues to thrust into his own climax.

Amid my trembling descent, I'm barely able to watch the expression of extreme gratification pass across his features before he collapses over me, still buried deeply inside.

His heavy breathing tickles my ear, and I numbly run my fingers over his slick back, savoring the feel of his damp skin.

"Well, that didn't suck," I joke. Bryce pushes himself up over me, a bemused expression on his face as he starts laughing. I can't help but laugh too, until the sensation causes his receding manhood to shift, tickling me in a whole different way. "Eek, don't make me laugh!" I wriggle under him as he tumbles out, laughing harder.

He rolls onto the bed next to me, still chuckling. "Give me a few minutes," he breathes. "Maybe I can do better next time." His head lolls toward me and I can see that he's smiling.

"Baby, I don't think it gets any better than that," I reply, gently kissing his bottom lip.

He strokes my arm thoughtfully. "That sounds like a challenge," he responds. He looks down at himself, but he's still, understandably, no longer at attention. "Hmmm, might need a bit longer actually."

I shake my head and laugh at him. "Were you a porn star in another life or something?" I ask teasingly. He grins. "You may be ready to go soon, but I'm going to need a break. I can barely move." I demonstrate by trying to lift a shaking arm from the bed and flopping it back down dramatically.

"Good," he replies, scooping me into his arms. "Then you're at my mercy."

He runs his nose over my neck, ears, and jaw, stopping to plant kisses along the way. Each point of contact leaves a hot flush under my skin, adding to my general feeling of being a pleasurable pile of jelly. Eventually the deep relaxation seeps out of my limbs, and I feel like I may actually be able to walk again. But lying here in Bryce's arms is its own kind of heaven. A reprieve from all the pain, sorrow, tension, and strife that we've both been through. But something is still niggling at me, even through the bliss.

"I don't want to spoil the mood…" I start.

Bryce pulls his head back and cocks an eyebrow. "But?"

"But while I'm glad most of this is over, there's still the issue of whoever is after Alessandro. They're still out there, trying to get at him through me." I pause, unsure of how to voice my concern. "The bodyguards have been a huge weight off my shoulders, in one sense. But this whole week I think it's contributed to me isolating myself. I can't imagine living a normal life being followed by armed guards, waiting for someone to try something. Even with them here I feel like I'm constantly waiting for the other shoe to drop."

"You'll get used to them being here," he assures me, sliding a leg between mine and using it to hook me and pull me closer. "And trust me. These goons who are after you have been biding their time, trying to catch you alone. Once they figure out that there will always be a guy with a gun between you and them, they'll give up."

I try to ignore the feel of his leg between mine, our hips lightly touching. "I get that having guards here is a trade-off. But I feel like I have to play hostess all the time," I object. He starts to contradict me, but I shush him. "I know they don't expect me to. But it's how I am. I can't help it. And it's nerve-racking."

Bryce looks at me, and I can tell he doesn't understand, but he's heard me. He strokes my thigh reassuringly. "Okay," he replies. "No more guards in the house."

I look at him quizzically. "Where are they going to stay?" I ask skeptically.

He shrugs. "They're not. Someone can pick you up each morning and be on call while you work. Then at the end of the day, they go home," he explains. "With one catch."

Ah. Yes. It sounded too easy.

"Which is?" I ask suspiciously.

Bryce's mouth twitches. "I stay," he says simply, grinning.

"I thought you weren't my personal security guard?" I ask, eyeing him skeptically.

"I'm not," he agrees. "But you're safer with me anyway. Right here. In your bed." He kisses my neck persuasively.

"Mmmm, using your newfound powers over my body is fighting dirty," I respond. I can feel him smile into the crook of my shoulder as his kisses go lower.

"I told you, that's how I do it now," he replies, amused. His tongue finds my nipple and I'm momentarily breathless.

"But won't that be a huge pain? Trucking back and forth all the time?" I ask.

Bryce releases my nipple and laughs. "Wow. Seriously, Sera. For someone so smart, you can be very dense." He shakes his head at me, and his expression becomes serious. "I'm saying we should live together."

My eyes go wide, but his amused expression returns despite, or perhaps because of, my obvious shock. "Isn't that kind of fast?" I squeak.

His hand travels to my backside, gently stroking it in a way that's both distracting and relaxing as he thinks about what he wants to say next.

"Not really," he eventually replies. "I mean, it doesn't have to be permanent. Not that I'd object if it was. But if it's too soon for you, I understand." He takes in my doubtful expression. "Listen, gorgeous. We've known each other for months. And I knew from the beginning what I wanted. And even if this part of our relationship is only starting, I'm still solidly on the side of the line where I'll take as much of you as I can get."

"Don't you think you'd get sick of me?" I ask.

"No," he promptly replies. "We've been through a lot, Sera. More than most couples who have been together for years. And we've fought. And made up. And so much more. I have no doubt that we can do this. I'm here because I realized all my doubts were about me. I have no doubts about you."

"I don't have any doubts about you, either." The words are out of my mouth before I even remember forming them.

He looks as surprised as I am. "Really?" he asks incredulously.

I chew on my lip. Really. I really don't. Bryce has always been there for me. Even when he was unsure how to behave around me. He was always the one wanting to persevere, to have the difficult conversations when I was running away. Which I only did because I was hurt, because I thought he was over me.

But the idea of living with him, of waking up every morning like this. Of spending weekends lazily making love, eating together while he reads the newspaper, and actually being able to go out as a couple. I realize there's a part of me that's always known that if I met Bryce first, we would have been here already. And I'd be safe, and always loved and cherished at his side. And of that I have no doubt.

"You said you knew from the beginning what you wanted," I hedge.

He nods reluctantly.

"What do you want?"

He inhales deeply, his eyes dark and serious.

"You. All of you. Forever," he admits. He regards me anxiously after the intense declaration.

And I should be scared. But I'm not. Because in the deepest, purest place in my heart, it's exactly what I want too. I feel the smile spreading across my face.

"That sounded an *awful* lot like a proposal," I tease him.

He strokes my face seriously. "Well, I guess that depends on what your answer would be if it were," he replies carefully.

I raise an eyebrow and laugh. And then I kiss him passionately, unable to put words to the love overflowing my heart. When I break away, he looks happier than I've ever seen him. As happy as I am.

"All of me," I agree. "In exchange for all of you. Forever."

And I know the answer before he gives it. Before we agree to join our lives. Before he makes passionate love to me again, over and over. Forever.

NEVER FORGET

PART I

"And think not you can direct the course of love, for love, if it finds you worthy, directs your course."
—Khalil Gibran

ONE

"Hmmm, forever is a long time," Bryce hedges. "I think I'll give you some time to get sick of me before I propose for real."

I can't help but laugh. "Seriously? I admit that I want to be with you forever too and that's all you've got?" I shake my head and poke him in the stomach.

He gives me a lascivious grin and rolls on top of me so suddenly it takes my breath away. "That's not even *close* to all I've got," he promises in a whisper as he nuzzles my neck, his warm breath tickling my ear. He pulls back suddenly and climbs out of bed, giving me an eyeful of his six-foot-four, ridiculously well-muscled body. "But first, breakfast."

"Naked breakfast?" I ask hopefully as he walks away.

He laughs and shakes his head, retrieving his boxers from the floor. "Just based on the ravenously horny look on your face, I'm going with no," he teases. "You know, because I actually want to eat. Food." He runs a hand over his short, chestnut brown hair, his blue eyes sparkling mischievously.

I pretend to pout a little. "Have it your way," I reply nonchalantly, making a show of stretching widely and letting the sheet slip off of me. I watch his eyes rove over my full chest and soft curves and I try not to let it excite me. But my stomach rumbles loudly and, as usual, he's right. I definitely need food.

Still, I take my time slowly sliding out of bed and pulling an oversized shirt from my bottom dresser drawer — which I bend down slowly to retrieve. Once I'm covered I saunter casually past him. He shakes his head and laughs, following me down the stairs.

I make a stop at the bathroom. My long, wavy brown hair is an absolute mess, so I take a moment to untangle it with my fingers before meeting Bryce in the kitchen.

I note that he's already started a pot of coffee. While it percolates, I examine the pitiful contents of the fridge and cupboards.

"Your choices are cereal and cereal," I announce.

Bryce smirks at me as he pours himself a cup of coffee. "Cereal it is," he agrees. "But we're going grocery shopping today." He passes by on his way to the dining room and plants a kiss on the top of my head.

I watch him sit down and find myself welling up a little.

He notices and gives me a quizzical look. "Everything okay?"

"Perfect," I admit breathlessly. Utterly. Fucking. Perfect. It's everything I've hoped for since I opened my heart back up to love not many months ago. And with all we've gone through to get here, I can't help being anything but blissfully happy.

I join him at the table with the food and we munch quietly, shooting each other furtive smiles, the freshness and excitement of our new relationship coursing through me.

"What else is on the agenda today?" I ask as we finish.

Bryce leans back in his chair. "Well, if I'm going to be staying here, I'm going to need to get some stuff from my place," he replies.

The thought is still a little overwhelming, but I'm thankful it'll be Bryce here with me instead of the personal security guards I'd had twenty-four-seven due to recent events. Though I'll still need them at least part of the time until the danger has passed. Whenever that is.

"What do you need to do today?" he asks.

"I have some phone calls to make," I admit sheepishly. "I wasn't just ignoring you and Emily this week."

During the epic pity party in which I thought I'd be alone forever, Bryce's sister had paraded over unannounced the night before last, tired of being ignored and raring to convince me into chasing her brother down. Fortunately, confiding in her led him to me. And I'm sure she'll be happy to hear that. But I should really call my mother, father, and my best friend, Allie.

"Funny you should mention Em," Bryce replies, taking our dishes into the kitchen. "Because we're seeing her tomorrow for brunch." His feigned casualness rouses my suspicion.

"Brunch?" I ask sharply, following behind him.

He turns away from the sink, wrapping his strong arms around me and gently stroking my backside. "At my mom's house," he replies, again too casually, but I can see the worry in his eyes. "That okay?"

"You know I love your mom," I reply. "But if you don't want to introduce me as your girlfriend yet, I completely understand."

Bryce pulls a face somewhere between offended and confused.

"You looked worried," I explain.

Understanding dawns on his face at my explanation. Bryce huffs a laugh and shakes his head.

"Baby, I want to shout it from the goddamn rooftops," he replies, looking intensely into my eyes. "But from now on I want this to go at your pace. Not mine. That's all."

I can't help but smile. This man. He's always looked out for my feelings first. Even when that meant watching me date a selfish, lying charmer of a man. Hell, not just watching, but helping me find the bastard when he "went back to Italy" or, as it actually happened, San Francisco. Only to stop hearing from him after a month when he did actually go back to Italy after all, but not because he'd planned to. The whole chain of events ultimately led to my being stalked and attacked by whatever criminals were after him, trying to get to him through me. Luckily, I'd already realized by the time he reappeared that my feelings were better spent on the man who'd always been there for me. This man.

I slide a hand over his gorgeous, taut chest, looking up at him from under my eyelashes. "I'd love to go," I respond. "Though I can't promise I'll behave." I slide my hand down, running a finger along the waistband of his shorts.

He laughs and shoves me backward, pressing me against the fridge. His soft lips run over my collarbone, his hands roving under my shirt. As his fingers find the tips of my breasts, his mouth presses over mine. I revel in the taste of him, the sweetness of being tangled together, getting to touch him in ways I'd only dreamed of before. But he pulls away before it can go very far.

"I see I'm not the only one who likes to play dirty," he says huskily.

I bite my lip to suppress a smile and he sucks in a sharp breath, his pupils dilating and fixing on my mouth.

"I'm going to do all kinds of amazing fucking things with that mouth later. But right now," he says, kissing me on the top of the head, "you need to get ready to go."

"I don't know where you get all this self-control," I mutter.

Bryce barks a loud laugh and runs a finger down my jaw. "Lots of practice," he replies.

I blush to the roots of my hair, and it just makes him laugh again.

"Sera, baby, please don't be embarrassed. It all worked out. And good things come to those who wait." The look on his face is full of promise and desire, and it's all I can do to keep breathing. And standing. He releases me slowly, leaning back against the counter behind him.

Somehow, I tear myself from him and drag ass back upstairs to take a shower. A very cold shower.

∾

WHEN I MAKE MY WAY BACK DOWNSTAIRS, BRYCE IS STANDING IN THE LIVING room, dressed, with his phone pressed to his ear and a frown tugging at the corners of his mouth. I sink into the oversized white sofa, watching the dim sunlight that has broken through the clouds sparkling on downtown Seattle outside of the large wall of windows that makes up one side of the living room. Bryce doesn't say a word, simply listens for a few more moments before slipping his phone into his back pocket and sinking into the couch next to me.

Slinging one arm on the couch behind me, he runs his other hand over my leg. "I have to go into the office today," he conveys grumpily. "But hopefully it won't take long."

I fold my hand over his, dipping my head so he doesn't see the disappointment on my face. "Everything okay?" I ask, tracing the veins in the back of his hand lightly.

He flips his hand over, squeezing mine. "It will be," he assures me. "It's nothing too out of the ordinary. Part and parcel of being in charge now. But it's not something I can really discuss. Corporate security issues and all." He winks at me.

I smile vaguely, curious but knowing I shouldn't press. It's how we met, after all, months ago when my own company was facing security issues, and he swooped in like the knight in shining armor that he is. But now that his father is gone, it's up to Bryce to actually run the corporate security company his grandfather created. It was a natural fit for him after leaving the Navy SEALs. Though I knew he was reluctant to accept the burden so soon, and with it already encroaching on his weekends I can understand why.

"Does that mean one of my bosom buddies will be back?" I ask warily.

Not that I necessarily mind any of my guards, but I'd much rather have some time alone, all things considered.

"Unfortunately, yes," he replies. "I'll call Tristan. I'm pretty sure he's available today."

I smile, perking up a little at the thought.

Bryce laughs. "I can see that you approve. I don't have anything to worry about, do I?"

I shove him lightly, not sure if he's really jealous or not. "Of *course* not," I reply. "We just get along well. He's a nice guy."

Bryce cocks an eyebrow at me. He's got eyeballs too, so I'm sure he knows how ridiculously attractive Tristan is with his blond hair, green eyes, and charming personality. And by charming personality, I also mean amazing body. Though not quite as amazing as Bryce's, admittedly.

"Well, as long as you don't get along *too* well," he replies, pulling his phone out of his pocket.

I give him a funny look and put my hand over his phone. "You know he's gay, right?" I ask.

Bryce's eyes widen. "Now I do," he responds. "I can't believe I didn't realize that."

I laugh and let go of his phone. "Hmm, I guess your know-it-all security guy superpowers have their limits," I tease him.

He sticks his tongue out at me and places the call. I arch my eyebrows and resist the urge to make a comment about his tongue. His wicked, amazing tongue. Shuddering lightly, I get up to retrieve my own phone.

It's not long before Tristan arrives, once again in his fitted black suit with matched, skinny black tie over a crisp white shirt. With fall arriving, it's cooler, but I can't imagine how they wear those suits in the heat of summer.

"Are you going out?" Bryce asks as we say our goodbyes at the door.

"No. I can order groceries to be delivered. Anything particular you need?" I respond.

"Eggs," he responds. "Lots." He leans in and plants a chaste kiss on my lips.

I scrunch up my nose grumpily. "That's all?" I pout.

His eyes flick to Tristan, who is looking out the window wall with his back to us, politely giving us space. Bryce's mouth drops to my ear.

"I've only got so much self-control. Any more and I'll end up doing what I've been imagining doing to you for the last fifteen minutes. And I think it would be inappropriate if I took you against the windows right now," he murmurs. "Tristan might notice."

A low gasp escapes my lips as my insides clench.

Bryce smirks and uses the opportunity of my speechlessness to leave with a wink. "Bye, Sera."

The door clicks shut softly behind him. But it takes me a few more moments before I catch my breath enough to return to the living room.

I take a few minutes to chat with Tristan before excusing myself and heading upstairs to my makeshift office, where I place an order for groceries to be delivered in an hour. If I'm not going out, I'm going to need the food for lunch. And I'm sure Tristan will appreciate it too.

Next, I hunker down and try to decide who to call first. I realize quickly that it's a no-brainer. I don't even really want to talk to my mother or father, and it's been nearly two weeks since I've spoken to Allie. And she's had enough of her own problems to deal with that I realize I've, once again, gone bad friend. So I call her immediately.

"Hey, stranger," she answers, sounding decidedly cheery.

I'm instantly grateful that she doesn't seem upset with me. "Hey, Allie," I greet her. "I'm so sorry it took me so long to respond to you."

"Let me guess. A lot has happened?" she replies with a smile in her voice. "Yeah, after our brunch two weeks ago, I figured that might be the case. Again."

"Yes," I agree softly. "A lot has happened."

"Give me all the juicy details," Allie insists.

I can't help but laugh. "It's not all sunshine and roses," I amend. "But okay."

Might as well lead with the least pleasant stuff. So I start by telling her how I was followed two nights in a row the week after we had brunch. I also explain suspecting Bryce was seeing his ex, Madison, then having it confirmed when I went to see him last Saturday night. But unable to face it, I ran out of his apartment building, not wanting to have to compete with Madison for his attentions. And unfortunately ended up being attacked. Which requires me to then explain *why* I was attacked, which in turn requires me to explain finding Alessandro at my door the next day, since it was ultimately his drama spilling over into my life.

I find having to talk about Alessandro Giordano bittersweet, to say the least. I'm hard-pressed to think of him as a selfish, lying bastard. Even though he is. He's also charming and he loves me, though in the end not enough to get over himself. And I loved him. But when he returned after weeks of not speaking to me to tell me he wanted me to leave with him, so he could protect me, so we could be together, it's no surprise to Allie when I explain I just couldn't. I couldn't leave my home, my friends, my work, and the man I'd realized I truly belonged with.

"Well," Allie says, finally breaking her silence. "At least you got some closure?" I hear her take a deep breath. "That's some heavy stuff, Sera. So what happened with Bryce? Is he still seeing his not-so-ex?"

"Ex," I reply firmly. "He ended it with her the same day I saw Alessandro. As it turns out, it was mostly a mistake. He'd lost his father, made a bad decision in his grief, and it took some time for him to disentangle himself."

"Well, that's a relief," she replies. "Are you okay?"

"There's more," I admit.

"Of course there is," she groans, laughing.

"I hired personal security guards after Alessandro left. Just in case. It really led me to isolate myself this week. That's why I wasn't responding to calls or texts. That made some people impatient. Eventually Emily marched over here demanding to know what my problem was," I explain. "Once I told her what happened, naturally, she told Bryce."

"Bet he's happy to see the back of Alessandro," Allie replies wryly.

I hadn't even thought of that aspect. Bryce has always disliked Alessandro. Now that I've got some distance, I can't really blame him.

"Probably," I agree. "But he came to tell me he still loves me." I flush at the memory of his admission, and everything that came after.

"Oh, Sera," Allie breathes. "Did you tell him you love him too?"

I snort. I'd never dared to admit to Allie the feelings I'd been developing for Bryce for a long time, though I probably shouldn't be surprised that she saw right through me anyway.

"Is there anything you don't know about me?" I ask bluntly.

Allie laughs. "I'm pretty sure some things I know about you before you know yourself," she teases.

It's hard to deny. Especially when it comes to feelings. I've always been purposely obtuse, having completely closed myself off to even the possibility of love for the better part of a decade. Some hurts run so deep that they can take what feels like a lifetime to heal.

"Yes, I told him I love him too," I admit. I hear her clap her hands with glee.

"Yay!" she squeals. "I was so rooting for you two."

I laugh. It's good to hear her so happy. And I decide instantly that I'm not going to bring up what she's going through, at least not directly. If she wants to talk about the deep depression she's struggled to overcome since losing her first pregnancy earlier this year, she knows I'm here for her. But she sounds so normal, and I'm just glad we're both in a better place.

"Enough about me," I insist. "What's new with you?"

"I'm glad you asked," she replies perkily. "David and I have decided to take that second honeymoon. We're going to Fiji!"

"Holy crap!" I exclaim. "That sounds amazing. When? For how long?"

"We leave in two weeks, and we'll be gone for ten days," she replies. "I would love to see you next weekend before we go."

"Of course," I agree. "Sunday brunch again?"

"It's a date," Allie affirms.

Downstairs, the doorbell rings, heralding the arrival of food. And I suddenly realize how hungry I am.

"I've gotta go, Al," I tell her. "But it was so good talking to you. Talk soon, okay?"

"You betcha," she responds. "Bye, Sera."

∾

AFTER LUNCH, BRYCE CALLS TO SAY HE WON'T BE BACK UNTIL DINNERTIME. Realizing that means I have no excuse, I call my mom. I decide beforehand that I'm going to keep things very high level. On top of already being emotionally exhausted, my mother and I have only recently forged a closer relationship. Most of my life she'd been passive aggressively critical and overbearing. But one of the few bright sides of my relationship with Alessandro was that it outed *why* — that my father, who left when I was twelve, had cheated on her in a spectacularly awful way.

Still, when I manage to get her on the phone, I do share that I saw

Alessandro and ended things officially and completely. I can tell she's relieved. She suggests coming for a visit, since we haven't seen each other in some time, but I bristle at the idea of revealing my new relationship with Bryce. She's already met him, but not as my love interest. And I just don't think I'm ready for that. So I make vague promises of a visit sometime in the future and steer the conversation away from me. Since she's always happy to talk about herself, it's not hard.

But once I'm done talking to her, I'm spent. And I have no desire to call my father. Having only recently spoken to him for the first time since I was a teenager, it just feels like a conversation I'm going to need more strength for.

Instead, I troop downstairs to the kitchen to throw together dinner. Bryce will be home soon. And the thought perks me up considerably.

⁓

I'M JUST ASSEMBLING A SALAD TO GO WITH THE LASAGNA THAT'S IN THE OVEN when Bryce returns carrying two large duffel bags. Tristan helps him bring them in, and Bryce sees him out before coming to me.

"Hey, you," he greets me, wrapping his arms around me from behind and kissing my neck. "Sorry I had to be away all day."

"I missed you," I reply, turning my head to kiss him.

As I wasn't quite done with the salad, I'd only intended a quick smooch. But he kisses me hungrily, holding my face to his with a strong hand. My body responds, and heat rises quickly in me. I drop the salad tongs and turn to face him without breaking the fervent dance of our lips.

His tongue gently teases mine as he slips his hands around my hips, pulling me toward him. I push into him hard, wrapping my arms around his neck for leverage. I can feel his readiness against my hip, and a small moan breaks out of my throat through our kiss. When he finally pulls his mouth from mine, we're both panting and aroused.

"I missed you too," he responds. He looks down at my frilly white apron. "And I'm going to fantasize about coming home to you making dinner in nothing but this apron."

"You're killing me with the dirty talk," I moan, pushing him away so I can finish making dinner. He grins and leans back against the counter opposite me.

"You don't like it?" he teases, his blue eyes bright and sparkling.

"I like it. Very much. You have no idea," I reply. "Now sit your gorgeous ass down so we can eat."

He laughs and moves to the dining room, popping open the bottle of wine I'd put on the table. "I'll keep that in mind," he responds.

I hand him the salad bowl over the counter and remove the lasagna.

"Anything else I do that you like very much?" he asks.

I shoot him a look as I bring the casserole to the table. "Plenty," I assure him. "But if I start talking about it, I just know I'm going to end up with lasagna on my back. So let's eat. Then I can *show* you."

Bryce laughs and concedes by sitting down. "I look forward to it," he replies suggestively, taking a sip of wine.

Dinner is full of silence and tension. But the best kind of tension. The feeling of Bryce's eyes on every inch of me as I eat is tantalizing. And I can't keep my eyes off of him either. Every movement is laden with suggestive undertones. By the time we are done, and the last dish is washed, I'm so turned on I can barely think straight.

Bryce leans back against the stove, eyeing me speculatively.

"That was good," he remarks casually, crossing his arms over his broad chest.

I shift my weight from one foot to the other. "Thanks," I reply softly.

His eyes drink me in, darkening as the tension builds.

"Damn, baby, if your eyes could talk," he mutters.

The corner of my mouth quirks up in a knowing smile. They'd be saying, *Take me already, damnit*, I think to myself.

"Mmmm," I reply noncommittally, unwilling to admit what I'm thinking. "Is this the part where we let things go at my pace?"

Bryce chuckles and pushes himself upright. "If we went at your pace, I have a feeling we'd already be done by now," he remarks. He saunters past me and I watch him slowly climb the stairs. He pauses before he gets too far and crooks a finger at me. "Coming?"

TWO

y heart pounds in my chest, my feet stubbornly refusing to move. Or unable. I'm suddenly very weak in the knees at his invitation.

I take a few deep breaths and find the will to move before slowly following him up the stairs and into the bedroom. I find Bryce stripping, until he's left in only a white T-shirt and his boxers. My eyebrows fly up, and I freeze in the doorway. He looks back at me, grinning while he tosses the clothing he's removed into a laundry bag.

He stretches out on the bed, lying on his side, and pats the other side of the bed invitingly. Slowly, I join him, lying down to face him.

After a few minutes of staring lustfully at each other, Bryce reaches out and strokes my face gently. "I hope I didn't offend you," he murmurs. "I like your pace. But we've got all night. There's no need to rush."

I cock an eyebrow and kiss his finger as it slips by my mouth. "We do have all night," I agree. "So fast or slow, I bet you that we could easily manage twice." I kiss his fingers again as they pass. "Or maybe even three times."

Bryce laughs. "That's one way to go about it," he allows.

"Now you have me curious about the other ways," I reply.

He grins and slides toward me. "Oh, good, we're to the showing part," he responds.

He reaches a hand out and runs it down my temple, the side of my face, his thumb grazing my lip gently, then down my neck. He lightly brushes his fingers along my collar bone and back, then continues running his hand down my chest, over my T-shirt, stopping at the peak of my nipple visible through my shirt. He circles and pinches it, causing a moan to escape me. He does it again, harder, until I moan louder. He brings his other hand up, pinching both nipples simultaneously until it's a pleasurable pain that has me writhing and moaning. Seemingly satisfied, his leisurely stroking continues down my stomach, over my leggings, stopping on my hips.

He grips me tightly, pulling our bodies together. His lips meet mine for one hot second, his tongue doing a quick sweep of my mouth before he slides down me, his lips and nose grazing my nipples on the way. His head comes to rest at my hips, his hot breath mingling with the heat between my legs. He uses his lips and nose to caress at the spot while his hand roves over my backside, down my leg, and cups underneath my knee. He holds me there while he nuzzles me, breathing deeply of the scent of my wetness. I'm so turned on I can barely move as I watch him.

"You smell fucking amazing," he groans.

With his mouth still in contact with my body, his words reverberate through me in a way that makes me even wetter than I was before. As if he knows, he rubs two fingers along the seam of my leggings, sighing happily at the dampness he finds.

Slowly, he peels off my leggings and underwear. I'm so hot and wet, that when his tongue hits me it almost feels cool. Temperature aside, his slow, deliberate strokes send tremors through me. But unlike the previous night's steady acceleration, Bryce continues his gentle, methodically unhurried exploration. It feels so amazing that I can't even form words to ask him to go faster, harder. It's pleasure unlike anything I've ever experienced before. Pleasure for the sheer sake of pleasure. Not to hurtle toward the finish, but just to revel in it. And I find I don't want it to stop — but I do want to do the same to him.

"Bryce," I manage to whisper.

It works, and he stops, pulling back and resting on his haunches at the foot of the bed. I push myself upright, tugging off my shirt and bra in one solid movement. His mouth opens a fraction, his eyes fixed on my erect nipples. Remembering my mission, I lean forward and pull his shirt over his head, directing him with my hands to lay back on the bed. I tug his shorts off, his massive erection springing free. I groan with approval but focus through the lust screaming in my veins.

I kneel next to his head and he looks at me questioningly. "I want to do that to you," I explain. "While you do that to me."

"Oh, fuck yes," he breathes, his pupils dilating massively.

Smiling, I swing a leg over him, allowing him to pull me into position. He places my knees above his shoulders and pulls my hot, wet center back into range of his mouth. As soon as I feel the first lick, I take him in my mouth. He shudders beneath me as I slide him in as far as he'll go. Keeping him there, I work my tongue over him as I grab his sack with my free hand and pull it toward his shaft, massaging both as I swirl my tongue firmly around him. I feel his tongue stop, so I ease back, moving from root to tip with a light grip and feathery swirls of my tongue. He resumes, and we both gently work each other simultaneously until the feeling of utter hedonistic, numbing pleasure seeps through me completely.

Deciding he's been too quiet for my liking, I abandon my pursuit of simultaneous gratification and focus on taking him to a level where he'll forget his own name. My feathery swirls accelerate quickly to deep suction, my light grip to a slick pump, working him into a hard, quivering frenzy. Predictably, his head drops back as the change registers, and he moans loudly.

"Shit," he cries. "That's … oh, god…"

As he loses his words, I ease up and climb off of him. He springs up and knocks me over, his mouth consuming mine frantically. When he breaks free for air, I can't help laughing.

"Sorry," I chortle. "I know you wanted to go slow. I just couldn't help myself."

He wipes at his chin, chuckling with me. "Don't apologize," he replies. "That felt fantastic."

I run my hands over the well-developed muscles of his arms.

He nuzzles his nose against mine. "How can I make you feel fantastic?"

I bite my lip. "Take me from behind," I breathe, squirming to get enough room to roll over.

"Goddamn, baby, you know just what to say," he groans. He rears back and reaches one arm under my hips and, with one pull, simultaneously rolls me over and raises my hips into the air like I'm a doll.

As if I wasn't immensely turned on before, all of my nerve endings come alive and I'm acutely aware of every square centimeter of our flesh touching as his knees open my legs and he runs his hand along my dripping core.

I feel his tip nudging at my opening and the sensation makes me clench in anticipation. He eases in slowly, and my body quickly responds, like it wants the deep, full feeling of him just as much as I do. And he doesn't disappoint. Though I can't feel his hips against my backside, so I know he's not even fully in. I lift myself up so I'm on all fours, stretching myself out and buying him a little more room. It's enough, and he slips in to the hilt, causing us both to moan appreciatively.

I look back at him, and the sight of his amazing, muscular frame behind me, his exquisite features set in a mask of pure bliss, and his manhood buried completely in me almost makes me come on the spot. Mastering myself, I reach an arm back to grasp his hand, to anchor us both for what comes next. He grips me back and takes the cue. His first thrust is painful, and not in the best way. But I don't make a sound. On the second thrust, I start to acclimate to his sheer size. And by the third, the pain is but a welcome compliment to the pleasure of his massive member stimulating every sensitive spot I have. It's not long before I want more.

I bite my lip and catch his eye. "Harder," I beg, whimpering.

He throws his head back for a moment, clearly unhinged by my plea. But he gets it together quickly and complies, ratcheting up the intensity of his thrusts. His eyes drop to my breasts, which are now shaking furiously under the force of our bodies colliding. The pure lust on his face drives me crazy.

So, I beg him again. "Harder, baby, please."

And this time, when he lets go, I have to turn away and use both arms to brace myself for the best fuck I've ever had. He slams furiously into me, and waves of pleasurable pain crash through me. It feels like only moments later when I feel the familiar tightening, each spearing thrust of his massive cock building to the ridiculously powerful climax that follows. He continues to thrust into me through the guttural screams that rip out of my throat and through my arms giving out. Through it all, he keeps my hips locked in his tight grip, riding me over wave after wave of incredible release that just keeps going and going. Finally, when I feel as if I'm about to black out from pleasure, he eases off slowly, sliding out so I can collapse onto the bed.

He lays down next to me and I look up at him. His cock is red and still alert, with no sign of his massive erection abating.

"You didn't finish?" I ask incredulously.

He shakes his head, sweaty and panting. Knowing that, plus the look of utter satisfaction on his face, and suddenly I have a second wind. I pull my shaking body up and climb over him, sliding him into me once more. He looks up at me, bewildered. But I ignore it and start riding him.

"You're incredible," he moans.

I'd laugh, but I'm too focused on his pleasure now. I take his face in my hands and kiss him deeply, but it slows me down. So I let him go, moving his hands to my breasts. He kisses and strokes them as I return to grinding my hips over him.

I run my hands over his hair, relishing the feeling of his lips all over me as I ride him. I should be sore and spent, but instead I'm finding it just as pleasurable as he seems to be. I look down into his eyes. And I've never seen anyone look back at me the way he does. Like he sees me. Adores me. Would do anything to please me.

"God, I love you," I breathe.

He trembles underneath me, pushing to encourage my hips to go faster as he approaches climax.

I pick up my speed. "I love you," I repeat.

His breathing accelerates to a fever pitch.

I brace my arms on him as I slam into him as hard and fast as I can. "I love you," I moan one, final time.

He bellows his release, and I feel him coming, warm and slippery, and it pushes me over the edge. I focus on continuing to ride him through our orgasms like he did me, and amazingly feel him continue to come inside me for far longer than should be possible.

As we both descend, I allow him to slide me onto the bed next to him. He holds me in his arms, placing light kisses on my lips, cheeks, and chin.

"You okay?" he asks.

I look up at him in awe. "Amazing," I admit. "Though I might be walking funny tomorrow."

He grins. "Ditto," he agrees, and we both laugh. "Seriously, though, that was…"

"The best fuck ever?" I offer.

"That's one way to put it," he agrees. "Though I thought most women liked to call it 'making love.'"

I consider that for a moment. "It was that too, I suppose," I finally allow. "But I've always associated that phrase with tender, sweet sex. Which, if it wasn't obvious, isn't really my preference."

"Just a good, proper fuck, then?" he asks huskily.

The question causes me to tighten, despite recent activities. "Even hearing you *say* it turns me on," I admit, grinding up against him.

He laughs. "I never would have guessed," he replies. "But I'm glad. It's what I like too, but I don't usually let go like that. I don't want it to be painful."

"It was, at first," I acknowledge. "But that didn't last long. And then it was amazing." I bite my lip and shudder with pleasure. "I've never had an orgasm like that."

He smiles, clearly pleased, and kisses my forehead. "Me neither," he agrees. "But then, I don't think I've ever lost myself in someone so completely for so long."

I look at him quizzically and roll my head back to look at the bedside clock. "Holy shit, we were going at it for more than two hours?" I exclaim.

Bryce chuckles. "Didn't feel like that long, did it?" he asks, nuzzling my neck. "If we call it an early night we might be able to do it again in the morning." His lips trace a path up to my ear, his breath simultaneously tickling and turning me on.

"I both can't believe I have to wait that long and am worried I won't be able to keep up with you," I joke.

"Something tells me it's me who will be keeping up with you," he replies suggestively. "So tell me how far this goes. Rough play? Bondage?"

"Why, are you into those?" I ask him curiously.

He shrugs. "Not really, but if you are, I'm willing," he replies.

I laugh and kiss him gently. "You are too much," I murmur, looking up into his eyes. "No, I'm not really into those either. Just a good, deep fuck. And you have a distinct advantage on both counts. But I hope you're ready to push the boundaries of just how deep and hard you can fuck me." And I'm incredulous when I feel his cock twitch between us. I look down in shock.

Bryce laughs. "I think that was him accepting the challenge," he offers. He stares at me for a minute. "I'm glad I didn't know about this before. Or I wouldn't have played it so cool all those months knowing I could be testing the limits of how hard a fuck I'd really enjoy, with the most amazing and gorgeous woman I've ever met."

"Pillow talk," I tease him accusingly. "Post-orgasmic exaggeration. But I'm glad things worked out too."

Bryce levels a serious look at me. "I mean it," he insists. "You know I've been crazy about you from the start."

I can't help but be self-conscious. It's hard to believe someone like him would think that about someone like me. "You're lucky I know how smart you are," I tease, attempting to make light, "or I'd question your intelligence for that."

He shakes his head and huffs an unamused laugh. "You don't see yourself, Sera," he replies seriously. "So I'm going to keep telling you until you believe me." He hooks a finger under my chin, forcing me to look into his eyes. "Never forget how much I love you."

THREE

The next morning, as soon as I wake up I know my prediction was dead-on. Even rolling over to look at Bryce causes me to feel the rawness between my legs. It actually makes me giggle.

"Was I talking in my sleep?" Bryce asks, opening his eyes.

"You talk in your sleep?" I ask, sliding into his arms.

He kisses me on my head as he pulls me to him. "I like waking up next to you," he dodges.

I shove him playfully. "Uh-huh, way to avoid that one, tiger," I tease him. "I was laughing because I'm so sore I swear I still feel you in there every time I move."

He laughs. "Yeah, the sheets are kind of chafing me," he admits. "Guess we'll have to heal up before we give it another go."

"Now we just have to practice not looking like we fucked each other silly for hours," I giggle. Suddenly, something occurs to me. "Does Emily already know? About us?"

"No, I've been a little busy," Bryce replies with a smirk. "Why?"

"Well if she doesn't, she's going to the second she sees us both walking funny," I explain.

Bryce barks another laugh. "Oh, well," he replies. "Not much to do about it now." He sits up and slings his long legs over the side of the bed.

And I get a nice view of the firm, well-defined muscles of his back. I lean over and trace my fingertips over his lower back muscles. He looks over his shoulder curiously. I grin up at him.

"Sorry, couldn't help it," I say, letting my hair fall over my face to hide my embarrassment.

He turns around and flips me over, climbing on top of me. "You've got to stop looking so sexy. It literally hurts," he murmurs into my neck, kissing his way down to my chest.

"Mmmm," I groan. "Funny, because as it happens I hurt *less* when I'm turned on."

"Don't say things like that," Bryce moans. He drops a hand between my legs, lightly skimming my sex.

Even the gentle touch is too much, though and I suck in a breath sharply. "No hands," I chastise him.

He raises an eyebrow. And I realize it was the wrong thing to say. His head drops between my legs and, before I can stop him, his silken tongue is pushing between my lips, stroking the extra-sensitive bundle of nerves hidden inside. It stings at first, but like last night's escapades, that melts into pleasure quickly. And he doesn't stop until I'm coming in his mouth. Again.

∾

As we pull up to his mom's house a few hours later, I'm still pouting that he wouldn't even let me try to return the favor.

He kills the engine and looks over at me. "You're not still sulking, are you?" he teases me.

I feign a glare at him. "No," I snap jokingly.

He chuckles and gives me an amused half-smile.

And I can't keep it up, cracking a smile of my own. "Yeah, laugh it up, baby. You'll get yours later."

Bryce leans over to whisper in my ear. "I've already got everything I need," he murmurs, kissing my neck. It's unexpected sweetness. Usually when he's whispering in my ear, it's something dirty.

I find I like it anyway. He shoots me a grin and climbs out of the car, so I follow suit. As soon as I round the car, he takes my hand. Feeling his rough, warm grip makes me feel a whole other level of safe than I even used to feel in his presence when he was simply my overprotective, close friend. And I can't remember ever being so happy.

He leads me into the house. We can hear Emily talking before we even enter the living room. But a hush falls over the room as we walk in, still hand in hand. Three shocked faces take us in — Emily, their mother, Rebecca, and their Aunt Charlotte. And I don't know who looks more thrilled to see our obvious couple-dom. Bryce smirks down at me, clearly amused by their astonished silence.

"Hi, guys," Bryce greets them, letting me go to kiss his mother and aunt on the cheek. He then sits down on the smaller of the two couches in the room, pulling me down next to him. He's so relaxed and casual, you'd think we'd always been showing up to brunch at his mom's house as a couple.

But Emily's having none of it. She tugs dramatically at her long, chestnut waves, her blue eyes brimming with excitement. "Yeah, hi, hey, nothing going on here," she intones sarcastically. "Just my brother. And my friend. *Together*. Unless you've just started holding hands with all our friends."

"She was my friend first," Bryce reminds her, putting his arm on the couch behind me and crossing his legs.

I suppress a smile. I'd get on his case for torturing his sister, but she's meddled in our relationship so many times lately, it's kind of fun to watch him take a little revenge.

"How are you doing, Mom?" he asks nonchalantly.

His mother gives him a look that's somewhere between disapproving and amused. I imagine Emily drives everyone a little crazy. But I know she means well, and she's got a heart of gold. She's been a good friend to me since we met and became close while I was helping with their father's funeral. So I almost want to spare her. Almost.

"I'm fine, darling, thank you," Rebecca responds. "It's so nice to see you, Sera. How are things with you?"

"Oh, no," Emily insists. "Nuh-uh. First you have to tell us: Are you or aren't you together?"

I give Bryce an overly affected look of bemusement. "We did come here together, didn't we?" I ask innocently.

He can barely contain his smirk. "Yep. Seemed a waste to drive separately," he replies airily.

And I swear Emily looks like she's about to punch us.

"Oh, for heaven's sake, Emily Rose Hoyt," Charlotte chides her. "They're obviously a couple. Unclench."

Bryce laughs.

Emily doesn't. She pouts openly, pointing it my direction first. "Sera, you pinky swore to be my friend no matter what," she reminds me. "Don't leave me hanging."

"Em," I sigh dramatically. "If your boyfriend wanted to mess with his meddling sister a little, wouldn't you let him?"

She takes my meaning immediately, squealing loudly as she jumps out of her seat to hug me.

I laugh as she embraces me. "But I'm with Charlotte on this one, anyway. Wasn't it obvious?"

"Always get the story straight from the source," she responds. "I don't assume."

I mash my lips together, suppressing a sarcastic response about her gossipy tendencies.

"Speaking of stories," I say, diverting the subject away from Bryce and me. "Rebecca, would now be a good time for us to talk about Landon? I meant what I said a few weeks ago. I really do want to hear more about your husband. You've all come to mean so much to me, and I'm sad I wasn't able to know him before he passed."

I'd already discussed doing exactly this with Bryce a while back, but he still looks surprised. I give him a look, wondering if it was okay to ask. He pulls me toward him and kisses me softly on the cheek. And I know it was.

Rebecca smiles sadly but, to her credit, flawlessly maintains her composure. Her husband only having passed a month or so ago, even though it wasn't unexpected, I'm in awe of how well she's doing.

"I think I'd like that," she replies softly. "Let's go eat and we can all share our favorite memories of him."

The meal is exquisite, and the reminiscing flows well beyond brunch. When Bryce and I say our goodbyes late that afternoon, I feel more like a part of his family than I even do of my own. Not that that's saying much, about my family anyway. And I can see how happy Bryce is for it too.

As we descend the front steps, he wraps his hand around mine once more. He walks me to the passenger side of the car, where he gathers me into his arms.

"They all love you," he says, looking down at me adoringly.

"Good," I respond, wrapping my arms around his neck and going on my tiptoes to kiss him. "Because I love them too."

He smiles and nuzzles his nose against mine.

I look seriously into his eyes. "Now take me home so I can do naughty things to you."

Bryce laughs and releases me, opening the car door so I can get in. "Yes, ma'am," he replies, grinning as he closes the door behind me.

∽

BUT ONCE WE'RE HOME, WE ACTUALLY END UP ON THE COUCH, LAYING DOWN holding each other and talking about all sorts of things. It feels like now that I'm getting to know him as a lover and partner, I need to relearn everything I already know about him from that slant. And he seems to feel the same. Our talk is much more hopes-and-dreams oriented, and we're just as in sync as we were as friends. Though it's hard not to expect something to crop up that will make this come crashing down around my ears.

But I decide, as I lay in his arms, looking into his gorgeous blue eyes and talking about our future, that I'm going to try to just be happy. It's against my nature and what life has taught me so far, but I'm so ready for hope. And Bryce Hoyt, with his sunshine smile and fierce loyalty, is just what I need.

We talk late into the evening, not even stopping through a light dinner. It's not until we realize it's past our usual bedtimes that we head upstairs. But I make good on my promise, seeing to his pleasure just as thoroughly as he saw to mine this morning.

∽

WHEN I WAKE TO MY ALARM THE FOLLOWING MORNING I FIND MYSELF ALONE IN bed. But I can hear the shower running. Bryce must be done with his workout. Gleefully, I slide out of bed to join him.

The bathroom is steamy, but I can just make out his tall form. And as I get closer I can see more of his gorgeous body. I'm instantly as wet as his glistening skin.

I knock on the glass door. Bryce turns, looking not terribly surprised to see me.

"Did you wait to take a shower until you knew I'd be getting up?" I ask suspiciously.

One of his eyebrows waggles suggestively and I laugh, sliding open the foggy door and stepping in. He's on me immediately, pulling me into the hot stream of water, his mouth pressing into mine insistently. My hand slips to his cock to stroke him into readiness, but I find there's no need. He's already there. I groan softly into his mouth as my own wetness is made redundant by the moisture that's engulfed us.

"Good morning, gorgeous," he says into my ear. "If it's okay with you, I'm going to fuck you. Hard."

I groan, leaning into him. I can't even speak, so I simply nod. Bryce turns me around, pressing on my back until I'm leaned forward and braced against the wall. And with a tilt of his hips, he's pressed himself into me from behind. I gasp at the suddenness of our joining, and he gives me the smallest fraction of a moment to adjust before his hands grip my breasts and he begins thrusting roughly into me. It's only painful for a second before I'm moaning in ecstasy. With Bryce groaning behind me as he holds nothing back, and every part of me still sensitive, it's not long before we both come apart with pleasure.

I turn back around, returning my lips to his for a final kiss before I playfully shove him out of the shower. "Thanks," I say, waving at him as I close the door.

He laughs and shakes his head. "That's cold, Sera," he teases.

I shrug and start to lather up my hair, pretending to ignore him. He laughs again as he dries off. When he leaves to get dressed I watch his unbelievably smoking hot backside as he walks away. And it's all I can do to concentrate long enough to finish showering.

∽

It takes me until mid-morning to fully get my head into work. Which is good, because I have a late morning meeting with Charles Sutton. I decide to drop in his office ahead of time to check in with him, given the understandable tension in the office these last weeks. Understandable because his son is pending trial for sexually assaulting one of my former employees. And the whole office has been buzzing with theories and gossip, to the point that I know even Charles must be hearing them by now.

I knock softly on his door.

"What?" his commanding, voice calls sharply.

Steeling myself, I poke my head in the door. "Good morning, boss," I greet him. "Mind if I come in?"

He turns from his place by the windows, his hands behind his back, a worn-out expression on his stern features. "Yes, of course, Sera, please," he replies, returning to his desk chair.

I take a seat opposite his desk, crossing my legs nervously after I'm seated. "How are you, Charles?" I ask.

He drums his thumbs on the armrests of his chair. "Managing," he replies. His dark eyes meet my own, and I see a great sadness in them. "What about you, Ms. Evans? My company absorbed yours not quite two months ago. Even aside from the issues with my son, I know it's been a difficult time for you."

I huff an ironic laugh. It's hard not to feel like the drama in my own life has invited it into Charles Sutton's. Not that his son's behavior is in any way my fault, but our contentious relationship before that even came to light made the transition difficult.

But then, I'd run my own real estate consulting services company for nearly five years. And Charles Sutton brought me into the fold with the express, though undeclared, purpose of mentoring me to become his successor, having deemed his eldest son's disposition a poor fit for the job. In hindsight I should have expected the epic clash of wills between Daniel and me. And if I hadn't personally been going through so much, I might have been able to contain myself better.

I heave a deep sigh. "It's been tumultuous, to say the least," I admit finally. "But I can't help feeling there's a reason for everything. And I have no regrets about coming to work for you or about folding Evans Realty Services into Sutton Developments. Being exposed to more of the industry, harnessing the power of our combined companies, I understand why you wanted this. I imagine it's what my grandfather would have wanted. For both of us."

Charles steeples his fingers under his nose, as he is wont to do, but I also notice tears in his eyes. And I realize they're in mine too. Perhaps it's the reminder of Grandpa Tyler, the bond that ultimately brought Charles and I together. He mentored us both, after all, and is the reason I became a real estate agent and started my own company. Not that I needed to with the immense fortune he left behind from his own investments, but because it's what I wanted. And working for Charles has been a natural extension of that journey. The bond we've already formed is irreplaceable, and perhaps also a contributing factor to my emotional response.

"No doubt," Charles responds softly, smiling. "Thank you for saying that. All of it. You are resilient as always, my dear, and I'm glad to hear you're happy to be here despite everything else."

"How is the rest of your family faring?" I ask curiously. I don't know much about Charles' wife or his other two sons. But I imagine this is just as difficult for them.

Charles gives a small shrug. "His brothers are, as I was, unsurprised, given Daniel's past issues. My wife has been struggling," Charles admits, sighing deeply. "It's been hardest on her, I think."

"I can't even imagine," I murmur, looking down into my hands.

"I'd like you to meet them one day," Charles responds.

I look up, startled, though I shouldn't be. I know he has big plans for me so it would only be natural.

"But not now. For now, we have enough to be getting on with, I think."

I glance at my watch. "Speaking of which," I prompt him.

He looks at his own watch, nodding in agreement and rising from his chair. "Shall we?" he asks.

I smile widely, despite my lingering sorrow. "Lead the way," I reply.

He laughs, nods, and does just that. And perhaps it's my imagination, but the rest of the day seems to go more smoothly.

∿

When Tristan drops me home in the evening, Bryce is already there. And he's making dinner.

"The only thing that could make this better is if you were shirtless," I tease him by way of greeting.

He looks up from chopping carrots and smiles. "Hey, you," he replies, smiling back with his patented sunshine smile. "How was your day?"

I kick my shoes off and drop my bag on the counter, sinking into a chair at the bar. He leans across the counter to kiss me.

"Better than I expected it to be," I reply when he pulls away. "How was yours?"

He huffs a forced laugh. "A laugh a minute," he replies sarcastically. "I'm starting to get why you were over being the boss."

"That bad, huh?" I ask with a grimace.

He stops his chopping again to give me a look. "I probably shouldn't complain. Things are going surprisingly well, considering," he allows. "I didn't think I'd be as on top of things as I am after just a month of running the company without Dad."

"I told you. You're the most capable guy I know," I assure him. Then I add, with a sly smile, "But I think you need a massage after dinner. Full body."

He doesn't look up, but a smile slowly spreads across his face. "You're just trying to get me to chop off a thumb, aren't you?" he teases.

I put my hands up in defeat. "Fine, I'll leave you to it then," I accede. "I'm going to change." But as I head up the stairs, I can't help pausing and watching him work. And wondering how I got so damn lucky.

∽

AFTER DINNER, BRYCE IS SPLAYED OUT ON THE COUCH WITH HIS FEET IN MY LAP as I rub firm strokes up and down his soles.

"So I forgot to mention something," he murmurs, opening his eyes. "They set a trial date today. For Daniel Sutton."

My eyebrows shoot up. "And you're just now telling me? When?" I demand.

He shrugs. "Sorry, it slipped my mind. And then you started rubbing me," he smiles provocatively. "It starts in two weeks."

I continue working his instep as I process that. "I should check in with Heather soon," I murmur. I haven't talked to Heather Irving, my former employee and Daniel Sutton's victim, in a few weeks. I'm a little surprised I haven't heard from her actually, but I'm sure she's got enough on her plate.

Bryce nods. "Probably a good idea," he agrees. "But for now, I have other plans." He gently pulls his foot out of my grasp and sits up. He scoots along the couch until he's right in front of me. Slowly, he leans in and nuzzles his nose against mine.

I can't help grinning like an idiot. "Hi," I say shyly.

"Did you know your eye color changes from light brown to hazel to pretty much full-on green?" he asks, looking deeply into my eyes.

I laugh. "It's like a mood ring," I reply. "Or a happiness scale, actually."

"I hope green means happy, because that's what they are right now," he says.

"It might," I say evasively, blushing.

"Hmmm," he says thoughtfully. "Let's see how green they can get." He kisses me softly, and the feeling of his mouth on mine wipes all thought from my brain. He pulls away and stares into my eyes again. "Not bad, but I think we can do better." Suddenly he grabs me, lifting me over his shoulder and rising from the couch. I squeal with surprise as he carries me out of the living room and up the stairs.

"Bryce! Holy crap!" I shout.

He smacks me playfully on the backside. "You know you like it, woman," he responds. But he sets me down at the top of the stairs anyway.

At first I think he's acknowledging my obvious displeasure at being moved bodily, but I quickly realize as he starts kissing me and pulling at my clothes as he pushes me toward the bedroom that it was a necessary step toward getting me naked as fast as possible. And that, I don't mind.

FOUR

When I get home from work on Tuesday, Bryce is still at the office, so I take the opportunity to check in with Heather as Tristan hovers unobtrusively near the window wall. I note that he seems to like it as much as I do as I listen to the line ring. Though who wouldn't — day or night, the view of downtown Seattle and Elliott Bay is spectacular. But as I continue to wait, Heather doesn't answer, and I eventually get dumped into her voicemail.

"Hey, Heather, it's Sera," I start. "Just wanted to check in and see how you're doing. I heard about the trial date. Maybe we can get together before then. If not, just let me know if there's anything you need, okay? Talk soon. Bye." Feeling awkward, I hang up.

Behind me, I hear the front door open and turn to see Bryce striding in, looking like hot business as usual in dark slacks and a baby-blue button front shirt. He gives me a huge grin, and I can't resist running to greet him.

He scoops me up gleefully and kisses me deeply. "Second best possible greeting," he murmurs, letting me go.

"What's the best?" I can't help asking.

Bryce's eyes flick up to where Tristan stands by the window and he mouths the word *apron*. I roll my eyes and shove him lightly. Tristan strolls casually toward us.

"You guys are disgustingly cute," he teases us. "I'm going to go home and throw up now."

I stick my tongue out at Tristan and Bryce calls after him, "Don't let the door hit you in the ass on the way out."

Tristan throws up a final wave without turning around. "'Night, boss."

We both laugh as the door closes behind him.

"Now, about that apron," Bryce says, turning to me.

I shake my head and huff a laugh. "Can you eat an apron? Because I'm hungry," I reply airily, heading for the kitchen.

And though Bryce doesn't say anything more on the subject, I can tell just how much he's salivating to see me in *just* that apron.

⌒

I LEAVE WORK EARLY ON FRIDAY TO PUT OPERATION APRON INTO EFFECT. I prepare an elaborate dinner and have it all laid out on the table before I get a call from Bryce's assistant that he's headed home.

Grinning like the cat that ate the canary, I let Tristan know that Bryce is on his way home. And that I'd like him to wait outside the front door until Bryce gets here, and then he can leave. Tristan laughs and shakes his head but does as I ask. And I go upstairs to change. Or strip, as it were.

So when Bryce walks through the door not quite fifteen minutes later, his look of confusion due to Tristan's unusual position rapidly disappears as he catches sight of me next to a tableful of food. Wearing sky-high red heels, a matched red lip, and the apron. And nothing else.

His jaw drops as he takes in the small sheet of fabric that's by no stretch of the imagination covering my generous curves. Free of a bra, my breasts topple out the sides, and it only just skims the bottom of my hips. I hold out a glass of whiskey.

"Welcome home, baby." My voice is husky with desire. Being mostly naked and waiting for a gorgeous man has made me as ready for what comes next as he is.

But instead of the pouncing I expected, he methodically sets his keys and wallet on the table by the door. As he slowly advances on me, he undoes the top two buttons of his shirt. He stops in front of me, casually accepting the proffered glass and taking a measured sip. And even though I'm wearing four-inch heels, he still towers over me.

I discreetly take a deep breath and I cock an eyebrow at him, marveling at his control. It's all I can do not to shake with anticipation. "How was your day?" I ask as nonchalantly as I can. And I manage to sound much calmer than I feel.

Bryce carefully sets the whiskey down on the table behind me and rolls his broad shoulders. "It's about to get a whole lot better," he murmurs, looking deeply into my eyes. His gaze is fire itself, burning me from the inside out.

My lips part and a small breath escapes me.

A smile flits across his features, and he uses his thumb to stroke firmly from my bottom lip, down my chin, to my neck and chest. "Where do you want me to fuck you, Sera?"

My whole body tightens in anticipation, heat pooling between my thighs. I don't trust myself to speak, so I simply look over at the couch. He gives a small nod. Grabbing my hand, he leads me the few steps into the living room and sits down on the overstuffed white behemoth. His eyes never leave mine. With a tug he spins me around and pulls me into his lap, so my back is pressed against his chest.

He brushes the hair away from my neck, his breath hot on the sensitive flesh. Tilting my head with one hand, he presses his mouth into the place where my neck meets my shoulder, then runs his tongue up to my ear. I gasp in surprise and lean back into him. His other hand reaches around, firmly grasping my breast under the apron, my nipple pinched between his unforgiving fingers. As he sucks and twists at me, I writhe against him, racked with desire. I grab at the hand working my breast and pull it out from under the soft fabric. I guide it under the bottom of the apron, between my legs.

His mouth breaks away and a low moan escapes him. My hips buck at the sound and he tames them with his hand. His fingers slide down and into the soft mound of flesh between my legs, finding their target quickly. And he works the vulnerable nub between two fingers just as he did my nipple. As my breath quickens and I loudly affirm my enjoyment, his other hand works under me, undoing his pants. And I feel it when his cock springs free, hard and hot.

I turn my head, my lips finding his, and our tongues do a feverish and lust-filled dance for a few moments before he pulls away, sucking my bottom lip on the way. He wraps an arm around me and lifts me slightly, then uses the other hand to slip himself inside me. And I can't help but gasp loudly and spasm at the sudden filling, my whole body tight and quivering in response.

Determined to be his every fantasy tonight, I push his pants to the floor, then spread my legs for leverage and brace my hands on the couch between his open knees. And I put all my concentration into raising and lowering my hips over him. At the first thrust, both of Bryce's hands drop to my hips and he groans loudly.

"You feel..." he pants through the words, "...so fucking good."

I pump again and this time he rises to meet me.

"Yes, Sera. Don't stop. God, don't stop."

I put everything I have into managing the almost overwhelming feeling of him inside me, every nerve ending screaming with pleasure. And I focus on the ride, up and down, and again. Until I'm sweating, shaking, screaming. Or perhaps it's just him screaming as his hands grip my sides, his hips rising to meet mine hard on every thrust, crying out loudly with every gratifying plunge into my slick center.

When I feel like my arms will give out I lean back with him still inside me.

He turns my head roughly, the fire of his passion erupting as his mouth roughly claims mine. His hips slide downward, off the couch, and his hands slide under my thighs, holding me in place. Using his arms to support me in position, he uses the freedom of his lower half hovering off the couch to start thrusting wildly.

And it's pleasure like I've never known, with me totally at his mercy as he balances me over him, spread open as he plunges deeper than I thought possible. A low ache begins to build and a desire to shatter into a million pieces pours through me but is just out of reach. I suddenly remember a move he made our first time, and I slip a finger between my legs. With a small touch I find the catalyst I was looking for. So I press harder, faster, until I'm keeping rhythm with him. Until I'm coming so hard that I've lost control over myself. But he doesn't stop, and the orgasm continues until Bryce can't hold the position anymore.

He sinks carefully onto the floor, laying me on the plush rug between the couch and the coffee table. He hovers over me, panting and just as slick with sweat as I am. His mouth descends on my nipple, his teeth pulling at it through the thin fabric. And then the other. I'm so spent that I can barely arch my back into the pleasure, but my hands pull at him nonetheless, desperate to have him inside me again. He smiles down at me.

"So impatient," he teases, sliding into me slowly.

I groan and wriggle under him.

"You just." He thrusts slowly. "Need." Again. "To." Again. "Relax." He keeps the rhythm, running his nose up my neck and kissing me as softly as he takes me.

I do as he says and relax into it. And I'm not sorry. The slow, sensual pace allows me to feel every inch of him and he of me. I close my eyes and bite my lip, intent on savoring the drawn-out ascent.

It's not long before I notice him speeding up. And not long after that I hear his breath hitch, and he nuzzles his face into my neck before his final shift back into an earth-shaking, orgasm-inducing frenzy. His thrusts are as shallow and fast as his breathing, and I focus on letting my climax wash over me before he loses it. And when it does, I grip him to me and tighten around him, pulling him in with me. His guttural groans spur on the continued contractions of my muscles as I ride the peak, causing him to shudder and quake over me, in me. I feel his release, hot and wet, spilling into me. Almost crying with gratification, I release him, and he rolls off of me.

He laces his fingers tiredly in mine, and we lie there in silence for a long while. When I feel like the world has stopped spinning with mad desire and lust, I roll toward him onto my side, propping my head on my hand.

"So did that live up to the fantasy?" I ask, tracing a finger down the muscles of his chest and stomach through his shirt. His answering smile is one of pure, exhausted bliss. He fingers the ruffled edge of the apron fondly.

"It turned the fantasy on its back and fucked it seventeen ways from Sunday," he responds matter-of-factly.

I chew my lip thoughtfully. "Do you have any other fantasies?" I ask curiously.

Bryce's eyebrows shoot up and he rolls onto his side to face me. "Four months," he says.

I look at him questioningly.

"That's how long I've know you. Wanted you. I could write a book — maybe even several books — about all of the fantasies I've had of you."

I press my lips together to suppress my amused smile. "For instance?" I prompt.

His eyes flick to the window wall behind us.

"Ah, yes, you mentioned that one recently."

He leans in and kisses me softly. "We can take mine one at a time," he replies. "How about you? Did you ever fantasize about me?"

I can't help giving him an incredulous look. "Um. Yeah," I say in a tone that implies that should've been obvious. "Have you seen yourself?" I poke him in his ridiculously large bicep. "I even had a dream once about us having sex that gave me an actual orgasm," I admit.

Bryce looks impressed. "Damn, that's pretty awesome," he says. "Well, whatever I was doing in that dream, I'd be happy to make it a reality."

And it hits me again. This man. Over and over he's proving to me that I've made the right choice. That I can trust him completely. That he adores me completely.

"My fantasies. Your fantasies. I want to do all of it," I admit. "I trust you, Bryce. Completely."

His face is inscrutable for a moment until he presses his lips to mine tenderly. He of all people knows how much that means for me. How closely I guarded my heart for so long.

He breaks the kiss but moves only far enough away so he can look into my eyes once more. "And I trust you completely," he replies. "No matter what life brings us, Sera, never forget how much I love you."

～

By Saturday afternoon we still haven't made it out of bed for more than a few minutes here and there. I know it won't always be this way, this new and exciting. So I want to enjoy every moment of wanting and being wanted so badly that things like food, sleep, and the outside world don't seem all that important. But even on top of that, there's a depth to being with Bryce that I've never experienced. And I know it's borne of the solid friendship we've created over the last months. So it's hard to regret anything that's happened to lead me here.

But I'm somewhat brought back to reality when Heather returns my call late that afternoon. I slip into a robe and leave the bedroom, going downstairs so I can talk to her in private. But she sounds distant and doesn't want to talk much, though we do manage to make plans to have dinner next Wednesday. When I hang up, I feel perturbed. I stare out the living room window wall into the grey mist of the day, wrapping my arms around myself for warmth and comfort.

"Everything okay?" Bryce asks from behind me.

I turn to see him sauntering toward me from the stairs, finally dressed in grey sweats and a white T-shirt. It doesn't make me want him any less. Though the sense of discomfort that still lingers from my brief chat with Heather puts a pretty big damper on my libido.

"I don't know," I reply honestly, sinking into my favorite chair.

Bryce takes a seat on the couch next to me and silently waits for me to explain.

"It seemed like Heather was doing so well for a while there. Her new job has been going well. She's getting therapy and has plenty of support leading into Daniel's trial. But she sounded off. I can't quite put my finger on it."

"Scared? Nervous? Doubtful?" Bryce offers patiently.

"Yes," I reply sweepingly. "All of that." I shake my head sorrowfully. "I just hate that one heinous, unspeakable act can continue to victimize her. And probably will for the rest of her life."

Bryce considers me thoughtfully for a moment. "Well," he starts carefully. "You of all people know what that's like. If anyone can help her through this, it's you."

I meet his concerned gaze. We don't talk much anymore about how, three months ago, he saved my life from a deranged employee with a massive grudge against me. How she kidnapped me, beat me, and almost shot me before Bryce showed up, Alessandro in tow, causing her to turn the gun on herself.

I rub my eyes as if it'll remove the image of the back of her skull exploding from my mind. "I don't know what I'm supposed to do," I admit. "I still have nightmares myself. Elevators still scare me sometimes." Once you've been kidnapped at gunpoint in one, it's hard to forget. "But even that pales in comparison to being violated the way she was. I can't even begin to imagine what she's going through."

Bryce leans forward with his arms resting on his massive thighs. He looks into his hands for a long while. Finally, he looks up at me seriously.

"Between serving in the military and running a company that profits off the vulnerability of others, I've seen a lot of different kinds of pain," he says. "But

I've also seen hope. And perseverance. It's normal to have doubts, to wonder if it'll ever get better. If continuing down a path is worth the cost. The ones who make it through have a good support system. It's the ones who try to pretend like bad things aren't happening or refuse help that suffer the most in the long run. Heather has her parents, us, her therapist, and hopefully other friends and family who are helping her through this. She's dealing with this and moving forward. But I think even she knew that path was going to be harder in the short term than doing nothing. But Daniel *will* be convicted. And Heather *will* get through this." He reaches out and folds his hand over mine. "And so will you."

His words strike such a chord in me that my eyes fill with tears, and it takes me a moment to figure out why. I blink back the tears as I finish putting my thoughts into words.

"The day I called you, when we hadn't spoken in more than three weeks," I say softly, looking to him to see if he remembers. Though I'm certain he does.

"Yes, after I'd stupidly yelled at you for not dealing with things that were difficult. Like the attack. Our feelings for each other. Your trust issues." His expression is grim and remorseful. "I should've called you first." He leans back into the sofa, running a hand over his hair.

"I didn't accidentally call you that day," I admit.

He huffs a dry laugh. "I know," he replies with a wry smile.

I shake my head. "What you don't know is how low I was," I respond. "Alessandro had stopped calling and was doing god-knows-what in Italy without any sign of ever returning. Daniel was making my transition to Sutton Developments hell. My half-brother decided he didn't want to meet me. Allie had lost her baby and crawled into her cocoon of depression. And you were hurting, and I *was* denying that I had feelings for you. When we stopped talking, and all of that was going on, I almost gave up hope."

Bryce looks at me quizzically. "But you didn't. And you got through it. And Heather will too, with your help," he reiterates.

I shake my head. "I didn't get through it. *You* got me through it. Before you came along, I didn't know what it was like to be loved by someone who was always there for me, even when their own world was falling apart. Not even my parents, for fuck's sake," I admit. "Whether I wanted to admit my feelings or not, I always knew you would be there for me. Even when we weren't speaking, I knew if I needed you, you'd be there."

"I was," he agrees, smiling at me sadly. "I am."

I nod, pulling my knees to my chest. "I know."

We stare at each other for a few moments, an understanding passing between us, a recognition of how truly deep the bond we share is.

"What does this have to do with Heather?" he asks, tilting his head.

I can't help but laugh. "Nothing," I admit. "What you said just made me realize that I'm no longer an island. And I'm glad for that. That on some level I always knew how much you love me. And that's what got me through everything I went through. Even if I wasn't ready to love you back. So thank you. For that. And you know, everything else." I give him a sheepish smile and he laughs.

"Anytime, gorgeous," he replies. "To that end, think of the Heather and Daniel situation from that slant. You'll do what you can to support Heather. And the whole thing will be difficult for you too. But we'll get through it, just like we've gotten through everything else."

"Yes," I agree, my eyes once again sparkling with tears — this time of joy. "*We* will."

FIVE

On Sunday morning I find it insanely difficult to tear myself away from Bryce to meet Allie for brunch. But since it has been three weeks since I've seen my best friend, I know I need to dig deep. Bryce doesn't make it easier, lounging half-naked on the sofa as I look for my keys, then begging for more kisses as I try to depart.

But finally, I manage to get myself there, where I find Allie already waiting at the restaurant. In stark contrast to the summery outfit she wore last time, she now wears a charcoal grey long-sleeved tunic over thick black tights, her strawberry blond hair hanging in loose waves around her shoulders. And she looks really happy.

"Sera!" she squeals when she sees me, pulling me into a tight hug.

"Hey, babe," I reply grinning and squeezing her back.

She presses me away to arm's length and scrutinizes my face. "You're glowing," she remarks suspiciously. "I'm guessing things are going well?"

My grin turns maniacal as I follow her into the restaurant. "You could say that," I reply coyly.

"Oh lord, you're going at it like rabbits, aren't you?" she asks, rolling her eyes as we're seated at a booth.

I cackle. "Maaaaaybe," I admit.

She shakes her head and laughs. "I forget what that part of the relationship is like," she responds. "At least I can relive it vicariously through you."

"Won't you be *actually* living it pretty soon in Fiji?" I tease her.

Allie smiles shyly from behind her menu. "As it happens, even the thought of a romantic vacation has made things a little more exciting recently," she admits.

"Oh, really?" I ask. "How *much* more exciting?" I'm teasing her mostly, since I know she's too shy about that sort of thing to actually tell me.

She laughs and waves me off. "It's probably not as exciting as I'm making it sound. Mostly things are back to how they were before," she replies. "When you live with someone and have regular access, it's just not as interesting, even at the best of times."

I suddenly realize I didn't tell Allie that Bryce and I are living together. And unfortunately, I'm not able to wipe the guilty look off my face before she notices.

"What are you hiding?" she asks sharply.

"God, Allie, I forget what a bloodhound you are," I mumble.

Thankfully, the waiter shows up to take our orders, so I have a moment to regroup.

When he's gone, I sigh heavily and approach the subject cautiously.

"You know how I told you I had personal security because the people who are after Alessandro are trying to get at him through me?"

"Yes," she replies, clearly unsure of where I'm going with this.

"And how having them around made me isolate myself?" I continue.

Allie nods, but waits for me to continue with a wary look on her face.

"Well, Bryce agreed to let me back off the security to just to and from work, but only if he moved in with me." I brace myself.

"So you and Bryce are living together. And going at it like rabbits," she deduces drily.

I nod.

She looks at me disapprovingly for a moment before sighing and shrugging. "Well, at least that gives you easy access."

"It's not permanent," I hedge.

"Pfff," Allie responds. "We'll see." She looks at the nervous expression on my face. "Oh, Sera, don't worry about what I think. As long as you're happy, that's all that matters to me. You know that."

"Thank you," I reply. "But in some ways, it even feels fast to me."

She levels a look at me. "You know, don't you."

It's not really a question, and I'm not sure what she means. I give her a puzzled look. "I know a lot of things," I reply slowly. "To what, exactly, are you referring?"

"That he's The One." She says it matter-of-factly, like she's just remarked that I know he likes to wear blue shirts.

I chew on my lip, trying to decide if I should attempt a denial. But in true Allie form, she sees right through me before I can even get that far.

"If you haven't realized it yet, that's fine," she replies airily, sipping the glass of water in front of her. "But I've known for a long time."

And I can't help but laugh at that. "Seriously? You knew that I wanted to spend the rest of my life with him before I did?" I reply sarcastically. And then realizing what I've just admitted, I clap a hand over my mouth.

Allie grins triumphantly. "See? That wasn't so hard," she says with a wink. "I'm happy for you."

"I'm happy too," I admit. "Ridiculously, rainbows-sunshine-and-unicorns happy."

Allie laughs, though her attention is quickly diverted as our food arrives.

After a few minutes of silently stuffing our faces, Allie swallows enough of her food to continue the discussion.

"Is he as hot with his shirt off as he is with it on? No wait, of course he is. I'm sure he's even hotter. How much hotter are we talking here?" she presses.

"It hurts thinking about it," I reply with a lascivious grin.

She lets out a frustrated groan. "What's wrong with this guy then? Is he…" she leans forward and lowers her voice, "lacking in the size department?"

"Allie!" I reply, shocked. "I've never heard you talk about this stuff, much less ask those kinds of questions." I examine her for a moment. "What happened?"

She blushes furiously. "I went off the depression meds at the suggestion of my therapist," she admits. "And it's been great. I'm great. I feel alive again. So I guess things have just started working again." She grins like a schoolgirl.

I almost want to cry with happiness. "That's so great," I breathe. Then after a pause, "Does this mean you might come back to work?"

She presses her lips together. "I think so," she replies. "After vacation, David and I are going to decide."

I want to jump up and hug her, or clap, or dance. But I hold it in, not wanting to pressure her. But I think she gets how happy that makes me anyway.

"Now, are you going to answer the question or what?"

A shit-eating grin splits my face. "Exactly the opposite of lacking," I reply, biting my lip thinking of it. "His only flaw is being too fucking perfect."

Allie laughs. "Yeah, we'll see about that. Let this phase wear off and every time he forgets to replace the toilet paper roll or pick up groceries on his way home, you'll be ready to tear his head off," she assures me.

I laugh in return. "Probably," I agree. "And not that I've ever been in a relationship long enough to know, but I'm sure you get past that phase too."

Allie nods sagely. "Oh, yes. Once he's realized that everyone is much happier if he just stops doing things that piss you off," she replies.

I look at her skeptically. "Seriously?" I ask.

Allie bursts out laughing. "Hell, no. You just give up after a while and stop giving a shit," she chortles. "And it's great."

"Ah, such high praise and hope for the romantic future I have ahead of me," I reply with feigned wistfulness. But then, dropping back into my usual tone, "Consider me warned. I'm going to enjoy the going-at-it-like-rabbits phase while I can."

"Then you better finish those waffles," she replies looking pointedly at my mostly uneaten food. "Sounds like you're going to need your strength."

∾

AT HOME LATER THAT EVENING, WHILE BRYCE AND I ARE LAZING IN BED — dressed and watching television, for once — my dad calls. I show Bryce the caller ID.

"You going to answer?" he asks curiously, stroking my thigh reassuringly.

I shrug. "Might as well," I reply.

While I feel readier to deal with it now, I'm not sure when, if ever, I'll be totally comfortable talking to my father, as he was absent for so long and for some reason has picked this tumultuous time in my life to want to reconnect. The single lunch we shared was awkward enough. I'm not sure how many more uncomfortable conversations I can handle.

"Want me to leave?" Bryce asks considerately.

"No, it's okay," I reply with a smile. I take a deep breath and pick up the call. "Hello?"

"Sera," Kent Evans' voice breathes in a sigh. "I'm so glad you answered. I was starting to get worried about you."

I roll my eyes. "I'm fine," I reply. "There's just been a lot going on. How was your business trip?"

"Productive. But I'm glad to be back home," he replies genially. "What's been going on there?"

I glance over at Bryce, not sure if I want to get into it with both men able to listen. "You know, I was just getting ready for bed," I fib. "How about we have lunch next weekend and we can talk about it?"

"Yeah? Are you sure? I mean, I'd love to see you, but I was worried after Hunter and I cancelled at the last minute before."

As if I needed a reminder that my half-brother clearly has no interest in meeting me.

"It's okay, really," I interrupt. "I'd probably have done the same in his shoes."

"He feels bad about it," Kent replies.

I'm shocked, and skeptical, but he sounds sincere. So, he believes it, anyway.

"He said that he'd come next time, but only if you were okay with it."

I frown at the obviously manipulative tactic. Because if I say no, now I'm the asshole. And I'm sure he expects me to say no, or he wouldn't have made the offer.

"Of course I'm okay with it," I lie.

Bryce gives me a look. I know he can't hear Kent's side of the conversation, but Bryce knows a lie when he hears one.

"Well! That's great, Sera," he replies, sounded beyond happy and relieved. "Same time and place?"

"Yep," I respond, eager to hang up. "See you next Saturday at noon."

"Goodnight, Sera."

"Goodnight, Kent." I hang up and groan loudly.

Bryce smirks unreservedly. "So I'm meeting your dad next weekend, huh?"

I shoot him a glare. "I'm going by myself," I respond snappishly. And I immediate feel bad for it. "I'm sorry. I don't know why I suggested we have lunch. Ugh. But it really is something I'd rather do on my own."

Bryce gives me a patient look. "I hate to break it to you, but I'm either meeting your dad, or you get to explain why Tristan has to stand within three feet of you at all times," Bryce replies. "Your call."

My eyes widen with realization. "Why did I get to go by myself to meet Allie today then?" I ask petulantly.

"Because it was three blocks away, and it's Allie," he replies drily. "But I can't let you go across town to meet a man I don't know by yourself."

"Fuck," I swear.

Bryce laughs. "I'll behave, I promise," he says, still chuckling.

"They're probably going to like you more than they like me," I grouse.

Bryce smiles his sunshine smile, and I immediately find it's impossible for me to be cranky any longer.

I pick up my pillow and whack him with it. "Stop." *Whack*. "Being." *Whack*. "So." *Whack*. "Perfect." *Whack*. "Damnit!"

Bryce shields himself half-heartedly from each blow, and on my last swing captures both me and the pillow. He throws the pillow off the side of the bed and pins me under him, planting kisses all over my face. I squeal and wriggle in protest, ultimately dissolving into indignant giggles.

But he abruptly pulls away after a moment. "Wait. They?" he asks.

I sit up, adjusting my camisole. "They," I confirm. "My father and my half-brother."

Bryce leans back into his pillow with his arms behind his head, considering that. "Well, that ought to be interesting," he replies thoughtfully.

"You promised to behave," I remind him.

He shoots me a sly grin. "Oh, I'll behave. At lunch anyway," he replies. "But I make no promises until then."

I only have a split second after I realize he plans to resume his attack to get away, but I'm not fast enough. Not that I mind since, as always, it quickly evolves into much more naked and pleasurable play.

SIX

I also find I don't so much mind the dawning of the workweek anymore now that Bryce is living with me. Shower sex after his workout has become the norm, and it leaves me happy, if not a bit distracted, for most of the day until we can get back to it before bed.

Work itself has slipped back into a steady, drama-free rhythm. Though without Daniel, I'm far more loaded with responsibility than I'd like to be. But it's still mostly manageable, and I'm just not as easily fazed these days, being at a zero stress level physically and emotionally.

But on Wednesday I get a one-two punch that knocks me back. First, Bryce calls to tell me that Daniel's trial has been postponed until further notice, mentioning something about a procedural error. Not long after, I get a text from Heather saying she can't make dinner and she'll let me know when she's able to reschedule. I text her back asking if she's okay, knowing that she's likely not in light of the news, but get no response. And for the rest of the day, I can't shake my concern for her.

Predictably, Bryce encourages me to let it go, that only she can decide to reach out, and to give her space if that's what she needs. It doesn't make me any less worried, but I decide that he's at least partly right — there's nothing I can do about it. So I bury myself in my new routine of work and Bryce, and by the end of the week it's mostly stopped niggling at me. Mostly. But when I realize that's happening, it starts niggling at me that it's not niggling at me, so I decide to just go back to worrying. Even though there's nothing I can do. Understandably, it drives Bryce a little crazy but, as with everything, he takes it in stride with immeasurable grace and patience.

When Saturday dawns, and I mentally prepare for lunch with my father and half-brother, I wonder briefly how far Bryce's Zen will go. Not that I know exactly what to expect, but I'm bracing for the worst. Though still hoping for the best.

I'm a little surprised when Bryce comes downstairs in dark slacks and his favorite cerulean blue button-front shirt that makes his eyes look the same, bright shade. He looks ridiculously handsome, of course, but he's normally a jeans and T-shirt kind of guy on the weekend. I'm wearing my usual uniform of shirtdress and leggings, opting for a deep purple long-sleeved dress with black leggings. So I don't look underdressed next to him, per se, but it does make me wonder.

"Why so fancy?" I ask him teasingly.

He cocks an eyebrow. "You don't think I look nice?" he asks, running a hand over his chestnut hair. I stand up and reach up to do my own pass, noting that it's long enough to really run my fingers through again. He sighs happily and slouches to let me massage my fingers along his scalp.

"You're gorgeous and you know it," I murmur. "But it's just lunch, at a bistro. There's no dress code." He straightens up and runs his fingers along my arms.

"Maybe not for the restaurant," he allows. "But there's an implied meeting-the-father dress code."

I laugh. "You're worried what my father will think of you?" I ask incredulously.

He shrugs. "Doesn't hurt to look nice," he replies.

I have to bite my lip to contain myself. "You are too cute, Bryce Hoyt," I respond.

He frowns exaggeratedly. "Not cute," he replies, deepening his already low voice. "Manly." He kisses me ferociously, his hands pawing at every inch of me, his hips pressing into mine.

When he pulls away I'm gasping for breath. "Careful there, tiger, or your manliness will be a little *too* obvious," I joke.

His eyes sparkle mischievously as he lowers his mouth to my ear. "Wouldn't want that. It might be…" he runs his nose down my ear and neck, causing that entire side of my body to tingle, "distracting." He kisses my clavicle softly, then pulls away, grazing a nipple with his fingertips as he goes. And then he walks nonchalantly to the kitchen bar to grab his wallet.

It takes me a full minute before I'm composed enough to move. He grins back at me over his shoulder, perfectly aware of the effect he's had on me.

"Ready?" he asks, turning back to me.

I shake my head at him. "If you're ready to start behaving, I'm ready to go," I qualify.

He laughs. "Fair enough."

∽

WE ARRIVE AT THE RESTAURANT RIGHT ON TIME. BRYCE, EVER THE GENTLEMAN, holds the door open for me. He's practiced at discretion, but I've started to notice how he scans a room whenever he enters it. And I'm glad we don't go out more often, because it's a reminder of the still present potential for danger. I sigh inwardly, wondering how we'll ever know to stop looking over our shoulders.

But I'm quickly distracted from my own thoughts as I spot my father waving at me from a table off to one side of the restaurant. I can see the appraising look he throws Bryce as we approach, and I realize I'd forgotten to tell him I wouldn't be alone. But, since he isn't either, he'd already gotten a table that could seat four.

And for the first time, I notice the half-brother I've never met. The product of my father's secret other "wife." A wife only in practice at the time, as he was still married to my mother. But all I know about my sibling is his name — Hunter — and that he's seven years younger than me. And, at around twenty-three years old, he still looks mostly like a kid. At least to me. And I can tell by the look Bryce is giving him, he feels the same way. I remember suddenly that Bryce, in his once nonstop quest to gather intel on everyone I associated with, mentioned Hunter having anger issues, and I regret never asking what he'd meant.

As we arrive at the table and they both rise to greet us, Hunter looks even younger as my eyes flick from him to Bryce. Bryce, at thirty-four years old, has a distinct air of commanding confidence. It helps that he towers over all of us, broad and strapping, his hard body still completely evident under his well-tailored clothing. He's the epitome of the manly protector. Hunter looks like a man-child in comparison. Though he actually also looks much like my father, with the same sturdy but otherwise unremarkable build and the same light brown hair as both my father and me. Hunter is also only a few inches shorter than my father's six feet, putting him right around my height. It all contributes to the air of youth about him.

"Sera," my father greets me. "It's so nice to see you. I didn't know you'd be bringing someone."

"Sorry," I reply sheepishly. "I forgot to mention. This is Bryce Hoyt. Bryce, this is my father, Kent Evans."

Bryce extends a hand, which my father shakes firmly. "Nice meeting you," Bryce says, his voice low and measured.

"And you are?" There's a challenge in my father's eyes that irks me.

"Bryce is my boyfriend," I interject.

The corners of Bryce's mouth twitch as he takes in my irritated tone.

I reach a hand out to my half-brother. "You must be Hunter."

He glances down at my hand before taking it. His handshake is surprisingly solid. "Yeah," he says dismissively. "Nice to meet you."

My father shoots an annoyed look at Hunter. "Please, sit," he offers, taking a seat himself.

Hunter sits down next to him, so Bryce and I take the seats across from them. There are only three menus, but having been here before with my father, I already know what I want, so I pass mine to Bryce. Likewise, while Hunter peruses his menu, my father's stays folded in front of him. And he's staring at Bryce.

"I'm sorry it took me so long to get back to you," I say to my father, attempting to draw his attention away from Bryce before he notices.

Kent's eyes jump to mine, and he seems to snap out of it a little. "It's okay, I'm just glad we were able to get together," he replies. "How did everything go with your, er, merger, was it?"

"Yes, the merger," I confirm, loosing a breath. I hadn't realized how long it's been since we saw each other. And so much has happened since then. Not that he needs to know about most of it. "It was rough going for a while there. But things seem to be mostly in a good rhythm now. I've taken on a lot more responsibility, but I'm also learning a lot."

"More responsibility than running your own company?" he asks skeptically.

I smile vaguely. "Well, no," I admit. "It's just different, I guess. When it was my company, I had to do a lot of tasks I didn't really enjoy but were necessary. Now I mostly get to stick to the real estate-related stuff — project selection, negotiation, goal setting, that sort of thing."

I think hard for a minute trying to remember what my father actually does, if he'll even understand where I'm coming from. He used to change jobs a lot when I was a kid, and I know he talked about his current job at our last lunch, but I'm having trouble recalling exactly what it was. I seem to remember it being related to the legal field, but for some reason it's eluding me at the moment.

"What do you do for a living, Mr. Evans?" Bryce pipes up, and I want to kiss him for asking.

I hadn't noticed, but his menu is now folded on the table in front of him and he's leaned back in his chair casually, one hand resting on my knee. I also note that Hunter is still studying his menu, though I'm beginning to think it's to avoid participating in the conversation.

My father shifts imperceptibly under Bryce's cool gaze. "I'm a process server," he replies.

Ah. Yes. That. Bryce suppresses a smile and purposely avoids looking at me. He obviously finds that funny, and I'm not sure why.

"What is it that you do, son?"

"I run a corporate security firm," Bryce replies matter-of-factly.

My father frowns. "Hoyt, did you say? That wouldn't be Hoyt Corporate Services, would it?" he asks curiously.

And I'm sure the surprise shows on my face.

"You've heard of us," Bryce replies with an amused smile. "How nice."

"Yes, well, your company has been around a long time," Kent hedges. "You seem a bit young to be running the operation, though."

I can't help the indignant look that breaks across my face. "Um, hello? I ran my own company for years, and I'm younger than Bryce," I pipe up.

"Sera, I apologize," my father replies, blushing. "Obviously, you were doing very well. It's just Hoyt Corporate Services has quite a reputation. And some very high-profile clients."

"What he means is, my company protects some of the largest and wealthiest companies in the Seattle area," Bryce interjects. "And those companies are run by people with high standards. They expect their affairs to be handled by someone who knows what they're doing. Someone with experience."

Now my father is beet red. And I notice that Hunter has put his menu down and, while still silent, is watching with amused interest.

"Well, yes," my father replies, clearly beyond embarrassed. "But I didn't mean to imply anything bad about you, Bryce."

"It's all right, Mr. Evans," Bryce responds in a calm tone. "I didn't expect to be running the company so soon, either. But my father recently passed away, so that's just how it went. I have both undergraduate and graduate business degrees, had been training under my father for the better part of two decades, and was deployed multiple times as a Navy SEAL security specialist. So I assure you I'm more than qualified."

And Bryce is such a humble person, that he says it as if he were simply talking about the weather. But I can't help giving a smug grin. And Hunter looks positively gleeful.

"Badass, dude," he says seriously to Bryce, raising a fist.

Bryce laughs and reaches out to reciprocate the fist bump. "Thanks," Bryce replies, still chuckling.

My father is spared responding as the waitress arrives to take our orders.

"How long have you two been dating?" my father asks after she's gone.

And while I'm thankful he's moved on from questioning Bryce's qualifications, I'm not sure I like where this new line of questioning is going, either.

"Well, we've known each other for months," I reply carefully. "But we've only been dating a couple weeks now." Lordy. Saying it sounds odd. It feels like we've been together for so much longer.

"Oh, well, that's nice," my father responds, clearly relieved that Bryce wasn't just a secret I'd been withholding from him.

"What about you, Hunter?" Bryce asks, leaning forward onto his arms. "What do you do with your days?"

Hunter shrugs noncommittally. "Haven't been able to find a job since I graduated," he replies, sounding bored.

"Translation: he plays video games when he isn't out vandalizing public property with those—"

"God, Dad, could you please not?" Hunter interrupts my father. Our father. Hunter doesn't look mad, just embarrassed.

"What did you get your degree in?" I ask Hunter kindly.

"Art," he replies simply, finally looking me in the eye.

And I'm extremely surprised. I look over at Bryce to find him studying Hunter with an appraising look. This was news to him too. And that kind of amuses me, considering Bryce usually knows that kind of information. Again, at least when it comes to people I might spend time with.

"Also known as a 'Would you like fries with that?' degree," my father jokes.

But nobody laughs. Hunter shifts uncomfortably in his seat. I almost ask Hunter what kind of art he does and what sort of job he is looking for, but I don't want to give my father more opportunity to make jokes at his expense, so I opt for changing the subject instead.

"I'm sure he'll find something great," I respond to my father. "I don't think you ever mentioned what your wife does." I suddenly realize I have no idea what Hunter's mother's name is.

"Barb is a beautician," Kent supplies.

"Oh," I respond, not quite sure of what to say. "That's great."

Awkward silence descends upon the table for a moment until Bryce breaks it.

"You guys 'Hawks fans?" Bryce asks.

Hunter shrugs, but my dad lights up. "Hell, yes," he responds vehemently. "I can't wait to watch us kick Dallas' ass tomorrow."

"I don't know, we're pretty evenly matched," Bryce replies. "Should be a good game."

"Evenly matched? Please!" my father scoffs.

And for the bulk of the rest of lunch, they proceed to break down each team's strengths and weaknesses and make predictions on tomorrow's game. I'm not a huge football fan, but frankly I'm just glad there's something to fill the conversation. And by the time we're done eating, whatever tension that existed between my father and Bryce is long gone.

I also realize I didn't really get much of a chance to talk to Hunter. So as we are leaving, and my father and Bryce are still chatting animatedly about all things football, I slip Hunter my business card.

"My cell number is on there," I explain quietly as we walk a bit behind the others. "I'd like to get to know you better, but I don't think we'll get to do that with these two around. Give me a call sometime, okay?"

Hunter turns the card thoughtfully in his hands before carefully slipping it into his pocket. "Sure thing," he responds. While his response is as taciturn as he has been all afternoon, he at least seems less bored and standoffish than he had at the beginning of lunch, so I take it as a win.

Once Bryce and I are alone in the car, I'm quietly processing the afternoon when he touches me lightly on the knee without taking his eyes off the road.

"You okay?" he asks gently, returning his hand to the steering wheel.

"Yeah, definitely," I assure him. "Though I think it's going to take me a while before I can get a good enough read on things to decide how I really feel about it all. What did you think?"

Bryce laughs. "It doesn't matter what I think," he replies with a grin.

"Oh, please," I respond. "Of course it does. You're the best judge of character I know. I take it you weren't impressed then?"

He looks over at me briefly, obviously flattered by the praise. "I don't want to say anything negative about your father. You've probably heard enough of that to last you a lifetime," he says carefully. "And in general, it seems like he honestly wants to make amends and get to know you."

"But?" I prompt.

Bryce presses his lips together and shakes his head.

"Spill it, Hoyt. Does this have anything to do with him being a process server? I saw that look on your face."

Bryce bursts out laughing. "Yes and no," he admits. "I don't have anything against process servers. But given your father's history, it just cracked me up. Because it totally fits."

I give him a bemused look. "And why is that?"

"Process servers deliver, or serve, legal documents and summons to people. Often people who don't want to be served. So they have to be, let's say, *creative* at times," Bryce explains. "So it's funny because your father has always been a sneaky bastard, but now he's actually getting paid to be one."

"That is strangely appropriate," I agree. "I notice you didn't mention having anything negative to say about Hunter. I thought you were concerned with some sort of anger issue he supposedly has."

Bryce glances askance at me. "So you *do* listen to me occasionally," he jokes.

I give him a sharp look.

"Okay, okay. I may have been wrong about Hunter. The kid seems harmless. In fact, I'm surprised he's not more of an ass given what a jerk his dad is to him. So whatever happened, I think there's some serious context missing."

"What happened?" I ask.

Bryce doesn't answer for a moment. "If I suggested that you wait until he tells you, would you be upset?" he asks tentatively. "Like I said, I think it needs context, and I don't want it to negatively affect your opinion of him if it's what I think it is. And it looks like he could use you in his court."

"When you put it that way, I guess I can wait," I agree. "Do you get sick of being right all the time?" I want to be grumpy about it, but his answering laugh is all sunshine, and I find it hard not to smile.

"Baby, I wish I were," he replies. "But we're all wrong sometimes."

SEVEN

I don't have to wait long to satisfy my curiosity about Hunter's past. On Wednesday morning, in the middle of a rather unremarkable workweek, I get a call from an unknown number on my cellphone that turns out to be my half-brother.

"Hey, Sera, it's Hunter," he starts, sounding awkward and uncomfortable.

"Hunter!" I say, trying not to sound as surprised as I feel. "I'm glad you called. What's up?"

"I'm catching a ride with a friend into Seattle for a thing tonight," he replies. "I thought we could hang out. Or whatever."

"Ah, well, that sounds good and all, but I have to work until around six," I reply apologetically. "And I don't want to interfere with your plans for the evening."

"Oh, no, that's not until, like, way later," he replies. "Like ten or eleven tonight at least."

Ah, to be young again.

"Well in that case, we can grab some dinner. Or you can come over to my place," I offer. "I usually cook anyway. The more the merrier. You can even bring your friend if you want."

"My friend has other plans today. If you text me the address I can walk or take the bus there," he says.

"Where are you coming from?" I ask, curious.

"Uhhhh, I think we're staying at a place in Burien?" he hazards.

"That's not really walkable. In fact, it's even kind of far to take the bus," I inform him. "How about I have my driver come get you before they pick me up?"

"You have a *driver*?" he asks incredulously.

"Heh, yeah," I admit. "It's, um, kind of a thing. I can explain later. Just text me your address and I'll let you know when they'll be there to get you."

"Awesome, sounds good," Hunter says agreeably, sounding much more enthused. "See you later then."

"Yep, bye," I respond.

After hanging up, I sit at my desk wondering if inviting him over was the best idea. Because it'll give him a front-row seat to a number of things I'm not sure I want my dad to know. Like the fact that I have round-the-clock protection. Though, since Bryce is half of that equation, maybe it won't be so noticeable. But it'd be hard to miss that Bryce lives with me. I shake it off as, for the most part, I realize it doesn't much matter what my father knows. It won't change whatever I decide I want our relationship to be.

I call Tristan and Bryce to let them know the change in plans for the evening and text Hunter with the arrangements. And then I do what I do best and ignore my reservations by burying myself back in my work.

⌒

JUST AFTER SIX THAT EVENING, I'M EXITING THE BUILDING WHEN I GET A TEXT from Tristan that they'll be about ten minutes late due to traffic. I sigh resignedly as I step out into the autumn chill. Since it's not raining at the moment, I have a seat on the wooden bench in front of the building.

The late September air is crisp and moist. With sunset less than an hour off, the light has begun to dim and glow around the bright green leaves of the cherry tree I'm sitting under. It's really quite beautiful.

A flash of movement in my peripheral vision catches my attention, and I swing my head around. A tall, dark man exits a dark blue sedan not thirty feet away. And he's staring at me. And approaching quickly. On gut instinct, I rise and bolt back into the building.

"Penny," I pant as I dash into reception.

Penny Westchester's blond curls bounce as her head snaps up, her brown eyes filled with concern at the obvious alarm in my voice. "Sera, everything okay?" she asks, rising from her desk and coming around to meet me.

I glance over my shoulder, but there's nobody there, inside the building or in front of its wide, glass façade. But I see the tail end of a dark blue sedan turning out of the entrance to the parking lot, and a shudder rolls through me.

"It is now," I reply tensely, giving her a forced smile. "I just got spooked waiting for my ride. But everything's okay."

Penny looks at me skeptically. I don't know her well, and she certainly doesn't know about my protective detail or the circumstances that necessitated it.

"Okay, well, if you're sure," she responds. "If you need anything, just let me know."

I nod gratefully. "Thanks," I reply. "I think I'll just wait for my ride in here."

Penny nods and returns to her seat, glancing up at me regularly, probably to make sure I'm not continuing to spiral into panic.

I sink into a black plastic chair in the waiting room where I can see the front curb and focus on breathing normally. Thankfully, it's not long before the black town car pulls up.

I give Penny a small wave and stride purposefully out to meet Tristan as he unfolds himself from the front seat. I'm out the door and jogging to get to him before he can open the back passenger door to admit me. I know Hunter is back there, and I don't want him to hear what I have to tell Tristan.

Tristan looks at me questioningly as I throw a hand up against the door, blocking his path.

"Hey, Sera, everything all right?" he asks, suddenly on alert.

I shake my head and blink back tears I hadn't realized were there. "Someone was here," I say tensely, in a low voice. "I came out to wait for you and they approached from a dark blue sedan, just there." I gesture to the spot the car had occupied.

Tristan's eyes widen at the closeness. "Why were you even out here by yourself in the first place?" he demands, clenching his fists in frustration.

"I'm sorry, Tristan, I wasn't thinking," I respond. "Things have been quiet. I just forgot for a minute. Please, don't say anything around Hunter, okay?"

"What did he look like?" Tristan asks, ignoring my plea.

I sigh heavily. "He was tall. Maybe six-three. Short, black hair. Dark eyes. Thin build. Menacing looking. Probably Italian," I admit.

Tristan looks at me somewhat skeptically. "So he just approached you? What makes you think he was actually after you?"

"Because when I bolted, he turned tail. I saw his car leaving the lot as soon as I was inside," I reply with thinly veiled anger. "And no, I didn't get a look at the plates. But he was here for me, Tristan. I know it."

I hadn't even stopped to consider I might have been paranoid. I *felt* that this guy was coming for me. But it's the first time I've gotten a look at one of my pursuers. Well, it's Alessandro they're after, really. I'm just a fucking pawn. It all makes me so angry. Apparently, even not being with him anymore hasn't changed anything, which he himself predicted. It's maddening.

Tristan considers the information grimly. "Get in," he finally replies in a clipped tone. "I'll talk to Mr. Hoyt when we get you home."

Which means Bryce is already back at the condo. Fuck. I'm not sure how to keep this from turning into a shit show in front of Hunter. I shake my head, still angry, and allow Tristan to open the car door for me. As I slip in, I put on my best game face.

Hunter is sitting behind the driver's seat with a bemused look on his face. I give him my best "everything is great" smile.

"Hey, Hunter," I greet him.

"Hey, Sera," he replies. "I like your ride."

I laugh. "Thanks," I reply shortly. "How was your drive down from Bellingham?"

Hunter shrugs. "Fine."

I smirk. It's like talking to a surly teenager. "So what's this thing you're here for?" I ask him.

Hunters looks at me but flicks his eyes away quickly. "It's an artist thing," he replies vaguely.

"Oh, like a gallery opening?" I ask curiously.

His answering smile is amused. "Something like that. So like, what about you? What do you do again?"

I consider how to explain it simply to Hunter without making him think I think he's stupid. "I work for a company that builds stores, apartments, that sort of thing," I respond. "Upscale ones, usually. They bought my company since we have a lot of expertise in putting together those sorts of deals." It's the barest bones explanation I can think of to avoid confusion or overexplaining.

"Do you have people that design the aesthetics of the spaces?" he asks. "You know, to make them feel upscale?"

I smile at the shrewd question. "We do," I reply. "Several, in fact, and we work with a lot of companies on interior and exterior visual design and materials. It's not something I'm particularly involved in the details of, but the finishes on the spaces we build are very important to the perception of our brand."

Hunter nods knowingly.

"Is that the sort of thing you're interested in doing?"

"Not really," Hunter replies. "I'm more into freestyle art."

"What does that mean?" I ask.

Hunter smiles cryptically as the car pulls to a stop in front of my building, effectively halting the conversation.

Hunter is quiet on the way up because, well, he's just kind of a quiet guy, it seems. Tristan is quiet too, but I can feel the tension rolling off him in waves. And I'm quiet because I'm dreading how this will unfold when we get inside.

We enter the condo to the amazing smell of barbeque and Bryce in the kitchen, clearly slaving on whatever masterpiece of meat and sauce he's created. He comes to meet us in the entryway, wiping his hands on a towel. He's already changed into jeans and a white T-shirt. He looks so handsome, and so happy, that it's all I can do to keep myself from collapsing tiredly into him.

"Hey, baby," he greets me with a perfunctory kiss. "Hunter, nice to see you."

"Hey, man," Hunter responds, looking around the condo in awe.

Tristan gives me a pointed look. "Sera, why don't you show Hunter around while Mr. Hoyt and I touch base?" he suggests.

I nod and lead Hunter to the window wall.

Hunter glances back over his shoulder. "Is Bryce that dude's boss?" he asks observantly.

"Yes," I reply. "Bryce's company does private security."

"Ahhh, so that's why you have a driver and a bodyguard and stuff," he replies, following me through the living room.

I cock my head, intrigued by the opportunity. That's as good an explanation as any. At least, besides the actual explanation. But I don't like lying, so I just let the assumption hang in the air.

"Make yourself at home," I encourage Hunter, gesturing to the couches. But I brought him to this side of the living room because it's impossible not to be drawn to the panorama behind us. And I'm not disappointed.

"Shit," Hunter swears, looking out over downtown and Elliot Bay. "People actually live in places like this?" He shakes his head, dumbstruck by the view.

While he's distracted, I glance back nervously at Tristan and Bryce, who are still standing in the entryway. Bryce is now glowering, staring at a spot on the floor while Tristan speaks lowly. He's rolling his massive shoulders anxiously, the muscles of his back clearly tensed. And as if he senses me staring, Bryce's clear blue eyes snap up to meet mine. And his gaze is so filled with love and concern that I have to look away before I cry.

"I actually didn't live like this until recently," I admit to Hunter. "But I couldn't help myself. I just fell in love with it."

"I can see why," Hunter murmurs, continuing to stare silently out the window.

I hear the front door open and close. "Hey, I need to go talk to Bryce for a minute," I tell Hunter. "Be right back."

Hunter nods mutely and I slink away.

Bryce is still standing in the same spot, waiting for me. "You okay?" he asks, gently gathering my hands in his and kissing them lightly.

"I was a little shaken at first, but I'm okay," I admit. "We knew this could still be an issue."

Bryce nods grimly in agreement. "I was starting to hope it was passed, but it is what it is," he replies somberly. "What do you need?"

I close my eyes, letting my emotions wash through me for just a moment, searching for the answer to his question. With startling clarity it hits me. I open my eyes, staring boldly up into his. I lean in so only he will hear me when I answer.

"I need you to fuck me up against the windows tonight," I reply huskily glancing over at the window wall. "Until I can't think of anything but riding you until you're screaming my name."

And what I've learned about my man is that his stillness in moments like these is a sign of his deep well of self-control. Because I can see in the slight flare of his nostrils and his dilated pupils that he likes it. No. He fucking *loves* it.

He takes a step forward so he's calmly towering over me. "I think that can be arranged," he promises with a glint in his eye. "Oh, and don't think I didn't notice that you hung that frilly little apron in the kitchen. It gave me a hard-on just looking at it." His words send a jolt through me, and I bite my lip to suppress the lustful grin threatening to break across my face. His eyes keep hold of mine for another heartbeat before he steps away, breaking the spell. "Hey, Hunter, you hungry?" Bryce's head snaps up to look over at my half-brother, still standing by the windows, and the vibe in the room mellows into casual relaxation.

I shiver lightly at the power of Bryce's emotional control over not just himself but everyone around him. And finally I feel safe again.

I saunter into the kitchen to get what I need to set the table and am joined shortly by Bryce to finish the usual trappings of dinner. It's not long before we're all seated and diving into Bryce's self-proclaimed "best barbeque ever."

"You know, I thought you were full of shit," I mumble through a mouthful of the ridiculously delicious meat. "But this is amazing."

Bryce smiles happily and leans over, using his napkin to wipe sauce off my chin.

Hunter laughs, and we both turn to him, a little surprised. "What?" he asks, shrugging. "It is good."

I shoot Bryce a furtive look but say nothing. We continue to make small talk, and Hunter progressively comes out of his shell. Finally, Bryce asks the same question I did earlier.

"So what exactly is it that you came here for?"

Hunter considers Bryce for a moment. "A bunch of artists are getting together to make an … installation of sorts," he admits.

Bryce raises an eyebrow. "Is this the kind of 'installation' that's created at night because it's done publicly, and," Bryce clears his throat, "not exactly legally?"

The look of shock on Hunter's face is priceless, and Bryce's instincts pay off once again.

"How could you possibly know that?" Hunter asks in disbelief.

Bryce smiles and I know what's coming. He points his thumbs at himself. "Security consultant."

And I can't help but bust up laughing. Hunter gives an embarrassed smile.

"But seriously, Hunter. I think you know how I know. Do you want to tell her or should I?"

My brother rolls his eyes and squirms uncomfortably in his chair. "I was arrested twice last year," Hunter admits. "The first time for vandalism and resisting arrest." He pauses, frowning. "The second, for assault."

"Do I want to know why?" I ask, looking between the two men.

Bryce shrugs and leans back in his chair, with a distinct air of staying the hell out of it now that he's opened the flood gates.

Hunter heaves a sigh. "I'm a guerrilla artist," he explains. "I was part of a team, actually. We did location-specific perception-altering pieces."

"English, please?" I ask, looking helplessly at Bryce.

"They go outside and make everyday things you see on the street look like something else," Bryce explains. "Sometimes intended to cause public harm."

"No," Hunter protests. "We didn't pull that kind of shit."

"So you didn't paint a wall to look like an alley? And then lure a cop car toward it at night so he rammed it at thirty miles per hour?" Bryce asks sharply.

Hunter pales at the depth of Bryce's knowledge.

"In case you hadn't noticed, you shouldn't attempt to lie to this man," I inform Hunter.

Hunter's eyes shift from Bryce to me. "My crew didn't do that," he insists.

"I'm listening," Bryce says patiently.

"I don't owe you any explanations," Hunter says tightly.

Bryce smiles indulgently. "No, I suppose you don't," he agrees. "But where you end up tonight may depend on it. See, I'm close, personal friends with at least a third of the police force in this city. One phone call and you and your friends may have a much more difficult night than you planned."

"*Bryce*," I gasp, surprised. I'm still reeling as Hunter's world is a whole new beast to me. But I don't want to scare away the only sibling I have and make him feel like he was lured to my house only to be threatened.

Bryce sighs and picks up our dinner dishes, ferrying them into the kitchen. "Look," he says on his way back. "I don't want to get you and your friends in trouble. I'm pretty sure you're not lying. But I want to know what really happened, so I know for sure I'm not turning a blind eye to dangerous criminals."

"That's a little harsh, don't you think?" Hunter asks accusingly. "That was just a prank. That my crew *didn't pull*."

Bryce's eyebrows shoot up. "If you think vandalism, destruction of public property, and endangering the well-being of a police officer are *funny*, then you've got a lot to learn," Bryce says dangerously quietly.

Hunter, at least, seems to get finally that he's walking a precarious line as it's a while before he responds.

"We did shock-value pieces," he finally admits. "We would draw people hanging out of high windows that looked realistic from the ground. We'd put down fake blood trails leading to cemented-in pieces made to look like bodies. That sort of thing. We didn't hurt anyone or destroy property." He glares at Bryce.

"Then who did you assault?" I ask softly. I want to ask *why*. Why do they do what they do at all? It certainly doesn't make any sense to me. But odd, random art in public places isn't the end of the world. Assaulting someone, however, is a whole other matter.

Hunter leans forward on his arms, twisting his fingers together. "My crew wasn't the only one in our neighborhood," he replies quietly. "The other crew, they were the ones that would go for destruction and chaos. We ran into them one night. Words were exchanged. One of their guys called me … well, he said something pretty bad, then pushed me from behind. I turned around and lashed out. But I had a crowbar in my hand. I practically took off half his face." Hunter shakes his head sadly. "In case it doesn't go without saying, I didn't mean to hurt him like that. It was a horrible mistake."

I'm so mesmerized by Hunter's story that I don't realize until he stops speaking that my hand is clamped over my mouth in horror. He nearly took off a guy's *face*. Bryce's expression is ominously blank.

"Wait a minute," I pipe up. "You said that all past tense."

Hunter smiles vaguely. "That's right. Both crews disbanded after that night," he replies.

"Then who are you meeting tonight?" I ask.

"It's a gathering," he explains. "Of all of us in western Washington, to do one, huge piece together. Peacefully, and not to cause harm." He glances reassuringly at Bryce. "But I haven't done anything public since that last time we were out. And I probably won't again after tonight. I just feel like I need the closure. And this is huge. I guess I wanted to be a part of it all one last time." His expression is so forlorn I want to hug him. But I'm still so appalled by everything I've heard.

"Does Dad know?" I ask, my voice barely above a whisper.

"No," Hunter responds sadly. "Not really. He thinks I'm in a gang, or a drug dealer, or a drug user, or all of the above. He thinks I'm just a violent, vandalizing thug. A lost cause. Worthless."

And this time I can't help it. I rise from my chair and go to him, leaning down and wrapping my arms around him from the side. I don't say anything, I just squeeze him with everything I've got. After a moment he lays his hand over mine, squeezing it gratefully.

"So you gonna call your cop friends on us?" Hunter asks Bryce warily.

Bryce shakes his head. "No," he replies. "I think you've had enough trouble with the law to last you a lifetime. Just be smart tonight and stay safe. And call us if you need anything."

The relief on Hunter's face is obvious. "Thanks, guys," he replies.

I finally let Hunter go and sink back down into my chair. "Thanks for being honest," I respond. "Brother."

Hunter's eyes lock with mine, and my heart shifts. And I see in his eyes that he feels it too. And that neither of us are used to having a real family. But looking between Hunter and Bryce, I'm thankful to be making my own.

EIGHT

Once Hunter is gone I sink into Bryce's lap on the couch. I rest my forehead against his as he traces light circles on my thigh with his thumb.

"Heavy night," Bryce murmurs, his eyes probing mine. For what I'm not sure. Signs of cracking, probably.

"Yes, but it wasn't all bad," I reply thoughtfully. "I think my brother and I have a real shot at getting to know each other. To be there for each other like our parents haven't been for us."

"You called him your brother," Bryce points out.

"So?" I ask, frowning. "That's what he is."

Bryce's strong fingers run over the length of my leg. "You've only ever called him your half-brother before," Bryce responds.

"I guess I'm feeling like I'm surrounded by family now," I explain. "Real family. The family I'm choosing."

Bryce looks at me, his eyes sheening in the moonlight now trickling through the windows. He wraps his arms around me, laying me on my back on the soft cushions. His arms braced by my sides, he hovers over me, hungrily drinking in my face with his eyes as if he wants to memorize every pore.

I gaze up at him, slightly confused, but tingling with anticipation. "I thought you wanted me up against the windows," I tease him.

His mouth swoops down to mine, his lips like wind on the fire building in me. He pulls back before I'm ready to let him go and I whimper in protest. He smiles down at me indulgently.

"Some other time," he promises. "Tonight, I'm going to make love to you right here."

My breath catches in my throat at his husky tone, his tender words.

He undresses me slowly, his tongue and lips tenderly caressing me as he goes. When I'm naked and trembling beneath him, he sheds his own clothes much more quickly, and I note he's already full and long. And if I was ready before, the sight sends a rush between my legs that has me aching and approaching the edge already.

His mouth reaches for mine and his torso sinks into mine. I wrap my arms around him, desperate to pull him onto me completely, into me. As his tongue dances with mine, he finally allows it, sinking into me slowly. We both moan into the pleasure before our hips dance, same as our tongues, slowly stoking the fire.

I run my hands down the strong muscles of his back, feeling him flex into me with every thrust. His lips drop to my neck, and I'm free to unleash my moans into his ear. I feel him harden sharply in me, his breath quickening. I dig my heels into his sides, encouraging him. But the sharp press has an altogether different effect, and he slides his hands under me, rolling over abruptly so I'm pressed on top of him.

He holds me to him, his mouth at my ear. "I love you, Sera." He drops his head back, so he can look into my eyes. "Never forget how fucking much I love you."

I lean into him, pressing my lips to his briefly, sweeping my tongue over his bottom lip as I rear up. "I love you too," I breathe, sinking him back into me.

With hands clasped, I tilt my hips over him, softly at first, then harder and harder, building methodically until we're both approaching climax.

"Come for me, baby," I encourage him.

My words are like throwing gas on the fire. His face and body contort with pleasure, and he bucks wildly beneath me as he explodes in fiery passionate bliss. I feel his seed, hot inside me, and the combination of hot, wet, and writhing sends me tumbling into ecstasy. My screams of pleasure outlast his, the fire in me finally quelled. And when I look down at him, he's half laughing, half dizzy with gratification.

I sink onto the sofa next to him, nearly swooning from the effort of bringing us both to climax. My hand finds his and our fingers intertwine.

"Let's buy a house," Bryce's voice abruptly cuts through my post-orgasmic stupor.

I shoot upright, aghast. "Excuse me?"

Bryce sits up next to me, leaning back against the cushions. "You heard me," he replies. "I love living with you. But this is *your* place. We should have an 'our' place."

"Bryce, we haven't even been dating a month and you want us to make one of the biggest commitments people can make?" I ask incredulously.

"I'm not proposing," he clarifies.

I laugh. "I don't mean to be blasé, but real estate is a much bigger commitment than marriage. Especially these days," I remark.

"I hadn't thought about it like that," he admits.

"I don't think you thought about it much at all," I reply. "If it's all the same, I think we should chalk that suggestion up to after-sex stupid."

Bryce arches an eyebrow at me. "Call it what you want, but there are other reasons it's a good idea," he replies stubbornly.

And I get the sense that I've offended him. "Such as?" I prompt.

"Well, we've determined you're not out of the woods yet. Moving would be a good opportunity to make you safer," he responds. And I have to admit to myself that he's not wrong. But it's a shit reason for us to buy a place together.

"We've already demonstrated the security here is good," I remind him. "So I don't think they'll try anything here again."

Even Bryce can't argue with that. But he still pouts nonetheless.

"Baby," I plead. "I don't want us to take such a big step just because something like this is hanging over our heads. Again. And it's not something I'd want to do until we're married."

Bryce cracks a smile. "You said 'until,'" he replies, slightly mollified.

I crawl between his legs, pulling his arms around me. "I did," I agree, looking up into his eyes. "I can't believe I'm the old-fashioned one here."

Bryce laughs, his sour mood gone. "I just can't bear the thought of wasting one minute of our new life together," he replies huskily. "But you're right. We're going to do this the right way. You deserve that."

"*We* deserve that," I correct him with a smile.

He nuzzles his nose against mine in agreement, and I sink happily back into his embrace.

❧

ALMOST A FULL WEEK FLIES BY WHEN, THE FOLLOWING TUESDAY, I HEAR FROM Allie, who is back from her vacation. She wants to meet for brunch as soon as possible, so we schedule for the coming Saturday. She sounded so relaxed and excited that getting to today was torture.

But as I go to meet her for brunch, I work on containing my own nerves, my imagination having gotten somewhat away from me over the last few days. For some reason I've settled on expecting to hear that they are moving to the tropical paradise. That it's best for Allie's stress levels and David will just work remotely. I know it's a silly and irrational fear, but I can't imagine what else would have her so excited to come *back* from vacation.

For once I'm thankful Bryce had to go into work today, so I couldn't nag him all morning with my fears. Because somehow it's easier to be a neurotic mess in front of Tristan. Not that Bryce doesn't handle it well, but I hate troubling him with it. Tristan ... well, it's kind of his job. And he'll get to go home at the end of the day.

I get a booth for Allie and me even though she hasn't arrived yet because it's starting to get busy. Tristan requests a separate, small table within sight distance, insisting his presence will just keep us from talking about "girlie things." I don't give up, but he continues to insist. He hasn't relented by the time Allie arrives, so I just leave him to his lonesome meal.

And Allie looks ridiculously fantastic. She's lean, tan, and beaming with happiness. After giving me a greeting hug, she slides into the booth with a satisfied sigh.

"So I'm guessing Fiji was everything you'd hoped for," I tease her.

"Oh, Sera, you have no idea," she replies dreamily. "I could have happily stayed there for the rest of my life."

I freeze for a moment.

"What? What did I say?"

"Nothing," I reply, dismissively waving my hand. "You just sounded like you had news and..." I trail off, unable to admit to my fear.

"And?" she prompts inquisitively.

"I got it in my head you wanted to move to Fiji," I admit, blushing furiously.

Allie laughs. "Oops, sounds like I stepped right in it then, didn't I?" she asks, beaming. "I'm not moving to Fiji, Sera."

And I shouldn't feel as relieved as I do, since I knew it was silly to start. But I do. "Thank God," I breathe.

"But David and I did agree to start trying again. For a baby," she responds candidly.

"Allie! That's fantastic!" I exclaim. "I'm so happy for you."

"Thanks," Allie replies sheepishly. "Also, I'm not going back to work. I'm quitting permanently."

That stops me short. I'm torn between supporting her and missing her. "Oh, Allie, you know I love you, babe," I reply sincerely. "And if that's what's going to work best for you, then that's great."

"I appreciate that," Allie responds just as sincerely. "I realized that I started working for you not knowing where it would lead, and in the end, it just isn't what I want for a career. Though I'll be honest — I'm not sure what I *do* want."

"That's totally fair," I concede. "And I'm sure you'll figure it out. Now. Tell me all about Fiji."

"Sun, beaches, sparkling clear blue water, blah, blah, blah," she jokes. "I'd really rather hear about what's new with you. How are things with Bryce?" A shit-eating grin splits across her face.

I glance furtively at Tristan across the restaurant, but I'm confident he can't hear me. Not that it really matters.

"Amazing," I reply with a sigh. "It feels like we've always been together."

"Do you think you always will be?" she asks shrewdly.

"It seems like it should be too early to talk about that kind of thing," I respond tentatively. "And yet we have. Several times."

"How so?" she presses.

I shrug. "When it happens, it's always a given. When. Not if. And it feels so natural, honestly," I admit. "I feel like I should be scared. Or I should have reservations about moving too fast. But Bryce and I have always connected on another level. And it's like now that's complete, and nothing can stop it or take its place."

"Wow," Allie says slowly. "That's intense. Great, but intense."

I nod. "I agree completely. But, I'm also happier than I can ever remember being. He feels like my family, same as you." Talking about it this way I feel laid bare and vulnerable. And it's finally making me a little uncomfortable.

Sensing that, perhaps, Allie changes the subject. "Hey, I meant to ask you what you want to do for your birthday," she says with a mischievous glint in her eye.

I groan loudly. As usual, I'd forgotten that was coming. But she's right. Next Friday I'll turn thirty. "Nothing," I grouse. "We don't even need to tell anyone it's my birthday."

"Awww, don't spoil my fun," Allie insists. "At least let me take you out to dinner or something? You're turning thirty. Before me, thank God. We need to celebrate. Say goodbye to your twenties. Preferably with booze. And cake."

I can't help but laugh. "I'm down with the booze and cake," I admit. "Or maybe a booze cake. But nothing too crazy."

Allie claps her hands giddily. "Yay!" she squeals, bouncing in her seat.

"Already too crazy!" I warn her jokingly.

She quiets and bounces lower, clapping softly.

And it makes me laugh again. "You're nuts. I missed you."

She smiles brightly. "Missed you too, babe," she responds.

∽

A FULL MEAL AND MORE THAN AN HOUR AND A HALF LATER ALLIE HAS GONE home, and Tristan is walking me out of the restaurant.

"You look happy," he remarks as we round the corner to the small parking lot sandwiched between the restaurant and the building behind it.

"I am," I admit. "It's great seeing Allie, well, Allie again. She..." I'm stopped short as we approach the car.

A man leans against the trunk casually, picking at his fingernails. He's medium height and build, with dark hair and olive skin. Tristan follows my gaze and, before I can so much as blink, he's shuffled me behind him and drawn his gun.

"When I tell you to, run back to the restaurant and call Bryce," Tristan instructs in hushed tones.

The man leaning against the trunk of the car catches sight of us and stands.

Tristan raises his gun and addresses the man. "I'd advise you to leave. Now."

"Nobody is going anywhere."

My skin crawls. The voice comes from behind me. I turn, my back against Tristan's, to find a second man, with his own gun drawn and pointed at me. It's the man who tried to approach me last time just outside of my work, once again staring me down menacingly. Tristan keeps his gun trained on the first man and glances back at the second.

"Drop your gun now or I will shoot," Tristan instructs.

My heart is beating so loudly in my ears that I barely hear him.

The second man laughs. "Not unless you want her dead," he scoffs.

But even I hear the bluff. Though even if he was the best liar in the world, I know they'll want me alive if they plan to use me against Alessandro. Not that I intend to be taken. But Tristan is already ahead of me. He doesn't say another word or give any further warnings. His foot finds mine and I know what to do. When he steps down on my toes, I drop to the ground. Tristan swings around, lightning fast, and shoots the second man between the eyes. And just as quickly points his gun back at the first man.

"Run," Tristan commands me without looking back.

So I do. And I don't look at the crumpled body as I jump over it. But I do notice the blur as the first man bolts and Tristan follows. Not that that stops me — I do exactly as Tristan instructed and run back into the restaurant.

The hostess looks shocked as I burst through the door, clearly terrified.

"Call 911," I insist, searching my purse frantically for my phone. "Someone has been shot in the parking lot, and my bodyguard is in danger."

The hostess pales and nods, picking up the phone on the podium and placing the call. Finally locating my phone, I frantically call Bryce.

∾

As I sit in the back of the squad car, Bryce paces the bit of pavement next to me for the thousandth time.

"He's okay," I assure him. "I know it. You didn't see how fast he moved. There's no way that guy got the drop on him."

Bryce waves a hand in the air, frustrated. "I know he's fast. But he shouldn't have pursued. He should have stayed with you."

Ah. So Bryce isn't worried for Tristan's safety. He wants to yell at him for leaving me.

"But I'm fine," I insist. "Thanks to him."

Bryce stops abruptly and squats in front of me. "You're not fine," he seethes. "These motherfuckers are coming after you head-on. No more subterfuge, no more stealth. They approached you directly, in daylight, with guns. They must be pretty fucking desperate to be this bold, this careless. It's *dangerous*, Sera."

A police officer appears at the back of the squad car and Bryce stands up, facing him. "They've found Mr. Thomas," he informs Bryce. "He lost the suspect and is on his way back now. And the body has been removed. Scene is clear. We'll meet you down at the station."

Bryce nods to the officer and extends a hand to me. He silently leads me to his car, putting me in the passenger seat and leaning against the door in wait. It's not long before Tristan appears.

"Get in the back, we're going to the police station to give a full statement," Bryce instructs Tristan sharply, without so much as asking if he's okay.

Tristan does as instructed and, before Bryce can get in, I turn to Tristan and mouth, "Are you okay?"

He nods briefly, his eyes on Bryce as he opens the driver's side door.

I mouth "thank you" as discreetly as I can before facing forward again.

❧

WE SPEND FAR LONGER THAN I'D LIKE AT THE POLICE STATION. I GET THE feeling it's because Bryce feels like it might be one of the only places in the city that I'm truly safe. My suspicion is confirmed when we're given a police escort home.

As we quietly enter the condo, I can't find words that I think will make any difference. I know Bryce is furious, and not really with Tristan, but with his inability to fix this. To end the danger I'm in. We're in. And there's nothing I can say or do that will help.

I go upstairs to take a shower. As I strip off my clothes, it feels like the armor I've had to sheath myself in to keep it together falls away with them. Exhausted, emotional, and naked, I sit on the floor of the shower and let the water flow over me. But it doesn't soothe me, and soon hot tears join the stream as my body shakes with sobs. I feel, rather than hear Bryce approach, but I don't look up.

I do, finally, hear a broken cry escape him as he realizes I've come apart. He climbs in with me, fully clothed, and wraps his arms around me. His body shakes with mine, despairing with me. I unwrap my arms from where they held my legs against my chest and slide them around his soaked shirt. And we hold each other like that until the water starts to run lukewarm.

We don't speak even as we dry off and, both naked and exhausted, climb into bed and know no more.

NINE

S unday morning arrives, and for early October there's far too much light in the room for my liking. But then, my eyes are puffier and more sensitive than usual. And the reasons why come flooding back. I breathe deeply, fighting down the tide of emotion. I roll over, not really expecting to find Bryce still abed this long after dawn, but he's there nonetheless, awake and contemplating the ceiling, one arm tucked under his head.

He turns his head to meet my gaze and gives me a small smile that doesn't reach his eyes.

"Good morning, sunshine," I greet him, attempting my own half-hearted smile.

He rolls toward me, stroking along my arm with his free hand. He leans in, touching his lips softly to mine.

"Hey, gorgeous," he replies. "How'd you sleep?"

My instinct is to assume I didn't sleep well after yesterday's events. But I realize that I actually did. I slept hard, and for a long time. And had not a single nightmare. I'm struck dumb, as nightmares were such a constant companion for so long as I went through these last months. But they've stopped. And it occurs to me that that's been true since I've shared a bed with Bryce.

"Surprisingly well," I admit. "How about you?"

He strokes my face gently and smiles sadly. "I always sleep well next to you," he replies. "Oh." He looks as though he remembered something, and he rolls to reach the nightstand on his side of the bed. He pulls something out of the drawer and turns back to me, something tucked inside his large hand.

"What's that?" I ask warily.

Bryce smiles, much more openly this time. "It's a gift. For you," he replies. "I'm not usually one to remember this kind of thing, but this is different. We're different. Because one month ago today, you changed my life forever." He lays his palm flat to reveal a small, black velvet box.

And the girlie girl inside me wants to squeal with excitement. But I settle for an eager grin. "Oh, baby, you didn't have to do this," I chastise him. I didn't even realize the date, or think to commemorate such a thing, but I know he wouldn't want me to feel self-conscious.

"I know," he allows. "But because you're not the type to expect it, it's all the more reason to give it to you. I'd give you the world if I could, Sera."

I snuggle up next to him and press my lips softly to his. "You're my world, Bryce Hoyt."

He kisses me passionately for a moment before pulling away gently. "I'll just take these back then, I guess," he replies airily, leaning back to put the box back on his nightstand.

I playfully smack his chest. "You'll do no such thing!" I admonish him. "Gimme."

He laughs and hands me the box. I open it gingerly, part of me wanting the anticipation to last, like I'm a little girl at Christmas again. But the reveal is just as satisfying. Even in the dim daylight, light bounces off the dazzling square gem earrings. They are delicately beautiful in their simplicity, and absolutely breathtaking.

"Diamonds?" I ask in shock.

"Diamonds," he confirms. "Though they're still not half as gorgeous as you are."

I don't even have words to express to him how thoughtful he is, how sweet, how wonderful. So I put the box on the nightstand behind me and show him instead.

❧

AFTER BREAKFAST, I'M SITTING IN MY FAVORITE CHAIR, WRAPPED IN A BLANKET and sipping coffee. Bryce sits at my feet, leaning against the chair and reading a book. It's such peace after the chaos of the day before. But I still turn the day over and over in my mind, looking for clues. I also spend a considerable effort trying to think of ways to end it. But I come up wanting.

"What if we went somewhere?" I ask abruptly, breaking the quiet. Bryce slips a bookmark into his book and closes it onto his lap, turning to look up at me.

"Where?" he counters.

"I don't know," I admit. "Just away. For a while. So they can't find me. Until enough time has passed, and they just stop trying."

Bryce sighs heavily. "I'm all one for a good vacation, but I can't just leave for long periods of time, Sera," he replies. "I have a company to run. And you have a job here. We have lives here."

"You're right. I just don't know what else to do. But after yesterday, the thought of just going on with my life as usual seems impossible. I feel like I'd only just stopped looking over my shoulder," I explain, tears welling in my eyes. I wipe at them angrily.

Bryce climbs to his knees, taking my face in his strong hands. "I'm going to do everything in my power to keep you safe," he says, looking me squarely in the eye. "Know that." He pauses, looking somewhat hesitant to say what he's thinking. "I've started my own investigation. I am going to get to the bottom of this, no matter what it takes. But it's going to take time. And it will be dangerous. And while I don't want us to be apart, if you'll feel safer away from here, I can make arrangements."

My mind swims with questions, but moreover the suggestion that I leave him is unbearable, and I feel the need to shut that down first and foremost.

"I don't want to leave you, either," I respond.

A look that's half pained and half adoration crosses Bryce's face. "I figured you'd say that," he replies. "And part of me wants to get you away from all this. But the thought of you being somewhere I can't be, where I can't protect you…"

I press a finger over his lips and shake my head. "Stop worrying," I say. I remove my finger from his mouth and pull his face to mine. When I kiss him it's full of sorrow and angst, but most of all love. Always love.

⌯

THE NEXT MORNING I HAVE TWO GUARDS ACCOMPANYING ME INTO WORK. AND they don't leave for the day like Tristan normally would. The new guard takes a desk near my office while Tristan takes a desk near reception. It's all been cleared through Charles, but I'd asked that nobody else be told the details. Needless to say that doesn't stop the office gossip. Especially as the new guard, Marcus, follows me around silently all day, never more than ten feet away.

When I talk to Bryce at lunch he has news. Daniel's trial has been rescheduled for two weeks from today. I frown, wondering if Charles has already heard. If he had, he showed no sign of it this morning, though I may have been too distracted by my own problems to notice. I decide to check in on him again just in case.

Charles' assistant, Anabelle, waves me past, looking furtively at Marcus as we pass. I knock and wait for Charles' invitation to enter, asking Marcus to wait outside.

Instantly, I know Charles has heard that Daniel's trial is, indeed, back on. In the privacy of his own office, his face is drawn, his shoulders slumped. He rises as I enter, and I can't help but going to hug him.

"Thank you," he says huskily. He gestures to the chair opposite his desk, which I take.

"It looks like we're both having a pretty shitty time," I reply honestly.

Charles chuckles drily. I'd given him a high-level overview of my situation, but there wasn't time to discuss it in any depth. And despite my own feelings, I am curious to hear what my mentor thinks of it all.

"I've been through much worse, my dear," he responds. "But you can't seem to catch a break. How are you holding up?"

"Honestly? I'm terrified. And so over it," I grouse. "I wish to hell I'd never got involved with the bastard who brought this on me." But despite my rancor, I don't really mean it. Part of me still loves Alessandro, even. I'm just so angry.

"I'd love to reassure you that everything happens for a reason," Charles parries wearily. "But honestly, bad things happen all the time to good people who've done nothing to deserve them. Only you can choose how you handle it. Whether to press through and overcome it or succumb to self-pity."

I blush furiously. He's right, I'm wallowing.

"Well, when you put it that way." I sigh. "You know me. I'll get through this. Some days are just harder than others."

"Indeed," Charles agrees.

"What would you do, if you were in my shoes?" I ask curiously. His eyebrows shoot up.

"I'd be hard pressed to truly understand what you're going through, Sera," he hedges. "But the most important thing is safety. If it were me, I'd do whatever I had to, whatever I could to make myself, my loved ones, safe."

∽

For the rest of the day, Charles' words seep into my consciousness. And by the evening, the beginnings of a plan have formed in my head. Realizing how selfish it is to keep everyone else in harm's way, I know I must remove myself. Go somewhere nobody knows where I am. Who I am.

I could never forgive myself if something had happened to Tristan, even though it's a known risk of his job. Or, God forbid, Bryce. I can't even think about that possibility. And with the new investigation he's launched, the odds are so much higher that something will happen to him. That thought pushes me over the edge, and I know I must disappear.

And while I have the means to do so, I don't have the connections. And it's obviously not something I can ask Bryce to help with. I'm sure he'd have the kinds of contacts that could create a new identity under which I could travel, but I'm also sure he'd never let me go alone. And I don't want anyone to catch wind of my plan, to try to stop me.

Thankfully I have enough knowledge on how to be untraceable online to find the answers I need. So that night I go looking for someone who *can* get me what I need. It doesn't take long to find. It takes longer to arrange untraceable payment, actually, and to arrange a way to receive the documents and other items I'll need without tipping off my bodyguards or Bryce.

But by Friday I've managed it, though not without laying out considerable sums of money in the process. As it's also my birthday, I've gone home early under the guise of getting ready for my birthday dinner with Allie, which Bryce will, of course, also be accompanying me to. But my real plan is to finish my preparations. Because once Bryce is asleep, I'm leaving.

I stow my small packed bag behind some boxes in the coat closet downstairs. I don't take much. I can always buy what I need once I reach my destination, and the less I pack the easier it will be to leave unnoticed, to travel unnoticed.

I take the letter I've written Bryce explaining everything and bring it into the bedroom. I settle on placing it in his nightstand drawer, as he rarely uses it. In fact, the only time I've seen him use it was when he pulled my "anniversary" gift out of it.

I slide it open. Only one object sits in the drawer — another small, black velvet box. It only takes me a moment to realize it's probably my birthday present, and that I'll need to find another place to hide my letter. I start to close the drawer, but curiosity gets the better of me. I set the letter aside and slowly pick up the box.

I hesitate, not usually the type to snoop, feeling guilty for potentially spoiling Bryce's surprise. But my inquisitive nature gets the better of me, and I open it anyway.

A diamond engagement ring sparkles back at me. Princess cut, just like the earrings, but much larger, and perfectly beautiful in its simple, platinum setting. My vision clouds as tears fill my eyes. And my resolve is hardened knowing I can't possibly put someone who loves me this much in danger. I close the box and return it to its exact place in the drawer. I decide I'll put the letter on the kitchen counter as I leave.

I dress carefully for dinner, donning the gorgeous earrings Bryce gifted me. Then silently, I master myself and descend the stairs. I shove all of the emotions the sight of that ring brought up deep back down. I can feel it all later. Bryce will be home soon. And I need to play the delighted birthday girl. The happy girlfriend. If only for just a little while longer.

TEN

e get to the building where the restaurant is, but we have to take an elevator to the twenty-first floor. Exiting to the top floor restaurant, we wait just outside the entrance for Allie and David. I can tell it makes Bryce nervous to be out in public with dangerous people still out there looking for me.

Having gotten home late, he didn't have time to change, so he's still wearing the khaki slacks and black button-down he wore to work. He catches me looking at him and pulls me close. His normal smell of evergreen and summer, mixed with his natural musk from the day, fills my senses and makes me a bit heady. He brushes my hair back from my face and looks searchingly into my eyes.

"You're wearing the earrings," he murmurs approvingly. "They look fantastic on you."

I finger the sparkling gems lovingly. "They remind me of you," I reply fondly.

He smiles, not quite his sunshine smile. He's still worried. "Then you should wear them all the time," he responds. He leans in close, nuzzling his nose against my ear and dropping his voice. "And I'd like to see you wearing nothing but those earrings later." His hot breath on my ear and neck, along with his words, sends shivers down my spine.

I relish it, trying not to think about it being one of the last times for what may be a long time.

I'm saved from the bittersweet moment by Allie and David's arrival. Hugs or handshakes are had all around, along with loud birthday wishes. Blushing, I duck into the restaurant, eager to get to the part where there's cake and booze.

Allie teases me the whole way to the table, making sure to loudly remark that we are here for my birthday. She knows how much it embarrasses me, but that's clearly part of the fun for her. Thankfully, once we're seated and looking at our menus, it dies down.

"You okay?" Bryce leans in to ask.

"I'm fine," I whisper. "It's only going to get worse once she's gotten some drinks in her, though."

Bryce laughs. "Then we should get a few drinks in you, so you care less," he teases.

And now I laugh.

"What are you two lovebirds tittering about?" Allie demands from across the table.

Bryce and I snap back upright, grinning. "Oh, you know, where would be the best place in the restaurant for a quickie," I joke.

David laughs, but Allie pulls an unamused face.

"At least David thinks I'm funny."

Allie sticks her tongue out at me and I return the gesture. The men roll their eyes at each other conspiratorially.

As we make small talk about our workweeks, I realize I never told Allie what happened after she left the restaurant last Saturday. And I don't think now is really the time. But she's going to be more surprised than most when I leave. And mad, of course. Not for the first or last time tonight, I suppress my thoughts and try to focus on the conversation.

And the food, which is amazing. As total carnivores, Allie and I had agreed a steakhouse was our only option. And as I dive into my ridiculously melt-in-your-mouth filet mignon, I know we made the right choice. Everyone seems pretty happy, in fact, and it's one of the only times everyone sinks into truly companionable silence.

But the inevitably of the birthday song arrives. And Allie, predictably, sings the loudest and most off-key. I can't help laughing, though, as I feel the love of those closest to me. There are worse ways to turn thirty, I decide. And the chocolate bourbon cake doesn't suck either, making good on Allie's promises of booze and cake. And booze cake.

All in all, as the dinner wraps up, I decide it was the perfect birthday get-together. Small, low key, good food, and the people I love. And blessedly few jokes about aging. What more could I possibly ask for?

Bryce and I stick around for a few minutes, lingering in the lobby so I can enjoy the view. The city lights twinkle around us spectacularly. And I know my dawdling is making Bryce even more nervous, but I feel like I need to take it all in one last time. He waits beside me as patiently as he can, though, his fingers entwined with mine. And I can feel him staring at me.

I glance over at him leaning with his back against the windows, simply taking me in. He doesn't look worried or impatient right now. He's exquisite in this moment, perhaps more so for my desire to drink in my last looks at his handsome face.

"What are you thinking about?" he asks.

I wonder if it's a general question or if he senses what I'm preparing to do. Probably the former, or he'd be a lot less calm.

"How grateful I am for this life," I reply honestly. It's part of the truth, anyway.

He's silent for a moment, his blue eyes bright and shining. And I know exactly what he's thinking, so I beat him to it.

"Never forget how much I love you, Bryce Hoyt."

And his true sunshine smile splits across his face, melting my heart even more than it already was. "You stole my line," he teases. His eyes darken with intensity. "I love you too. Now let's go home."

"What, no dirty things you want to whisper in my ear first to drive me crazy?" I tease, letting him lead me to the elevator.

He glances around at the empty lobby. "It's not as much fun when there aren't other people around," he remarks.

I laugh, and it feels good. "You're incorrigible," I chide him as we step into the elevator.

Once the doors close behind us, and we're completely alone, he presses me roughly against the back of the elevator, towering over me. A thrill shoots through my body, warming me from my core to the tips of my fingers and toes.

"You have no idea," he murmurs, finally dropping his lips to mine. The force of his kiss takes my breath away.

I wrap my arms around his neck, drawing him into me as close as I can get him. But the elevator doors ping open before I expect them to. Never one to be rude, Bryce pulls away, turning to face forward.

But we're both stopped short at the three large, dark-haired men facing us in the elevator as the doors slide closed behind them. I can feel Bryce stiffen next to me. The one closest to the panel pulls the elevator's red "stop" switch, and Bryce steps in front of me as the man in the middle takes out a gun. I try not to throw up as panic overtakes me. All I can think is, *Not again*. Not another gun, in another elevator, another kidnapping. But Bryce wasn't with me last time. I watch him slip his hand under the back of his shirt and wrap around his own gun, flicking off the safety.

"Don't do anything stupid," the man on the left says. "Just give us the girl and neither of you will be hurt."

"You're not taking her, so get out now. That's my only warning." Bryce's voice is full of quiet, barely controlled rage, and I've never heard him sound so terrifying.

And large though these men are, none of them are as big as Bryce. But while he's got the intimidation factor going for him, there are still three of them. I press my lips together, trying to stay silent and will away the tears threatening at the back of my eyes.

The man in the middle with the gun laughs. He turns his head to the man who spoke first. "This guy thinks he can…"

Bang! The loud sound of a gunshot goes off in the small space and the man in the middle drops. Before I can even process what happened, another deafening crack reverberates through the elevator and the man on the left drops. As I start to register the pain in my ears, I realize Bryce's gun is drawn and is trained on the third man. Like the now-dead men, I wasn't fast enough to notice Bryce draw and fire his gun. Twice.

But the third man, the one who'd stopped the elevator, apparently did. Because he now has a gun that is pointed back at Bryce. A very large gun. Bryce eyes it tensely but doesn't shoot.

"I think you know what happens if I fire," the man says calmly.

Reluctantly, Bryce nods. Leaving me to assume he knows we'd both be dead if the guy got off a shot. Because I know Bryce would sacrifice himself in an instant if he thought I'd be safe. And at that thought I can't fight the tears back any longer, letting them spill silently over.

"Good. Now, I assume you also know that I have no desire to kill her. She's of little use to me dead. So let's get this over with quickly before we have company. Drop your gun now or I shoot."

Even before Bryce complies, I know he will. And based on the speed of his first attack, I also know what's coming next. But so does the dark-haired brute with the big gun. Bryce opens his hand, dropping his gun, and attacks simultaneously. But the bastard is already pulling the trigger. Given the proximity, though, Bryce manages to cross the short distance in time to knock the gun upward, deflecting the shot into the ceiling.

But our attacker seemed to be prepared for that, too, as his knee is already flying up, dislodging Bryce from the grasp he has on the gun. It's not enough for the man to keep his own grip on the weapon, however, and the gun tumbles out of his hands onto the floor. Bryce's attack continues relentlessly, his fist swinging for the man's stomach, chest, and head, only to be blocked each time. I can only watch in horror as the two, dangerously evenly matched, trade attempted blows.

My eyes flick to the ground, to the pools of blood spreading and joining under the two bodies. Fighting another wave of sickness, I try to concentrate on finding one of the guns on the floor. But before I can focus long enough, Bryce grunts in pain, causing my eyes to snap back up to the fight. The third man looks to have landed a hit to Bryce's face. Bryce is reeling back, blood spurting from his nose as the man dives for his gun.

"No!" The cry escapes my lips before I can stop it.

It's all happening so fast. Too fast. I throw myself to the ground, desperate to get my hands on one of the fallen weapons as I watch our attacker reel back up with his own, spinning around on a dazed Bryce. But he's too close to shoot as Bryce lurches at him, catching him in his midsection and pushing him hard into the side of the elevator.

Unfortunately, the humongous gun is still dangerous. I watch in horror as he brings it down on Bryce's skull. A loud *crack* echoes as it makes contact, and Bryce slumps to the floor, unconscious. The man huffs a short, satisfied laugh. And then kicks Bryce in the head with enough force to flip his large body away. I tuck my head down, into the floor, unable to look at the blood streaming from Bryce's face, and the reality of what just happened. My stomach lurches and my head spins. I can feel darkness tugging at me, and I know I'm close to fainting. My hand finds something hard and cold under my midsection. I grip it, trying to anchor myself to the feeling, to awareness.

"Well, ain't this a pickle," I hear the man murmur through the ringing in my ears. "It's gonna be tricky getting you out of here fast enough."

I feel the elevator jolt and resume its descent. A hand grips the hair on the back of my head hard, drawing me to my feet. The man's cold, dark eyes meet my own.

But I look down at my hand, still holding whatever it is I'd picked up from the floor. I want to weep with relief when I see that it's Bryce's gun. He looks down too. But too late. I fire into his face. The recoil throws me back, but I know from the warm, coppery spray that hits me that I didn't miss. And I at least have that satisfaction as I rapidly lose consciousness.

ELEVEN

Waking up in the hospital this time is much different from the last time. The first thing I see is a trio of concerned faces. Allie, David, and Emily all peer expectantly at me. But I can only think of one person.

"Bryce," I croak, my mouth dry. "Is he okay?"

Allie rushes to my side, slipping her hand in mine. David steps up beside her and gives my leg a reassuring squeeze.

"He's alive," Allie offers. "But he's not in good shape, Sera. They won't know more for a while."

I reach my hand out for Emily, knowing she must be as heartbreakingly worried as I am. She rushes to me, her eyes filled with tears, and Allie and David step aside to let her embrace me.

"Oh, Sera, I'm so glad you're safe," she murmurs, embracing me carefully and stroking my hair.

When she pulls away, I look down, trying to figure out why she was so particular in the way she held me, to see if I'm injured. But while there is a good amount of blood on my dress, I can't feel any pain. And knowing I'm whole makes my worry for Bryce all the more pressing.

"What's happening, Em? Why don't they know?" I ask, tears streaming desperately down my face.

"They said he sustained severe head trauma," Emily replies, the tears slipping down her face now as well. "He's still in surgery."

"How long have I been here? When..." I'm interrupted by a nurse bustling in through the door.

"Okay, everyone, let's please stop upsetting the patient," she snaps testily. Everyone takes a huge step away from the bed and gives her a wide berth. "Ms. Evans, I'm Nurse Kettleman. You don't appear to have sustained any physical trauma, but you were brought in unconscious approximately two hours ago. I'll need to check your vital signs now, okay?"

I note that the ringing in my ears is gone, and though tired and emotional I think she's right. I think my trauma is purely mental. So I nod, too tired to resist, and knowing I won't get answers from a hospital bed anyway. After a few minutes of questions and poking, she declares me fit to be released and hustles out the door to get the doctor.

I sit up and swing my legs over the bed, hopping down. "What else do we know about Bryce's condition?" I press, looking hard at Emily.

She shakes her head sadly. "Just that it's too soon to know," Emily replies. "That's it. Mom and Aunt Char are in the waiting room. They didn't want to overwhelm you."

"Has anyone spoken to the police?" I ask.

Allie and David share a look at my sharp tone.

"Of course," Emily responds. "And they're already on it. They know what happened from the video feed in the elevator, and they're trying to identify the bodies."

"That's good, but is there a police officer here now?" I demand.

While I'm terrified for Bryce, I haven't forgotten the reason we're here. And why I'd planned to leave. But with that out the window, and the boldness of tonight's attack, I know I'm more vulnerable than ever, but leaving is out of the question.

"Yes," Allie replies. "There are two in the waiting room. But the bad guys are dead, aren't they?"

I sigh heavily, not wanting to answer for fear of making them worry more. "Let's talk about this later. Right now, I need to get out of this damn hospital room," I reply.

"Well, then it's a good thing I'm here," a voice answers from the door.

I look up to see a fit, middle-aged man in scrubs.

He extends his hand. "I'm Dr. Miller. And from your chart and your attitude, I'd say you're fit to be released. If you have any trouble or black out again, please come back, okay?"

I don't take his hand, but he smiles warmly at me nonetheless, and instead signs and offers up a copy of my paperwork.

"Thank you, doctor," I respond. "But I'm not actually leaving the hospital." I take the proffered discharge slip and storm out the door.

Allie, David, and Emily follow, directing me to the surgical waiting room. I stop on the way to clean myself up as best I can. There's blood spatter on my face and chest, and a little in my hair, that I'm able to remove. The stains on my clothing will just have to wait.

Continuing into the waiting area, we find Rebecca and Charlotte, who stand as we enter. I go to Bryce and Emily's mother first, wrapping her tightly in a hug.

"Rebecca," I breathe as she embraces me in a way that only a mother can. "I'm so sorry." I bite back the guilt, the tears, and I let her go.

"I'm just glad you're okay," she replies, her eyes shining with tears. "Don't worry, Sera. Bryce is strong. And stubborn. Always has been. He'll be okay. I can feel it."

I don't respond, but hug Charlotte instead. She gives me an encouraging smile as well. At a different time I'd be saddened by how warm and reassuring Bryce's family is, as opposed to my own selfish and critical parents. But right now I'm laser-focused on what I can do. What I must do.

I step away from the women and over to where Allie and David are.

"Thank you, guys," I say. "For coming. I know this is probably scary and confusing. But I'll be okay. You can go home."

"Are you sure?" Allie asks skeptically. "We can wait here with you until Bryce is out of surgery. Or as long as you want."

I smile sadly and pull them both into a hug. "There's no need, really," I reply. "I should talk to the police and be here for Bryce's family. I'll let you know if I need anything, though, okay?"

"If you're sure," Allie responds, still obviously unconvinced.

I grab her hands in mine and squeeze them, giving her my best impression of calm confidence. "I'm sure. Love you guys," I say. "I'll let you know when we hear something."

After a few more reassurances, David finally manages to pull a clearly still uncertain Allie away. Once I'm sure they're gone, I approach the two police officers on the opposite end of the floor. I recognize one of them from the night I was attacked outside Bryce's apartment. And as I approach, I see the clear glint of recognition in his eye as well.

"Officer Abbott," I greet him. "I need your help."

"Ms. Evans," he responds. "I'm so sorry to meet again under these circumstances, but I'm at your disposal. We've actually been waiting to see if you needed us. What can we do for you?"

"Is there a detective assigned to the case yet?" I ask.

"There is," he replies slowly.

"Good, then I need to talk to him. Here. As soon as possible," I insist.

He considers me for a moment. "Sure thing, ma'am, I'll call him right away," he finally agrees. "And please know that all of us on the force are going to do everything we can to help," he glances at his partner, who nods in agreement. "Bryce is practically one of us."

"I appreciate that," I respond softly. "I'll be in the surgical waiting area. I need to make another phone call."

As I return to Bryce's family, I call the next person I'm going to need for my plan. Given the hour, I'm not surprised when he doesn't pick up right away. But eventually he does.

"Sera?" Tristan's voice is laden with sleep. "Everything okay?"

I look up at the ceiling, blinking back tears and concentrating on speaking as calmly as I can. "No. Bryce and I were attacked tonight. I'm okay, but Bryce is in surgery. And I'm afraid we're still in danger. I need your help, Tristan."

"On or off the books?"

His question brings a grim smile to my face. Because I know he's asking if he should ditch his GPS tracker. The loyalty his question demonstrates, at any other time, would warm my heart. But right now all I feel is cold fury.

"I would never ask you to do something off the books, Tristan," I respond. "But thank you all the same. Just come down to Swedish First Hill and we'll talk."

"I'll be there as soon as I can," he assures me.

∽

BRYCE IS STILL IN SURGERY, AND I'M GIVING A FULL HISTORY TO DETECTIVE Jacobs when Tristan arrives. He waits patiently while I finish filling in the tall, wiry detective on the situation. He's seen the police reports from my previous issues where I was followed twice and attacked on two separate occasions as well, including the attack of last weekend, but I'd never brought up Alessandro in my reports. Never hinted that there could be something bigger behind it. Until now. And now I've told him what I know, damn the consequences. Including that Bryce himself had launched an investigation. I can only hope it's enough.

But if it's not, I have a Plan B. Which is where Tristan comes in. As soon as the detective is gone, I find a quiet corner of the waiting room.

Tristan gives me a brief hug, which I gratefully accept. And I catch Tristan up too. Because he's only been told bits and pieces here and there, and if he's going to help he needs the whole story.

"Wow," Tristan murmurs as I finish. "That's a lot, Sera."

I close my eyes and give a brief sigh. "I know, but I need to focus right now," I reply. "Or I'm going to fall apart. I need to find Alessandro and get him to put a stop to this. And the only way I can think of to potentially reach him is through Marco Rossi, who took over his company here in Seattle. They're practically family, so Marco will almost certainly know where Alessandro is. Unfortunately, the number I have for Marco isn't working anymore. But honestly, I want to do this in person anyway. So I need you to find him for me and take me there once Bryce is out of surgery."

Tristan considers that, then nods. "Okay," he agrees. "I'll let the officers know that someone should stay here with you until I get back. And I'll get another guard to join me for first shift. I don't want to take any chances."

"That's probably a good idea," I reply.

And for once, none of my reservations about having the guards around matter — the thought of not having them is far worse. I can only hope this gets resolved quickly. And I'm furious with myself for letting it get to this point before going on the offense.

With Tristan gone, I return to the waiting room with Bryce's family to, well, wait. And hope.

It's several hours before a surgeon emerges, looking grim. We all jump up, snapping abruptly out of our half-asleep stupors.

"Mrs. Hoyt?" the surgeon asks.

Bryce's mother steps forward. The surgeon extends a hand, which she takes timidly, clearly terrified.

"I'm Dr. Barnes. Your son made it through surgery and is in recovery. We were able to repair the damage. Now all we can do is keep an eye on him to make sure the swelling goes down. The rest is up to him. Chances are good he'll wake up, but with this kind of head injury, it's impossible to know what the aftereffects will be."

"Thank you, doctor," Rebecca manages. "But what does that mean?"

"A traumatic brain injury often affects speech, cognitive function, mobility, and so on," he admits.

We all exchange horrified glances.

"But," he hedges, "as I said, there's no way to know if he'll have any of those issues or to what extent. And with rehabilitation there is a high success rate for recovery."

"When will he wake up?" Emily asks, gripping my hand tightly.

Dr. Barnes shakes his head. "We don't know. But we will keep him sedated for a while longer to give him time to heal. I'd recommend you go home and get some rest. We will call you if there are any developments," he replies.

I let out a frustrated gasp. "We can't see him?" I ask.

Dr. Barnes' eyes meet mine, and I see the compassion there. "I'm afraid not," he responds softly. "Not with this kind of injury, and the type of surgery that was done. Once the antibiotics have had a chance to take hold, you'll be able see him."

I try to fight back the rage and sorrow brewing in me before saying anything more. But Charlotte beats me to it.

"And when exactly will that be?" Char snaps uncharacteristically.

Dr. Barnes is clearly used to dealing with distressed loved ones, as he takes it fully in stride. "Twenty-four hours," he replies.

I sink into the chair behind me, no longer able to stand. Emily sits next to me and wraps an arm around me. I look up through tears at the doctor.

"So there's a chance he won't wake up?" I ask thickly.

The doctor looks down sadly at me. "There's always that chance, but I believe he will," he replies.

"But if he's fighting for his life, won't it help to hear our voices?" I press. I don't even think of asking what happens if he starts to lose that fight, if we'll be permitted to say goodbye, or even have time. But thankfully my question seems to have given Dr. Barnes pause.

"I'm a firm believer that that's true," he finally replies. "Come back this afternoon. If you're willing to go through the sterilization process, you can see him and talk to him, one at a time."

I jump to my feet and hug him before I can stop myself. "Thank you," I breathe.

He gives me a small, reassuring pat before stepping back. "Just check in at the nurse's station if you have any questions and to leave your contact information," he responds, then disappears through the swinging doors behind him.

I turn to the other ladies. "I hate to have to bring this up, but someone should notify Bryce's company of what's happened," I say tiredly.

Rebecca nods. "I already did, dear, don't you worry about anything," she replies.

I look at her in surprise. Having so recently dealt with the death of her husband, I finally realize how calm she's been through this so far. And I'm grateful, as that makes it easier for me to keep it together. I reach out and squeeze her hand.

"Thank you," I reply sincerely. "But unfortunately there are other matters I *will* need to worry about this morning. But please call me the instant you need me, and I'll drop everything. Okay?" I look at each of them in turn and they all nod. Out of the corner of my eye, I see Tristan and Aiden, one of my other former bodyguards, hovering. I embrace each of the women and say my farewells.

When I make my way over to Tristan and Aiden, I'm surprised when Aiden hugs me warmly.

"Thank you, Aiden," I say in surprise.

He gives me a sad smile. "My pleasure, ma'am," he replies. "What news?"

I sigh deeply. "Bryce is out of surgery and in recovery. We won't be permitted to see him until this afternoon, but the doctor sounded relatively optimistic at his chances," I reply, leaving out the part about potential issues and recovery. I just can't right now. "But there are other pressing matters at hand. Tristan, did you get the information I asked for?"

Tristan nods grimly. "Yes, ma'am," he replies.

I press my lips together, determined. "Good. Let's get moving, then. I'd like to stop home and change, and then go directly there," I instruct.

Tristan glances at his watch. "It's just past six a.m.," he points out softly.

I give him a sharp look. And never mind the fact that he's five inches taller than me and is far stronger, he wisely snaps his mouth shut in response.

"He'll be up. Or I'll wake him up. In either case, I'm not concerned," I spit angrily. And I can only hope Tristan knows I'm not angry with him, nor with Marco, really. And not even with Alessandro. I'm just angry with the world right now, for doing this to Bryce. He doesn't deserve it.

I turn heel and march out of the emergency room, my two guards scrambling to keep up behind me.

TWELVE

I t's not quite seven a.m. when, freshly showered and changed, I bang on the door of Marco's tiny house in Fremont. Tristan and Aiden flank me, exchanging a nervous look behind my back. I don't think either of them have ever seen me on the warpath, but I don't much care.

Marco answers the door, looking casually bewildered in blue flannel pants and a black T-shirt.

"*Buongiorno,*" I greet him. "I'm sorry to show up like this, Marco, but I need to speak with you."

"Sera, *buongiorno,* of course, please come in," he replies, bemused as he stares at the two men with me. He steps back, allowing us all to cross the threshold into the small living room behind him.

Marco pulls a few stray papers off the couch, gesturing for us to sit as he takes a chair. His wife, Angela, pops her head in from the kitchen.

"Serafina! *Buongiorno! Come stai?*" she greets me.

How am I? I suppress an ironic laugh as I rise to hug her.

"Angela, *buongiorno. Sono stato meglio. E tu?*" I return. "I've been better" is probably the understatement of my year.

"*Bene, bene,*" she assures me.

Well, I'm glad at least one of us is good.

"Cappuccino? Espresso?" She looks around at each of us, but we all shake our heads.

"I only need a word with Marco, *per favore,*" I reply.

"*Sì, naturalmente,*" Angela responds kindly, smiling and ducking back into the kitchen.

Marco shifts nervously in his chair. "Well, it must be something very urgent if you've come to see me. What can I do for you?" Marco asks with a note of suspicion.

"Where's Alessandro?" I ask bluntly.

Marco squirms, and I don't miss his eyes darting to the small set of stairs in the entryway.

"You've *got* to be kidding me."

"Sera, you must understand…" Marco starts, but I cut him off with a growl.

"I must understand nothing," I reply tartly, rising and going to the bottom of the stairs.

Tristan hops to his feet, clearly unsure of whether or not to follow. Marco eyes the gun now exposed as Tristan's jacket shifts.

Ignoring them both, I yell up the stairs as loud as I can. "*Alessandro Vittorio Giordano, you'd better get your ass down here right—*"

He appears at the top of the stairs before I can even finish. But he's not the man I remember. Thin and pale, his dark hair hangs long and limp around his face and unkempt beard. Even from this distance I can see the dead look in his dark eyes. And his tired sweats and T-shirt look like they could use a good washing. He's a far cry from the dynamic, fiery, and well-coifed man I loved.

"*Buongiorno, mio tesoro,*" he replies in greeting, his voice hollow and tired. He starts slowly descending the stairs as if every step is painful.

Marco appears at my side. "Be kind, Sera, you don't know what he's suffered," Marco says softly.

I bite back an angry reply, knowing it will do no good. He ascends the stairs, Angela following behind him as Alessandro finally makes it down.

"I'm glad to see you're safe," Alessandro remarks, taking note of Tristan and Aiden's presence.

And I can't help it. My hand flies up and I smack him across the face. Hard. He runs a hand over his lip, not even looking angry.

"I deserved that," he admits.

"And so much more," I seethe. "I may be safe for now, but Bryce wasn't so lucky." I practically choke on the words.

Alessandro raises an eyebrow. "I thought you said the giant was out of the picture?"

"No, I said it wasn't an option for me to go to him when I last saw you," I retort. "But he's very much in the picture. Assuming he survives. We were attacked last night, and not for the first time. And now Bryce is lying in a hospital bed, fighting for his life, because of *you.*" My eyes fill with angry tears. "*Why?* Tell me why, goddammit, and what you're going to do to stop this before they take everything from me."

Alessandro doesn't answer. Instead, he trudges into the living room, sinking defeatedly into the chair Marco just vacated.

"Did you realize that you loved him before or after he was hurt?" Alessandro asks.

I'm dumbfounded at the seeming indifference of his response, but I answer anyway. "Before."

Alessandro huffs a small, unamused laugh. "Lucky him, then," he murmurs. He rubs his hands roughly into his eyes. "I don't know where to begin, Serafina."

I look to Aiden and Tristan. "May we have privacy, please?" I ask them softly.

They rise and head out the front door. "We'll be on the porch. If you call out, we'll hear you," Tristan assures me as he leaves.

"Thanks," I reply. As soon as they're gone, I sit on the couch nearest to Alessandro's chair. I consider him carefully for a moment.

He's a shell of the man I knew. What could rob someone so strong-willed, so vital, of their spirit, their hope, and their health in such a short time? I almost don't want to know. But unfortunately right now I need to. Because if he can't, or won't, I need to be the one to figure out how to stop this.

"I'm sorry," Alessandro finally offers into the silence. "I've failed everyone."

"What are you even still doing here, Alessandro? Have you been here since I last saw you?" I press.

He shakes his head sadly. "No, *amore*. I went back to do what had to be done. But it wasn't enough. So I came back to make sure you were okay. For all the good it did," he spits venomously.

"Clearly, they didn't need me to accomplish your undoing," I reply sharply.

He looks up and catches my eye. "True," he agrees. "But that's not really what they were after, unfortunately."

"It's time to tell me the truth. It's time I know what's going on. If you can't end this, I'm going to help you to," I push. "So tell me: Who is after you, and what do they want?"

Alessandro sighs heavily. "What do they always want? Money," he replies, dodging my first question.

I tap my fingers impatiently on my knee. "How much money?" I ask.

"Nearly three million dollars, at last count," he replies.

I can't help but huff a dry laugh. "That's all?" I ask incredulously.

He levels a tired look at me. "That's all that's left, yes," he replies. "But for all I've already given." He looks at me miserably, and suddenly, somehow, I know he's still trying to protect me. Even now, in his seeming impotence, from whatever it is that has brought him to this state.

And it's hard to forget how much I still care for this man. Sliding off the couch, I sink to my knees in front of him and take his hand.

"Unfortunately, I'm not exactly in a position to seduce it out of you this time," I tease him gently. "So you're just going to have to tell me on your own."

He smiles, and it makes him look more like himself. "As you wish," he consents. He takes a deep breath. "You asked me once why I left Italy, and I'm afraid my answer wasn't very satisfying."

I nod, recalling the conversation.

"I went into real estate because it's what my father did. But I wanted to make my own way, so I didn't join him, and it angered him. My older brother was already working with him, though, so I didn't understand until much later why. But he more or less disowned me. It was not the best way to start out in life, but it made me work harder, and I think it's part of the reason I was so successful." He pauses to rub a finger along his chin.

"What did your mother think?" I ask curiously.

His sad eyes meet mine for a brief moment. "My mama wouldn't have cared, I know, but once he stopped speaking to me, she couldn't either without angering him," he replies. "It was bad, for everyone. But as the years went on, and I started to do well, I thought about it less. Until my brother started coming to me for money, with this excuse and that."

I raise my eyebrows delicately. "And you gave it to him?" I infer.

He nods. "I'm not usually one to suffer wastrels, but I was already at odds with my parents. I couldn't stand not being there for my brother," he admits. "But as I earned more, he asked for more. So, at some point, I stopped. But my mentor, he jumped in with my brother to guilt me, to say I had no loyalty to family."

"You mentioned your mentor changed," I recall. "You said he was limiting? Is that what you meant?"

"Ah, that," Alessandro responds. "No, that was something else entirely. He started steering me away from certain projects and toward others and throwing his weight around when I disagreed. It was quite strange at the time. Between all of it, though, I'd just had enough. So I left. I went somewhere I could make my own way."

"San Francisco," I supply.

He nods. "*Sì*, San Francisco," he agrees. "And it wasn't long before I met Peyton there. Which, as it turned out, wasn't a coincidence at all."

"How's that?" I ask.

He shifts uncomfortably in his chair, and I give his hand a reassuring squeeze to settle him.

"When Peyton was in college, she studied for a year abroad in Italy, which I knew," he responds. "What I didn't know is that during that time she met and fell in love with Antonio, my brother. It was he who first mentioned San Francisco to me, as a land of real estate opportunity. I remembered that when I learned he'd sent her after me, to do whatever was necessary to keep my money flowing back to him."

"Holy shit," I gasp. "Why did he need your money so badly?"

Alessandro closes his eyes, but the tears still find their way through, sliding slowly down his hollow cheeks. "They were all *Cosa Nostra*," he replies quietly. He opens his eyes to my confused expression. "Made men, as Americans say. You even joked once, about my having mob ties, and I laughed at you. Turns out it wasn't so funny after all. My father had gotten into it when we were little, when his business was struggling. And he brought my brother in when he came of age. That's why he was so angry — he knew I was smart, and that I'd help him do well. And then I refused him." Alessandro shakes his head sadly. "They made a bad investment with mafia money. Lots tens of millions of euros a few years before I moved to the States. That's why my brother needed money. And why my mentor was even my mentor in the first place — he was one of them, sent to watch me, make sure I was doing everything I could to make back their money and give it to my brother. So as long as my money kept coming, through Peyton, everything was fine."

I stare at him, open-mouthed, in utter shock at the situation. In the last months he's learned that his father and brother are mobsters, his ex-wife only married him out of love and obligation to his brother, and his mentor is a mob goon only there to see a debt repaid. And I'm starting to understand the change that has come over him.

"So the divorce..." I start.

"Yes, the divorce. It stopped the money. And they weren't used to having to make their own anymore, or perhaps were never all that able. So they got desperate, and their debtors anxious," he replies. "They were given a deadline. And when they didn't meet it, they killed my father." More tears slip from Alessandro's dark eyes.

"Oh, Alessandro, I'm so sorry," I reply. "What about your mother? Your sisters? Are they okay?"

"They are," he confirms. "The older of my two younger sisters, Adriana, is *Carabinieri*. Military police. She is trained in hiding. She fled the country with my mother and my youngest sister. So at least I know they are safe."

"When did it happen?" I ask softly.

"Just before I went back," he replies. "While I was following Peyton. So it's no surprise that after tipping my hand to get more information once I arrived in Rome, my brother found me quickly. He told me everything and begged me on behalf of their unborn child to help them."

"She was actually pregnant?" I ask, surprised.

"So he said," Alessandro replies dubiously. "The web of lies was so great, there is really no knowing. But I highly doubt it. In all the time I was watching her, she showed no signs."

"If she was pregnant and they needed money so badly, why did she agree to the divorce?" I ask, confused.

Alessandro smiles vaguely. "Because she's not very bright, Serafina," he responds. "She didn't realize I could push it through if she didn't answer my petition. And she thought she could plead her sob story to a judge."

"Oh, god, what did she say?" I ask.

"That I abused her, was a cheating bastard, and that I was in love with another woman," he rattles off. "In the heat of the moment I admitted to, at least, being in love with another woman, but of course denied her other lies. She was happy to have me out of her life not long after we married, and now I know why. But none of that mattered. Even if the judge didn't see right through her, which he did, she'd had her chance to respond to the paperwork and didn't. So it was done."

My hand flies to my mouth as a horrible realization dawns on me. "That's how they found out about me, isn't it?" I whisper.

Reluctantly, Alessandro nods. "My brother used that. Told me they'd come after you too if I didn't help him," he admits. "So I had no choice. I gave them everything I had. But it was not enough. So I promised to help Antonio find or make the rest of the money. But the timeline was short. And we weren't fast enough." Tears fill his eyes again and he presses them away angrily.

And I know whatever it is that happened next must be horrible, but I can't help asking. "What did they do?"

His dead eyes meet my own. "They killed Peyton. Right in front of us. And they told me they'd found you. And if they didn't get the rest of their money within a month, they'd kill you in front of me too. That's when I came back for you."

I gasp, doing the mental math quickly. "Alessandro, that was six weeks ago."

He leans forward, gathering both of my hands in his now. "I know," he replies. "And when they stopped hearing from me a couple of weeks ago, I knew it would get worse. Much worse. But I've been paralyzed. Too afraid to go back, too afraid to tell you. And my inaction cost my brother his life." His tears flow unreservedly now, dropping on the light carpet between us.

I slide a hand out of his grip and lift his face so he's looking into my eyes. "Your brother was responsible for his own life," I say firmly. "And you should have told me all this sooner. Much, much sooner." I let him go and rise to my feet. "If we pay them, will this stop? Will it be done?"

Alessandro looks up at me skeptically. "Yes, I believe it will," he replies uncertainly. "They have no use for me, and everyone else is either dead or out of their reach. But if I had that much money left, it would already be done."

I pause and wonder, did I really never tell him? Exactly how much money I have, the extent of the legacy my grandfather left? A great sadness wells in my heart knowing this could have been over long ago. That Bryce didn't have to be affected by this. That my and Alessandro's safety didn't have to be at risk. I stop myself from thinking about the others. Who knows what would have been changed if I'd just known the truth from the start.

"Call them. Ask them how much they need today to end this. And that it will be done," I instruct him.

"Serafina, I can't ask..." he starts.

I whirl on him furiously. "You're not asking. I'm telling you what's going to happen. The man I love is fighting for his life right now because of this, Alessandro. And neither of us will be safe until the debt is paid. So make. The. Fucking. Call."

And for once, he does as I ask.

∾

By midday, it's done. All of it. The money transferred, vows given that release us from the unknowing hell we've both been hostage to. I'd feel relieved if I still wasn't so worried for Bryce.

We drop Alessandro back off at Marco's. While Tristan waits to escort Alessandro to the door, he turns to me.

"I hope Bryce is okay," Alessandro says sincerely. "Truly. He protected you when I didn't. And for that I'll always be grateful."

I fight back the tears, not wanting to spend any more emotion on this man. "Take care of yourself, Alessandro," I reply stoically.

He looks at me as if he wants to say something else, but wisely doesn't. And then he's gone. Maybe someday we'll be friends again. But not today.

As soon as Tristan climbs back into the car, I give the order to return to the hospital. And then I let myself fall apart quietly in the backseat, while I can, knowing I'll need to keep it together again too soon.

THIRTEEN

When I arrive at the hospital I find Rebecca, Charlotte, and Emily in the waiting room, their faces shrouded in worry. I embrace them each in turn, trying to project an air of assurance that I don't really feel.

"When do we get to see him?" I ask by way of greeting.

Rebecca and Charlotte exchange a glance, and Emily pulls a nasty face.

"What? What's going on?" I can feel the blood drain from my face at their taciturn response.

"They say only one of us can go in," Emily pouts.

Charlotte throws her a sharp look.

"We've decided it should be you," Rebecca addresses me softly.

I'm taken aback. "I appreciate that, but you're his mother. I really think you should go," I reply.

Rebecca shakes her head. "I gave him life. But in his thirty-four years I've never seen him love someone the way he loves you. You're his life now," she says to me. "And I'm thankful for that. If he's going to fight for anyone, it will be for you."

Any hope I had of maintaining composure crumbles at her words, and I melt into her arms, sobbing. When I'm able to collect myself, I nod gratefully. "Thank you," I whisper.

They lead me to the nurse's station, and a short wisp of a woman in scrubs leads me to a room to undergo the sterilization procedure.

I emerge into the clean area a while later, scrubbed, stinging, and wrapped in garments that keep my bodily elements out of the environment around me. I feel like I'm wearing a space suit, but at this moment I don't care. I'd dress like a giant hot dog if it meant seeing Bryce.

I follow the directions I was given around the corner and into a room with no door. There's only one occupant, lying in a hospital bed, surrounding by tubes, wires, and machines that hum softly in the otherwise silent space.

I approach as close as I dare, stopping inches from the edge of the bed. There are tubes from his head, nose, mouth, and arm that snake over the great expanse of his chest and the side of his bed. I'm afraid to even be near them, should I accidentally bump anything.

When the initial fear has passed, I spend a minute just looking at him. His head has been partially shaved toward the back, his handsome face obscured by the tubes and tape. But I can see the bruising that spreads over his nose, chin, and cheek. Tears fill my eyes remembering how he got them.

I take a deep breath, fighting hard to stay calm. So that when I speak he hears me, and not my anguish.

"Hey, baby," I greet him. "I'm here. I'm sorry I couldn't come sooner. You had surgery, and they didn't even want to let anyone see you until tomorrow. But I couldn't wait that long. You know me, always impatient."

A flash of memory of the last time he called me that slips through my defenses. We were both naked. I blink the tears away hard and breathe deep to suppress the memory.

"The doctors say you're going to wake up. And that there's a good chance that you'll fully recover. And I'm going to be here for you every step of the way. But there's something else you should know."

I pause, not sure how much I should say, if it could somehow stress him further. So I couch my words carefully and explain how the threat against me, against us, is over. His face, his limbs, and his long frame are still throughout, not a hint of change in the beeping of the machines around him. But I persist.

"We're safe now," I conclude. "Even if it was too late to stop this. I'm so sorry, Bryce." My voice cracks at saying his name. I'm saved an imminent breakdown when a small speaker by his bed crackles to life.

"Ms. Evans?" the nurse's voice floats softly into the room. "Time is almost up."

I nod mutely, even though I know she can't see me, and my throat constricts with everything I want to say to him.

"I've got to go," I say apologetically. "But starting tomorrow I'll be able to visit more. We all will." Throwing caution to the wind, I step forward and slip my gloved hand over his, squeezing gently. "Never forget how much I love you, Bryce Hoyt." I turn and leave, barely holding back the tide of emotion.

∾

Even though we aren't allowed to visit Bryce until the following morning, we spend most of the time at the hospital anyway, sharing shifts in case there is news or he wakes up. Once they transfer him out of the clean area, his family is allowed to visit a fair amount, but non-family visits are more restricted. Still, I spend as much time as I can by his side, quietly reassuring him and calling him back to me.

As Sunday draws to a close I realize there is no possible way I'm going to be able to work while he's in this state. I call Charles to let him know and, thankfully, he completely understands, sends his best wishes and tells me to call if I need anything.

But I forget even my most basic needs until Allie shows up, all but forcing food and rest on me. I'm exhausted, and though I'm not hungry, I notice the impact of not eating much. The copious amounts of coffee I consume hit my stomach like lead, and my head pounds. By Monday night, I start to wonder how much of this I can take.

And by Tuesday morning the sentiment has spread, as I can sense the nurses and doctors are tiring of reassuring us that it's not abnormal for someone to be unconscious this long under the circumstances.

But on Tuesday afternoon, when I'm getting my umpteenth cup of coffee for the day, Emily comes shooting down the hall.

"He's awake!" she cries as she approaches.

And thankfully the cup of coffee is still filling in the machine, or I would have dropped it in my haste to get to him.

But before I can get far Emily has planted a hand firmly on my chest. "We can't see him yet. The doctors are with him now."

I pull back, frustrated. "Were you there? What happened?" I demand.

Emily shakes her head. "It was Mom. I don't know. She said he seemed disoriented, and she called for the nurses right away. They asked that she leave while they tend to him and get him checked out," Emily replies.

I frown and turn to get back to the waiting room, to talk to Rebecca directly. I find her beside a pacing Charlotte, both women twisting their hands together frenetically.

When Rebecca spots me, she approaches and wraps her arms around me. "He's awake. Focus on that," she says. Her tone worries me, but afraid to ask, I say nothing and we all take seats in tense silence.

What feels like hours later, a doctor asks Rebecca to go with him to see Bryce. Another long, anxious, stretch of time passes before she emerges, white-faced.

"Well?" Emily demands.

Rebecca looks up at her dismally. "Physically, he's doing quite well. He has all of his motor functions," Rebecca responds carefully. "And he seems in decent spirits, despite still suffering a considerable amount of pain, even with the medications he's on. So they're adjusting those doses."

"But?" I press, knowing there's something she's not saying. Something big.

"He seemed confused. He asked for his father," she admits. My heart sinks in my chest. "The doctors told him he needs more tests, and rest, before he sees *anyone* else. The privately told me not to break any kind of news to him right now, that they need time to assess the extent of his issues."

I start clutching my midsection as sharp pain shoots through me like I've been kicked. Rebecca reaches out and grabs me by the arms.

"Don't worry yet, Sera, please," she begs. "It's too soon. He's awake. And I can tell you right now, he's still our Bryce. Let the doctors look at him. One step at a time."

I should feel comforted. Because she's right. So even though I can't help but worry, I sniff deeply and nod. Rebecca and Charlotte step to the side to talk quietly, and Emily approaches me, wrapping me in a tight hug.

"I'm here for you, Sera," she assures me. "Remember, we pinky swore. No matter what happens."

I can't help but laugh. "Thanks, Emily," I reply. "Ditto."

She lets me go and we sink into the hard, plastic chairs in the waiting room. And we wait.

No news comes, and not long later a nurse lets us know that we should go home and come back tomorrow.

I return home reluctantly, and without my security guards for the first time. There's nothing to fear anymore. Well, nothing outside of the hospital, anyway.

∽

THE NEXT MORNING, I PACK A BAG FOR BRYCE WITH SOME SWEATPANTS, SHIRTS, his house slippers, and some hygiene items. As I pass the kitchen, I'm momentarily tempted to pack the frilly white apron that still hangs by the fridge. I resist, but somehow it gives me hope. Because it reminds me how much he loves me. And in love, there's always hope.

I meet Rebecca and Emily in the waiting room by eight per our usual routine, but Charlotte has gone back to work with the worst of the danger passed.

"I brought him some of his clothes and things," I say. "I didn't know how long he'd be here."

Rebecca smiles warmly. "The nurse says the doctor has some information for us. He'll be out shortly," she replies. "So hopefully we'll know soon."

I nod meekly, nervous. Thankfully, we're not made to wait long. A shorter man in a lab coat and glasses comes out and heads straight for Rebecca.

"Mrs. Hoyt?" has asks kindly.

She nods.

"I'm Dr. Farber."

"Call me Rebecca, please," she responds. "This is Bryce's sister, Emily, and his girlfriend, Sera."

"Ladies," he replies with a dip of his head. "Bryce is doing quite well, physically. But we are still a little concerned with his cognitive functions and his memory. Despite the reduction in swelling, he's still struggling with both. But please be assured that that's completely normal. He should make a good deal of progress in the next few weeks, but it could be up to a year before his recovery is complete."

"When can we see him?" I ask.

"He's perfectly fit for visitors, but be aware that he's currently unable to remember anything within approximately the last eighteen months."

We all three of us let out a collective gasp. None of us imagined it was that extensive. I try my best not to panic, but it's practically impossible.

Bryce won't remember me. My ears ring as the conversation continues, and I have to push myself hard to listen.

"Eighteen months?" Emily spits out incredulously. "Will that get better?"

Dr. Farber holds up a hand. "As I was going to say, he should not be pressed to remember anything he can't at this time. He's been made aware of it, but nonetheless it's dangerous for his healing to push him. And we're going to keep him for a few more days to make sure the swelling continues to go down and he's weaned off of the majority of the medicines we've had him on," Dr. Farber hedges. "But yes, his memory should improve. Though there's no telling how much. Regardless, until his cognitive functions return to normal levels and his short-term memory is repaired, he should take it easy. No work, no major decisions, no trying to force progress."

"And, on average, when do you expect to see that kind of improvement?" I ask quietly.

"He could be ready for work in a matter of weeks, months at most," Dr. Farber responds. "But he'll need to work with a rehabilitation therapist to aid his healing. After a year, whatever progress he's made is likely to be where he stays."

I rub the back of my neck, unease creeping through every pore in my body. "I've only known him for five months," I admit. "Is it okay if I go in? Just in case it jogs something?"

Dr. Farber looks like he wants to say no, and I press my lips together, willing him to at least let me see him. If for nothing else than to see for myself that he's himself, mostly. That's he's okay.

"Normally, I would advise against it," he hedges. "But if you don't introduce yourself as his girlfriend, and you respond to his lead, I can allow it. He can't be subjected to strong emotion right now, though, so if you need to, please leave the room rather than upset him."

I nod, simply thankful for the opportunity. "I can do that," I agree.

Dr. Farber looks around at all of us. "That really goes for everyone, until he's improved. Let him lead. Watch him carefully for signs that he's had enough. Know when to back off. The nurses will help you," he assures us. "Any other questions?"

Rebecca looks to Emily and me, and we shake our heads. "Not right now, doctor, thank you," she responds.

"Then follow me," he responds. He grabs a nurse along the way and leads us to Bryce's room.

Emily pulls me aside as Rebecca enters with Dr. Farber and the nurse. "I'm here if you need me, Sera. Just remember the long game," she encourages me. "Even if he doesn't remember you right now, that doesn't mean anything. It's early."

I nod, swallowing hard. "I just want to know he's okay," I respond.

Emily nods, and slips her hand in mine. The warm, soft reassurance is more than welcome.

Dr. Farber exits, eyeing us as he goes, but saying nothing. I take a deep breath and let Emily lead me in.

The nurse stands by Bryce's bed, checking his vitals. Rebecca sits on the edge of his bed, holding his hand. And he's sitting up, completely free of tubes and wires. And he's smiling. My heart almost breaks with relief and gratitude. Because even if he doesn't remember me, he's *alive*. And he's going to be okay.

When he sees Emily, his smile widens into his classic Bryce sunshine smile, and I have to blink back bittersweet tears.

"Em!" he exclaims opening his arms to her. She drops my hand and rushes forward to embrace him warmly.

"Bryce," she replies. "I'm so glad you're okay." She pulls back. "Love the haircut, bro."

He laughs and runs his hand gingerly over the partially shaved patch. "I'll just shave the whole thing later," he assures her. "Nothing can stop these good looks, though."

Em laughs. "Boy, a traumatic brain injury can't even dent your ego," she teases. "Is it wrong that that makes me feel relieved?" Emily rounds the bed, dropping into one of the metal chairs on the other side.

And Bryce looks up and sees me for the first time. He does elevator eyes over me, and a shiver runs through me. He turns and looks questioningly at Emily, realizing I came in with her.

"Who is this?" he asks blankly.

And I can't help it. Even though I was expecting it, my heart breaks at his question, and I have to work to keep myself calm and my expression neutral.

"That's my friend, Serafina Evans," Emily responds carefully.

"Oh," he responds happily. "Nice to meet you, friend Serafina Evans." He extends a hand and something in me shifts again.

I identify the feeling this time — it's like a tiny death of a fraction of my hope.

I extend my right hand, shifting his duffle bag to my left. "You can call me Sera," I respond as evenly as I can.

His hand is rough and warm, and wonderful. He lets go far sooner than I'd like. "I take it we've met before," he responds drily.

I look at him in shock. "Yes, actually," I admit. "But how did you know that?"

He smirks and points at the duffle bag in my hand.

I blush furiously. "Oh. Yes, that. Sorry. I brought some of your things. Sweats, shirts, slippers. And your toothbrush and shaving kit. Probably a few other things. I don't know." I hand over the bag dumbly, embarrassed by my verbal incontinence.

Bryce raises an eyebrow. "You brought those, huh?" he asks, confused. "Do I want to know why you had them in the first place?"

We all freeze for a moment, and it's all I can do to keep my jaw off the floor. He sure as hell doesn't seem like he's got any cognitive issues. He seems just as observant as ever.

"Um, it's a long story," I reply. "I'm sure Emily will tell it to you later."

Bryce nods, obviously placated. So maybe he's not as sharp as usual.

Bryce turns to his mom. "Has anyone told Madison I'm here?" he asks innocently.

A brief hush falls over the room as we all realize if the last thing he remembers is a year and a half ago, he's still the Bryce that was with Madison. The Bryce that was about to *propose* to Madison, if I remember the timeline of the downfall of their relationship correctly. Suddenly, I feel like throwing up.

Rebecca shoots me a furtive glance. "No," she admits. "We can worry about that later."

I swallow a lump in my throat. Rebecca and Emily continue shooting me sympathetic looks. And I know I need to leave. So I don't fall apart, and their response to me doesn't tip Bryce off that something is amiss. Especially if Madison is going to come parading in here soon.

And the thought of her being here while he's in this state makes me want to punch something. But I shove it all down.

"I should go," I interject. "Bryce, I'm really glad to see you're doing so well. I hope you keep getting better, okay?"

He nods happily. "Thanks, Sera, it was nice to … er, see you," he chuckles.

I catch Em's eye. "I'll talk to you soon, right Em?" I ask.

"Count on it," she assures me quietly.

"'K. Bye," I reply, ducking out as quickly as I can. And before I completely lose it, I call Allie and ask to come stay with her. Because I know being alone in the house I shared with Bryce is a recipe for a complete breakdown.

FOURTEEN

Staying with Allie was a good call. Since she's still not working, she's around constantly to be a sounding board, distraction, and source of comfort as needed. Especially since I decide to take the rest of the week off, unsure whether I'm in control enough of my emotions to make it through a workday.

Emily calls on Saturday to let me know Bryce is being discharged and will be going to stay with their mother. She blessedly doesn't mention Madison. She does say that Bryce has slowly started asking questions about his life these past eighteen months, and that they're carefully answering them. Since it was kind of difficult to avoid, they did have to break it to him that his father had passed, which has forced them to back off everything else as he absorbs that news.

It's the only thing she tells me that plunges me back into despair. And not for myself, for Bryce. Because I was there when he dealt with it the first time, and I remember how much it affected him. He needed me so desperately then, and it caused the chain of events that led me to realize how deeply I cared for him. But it's also what drove him back to his conniving ex, Madison, if only temporarily. I can only hope they're encouraging him to be cautious on that front. Because despite repeated attempts at suggesting I visit, they've made it clear that Bryce's mental state is still too delicate.

I return to my own home and to work the following week and bury myself deeply in the myriad of development projects I'd dumped on Suraj's desk with my absence. It's a reminder of how lucky I am to work with Charles, Suraj, and everyone at Sutton Developments. My absence would have had a much bigger impact had I still been running my own company.

It's not until Tuesday evening, when Heather calls, that I'm reminded Daniel's trial started yesterday.

"Heather," I answer. "Hi. I'm so glad to hear from you."

"Hey, Sera," Heather replies. "Sorry I've been out of touch. With the trial coming up I just needed some time to prepare myself, I guess."

"I totally understand," I reply. "How is it going so far?"

"Slow," she admits. "But being in the courtroom with him isn't as hard as I thought it would be."

"I'm glad to hear it," I respond, unsure of what else to say. I want to be there for Heather, but I've had to shut down my emotions so much lately it's hard feeling anything, for anyone.

"Officer Ramirez told me what happened to Bryce," Heather says. "I'm so sorry, Sera. Are you okay?"

"I'll be fine," I assure her. "You have enough to worry about. Is there anything I can do for you?"

"Oh, Sera," Heather sighs. "I'm an expert at deflecting, so I know it when I hear it. You don't have to do that. I have a great support system. Don't worry about me, or the trial. I'll let you know how it goes, okay?"

I breathe a sigh of relief, though part of me feels guilty. I've always been in the role of boss or mentor for Heather. It feels odd to have her looking after me. But I almost have no other choice than to accept it. I don't think I could handle being involved with Daniel's trial right now, even if I wanted to.

"Thanks, Heather," I respond gratefully. "I'll talk to you soon."

"Bye, Sera."

Once she's hung up, I realize Charles hadn't said a word about Daniel's trial these past two days, either. As his father, I can imagine this is almost as hard on him as it is on Heather, though obviously in a very different way. I vow to check in with him the next day and call it an early night.

∿

CHARLES IS UNCHARACTERISTICALLY UNAVAILABLE FOR THE REMAINDER OF THE week. I take the hint and leave him alone. I myself, having perfected the art of burying my emotions in work, can hardly fault him for it.

But I'm shaken from my own determined head-down stance on Friday afternoon when Emily calls.

"Hey, Em, what's up?" I answer warily.

"Hey, Sera," Emily replies, already sounding reluctant. "Would it be possible for you to bring the rest of Bryce's things to Mom's tomorrow?"

Something tugs sharply inside my chest. "Of course," I reply. "Am I going to be able to see him?"

"That's actually kind of the point," she responds. "Bryce has started asking about the accident. There's so much that opened up, and he wants to talk to you."

I freeze in my chair. "What does he know?" I ask tensely.

"That he was protecting someone in an elevator when he was attacked," she responds. "Naturally, he wanted to know who. So we told him it was you. He actually seemed more satisfied by that answer than I thought he'd be. I think he thinks that's why you were at the hospital last week. That you were a client."

I laugh humorlessly. "Well, technically speaking, I was," I reply. "You really didn't tell him anything else?"

"Not yet," she admits. "He's still taking a lot longer to process things. We've been careful not to overwhelm him. But the doctors say he's already improved a ton, so I think he can handle more."

"Has he been seeing Madison?" I ask bluntly.

"Do you really want to know about that, Sera?" Emily asks timidly.

"I need to know where he's at if I'm going to talk to him," I reply snappishly.

Emily doesn't respond for a long while. "They've talked a few times," she finally discloses. "But he's agreed not to jump into anything. Or back into anything, from his point of view."

"Okay," I say, trying not to die inside that he's talked to Madison multiple times, but I haven't been allowed anywhere near him. "I'll talk to him. What time?"

"Ten?" she offers.

"Fine. I'll see you then," I respond tersely.

"Thanks, Sera," Emily replies, sounding relieved. "I know it won't be easy for you. I appreciate it."

"I love you, Em, but I'm not doing it for you. I'm doing it for Bryce," I say tiredly.

"I know," she agrees.

When I hang up, I find going back to work impossible, so I trudge home to pack Bryce's things. And that night, the nightmares return.

∽

ON SATURDAY MORNING I FIND MYSELF TOO NERVOUS TO EAT. AND TIRED AS I am, I try to limit my coffee intake so as not to be a shaky mess. Though coffee or not, I end up a twisted ball of nerves as I unload the duffel bags from the car, lugging them individually to the door before ringing the bell.

Emily answers, looking as nervous as I feel.

"Hey, Sera," she greets me, pulling me into a warm hug.

I squeeze her back hard, gratefully accepting the last shot of comfort and warmth before I enter the house. We each drag one duffel bag into the foyer, leaving them there to be dealt with later.

"Where's your mom?" I ask curiously as she leads me into the living room.

"She's out shopping with Aunt Char," Emily responds. "She thought it might be less overwhelming if there were fewer of us here."

I sigh inwardly, unsure of whether I agree, but realizing ultimately it doesn't matter. "And where is he?"

"In his room," Emily replies softly as we settle on the small, grey-blue settee in the lush living room. "Are you really up for this?" Her blue eyes look probingly into mine, and I avert my gaze quickly.

"Yes," I reply tersely, unwilling to admit exactly how much I *need* to see him. How much I miss him. "How is he doing?"

"They were way off on his cognitive skills," she responds. "Or he just recovered that quickly. He has trouble with complicated sequences, but if they weren't testing him I'd never know there was anything different. Except the memory thing, of course."

"Of course," I allow. "And how is that?"

Emily gives me a heartbreakingly sad look. "Still no change," she replies. "He accepts whatever we tell him, but as far as he's concerned, it's July of 2017."

"Wait, I thought he was eighteen months behind? That's only fifteen," I respond, confused.

Emily shrugged. "We were wrong. He's been able to be more specific about his last, complete memories, and they end around July of last year," she replies.

"Is that better?" I ask.

Emily shrugs. "The doctors say yes, a little. Less to get back anyway. But still not enough," she acknowledges.

"No," I agree. "Still not enough. Anything else I should know?"

Emily eyes me warily. "He gets pretty agitated when we tell him too much at once. When he can't remember important things. It's why we haven't tried to get you two talking again. So just be careful, okay?" she asks.

I nod and take a deep breath. "Well, let's do it then," I say.

She leans over and gives my hand a reassuring squeeze before rising and striding purposefully from the room.

In no time at all, a heavier set of footsteps approaches. I don't dare look, holding my composure around me like a shield as long as I can. I only look up as he settles into the larger settee across from me.

He looks so normal. His chestnut hair has been buzzed down, and he's leaned out a bit. I'm sure they're not allowing him to exercise yet. But he looks healthy, and more relaxed than I'd expect given what he's learned recently. His blue eyes fix on mine, but with none of the fire and warmth I'm used to seeing in them. It hurts, on some level, but I ignore it.

"That's your mom's spot," I say reflexively.

His mouth tugs up into a small smile. "You've been here before," he responds. His smile quickly fades, and I can see the air of grief about him.

The sunshine around him when he woke has been dulled by his expanding awareness of reality. Of the loss of his father. But he's nowhere near as devastated as he was the first time. Though there was so much else going on then.

"For your father's funeral," I admit in partial truth, baldly addressing the elephant in the room. "I'm so sorry, Bryce."

"Thank you," he responds quietly. He runs a hand over his buzz cut in such a Bryce way that there's another sharp tug of pain at my insides. "It's a lot to take in, even outside of everything else that's going on."

"How are you doing with all of this?" I ask him, gesturing around me metaphorically.

He shrugs. "In some ways, it's fine. I'm a roll-with-the-punches kind of guy. But knowing something and accepting it are two different things," he responds. And instinctively I realize he's talking about his company. That he'll once again need to accept running Hoyt Corporate Services at some point.

"Bryce, not only do you not have to, but you shouldn't worry about anything right now," I say, catching his eye. "Dealing with the loss of your father is enough. You don't have to think about everything that follows. I talked to your mom. The company is in good hands — your VP seems perfectly capable. I think everyone understands you need time to heal and figure out what's right for you in this new life of yours."

Bryce looses a deep breath. "Thank you," he replies. "That actually helps." He looks at me curiously. "How did you know that's what I was worried about?"

I consider that and decide to be as honest as I can. "Because I was around when you dealt with this the first time," I admit. "And I knew you pretty well, once."

"Really?" he asks skeptically. "Because I couldn't have known you more than a year or so."

I huff a dry laugh. "We've actually only known each other for five months," I admit. "I hired you during a rather difficult situation at my own company."

"Ah, so you are a client," he responds. "And not a friend of Em's."

"Oh, I'm friends with Emily," I correct him. "But yes, I'm a client of yours. Or was, anyway."

"So I stopped the bad guys?" he asks with a grin. "I'm glad it wasn't for nothing then."

"You protected me," I agree. "More than you know. And I'll be forever in your debt."

Bryce leans forward, his smile mellowing into something more thoughtful. "We were dating, weren't we?"

His expression is still so casual, I know it's not a memory. Just Bryce, putting the pieces together like he always does. In a way it's reassuring. In a way, another small fragment of hope dying.

"Yes," I admit.

Bryce nods. "Every time I asked Emily where my things were, she dodged the question. And then you show up with them, again. So I figured as much, but thank you for being honest with me," he responds.

"You're welcome," I reply slowly. "But I don't know any other way to be."

Bryce laughs. "That's refreshing. Everyone around me right now seems to want to shield me from the truth," he remarks. "Don't get me wrong, I understand why, but it gets old fast."

I smile vaguely in response, and at the knowledge of all I'm not telling him. "I can understand that. But being honest and telling the whole story are two different things. Though when you're really ready, I'm happy to do both," I reply. He leans back again, considering me thoughtfully.

"Are you, now?" he murmurs. The question and its tone remind me of things he used to whisper in my ear and my insides clench in response, but not in the good way. "How about most of the story?"

I spread my hands in invitation. While in some ways talking to him is difficult, in other ways it still feels like the most natural thing in the world, as it's always been between us. Except that I can't sit with him, wrap myself around him, taste his lips on mine. I shake myself, refocusing.

"How long were we dating?" he asks.

"A little more than a month," I reply.

"And I was living with you?" he asks archly.

The shock in his tone should hurt, but it doesn't. Even I always thought it was fast. But then, I fought against my feelings for him for so long it's not like we didn't know each other, not like if we'd just met and decided to shack up after days.

I shrug. "It made sense. You were protecting me," I explain. And so, so much more.

He eyes me skeptically. "I don't usually move that fast," he replies pensively.

"Me neither," I admit with a small, sad smile.

"Then why?" he asks curiously.

I can't think of a way to answer his question that doesn't require me laying my heart on the floor for him to stomp on with his lack of memory, his inability to reciprocate. And the longer I try, the less comfortable this becomes, the more like a poignant reminder of our current situation.

I shake my head, throwing off the pain. "That's not something I can explain," I respond. "If you remember someday, you'll understand. And if you don't, then it's moot anyway."

But meeting his gaze, I can tell he knows why. That we must have loved each other.

"Is any of this helping?"

"If you mean, is it making me remember, I'm sorry to disappoint you, but no," he admits. "But it's helping me to understand what happened and why. So thank you."

"You're welcome," I reply simply. "Do you have any other questions for me?"

"Not right now, no," he responds. "I think I just need some time to process all of this."

I rise from the couch. "I understand. You'll be fine," I assure him. "You always know what to do, Bryce. Just trust yourself, and you won't go wrong."

He looks at me curiously. "I can see why…" he murmurs, then shakes his head. "I'm sorry. I'll walk you out." He rises and takes a step toward me.

But looking up at him, into his gorgeous face, his body as close to mine as it has been since that night, it's all too much. I put up a hand, afraid of him coming closer. He's exactly my Bryce, still. Observant, logical, considerate, kind, and heart-breakingly handsome. It's too much to bear.

"I know the way. Take care, Bryce." And without another word I turn and leave.

FIFTEEN

I stumble through the rest of the weekend, a prisoner to my own malaise. Before it's over, I decide to preemptively make plans for the following weekend to stave off further wallowing. I haven't seen or even really talked much to my mother in a while, so I make plans to visit. And, as an afterthought I ask Hunter if he wants to get together. That set, I dive back into protection mode, deeply burying myself in work.

And it's a good thing too, as after being in and out of the office so much these days, there's plenty to do. I find myself getting in early and staying late every day. Charles is happy for the relief and progress, and I don't have to think about anything but zoning permits, building materials, and the like.

On Thursday afternoon Heather calls and asks me to meet her for drinks the following day. Since I wasn't planning on heading up to my mom's place until Saturday morning, I agree. Besides which, my interest is piqued as she won't say anything about the trial, and I haven't dared talk to Charles about it since he's made it obvious he'd rather pretend like it isn't happening. I try not to think about the fact that Bryce doesn't remember any of it.

When I stride into the bar on Friday evening, I find myself anxious to hear whatever it is she has to share. I spot her waving at me from a small table on the far side of the room, her long black braids twisted prettily into a bun atop her head. And based on the barely suppressed grin on her face, I know she has good news.

I rush over to her, throwing my arms around her. She embraces me back fiercely, laughing and crying.

I pull away, keeping a firm hold on her shoulders. "Good news, then?" I ask brightly.

She squeezes my arms and nods. "The best," she responds. "Guilty. On all counts. Unanimously. They recommended the maximum sentencing, and he was given a sentence of seven years at a hearing this morning."

I sink onto the barstool, relieved that at least *something* is going right. "Oh Heather, I'm so glad," I admit. "You must be so relieved."

"Beyond," she acknowledges. "I was afraid, at first, that since neither you or Bryce..." a deep blush appears on her dark skin. "I'm sorry, Sera, I didn't mean to..."

I hold up a hand. "It's okay," I assure her. "I know it must have been disheartening that neither of us were there. But I'm glad it worked out, and you've come out on the other side all the same."

"Me too," she confesses. "And I'm sorry, again. I know he probably doesn't remember how much he helped me, but I wish I could thank him anyway."

I swallow against the lump forming in my throat. "Me too," I reply softly. "Someday, perhaps."

Heather considers me carefully for a moment. "Shall we talk about something else?" she asks quietly.

"Yes, please," I respond, smiling. "And alcohol. Lots of alcohol."

We both laugh, and I go to the bar for our drinks. And we spend the evening drinking and talking about what a bastard Daniel was at the trial, Heather's job, my job, and everything in between. It's a welcome reprieve from, well, everything else.

∾

It was so nice, in fact, I don't even regret waking up slightly hungover on Saturday morning. And the pain in my head is easily put aside with a good breakfast, coffee, and a handful of ibuprofen. By the time I'm halfway to Bellingham, I find I'm actually even able to enjoy the ride.

Despite the early November chill in the air, the clouds have parted, and the sun plays spectacularly on my pastoral surroundings as I make my way between towns. I always forget how calming this drive can be, and all the little sights on the way that remind me of going home — the expansive garden store Mom and I always liked to trek to on the odd weekend, the apple cider barn where we spent fun fall days, and the vast, marshy fields filled with huge, white geese at certain times of the year.

By the time I arrive at my mom's house, I'm feeling more relaxed than I have in weeks. A twitch of the curtains tells me I've been spotted, so I'm not surprised when my mother comes rushing out the front door.

And I do something I don't think I've ever done. I leap out of the car and race into her arms. She holds me tightly, only letting go at my signal.

"Welcome home, darling," she says.

The love in her voice wraps around me, warming my aching heart. As I'm still holding her closely by the arms, I notice for the first time her hair, once a few shades darker brown than my own light brown, is now streaked more gray than not. And her hazel eyes, which are just like mine, are couched with creases. I realize she must have looked something like this for a while. But there had always been distance between us, even as we've grown closer lately. I'm ashamed it's taken such tragedy for me to be this close to her, to really see her.

"I love you, Mom," I declare spontaneously.

"Oh," she replies in surprise. "Well, I love you too."

Her smile causes me to pull her in for another tight hug.

"What brought that on?"

I pull away and go to retrieve my bag from the car. "Life is too short," I reply. "Too precious not to say it." I close the trunk and approach her. "I'm sorry it took me so long to realize that."

My mom shrugs and holds the front door open for me. "I can't say I blame you," she admits, following me into the living room. "Our relationship has never been easy."

I huff a dry laugh. "That's an understatement," I agree, smiling. I drop onto the old, flower-patterned couch with a sigh.

My mom takes a seat in the armchair next to me, eyeing my warily.

"But I'm glad I'm here now."

"Me too," she replies. "You've been pretty tight-lipped about everything that's been happening. I've been more worried than I cared to admit. But I didn't want to press."

I nod. I know I've been withholding all but the necessary information from her for some time. And though I'm learning to trust her again, it's all been a lot. And I've barely spoken in depth about it to anyone. Even Allie, with everything she'd been going through, I'd kept at a certain distance. My main confidant of late had been Bryce, or occasionally Emily, but obviously the former is no longer an option and the source of most of my sorrow, and the latter, well, now it's so very complicated. So really, it's a good time to let my mother in a little more. Because I need it. And I think she might too.

"I appreciate that," I respond. "But I'm ready to let it all out. I think I need to, so I can move forward."

My mother raises an eyebrow. "You've given up hope," she guesses. "That he'll remember."

I blink back tears. "I'm starting to," I admit. "And I know it hasn't even been a few weeks yet, but there's *nothing*. No indication that he remembers me at all."

"Maybe you should give him a chance to get to know you again," she suggests.

"I just don't think he's there," I reply. "He's got so much to absorb. And honestly, I don't know if I have the strength to love him like I do, to want him, when he barely even knows who I am." I shake my head and laugh through the tears that have started falling. "I don't know how he did it for so long. Hell, he had it worse — he had to watch me be with someone else first."

My mother's hand slips over mine. "This is different," she says. "He was in love with you, and that's a very theoretical thing. He didn't know what it was really like to be with you. For you, well, you two were in love and together, completely. And now you know, really know, what it is that you're missing."

Her words break my heart on a level I can barely handle. Tears fall unreservedly down my face at their truth. And I know I'm not strong enough to go from what we were, to what we'd have to be. I shake my head, trying to throw off the tears, the sorrow, but they just keep coming.

I feel my mother slide onto the couch next to me and wrap her arms around me.

"Let it all out, baby," she encourages me.

So I bury my face in her chest, and I do.

∽

After a comforting day and night with my mother, Sunday dawns and I prepare to meet Hunter at a local diner for breakfast. Still plagued by nightmares, I'm exhausted and defeated, but somehow looking forward to spending time with my half-brother anyway.

I pick him up from our father's house, purposely avoiding going in. Thankfully, Hunter bounds out and hops in the car before either of his parents catch on.

"Hey, Hunter," I greet him, pulling quickly away.

"Hey, Sera," he replies. "Figured you wouldn't want to deal with the old people."

I laugh drily. "Thanks," I reply. "What's new? Got a job yet?"

"Nah, there's really not much here," he replies.

"Oh," I say, unsure of how to respond.

"Where's Bryce?" Hunter asks curiously.

Thankfully, I was prepared for that question. I'd purposely arranged our meeting via text, so I had time to figure out what I wanted to say.

"Bryce and I aren't together anymore," I reply evenly. And I leave it there. I know he won't question it.

"That sucks," Hunter remarks. "I liked him."

"Me too," I reply softly.

Over breakfast, Hunter tells me about how he's moving to "confined" art — aka actual canvas or space that's *meant* to be painted. He thinks he might want to be an art teacher or something along those lines, so it's his attempt at going "mainstream."

I'm so not an artist, but the conversation is entertaining in a way I can't even quite explain. But in any case, it's clear that Hunter is tired of his dead-end life and he wants out. And as we finish eating, something occurs to me.

"You know, there are bound to be a lot of opportunities in Seattle," I bait him.

Hunter pushes his empty plate away and nods. "There is a really great artist's community. I've thought about moving there, but I don't really want to have to work at a fast food place just to be able to afford to share a place with twenty other dudes," he replies.

I smile mischievously. "Then I have the perfect solution," I respond lightly.

He looks up, brushing his hair out of his eyes.

"You should come live with me."

His eyes widen. "In your condo? Seriously?" he asks disbelievingly. "I don't think I could afford the rent."

I laugh. "You don't have to pay me anything," I clarify. "Just pull your weight. I could use the company. Really." I hope I'm not inviting something painful and awkward, but it seems like a pretty great solution for both of us right now. "And if it doesn't work out, no harm done."

He considers me pensively for a bit. "You do seem like you could use an assistant," he allows.

I chuckle at the idea. "How so?" I ask curiously.

"Well, you work a lot, right?" he asks.

I nod in agreement.

"So you could probably use someone to like, do your grocery shopping, pick up your dry cleaning, that sort of thing, right?"

"Yeah, I guess I could," I admit. "Think you're up for the job?"

Hunter, uncharacteristically breaking his carefully cool façade, grins eagerly. "Hell, yes!" he exclaims. "When can I move in?"

"Whoa there," I caution him. "Don't you want to talk to your parents first?"

"Sera, please," he scoffs. "I'm twenty-three. I don't need their permission."

I suppress a smile. "All righty then," I allow. "I'm going back later this evening. You can join me. Or I can come pick you up next weekend." But I already know which he'll choose.

Hunter has regained his carefully indifferent pretense. "Might as well go with you when you're already here," he replies with a shrug.

I bite back a laugh. "It's a plan, then."

∾

WHEN I TELL MY MOTHER THAT AFTERNOON SHE IS, UNDERSTANDABLY, skeptical of the arrangement, but true to her word that she wants to support me on my terms, she doesn't say much. Neither does my father, to whom I say very little as he helps Hunter load his few possessions into my car. Thankfully, I somehow manage to avoid meeting Barb, Hunter's mother. I've been through enough lately, and that's not really something I'm ready to do yet.

Hunter and I banter about the various things to do in the area, though he's clearly already got his own agenda.

When we get home, I get him settled in the guest bedroom, give him a key, and show him how to work the security system.

As I go to sleep that night, I'm hopeful for the first time in a while that the future holds something besides the painful recovery I know I still have before me. But it's not enough to stave off the nightmares.

I wake in the dark, panting, a garbled cry dying on my lips. I hold my breath for a moment, hoping I didn't wake Hunter. But his room is far enough away that, after a few moments, I decide he likely didn't hear me. As my dreams, and my reality, catch up with me, I roll over and cry myself back to sleep.

SIXTEEN

s the week dawns once more, I hunker down into work but try to keep more reasonable hours. Hunter seems to be just fine on his own, but I don't want him to feel like I've forgotten him. He's surprisingly easy to live with, and just as he promised, has done all manner of chores and errands from go. So I'm thankful when, early in the week, I have an idea that takes practically no effort to implement, that I'm hoping will make him feel like it's really his home.

There are four bedrooms in the condo — my own, my office, the guest bedroom now occupied by Hunter, and the nearly empty fourth bedroom. I clear the few boxes and forgotten pieces of exercise equipment out of the last room, leaving it bare. And the next day at lunch I go to an art supply store and pick up a range of canvases, brushes, and paints.

It takes some stealth to get it all into the room without Hunter noticing. I have to wait until he disappears on Wednesday evening to grab a few things from the convenience store down the block to set it all up. Once he's back, I giddily lead him upstairs.

"Dude, you're like totally freaking out," Hunter laughs as I pull him toward the room.

"You will be too," I singsong at him as I open the door.

He walks in, his mouth dropping open instantly at the spread of supplies. "This is for me?" he asks, clearly astounded.

"You deserve a place to work," I say, shrugging. "This is your studio now. Do whatever you want with it."

He looks at me skeptically over his shoulder. "Can I paint the walls?" he asks slyly.

I laugh. "Go for it," I reply. "This place could use some color."

Hunter smiles deviously. "Be careful what you wish for, Sera," he singsongs back at me.

It might be the first time he's joked with me, and I can't help but burst out laughing. And it feels damn good to really laugh again.

∽

But as it always seems, I'm abruptly brought back down to Earth on Thursday when Bryce calls. Reflexively, I answer, kicking myself almost immediately.

"Hello?" I say tentatively, hoping maybe it was an accidental butt-dial.

"Hi Sera, it's Bryce Hoyt," he responds.

As if I could ever forget his deep, calm, and sexy voice.

"I know. Hi, Bryce, how are you?" I ask warily.

"Good," he replies. "I'm cleared to resume normal life, mostly. So I've moved back to my own place."

My heart sinks. His apartment is barely ten minutes from mine. Knowing he'll be that close again has my pulse racing, and not necessarily in a good way.

"Oh?" I ask as calmly as I'm able. "Does that mean you're going back to work?"

"Yes, though only part time at first," he responds. "On a trial basis."

"That's good?" I hazard. Something inside me snaps at the superficiality of the conversation. "I'm sorry, why are you calling, Bryce?"

He doesn't respond immediately, and my throat starts to constrict in a way that's becoming all too familiar.

"I was hoping we could talk this weekend. Face to face," he explains.

I note that he doesn't say why, and it makes me wonder just enough.

"Okay," I agree. "When and where?"

"My place okay? Saturday morning? Does nine a.m. work for you?" he offers.

"Yes. I'll see you then," I agree. "Bye, Bryce."

"Bye, Sera."

∽

Needless to say, the rest of Thursday and Friday are torture. I barely sleep on Friday night. Dressing on Saturday morning, I feel like a shell of myself. I pull on a dark, woolen sweater dress over black tights. Dark clothes for a dark mood. I don't bother dolling up, but as I come across the diamond earrings Bryce gave me, I can't help putting them on. It's a small bit of what we were that I can cling to through whatever happens.

By the time I get to Bryce's door, my feet are practically leaden, every step requiring immense effort, as if my whole body is protesting against the emotional torture of seeing him again.

I knock dully, and he answers, wearing jeans and a white T-shirt, looking wholly like himself again. Even the muscle definition in his arms has returned, his short hair lengthened ever so slightly.

"Thanks for coming," he greets me, stepping aside to let me in.

I stop awkwardly just inside the door, afraid it's presumptuous to do anything else.

He walks around me, but stops and turns back, as if he were about to extend an invitation to sit down. But something halts him, and he pauses, too close, looking down at me.

His right hand reaches up and, before I can even register, fingers the diamond stud in my left ear. He stares at it intensely for a moment. Frozen in place, all I can do is watch him, his beautiful face so close, his blue eyes dark and penetrating. I wonder suddenly if he recognizes them, if he's remembered, and my breath catches in my throat.

But too soon, he shakes himself, stepping back. "Those are beautiful earrings," he remarks nervously. "They suit you."

And I can only think of the last time he noticed them, when he told me he wanted to see me wearing nothing but these earrings.

But when he looks at me again there is no hint of recognition, none of the fire that was there that last time. And I'm still too frozen to respond.

He gestures to the living room. "Please, sit down."

He seats himself in the leather armchair, so I take the couch next to him. But far enough away for comfort.

"You look well," I offer. "How is your rehab going?"

He runs a hand over his hair, and I have to look away. Some gestures are just so *him* it hurts. Not just because of the reminder of what he was, but that damn undying hope that, if he still acts like himself, that his memories are still in there somewhere.

"Cognitive skills are all back," he responds. "But zero on the memory front." And there it is. A month later. Confirmation that my Bryce hasn't come back and may never.

"What's the prognosis?" I can't help asking.

Bryce shrugs. "It's a coin toss. But they're concerned that *nothing* has come back yet," he admits. "Usually *something* does. And then piece by piece, more will."

"What does that mean? Is it all just … gone?" I press.

Bryce leans forward. "They won't say that," he replies carefully. "But Mom, Char, Em, you … I see the disappointment on all your faces. And for that reason alone I won't give up."

"What about Madison? Does she seem disappointed?" I ask pointedly.

Bryce's eyebrows shoot up. "Ah. So you know about Madison."

I roll my eyes. "Of course I do," I reply tersely. "And if you don't remember anything before sixteen months ago, then your brain still thinks you've been dating her for the last three years."

Bryce runs a hand over his mouth. "Yes, it does. And not just my brain. There are still feelings there," he admits.

I huff a joyless laugh. "Good ones?" I ask sarcastically.

"Mixed ones," Bryce allows. "And if I'm being honest, Sera, while I can't remember you, when I look at you…" He trails off, but he has my full attention now.

I press my lips together, not trusting myself to speak.

"There are feelings there too. But without the memories, it makes no sense. It's like trying to grab smoke."

And I know what he's saying. "But you do have memories of Madison," I respond with a snort. "Except the ones that caused you to break up with her in the first place."

Bryce spreads his hands out in front of him. "I can't help that," he replies. "And I don't know what will happen with my memories. All I can do is react based on what I know."

I nod, understanding. He's going back to Madison. And I don't even need to ask if she'll take him back. She will. The conniving, superficial, gold-digging bitch.

"You're a good man," I respond, looking down into my hands, avoiding my eyes. "Better than she deserves." Tears well in my eyes and I feel so sick it's all I can do to sit here, still and quiet.

"I'm sorry," Bryce says softly. "I don't want to hurt you. But I'd rather regret doing something than doing nothing."

My eyes snap to his, unable to believe that I just heard those words come out of his mouth. The very words I spoke to him when I went after Alessandro.

Insane laughter bubbles out of me. I shake my head, a few tears spilling out. "I'm sorry," I gasp, reining myself in. When I've managed to collect myself, I look back up at him. "The universe has a very sick sense of humor. Why did you ask me to come here, Bryce? Because I know it wasn't to tell me that you're getting back together with Madison. I mean, obviously you are, but I'm sure that's not why you wanted to talk to me."

"No," he agrees. "And after telling you that, I feel like a complete asshole for even asking, but I was hoping we could be friends."

I twist my fingers together, choosing my words carefully.

"You're not an asshole," I respond. "But I'm not capable of being your friend right now, Bryce. Please understand that, while the thought of losing you is unbearable, to me it feels like I already have. And to be reminded of that over and over, well, I'm just not that strong. I've been through too much."

Bryce nods understandingly. "I went through your file," he admits. "And I know that what I'm asking isn't fair." But he looks at me pleadingly nonetheless, and I nearly crack.

"I think it would be better for both of us," I reply. "If I weren't around, pining for what was. Because I can't look at you without thinking about it. Not after everything that we've gone through. Everything that we were to each other."

"I'm sorry, Sera," he says again, and I know he means it. "I wish I remembered."

I laugh, wiping at the tears that have slipped over my cheeks. "Me too," I agree. "But you don't. And that's not your fault. But I'm at my limit, and I need to safeguard my heart again. I'm sorry I'm not stronger."

He looks like he wants to reach for me, but he stills himself. "I may not remember anything," he murmurs, "but I do know you're incredibly strong. What you've been through most people wouldn't survive. So I understand that you're doing what you need to do to."

"Thank you," I respond, rising from the couch. "Take care of yourself, Bryce, and be happy."

He follows me to the door. I pause at the threshold, looking back up at him. And I just can't help myself.

I slip against him, and before my arms are even around him, he's already wrapped his around me. While we hold each other tightly, I take one last, deep breath of his evergreen summer scent, listening to the steady and familiar beat of his heart under my cheek. And for one small moment, I'm home in his arms. But it's not long before I remember that he's not my home anymore. And the reminder that this man doesn't remember me, is just humoring me, causes me to extract myself, finally.

I drink in one last look at his face. "Goodbye, Bryce," I whisper.

"Bye, Sera," he murmurs.

And before I can do anything stupid, I go.

⌒

Unfortunately, Hunter is in the living room when I get home, and there's no hiding my agony.

"Hey, Sera," he greets me.

"Hi," I reply tersely.

He studies my face for longer than I'm comfortable with. "Come on," he says, gesturing for me to follow him.

I contemplate protesting but decide I just don't have the energy. So I follow him up the stairs and into his studio.

Nothing could have prepared me for what I find. He must have bought more paint. Every canvas, every inch of wall is covered. And it's unbelievably gorgeous. It's a dark mass of blacks, blues, and purples with the occasional spots of bright color here and there. There are some recognizable motifs — a woman and a child, holding each other crying; an old man playing chess — all connected by abstract whorls, matrices, and lines.

It's a story of human emotion in three-hundred-sixty degrees, I realize as he shuts the door. I turn on Hunter, who is gazing at a portion of the painted wall as if it's nothing at all.

"This is unbelievable," I whisper. "You did all this in two days?"

Hunter shrugs and smiles. "I haven't really painted in a long time. I forgot how much fun it is," he replies nonchalantly.

I approach one of the canvases. Its colors are brighter than most of the surrounding areas. It speaks of warmth, love. And it breaks my heart.

"We're going to need more paint," I mutter.

Hunter nods. "We can paint it all over tomorrow and I can start again," he suggests.

I turn to him and shake my head. "No," I reply. "We're going to paint the rest of the house."

Hunter raises an eyebrow. "We?"

"If you'll teach me how to paint," I reply. "Yes. We."

He looks at me thoughtfully. "Painting, art, is literally pouring your soul out onto something," he says slowly. "Are you ready for that?"

I infer from the question that he understands how I'm feeling much more than I gave him credit for.

I close my eyes, roiling in the swell of emotion flowing through me. "I think it's exactly what I need."

∾

ON SUNDAY AFTERNOON, WHILE HUNTER AND I PAINT THE LIVING ROOM WALLS, my phone rings. Since I'm completely covered in paint spatter, it takes me a moment to find something to wipe my hands clean with before answering.

I don't actually make it in time but notice it was Allie, so I call her back.

"Hey, Allie, sorry I haven't called in a while," I greet her once she answers. I realize it's been a couple of weeks since we've spoken, which isn't usual for us.

"Oh, Sera, it's all good," she squeals.

548

"Whoa, you sound happy," I reply with a laugh. "What's up?"

"I'm pregnant, Sera," she shouts happily.

"Omigod!" I screech. "Congratulations, Allie!"

"Eeeee!" she squeals back. We both dissolve into giggles.

"This calls for a celebration. I'm taking everyone out to dinner tonight!" I exclaim.

"Yes!" Allie agrees.

"Great, I just need to get all this paint off of me," I reply, coming down off of the high of the news.

"Paint?" Allie asks, confused.

"I'll explain later. Um, Hunter will be coming with me too, which I'll also explain later," I reply.

"Okay, well, let me know when you're ready," she replies.

"Will do," I agree. "Bye."

"Bye, babe!"

I hang up, staring at my phone. The initial shock worn off, I realize it's going to be an evening of watching a happy, married couple celebrating their joyous news. And while I'm thrilled for them, it's like the final death of whatever hope had remained. Like embers bloomed back into fire, my heart burns with love lost. But I have to lock it up, cut off the oxygen. And safeguard my heart from the flames.

PART II

"Ever has it been that love knows not its own depth until the hour of separation."
—Khalil Gibran

NINE MONTHS LATER

SEVENTEEN

The small, pink fingers wrap around my thumb. I marvel at his tiny strength, my heart overflowing with love.

"Look how hard he's squeezing!" I squeal, trying to balance my phone in the other hand and get Allie's attention.

"God, Sera, I think you have more videos of our kid than we do," Allie replies drily, coming over to observe baby Brian's tiny fist gripping me tightly. "He's only four weeks old. Too much radiation isn't good for him."

I scoff at her, even though I know she's just teasing. "Oh, please, it's a *cell-phone*," I reply. "I'm not taking him on a walk through Chernobyl."

Brian squeals, drawing my attention back to him, and I can't help but make silly faces until I think he's smiling. At this age it's so hard to tell. But I soak up every moment of it.

"So this is pretty much how I spend my week," Allie laughs. "How was yours?"

I glance up at her. "I saw Alessandro," I admit. "We had lunch."

Allie's eyebrows shoot up. "Well, that's something. It's been a few months, hasn't it? How's he doing?" she asks curiously.

I shrug. "Better," I respond. "Since he's taken Buone Case back over, he's got them on track again. He's back in his own place now too."

"He didn't ask you out again, did he?" she asks.

I huff a small laugh. "No. I think he's gotten the message," I reply.

"Who's gotten what message?" David asks, entering the room. He immediately starts cooing over Brian, though, and I doubt he'd hear a response even if I gave it.

I slide back onto the couch behind me and let him pick up the baby and take him to be changed. Being an aunt comes with the privilege of non-mandatory diaper changing services. And, you know, getting to sleep through the night.

"I swear, he's got the attention span of a gnat these days," Allie jokes as David leaves the room.

"Can you blame him? I dare anyone not to be distracted by that kid's cuteness," I reply.

Allie rolls her eyes. "So you and Alessandro, you're really just going to be friends?" Allie presses.

"Yes, Allie, I'm really not looking for anything right now, and our differences were way too fundamental," I reiterate for the thousandth time.

"If you say so," she replies, shrugging. "But I think it's about time you got back in the dating pool, one way or another."

I press my lips together impatiently. "Well, I'm going out with Em tonight, so maybe someone will manage to woo me before I get stinking drunk," I reply wryly.

Allie shoots me a dirty look. "Maybe ease off the booze and someone will *want* to woo you," she shoots back.

"Ah, see, there's the crux," I reply. "Maybe I don't want to be wooed. I'm doing fine on my own, thank you very much."

"You're not on your own. Your twenty-four-year-old brother lives with you," she reminds me. "Which, by the way, is also a huge deterrent for any would-be-wooers."

"Is 'wooers' a word?" I ask contemplatively. "It doesn't sound like a word."

"Deflecting," Allie says accusingly.

"Oh, look, a shiny object," I say, rising from the couch and grabbing my keys. "Gotta go, Allie!"

"Cute, real cute, Sera," she calls after me.

I wave dismissively over my shoulder. "See you for dinner tomorrow," I reply, then call down the hall. "Bye, David!"

"Bye, Sera!" he calls back.

And I leave before Allie can continue telling me how to run my love life. Or lack thereof.

❧

I'M TWO DRINKS IN, HAPPILY BUZZED, AND WELL ON MY WAY TO STINKING drunk when Emily finally finds me at the bar on Capitol Hill.

"Hey, stranger," she greets me, wrapping me in a hug. "What's it been, like a month?" She slides onto the stool next to me.

"I've had a cute baby to fawn over, so sue me," I reply with a smile. "Wanna see pictures?"

Emily laughs. "Maybe later," she replies. "How are you?"

I shrug. "Okay. Work's great. Hunter is really coming along. The other designers say he's got real talent," I reply.

"Hmm," she replies noncommittally. By the look on her face I know she's in Allie's boat, wishing my summary included a man.

"How about you? How are things going with John?" I hazard, trying to remember the name of the guy she was dating last time we met up.

"*Jack* and I are actually still seeing each other," she corrects. "Still pretty casually. It's only been a couple months."

"Sometimes that's all it takes," I respond, memories unwillingly pushing their way through my defenses. I shove them back, and we continue to make idle conversation for a while.

After another hour and a few more drinks, though, I can't stem the tide any longer.

"So how is your brother doing?" I ask, doing my best impression of barely interested. But Emily isn't fooled.

"He remembered a few more things," she admits. "But nothing major." I shrug, unsurprised. The few updates Emily has shared have all been the same. He remembered some paperwork or other that he'd stashed during the missing memory months. Or a movie he'd seen. Or the name of a client he'd spoken to back then but not since. But never anything about me. About us.

"Well, sounds like he's doing pretty all right then," I grouse. I hate talking about this, which is why I usually avoid it. I must be in a more masochistic mood than usual.

"While we're on the subject, there's something else I've been meaning to tell you," Emily admits nervously. Something about her tone makes me down the rest of my margarita in one go.

"Go ahead," I reply warily.

Emily gives me a brief disapproving look. I suppress my annoyance, knowing deep down all the concerns about my drinking are not wrong, but too ruined to care.

"Bryce and Madison are getting married," she says quickly, flinching as the words tumble out.

My throat goes dry and my stomach churns. I fight a short battle with the urge but realize quickly that I'm going to lose.

"I think I'm going to be sick," I admit, bolting for the bathroom. I barely make it into the tiny two-stall bathroom, tumbling into the closest stall as the contents of my stomach reappear. I hear Emily come in behind me, and I feel the cool touch of her fingers against my neck as she gathers my hair in her hands, holding it back as I retch into the toilet.

When I'm finally spent, I sink onto the dirty, disgusting floor next to the toilet, a testament to the painful oblivion her revelation has caused. Emily crouches next to me, stroking my hair gently as I sob.

"I'm so sorry, Sera," she says soothingly. "I knew it would be hard, but I thought you'd moved past it. You barely ever ask about him anymore."

I shake my head violently. "I don't want to talk about it," I reply.

"Please, Sera," Emily begs. "I had to tell you. I need your help. He won't listen to me and you *know* Madison. She doesn't care for him, at least not more than share cares about his money, his reputation. She's manipulated him into this. We can't let—"

"*Stop*!" I screech, throwing my hands over my ears. "I'm sorry I asked. Because I don't really want to know. Any of it." I rise from the floor, swaying dangerously.

"Okay," she relents. "I'm sorry. Let's just get you to my place so you can sleep it off, okay?"

And I want to protest, but my world is still spinning, in so many ways. So I grunt my assent and let her lead me out of the bar, into a cab, and ultimately onto her couch. Where I promptly surrender to blissful nothingness.

∾

I WAKE THE NEXT MORNING TO THE SMELL OF COFFEE. COTTON-MOUTHED AND heavy-headed, I rise gingerly, wincing against the pain.

Emily drops into the armchair next to me, handing me a large cup of dark coffee. I guzzle it gratefully.

"I'm sorry about last night," she apologizes softly. I look up at her. Her hair is wet, and she's wearing a matched pink sweat suit. And she looks as contrite as I've ever seen her.

"No, I'm sorry," I admit. "I reacted poorly."

Emily laughs. "That's putting it mildly," she replies.

"When?" I ask softly.

Emily is silent for a moment, and I know she's debating whether or not to answer.

"October twelfth," she finally replies.

My head snaps up in disbelief. That's barely more than two months away. But it's the exact date that horrifies me.

"They're getting married on the anniversary of the fucking attack that did this to him?" I ask incredulously. "On my *birthday*, for fuck's sake?"

Emily cringes and nods. "I pointed both of those things out in front of Madison. They picked it because of the attack. Supposedly to celebrate that he survived it, to turn it to something good," Emily spits. "But when she learned it was also your birthday..." Emily's hands curl into fists. "The bitch looked *smug*, Sera. I wanted to punch her."

I have no words, I simply shake my head, looking grimly into the dregs of my coffee cup. Eventually, I say the only thing I can. "He's his own man, Em. If he wants to marry her, what could I possibly say to change his mind?" I look down at my crumpled, smelly dress. "I need a shower."

Emily gestures to the bathroom. "Have at," she replies morosely. "I'll dig out some clothes for you."

"Just as long as it's not a matching purple sweat suit," I tease her.

She sticks her tongue out at me as I head to the bathroom.

The heat of the shower goes a long way to unraveling my tightly coiled nerves. And as I dry off, I spot the powder blue sweat suit, matching panties and all, that Emily left on the counter. I burst out laughing.

"Emily, you're a nutcase!" I call out. I hear her laughter floating under the door from the kitchen. I dress quickly, throwing my dirty clothes into a plastic bag, and emerge back into the living room.

But Emily's not alone. Bryce sits on the couch next to her. The sight of him is like a fist to the gut. He looks beyond handsome, bulkier than when I last saw him, his chestnut hair longer and curling around his collar just as it did when we first met. When his eyes meet mine, it roots me to the spot. My eyes flick to Emily, trying to convey my terror. But Emily looks so guilty that I know she planned this. And that she's not about to rescue me. She disappears back into the kitchen, leaving us alone.

"Hey, Sera," Bryce greets me softly.

"Hello," I reply quietly. I drop the plastic bag next to the couch and slink into the kitchen. I get right up next to Emily and poke her, hard.

"Sorry," she whispers. "I told you, I'm desperate."

I shake my head violently. "You can't do this to me, Em," I whisper back.

"Please," she begs. "Just try?" She looks so miserable, despite the angry pit in my stomach I shrug noncommittally, giving the tiniest of nods. She wraps her arms around me briefly before turning back to the food she's preparing.

I return to the living room, taking a seat on the small couch with Bryce, but as far into the corner as I can, so there's at least some distance between us.

"I made waffles," Emily announces, hopping up from her chair and waltzing into the kitchen.

Bryce gives me a side glance. "You didn't know I'd be here, did you?" he asks shrewdly.

I shake my head mutely, a thousand emotions swirling inside me. I'm not sure I could hold a waffle down right now if I wanted to, so when Emily returns with a plate, I surreptitiously slide it onto the coffee table, untouched.

"I'm going to get more coffee," I announce, already unable to keep still in his presence. "Anybody want?"

Emily shakes her head, but Bryce puts down his plate and beats me to it. "I've got it," he replies, plucking my mug from my hands and striding easily into the kitchen. He returns shortly, handing me back a full mug. "Cream, no sugar."

I stare up at him, open mouthed. Emily looks at me questioningly.

"You … you remember how I take my coffee," I stutter.

Emily's mouth drops open.

Bryce looks unnerved. "I guess I do," he replies. "I didn't even think about it, I just did it." He shrugs and returns to his waffle, but the atmosphere in the room has changed to tense silence.

My eyes drift to the balcony, remembering the last time the three of us where here together and things were tense. I put my nearly full coffee mug down, unable to handle it any longer. "I should go," I say quickly, rising.

"Oh no, please, don't," Emily begs.

"Really, I have a lot to do today," I lie. "But thanks for breakfast."

"I hope you're not going on my account," Bryce pipes up. "I didn't mean to—"

"No, really, it's okay," I interrupt. "But hey, congratulations. Um. On your engagement."

Bryce blushes and I pause awkwardly.

"Yeah, so, see ya."

I grab my purse and the plastic bag and bolt out the door as fast as I can walk. Running seems too obvious. But before I can make it to the stairs outside her door, I sense someone behind me even before the hand grabs my wrist. Large and warm, I know who it is without turning around.

"Hey," Bryce calls, pulling me to a stop. "I'm sorry. I didn't know Emily hadn't told you I was coming over."

I pull my arm out of his grasp, wrapping my arms around myself self-consciously. "It's okay," I assure him. "I just really need to go."

"Sera, if you knew me as well as you once said you did, you know I can tell when people are lying," he teases.

I smile vaguely, not taking the bait. "Was it your idea or hers?" I ask curiously. "Breakfast, I mean."

"Em's," he admits. "She said you wanted to talk to me."

And before I can stop it, a sarcastic laugh slips through my lips.

"Guess not, then."

"She wanted me to talk to you," I clarify. "To talk you out of marrying Madison, more specifically."

Realization dawns on Bryce's face. "Ah," he says. "Yeah. She's, uh, not too happy about that." He scratches the back of his head self-consciously.

I shrug. "Well, you're a big boy," I reply. "I'm sure you can handle her. And I should really get home."

"Yeah, of course, sorry. Good seeing you, Sera," he replies. His eyes search mine for a moment, and I'm almost distracted out of leaving. He too, looks lost in thought.

"Bye, Bryce," I say before I totally lose my nerve. I turn toward the stairs.

"Bye, gorgeous," he calls after me.

I stop short, whirling around to face him.

He looks as shocked as I am. "I'm sorry, I don't know why I … that was totally…" He presses a hand to his head.

"Are you okay?" I ask, taking a tentative step toward him.

He rubs at his temple for a moment. "I'm fine," he replies. "I just don't know why I said that."

"You used to call me that," I reply simply.

He looks down at me, clearly still struggling. "Then it was probably just a reflex," he replies, clearly embarrassed. I blush and look away, reading between the lines — he doesn't want me to think it meant anything and get my hopes up.

"Yeah, probably," I agree. "No worries. I'll, um … bye." I wave nervously and disappear down the stairs as fast as I can, my heart hammering in my chest.

∾

When I tell Allie the story at dinner, she's understandably shocked.

"Holy *shit*, Sera," she gasps. "His memories are coming back."

I shake my head vehemently. "After all this time? No. Nuh-uh. It's exactly as he said. A reflex. It's been ten months, Al, he's not going to start remembering now," I insist.

Allie looks at me skeptically. "Who are you trying to convince, sister, me or you?" she asks, smirking.

I glare at her. "I'm not putting myself through this," I insist. "I'm steering clear of all things Hoyt until after Bryce is married. I can't do this, Allie."

"Geez, okay, okay," Allie mutters. She gives me a sad look. "I guess I get it."

"Thank you," I reply.

But she's not completely wrong. I repeat the story to myself over and over again. Because eventually I will believe it.

EIGHTEEN

On Monday night, Hunter and I sit quietly at the table eating dinner. I'm so lost in my own thoughts, unable to stop replaying the conversation with Bryce in my head, that I don't notice Hunter openly staring at me.

"You okay?" he finally presses gently.

My eyes flick up to his. "No," I admit, dropping my fork. "I saw Bryce yesterday." I'd long since confessed the full situation to Hunter. It'd be impossible not to, having lived with him the last nine months, as well as working at the same company for most of that time.

"Shit," he replies.

I chuckle. "Yeah, that about sums it up," I agree.

"What happened?" he asks simply.

I shift uncomfortably in my chair but decide to just go with it. So I tell him what happened.

"Hmm," is his only response.

"You've got to give me more than that," I reply drily.

Hunter finishes his pasta and pushes his plate away. As he's wont to do, he sits silently for a while.

"We're more alike than you know," he finally replies, leaning back in his chair and meeting my curious gaze. "I have to protect myself too."

My brows scrunch together. "I don't understand," I admit.

Hunter sighs. "At this point it's hard to believe Bryce is actually getting better," Hunter clarifies. "So it's safest to protect yourself. Because even if he is, he's still getting married. So I get it. I get why you're holding back."

"What do you hold back?" I press curiously. I suddenly realize in the months Hunter has lived with me, he's never said a word about dating anyone. Perhaps he's as closed off as I once was. Or, am now, as it were.

An anxious, determined look spreads over Hunter's face. "You can't tell Dad."

I laugh. "Oh, Hunter. You know I can barely stand the man. I've only seen him twice since you moved here, and only because he insisted," I reply. "I hope you know you can trust me."

It kind of stings, thinking he might not, after all this time. And while we haven't exactly stayed up late talking about life and love and braiding each other's hair, the quiet bond we've shared painting and repainting the condo ad nauseum has been special to me. And so necessary for me to deal with everything. But maybe we're not as close as I thought we were.

"I know," he replies quietly. "There are just things I don't tell anyone. Well, one thing."

My finely-honed intuition on when to stay quiet tingles. So I do. And as usual, after a stretch, it pays dividends.

"I'm gay, Sera." He studiously avoids my gaze.

And I find myself unsurprised. I'd thought perhaps he was asexual, but it never really mattered to me one way or the other. I'm certainly the last person to criticize anyone's love life, or lack thereof.

"Are you seeing anyone?" I ask nonchalantly.

Hunter looks at me. And I almost laugh. His expressions are all so similar, but I've come to know the subtle changes in his features well. The ever-so-slight arch of his left eyebrow betrays his shock.

"Oh, come on. It's 2019. So you're gay, who cares?"

"Dad would," he insists. "And there's already enough crap between us."

But his protests are a diversion. I don't miss that he didn't answer my first question.

"Who is he?" I push.

The corners of Hunter's mouth twitch as he rises and collects our dishes, taking them into the kitchen and loading them into the dishwasher. When he's done, he starts heading upstairs.

"Goodnight, Sera," he calls without turning around.

"I'm gonna find out!" I call after him.

I can hear him chuckling as he disappears into his studio. And I can't help laughing a little myself. And it snaps me out of my funk, if only a bit.

∾

I watch Hunter closely over the week that follows, but he's either the stealthiest motherfucker on the planet, or he's really not seeing anyone. I decide to follow him out of the house the following Saturday in one last-ditch effort to catch him at it. Even though I know I shouldn't. But I just can't help myself.

As I follow him into a busy coffee shop, I'm distracted out of my pursuit as I run smack into Alessandro.

"Serafina!" he exclaims in surprise, pulling back the lidded cup in his hand to keep it from sloshing. "*Ciao*. I didn't expect to see you again so soon." He gives me his most charming crooked smile, and I have to laugh.

"*Ciao*," I reply. "*Come stai?*"

"*Bene*," he replies. "May I join you for a coffee?"

"Oh, but I don't want to keep you. It looked like you were leaving," I offer.

In truth, I'm not sure seeing him so often is a great idea. While he didn't press last time, I know he still holds out hope that he can win me back. It's admirable, if not a little annoying. And a good reminder why I don't go out very often. It's too easy to run into people you aren't expecting to see.

"Not at all," he assures me. "I have no plans today, just enjoying the beautiful weather. We must soak it up while we can."

I laugh. That is the Seattle way. We are hermits nine months of the year, sunflowers the other three.

"Okay," I relent. "Let me get a cappuccino and I'll meet you outside." As I approach the counter I also realize I'm starving, so I add a breakfast sandwich onto my order. Once I have my food and coffee, I wander onto the patio, looking for Alessandro. I spot him on the street side, people-watching.

I take him in for a moment as he's distracted. He really is every bit as handsome as he ever was, his dark brown hair now once again perfectly coifed in that messily styled manner, his beard tamed into a perfectly groomed accent to his sharp jaw and straight nose. Truly, he's the epitome of the gorgeous Italian man. Stubbornness and borderline narcissism included. Shaking my head, I proceed to the table to join him.

As I sit eating my breakfast, talking shop with him in the warm, sunny morning, I'm reminded though that sometimes it *is* nice to just enjoy someone's company on a beautiful day. It's been a long time since I've done something so normal. And, thankfully, he seems settled into the notion that a relationship of any kind is off the table, for now at least.

He's telling me a story about his new assistant when he stops cold, his eyes narrowing at something in the distance.

"Serafina," he says with a caution in his voice. "Are you speaking to the giant?"

I'm so taken aback by his question that I can't help but turn and follow his gaze. And I freeze when I see that Bryce is, in fact, approaching, walking hand in hand with Madison, his perfect five-foot-six, slim, blond beauty queen of a fiancée. My breakfast churns uncomfortably in my stomach.

"Fuck, fuck, fuck," I whisper, whipping my head back around.

"I'll take that as a no," Alessandro replies drily. "Maybe if we just…"

"Sera?" Bryce's voice cuts across Alessandro's attempted avoidance.

I sigh one last silent *fuck* in my head before plastering a smile on my face and turning around.

"Bryce!" I exclaim with false enthusiasm. "And Madison." I nod curtly at her. I don't miss that she wraps her arm possessively around his waist.

Bryce's eyes shift to Alessandro and his whole countenance changes. He narrows his eyes, his jaw clenched, his hand curling into a fist at his side. Alessandro looks at me confused, and the question in his eyes is clear, as I'm thinking it too. *He can't remember me, can he?*

"Bryce, this is my friend Alessandro Giordano," I say. "Alessandro, this is Bryce Hoyt, and his fiancée Madison Connolly."

Madison looks smug and well pleased that I know of their betrothal. She extends a hand to Alessandro, batting her eyelashes.

"*Piacere*," she says sweetly.

"*Piacere*," he replies genially, but uncharacteristically doesn't offer anything further. He looks to Bryce.

"I'm pretty sure we've met before," Bryce says thinly.

Neither man offers a handshake after Bryce's icy acknowledgement. Madison gives him a stern look, but he ignores her, keeping his eyes fixed angrily on Alessandro.

"Well, it was so nice running into you, but we have to be going," Madison declares, awkwardly pushing Bryce onward. "Ta!"

I flutter my fingers at their receding backs. "Bye now," I murmur.

"What the hell was that?" Alessandro asks, voicing my exact thoughts.

I look back at him, bemused. "I have no clue," I admit. "That was bizarre. He can't possibly remember you. He doesn't even remember *me*."

Alessandro looks at me appraisingly. "Are you sure about that?" he finally asks. "Hate is a very strong emotion. Sometimes stronger than love. It can be very hard to forget."

"Oh, please, Bryce never hated you," I respond reflexively. But suddenly I'm not so sure. "Did he?"

Alessandro laughs mirthlessly. "Yes, undoubtedly," he replies. "He made that quite clear."

I raise my eyebrows, but I don't ask. "I don't want to know," I respond. "And it doesn't matter anyway. It's all water under the bridge."

Alessandro shrugs. "If you say so, *bella*," he murmurs. He looks at his watch. "In any case, it was lovely seeing you, but I must get going."

We clean up our table and head out. And with a friendly embrace, we go our separate ways. Though I'm still bewildered and disturbed. But moreover,

I'm concerned that we may have upset Bryce, so, against my previous decision, I decide to call Emily and see if she can shed any light on it.

"He what?" she asks incredulously after I've explained what happened. "That's very weird. And very un-Bryce. He's never rude. To anyone. Even if they deserve it. *Especially* if they deserve it."

"Exactly!" I exclaim, satisfied that she's put to words what I for some reason couldn't. "I mean, maybe Alessandro is right? Maybe it's easier to remember someone you hate?"

"That makes no sense," Emily replies. "But I'll see if I can find out what it was all about without making it worse."

"Yes, please," I respond. "I may not be up for being bosom buddies with Bryce, but I certainly don't want to upset him, either."

"I'll let you know," she responds.

I thank her and hang up, still unable to shake my unease as I return home.

When I get back in the condo, Hunter is waiting for me with a grin.

"Boy, you must have gotten really lost after I ditched you at the coffee shop," he remarks airily.

Snapped out of my reverie, I laugh heartily. "You're a sneaky bastard, I'll give you that," I reply.

"What were you hoping to find?" he asks.

I shrug. "I'm curious, I guess. I just wanted to know if you're seeing someone or not. And obviously I'm not as stealthy as I thought I was," I allow. And I'm silently thankful that Hunter doesn't seem upset.

"In all fairness, I did dodge a direct question. I was practically begging to be followed," he responds.

"I take it then that there is a special someone?" I ask.

Hunter blushes, confirming my suspicions.

"You should bring him around sometime, then. I'd love to meet him."

"Okay, maybe I will," he replies cryptically before heading upstairs.

My curiosity about Hunter's beau fades quickly, the bewilderment at today's encounter slipping back to the forefront of my mind, despite my best efforts.

❧

I DON'T GET RESPITE FROM MY CONCERNS UNTIL THE NEXT DAY WHEN EMILY calls back after lunch.

"Soooo, I talked to Bryce," she opens.

"And?" I press.

"He doesn't know why he reacted that way," she replies, clearly frustrated. "He didn't really want to talk about it much. All he said was, and I quote,

'There was just something about the guy that rubbed me the wrong way.' As if that explains everything."

"And it doesn't," I agree. "Alessandro was just sitting there. He hadn't even spoken a word before Bryce got his panties in a twist."

"The doctor talked to us about lingering reflexes," Emily offers. "Sometimes, they're just there. And they don't necessarily mean you'll remember why you speak or react a certain way."

If any of Bryce's behavior had stirred hope in me, it's crushed completely at her words. It's been my own mental justification, but to hear that the doctors agree it doesn't mean anything is a finality I wasn't prepared for. And it tells me that despite my determination to keep my heart locked away once more, I haven't been all that successful, because I'm disappointed.

"That's good to know," I answer edgily. "Thanks, Em."

"Sorry, Sera," she replies softly.

Closing my eyes, I focus on staying calm and logical. "There's nothing to be sorry for, Emily. I just wanted to make sure Bryce is okay," I say. It's not untrue. "Take care, okay? I'll talk to you later."

"You too," she responds, sounding wholly unconvinced. "Bye, Sera."

After I hang up, I realize quickly that it's going to be nearly impossible for me to turn my brain off. And I don't feel like painting. So I go to my other standby, and pull a bottle of whiskey out, settling into my favorite chair by the window wall to drown the memories. It takes a lot of alcohol, but eventually I get there. Not the best choice for a Sunday night, but I reason that the alternative is worse.

Later, as I stumble drunkenly to bed, I say a silent prayer that I figure out how to move past this. Before it kills me.

NINETEEN

On Monday night the universe flips the bird to my silent plea when, three glasses of wine into my new nightly drinking ritual, my doorbell rings.

Hunter is out doing god only knows who or what, so I'm left to stumble out of my chair and answer it. And I'm not pleased at what I find waiting on the other side of the door.

Madison stands on my doorstep in teetering heels and a tight, red dress that leaves little to the imagination, her blond hair piled carefully atop her annoyingly perfect head.

"I'm sorry, I don't think we placed an order for a conniving bitch," I say by way of greeting and dismissal, starting to swing the door closed.

Madison levels a glare at me and sticks her foot in the door, preventing me from slamming it in her face.

"If you care about Bryce at all, you'll want to listen to what I have to say," she snaps.

I pull the door open angrily. "And if you cared about Bryce, you'd leave him alone and go crawl back into whatever hole you crawled out of," I retort hotly.

Madison folds her arms across her chest smugly, still leaving her foot in the door. "I'm his *fiancée*," she reminds me. "You, on the other hand, are confusing him. He's a mess, no thanks to you and your boyfriend."

And despite myself, guilt weighs on me. "What do you mean, he's a mess?" I ask tensely, not even bothering to correct her about Alessandro.

"Seeing you two the other day, reacting the way he did, it bothered him so much he can't stop talking about it, thinking about it. He convinced something didn't heal properly, that he's having some sort of aftereffect that's going to give him an aneurysm or something," she spits angrily.

I narrow my eyes at her appraisingly. "You're not worried about Bryce," I reply accusingly. "This is about the wedding, isn't it?"

She throws her hands in the air. "Of course it's about the wedding," she says sharply. "He wants to *postpone* it, for fuck's sake! Until he's sure nothing is wrong. At least, that's what he says. But I think he's just waiting to remember something. And I am not going to—"

"What, let him out of your trap?" I cut her off with a laugh. "Of course not. Couldn't have him coming around and realizing you're only marrying him for his money."

"I'm not *only* marrying him for his money," she replies with deadly calm, leaning forward and lowering her voice. "You've fucked him, Sera. So you know how good he is. Why would I give that combination up?"

My palm itches with a desire to smack the smug smile off of the bitch's face. She's a special kind of fucked up to care more about her wedding than the health of the man she's marrying, not to say anything about his happiness. But tipsy as I am, I still rein myself in, knowing it will only hurt Bryce if we fight.

"Yes, I know how *good* Bryce is. In a way you never will. And I don't know how you found out where I live," I seethe through clenched teeth. "But get the fuck out of here and don't ever come back."

Madison straightens up, laying one last icy glare on me. "I'll go," she accedes. "But if you come near Bryce again it will be the last thing you ever do. You are not going to stop me from marrying him. Even if I have to force him down to the courthouse tomorrow."

I'm so disgusted I can barely look her in the eye without losing it. "Do you even love him?" I can't help asking.

And she laughs. The bitch *laughs*. "Who needs love when he's as rich and good looking as he is? And he's *so* eager to please. So don't even think about trying anything. I've got that man wrapped around my little finger, among other things," she says with an evil glint in her eye. "Just stay. The. Fuck. Away." She turns on her heel and marches down the hall.

I slam the door as hard as I can, rattling the frames on the walls. I walk back to the dining table where I'd placed my wine glass, gripping it nearly to the point of breaking as the anger boils over inside me. And before I know what I've done, I fling the glass into the kitchen, shattering it on the fridge, where the dark, red liquid drips ominously down the stainless steel.

I pace in front of the window wall angrily. A glance at the clock tells me it's too late to call Allie. And I decide immediately to stick to my first instinct and stop talking to Emily until this is all over. Because despite not wanting to give

Madison the satisfaction of knowing it, I just want to hide from all of them and wait for it all to pass me by.

But what I really want more than anything right now is to punch something. Even though it's after nine o'clock at night. There's only one place I can think of to do that. And maybe it'll be exactly what I need to exorcise my demons. Or exercise them. Either way is fine with me.

I don't bother cleaning up my mess. I simply grab my keys, wallet, and phone, calling for a cab on my way downstairs.

It's not until I'm dropped off in front of the gym where Bryce taught me self-defense that I realize this may have been a stupid, drunken idea. But somewhere deep inside I can't shake the feeling that this is where it started. Where he drew the line, asked that I choose him with all of me. And this might be where I can take that part of me back, so I can just get on with my life. It's worth a shot, anyway. And if it doesn't work, maybe I'll at least get out some frustration.

I take a deep breath and go in, striding confidently toward the guy behind the front desk. He's big and bulky and covered in tattoos, much the same as the few guys scattered around the gym.

"Hey," he greets me. "What can I do for you?"

I chew on my lip self-consciously. "I have to ask you for something. And it's going to be weird."

Turns out it wasn't so weird, and front desk guy has me set up in the room with the mats, a freestanding punching bag, and a pair of boxing gloves in no time. He leaves me to it with a grin and a shake of his head, and I wonder what kind of shit goes down here that he didn't even bat an eyelash at my request.

I throw my things into a corner and use a hair tie to pull back my long, wavy hair. I'm suddenly thankful I'd already changed for bed into capri yoga pants and a loose T-shirt.

I slip the gloves on, tightening the laces like he showed me, and square off in front of the massive black bag. I close my eyes and breathe deeply, picturing Madison's face. And I punch. And again. And again. Until I'm sweating and breathing heavily.

I step back to take a break. And once I've caught my wind, I let all the sorrow, all the angst, all the fear I've felt these last months pour out of me in an attack of such intensity that, were I in my right mind, would scare even me.

"Remind me never to piss you off."

I practically jump out of my skin, whirling around to the voice that came from the door. My jaw practically hits the floor when I see Bryce, leaning against the frame, the casual tone of his greeting betrayed by the tense set of his jaw, the downturn of his gorgeous mouth.

And I'm too tired, too emotional for this. "What the fuck are you doing here?" I sputter, still winded, ripping off the gloves.

Bryce pushes himself up, striding slowly toward me. "I could ask you the same thing. How do you even know about this place?" he asks. "You're not exactly their usual clientele."

I look at him, bewildered on so many levels. I shake my head, unable or unwilling to answer.

Thankfully, he doesn't press, but he looks at me silently for a full minute. "Madison came home angry tonight. And I got out of her that she went to see you for a little chat."

I snort derisively. "That's one way to put it," I scoff. "I'd call it delusional ranting threats from a scheming bitch."

He looks thoroughly confused and it makes me laugh.

"Did she tell you she just dropped by for tea and scones and to make sure my invitation to the wedding hadn't gotten lost in the mail?"

He stops in front of me, looking down at me disapprovingly. The proximity is more than I can handle, and my head swims.

"I don't know what happened between you two, and I don't really need to. I told her she had no right to disturb you. That you'd been through enough," he replies coolly.

"Damn fucking straight," I say emphatically, my anger clearing my senses. "But I didn't need you to track me down to make sure she didn't hurt my feelings. I'm a big girl. I'll get over it."

I make to step back, but he grabs my wrist, holding me in place. His tight grip betrays the emotion stirring under his cool exterior.

"Why here?" he demands. The intensity radiates from every pore of him, the heat from his fingers sizzling up my arm.

I want to ask him to stop touching me, but the masochist in me never wants it to end. I feel like I'm coming apart at the seams, and I can't stop it. Unable to rein it in, my composure finally slips.

"Because I'm torn in pieces again," I sob. "And this time I choose me. It's the only choice I have left."

His eyes go wide, staring into the distance, and his hand springs open. I pull my wrist to my chest, rubbing it with my other hand as if it could remove the effect he's had on me.

"Torn in pieces..." he mutters, his eyes glassy. He looks over at me, his eyes focusing rapidly. "I won't settle for anything less."

My heart stops in my chest and all the breath goes out of me. "Yes," I breathe. "That's what you said to me here. That if I chose you it had to be with all of me. That you wouldn't settle for anything less."

"Yes," he agrees, his stare going glassy again, his eyes unfocused. "I was teaching you to defend yourself." His eyes snap back again, and he steps forward, closing the distance between us. "Sera …"

Before I can even take a breath, his mouth is on mine, the familiar feel of his warm lips, the taste of his breath clouding my senses. I react instinctively, leaning into him. His hands find my hair, tugging the hair band out so he can run his fingers through the tangled waves.

It takes all of my strength to push him away. "No."

And my quiet protest causes a shift in him. "I'm sorry, I don't know why I…" he stutters and stops, clearly at a loss. Clearly horribly confused.

"It's just a reflex," I respond wryly. "It will pass."

He shakes his head. "No," he objects. "That was an actual memory." His eyes meet mine. "A complete one. But it's like … looking at a small piece of a big puzzle that isn't there." The sorrow in his voice practically incapacitates me.

And despite my own pain I find myself wanting to comfort him. But I remind myself he's not mine to comfort anymore. And despite coming into his first real memory of me in the ten months since his attack, it's one of the worst ones he could remember. Because it's a reminder of the day he thought I was still trying to dick him around, not realizing how much I was already in love with him. Not that I'm sure I realized it then, either.

"Go home," I respond dully. "Fuck your fiancée. It'll make you feel better. And forget about puzzles and memories. They'll just drive you mad." I grab my things from the corner and make for the door. Under my breath I mutter, "Trust me, I should know."

He huffs a sad laugh and I know he's heard me. But he doesn't try to stop me as I leave.

∾

THE NEXT NIGHT I GO TO ALLIE'S AFTER WORK, UNABLE TO BEAR THE THOUGHT of another miserable night of drinking. Plus, I figure Hunter will be happy to have the place to himself for a change.

And bouncing baby Brian on my lap is just about the only thing that's made me feel halfway normal in a while. I've finished catching Allie up on all the latest between tummy tickles and cooed adoration of Brian's cherubic cheeks.

"So what now?" Allie asks. I look up at her. She looks exhausted.

"Well, you could go take a nap while I hang out with this handsome little guy," I reply, tapping the baby on his adorable little nose.

Allie smiles. "Thanks, but I don't think I could sleep right now if I tried. I can only sleep when it's least convenient," she responds drily. "It's a whole thing."

"If you say so," I shrug.

"Seriously," Allie presses. "Are you going to be okay?"

I sigh heavily and set Brian down in his bouncy chair, rocking it lightly with my foot to soothe him. "Of course," I mutter. "I'll be fine."

"Fucked up, insecure…" Allie starts.

"Neurotic and emotional," I finish. "Yeah, yeah, yeah." I wave a hand at her dismissively. "Their wedding is in two months, Al. It's practically a done deal. And I'm so over it all. Hopefully, now that Madison has had her say they'll leave me alone."

"But what if they don't? You should really—"

"Hey, so, Hunter's gay," I interrupt, desperate to change the subject.

Allie's mouth pops open. "When did you find *that* out?" she demands.

I internalize a smug high five with myself for successfully changing the subject with zero tact. "Just a few days ago," I assure her. "He's bringing his boyfriend home for dinner this Friday."

"Wow," she mouths. "That's big." I nod.

"I was pretty thrilled he trusted me enough to tell me," I admit. "It kind of explains a lot, actually. He's worried about telling our dad, though. He said he didn't want him to know at first, but he finally admitted he doesn't want to have to keep it a secret forever, either. So, you know, I'm going to try to help him with that."

"Does his mom know?" Allie asks.

"No, but he's not worried about that part," I respond. "I mean, I understand why he's nervous. It's his dad. I wish I could lend him my ability to not give a shit what my parents think." Allie laughs.

"That would sure help," she agrees. "But he's lucky to have you in his corner."

"It's been good for me too, having him around," I admit. "With my luck his boyfriend will be fabulous, and they'll be getting married and I'll be all by myself again."

Allie reaches over and squeezes my hand. "You've always got us, babe," she assures me.

I squeeze back, smiling. "I know. Thanks," I reply.

But I suppress the urge to tell her it's just not the same. And I wonder if I'll ever have what Allie has. I look down and Brian is happily sleeping in his chair, sucking on the back of his sweet, pudgy little fist. I decide in that moment that, if nothing else, I'm going to be the best auntie there ever was.

TWENTY

unter's boyfriend, as it happens, is *not* fabulous and obviously *not* ready to follow my brother down the aisle into wedded bliss. Which actually is a good thing, since Hunter is only twenty-four.

It turns out his boyfriend, who is ten years his senior, is also the annoying IT guy at Sutton Developments, Graham Forrester. Will, the head of IT at the company I once owned, is now peers with Graham and complains about him to me all. The. Time. So it's unfortunately with preconceived notions that I welcome him into the house as my brother's boyfriend. And I'm a little ticked at Hunter for not warning me. I pull him aside as Graham gazes in awe at the window wall.

"What?" Hunter hisses as I pull him into the kitchen. "It's not against the rules to date a coworker, right?"

"No," I respond, exasperated. "But did you have date *that* coworker?"

Hunter smiles and shrugs. "Yeah, okay, so he's a little obnoxiously nerdy," Hunter allows. "But he's a cool guy when you get to know him. Just try, okay?"

I sigh and fold my arms over my chest. "Oh, I have," I reply. "But I'll play nice because you're my brother and I love you."

Hunter looks startled at the declaration. "Thanks," he mutters, blushing.

And for the first time, I feel like giving him a sisterly noogie. But I resist. I mean, I am thirty years old, after all.

Unfortunately, the evening goes about as well as I expect. That is to say, not well at all. Our conversations are forced and awkward, and Graham and I don't have much in common besides Hunter. And Will, of course, who Graham doesn't seem to like as much as Will doesn't like him. And Hunter isn't exactly a rife topic for conversation as he's always so taciturn, and it's hard to tease him.

But somehow, we make it through, and by the end of the night I find I don't dislike Graham quite as much as I thought I did. Hunter obviously cares about him, so that helps his case considerably. And when I wish them goodnight, going up to my room earlier than I ever would to give them some privacy, I don't miss the sweet smiles they share. And I'm happy, at least, that Hunter is happy. At least one of us is.

FOR SOME REASON I FIND MYSELF AGREEING TO HAVE DINNER WITH Alessandro the following weekend. Normally, I restrict our meetings to lunch only, to keep it friendly and casual. But he's tempted me with a feast at Marco's parent's restaurant, and I'd be an idiot to say no. Having taken me there once before, back when we were together, I remember it being like nothing I'd ever experienced, or have experienced since.

So I dress with care, selecting a silky black dress with red heels. I let my hair flow freely around me, perfectly shining and curled. I need to feel pretty again, but I carefully stay just this side of the line, so it doesn't scream, "You're getting lucky later." Hopefully, Alessandro has truly given up that pursuit.

Though when I answer the door that evening, he looks awfully tempting in a black suit, his white shirt open at the collar, his trademark sideways smile hanging on his full lips.

"*Buona sera,*" he greets me roguishly.

"*Buona sera,*" I respond, chuckling. "If you're trying to charm the pants off of me, you're wasting your time. I'm not wearing any." And with a wink I take his arm and let him lead me to the elevator.

"So I see," he remarks. "It's a good look for you."

Our flirtation continues all the way to the restaurant. I can sense it's completely harmless, as he seems happy just to see me smiling for once. And I realize it has been a while since I enjoyed myself so thoroughly. I decide to surrender to it.

We end up seated on our own, the restaurant arranged in its normal configuration.

"There's no event tonight?" I ask as he sees me into my chair.

"No, I just wanted to do something special. You deserve it. And I remembered how much you enjoyed being here the last time," he replies while taking his own seat. He starts examining his menu, and I can't help but stare at him for a moment, in slight awe of the sweetness of the gesture.

"*Grazie mille,*" I say to him. "Really, Alessandro. I forget how thoughtful you can be."

He looks up and shoots me a wink. "Then perhaps I need to remind you more often," he teases.

"Perhaps," I muse. "Or perhaps I'm just suffering from cabin fever. I can't remember the last time I went out in public."

The waiter arrives, and Alessandro orders for both of us. Anywhere else, with anyone else, I would never allow it. But it only makes sense here, in his extended family's restaurant, that he does so.

"So I trust the giant is over whatever it was about me that troubled him so," Alessandro offers after the waiter leaves.

"I imagine so," I respond. "They supposed it was a reflexive reaction. He doesn't really remember you."

"Nor you, it would seem," Alessandro replies.

"For the most part," I agree. Alessandro raises an eyebrow.

"And the least part?" he asks curiously.

"He had one memory surface. But that was a couple of weeks ago. I've made it a point to avoid the lot of them since," I admit.

"I see," Alessandro replies, folding his hands in front of him contemplatively. "Is that why you've holed yourself up lately?"

I weigh his question for a moment before answering. "Yes, I suppose it is," I allow.

"*Bella*," he starts, and the concerned tone in his voice already has me on my guard. "I hate to see you so affected. Listen. It may be presumptuous, but I'm going back to Italy in a few weeks. You should come with me. Take some real time off, have a vacation."

I can't help pulling a skeptical face. "I don't think going on a holiday with you is a good idea," I respond dismissively. He holds up a hand.

"Hear me out," he urges. "I'm meeting friends at the Amalfi Coast. Lots of beaches, sun, sand. Very relaxing. You can stay in your own room, come and go as you please. No expectations."

I have to admit, it sounds pretty good. And I can't even remember the last time I took a real vacation. "I'll think about it," I concede.

A wide grin breaks across his face. "*Bene*," he says happily, clapping his hands together.

The food arrives, and we move on to less serious topics as we enjoy our meal.

It might be the food, or the wine, or the enjoyable company, but at the end of the night, when Alessandro drops me off at my door, I do something I rarely do and throw caution to the wind.

"Alessandro?" I ask, turning back to him with my keys in my hand.

"Hm?" he murmurs.

"I'll do it. I'll go to Italy with you," I declare.

He smirks, and though he's not trying to be sexy, well, he is. "I thought you might," he replies. "I'll send you the details tomorrow, so you can make reservations." He slips his hand in mine, lifting it to his lips to place a tender kiss on my palm. "*Ciao.*"

"*Ciao,*" I whisper in reply.

And I don't want my heart to race at his touch, but it does. And he knows it. Smiling, he walks away. And I let myself into the condo wondering what the hell I just agreed to.

∿

BUT THE NEXT MORNING, HE'S SENT ME THE DETAILS AND I FIND MYSELF booking a flight to Naples just short of three weeks away. When it's done, I feel a sense of freedom and anticipation I haven't felt in a long time. Possibly ever.

For about fifteen minutes, that is. Until my phone rings. And I notice it's Bryce. I curse loudly.

"Are you fucking joking?" I answer. "Bryce Hoyt, are you *tracking* me?"

"Don't go," he responds. "To Italy. With him. Please. I know I have no right to ask."

"*None,*" I reply emphatically. "And best not to let the future Mrs. Hoyt know you're speaking to me. As I recall she threatened that coming near you again would be the last thing I ever did. And I don't know if talking on the phone counts, but I'd really rather not find out."

"She seriously said that to you?" he asks.

"I thought you said you didn't need to know what happened between her and I," I remind him. "Look, I can't do this. I can't get pulled back into your web of confusion. I find it fascinating that you even care, considering you only have one memory of me from before."

"I may not remember us," he admits. "But I can't shake my feelings about that guy. And that tells me he's bad news, and you shouldn't be with him. Please, Sera. I know how this must seem to you, but I can't help how my brain is piecing all of this together."

"Just stop," I beg. "I get that you're still healing, and that this all must be very difficult for you. But you've made your choices. And I've made mine. If it makes you feel any better, I'm not involved with Alessandro. Not that way. I just need some space. I need to get away. That's all." Every word I utter frustrates me more. I don't owe him any explanations. "Seriously, I should go. I don't want to get you in trouble."

"You won't," he replies simply. "I ended things with Madison."

"Seriously?" I ask incredulously.

"Seriously," he confirms.

"Why?" I ask suspiciously. "Did you remember something?"

He snorts. "I wish. No. I finally listened to Em. And I asked Madison point blank why she wanted to marry me. I guess I'd never questioned it before, when she had the opportunity to say things in her own way to make me believe what she wanted me to. But head on, she's not a good liar," he replies.

"So you know she was just after your money," I reply bluntly, not really believing he knows the full truth.

"Yes," he responds plainly. "I'm sure she cared for me in some way, but not the way I cared for her once." He sighs in frustration. "Honestly, I think I knew it all along, because I knew it then. She's not a giver."

His words pull at that stupid thread of hope in my heart, but I won't be sucked back in so easily.

"Well, I'm really glad you figured that out before it was too late," I say dully.

"I didn't just call about the trip. I had to try one more time. Please, Sera, is there any chance we can try to get to know each other again?" he asks hopefully.

My heart twinges painfully in my chest. Hope dies last, but I can't let it override my survival instincts. Not again.

"I'm afraid not," I say, my voice low and tired. "See, I already know you, Bryce. So in this case I would be the one who cared far more. And that's just not something I can handle. I can't suffer the thousand tiny rejections that doing that would mean, especially not when it could very well end with you never remembering any more about our past, and never developing those feelings again in the future. It's a bigger risk than I'm willing to take. I'm sorry."

"No, I'm sorry," he says softly. "But you can't blame a guy for trying."

"I understand. Take care, Bryce."

"Take care, Sera."

∾

Back at work the next day, I clear the vacation time through HR. Once that's done I let Hunter know I'll be out of town those weeks. He practically does a happy dance knowing he'll have the place to himself for a while. I stop myself from requesting that he not have sex in my bed. Hopefully, it goes without saying.

Graham, fortunately, seems just fine pretending he's not dating my brother whenever I see him around the office. But he starts hanging around the condo more, and I often see him disappearing out the front door as I come down for breakfast in the morning.

My slight annoyance at his constant presence is outweighed by Hunter's clear happiness. I mean, I've never seen him so giddy. He practically speaks in full sentences these days.

On Wednesday I get a call from Emily, which I promptly ignore, sending it to voicemail. She leaves a lengthy message pleading with me not to go to Italy, and I'm thankful I don't have to suppress my eye rolls and sarcastic responses. Those two are exactly the same as ever with sharing behind my back and meddling. I'm thankful I don't have to deal with it anymore. And that I'm spared the trouble of explaining to Emily how sick I am of hurting and hoping. Because through it all, Bryce's memories really never came back. And I know that's just as hard for him as it is for the rest of us, though in a different way. But I want to spare him that nonetheless. So instead of explaining that we should all just move on, I focus on just doing it.

TWENTY-ONE

The end of the workweek arrives, but it hardly feels that way as, when I get home, Graham and Hunter are on the couch making out. Not that they make out at work, but I'm still getting used to Graham's presence, and it's hard not to think about work when I see him. Even if it's while his tongue is shoved down my little brother's throat. Shaking it off, I grab a bottle of water and some food from the fridge and go hide in my room.

I make a few phone calls to let my mother and Allie know about my vacation plans and to catch up. And then I do something I haven't done in ages — I read. I find a trashy romance novel to download and sink deeply into my soft bed, losing myself in the kind of action I haven't had in a long time.

It seems to be the theme of the night, though, as around eleven I hear Hunter and Graham *giggling* as they make their way upstairs. And I thank the stars I won't be able to hear them from my room. Nonetheless, I take the opportunity to go downstairs and get a drink. After a short consideration, I opt for a glass of wine, hoping it will knock me out long enough to chase away the bulk of the nightmares.

Taking my glass, I turn off the lights and settle into my favorite chair in the dark, gazing contemplatively out the window wall. The dark sky is a solid mass of grey, the lights of the city reflecting off the low, late summer cloud cover. The humidity has been high lately, and I wouldn't be surprised if a thunderstorm rolled through soon.

I sip the wine slowly, enjoying the warmth that spreads through my face and chest as it does its work. By the time I'm done, it's definitely taken the edge off and I'm more than ready for bed. Alone. I heave a sigh and push myself out of the chair, arming the security system before I head back to bed. If I'm really lucky, I might even manage to sleep in.

∽

I'M WOKEN BY AN ALL-TOO-FAMILIAR CACOPHONY OF SOUND. THE ALARM blares obnoxiously through the condo. I sit bolt upright in bed, realizing the sky is already lightening, so it must be close to sunrise. I grab the bat under my bed and approach the alarm panel at the top of the stairs. It tells me the front door has been breached. I stand on the landing at the top of the stairs, peering around the wall down into the foyer.

Graham and Hunter are at the alarm panel nearest the front door, with the door itself cracked open behind them while they desperately punch codes into the system. Realizing there's no danger, I fly down the stairs as the alarm continues to blare obnoxiously.

"What happened?" I yell over the noise.

"Graham was leaving and set it off. He panicked and tried to turn it off, but we're locked out now!" Hunter yells back.

He points at me and then at the alarm panel. I shake my head. If we're locked out, only building security can fix it.

The alarm continues to blare overhead, likely waking everyone within a few floors. I prop the bat against the wall and grab my cellphone, heading into the hallway so I can hear.

But I find a security guard already rushing toward me.

"Everything okay, ma'am?" he asks.

"Yes," I assure him. "My brother's boyfriend accidentally set it off. He tried to turn it off, but it locked him out. Can you stop it?"

The guard's eyes go wide. "I'm afraid I don't have those codes. I'm not usually on this post. I'll have to call in for another guard. It might take a few minutes."

I throw up my hands in frustration. But he continues to stare at me.

"Well, do it!" I snap at him.

He jumps, pulling a cellphone from his pocket and heading to the other end of the floor where it will be easier to hear. I feel slightly bad for snapping at him.

And unfortunately, he wasn't kidding. It takes nearly ten minutes for someone to come turn off the alarm. I make the mistake of waiting in the hall, nervously willing someone competent to come save me from the murderous looks my neighbors are now throwing me as they peep out of their doors. I can't say I blame them. If one of them had woken me up before six a.m. on a Saturday, I'd be pretty pissed off too.

Finally, a guard with the proper access comes and has the alarm off in moments. Graham and Hunter have the good grace to look horribly ashamed. The guard slips out and Graham makes to follow him.

"Oh, no, you don't," I caution.

Graham leaves the door where it is, sulking back in to stand by Hunter. "Sorry, Sera," he says glumly. "I was just trying to head out, like I always do."

I glare at Hunter. "Have you been leaving the alarm off?" I accuse him.

Hunter shrugs guiltily. "Maybe," he admits. "It's just easier."

I squeeze the bridge of my nose. "Hunter, you know what I've been through. We can adjust the settings if you need, but..." I trail off as Hunter's stares past me, his eyes widening to the point where it's almost comical. I turn around and follow his gaze to the half-open door.

"I got a call." Bryce steps into the room.

And I realize I'd never taken him off as my emergency contact, so he must have automatically been notified when the alarm went off.

Graham takes the opportunity to slip by Bryce and out the door, pulling it closed behind him. Hunter conveniently disappears upstairs. I'm left standing there, in leggings and an oversized T-shirt, staring dumbly at Bryce.

"I'm sorry you were disturbed, but everything is fine," I reply, finally finding my voice again. "I forgot to take you off as emergency contact. I'll fix that as soon as I can." I'm suddenly extremely conscious of the fact that I'm not wearing a bra, and my hair is probably a tangled mess. I tug my fingers through it, trying to tame the worst of it.

"Since I'm here, do you mind if we talk?" he asks, taking a step forward.

I subconsciously take a step back. "I don't think that's a good idea," I reply, folding my arms over my chest protectively.

He runs a hand through his hair, and I note it looks damp — he's probably fresh from his post-workout shower. Same old Bryce. Except not. My insides twinge.

"Fine, I'll talk, you listen," he replies. "I can't stop thinking about you. I know you said you can't be friends, but I don't know if I can stay away, Sera. It's like you're a magnet, and I'm being pulled toward you whether I want to or not."

A derisive laugh escapes me. "It's too early for this," I mumble, shaking my head and heading for the kitchen. I'm going to need coffee if I'm going to deal with this shit.

Bryce stands awkwardly between the front door and the dining room, unsure of where to go as I knock around in the kitchen, getting a pot of coffee on. After a few silent and uncomfortable minutes, I emerge with a tray carrying two mugs and set it on the dining room table. He takes the hint and sits down across from me.

"Thanks," he says softly, grabbing the cup I made for him. He takes a sip. "Looks like you remember how I take my coffee too."

I close my eyes briefly and drink deeply, letting the beverage's warmth imbue me with strength. "So this magnet thing," I say. "Let's demagnetize it."

Bryce arches an eyebrow. "And how exactly do we do that?" he asks.

I can't help cracking a small smile. "Well, the traditional ways are heat, electric current, or banging on it real hard…" I trail off, my eyes going wide when I consider what I've suggested.

Bryce laughs. "Sounds kinky."

There's a sparkle in his beautiful blue eyes that I haven't seen in a long time. But then, I've purposed not to see him, despite how he manages to keep popping up.

I blush furiously. "It was supposed to be a metaphor, but I didn't think it through. Gimme a break. It's early," I reply.

"Look, I know I should take no for an answer—"

"It's okay," I interrupt him. "I wouldn't either if I were in your shoes."

"I'm just asking that we be friends, Sera," he replies softly. "Spend some time together. See if it shakes anything loose."

I set my mug down in front of me. "It's not that I don't want to on some level," I allow. "But you don't remember, Bryce, so you don't know how hard it was for me. To get where we were. It was a long and winding path. And it *was* worth it. But it's not something I can do again, not knowing whether it will be worth it in the end this time."

He stares at me intently. "You're scared," he observes.

A small sound of agreement escapes my lips. "Yes," I admit. "I'm scared." I pause. "You once accused me of avoiding a relationship with you because I was terrified of having to really trust someone enough to be close to them." I meet his eyes. "I keep talking about you like I know you out of habit, I think. But I really don't. You're not the person I was in love with. Yet you are. Sort of. You're a new version of you. And I'd have to learn to trust you all over again. I don't know if that's something I can do."

Bryce knocks his knuckles against the side of his head. "That guy is in here somewhere," he assures me. "I think that's where this is coming from."

"Maybe," I allow. "But then again, maybe not. I'm not a risk-taker. It took me a long time and a lot of pain to admit that I loved you, Bryce. You don't know what you're asking of me. I'm not like you."

"Oh? And what am I like?" His question is sincere.

"Just like this," I supply. "Always wanting to keep trying."

"So I must have convinced you to do the same before," he challenges.

It makes me laugh, because he's not wrong. "Yes, but then we were in a place where we were both in love with each other," I reply.

"And are you still in love with me?" he asks.

It's a question I wasn't prepared for. And it requires a level of honesty I'm not sure I possess at the moment.

"I'm going to need more coffee before I can even think about unpacking that question," I admit, grabbing my mug and rising from the table. "Need a refill?" I slip back into the kitchen and top off my mug.

"Sure," Bryce replies, following me in.

But he freezes by the fridge, his eyes fixed on something next to it. I take a step back, so I can see what he's looking at and spot the frilly, white apron, still hanging from its hook on the wall. Bryce sets his mug on the counter behind him and reaches a hand out, letting the silky fabric of the apron run through his fingers before gripping the bottom, fingering the flowing edge of the fabric. I watch, frozen and fascinated, as he lifts it to his face, breathing in deeply.

"I remember this," he says.

My throat constricts. I don't want to ask. I don't want to hope. But I can't help myself. Ever the masochist, I reply. "Tell me what you remember."

He turns in place to face the dining room. "I came home from work and you were there," he points at the table. "Red heels. Sexy as sin."

I shudder as he describes the scene, remembering it all too well.

"But I had you there," he points at the couch. "And then there," he points at the floor. "And then..." He stares intently at the window wall.

"Not there," I say softly.

He turns to look at me. "I wanted to."

But looking into his eyes, I don't see recognition and love. I see pain and confusion.

"Yes, you did," I agree.

He takes a tentative step toward me, his torment written all over his face. I instinctively pull back.

"Don't," he pleads. "Just hold still." Something in his voice freezes me in place.

But I can't look, so I close my eyes. I feel him stop in front of me, and he must be very close because I can feel the heat radiating off of him.

"Look at me, Sera," he commands.

And I'm powerless to resist his husky tone. I open my eyes and look up into his beautiful face. I let my mind go numb, surrendering to whatever it is he needs to get out of his system, hoping it doesn't crush me too badly.

He raises his hand and runs it down the side of my face, along my chin. He tips my head up, lowering his face to my neck, inhaling deeply. His nose lightly grazes my ear, and a shudder ripples through me.

He pulls back abruptly, feeling the shaking of my body. "I'm sorry," he murmurs. He steps back, and then out of the kitchen into the living room. He strides to the window wall, looking out over the city.

I follow, stopping a few paces behind him next to my chair. He turns, leaning against the glass and facing me, surveying the room.

"You like to sit there," he nods at the chair.

I huff a dry laugh. "That's obvious. The cushion is shaped exactly like my ass," I joke.

"And you drink too much when you're upset," he continues. "Wine, mostly, whiskey when things are really bad."

I swallow hard and nod, wondering if it's really coming back to him, or if it's just a reaction to familiar objects. Still not quite daring to hope.

His eyes rove the paintings that now cover the walls. "Those are new."

"My brother taught me to paint," I explain. "When we ran out of canvas we just … kept going."

He walks to the wall and slides his long finger over a dark swirl. "The guerilla artist, confined," he mutters.

"Yes," I gasp. "Hunter. He was a guerilla artist. Though he's gone traditional now. And he works for me."

Bryce looks back at me curiously. "Doing what?" he asks.

"Trim work. Interior design. That sort of thing," I admit. "He's got quite an eye."

Bryce pales and grabs back the back of the couch. "I feel a little lightheaded," he admits.

I rush to his side and let him lean on me. "Lay down on the couch," I insist.

He allows me to help him onto the overstuffed cushions, sinking gratefully onto them, lying on his side.

I grab a throw pillow and use it to prop up his head, then I fold myself onto the floor next to him. "Better?"

"Yes, thanks," he replies quietly.

"You're worrying me," I admit. "Are you okay? Should I call someone?"

Bryce takes a deep breath through is nose. "No, I think I'll be okay. My head just feels backwards," he replies.

I chuckle. "It looks like it's on straight to me," I tease him. "I'm going to make some breakfast. You hungry?"

He nods, so I head into the kitchen. As I throw together a quick meal, I keep one eye on Bryce. After a few minutes he sits back up, looking considerably less pale and in shock. But I bring the plates out to him anyway, handing him a dish stacked with eggs, bacon, and toast.

"You used to feed me a lot," he remarks. It's not a question.

"You're a hungry guy," I reply with a shrug. "So are you really remembering, or are these all just reflexes?"

Bryce stares at me as he polishes off his toast. "Em told you about that, huh?" he asks.

"Yep," I reply, avoiding his gaze.

He doesn't speak again until his plate is clean. Setting it down on the coffee table in front of him, he dusts his hands on his jeans.

"They're not reflexes," he finally replies.

I set my plate aside, even though I'm not finished. "How can you be sure?" I press.

Bryce smiles. "The reflexes are just that — I see something, I react. I don't really understand why or feel much of anything. Well, except with the Italian," he allows. "It was hard to tell the difference between those and the real memories until recently."

"Why's that?" I ask curiously.

He levels a look at me. "Because my first real, full memory didn't come back until I saw you at the gym," he admits. "And I haven't had any more until today. Just small bits here and there."

Suddenly I'm questioning if I should've skipped eating as my stomach roils. "Is that normal?" I probe.

"There's not really a 'normal' when it comes to this kind of thing," he hedges. "Some people get everything back quickly, some never get anything back." He leans into the couch, crossing his legs, something in his manner changed. "And I don't want to scare you, Sera, but I remember now. Well, enough anyway. More than I did."

And I can't handle it. I grab our plates and return them to the kitchen, eager to turn away from him so he can't see the heat and panic rising on my face. "How much is enough?" I toss over my shoulder as nonchalantly as I can manage.

He laughs and follows me to the kitchen, leaning over the bar as I scrape off the plates. I look up into his eyes, noting they're back to their clear, sparkling blue. And he looks coolly confident, and smug.

"I don't think you're going to believe anything I say," he replies cryptically.

"You're probably right," I admit with a meager smile, wiping my hands on a towel. At least he's finally catching on.

"So how about I prove it to you?" he challenges. I look at him, confused.

"Well, I guess you already proved you remember some things," I allow. "I'm not sure what else you mean."

"I mean, how about I prove that I remember the way I feel about you," he clarifies.

Suddenly, I'm having trouble breathing. "You remember how you feel about me?" I ask incredulously. "After all this time? I find that hard to believe."

Bryce smiles and shrugs. "Maybe I just needed the right environment. The right frame of mind," he replies. "But I do remember. The important stuff anyway. I'll admit I'm still a little fuzzy on the details, though."

I don't ask what the important stuff is. Because I know what he thinks it is, and I can't bring myself to trust that it's true.

"It sounds like you've made some good progress," I reply, dodging the bait. "Maybe we should call it a day before you hurt yourself."

He snorts, shaking his head. "You mean before I hurt you," he replies. "Not gonna happen, Evans." He suddenly seems very sure of himself, so I decide to call his bluff.

"Okay, prove it," I reply.

Smiling, he holds up a finger, then turns and bounds up the stairs. He's not gone long, returning with something clutched in his fist. He sets it on the counter in front of me. It's a small, black velvet box that I recognize all too well. It's the engagement ring I found in his nightstand on my birthday.

TWENTY-TWO

"I was going to give this to you that night," he explains.

I eye the box like it's full of poisonous spiders. "I can't take that," I reply, stepping back.

He raises an eyebrow. "You know what's in it," he accuses me with an incredulous smirk. He clucks his tongue in admonishment. "I never took you for a snooper."

"I'm not," I protest indignantly. "I was looking for a place to put something for you."

"Ah," he responds. "Did you read the inscription too, then?"

I shake my head. He opens the box, and the ring sparkles brilliantly, shooting rainbow reflections across the room. He holds it between his thumb and forefinger, angling it so I can read the elegant script written on the inside of the band.

"What have I always told you?" His voice is soft, filled with love and longing.

I look up into his eyes. I don't need to read it. The words are etched onto my broken heart. "Never forget how much I love you," I whisper.

He's right. He remembers the important stuff. A tear finds its way down my cheek, remembering all the nights I fell asleep remembering those words, wishing he would too. And now he has.

Bryce sets the ring back in the box and rounds the kitchen counter, coming to stand beside me. And despite him standing before me, it all feels unreal. "That's right," he replies. "Did you forget, Sera?"

I close my eyes and shake my head. "This all would have been much easier if I had," I reply honestly. I feel his finger slip beneath my chin, tugging it up in a familiar motion. I open my eyes and look at him.

"I know," he says softly. "And I can't undo that pain. But I remember you, finally, if not every detail of our life. But I remember this."

He drops his lips to mine, and it's more than familiar. The fire in his kiss is the fire in me that I thought had long since died. The fire that burned between us all those months ago. I burn with it, letting the feeling spread through me as his lips claim mine, truly, once again.

He pulls back, stroking a finger along my face, nuzzling his nose against mine as he used to do. "Do you believe me, that I remember you? Really remember you?" His eyes search mine deeply, begging me to accept him, to trust him.

The dam inside me breaks, emotions flooding my entire being. I nod, tears in my eyes. "Yes." It's all I can manage before needing to feel his lips on me again. I let the force of his mouth on mine drive away all the doubts, all the fear, all the pain I've felt. I can feel his own struggles melting in the purifying fire that burns between us. I can feel in his touch, in the response of my own body, how lost we've both been without this connection.

When our mouths part finally, I'm breathless and dizzy, and hopeful.

"So I guess that means you *are* still in love with me?" Bryce asks teasingly.

I press my knuckles into his strong chest and push myself backward a step. "Wouldn't you like to know," I tease back.

Bryce leans back against the counter, as in control as he ever was, now refusing to rise to my bait. His eyes flick to the clock on the microwave. "What I'd really like to know is if you'll let me take you to dinner tonight," he replies seriously.

I chew on my lip. My brain is still catching up, and I fight off the instincts I've been using to protect myself these past months. "Okay," I reply. "As long as there are no elevators."

Bryce snorts. "Deal," he agrees. "And I can't believe I'm saying this, but I need to leave. I have to go into work today. I'll pick you up at seven?"

"Deal," I echo.

He heads out of the kitchen, and I don't miss that he grabs the little black box, sliding it into his pocket on his way to the door.

I make to reach for the knob, but he shakes his head, stepping forward and using his bulk to pin me against the back of the door. He slides his hands over my hips, gripping me tightly and pressing himself into me. I breathe deeply of his scent before I look up at him.

As soon as I do, his lips capture mine, gently, sweetly, his tongue slipping between my lips, searching. It caresses mine lightly for a moment before he pulls away. And with another nuzzle of his nose, he's done, stepping back so I can open the door.

"I missed you so much," he says intently. "But I'll see you soon."

I nod. "Bye, Bryce."

"Bye, Sera."

Once he's gone I spend the rest of the day convincing myself it wasn't a dream. Well, except when I go back upstairs to yell at Hunter some more as I'd planned to do before Bryce showed up.

∾

Just before seven I'm waiting nervously on the couch, constantly running my hands over my blue wrap dress, anxiously tapping my high heels against the wooden base of the couch.

By five after I'm sure it was a dream, or that it was temporary, and his mind has slipped back to where it was, when he didn't know he'd loved me.

And by the time the doorbell rings at ten after, I'm practically in hysterics, having already fully convinced myself that he wasn't going to show up. Feeling ridiculous, I try to breathe deeply as I go to pull the door open. But it pops open in front of me, Bryce having unlocked it himself.

"Sorry I'm late," he announces, pocketing his keys. "But hey, I just remembered I still have a key."

An ugly sob rips out of me. He looks up and notices the anguish on my face. And he's there, holding me in an instant. "I'm sorry," I blubber, the tears pouring out. "It just seemed too good to be true. And then you were late, and I—"

"Shhhh," he says, stroking my hair. "It's okay, I'm here." I sniff loudly, trying my hardest to rein in the crazy. When I feel like the panic has subsided, I pull away, wiping at his ruined shirt.

"I'm sorry I got you all messy," I grumble.

Bryce forces my chin up with a finger, looking down with sparkling eyes. "You know you can get me messy anytime," he murmurs suggestively.

I smile feebly, not really in the mood to flirt. "I'm not sure if I can do this," I admit.

Bryce shrugs. "We can stay here and eat then," he replies.

I press out of his arms and stride back to the living room, sinking defeatedly onto the couch. "No," I respond with a sigh. I gesture between us. "This."

Bryce is so still for a moment that it makes me even more nervous than I already am. Then, he quietly takes his black suit jacket off and lays it over the back of one of the dining room chairs. He calmly rolls up the sleeves of his white dress shirt, still stained with my wet tears and a little bit of my makeup.

He saunters coolly up to me, sinking down to his knees on the floor in front of me. He unfolds my arms from around my midsection, gathering my hands in his.

588

"You've spent the better part of a year living in a world where I didn't remember you. I get that," he admits. "So if this is all too fast, too much, I get that too. I'm just so fucking glad you hadn't moved on, Sera, you have no idea. But if you need time, or space, then we can do this slow. I told you once that I wanted us to move at your pace. And I stick to that."

"God, Bryce, *I* didn't even remember your saying that until you just reminded me," I reply incredulously. "This is for real, isn't it? Your memories are really coming back."

He pushes up and slides onto the couch next to me, running a hand through his hair. "It's been a slow trickle, all day," he confesses. "Like the memories were just waiting for a crack of light to know where they could get out. You're that light, Sera. From the moment I met you, something inside me *knew* you. Knew that we belonged together. And even after I lost my memories of you, even though I was trying to do the right thing, the safe thing, something in me still knew it was wrong. I don't think it's a coincidence that I didn't start to get full memories back until I was with you again. Really with you, and not distracted by—"

"Please for the love of all that's good don't say her name," I interrupt. "In this house she shall forever be known as 'she who shall not be named,' got it?"

Bryce smirks. "My point is," he says, "I'm still solidly on the side of the line where I'll take as much of you as I can get."

And that one I remember. It's one of the things he said to me the first night we both confessed our love for each other. I scowl jokingly at him. "Well now you're just showing off," I scoff.

He grins, his true sunshine smile. "Is it working?" he asks eagerly.

And I laugh. "It's working," I assure him. "And while I can't promise there won't be times this all still scares the shit out of me, I'm in."

Slowly, a smile creeps across Bryce's face until he's grinning again. "All in?" he asks, running a hand down my arm.

"All in," I confirm, allowing the tingling sensation his fingers leave behind to stir me.

"Mmm," he murmurs. "Prove it."

I chuckle and raise an eyebrow. "And how exactly would you like me to do that?" I ask. Though I have a suspicion.

His eyes flick down my body. "Take off your dress," he replies.

And despite the thrill that runs through me at his words, I have to give him the "not a chance in hell" look.

"You do realize that my younger brother lives here now and will probably walk through that door with his boyfriend — one of my coworkers — at any moment now, right?" I remind him.

"Shit," Bryce curses. "No, you hadn't mentioned he actually lives here. Or the other bit."

"So you thought he was just hanging out here at six o'clock in the morning?" I tease.

He shrugs. "I was distracted. You weren't wearing a bra," he defends himself.

I roll my eyes. "Men. I swear."

"Okay, fine. Get your gorgeous ass upstairs, then take off your dress," he amends, rising and offering a hand. I take it, pulling myself up.

"Aren't you hungry?" I ask.

He drops his mouth to my ear. "Not for food," he murmurs, his deep voice tickling my ear, causing heat to instantly pool between my legs.

"I thought we were going to go slow," I reply, slightly breathlessly.

He laughs. "I said we'd go at your pace," he corrects me. "So if you don't want to go there, we won't." He takes a step back, but it doesn't stop what he's already put in motion.

"You fight dirty, Bryce Hoyt," I reply shaking my head.

But even looking at him is too much. I feel silly that a few light touches and suggestive words have me this worked up. Though I have to allow that it's been a very long time.

"You know you like it," he replies with a wink.

I do, but I pull a page out of his book and put on my best poker face, shrugging noncommittally. I stroll casually past him, to the bottom of the stairs, knowing the wall that's now between me and the front door will shield me if needs be.

And as if I'm simply getting ready to take a shower, I untie the front panel of my dress, opening it like a robe and letting it fall to the ground behind me. Leaving me standing there in lacy, black lingerie that leaves nothing to the imagination. A small moan escapes through his parted lips.

"I guess we will be eating out after all," I say lightly, turning and heading up the stairs, biting my lip to keep a shit-eating grin from breaking across my face. And giving him a full view of my backside.

But as my foot hits the third step I hear the front door open. Bryce's head whips toward it, open mouthed. And then he makes a break for the stairs as I start to flee up them. He reaches down to grab my dress on the way.

"Leave it," I hiss.

He gives me a funny look but chases me quickly up the stairs. I burst into my bedroom, giggling, Bryce toppling in after me. And I quickly slam the door behind him.

"Why'd you want me to leave the dress?" he asks.

I grab his hand, pulling him to the bed. The thrill of almost being caught has my adrenaline pumping.

"So I didn't have to leave a sock on the doorknob," I tease. When I feel my legs bump against the edge of the bed, I pull him to me, having to rise on my toes even in heels to kiss him.

And he takes no time returning the kiss and then some, lifting me up and laying me gently at the head of the bed. It's the last gentle thing he does.

I can feel the impatience in his kiss, the hunger. His mouth and tongue work with mine furiously, his hands kneading and working down my body roughly until he slips one hand between my legs, shoving my panties to the side and using his whole hand to stroke me. He lets out a low moan into my mouth when he feels how ready I am. His hand continues its work as his mouth cuts a path down my body to meet it, leaving a scorching trail wherever he kisses, licks, and nips.

And before his tongue even finds its final mark, I'm panting and moaning and gripping the bedspread, my hips rearing off the bed like they have a mind of their own. He sets a furious pace, as if he plans to consume me bodily, his tongue and fingers working forcefully to unleash the pent-up energy now roiling between my legs. And I don't know where the feverish sting of anticipation ends, and his hot, deft mouth begins. But in what feels like seconds I'm coming so hard I think I might pass out from the sheer effort it takes to keep from screaming at the top of my lungs. As I descend, he yields, and I stop holding it all in, letting my breath out in a great sigh.

But he moves up to cover my mouth with his once more, his taste now mixed with mine. Combined with the ferocity of his need, I'm plunged back into a dizzy frenzy. I barely register his hand as it works quickly between us to free his manhood before he nudges into me, sinking deeply. As he's still fully clothed, the sudden and unexpected move causes me to gasp in surprise. But he doesn't relent. He wraps an arm around me, bracing himself with the other, and pounds into me fiercely. It's only slightly painful for a moment before it's something so much more.

I throw my head back, not bothering or perhaps unable to stem the moans pouring from my throat as he rides me. As mine did, his climax comes quickly, the groans emanating from him rising rapidly to a crescendo. He shudders over me finally, then sinks into my embrace, still fully buried inside of me. His mouth finds mine once more, his desire still obvious, but the demanding edge now gone. Like a raging inferno dying to a low, slow flame.

When we break apart, he lets out a laugh. "I haven't fucked that fast since high school." He glances down at his watch. "We could probably still even make our reservation."

"Seriously?" I ask.

He throws me a mock sharp look, then laughs. "No," he admits.

I run a hand over his chest, wishing I'd gotten to see him naked. It's something I've dreamt of frequently. "It was quite different," I remark, looking at him from under my eyelashes. "But in a good way. Obviously, I was just as turned on as you were."

"It was more than that," he replies huskily, looking deeply into my eyes. "While I was going down on you, I remembered things. Doing that to you before. Doing other things to you before. You doing things to me. It took all of my strength to let you finish. So it's a damn good thing it didn't take you long either, or I may have exploded in my pants. Also something I haven't done since high school." His lips settle into a wry smile.

"Well, while I hope you eventually remember more than just our sex life," I reply, "right now, all I can remember is that I'm starving." My stomach rumbles loudly as if to prove my point and Bryce laughs.

"Then I guess you'd best clean up and find something else to wear," he suggests, reaching down to put his clothing back to rights. "Because as much as I'd love to watch you walk around in that sexy lingerie all night, I don't think your brother and his boyfriend would care much for it."

The reminder that they were likely here for our escapades makes me blush furiously. "Oh, god, they probably heard us," I whisper.

Bryce laughs. "I'm sure you've heard them," he replies with a shrug. "I wouldn't worry too much about it."

But as I dress, I still can't shake the embarrassment. I pick a pair of dark leggings and an emerald green sweater with a high neckline. At least fully covered I feel slightly less, well, exposed. We exit the bedroom, Bryce following behind me, and I say a little prayer that they didn't hear, or have already left again, as we descend the stairs.

As soon as I see Hunter and Graham, though, I know I'm out of luck. On both counts. The looks on their faces clearly say they heard it all. As we hit the bottom stair, I quickly retrieve the discarded wrap dress, tossing it self-consciously into the coat closet next to the stairs.

"Hey, guys," I say, attempting nonchalance. "You remember Bryce."

Bryce gives a little wave and goes into the kitchen and starts rifling through the fridge. They wave back, mystified.

"Whatcha doin?" I ask him as I wander in after him.

"Making dinner. Go sit down," he replies calmly with his head still in the fridge.

"Are you sure?" I ask tentatively.

He straightens up and fixes me with a look. "Yes. I used to live here, remember?" he teases.

"Yes, as I matter of fact, I do remember that. But the better question is, do you?" I tease back.

He narrows his eyes at me. "As a matter of fact, I think I do," he replies saucily.

I laugh. "All right, then," I reply. "I'll be in the living room."

He gives me a quick peck on the cheek, then swats me on the behind. I join Hunter and Graham in the living room, folding myself self-consciously into my favorite chair.

"Thank god," Hunter immediately says to me. "We saw the clothes and heard, well, you know. And I thought you might have gotten back with..." he drops his voice to a whisper, "the Italian guy."

I look at Hunter, confused. "Except you saw Bryce here this morning," I reply.

Hunter shrugs. "I thought maybe it upset you, so you went looking for comfort. I gotta say I'm glad it's not. That dude is bad news," Hunter grumbles.

"I remember liking you, Hunter," Bryce's voice floats over from the kitchen. He points a spatula at Hunter. "Good instincts."

"So you remember, huh?" Hunter asks. I can't help smiling.

"Starting to," Bryce admits. He looks at me and smiles back. "But I'm getting more back with every passing hour. Still don't know who this guy is though." His eyes flick to Graham.

"Oh, sorry, this is Graham Forrester," Hunter replies. "My boyfriend." Hunter shifts uncomfortably.

"Nice to meet you, Graham," Bryce replies, looking down at whatever it is he's chopping. "I'm Bryce. I'd shake your hand but..." He lifts his hands to demonstrate the knife in one and a pile of zucchini in the other. I hear a sizzle as he tosses the zucchini into a pan before going back to chopping.

"Nice to meet you," Graham replies uncertainly, still clearly wondering what the hell is going on.

Hunter also looks like he'd like an explanation. "So..." he prompts in a low voice.

I shake my head. "Later," I whisper.

"Okay. You guys need some privacy?" Hunter whispers back.

"Maybe later," Bryce calls. "Stick around. I'm making stir fry."

"God, that guy has got the ears of a bat," Graham mutters.

And I can't help but smile. "Some things never change."

TWENTY-THREE

Unsurprisingly, after dinner Hunter and Graham decide to go to Graham's place for the night. Bryce seems pretty happy with that. And as I sit in Bryce's arms on the couch, I'm feeling pretty good about it myself.

"So what else did you remember today?" I ask softly, lying back against his chest and trailing my fingers down the arm he has wrapped around me.

"Heather," he replies. "And Daniel. What happened there?"

"Ah." I sit up, turning around to face him. "He was convicted and sentenced to seven years. Heather is doing great. She's seeing someone now, and she seems really happy. She told me to thank you for your help, once you remembered."

"And Charles? How did he take it all?" Bryce asks.

I can't help but smile sadly that he's remembering, but the things he's remembering are so heart-rending.

"It was tough. But he's okay. He finally made an official succession plan. That's when I knew he'd really accepted it. And things have been better," I reply.

"So you'll be in charge of Sutton Developments one day?" Bryce asks.

"Yes," I agree. "How about you? Will you run Hoyt Corporate Services again?"

"I'd planned on it," he admits. "But I'm not so sure anymore." He pulls me close to him, running his hands down my arms. I press my palms against his chest, relishing the feel of his heartbeat under his warm, firm muscles.

"Why not?" I ask curiously.

He pushes my hair behind my shoulders and looks deeply into my eyes. "Well," he replies, "if we're both running companies, who is going to raise the kids?"

I laugh. "You mean Hunter and Graham?" I tease.

Bryce smirks. "I think you know full well I don't," he chastises me.

I press my lips together to suppress my smile. "Getting a little ahead of yourself, aren't you?" I ask. "Technically, you haven't even proposed. I mean, you flashed a ring and all, but that seems to have disappeared."

Bryce grins mischievously. "Do you really want me to propose to you on the same day my memories came back? You seemed pretty dead set on not letting me back in unless there wasn't any chance you'd be left hanging."

"Well, I let you back in, didn't I?" I reply.

"Hmmm," he says in mock thought. "So you really must believe me. Which means…"

"I might consider marrying you if you weren't such a jackass," I reply, smacking him on the chest and attempting to wriggle backward.

But he locks his arms behind me, making escape impossible. "You know you like it," he teases me, burying his face in my neck. His lips work my flesh, and all the fight drains right out of me.

"I do believe it," I respond, ignoring his teasing and wrapping myself around him. "I just needed a little time to absorb that it was really true. That you really remembered, and that it wasn't a reflex."

He gazes seriously into my eyes. "I really remember. Not everything still, though more is coming back all the time. But I know three things, Serafina Evans," he replies, kissing me lightly on the lips. "First, that I've loved you since the moment I saw you." He kisses me more deeply. "Second, that I missed you even when I didn't remember you, I just didn't realize that's what I was feeling until my memories came back." He kisses me again in a way that causes me to moan against him. "And finally, that life is too short, too precious to live another moment without asking you to be my wife." He slips out of my arms, crouching on one knee next to the couch, the ring mysteriously having appeared in his hand. "Marry me, Sera."

I'd only been teasing him about proposing. And even though I knew he had the ring, and that he'd planned to propose before he'd lost his memory, he's right — I never thought he'd propose the same day his memories returned. But this whole ordeal has also made me realize how fleeting everything is. How much I love him. And I'd be an idiot to say no.

"I know three things, Bryce Hoyt," I respond with a grin. "First, I love you more than I ever imagined I was capable of loving anyone." I kiss him lightly and he grins. "Second, yes, I will absolutely marry you." He lets out a small, choked happy noise as I kiss him again. "And third, I think we should buy a house together and fill it with little Hoyts."

A look of sheer joy settles over him, and this time he kisses me, nearly knocking me over on the sofa. I laugh as he pulls away and slides the ring onto my finger. And it's a perfect fit, just like we are.

Bryce cups my face in his hands, radiating warmth and love, and his mouth covers mine. I press him back gently after a moment, rising from the couch. I tug on his hand, leading him to the window wall.

"Actually, I guess I know four things," I amend. I go up on my toes to whisper in his ear. "I know I want you naked and fucking me against the window. Now."

"Goddamn, baby," Bryce groans. His hands fly down his shirt buttons, and I tug my dress over my head, flinging it away from me. As he takes off his shirt, I add my bra to the pile. And when his pants and boxers go, so do my panties and leggings. And in a clash of flesh, his mouth is joined to mine, his hands roughly teasing my nipple and between my legs.

I cry out as he primes me, sinking against him and feverishly stroking him. He spins me around, grabbing my hands and placing them against the window. He runs his fingers down my back, to my hips, lifting them into position as he leans down and seats himself at my opening. I can see him reflected in the glass, lovingly caressing my backside as he teases me. I groan anxiously.

"So impatient," he murmurs approvingly. How he loves making me wait.

But I know it'll be worth it. And instead of giving in to the urge to pounce, he enters slowly, torturously. And the moan that seeps out of me is nothing short of primal. He groans appreciatively, at the sensation of our joining or my clear enjoyment of it, I'm not sure which.

But even he can't take the disciplined torment for long. Our quick encounter earlier has only left us both hungry for the full experience. So I'm not surprised when he quickly accelerates to the deep, full thrusts that send my body soaring with pleasure. The sounds of his enjoyment mingle with my own, spurring us both on as he takes me. His hands reach under me and find my breasts, allowing him leverage to drive completely into me. He hovers there, using a slight tilt of his hips to move the head over *that* spot inside me. A familiar low ache begins to build. And having learned from Bryce how to make the climax all the more intense, I slip my fingers onto the sensitive nub between my legs, pressing with our rhythm until the ache consumes me, spreading its explosive fire through my body so fiercely that my arm loses its hold, my face and chest sinking against the glass as I come apart.

As I come down from the sensation, Bryce releases me and turns me to face him. His mouth finds mine, and I get a slight respite as I sink into him, enjoying the feel of our naked bodies touching. I press him back, running my hands over the smooth muscles of his chest, then the rippling muscles of his abs. My eyes drink them in hungrily, then move down to his throbbing cock.

I drop to my knees at the sight, descending on him with my mouth. He moans loudly, his hand resting lightly on the back of my head as I work him. I pleasure him with varying stroking and sucking, enjoying every noise that he makes. It's all I can do to let him stop me before I finish him.

He lifts me up bodily, pressing me against the cold glass behind me so our hips are aligned. And then he's inside me once more, pinning me with his torso and tilting his hips into me furiously as I cling to him with my arms and legs, enduring the intense pleasure caused by the contrast of the cool window, his warm body, and the deep, intense thrusts. His head is pressed against the glass next to me, his mouth hovering over my shoulder. So when his breathing picks up as he approaches orgasm, I hear it, and use what muscles I can to spur him toward his finish. When he feels me clamp around him, he cries out and explodes inside me.

We both sink to the floor, utterly spent and gratified, leaning our warm, sweaty bodies against the chilly glass, looking up at the dark, grey sky outside. After we've caught our breath, Bryce pulls me to him, kissing me lightly. His beautiful blue eyes find mine, his handsome face filled with love.

"I don't want to wait," he says. "To make you mine."

I smile shyly. "I'm already yours. I have been this whole time. I was just waiting for you to remember," I reply. "But now that you do, I don't want to wait, either."

"Really?" he asks, with a hopeful look.

"Really," I confirm. "I'll marry you anytime, anywhere, Bryce Hoyt. Just so long as we can do this, forever." I press my body against his.

His strong hands pull me into his lap, and I wrap my legs around him, my breasts pressed against his chest.

"God, I love you," he breathes. His words shoot through my heart, filling me with joy.

"And I love you," I sigh. "Never forget how much I love you."

He smiles. "Never again," he agrees.

TWENTY-FOUR

Two weeks later, I'm holding Bryce's hand in the kitchen at his mother's house.

"Do you remember we almost kissed here once?" I ask teasingly.

He backs me against the very counter I'd used to support myself in anticipation of that almost-kiss. "I do," he murmurs seductively. "And this time, Em isn't going to spoil it." He lowers his face to mine.

"Em isn't going to spoil what?" Emily asks, entering the kitchen.

And I can't help but burst out laughing.

"Shitty timing, as usual, sis," Bryce grouses. But he kisses me anyway, cutting off my laugh.

I sink into his embrace, not caring that Emily is watching.

"You know, this is your party," Emily grumbles. "You might want to help out a little. People will be here soon."

Bryce breaks away and shoots me a conspiratorial smile. "If you insist," he replies, helping Emily bring plates and cups out to the buffet table.

I sigh happily watching him go. There's not much he *doesn't* remember anymore, and the last two weeks have been a dream rediscovering each other, settling back into our relationship, and seeing him get back all that he lost. And then some.

Charlotte walks in with Rebecca, the former moving in to hug me first. "I'm so glad you decided to celebrate your engagement with everyone before you went on vacation," Charlotte says sweetly.

Rebecca embraces me next. "Yes," she agrees. "We couldn't be happier to be welcoming you to our family, Sera. I'm only sorry it had to be such a rough road here."

I press her away at arm's length with a smile, squeezing her shoulders gently. "I'm not," I admit. "It happened the way it happened, and in the end, it all worked out."

The older woman beams back at me, nodding in agreement. "You're right, of course," she responds with a smile.

Emily sticks her head in the kitchen. "Hey, Sera, your dad and his wife are here," she calls.

"Already?" I gasp, running out to find Bryce.

I spot him by the table setting things out.

"Baby, have you seen Hunter yet?"

He looks up at me, confused. "No, I don't think he and Graham have arrived, why?" he asks.

"Shit," I curse. "My dad and his wife are here."

Bryce's eyes widen. "I'll ask Aunt Char to run interference," he suggests.

I nod, and he runs to the kitchen to get Charlotte while I move to meet Kent and Barb. I find them hovering in the foyer.

"Kent," I call.

He looks up and his face floods with relief at the sight of me. "Sera, there you are," he breathes. He gestures to the tiny redhead next to him. "This is my wife, Barb."

I extend my hand out, which she grasps firmly in greeting. "It's so very nice to meet you, Barb," I say. I feel a hand slide on my back, and I turn to see Bryce has joined us. "This is my ... Bryce." I laugh.

Bryce extends his hand to my father first, and they have a friendly shake before Bryce shakes Barb's hand too. "Please, come in," Bryce encourages, leading us all to the living room.

Behind us, I see Charlotte dart for the door to field incoming guests, particularly Hunter. Because today, of all days, Hunter has decided to come out to our father. As if there weren't enough going on.

The next group to arrive is the Sutton Developments crowd — Charles, Suraj, and their spouses. Bryce and I position ourselves between the foyer and the living room in wait, while we watch Rebecca and Charlotte entertain Kent and Barb as Emily continues to run food from the kitchen to the buffet table. I knew the morning had been too calm — everything is in full swing now, though, so I take a deep breath as I prepare for another round of introductions.

I embrace Charles as he makes it to us, accepting his congratulations and introducing him to Bryce. It's odd seeing the two men shaking hands. They're both such a big part of my life now, and I don't miss the momentousness of the occasion. Charles introduces us to his wife, Diane, and then we repeat the whole process with Suraj and his wife, Mena. When they've all moved on to the living room, I turn back to Bryce.

"It's already weird seeing all these different people in one place," I whisper. "Was this a good idea?"

Bryce shrugs and drops a gentle kiss on my forehead. "Too late now," he murmurs in my ear. "Just focus on tomorrow. We'll be driving through the Italian countryside and eating gelato."

I let out a sigh of anticipation. "Mmmm, that was better even than dirty talk," I tease.

He smiles, but doesn't respond, gesturing to the door, where I see Heather and her boyfriend. She runs over and hugs me, introducing us to Sam, who seems like a really great guy. Though the huge smile on her face whenever she looks at him speaks volumes too. And Heather also takes the opportunity to thank Bryce personally for everything he did for her. Bryce is, as usual, gracious and humble, and every word out of his mouth makes me love him more. If that's even possible.

But it's back to it before I can spend too much time staring adoringly at him, as we welcome Tristan and his boyfriend, Max, my mother, and the Kramers all in quick succession. I spend a little extra time greeting Allie and David, fawning over Brian in his cute little sailor outfit.

But not long after, Alessandro arrives. And I watch Bryce tensely as Alessandro embraces me. Thankfully, he's on his best behavior, and he knows Alessandro and I have been through too much together not to remain friends.

Finally, Hunter and Graham arrive.

"You guys are the last ones in," I greet them. I look at Hunter. "Now or later?"

Hunter shifts nervously. "Let's just get it over with."

Graham squeezes Hunter's hand and disappears into the crowds in the living room to wait until Hunter signals him to return. Bryce approaches, bringing Kent and Barb with him.

Hunter hugs them both and they spend a few minutes catching up. I purposely keep my distance, waiting for a signal same as Graham, in case Hunter needs me. But I'm close enough to hear it when, apropos of nothing in particular, Hunter spills the beans. His declaration is met with stunned silence.

And after a time, this gem from our father: "Well, son, I'm proud of you anyway."

Barb has the good sense to smack him on the back of the head and reassure Hunter that they love him, and they just want him to be happy, whatever that means for him. Hunter catches my eye over her shoulder and smiles. I give him an encouraging thumbs-up and step away to give them privacy, pleased by their response.

A bit later I notice Hunter call Graham over. But it's then that I catch that

Bryce has been watching me. Our eyes lock across the room, and a shiver of anticipation runs through me. I hope quietly that I'll always feel this way when he looks at me across a roomful of people.

As conversations ebb and flow, I slowly make my way across the room to where Bryce is. I make sure to check in with my mom, having not much more than greeted her yet. But once I make it by Bryce's side, he tucks me protectively under his arm. I wrap my arms around his torso, looking happily up into his shining blue eyes.

"Ready?" he murmurs into my ear.

I nod, and he picks up a spoon, using it to tap his glass. The room falls silent and everyone turns to us.

"Thank you, everyone, for coming," Bryce starts. "Sera and I are touched that you were all able to make it on such short notice. You all know that I proposed to this beautiful woman two weeks ago, and she accepted."

Everyone cheers and Bryce smiles, holding up a hand after a moment to call for silence.

"But you may not know I actually bought the ring a year ago." He looks down at me lovingly. "And though fate prevented me from giving it to her until now, I've loved her since the day I met her. And I'm the luckiest bastard on the planet because she loves me too."

I rise up on my toes to plant a kiss on his lips and a collective "awwww" rises from the room.

"But if we've learned anything through it all, it's not to take for granted that there will be a tomorrow. So we promised each other that we would live each day with no regrets, without hesitation, without fear. Together. And because we didn't want to waste one more minute without joining our lives, we were married yesterday by a justice of the peace."

Gasps ring through the room.

"And so, I'd like to introduce you all to my wife — Serafina Hoyt." He raises his glass, looking down at me. "Thank you, baby, for bringing me back, and making me the happiest man alive. Never forget how much I love you." He slips his wedding ring out of his pocket, making a show of putting it on.

Grinning from ear to ear, I pull him to me once more, kissing him deeply this time, to cheers from all. "I love you too," I murmur back to him. But I wonder if he even heard me as our family and friends close on us, eager to hug and congratulate us.

I receive all of our friends and family in turn, accepting their congratulations, hugs, blessings, and everything else. My parents are both thrilled, having already come to adore Bryce. And thankfully there are few hurt feelings. Allie is really the only one who is ticked. I can see it written all over her face before she's able to corner me some minutes later after the initial wave of well-wishers has died down.

"You *didn't*," she sputters, handing baby Brian off to David. "Please, Sera, tell me you didn't get married *without me*."

I bite my lip, and I'm sure I look guilty as hell. "I'm sorry, Allie," I reply. "We wanted it to be just us."

"Oh, really? What about your witnesses?" she presses testily.

I shrug. "There was another couple there to get married. They witnessed for us," I reply. And instantly, I know it was the wrong thing to say.

"Strangers?" Allie replies.

She's so loud it catches Bryce's attention. David takes the opportunity to hand him baby Brian so he can talk Allie down.

"Al, come on, it's their wedding, their choice," David reminds her soothingly.

Allie whirls on him and he shrinks back. Bryce's eyes go wide, and he smoothly carts the baby off somewhere out of the line of fire.

"No. Just no," she says to David before turning back on me. Her anger melts, leaving an expression of pure hurt on her face. "You could've called me. I would've been there in a heartbeat."

I hold my arms out to her, hoping a hug will reassure her. She accepts it but doesn't seem terribly placated.

"Allie, I love you, you know that," I assure her. "But Bryce and I have been through so much. We just needed this to be apart from everything for a little while. Our own private moment that the world couldn't touch or spoil. Does that make any sense?"

Allie looks like a deflated balloon. "Actually, it does," she admits. She throws her arms around me and hugs me tightly again, for real this time. "I'm sorry, Sera, you're right. And really, I'm so happy for you both."

I squeeze her back tightly. "Thank you," I breathe. "You know that means the world to me."

She pulls back, nodding. "And hey, I figured out what I'm going to do with myself," she says brightly.

"Oh yeah, what's that?" I ask eagerly.

"I'm writing a book," she replies with a small smile. "About what I went through. It's really helping me work through a lot of what happened."

"That's great, Allie," I reply. "I can't wait to read it."

"Thanks," she says brightly. "Brian has been such a blessing, and he's really helped me look into my own heart to understand my *why*." She looks around. "Where'd he go?"

I laugh. "Bryce took him away when you started to go nuclear," I explain. "Let's go find him."

We mill around, ultimately finding Bryce in the kitchen holding Brian, with David nearby preparing a bottle. We hover by the door, taking it in. Bryce is looking down at Brian, cooing gently while Brian grips his finger with his tiny fist. The tenderness in Bryce's touch and the love and joy on his face split me open. It's heartbreakingly beautiful watching him fawn over the baby.

Allie rests a hand on my arm. "He's going to be a great dad," she whispers.

Bryce's eyes snap up, having clearly heard her.

I smile lovingly at him. "Yes, he is," I agree. I'm awarded with a sunshine smile in return, and it melts me that much more.

"We've got this," Bryce assures me in a gentle tone. "You guys go enjoy yourselves."

Allie gives me an impressed look and immediately pulls me back into the living room. We're headed to the buffet table to grab some food when Allie gasps and pulls me to a stop.

"Allie, what the hell?" I ask.

She shushes me and points into the foyer. I look up to see Emily leaned against the wall. Alessandro stands over her, leaned next to her, his face close to hers. He's obviously working his magic charm on her, as I know exactly what that sexy smirk means. And she's obviously enjoying it, toying playfully with the ends of her long, wavy locks and batting her eyelashes at him. I cover my mouth with my hand to hide my shocked laugh.

"Oh, Bryce is going to be *furious*," I hiss.

Allie laughs. "Then we best not tell him," she replies.

"He'll find out," I assure her. "And if he finds out I knew and didn't tell him…"

Allie stares at me in shock. "You're not really planning to tell him, are you?" she asks incredulously.

I consider Emily and Alessandro for a moment. Technically, I'm pretty sure Emily's still seeing what's-his-face. And Alessandro is probably not stupid enough to actually try dating Bryce's sister. I hope.

"They're just talking," I finally say slowly. "Right?" I give her a pointed look.

"Who is?" she asks dumbly, turning around and dragging me with her.

I laugh. "Better still," I respond.

After I've managed to sneak a few appetizers, I pop back into the kitchen to check on Bryce. Baby Brian is sleeping happily in his arms, having had his bottle, and Rebecca is gazing adoringly at him.

"I want lots of these," she says softly to Bryce. "You know, grandbabies."

Bryce chuckles softly.

"That's the plan," I interject quietly.

They both look up at me, and I catch Bryce's eye, smiling adoringly at him.

Rebecca looks between us. "Your news was timely, you know," she says to us.

Bryce's eyes move to his mother's. "Why's that?" he asks curiously.

She gestures around her. "This old place," she sighs. "I'm a widow now, Bryce. It's too much for me. I've been thinking it's time I downsize."

"No, Mom, you're not selling the house," Bryce protests.

Rebecca shakes her head. "Of course not," she scoffs. "I'm giving it to you."

Bryce's mouth drops open.

"That is, if you want it."

Bryce looks at me questioningly. I nod. I know how much he loves this house, and the timing really couldn't be more perfect. He wraps his free arm around his mother, pulling her close. His eyes shine with tears, and he seems unable to speak.

"We'd be honored by such a generous gift," I say for him. "And we would love to live here and raise our family here. Thank you, Rebecca."

Rebecca opens her free arm to me, and I join their huddle.

"Mom, can you take Brian back to Allie, please?" Bryce asks, letting his mother go.

Rebecca nods understandingly, gently transferring the sleeping baby to her arms and leaving us alone. Bryce takes my hands, pulling me to him. I slide happily into his embrace, tilting my head to look up into his eyes.

"You're really okay with living here?" he asks softly.

I smile happily. "Yes," I assure him. "And not just because I'd live anywhere with you. Or because you love this house. I love it too. It will be a constant reminder of the love in this family, for all the years they've been here. So your father will always be with us in a way. And your mother can still be here as much as she'd like."

His eyes are shining once again, bright blue and filled with happiness. "You really mean that," he whispers.

I nod.

"You are too good to be true, Sera Hoyt."

I grin at his use of my new name.

"No, I just hate house shopping," I tease him.

He laughs. "Whatever you say, Mrs. Hoyt," he mutters.

"You just really like calling me that, don't you?" I observe.

His sunshine smile breaks across his face, and it makes me sublimely happy seeing it so often. "Mhhhmmm, and I'm going to like calling you that in bed later too," he murmurs suggestively.

"Then I'd say it's about time we leave for our honeymoon," I reply. "But since there won't be any beds for a while..." I glance down the hall suggestively.

He looks around, considering for a moment before scooping me over his shoulder and bustling me down the hall to his room. He drops me on the bed, closing the door behind him.

I lay there, propped up on my arms, eyeing the tender look on his face.

"Are you going to make love to me now, Mr. Hoyt?" I ask him teasingly.

His eyes darken, and he rolls his muscled shoulders once before slowly advancing on me. When he reaches the bed, he leans over me slowly, planting his arms on either side of me so our faces are inches apart. I can feel the desire rolling off of him as he sizes me up.

"No, Mrs. Hoyt," he replies huskily. "I'm going to fuck you senseless."

"Promise?" I whisper.

He doesn't answer. At least, not with words.

HER DIRTY SECRET

ONE

"Do you ever want to get married?"

Chad looks up at me from the acoustic he's restringing. "You're the last person I ever expected to ask that question," he replies with a knowing smirk before going back to what he was doing.

"Hey, I might get married someday," I protest with a whine. "And you didn't answer the question." I lean forward on the glass counter, letting my feet swing freely as I await his reply. Not that I really care. But the shop is slow today, for a Saturday anyway, and the engagement party I'll be attending later is on my mind.

"I don't know. Maybe. I can't say I've given it much thought," he finally replies as he clips the newly wound strings and grabs a tuning fork.

I look him up and down. I've known Chad too long to think of him that way, but he's not bad looking. Mid-thirties, average height, average build, with sandy brown hair and light brown eyes. But he's one of the best guitarists I know, and chicks dig that. Well, chicks who haven't been there, done that, learned their lesson, got the T-shirt, and all that.

"Yeah, me neither," I agree.

He laughs. "Bullshit. All chicks think about it."

I frown, drop my feet back to the ground, and slug him on the arm as he tunes. "Don't be such a misogynist."

"What's this about, Emily?" he asks bluntly.

I'd cringe, but it's exactly what I like about having mostly guy friends. They don't beat around the bush.

"I'm going to my brother's engagement party today," I admit with a sigh. "I dunno. I'm happy for him. But it makes me realize I can't really see myself ever getting married. Is that weird?"

Chad shrugs as he finishes and puts the guitar back in the case. "Maybe you just haven't met the right person. Maybe go through another few hundred and you'll find 'The One,'" he replies with a cheeky grin.

"Fuck you, Chad."

"Heh heh," he chuckles. "Isn't that your flavor of the month's job?"

I glare daggers at him, but luckily he's saved from my wrath by a customer approaching the counter. He smiles serenely as I lead them to the pedals they're looking for, and I stick my tongue out at him as soon as their back is turned.

Probably better I didn't get to reply. Then I'd have to admit things with Jack went kaput last week. Like they always do, though this one lasted longer than most. Even though I wasn't all that interested in him. Not that I'm ever all that interested in any of them.

Most of the guys I meet are just guys. Little more than boys, and certainly not men. That's what I get for working in a music store. Hanging out with musicians. Being a musician. Hell, who am I kidding — I'm just as flighty and immature as most of the guys I date. But at least I don't pretend to be something else.

I shake myself, unsure of why I feel like such a Debbie Downer. I'm not usually this sad after a breakup. I push the thoughts out of my head and try to focus on the last hour of my shift. Before I have to put on a happy face for Bryce and Sera's party.

❧

I GET BACK TO MY APARTMENT WITH LITTLE TIME UNTIL I HAVE TO GET TO THE party, but I still take care primping. Even though I feel like crap, I decide I might as well look like a million bucks. I carefully wash and straighten my long, chestnut brown hair before applying the layers of makeup that will make the blue in my eyes really pop. Likewise, I pick a slinky, fitted dress that hugs my thin frame with splashes of bright spring colors, even though the cooling Seattle September air hints at the rapidly approaching fall.

Once I'm satisfied, I call for a car service and pick up my ukulele to practice while I wait. I'm not nearly as good on it yet as I am with a mandolin, but I'm getting there. It's hard to work in a music shop and not get distracted by all the cool instruments. My apartment is certainly a testament to that, with nearly a dozen littered around the living room. Not that I've ever spent much time getting particularly good at any of them. Much like in life, I flit among my instruments, playing whatever makes me happy at the moment.

My cellphone pings, interrupting my reverie, or practice, or whatever the hell you call it, and I head out to meet my car.

The drive through downtown and over the West Seattle bridge is uneventful. I glance out over the industrial district and watch a ferry chugging along slowly through the waters beyond. Not for the first time, I realize what a beautiful place I live in. But it hasn't stopped me from wanting to travel the world, if only for a little while.

I almost did, before my dad died unexpectedly. But then Mom needed me. And then Bryce had his accident, and he needed me. And now that he's healed, and he and Sera are getting engaged, I suspect there will be little nieces and nephews who need me soon.

As we start winding through the streets of my childhood, I put on my game face. *Time to act happy, Em, even if your own dreams are on hold. Whatever those might be.* I can't help laughing at myself a little. For a twenty-eight-year-old, you'd think I'd have my shit together better.

Once I'm out, the car peels off behind me and I trek up the front steps, taking a deep breath before entering. I head through the massive house to the kitchen, knowing it's where everyone probably is as they prepare for the onslaught of guests due to arrive shortly.

But I actually find Mom and Aunt Char in the living room, laying a tablecloth over a banquet table that's been lined against the wall. Bags of supplies sit behind them on the couches.

"Where are Bryce and Sera?" I pipe up.

Mom, who is facing me, looks up, but Aunt Char jumps a little in surprise. She turns around with a hand to her chest.

"Goodness, Emily, you startled me," she replies.

"They're in the kitchen, dear," my mother supplies.

I set my purse down on a side table and move toward my mother.

"Shouldn't they be doing all this?" I ask, planting a kiss on her cheek.

Aunt Char waves a hand. "Nonsense," she chides me. "We're here. Why wouldn't we help?"

With a shrug, I turn to head into the kitchen to give Bryce a hard time for resigning them to manual labor. Honestly.

As I swing the door open, I catch Bryce's huge frame wrapped around Sera in a corner of the kitchen.

"And this time, Em isn't going to spoil it," Bryce is telling her. He goes to kiss her, and I just can't help myself.

"Em isn't going to spoil what?" I ask unnecessarily loudly with the most innocent expression I can muster.

Sera looks up at me and bursts out laughing, letting her long, wavy light brown hair fall into her face. My brother's head whips around and he glares at me.

"Shitty timing, as usual, sis." And with that, he proceeds to ignore me, planting a far too steamy kiss on Sera. They go at it like teenagers, clearly not caring that I'm standing right here.

"You know, this is your party," I remind them. "You might want to help out a little. People will be here soon."

It takes a second, but they finally peel apart.

"If you insist," he replies, planting his giant, muscled self in front of me. I don't know why he thinks he can intimidate me like he does everyone else. I know exactly where to punch him to make him drop to the floor and cry like a girl.

With a smug smile, I pick up a stack of plates and cups. He does the same, following me back out to the living room.

As we lay everything out, I can't help poking at him a little. "Seriously, you gotta be more careful with the PDA," I tell him. "Would you want Mom to walk in on you guys feeling each other up like that?"

Bryce smirks down at me. "Jealous much?"

If I was teasing before, I'm annoyed now. "Uh, no."

He crosses his arms over his slab of a chest and raises an eyebrow at me. "Emily Hoyt, I think you *are* jealous," he teases me.

Something about my big brother and that tone of voice makes me want to stomp my foot. But I resist. Barely.

"Don't worry, little sis," he assures me, wrapping his huge arm around my neck. I give him a look that forbids the coming noogie, and thankfully he relents. "Someday, you'll find someone who is just as crazy about you as I am about her." He looks back at the kitchen wistfully.

It melts the fight out of me. "You two *are* ridiculously, adorably perfect for each other," I grudgingly admit. "But that doesn't mean I'm not just fine on my own."

"Of course you are," Aunt Char offers, coming back through the room with Mom behind her. "Emily has always been a free spirit. She doesn't need a man tying her down."

Mom shakes her head. "Says my never-married sister."

Bryce and I chuckle as they head into the kitchen.

"At least someone in this family gets me," I shoot at him.

Bryce narrows his eyes at me. "Oh, believe me, I get that you don't want to be tied down to anything traditional. The dozen times you've turned down working in the family business to pursue your 'music career' pretty much got that point across." He says it with a smile. And I realize I'm just being a grouch. Because if anyone gets me, loves me, accepts me for who I am, it's my steadfast big brother. He's always been the reliable rock of the family, even more so than Dad was. Dad was just as moody as I am. At least I know it's genetic. Not that that helps much.

But before I can apologize for being so snippy, there's a knock on the door. Bryce goes to answer, but I wave at him to continue setting up, and I head down the hall and into the foyer.

I open the door to a completely average-looking middle-aged man and a tiny redhead. The man extends his hand.

"Kent Evans," he introduces himself. "I'm Sera's dad. And this is my wife, Barb."

I shake his hand, wincing under his vice grip. "I'm Emily, Bryce's sister," I reply, offering my hand to Barb next. Her handshake is just as firm and uncomfortable. Yeesh. These two. I step back in invitation. "Please, come in." They enter, standing awkwardly in the foyer. Since I'm not sure we're ready for them in the living room, I decide to leave them here. "I'll just go get Sera."

I make a break for it down the hall and through the living room, where Bryce gives me a weird look as I dash by him into the kitchen.

"Hey, Sera, your dad and his wife are here," I hiss.

She looks up from talking to Mom and Aunt Char, clearly startled. "Already?"

Sera whips past me, heading out the kitchen door. Mom and Aunt Char look at me, and I shrug. Not a moment later, Bryce pops in.

"Aunt Charlotte, can you please man the front door? We're trying to keep Sera's brother and father apart until he's ready to, er, tell his dad something."

"Of course," she agrees, following him out.

Mom and I exchange a look.

"I think it's best if I go play hostess as well," Mom says wisely. "Why don't you start putting out the food, Emily?"

"Sure thing," I agree.

I start moving dishes from the loaded counters to the banquet table, which unfortunately doesn't allow me to catch much of the conversation with Sera's dad and his wife. I have to admit that I'm more than curious, since Sera's told me all about the double life her dad apparently lived with this woman while she was a kid, but I figure it's better not to be caught eavesdropping. And not to annoy Mom by neglecting to feed people. Heaven forbid.

Once everything is out, I note that the place is pretty packed. Looks like most people are here. I make the rounds, introducing myself to everyone, making sure they know where to find the food, and all that kind of stuff. Being fake and cheery isn't really my thing, and my dangerously low brain-to-mouth filter means that I need to avoid talking to anyone in particular for too long.

And when a couple with a baby arrive, I introduce myself briefly and then make sure I stay as far away as possible. It's something I would never admit to anyone, but babies freak me out.

I babysat a baby once when I was a teenager. That's all it took. The little hellion spent the whole time throwing up, peeing, pooping, or screaming. Sometimes more than one of those at a time. And when he peed *in my mouth* I swore from then on never again. No babies. No pretending to like people's babies. Probably not even having my own babies, a conviction that developed steam over the years. And even though this baby looks happy and cute in a little sailor outfit, I just can't. Traumatized for life.

So when I hear the doorbell chime, knowing Aunt Char is in the middle of a conversation, I more than happily trot down the hall and away from anything baby to answer it.

What I was in no way expecting is the Roman god standing on the doorstep. Lean and sculpted in perfectly tailored black pants and a black button-front shirt, with a perfectly styled head of gorgeous dark hair and a trimmed beard, brown eyes sparkling like he knows exactly how outrageously dazzling he is, I know without a doubt who this must be. The lying, cheating Italian prick who fucked with Sera's heart. Who my brother hates with every fiber of his being. Well, as much as Bryce Hoyt can hate anyone. When my mild-mannered, all-knowing big brother hates someone, that's saying something. But fuck me sideways if this isn't the most gorgeous man I've ever laid eyes on.

He stares at me expectantly as I stand there, speechless, looking me up and down in a way that makes it even harder to form a sentence.

I'm saved having to string words together in greeting when Sera appears behind me.

"Alessandro," she breathes, a little too happily.

"*Buona sera*," he offers in return, extending his hands as he steps across the threshold. My heart hammers in my chest at the voice that's just as sexy as he is. They greet each other with a hug, just as my brother walks in behind Sera, clearly struggling to hide his distaste at her obviously being glad to see him.

But as much as I hate the dude for what he did to her, I kind of get it. They've been through a lot together. And Sera's a smart chick, even if she does tend to overlook people's shortcomings. But damn, I might be willing to overlook his shortcomings too if he's half as good in bed as he is gorgeous. The odds are good as, from what I hear, he's had enough practice.

I blush furiously, banishing the thought as I watch them converse. I swear Alessandro's eyes wander to me more than is natural, but I could just be imagining it. Or I could just be staring so hard that I'm making him uncomfortable.

I realize suddenly it's been a long time since I've had good sex. I'm sure that's where this is coming from. Just horniness. I shake myself a little and make to head back into the living room when there's another knock on the door.

Since Bryce is closer, he answers, grabbing Sera's attention too, as it's her brother and his boyfriend. That leaves Alessandro on my side of the foyer. And apparently, I haven't stopped staring at him despite my intention to leave.

He turns to me and sizes me up once more.

"I'm sorry, I didn't catch your name," he says silkily. "Are you a friend of Serafina's?"

"How rude of me," I reply, finally finding my voice, and my manners. I extend a hand. "I'm Emily. And yes, I'm friends with Sera. Though I'm also Bryce's sister."

Alessandro accepts my hand, tilting his head and raising an eyebrow, a smirk playing at his mouth as he brings the back of my hand to his lips. His full, delicious lips. He places a light kiss there before raising his eyes back to mine.

"Are you, now?" he asks, still holding my hand in his. "Then perhaps I shouldn't find you quite so beautiful. I fear your brother already doesn't like me much."

I've been fed enough lines in my day to know an attempt to get in my pants when I hear one. Though I know that's probably exactly what he's doing, his words sound much more sincere than not. Or maybe I just find him that attractive. And it has been more than a year since he and Sera split. And she is engaged to my brother now. Would she really care if we had a fling? Though it's Alessandro's implication that's more to the point — my brother would care. And that, unfortunately, is an issue. I wander down the hall, and he follows.

"No, I'm afraid he doesn't," I agree. "And I wouldn't want to get you in trouble. I know Sera cares for you very much."

A feline smile spreads across his lips as we settle onto a vacant love seat in the living room. "Yes, we will always care for each other," he agrees. "And I'm glad to see her so happy. But still, I think I would happily face the giant to get to know you."

A peal of laughter escapes me. "You call him 'the giant'?" I ask, clapping in delight. "That's the best thing I've heard all day." It fits Bryce, to a T. He's such a towering, glowering fuddy-duddy sometimes. Especially when he gets in protective mode, which is not infrequently, and I'm sure something Alessandro saw a lot of.

Alessandro stares at me intently, looking like he wants to reach out for my face.

"What?" I ask self-consciously. "Do I have something on me?" I wipe at my mouth, suddenly worried there might be cheese dip lingering from the appetizers I snuck earlier.

"No," he replies lowly. "Forgive the cliché, but you're mesmerizing."

"Mhm," I reply, pressing my lips together in a skeptical glare. "I've heard about you. The whole handsome and charming shtick isn't going to work on me."

Now it's his turn to laugh unreservedly, and I can't decide which I like better, the stoic and sexy face, or the amused and joyful one. Mesmerizing. It's a good word, for him at least. I see why Sera was so hesitant about him in the beginning. He naturally just comes on strong. Luckily — or unluckily perhaps, for him — charisma doesn't really sway me. Because I'm not looking for a prince to sweep me off my feet into happily ever after. All I care about is having fun. Charisma isn't a requirement, though damned if he doesn't seem like fun too. If only it wouldn't give my brother the exact excuse he needed to do what I know he's been itching to do for the better part of two years and end the guy.

"Well, this is a first," he replies, still smiling.

"Oh? How's that?" I ask, honestly curious.

He leans in, his mouth hovering near my ear. "It seems you have the upper hand," he says softly. A shiver glides down my back. The accent, the heat emanating from him, his scent all prove him wrong. If he asked me to go upstairs right now, I'd be hard-pressed to refuse him. I fail to see how that gives me the upper hand.

"Mmmm," I hum, neither agreeing nor disagreeing.

The sound of tapping on a glass rips through whatever retort I was trying to form, and the room stills. Bryce stands on the other end, Sera at his side.

"Thank you, everyone, for coming," he says. "Sera and I are touched that you were all able to make it on such short notice. You all know that I proposed to this beautiful woman two weeks ago, and she accepted."

Cheers erupt, and a genuine smile crosses my face. I really am so happy for them. My brother holds up his hand to quiet the crowd.

"But you may not know I actually bought the ring a year ago." He shares a loving look with Sera that brings tears to my eyes. "And though fate prevented me from giving it to her until now, I've loved her since the day I met her. And I'm the luckiest bastard on the planet because she loves me too."

He pauses to kiss her, and something inside me rips. I suddenly feel like I need air. Unfortunately, he's not done.

"But if we've learned anything through it all, it's not to take for granted that there will be a tomorrow. So we promised each other that we would live each day with no regrets, without hesitation, without fear. Together. And because we didn't want to waste one more minute without joining our lives, we were married yesterday by a justice of the peace."

My gasp joins those around me. Including Alessandro's. As my brother continues, I can't help noticing Alessandro looks paler than he was. And I wonder if he's really over Sera, even after all this time. It helps me to not focus on my reaction to their news, which, if I'm being honest, isn't all good. It makes me uncomfortable in a way I don't want to think too hard about. It's nothing on them. They're perfect. But then, my brother has always been the perfect child. Me, not so much. And their perfect love for each other is a small, needling reminder of that.

"And so, I'd like to introduce you all to my wife — Serafina Hoyt." Bryce raises a glass, his eyes never leaving Sera. "Thank you, baby, for bringing me back and making me the happiest man alive. Never forget how much I love you." He slips a wedding ring out of his pocket, making a show of putting it on. And they kiss again.

God, my brother is married. This is so weird. I tear my eyes from them, looking back at Alessandro. He's still watching them with an inscrutable expression. I lay a hand on his arm.

"You okay?" I ask softly.

He turns to me, tears filling his eyes. "Yes," he manages. "I know it may seem strange to you, but they're tears of joy." I look at him, confused, and he laughs. "Really. I love her, truly, so how can they be anything but?" He squeezes my hand and slips away, joining the forming line to congratulate them. I watch for a moment in shock.

He sounds nothing like the selfish bastard I expected him to be. Big ol' flirt, absolutely. But there's something about his reaction that was so heartfelt and sincere. Knowing I won't be missed, that I can offer my congratulations later, I slip out the front door to absorb things alone. Sinking onto the steps, I stare up at the sky. Behind the bank of grey clouds, night has fallen. I breathe deeply of the cool air, letting it calm me.

It's hard to say what unnerved me more: that Bryce and Sera went off and did the deed, or Alessandro's selfless happiness for them. No, I know what is harder to come to terms with. To be fair, I only met the man myself tonight, but Sera confided in me at length over the end of their relationship. I was there to see what he did to her. Reconciling that with the man I saw crying for her happiness has shaken me.

I have to work to place my feelings. The closest I can get is that it gives me hope. That it's never too late to be someone else. Or maybe, even the person you always wanted to be. If Alessandro can change, grow, and move forward, then anything is possible.

It makes me realize that everyone around me is moving forward with their lives, while I've been stuck in the same place for years. In the same rut of partying, drinking, dating in the same crowd I've always run in. The wishers, the wanters, the dreamers. I'm all of those things. But I also want to be a doer. It makes me realize that it's time to start doing the things I've always hoped to do. To stop letting life derail me. Because if not now, when?

I rise and march back inside. And run smack into Alessandro.

"*Scusa,*" he gasps, grabbing me by the arms before I can topple over. I lean into the wall behind me to steady myself, and he lets go. But he doesn't move away. Staring up into his eyes, I decide he's one of the things I want to do. And

I won't let my brother derail me. It's none of his business, and in any case, I never bring home any of the men I date anyway.

"Sorry," I say breathlessly. "I didn't mean to—"

"No, it was my fault I—"

I reach for him, silencing him with a hand on his arm. "It's okay." The heat of his gaze makes me blush, and I retract my hand, dropping it down and playing nervously with the ends of my hair. The humidity outside has curled them, and I tug at my hair, futilely trying to smooth it back into submission.

"Emily," he says. My name sounds beautiful on his lips. But then, I imagine everything does. I look up at him from under my eyelashes to see he's smoldering down at me. It's almost too much to take.

"Yes?" I prompt, swallowing hard.

"I just came to see if you were all right," he replies, stepping back slightly. "I saw you leave but couldn't break away. You seemed upset."

There he goes with the selflessness again. He's either a pile of contradictions, or he isn't the same man he once was. Part of me wants to forget about him, to not take the risk. But part of me wants to know him, and not just to know if people can really change.

I breathe deeply and right myself, dropping the coy flirtatious act. "Thank you," I reply. "But I'm fine. Or I will be."

Alessandro smiles indulgently at me. "You're a tempestuous one, aren't you?" he asks, a note of teasing in his voice.

I laugh shortly. "Yes, I suppose I am," I admit. "You also seem a little…" I try to come up with a word to describe him.

"Passionate," he murmurs. "That's the word you're looking for." I swallow hard again. It's not exactly where I was going, but clearly true nonetheless.

We stare at each other for a moment.

"So you're really sure you'd be willing to deal with my brother just to get to know me?" I ask abruptly.

He gives me a mischievous smile. "Are you falling for the 'handsome and charming shtick' after all?"

I laugh. "Let's just say I've reconsidered. I realized I need be more spontaneous and stop sitting around wishing things would happen a certain way."

"Intriguing," he replies, rubbing his finger under his chin with a sparkle in his eye.

A noise grabs my attention, and I look down the hall at the crowd starting to break up and head this way. With a sigh, I realize I'm out of time for now.

"I should go congratulate the happy couple," I tell him. "And then call my ride home. It was nice to meet you, Alessandro."

His eyes sweep over my face. "It was my pleasure, truly, Emily," he replies, stepping aside to let me pass. I walk away, thoroughly confused and disconcerted by our exchange. I can't even seem to flirt properly these days.

With a sigh, I seek Bryce and Sera out, giving them hugs and congratulations. They remind me that they'll be leaving for their honeymoon later tonight, and it makes me yearn for the kind of trip they're about to embark upon. And when I see them sneak away, it makes me yearn for what I know they're about to do.

It's a few more minutes until everyone clears out, and I spend the time cleaning up so Mom and Aunt Char don't have to. I say my goodnights and step outside to summon my ride and wait in the cool of the evening, rather than keep Mom and Aunt Char up.

But there's still a car in the driveway. And Alessandro sits on the hood of the sleek, dark luxury coupe.

"If I owned a car like that I wouldn't sit on the hood," I remark drily, pocketing my phone.

He grins widely. "What good is it if you can't?" he replies, hopping down.

I laugh, shaking my head. "What are you still doing here?"

He gestures to the car. "You said you needed a ride. Your chariot awaits."

His choice of words freezes me on the spot. "I'm not a damsel in distress," I snap.

Alessandro presses his lips together, clearly amused by my change of mood. It pushes me further into annoyed and I fold my arms over my chest.

"Do you get tired?" he asks with a tilt of his head.

"Of what?" I brace myself, expecting the pickup line that's probably coming.

But he steps forward, prying my arms away from my chest, holding my hands in his. "Of fighting against what you really want."

He might as well have poured a bucket of ice water over my head for how shocked his words leave me.

"You're right," I whisper, more to myself than him.

His hand slips under my chin, prompting me to look up into his eyes. "I know."

I give him a mock frown. "And you're arrogant."

He laughs. "I know that too."

His honesty makes me laugh with him. "I'll let you drive me home on one condition," I say with a sneaky smile.

"Go on," he replies.

"Show me what this baby can do."

With a grin, he walks around and opens the passenger door for me. I slide into the buttery-soft red leather seat. And when he gets in and takes off, holy shit does it take off. It takes half the time it usually would to get home, and I can barely direct him there for laughing gleefully as he whips around at high speeds.

As he idles outside of my building, the adrenaline speaks for me.

"Come upstairs," I say.

He looks over at me intently.

"Any other time I would," he says carefully, "but I must be on a flight to Napoli in a couple hours."

Shit. That's right. The whole reason Bryce and Sera are honeymooning in Italy is because she'd originally planned to go on a group trip to the Amalfi Coast with Alessandro.

"Ah, yes, that," I reply. "Some other time then." I give him a wan smile. "Thanks for the ride." I turn to leave, but he leans over and covers the hand I have on the door latch with his. I turn toward him, and his face is dangerously close to mine.

"Give me your phone," he says urgently.

I only hesitate for a moment before handing it over. He quickly programs something in, then hits a button. His phone, tucked behind the stick shift, vibrates. He presses another button, then hands it back.

"Now you have my number, and I have yours. I'll call you when I have a moment," he promises.

That one I've definitely heard before. "Yeah, okay," I reply, unconvinced. "Bye then."

He laughs and shakes his head. "You'll see." He gives me a wink but doesn't stop me leaving this time.

TWO

EMILY

I'm not even in the apartment for five minutes when he calls.

"I'm an idiot," he says without preamble.

"I won't disagree with that," I reply. "A pretty girl asks you to have sex with her and you say no." I tsk at him.

He laughs loudly. "Well, I wasn't sure that's what you were asking, but I guess I am now."

I shake my head. "Is that why you called? To ask what I meant by, 'Come upstairs?'" I tease. "I know there might be something of a language barrier, but—"

"Come to Italy with me," he interrupts. And I'm rendered speechless. "I'm downstairs. You wanted to be spontaneous, no?"

My heartbeat thuds in my ears. I should have a million questions.

But I don't.

"Give me five minutes."

"Is that five minutes in real time or woman time?"

"You've already wasted thirty seconds asking me that," I reply in mock indignation. And I hang up.

I look around my apartment. Can I really do this? Can I really jet off to a foreign country at the last minute with a ridiculously hot Italian man I just met a few hours ago?

Even asking the questions in my head makes me laugh.

Hell. Yes.

621

I don't waste any more time thinking. I bolt into the bedroom, unearth my passport from the bottom of my desk drawer, thanking God I got one just in case, dig the suitcase out of my closet, and pack every loose article of clothing I can get my hands on, finishing with all of my toiletries and electronics. I also throw a few books into my purse for good measure. I race downstairs faster than I knew possible. And he's really there, leaning against the car.

When he sees me, he beams. "That was seven minutes, but I'll forgive you."

I throw him a mock glare. "You realize this is crazy, right?"

He crosses the distance between us quickly, taking the suitcase from my hand and hovering over me. He's just the perfect half a head taller than my five feet, seven inches. And his dark eyes are filled with fire. He looks deeply into my eyes, his warm breath making me dizzy.

"You realize that's what makes it so much fun, right?" he asks lowly. With a wink, he pulls away and neatly seats my suitcase in his open trunk, right next to his own.

And I do realize that he's right. This is hands-down one of the craziest and most exciting things I've ever done. And that's saying something.

As we slide into the car, he looks over at me. "You have a passport, right?"

I fish it out of my purse and wave it in the air at him.

"Good," he says, grinning. "Let's go."

As we drive, I pepper him with questions about the trip. I learn he's meeting a dozen or so friends, one of whom shares a house there, so there may be some bunking up, or I can always stay in a hotel. There will be no need to arrange additional transportation, as they're meeting in Naples and driving from there. And they'll be there a few weeks.

A few weeks in paradise. The more he talks, the better it sounds.

"You needn't stay the whole time," he assures me.

I wave a hand dismissively. "Spontaneous, remember? Let's get there and see what happens."

"If that's what you wish. But please don't do anything that could jeopardize your job on my account."

"They won't fire me," I assure him. "I work in a music store. They're all a bunch of flakes, and they're used to people pulling shit like this. Besides, it's not like I need the money anyway." I look out the window to hide the flush in my cheeks. I hadn't intended to say that last part.

"There's no shame in having money," he assures me, resting his hand briefly on my knee. "That you continue to work anyway says you're not content to waste your days shopping and tanning."

Shaken from my pity party, I turn to him and laugh. "Isn't that exactly what we're about to do?" I point out.

He smiles and shakes his head. "When you do it a little while, it's a holiday.

When you do it all the time, it's a lifestyle. Big difference." He lets that sink in but continues on when I make no reply. "What instrument do you play?"

I almost give him a hard time for assuming I play an instrument because I work at a music store. But he's called me out on that kind of bullshit once already, and the man *is* taking me to Italy.

"Mandolin, mostly. But I've taught myself a little of everything — guitar, banjo, lute, ukulele…" I pause, willing myself to open up. "And I sing."

He smiles over at me. "Are you any good?" I blush so deeply he laughs. "Okay, maybe you can just show me sometime and I'll be the judge."

"You're a devious bastard," I tease.

He waggles an eyebrow as he pulls into the airport parking structure.

"You have no idea," he murmurs.

He's right. But I can't wait to find out.

We get our luggage out and head inside. The first leg of Alessandro's itinerary is to Paris. There are no coach seats left, but there are two first class seats. He doesn't hesitate to upgrade, so I don't hesitate to go for it. The flight from Paris to Naples has available seats, though apart, but it's short, and getting a break from each other at that point might not be the worst thing.

With that settled, we make our way through security.

As soon as we're through, something occurs to me, and I stop Alessandro with a sharp tug.

"Are Sera and my brother on our flights?" I can't keep the note of panic out of my voice. Because deciding to do something my brother would be upset about and flaunting it in his face are two very different things.

"No," he assures me swiftly. "Serafina specifically told me she switched them to avoid that. They will fly into Firenze, then they'll be staying there and other places around the country, but not where we'll be."

I let out a deep breath. And I finally get excited. I'm going to Italy. Only having been out of the country to go to Canada, that's huge. Though our family was comfortable growing up, Mom and Dad didn't want us to be spoiled little rich kids, so most of our family trips were very modest. Disneyland, Yosemite, the Grand Canyon, that sort of thing.

While we wait to board, and after I've sent the necessary texts and emails to let Mom and work know I'll be traveling indefinitely, I ask Alessandro about growing up in Italy. He tells me a good deal about his country, his friends, and his family, but stops abruptly when he gets to his reasons for coming to the United States.

I lay a hand on his thigh. "It's okay," I assure him. "Sera gave me the highlights."

Alessandro grimaces. "Normally, I'd be unhappy about that, but I guess it's better that you know."

His words give me pause, because what I know about him isn't exactly roses and sunshine. Sera told me how he fled his family's pressure to use his talent at making money through real estate development so they could pay off mob debt. The same debt that eventually got them killed and almost killed Alessandro and Sera. But, while they both managed to avoid serious injury, it all ended with my brother in the hospital. That's some pretty heavy stuff, and it doesn't exactly help him where I'm concerned. Suddenly I kind of wish I didn't know all that about him. That we were simply two people who met, had an instant and intense attraction, and decided to run off together. Though I guess we are still that.

I examine his face as he rubs a finger under his chin. "You do that a lot," I tell him, pointing at his chin.

He smiles at me. "Yes, and you twirl your hair," he teases.

"I do not," I protest.

He points and I look down to see my hair wrapped around one of my fingers. We both burst out laughing.

We board shortly thereafter, and once we're settled I'm more than happy to have splurged on first class. Though when he starts asking questions about my life, it has me squirming. But considering the scales are pretty tipped, I try not to hold back too much.

When he learns my age, his eyebrows jump.

"What? I'm only two years younger than Sera," I point out self-consciously.

"True," he allows. "Though at times I swore Serafina must be older than I am. She can be so serious."

I shrug. "It's why she and I work as friends. There has to be balance in any relationship. If you're too alike, you'll drive each other nuts."

"Is that why your relationships haven't worked out?" he asks shrewdly.

I narrow my eyes. "Yes, as a matter of fact. How did you know that?"

He presses his lips together to suppress his smile. "Don't worry, Serafina hasn't told me anything about you," he replies. "You just seem like you bounce around a lot. If you weren't so grounded in your family, I imagine you would be a nomad, moving around the country whenever and wherever you want."

"Probably," I agree with a smile. "Why do I feel like you already know me so well?"

His answering smile is tender. "Because I'm afraid we're quite a lot alike."

I nod. "So we're doomed," I reply matter-of-factly.

Alessandro laughs. "I'm afraid so."

"Well, let's enjoy it while it lasts then," I say with an overly dramatic sigh.

He considers me for a while before responding. "I already am," he finally responds. "You remind me what it's like to want more, and I think we both needed to do something drastically different for a while."

His eyes are alight with the passion he used to describe himself earlier. It pulls at something inside of me, and I can hardly believe I'm sitting here, on my way to Italy, next to this impossibly gorgeous man who just twenty-four hours ago I had pegged as a selfish asshole. Which he may yet be, should the opportunity present itself. But I'm starting to realize that he's so much more complex than that.

We are alike in our changing moods. But I sense, also like me, Alessandro is loyal to those he cares about. And while I don't expect we'll come to care for each other that deeply, it makes him that much more attractive. Though I don't miss that he hasn't so much as kissed me, or the implication that it's my impulsiveness that inspired him to bring me along. Sure, he's flirted, but being just as big of a flirt, I know how empty that can be. Because I basically told the man I'd have sex with him, and he's done nothing about it.

If I were smarter that would reassure me. As it is, I can't help but feel a little disappointed. I push the feeling down, determined to enjoy myself no matter what this trip does or does not bring. To just appreciate the experience and go with the flow.

To that end, we spend a while longer getting to know each other. He's smart with a sharp wit, and is more of a balance between risk-taker and playing it safe than I am. But then, he outstrips me in both years and life experience. I can't decide if it's intimidating or sexy. But then, why can't it be both?

∾

I MUST HAVE DRIFTED OFF, BECAUSE THE NEXT THING I KNOW ALESSANDRO IS nudging me awake.

"We've landed," he says softly.

"Holy shit," I cry, springing up. "We're in Paris?"

Alessandro laughs. "You sleep like the dead. And yes. Have you been before?"

I lean over him to look out the window. "No," I reply softly. "This is officially the first time I've been out of North America."

Alessandro catches my face, turning it toward him. "Then I'm sorry we won't have time to see Paris. It's quite beautiful," he says softly, and in a way that makes me feel like it's not just Paris he's talking about.

"Some other time," I say without thinking.

A small smile flits across his face. "Some other time."

We collect our things and make the transition to our next flight seamlessly. And this time when we land, I'm wide awake. I can't drink in the sights around me fast enough.

As we take a taxi to the meeting point, I'm bouncing in my seat with anticipation. I barely have time to soak any of it in when we're out of the car and Alessandro is jumping into a hug with a huge group of people.

For a few minutes there's simply a lot of gesticulating, shouting, and back-clapping embraces. Amid the chaos I count eight men and three women. Two of the three women are clearly attached to men in the group. The third, not so much, at least not based on the looks and touches she gives Alessandro as they greet each other. It annoys me immediately. While I'm still not sure if anything would happen between us, I'm not that girl who competes for a man's attentions.

Before I can think too much more about it, Alessandro pulls me into the fold and introduces me. I'm horrible with names as it is, but I know I'll never remember all of them. Except her. Valentina. She's gorgeous in a way I'll never be, curved and feminine in all the places I'm flat and lacking. Being "willowy" has never made me so self-conscious.

We pile into three tiny cars. Alessandro sits beside me, rubbing my leg reassuringly.

"Will you all speak Italian the whole time?" I ask quietly.

He smiles so widely it crinkles the corners of his eyes. "*Mi dispiace*," he says. "I'm sorry. But yes, they probably will."

I smile vaguely. "Oh, well, I'm sure I'll be fine," I murmur.

He leans close. "Don't worry, they all can speak English. I've asked them to try to remember to speak it around you as much as possible." He kisses me on the forehead.

On.

The.

Fucking.

Forehead.

Bryce kisses me on the forehead. My grandpa kisses me on the forehead. Instantly, my mood flips.

"So, you and Valentina," I spit out. His eyebrows fly up at my asinine tone. "You dated? Dating? Or is she another wife you conveniently forgot to mention?"

The guy in the front passenger seat shoots a look back at Alessandro. His jaw tightens, and he shakes his head at me and looks away. I've clearly insulted him. I should be sorry for reminding him about the estranged wife he hid from Sera while they were dating, as it's so far in the past and had nothing to do with me, but I'm not.

So I spend my time looking out the window as darkness settles in. Thankfully, it's not a long drive.

When we get to the house where we'll be staying, I'm shown to a tiny room with one bed. At least I get my own room. I'm not left alone long when there's a knock on my door.

"Come in," I call.

Alessandro's lean frame appears in the door.

"We're leaving for dinner shortly, but I'd like if we could talk," he says quietly.

I gesture widely for him to go on. He enters, closing the door gently behind him, then settles next to me on the bed.

"Valentina and I have been together in that way, though many years ago," he admits bluntly. I cross my arms over my chest and look away. He sighs deeply. "But that's not what I'm here for."

"I'm an idiot," I say, laughing. "Do whatever you want, Alessandro. Fuck her silly if that's what you really want. That's what we're both about, right? Being spontaneous. Doing whoever and whatever we want." For the first time I admit to myself that the feeling I'd had when I saw them greeting each other, saw her obvious interest in him, was jealousy. I'm nothing to him, I know. And the short time we've had to get to know each other has barely made us friends. But I guess I didn't realize how one-sided the attraction between us is.

"It's not what I want," he says simply. "Now let's just go to dinner. Once we've had something to eat, we can come back here and sleep, and by tomorrow most of the jet lag will have passed, and we'll both be thinking more clearly."

I turn my head back to look at him. "What aren't you thinking clearly about?"

He looks hesitant. "Honestly? I may have made a mistake. I feel like..." he trails off, clearly unsure of how to say whatever it is he's trying to say, "... you're in a place of transition. And I don't want to take advantage of that."

I shake my head, furious, climbing off the end of the bed to avoid having to go directly around him. "I'm not a fucking kid," I retort. "I'm a grown woman, here of her own volition. But maybe I'm just a kid to you."

I consider that. How would I feel about dating a man as many years younger than me than I am younger than him? But the distance between eighteen and twenty-eight is so much more than twenty-eight to thirty-eight.

"I know you're not," he says before I can make it to the door. "Believe me, I know it." I spin around to see him staring at me. Really staring at me, as if he's trying to undress me with his eyes. "But maybe I'm not in the best head-space right now, either." The look on his face is so pained, so raw, it pains me too. And again, I'm reminded that we're probably more alike in some ways than I'd care to admit.

I tilt my head back and laugh toward the low ceiling. "You know what I usually do when I feel that way?" I ask. "I fuck someone I couldn't give a shit about. Just to feel something besides what I don't want to feel."

"I did that for a long time," he says. "It never worked out well."

I tip my head back down and look at him. "Well, then I guess there's always booze," I reply with a wobble in my voice.

He laughs, and rises from the bed, stopping in front of me. "Yes, there's always booze," he agrees. His hands rest on my shoulders, skimming down my arms, then back up until his hands settle on either side of my face. "But when I fuck you, *Cara Mia*, it will be because we both know it's right. Not because we can't stand thinking about what's wrong."

My stomach flips at the implication. Maybe it wasn't as one-sided as I thought.

"What about kissing me?" I ask, looking up at him defiantly.

"You just won't take no for an answer, will you?" he asks with a smile.

"No more than you would," I point out.

He runs a finger down my cheek. "You have a fire in you," he murmurs. "I know what that feels like. But there's no rush."

"Maybe. Maybe not. What if the world ends tomorrow and all we have is right now?" I say, half teasing, half wondering what his holdup is.

He shakes his head. "It's still not our time."

"What if I've got nothing to offer but right now?"

Alessandro looks at me sadly. "Do you really believe that?" He strokes my cheek with his thumb. "You have fire, you have strength, and you have everything to give. Don't ever sell yourself short for anyone. Especially not me." And with that he pulls away.

I want to argue. I want to convince him to kiss me, to take me, here, now. To live in the moment with me. I can't explain to him that I'm not selling myself short, I've just never been one to think about anything beyond today.

"Why did you bring me here?" I ask, closing my eyes.

I feel his hands slide into mine, and he pulls me to him, letting go so he can wrap his arms around me. It feels too good not to hold him too, so I wrap my arms under his and rest my head against his chest. The steady beat calms me.

"I don't know, I didn't think too much about it," he murmurs into my hair. "It just felt right."

I agree with him, but I hold back, already feeling exposed. "Well, it's a start." I take a step back. "Shall we?"

With a smile, he gestures for me to precede him out.

It turns out the house we're staying in is pretty far up the hill, so we walk in a loud, raucous group down to the closest bar to eat. The lot of them spend hours eating, talking, and drinking, and I do my best to keep up. Though exhausted, I learn one thing. It's practically impossible to get an Italian drunk. They drink more than I do, which is saying something, but they space it out, and eat enough to where it hardly seems to affect them. Though it might also be the jet lag that's causing the little I drink to hit me hard.

I look over at Alessandro, though, and he seems completely unaffected. I swoon backward into the booth we're sitting in, giving up trying to engage. Thankfully, Valentina sits on the other end the whole time, so at least I haven't had to contend with her flirting for his attention. She seems happy enough to flirt with the other half dozen available men. The tramp.

I hear my name being spoken amid the rapid Italian shooting around the table, then warm arms sliding under me.

"Time to go home, *Cara Mia*," Alessandro says, his deep voice rumbling in my ear. I look up, realizing my head is on his chest.

"I can walk," I murmur sleepily.

He laughs, and it makes me smile.

"Shhhh, *bella*," he hushes me. "I've got you."

Too tired to protest further, I surrender, my eyelids sliding shut.

THREE

EMILY

I wake up with more arms than I should have. Looking down, the one over my waist is significantly hairier. I crane my neck backward and see Alessandro tucked behind me.

I roll over with a smile, noting the small windows are open, and I can hear shorebirds calling in the early morning sunshine. It's plenty warm in the room, and I'm still wearing the slinky dress I put on for Bryce and Sera's party.

I examine Alessandro's face for a moment. He looks more his age when he's asleep, without the smile he usually has, but he's no less handsome for it. I stop myself from kissing him, or even touching him, though I want to do both. And a whole hell of a lot more.

"Like what you see?" he asks without opening his eyes. It startles me so much I jump back a little. He laughs, finally opening his eyes. "*Mi dispiace.* I didn't mean to scare you."

I push on his chest. "Yes, you did."

His answering sideways grin makes me wish we were wearing fewer clothes. "You're right, I did." He lifts his wrist to look at his watch. "*Perfetto.* It's almost nine. By the time we get cleaned up, there will probably be breakfast still."

He sits up, swinging his legs over the bed and unbuttoning his shirt to reveal a black undershirt.

"Don't you have your own room?" I tease him, propping my head up on my elbow.

He looks back at me with a sexy smirk. "*Sí, bella.* But I underestimated how tired I was last night, and I fell asleep here before I could make it there," he explains.

I give him a skeptical look. "Is that so?"

He tosses his shirt onto a chair beside the bed and turns back to me fully. "Quit laying there looking so sexy," he murmurs, not answering me. "This question may be the death of me, but I trust you brought a bathing suit?"

I narrow my eyes at him. "I'm starting to think you're just a big flirt," I reply. "But yes, I did. A two-piece, if you must know."

He looks mildly insulted, laying a hand over his chest in mock indignation. "Me? A flirt? Such accusations," he grumbles, teasing me. "There's a bathroom just outside in the hall if you'd like a shower. Then be ready in your suit. Preferably with something over it so I don't do anything untoward at the breakfast table."

I sit up, shaking my head. "See? There you go again with the flirting."

"It's not flirting if you're serious."

"Pfff. Says who?"

He grins. "Me." He winks at me.

I shove his chest a little as I climb by him off the bed. "You're impossible."

He grabs my waist before I can get away, dragging me into his embrace. This close, his smell is strong, as neither of us has showered in a while, but it's also overwhelmingly appealing, and as I look up at him, the intensity in his expression takes my breath away.

"So I've been told," he murmurs. His face dips toward mine, and my breath catches in my throat.

His nose gently touches mine, gliding up, then down again. His hot breath fills my senses, and breathing is still difficult. He's alluring in a way I've never experienced, intense yet somehow still playful, and the anticipation of his kiss is killing me.

I bring my hand to his face, stroking the coarse hair of his beard. A small sigh escapes him, and his mouth finds mine. His kiss is soft, sensual, and more polite than I'd like it to be. At least, at first. I slide my hand back into his hair, gripping it as he kisses me. His hands wrap around my back, and he pulls me completely against him, deepening the kiss.

Finally, his tongue pushes into my mouth, and I accept it eagerly. But just when it's getting really good, he pulls away.

"This is exactly why I knew better than to kiss you. Now I need a cold shower," he teases. He runs a thumb over my lip.

"Be careful, or you're going to get more than a cold shower," I caution him.

He laughs and stands up. "Fair enough," he replies. "When you're ready, follow the smell of coffee." And with a wink, he's gone.

I hurry through a shower, and dress quickly in a shamelessly skimpy pink bikini, covering it with a pair of cutoff jean shorts and a white tank top, finishing with a pair of flat, white strappy sandals. And then, just as he told me to, I follow my nose to the bottom floor, joining everyone in the kitchen as they sip at coffees and argue loudly. Well, it sounds like arguing, anyway.

Alessandro sits on a packed couch, across from another one, and they're all talking animatedly. He looks me up and down and gives me a wink as I pass by. I stick my nose in the air and pretend I don't see him. But I can see his amused grin in my peripheral vision. As I get breakfast, I chat idly with one of the other women, who kindly reminds me that her name is Bianca. She seems to be closer to my age, and her husband, Lorenzo, grew up with Alessandro and his brother. Soon she's telling me all sorts of stories about the trouble they'd get into as teenagers. As if sensing his secrets are being spilled, Alessandro wanders over and inserts himself into the conversation.

"Don't believe a word she says," he tells me with a deadpan expression. "Enzo made up all kinds of shit to impress her."

Bianca laughs. "As if I couldn't tell the difference," she chides him.

Alessandro laughs and looks down at me. I'm struck by his easy charm among his friends. He slides an arm around my waist. "Having fun?" he asks lightly.

"Very much," I reply, looking up at him. Wishing he'd take me back upstairs and finish what he started. But I'm also excited to explore. "What are we doing today?"

He chuckles and looks back to Bianca. "Americans, always in a rush," he jokes.

She shrugs. "I'm tiring of all this talk myself. Let's get out of here." She rises, fishing around behind the counter we were sitting at and producing a bag. Wrapping it around her body, she yells at her husband from across the room.

"Enzo, *andiamo!*"

He yells something back that I don't understand, and everyone laughs. I look at Alessandro.

He leans into me, whispering into my ear, "He called her his beautiful, bitchy alarm clock." My eyebrows jump, and he chuckles. "It's their way." He looks down at my outfit. "By the way, you look beautiful."

I narrow my eyes at him. "I bet you say that to all the girls," I tease him. In his bright blue board shorts and black tank top, he looks like a magazine ad for beachwear. His toned arms are tan, as is the bit of well-muscled chest peeking out the top of his shirt. With a pair of designer sunglasses hanging casually from his top, he looks ready to go. "But you don't look so bad yourself."

He plants a kiss on top of my head, then pulls me along. We take our time meandering down the hill. I don't mind the slow pace, as it gives me time to take everything in. It feels surreal finally being someplace so different from Seattle, someplace I've always wanted to go like this with its packed, colorful buildings, cobblestone walkways, and balmy sunshine. I don't bother with the hat or sunglasses I brought in my bag, letting the rays hit my face, soaking up every bit of their warmth.

We spend most of the day lying on the beach, tossing a frisbee around, splashing in the water when we get too warm. After lunch, the women lay out to tan, but it really ends up as a nap. Late in the day, we wander back up the hill, a final workout to top off a day of exhausting sunshine and laziness.

We cycle through showers and donning more appropriate clothes to go out for dinner, then head out to an actual restaurant, where we spend the rest of the evening and into the small hours of the next day.

Much as the night before, the food, alcohol, and laughter flow freely. I find myself participating more, all the while sticking close to Alessandro. It's hypnotic watching him slip so easily between English and Italian, his easy grace and warmth making me comfortable and happy by his side. By the end of the night, when I've spent most of my time watching him, I realize I'm way more into him than I was even this morning. No way I'm going to settle for "whatever."

Once we're all back at the house, he offers to walk me to my bedroom door, and I'm practically giddy with anticipation. Thankfully, he follows me in, taking a seat in the chair next to the bed as I remove my sandals. I sink onto the bed, suppressing a frown.

"You're awfully far away," I say, patting the bed next to me.

He raises an eyebrow. "Did you have good day?"

"Yes," I reply. "You seemed to enjoy yourself."

"I did," he agrees, crossing his legs. "It's been a long time since I've felt this relaxed." He rubs his chin thoughtfully. "You fit beautifully into the group. I expected it to be…" he pauses, searching for the word.

"Awkward?" I supply.

"Yes," he agrees, leaning forward. "Awkward."

"Like right now."

He laughs. "Yes, something like that."

"So are you going to spill or what?" I ask bluntly, folding my arms over my chest to demonstrate my impatience.

He slips off the chair and takes a seat next to me, brushing my hair back behind my shoulders tenderly. "Do you always say exactly what's on your mind?"

"Yep. Do you always avoid saying what's on yours?"

He considers that with a smirk. "Not always. Just when I think it will get me in trouble."

I roll my eyes. "That's exactly when you *need* to speak up."

"Even if it might upset you?"

I shake my head. "Are you really that scared of hurting my feelings? Yes.

I'd rather be upset and know, than sitting here wondering what the hell you're thinking."

"That's refreshing." He takes a deep breath. "I'm afraid of ruining this. I find you fascinating, *Cara Mia*. You seem to understand me so well. You're a little too observant at times, really. And then you just say exactly what you're thinking. It unbalances me. You unbalance me." He stares at me intently. I stare right back. "I've always jumped into romance, like you seem to want to do now. But this feels different."

"Can we not?" I ask. "Overanalyze this, I mean. You're different than anyone I've ever known too. And I never thought I'd be doing this, with you, here, so fast. But thinking too hard causes more problems than it solves, in my experience. Can't we just be whatever it is we feel like being?"

The silence that follows my words is painful. So much so, I can't stand it. And I'm not used to having to convince a man to be with me. With a shake of my head, I rise, going to my suitcase and pulling out a nightshirt.

"You're not going to need that."

I whirl in place to find he's standing behind me. The fire in his eyes answers the question that I'd asked, that had been lingering uncomfortably in the air. Finally. I drop the nightshirt and go into his arms just as he reaches for me.

This time when he kisses me there's nothing tender about it. His lips are demanding, consuming my answering kisses with a fiery passion that immediately sets my skin ablaze for him. He works his hands under my blush sundress, sliding them over my ass as he pulls me back toward the bed. I press him down until he's seated, mounting him as our mouths continue to work together, as I wrap my hands in his luscious hair. I pull at it hard, tipping his mouth away from mine.

"Do you have a condom?" I ask breathlessly. He nods. *Thank fucking God.* "Good. Now undress me."

"As you wish," he replies with a sultry smile. In one swift motion, he pulls the sundress over my head and discards it on the floor. His hands trace back down my chest, over my nude lace bra, down the matching thong. His fingers stroke me over the fabric, and I grip his shoulders as the hot fire of desire rises in me under his touch. His deft fingers reach around and undo my bra, and he discards it. His hands swirl over my breasts, pinching at my taut nipples, before tracing down my stomach. "You're stunning."

I look down at him. "And you're still dressed."

He slides me off his lap onto the bed, and wastes no time removing his clothes as I lay back against the pillows. "Better?" he asks, turning to me.

I slide a hand under my panties, stroking myself. I watch his sizeable cock harden as he takes it in. I lift my other hand, twirling my finger.

"Turn around."

He does so and I get a good look at his gorgeous ass. I slide off my panties and, unable to help myself, I sit up and run my hands over his rock-hard backside. Then I slip my arm around him, grabbing him and stroking firmly. His left hand reaches back and latches onto my arm. "Fuck."

"Condom?"

His right hand flicks up, the packet held between two fingers. I snatch it away from him, open it, and roll it over his hard length before turning him back around and pulling him onto the bed.

"What, no foreplay?" he teases.

I push him down onto the pillows and swing my leg over him, hovering above him. "We've had days of foreplay," I reply. "I need to fuck you before I go insane."

His head tips back slightly and his muscles tense. "God, yes," he breathes.

I reach between us, stroking him, lifting him into position. His throbbing tip grazes me and it takes everything I have to concentrate through these first few, sensitive touches. And as I slide him into me, I enjoy every goddamn inch of heat that licks through me. There's nothing so good as this moment. Well, not until the end anyway.

I look down at him, and I can feel the flush of my cheeks, the tightness of my nipples. He sees it, and reaches up, stroking and pulling at them. I shift gently, rocking him inside me. We both gasp at how good it feels. His hands drop to my hips, begging for more.

And I don't disappoint him. I rock slowly at first, until he's groaning beneath me, until I'm soaking wet enough to really ride him. Once I am, I lean into him, arching my hips to slide him in and out, faster, harder, until I feel my climax building. I sit up so he's fully buried in me and give myself a moment to watch his perfectly exquisite face contract with pleasure. Letting go, I grind into him, stimulating myself inside and out until my orgasm swirls inside me.

It's when the expletives start rolling off my tongue, and Alessandro grabs my nipples, pinching and pulling into my release. It sends the fire shooting between my core and my breasts and back again before exploding out into my limbs as I ride the wave of my climax. When I finally descend, I sink into him, a mewling, trembling mass of post-orgasmic bliss.

He shifts beneath me, holding me to him with one hand, using the other to hold my ass in place while he pushes up from the bed and continues to take me. I didn't expect it, and I gasp into the amazing feeling of him fucking me. But he can only go so deep from this angle. So, I roll to the side, and he rolls with me, pressing into me to stay inside.

He slips my legs up onto his shoulders, then braces against them, dragging my ass into his lap so he can take me hard and fast. Soon, my legs are trembling in anticipation of another orgasm. He drops one of my legs and presses into me, circling his hips when he's in to the hilt so he's rubbing against me with every thrust. I cry out, and he smirks down at me, knowing exactly what he's doing, how crazy it's making me. He slows, deliberately pulling all the way out, only to plunge back in fully again.

"Please," I beg.

"Shhhh," he responds. "Trust me."

And though I'm aching for release, I give myself to him. I surrender to his rhythm, allowing him to fill me only to leave me void over and over, slowly, torturously. Without warning, instead of burying his cock in me, he slips a hand between us, vigorously pumping into me. The switch-up has me arching off the bed, but before I can so much as gasp, his cock enters me once again and his mouth attaches to mine. Plunging his tongue in my mouth, he keeps his cock buried deep, rubbing in a way that brings me abruptly to the edge and hangs me there. My hands find his ass, holding on for dear life, encouraging him. His mouth drops to my neck, his heavy breathing tickling my ear.

I moan into him, and he moans back. I tilt my hips up, needing him as deep as he can go. It changes things just enough to tip me into climax, and I clench around him.

"Ohhhh, *mio dio*," he moans as his muscles tighten. "*Cazzo, sto venendo*." I can feel his orgasm shudder through him, and it turns me on so much it interrupts my descent, giving me one last jolt of pleasure.

As both of our bodies finally relax, he presses his forehead into my neck. It feels so good laying here with him still between my legs that I'm not ready to let go quite yet.

"What does, '*Cazzo, sto venendo*' mean?" I ask curiously, stroking his damp back.

Alessandro laughs. "Fuck, I'm coming." When I laugh too, he picks his head up to look me in the eyes and gives me a light kiss on the lips. "That was amazing."

"Mmm, yes, it was," I agree. "Teach me something else in Italian."

He leans back, pulling out, much to my dismay. After he's discarded the condom, he lays back down next to me.

"*Sei il miglior fra tutti quelli che mi sia mai scopate*," he says slowly.

I laugh but let him repeat it to me until I can repeat it back.

"*Sei il miglior fra tutti quelli che mi sia mai scopate*," I'm finally able to say. "What does it mean?"

He's unable to suppress his shit-eating grin. "It means, 'You're the best fuck I've ever had,'" he replies, bursting into laughter.

I pull the pillow from behind my head, rise to my knees, and proceed to whack him with it. "You arrogant bastard," I cry out. "I can't believe you seriously just made me tell you that." I continue beating him with the pillow as he laughs. I give him one, final hard whack in the face. "Honestly." I try to throw as much disgust into the word as I can, but I'm having a hard time not laughing.

He pulls the pillow away from me and puts it behind his head. "Maybe I was telling you you're the best fuck *I've* ever had," he replies.

"Maybe?"

"Or maybe not." He laughs again, acknowledging that I'm clearly not falling for it. "Am I?"

I narrow my eyes at him. "Maybe," I reply airily. "Teach me something else."

"Hmmm. Perhaps I need to teach you something that will help you answer my question," he says suggestively. I laugh, and gesture for him to continue. "*Leccamela tutta.*"

"That's much less of a mouthful," I remark. He bursts out laughing. "What?"

He shakes his head, wiping tears of laughter from his eyes. When he's regained composure, he looks at me, trying to keep the laughter at bay. "Just say it," he urges. "I promise you won't regret it. *Leccamela tutta.*"

I give him a stern look, not sure if he's trying to fool me. "*Leccamela tutta,*" I say.

An evil glint appears in his eyes and he prowls toward me. I don't flinch or move an inch. He pries open my naked legs, pushing me back onto the pillows. Then his head disappears, and I feel his tongue *there.*

"Holy shit," I gasp, realizing what he had me ask him to do. But as his tongue laps at the extra-sensitive folds between my legs, my brain fogs and heat builds in me, and I find I'm not able to protest. Scratch that, I don't want to.

While he sucks and nibbles at my nub, sending me into a trembling frenzy, his beard tickles my opening, his chin pressing into my sex in a way that has me wetter than I ever remember being. The erotic sounds of him lapping at me are unbelievable. In a slow build, he caresses me in ways I'd never dreamed of, and though I could languish in the amazing feeling forever, I'm soon coming on his face, whimpering my release, too overwhelmed to do anything else.

He sits up, looking extremely satisfied with himself. And damn well he should be. He wipes his face, removing as much of the moisture from his beard as he can.

"Well?" he teases.

I nod in defeat. "*Sei il miglior fra tutti quelli che mi sia mai scopate.*" He beams with pride. "You should teach classes on what you just did there."

He laughs, sliding down next to me. "I don't do that for just anyone, you know."

"Oh, so I'm special?" I tease back, turning toward him and running my hands down his chest.

He strokes my face, kissing me gently. "More than you know," he says seriously.

"And you were the best I've had even before the mind-blowing oral," I reply.

He lunges for my mouth with his, capturing my bottom lip between his teeth before plunging his tongue into my mouth. I wasn't expecting the intensity, but I'm finding the feeling of his mouth on any part of me to be very addicting, so I sure as hell don't mind.

We sleep together that night, wrapped around each other peacefully. As it happens, it's also the best sleep I've ever had.

FOUR

EMILY

On Wednesday morning, I wake nestled in the corner against the wall. I try to wriggle upright only to bump into Alessandro, who is spread-eagled in the small bed, taking up ninety percent of its surface.

I shake my head and start pushing him out of bed. What a pig. I decide a good, solid fall to the floor will be a fitting punishment. But he's heavier than he looks, being all lean muscle, and he starts to wake up before I can get him over the edge.

He grabs at me, rolling me onto my back. "That's not very nice," he chastises me, pinning me beneath him.

I wriggle violently. "Yeah, well, it's not nice to hog the bed, either," I reply, sticking my tongue out at him.

With a grin, he descends upon it, covering my mouth with his and joining his tongue to mine. Suddenly, I'm less mad and more horny. Noting with satisfaction that he's got morning wood, I twist suddenly and give a swipe of my leg to topple him onto the bed. Thankfully, he left his stash of condoms on the nightstand, so I grab one and suit him up before climbing on top of him. Unsurprisingly, he doesn't protest, watching me with amusement.

Until I sink down on him. Then he's throwing his head back in pleasure. And it feels pretty damn good for me too. I take my time riding him, testing to see what we both like best. He's being lazy this time around, letting me take control, simply watching me with his arms tucked behind his head. I have to say it's a pretty big turn-on.

The more intently he watches, the more turned on I get. I close my eyes, still feeling his on me, and I surrender to the moment. I work my nipples, then rub myself between my legs as I bounce over him. A few hard circles on my clit, and I'm groaning as I start to come. His hands find my hips, helping keep the pace as I languish in the orgasm, barely able to move while I explode in ecstasy. He gives a few ferocious thrusts and a groan that tells me he's finished too.

I sink onto him with a catlike grin.

"Good morning," I purr.

"Fucking amazing morning," he replies, kissing me deeply. "Let's just stay here and do this all day."

I laugh. "No dice, sir. I've had a taste of real Italian food, and there's none in this bed, so you're out of luck."

He laughs loudly. "Not even two full days in Italia and you're already spoiled," he teases.

I smirk at him and climb off of his gorgeous body, stretching widely. "I'm going to take a shower," I proclaim. He sits up on his elbows and raises an eyebrow suggestively. "*Alone*. I'd like to eat before noon."

With a sigh, he climbs to his feet and starts to dress. "If we must," he replies. He's dressed quickly and, with a smack on my ass and a kiss on my cheek, he leaves me to get ready.

I can't keep the smile off my face the whole time, either. Being with him definitely puts me in a good mood. Or maybe it's the setting. Or being on vacation. Bah, who knows, and who cares? I'm going to enjoy every damn minute of it.

As I descend into the main area, the smell of pastries is overwhelming, and my mouth starts to water.

"Ohhhh, who is my new best friend?" I joke as I step off the stairs.

Valentina looks up from the freshly opened bakery box she's obviously just set out and puts her hands on her hips.

"Ah. Never mind," I mutter. But as soon as she's taken one and wandered off, I sneak my own. I find the farthest seat from her and descend upon the delicious smelling pastry gleefully.

It's how Alessandro finds me minutes later, though it's almost gone, and I'm covered in chocolate glaze.

"You look like a chipmunk," he teases me, setting down two cups of coffee.

I chew quickly and swallow, grabbing at the cup nearest me and drinking greedily.

"Thank you," I reply earnestly.

"For calling you a chipmunk?" he asks with a confused look.

I roll my eyes. "For the coffee, dummy."

"Oh, I'm a dummy now, am I?" he asks.

I give him a stern look. "If I'm a chipmunk, you're definitely a dummy."

He shakes his head and laughs. "Fair enough," he agrees. "But finish quickly. We're leaving soon."

"Ooh, where to?" I ask eagerly.

"Driving a bit up the coast to spend the day at a different beach. But same plan. Lounging. Eating. Trying to sneak away to make love to you in the ocean," he says nonchalantly.

I wrinkle my nose at him. "We didn't do that last one yesterday."

He finishes his coffee, rises, and leans in to kiss me on the cheek. "Then we have some catching up to do," he murmurs into my ear.

Shivers shoot down my spine. I bolt down the rest of my food and follow him as fast as I can. Screw looking too eager. It's going to be a damn good day.

~

It turns out to be an understatement. The drive is so ridiculously beautiful, I'm practically crying by the time we get to our destination. And we spend the rest of the morning and into the afternoon lounging by the shore, playing in the water, and generally just enjoying the crap out of ourselves. After lunch, we return to the beach, where we vie for spots under umbrellas or in the shade to nap off the food coma. But it was totally worth it.

Alas, before I can drift off, Alessandro is tugging at my hand.

"Come," he urges quietly. I let him pull me up, and we walk quietly, hand in hand, down to the water's edge and along the shore.

Before long we pass a group of rocks. Alessandro pulls me between them, and we nestle into the soft sand, him leaning against a smooth rock, me leaning against his chest.

"If you brought me here to have sex, you're going to be very disappointed," I say softly. "I don't fancy getting sand in my private parts."

He laughs lowly. "No, *Cara Mia*. I just wanted you to myself for a while."

I turn my head to look up at him, and he lightly skims my lips with his.

"Tell me about your music," he prompts.

I huff a small laugh. "That's a pretty broad question," I hedge.

He shrugs, running his hands up and down my arms soothingly. "Okay," he allows. "What was the first instrument you learned to play?"

The memory so forcefully pops into my head, I can't help but smile. "Piano. My dad started teaching me when I was six." A pang of longing shoots through me.

"You miss him," Alessandro murmurs. I turn and look at him in shock. He squeezes my shoulders. "I could feel it. Here. And I can hear it in your voice."

"I do," I admit. "I try not to think about it much. He and I were so much alike." I shake my head.

"Was that a bad thing?" he asks.

I tuck my legs under me, playing with the hem of his board shorts. "Sometimes. But most of the time we just had a lot of fun together. Mom and Bryce are the serious ones. They thought we were nuts."

"You are a little nuts," Alessandro replies, smiling. "But in a good way. Mostly."

I turn and poke him in the stomach. "Be careful," I warn him. "I assume you still want to get laid later."

He puts his hands up in surrender.

"You know, music is one of my great loves as well," he admits.

"Oh, really?" I ask skeptically.

"Nothing can move me like a good piece of music," he asserts. "Though I'm hopelessly lacking musical talent. But I admire those with it greatly."

I shrug. "It's not a big deal. I'm sure there are things you're better at. You know. Real estate stuff."

He laughs loudly. "Yes, real estate stuff. I'm quite good at that."

"You're good at other things too," I remind him with a suggestive grin.

"Mmmm," he replies, his eyes locking on mine. "Are you asking for a demonstration?" His voice is thick with desire, and just the sound of it turns me on.

"Maybe," I whisper hoarsely.

He turns me back around so I'm against his chest, running his hands over my breasts, baring them to the warm air. His thumbs prime my nipples as his mouth runs along the shell of my ear, his hot breath unbearably sexy against my skin. One hand drifts down, skimming my stomach, slipping under my bikini bottoms. His fingers slip between my folds, stroking me gently at first.

"*Cara Mia*," he whispers in my ear. "You are unbelievably sexy." I moan into the stimulation. "Yes, let me hear you." His deft fingers stroke and slide, and I'm writhing in his arms. My hands go to his thighs, holding on for dear life as he rubs me into a frenzy. I try to keep the volume down, but I just know when I come, I'm going to scream.

He seems to know it too, because a moment before, he turns my head with his free hand, and my moans erupt into his mouth, muffling the sound.

As I drift back down to earth, he wraps his arms and legs around me. Once I've fixed my top, we settle in and watch the surf lap at the shore for a while longer. And when he unwraps himself, stands, and offers me a hand, I just stare. Because I want to etch this moment in my memory. I can't remember ever being quite this happy. And I know it won't last forever. It never does.

We rejoin our group just in time for the last round of post-nap beach antics before dinner. Dinner is, as usual, an all-night affair of eating, drinking, and talking. After which we drive home, and Alessandro and I have sex in the shower, then spend the last of our waking moments talking about everything and nothing.

He continues to amaze me with his ability to listen, share himself completely, and make me feel like I can tell him anything. And the fact that he's beyond amazing in bed doesn't hurt, either. As we drift peacefully to sleep after going at it one final time, I can't help but think to myself that this is like living in a fairy tale. And I'm already dreading the day I have to go back to reality.

~

THE NEXT DAY IS MUCH OF THE SAME, JUST A DIFFERENT BEACH, A DIFFERENT lunch spot. But for dinner, Alessandro steers me away as the others head to a nearby restaurant.

"I have something special planned, *Cara Mia*," he tells me with an excited grin.

"Oh? Is this the part where you finally get me alone and I find out you're really an ax murderer?" Just to be weird, I say it like I'm excited about it, and he gives me an impatient look.

"Yes," he deadpans. "You caught me." He rolls his eyes. "No, crazy. Come, I'll just show you."

He takes me by the hand and leads me away from the main tourist area, meandering up a side street that looks like it goes up a hill to nowhere. But as we turn the final corner, I'm surprised to find an old, towering restaurant tucked away on a cliff.

He gestures to the entrance. "If you think you love Italian food now, you're going to be in heaven soon," he explains. "Trust me."

I give him a look somewhere between surprised and sad. "You're too sweet to me."

He stops, a frown pulling at the corners of his mouth. Getting up in my face, he lifts my chin. "You deserve it," he tells me seriously, looking deeply into my eyes. "Don't ever doubt that."

I want to tell him I don't, but I don't want to argue and spoil his wonderful surprise. "Thank you," I reply sincerely. "For bringing me here. Now quit being so cute and feed me."

He laughs lightly but stays to kiss me for a moment before leading me inside.

And by the time we're done eating hours later, I couldn't argue with him if I wanted to. I'm too blissed out over the most amazing meal of my life. With the most amazing views. With an amazing man, whom I still can't reconcile with the selfish ass I'd pegged him as. I don't consider myself particularly romantic, but dinner with him was off-the-charts intimate.

As we walk home, I say the first prayer I've said in years that he's really this man. That I was wrong about him before, when all I had to go on was what someone else told me. But deep down, I have trouble believing it. It's so much easier believing the bad things.

Not even another night of amazing sex completely wipes away my fears. Because the better this gets, the more I keep expecting it to all come crashing down.

THE NEXT DAY, FRIDAY, BIANCA DECIDES WE'RE GOING TO HAVE A BONFIRE that evening. It's a slapped-together affair of convenience store food, which is still leaps and bounds better than the American kind, straight-up bottles of booze, and a few stray games and instruments they're able to find. So that night we do indeed find ourselves by a moderately large fire, though the night is still quite warm. It means, at least, I didn't have to change out of my bikini, shorts, and tank that have become my vacation uniform.

Seated on a blanket just outside of the main ring around the fire, I stretch my legs out and am considering how tan they've gotten in such a short time when Alessandro approaches with a guitar in hand.

"It's the best I could do. Will you play for me?" he asks.

I take it from him, weighing the acoustic in my hands. I check that it's in tune and strum a few chords.

"Couldn't hurt, I guess. Any requests?"

He leans down to kiss me on the cheek and then stretches out on the blanket to watch. "Whatever makes you happy," he replies huskily. I stare at him for a moment, his face in shadow, the light of the fire flickering against his back. I let the moment flow through me, sink in deep, and then I let it out through my fingers.

I close my eyes, surrendering myself to the music, not even sure exactly what I'm playing, but still hearing the music pouring out of the old instrument nonetheless.

As I finish the first song, I open my eyes. Everyone has settled themselves near us, intently listening to me play. I finish and give a laugh when they all start clapping enthusiastically.

There are various calls of "*Bravissima!*" and "More!" but I note Alessandro still lays on his side, staring at me, the fire now in his eyes. I know without a doubt that if we were alone, he'd be taking me on this blanket right now. I play more, but as far as I'm concerned, he's my only audience. He doesn't take his eyes off me as I continue playing a second, third, then a fourth song. Finally, my out-of-practice fingers need a break, and I thank everyone graciously for their applause.

I set the instrument gently down on the blanket next to me, and they all go back to what they were doing. Alessandro rises, offering me a hand.

"Walk with me?"

I take his hand without a word, and he leads me down the beach. We stop at a group of benches, settling in on one to watch the gentle lapping of the water at the shore.

"You play beautifully," he says softly.

"Thank you," I reply simply.

"Will I ever get to hear you sing?"

I look over at him in horror. "No. Um, decidedly not."

He frowns. "Surely, it can't be that bad."

I shrug. "It's not that. Singing in front of people is a level of vulnerable I'm just not ready for." I have to stop myself from saying "I'm not capable of." That would be a little too much honesty.

Thankfully, he lets it drop, and we sit, starting out at the dark water.

"I don't want this to ever end," I say softly.

He stares stoically at the ocean. "But it will," he assures me softly. "And then what?"

I make a noise of frustration and shake my head. "That's a question for another day."

He turns and catches my eye. "I'm asking now."

"No, you're treading into dangerous territory now."

"Nonetheless, I'm curious."

I heave a deep sigh. "I don't know," I reply honestly. "I guess we just keep going and see what happens."

"Is that what you want?" he asks plainly, turning toward me and pulling at the hem of my shorts.

"Yes," I say. "For now."

I didn't mean to say the last part and I can see it's not sitting well with him.

"So this is more a vacation fling for you?" he asks, hurt in his voice.

"Why are you suddenly so worried about this?" I ask.

"Because I found out today that I need to go back to Seattle on Sunday. My company needs me. And you're welcome to stay, but I want to see you once we're home. Though it doesn't sound like you feel the same," he replies genuinely.

"I'm surprised you do," I admit. "I figured this was just a vacation fling for you too. Surely you don't really want to piss my brother off. Or Sera. I'm not sure she'd be okay with this, either."

"I think Serafina would be happy for us," he responds. And though I'd never admit it, he's probably right. "And I thought you weren't worried about what the giant thought anymore."

"When he's not here to care, no." But it's so much more than that. I can feel myself fighting being with him. Still, my brother is the first and most obvious reason this just won't work.

Though it clearly was the wrong thing to say. Alessandro rises, fuming, and folds his arms over his chest. "Not wanting a relationship is one thing, but I didn't sign up to be your dirty secret, either."

"Oh, please, you're not my dirty secret, don't be so dramatic," I snap, rising to my feet as well.

Alessandro barks a laugh and runs a finger under his chin, clearly agitated. "Coming from you, that's ironic," he retorts. "Everything is drama with you. I can't even tell you I want to date you without you getting upset."

And just like that, I'm seeing red. I whirl on my heel, stomping away.

"Dammit, Emily, come back," he demands. But I don't listen. I stomp up the beach as he follows. The Alessandro of legend is finally making an appearance.

"Fuck off, Alessandro," I bark back at him.

He jogs up beside me, putting himself in my path.

"I won't," he says obstinately.

"You want to see drama? I'll give you drama," I spit at him. "I shouldn't have come here with you. My opinion of you before we met was dead-on, I just let your stupid fucking charm cloud my judgment. God, I should know better by now. I always date the same jerks, just with an accent this time. News flash: you don't get to make demands from me and then tell me who I am."

He throws his hands up in the air and I flinch away, my guard momentarily down. "Fine. You want to throw a temper tantrum? Be my guest." He steps aside, and I scurry off as fast as I can, away from his wrath, away from him, my heart pounding in my chest.

The arduous walk back to the house doesn't do much to cool me off. When I get back to my room, I pace around until I hear everyone returning. It's still early, so I hear them settle in downstairs to chat and, presumably, drink in the living room. I stop pacing, not wanting to draw attention to myself. Sitting on the bed quietly goes a long way toward calming me down, finally. And once I do, I'm able to admit to myself that I may have overreacted a little. But he's still got some apologizing to do too.

I trudge downstairs and peek into the living room, but there's not even half a dozen people there, and he's not among them. Assuming he's gone to bed, I head to his room.

I knock once, and nobody answers, but there's clearly a light coming from under the door. So I knock again.

"Alessandro, it's me. Please, I know you're angry, but we need to talk," I say through the door.

I hear shuffling, then, "We're busy, fuck off little girl." The voice is unmistakably a woman. And not just any woman. Valentina.

My heart drops, and I turn on my heel and run back to my room. Thankful that almost everything is still in my suitcase, I pack even faster than when I did to run here with Alessandro. Because now it's time to run away.

I flee back down the stairs in time to see Alessandro standing at his door down the hallway, looking at me in terror, realizing that I'm leaving.

"I hope she was worth it," I spit at him. But I don't wait for a response, I just keep going. Predictably, he follows.

"Can you please stop and talk to me?" he calls.

"No," I call back over my shoulder as I fly out the front door. "Why don't you go back and talk to your girlfriend?"

"Emily," he calls. "Ow!" I look back, and he's holding a bare foot in his hands, pulling something out of it. Good. I hope he really hurt himself.

Practically blind with the tears I hadn't realized I'd started shedding, I flee down the hill, looking for a place to hide and call a taxi. It's time to go home.

FIVE

SERAFINA

Two weeks later

"Hey, baby?" Bryce's head peeks around the stairs. I look up from my book.

"What's up?" I prompt, setting the novel down on the coffee table next to me.

The rest of him comes into view and, as usual, the sight of him still makes my heart race a little. My husband. Even the thought makes me want to throw him down on the couch and do naughty things to every inch of his gorgeous body. And that's a lot of inches. In every respect.

He stops at the foot of the couch, giving me the same admiring look I'm sure I'm giving him.

"Damn, you look good there," his deep voice rumbles, glancing at the stack of books on the floor next to me and the pile on the coffee table. "Like a sexy little librarian." His blue eyes sparkle mischievously, and I know he's thinking about doing naughty things to me too. And here I thought once the honeymoon was over, we'd be tired of going at it like rabbits.

"Thanks," I reply. "But what were you going to ask me?"

"Oh, right," he replies, his trademark sunshine smile splitting his face. "Have you talked to my sister since we got back?"

"No, why?"

He sinks onto the couch next to me, pulling my legs into his lap and stretching his out on the coffee table while he rubs lazy circles into the bottom of my foot with his strong hands. "Mom called. She hasn't heard from her since she got back from her trip."

"Mmmm," I reply, distracted by the foot massage. "Wait. Emily was on a trip?"

Bryce drops my foot and smacks himself in the head. "That's right, I forgot. Damn. I got a voicemail from Mom the day after we left. She mentioned Emily had taken off after the party on some last-minute vacation. I meant to tell you, but, well, you know…" He grins at me suggestively.

"Yes, you were more focused on taking me on every surface of our hotel room," I murmur. I'm sure Italy is gorgeous, but frankly we mostly only ended up seeing the inside of our hotel rooms. For two whole weeks. Except the gelato. I made sure we escaped for that at least once a day.

He runs a hand forcefully over his short, chestnut hair, and I know exactly what kind of agitated he is right now. My whole body starts to tingle in response, but I shove it down and try to focus. We really need to learn to be able to have full, normal conversations again at some point.

"So where'd she go?"

He shakes his head. "Don't know. She didn't say, and nobody has talked to her."

"I'd say that's out of character for her, but—"

"But it's not," he agrees. "Yeah. I'm more worried about why. I hope our getting married didn't have anything to do with it."

I can't help the look of surprise on my face. "Surely she would've said something. I mean, Allie was pissed too, and she sure let us know. Emily's never really been the type to hold back with me."

He shakes his head, a small frown tugging at his mouth. "Em's fine calling people out on their shit. But if it's anything serious going on with her, she closes up tighter than a camel's ass in a sandstorm."

"Bryce!" I reach out and smack him on the arm as hard as I can.

He laughs. "What?"

I shake my head at him. "Whatever. Should we be worried?"

"Nah, I'm sure she'll turn up when she's ready to talk," he assures me. He gives me a look and stills. "But you should be worried. That little smack you just gave me woke The Beast."

I press my lips together to suppress a laugh. "I'm still not going to start calling it that."

He turns toward me and climbs between my legs, hovering over me. "Oh, it'll rub off on you eventually."

"Pun intended?" I tease.

With a grin, he leans in and covers my mouth with his, wasting no time feeling me up under the grey shirtdress I'm wearing. I run my hands over his muscled arms, gently stroking his tongue with mine, waiting for him to realize what *isn't* under my clothes.

He gasps and pulls away. "Dirty girl," he whispers as his hand slides between my legs unhindered by the panties that aren't there.

"Please," I say into his mouth. "You know you like it." I grab his semi-hard cock through his sweatpants. "And I'd bet anything you're not wearing underwear, either."

"Baby, I'd walk around naked if you'd let me, just so I could fuck you silly the instant you wanted me."

I suck a sharp breath in through my teeth. "You sure know how to distract a girl." I lift my foot and use it to press against his massive chest until he's a safe distance away. But I'm sure it gives him a full display of what's under my dress, because he can't tear his eyes away. "Strip, Hoyt."

"Anything you say, Mrs. Hoyt." He hooks his thumbs into his white T-shirt and removes it in a flash. The sight of his chiseled chest and abs never gets old. A second later he kicks off his grey sweats, freeing his massive cock. And I have to admit, The Beast is a pretty appropriate name for it. Impressively huge and as insatiable as he is, it's definitely one of my favorites of his body parts.

"I'm so glad we decided to stay home this weekend," I murmur. Then, before he can respond, I lean forward and take him in my mouth, slowly teasing him. As usual, the noises he makes leaves me slick and ready. And when he enters me, I can barely stand how much he fills me, how I never seem to completely adjust to his size. And I'm glad for it.

But he goes slow, torturing me. I hook my leg around his backside, urging him to go faster, deeper. He grins and shakes his head.

"Always so impatient." He reaches down and strokes my breasts, then slips his hands under my hips. In a flash, he's holding me tightly by them and pounding into me so hard I think my building orgasm has its own orgasm before I eventually shatter into pieces.

When we've cleaned up, and the need to be wrapped in each other has subsided once more, or at least for the next hour or two, I pick up my phone and try to call Emily. But it goes straight to voicemail. I leave her a generic message, asking her to give me a call, but as soon as I hang up, something starts niggling at the back of my mind.

Bryce is now settled on the other end of the couch with his own book, and he looks up as I struggle to remember whatever it is I've forgotten.

"Everything okay?" he asks softly.

I shake my head. "I feel like there's something about Emily I should be remembering."

He closes his book on a finger to keep his place. "Did she say something about taking off before we left?"

I shake my head. "Not that I can remember." The harder I try to remember, the less defined the thought becomes.

"Don't worry, I'm sure she'll call one of us back soon. She just does this sometimes. Usually because of a guy. It's why I didn't try to figure out where she went. I didn't want to have to kill anyone," Bryce jokes.

And like lightning hits, I remember in a flash. I barely keep the words "Oh, fuck" from tumbling out of my mouth. Because while I don't know if Emily was still seeing the guy she'd been casually dating, I'm pretty sure she didn't care enough about him to be all that upset if they had broken up. But I do remember who she was flirting with at our engagement-turned-wedding party. Alessandro fucking Giordano. And that he was still supposed to be leaving that same night for his Amalfi Coast vacation.

"Right," I reply with an affected smile before I can freak out too badly. "Wouldn't want that."

Bryce goes back to his book, seemingly clueless as to the thoughts racing through my head. A million questions go through my mind. Alessandro wouldn't really pursue Bryce's sister, would he? And even if he did, he's not so impulsive as to try to whisk her off to Italy with him, is he? I don't even need to ask myself if Emily is impulsive enough to go with him. She totally is. Or if she'd find him attractive — she's got eyeballs. And damned if he isn't charming when he wants to be.

But I also remember her being the one to force me to admit last year that his selfishness was what was keeping our relationship from working. But then, I can't say I've ever heard of Emily dating a guy for all that long, much less being in a relationship. So maybe looking for a guy who's actually relationship material isn't that high on her list. Or maybe, just like I once did, she saw him as an opportunity for some no-strings-attached fun.

Shit. The truth of it slams into me. But before I can jump to conclusions, I work on settling myself. Because if I panic, Bryce's finely tuned radar will go off. And if it really is true...

I shudder lightly, pushing down the thought. One thing at a time. Alessandro is still my friend. Having been through so much together, we'll always have a unique bond. One that works better if my husband doesn't kill him.

As casually as I can, I pick up my phone and text Alessandro. Since Emily is clearly shutting everyone out, I highly doubt she's going to call me back. But Alessandro wouldn't dare lie to me again. I hope.

❧

ALESSANDRO IS A BIT MORE DIFFICULT TO PIN DOWN THAN USUAL, BUT HE eventually agrees to meet me for lunch on Wednesday. Since Emily is also still silent, both Bryce and his mother have tried her at her apartment, with no answer. Bryce even goes down to the music store she works at, only to find out she's quit. Thankfully, Bryce has been busy running his family's corporate security company, and I manage to keep my suspicions under wraps, though it requires a lot of distraction. Mostly the kind of thing we would've already been doing, so it's not a difficult line to walk. But it's only a matter of time before Bryce decides to find out where Emily went that week, and with whom, hoping to shake loose answers that will help him get her to contact him or their mother.

So I'm itching for answers by the time Alessandro shows up and joins me at the private booth I've secured at my favorite seafood restaurant.

As he approaches, I note from afar that he looks just the same as always, well-coifed in a dark grey suit and black button-front shirt open at the collar, his dark hair and beard styled perfectly. But as he gets closer, I can see it in his eyes. Hurt.

Still, he greets me warmly, with a hug and a kiss on the cheek. "Serafina," he says. "You're glowing. I see marriage agrees with you."

I give him a guarded smile and take my seat, while he takes his opposite me. "Thank you," I reply. "It does, very much. How are you?"

I can see him suppress a sigh as he fixes me with his usual sideways smile. But it has none of its usual charm.

"Work has been stressful," he replies. "But nothing I can't handle. How are things at Sutton Developments?"

"Same," I reply. "Charles is piling more on my shoulders every day. If I didn't know better, I'd think he finds it funny."

Alessandro gives a half-hearted smile. "Well, I imagine he wants to make sure you'll be ready to run things when he's retired. That's nothing to laugh at," he replies.

"Are we really going to sit here and talk about work?" I ask bluntly, unable to handle it anymore.

Alessandro uncrosses his legs and leans his arms on the table. "What would you prefer we discuss?"

"How was your trip?" I ask, not wanting to accuse him of anything directly.

He smiles faintly. "It was wonderful, until it wasn't. I had to cut it short and come back to work." He leans back in his chair. "How was your honeymoon?"

I give him a skeptical look and huff a dry laugh. "I'm entirely sure you don't want to hear about it," I reply. "I need to know something, but I don't know how to ask you, Alessandro."

He scrubs a hand over his face. "Then just ask."

I take a deep breath. "Did you bring Bryce's sister with you to Italy?"

He stares at me impassively. "Yes."

I'm not sure if I didn't expect the honesty, or if, deep down, I didn't really think I was right, but his answer is like a punch to the gut.

"How could you do that?" I bark at him.

The waiter chooses that moment to come back and take our orders. It gives me a moment to calm down, at least. Once he's gone, I give Alessandro a minute to respond, trying not to look like I want to smack him.

"Have you talked to her?" he finally asks.

"Not yet," I reply. "She's avoiding us. But I've known you longer, anyway, and I think I deserve an explanation."

"If it makes you feel better, she's avoiding me too," he says drily. "Though in my defense, I didn't think it would upset you."

"That you had a fling with my sister-in-law? That whatever happened upset her so badly she won't talk to anyone?" I have to work to keep from screeching the words at him.

The sadness in his eyes spreads, and his face falls. "I'm sorry," he replies. "I didn't intend for any of this to happen. But for what it's worth, it wasn't a fling. Not to me. Even if I didn't realize until it was too late that it was for her." And he looks so thoroughly miserable, I have no choice but to believe him.

"I may not be able to get ahold of her," I reply firmly, "but if this was just a fling to her, she wouldn't be this upset."

He raises his eyes to mine. "Do you really think so?"

The hope in his voice is evident, and I realize there's much more going on here than I imagined. "Alessandro," I gasp. "You're *in love* with her, aren't you?"

He shakes his head. "How can you be in love with someone who only thinks of you as their dirty secret?"

"You *are* in love with her." I'm in awe. I was sure after he'd given up on me that he'd gone back to dating casually, read man-whoring, wholly put off by relationships after everything we'd been through.

He sighs. "Yes."

"I'm seriously confused right now," I admit. "Let's back this up. What happened at our party?"

"I can't say it was love at first sight, if that's what you're asking. Even I'm not that clichéd. But as soon as I laid eyes on her, I *did* feel like I'd met her before. The feeling that I just *knew* her grew stronger with every minute we spent together." He sighs again, something I'm getting the sense he's done a lot of lately. "I think she was emotionally overwhelmed by your announcement and just needed to do something drastic. So when I invited her to come with me, I don't think it was because of me that she said yes."

"But you got close that week."

"I fell in love with her that week," he admits, shifting uncomfortably in his seat. "It's very strange, telling you these things. Knowing it upsets you. I didn't—"

I throw up a hand to stop him. "I was upset because I thought you were just working your charm on her, or using her for a good time or something," I explain. "I didn't know how you felt." I pause, thinking about what he's said. "Why do you think she thinks of you as her dirty secret?"

Alessandro smiles wryly. "Emily seems to believe she's got nothing to bring to the table in a relationship. Or, at least, that's what I thought was holding her back until she informed me she could never have a relationship with me because of her brother. That she only meant for us to be a 'vacation fling.' I'm afraid I said some things at that point that I'm not proud of."

Our food is delivered then, giving me time to process while we eat in silence. But I'm too distracted to care much about the food, and it's not long before I put down my fork.

"What could you have possibly said that would make her shut everyone out?" I muse out loud.

"It's not just what I said. It's also what she thinks I did."

My eyes meet his and he sets down his own fork.

"I was technically sharing a room with someone," he explains, "not that I spent much time in it. After our fight, I think she went looking for me there. As I understand it, a woman in our group I'd admitted to being previously involved with had been — what's the phrase? Ah, yes — shacking up with the other person sharing the room. Anyway, this woman and he were in the room, and she thought it was me in there with her. She left before I could correct the misunderstanding."

When he finishes, I'm gaping at him in disbelief. "So she thinks you had a fight, then went and fucked some other woman?"

He rolls his eyes to the ceiling and breathes deeply. "It sounds so much worse when you say it out loud."

"Well, it explains why she is so upset," I offer. "But it also convinces me you definitely weren't just a fling to her, Alessandro."

He looks back at me, again with that glint of hope. "You think?"

I laugh drily. "Yes, but I don't know that that helps you much. Because she wasn't wrong. Bryce is going to blow his lid. You'll be lucky if you survive long enough to convince her you aren't a disgusting prick."

Alessandro goes back to picking at his food. But I'm thoroughly done with mine. My brain has moved on to other things.

"We needn't ever upset him with the knowledge," he finally mutters. "What good would it do? She's even more stubborn than I am. She'll never listen. And even if she does, she made it abundantly clear that she doesn't feel the same about me."

I fold my arms on the table and lean forward. "Oh, we're going to tell him," I insist. "Because if we don't get him on board, Emily will never know what really happened. Until she does, you'll never know for sure what was possible. Is that what you really want?"

This time he tosses his fork down forcefully. "It doesn't matter what I want, dammit. Your husband is never going to let me anywhere near his sister after he learns of all this."

"He will," I assure him. "And then you're going to tell Emily what really happened. If she doesn't want to be with you after that, then at least you'll know it wasn't meant to be."

He stares at me for a minute, clearly confused and upset. "Why would you go to all this trouble?"

I grin gleefully. "Because once, when I'd given up hope, she was the obnoxious little thorn in my side. She meddled and meddled until Bryce and I got together. And now I'm going to return the favor. But I think the better question is, if you really love her, why wouldn't you?"

Alessandro smiles dimly. "Because she doesn't love me, Serafina. You may know her in many ways, but I've known her in a way you can't. She's still finding her way, and I think she's too scared of opening herself up to someone. I've been there. It's why..." he trails off, looking at me thoughtfully. "It's why all of us casually date, never letting things get serious enough to matter, never letting anyone affect us."

"Her walls aren't going to break themselves down," I reply firmly. "If she hadn't helped Bryce break mine down..." I shake my head, refusing to finish that thought. "If you'll let me, I'd like to do this. Please, Alessandro."

"I think it's cute that you're asking my permission. I know you quite well, Serafina, and I'm fairly certain you're going to do this whether I want you to or not," he replies with a wry smile.

That gets a laugh out of me. "Excellent," I reply, picking my fork back up. "Now let's eat. We're going to need the energy for what comes next."

He raises an eyebrow. "I sense I'm not going to like this."

I smile at him beatifically. "Not at first," I agree. "But you'll be glad once it's over." He looks at me, waiting for me to tell him what I've got planned. I shake my head and laugh. "I thought it would be obvious. We're going to tell Bryce everything."

SIX

SERAFINA

I've been nervous all afternoon since leaving Alessandro. Since promising to call him as soon as I'd prepared Bryce. But now, sitting on our living room couch, waiting for him to walk through the door, I still have no clue how to break this to him.

When the door clicks open just before six, I don't run to greet him like I normally would. I rise, unsteadily making my way to the entryway.

"Hey, baby," he calls, grinning at me across the open space. "How was your day?" He removes his suit jacket, revealing the gun holstered under his left arm.

"Fine," I reply vaguely. As I near, I point at the weapon. "Why do you still carry that thing? You're the boss now. Surely you don't pull security detail anymore?"

He raises an eyebrow at me. "It's never bothered you before," he remarks, undoing the holster and setting the whole thing down on the table next to the door.

Yeah, it's never bothered me before. But I'd rather not tell him something that's going to piss him off while he's packing heat.

I go up on my toes to greet him with a kiss. "I was just asking," I reply nonchalantly, pressing my mouth to his. I slip my arms around him and sink into him, hoping to put him in as good a mood as possible.

"Mmm," he murmurs. "I missed you today." His hands slip over my backside, pulling me into him tightly. "Want to join me in the shower?"

I press my hands against his chest. "Maybe later," I reply. "But first I need to talk to you about something."

He draws his head back, giving me a suspicious look. It's the first time in recent memory I've passed up the chance to get him naked. "Everything okay?"

I roll my lips through my teeth. "It's about Emily."

"Okay, what about her?"

I step out of his embrace, tugging him by the hand into the living room. Once we're settled on the couch with one of my legs crooked in his lap, holding his hand in mine, I look up at him and take a deep breath. "I think I know why she won't talk to us. But I need you to promise not to freak out if I tell you."

Bryce laughs and undoes the top two buttons of his shirt, then leans back into the couch while stroking my leg. "This is about the Italian."

My mouth drops open. And I realize I was an idiot to think he wouldn't already know everything. He always knows everything. After all, that's kind of what he does for a living. The sight of me gaping like a fish makes him laugh harder.

"Seriously, babe," he says, then hooks his thumbs back, pointing at himself. "Security consultant."

I shake my head. "But why didn't you tell me you knew? *When* did you know?"

He shrugs, giving me a small smile. "You have zero poker face, Sera. When I made that joke about killing someone this weekend, it was written all over your face. It took me about two minutes to figure out where she was on her little trip and who she must've been there with."

Fuck. I forget sometimes exactly how damn observant he is.

"So why aren't you more upset about this?" I press. "You hate the guy."

Bryce shrugs. "I don't *hate* him," he starts, but is stopped short as I fold my arms over my chest and give him the most skeptical look I've got. "Okay, fine, I'm not his biggest fan. But I've long since learned to stay out of Em's business. And I know it was probably just some impulsive thing she did anyway. She doesn't do relationships. No sense freaking out over something that's not going anywhere."

"What do you mean, she doesn't 'do' relationships?" I demand. Suddenly, I'm angry on Alessandro's behalf.

Bryce pulls a reticent face. "She has her reasons."

"Ones that make it okay to toy with people's emotions?" I demand.

His eyebrows jump. "The Italian has emotions? There's a newsflash."

"Bryce," I say, a warning in my voice.

He puts his hands up. "Okay, okay, I didn't realize he actually cared about her." He pauses. "*Does* he actually care about her?"

I take a deep breath. "Yes," I reply softly. "I've never seen him like this. I think he really loves her."

"Wow. Didn't see that coming." He looks pensive about it.

"Does that change the way you feel about them?"

"I don't know," he admits. "I'd already written it off. But regardless of how he feels, he's got a mountain to climb to even get her to listen."

"You're the first hill," I point out.

"Me?" he asks in surprise.

"Yes, you, you big scary dork," I snap. "She told him she couldn't really date him because she didn't want to upset you."

"Pfff," Bryce scoffs. "Please. Em does what she wants. That's a total bull-shit play."

"She may be your sister, baby, but I know a woman trying not to fall for Alessandro when I see one. I was that woman once," I remind him.

He grimaces. "Ugh, really?"

"Really," I confirm, not sure which part I'm validating. But the answer is the same for both anyway. "Why don't you tell me what's really holding her back?"

He sighs. "You and her are a lot alike," he grumbles. "Can't mind your own business, can you?" But by the small smile tugging at his lips I can tell he's not totally opposed to my meddling.

"Don't worry, I'll warn him that if he ever hurts her, you'll end him and all that crap," I promise.

He laughs. "Oh, don't worry about that," he assures me. "If he can get behind the walls of Fort Emily, I'll take care of that myself." He cricks his head to the side, cracking his neck. I roll my eyes at him.

"Whatever. Pissing contest later. Talk now."

But he still looks reticent. "She's going to be mad I told you."

I crawl into his lap, holding his face between my hands. "Don't worry about her right now. It's just you and me here," I say softly, grinding my hips into his. His mouth opens a fraction.

"You fight dirty," he breathes, running his hands down my back.

With a smile, I lean in, so my lips are hovering over his, my breasts grazing his chest. "I learned from the best."

With a smile, he plants a brief, chaste kiss on my lips, then pushes me back on his lap. "Short version? Emily's first boyfriend was bad news. And it didn't get a lot better from there."

"Which kind of bad news?" I ask delicately.

"The metalhead, drug-using, getting-locked-up-for-assault type," he replies grimly. "He hit her once. Only once, and that's what convinced her to leave. He was arrested for nearly beating a guy to death a month later."

I can't imagine a world where the feisty woman I know lets a guy hit her. Or where her protective older brother doesn't do something about it.

"What did you do to the guy?" I whisper.

Bryce shakes his head. "She was in college at the time, and I was deployed. By the time I came back, he was dead. Prison fight." The sorrow in his eyes is only a shadow of what I imagine Emily went through. "She's always been tough. But when I got home, she was even tougher than when I left. Doesn't take a lick of shit from anyone. Not sure how, but she's been in love twice since. Mostly just ended because the guys were too big of douches to be very good boyfriends. But ever since that first wreck, when she gets hurt or scared, she just withdraws for a while. Then she comes back like nothing ever happened. It just established some really bad patterns for her."

"I had no idea."

He runs his hands lightly down my arms. "She doesn't exactly open up to people, babe. It's not your fault you didn't know. Hell, it's not the Italian's fault either. If he really does have feelings for her, if he said something to her about it, that would be enough to send her running. She was just scared."

"Scared," I agree. "And hurt too." I relay everything Alessandro told me about their fight and her thinking he was with another woman after that.

Bryce lets out a low whistle.

"Yep, that'll do it."

"So what do I do?" I ask.

He considers me for a moment. "There's nothing you can do," he says simply.

"But I—"

He holds up a hand. "The Italian's got to. He needs to do what I should have done, instead of sending Emily in to do it for me."

I huff a small laugh. "Oh? And what's that?"

He sits up, drawing close, and looking deeply into my eyes. "He needs to do whatever it takes. Stand at her door shouting his feelings for the world to hear. Send her love letters through the cracks of her door all Harry Potter–style and shit. Let her see how fucking lost he is without her. That's what the dumb-fucks before him never did. Fight for her."

His thumb skims my cheek, and I realize he's brushing away tears.

"I thought about doing all those things and more," he whispers. "I gave you too much space. He shouldn't make the same mistake."

I laugh through my tears. "Don't beat yourself up," I reply. "It turned out pretty good for us, in the end."

He smiles. "Yeah, but only because my sister couldn't stay out of it. But if you try to do that to her, she'll close up more. I know her. It has to be him. And he has to be unflinchingly patient and steadfast. Trust me."

I close my hand over his. "I do. Though I'm still not sure why you'd want to help Alessandro win her back."

He frowns. "If that's what makes my sister happy, who am I to stand in the way?"

I run my finger along his pouting lips, then replace it with my mouth. This man. When I pull away, he looks considerably less upset.

"You are the most amazing man I've ever known. I love you, Bryce Hoyt."

He graces me with his sunshine smile. "Love you too, baby. Now, if we're done talking about my sister, I need to be buried in you. Now."

He flips me onto my back next to him, grinding against me as I giggle in protest.

"No! Don't! Stop!" I screech amid the laughter.

His hand slips under my panties, stroking me. The sudden assault has me bowing into him in pleasure.

"Ohhh, don't stop," I moan with another giggle.

His mouth moves to my breast, teasing my nipple through my shirt. And I can't remember for the life of me what we were talking about.

Later that evening, though, when I'm no longer distracted, I call Alessandro. I can tell he's in shock that Bryce would so readily approve. I don't bother explaining that it's not exactly approval. But that if he really wants to get through to Emily, Bryce isn't standing in the way. And I relay exactly what Bryce told me he'd need to do. While I'm tempted to share why she's holding back, it's not my place. But I warn him that she's been hurt before, that it might take time, but not to give up if she's what he really wants. Unsure of whether he actually plans on pursuing her, I realize it's time for me to step back. The rest is up to Alessandro.

SEVEN

I stare at the plate of food for a full fifteen minutes before dumping it in the garbage. Can't say I haven't been trying. I take another sip of vodka from the bottle on the counter. It's worse this time. So much worse. I barely hear it when they knock anymore. Mom. Aunt Char. Bryce. Chad.

I settle onto the couch, absently picking up the guitar sitting there, strumming mindlessly. I can't bring myself to play anything else lately. Endlessly replaying that night.

Sometimes it makes me angry. Sometimes it makes me sad. But right now, I'm just numb. Thank you, vodka.

I think about leaving. But with no car, that leaves me with airplanes, boats, or trains. And I hate trains. Slow, cramped, and smelly. And airplanes are out of the question. Too many memories now. Maybe boats. But that would take effort I don't have to give right now. Damned in any case.

A sharp pain wakes me, and I look down. My index finger is bleeding from the endless strumming. I almost laugh. Good. Bleed, little finger. Let it all out.

I know I need to talk to someone, anyone. But to be honest with them, I'd have to be honest with myself. And that's just not worth it. None of it is worth it. Especially not him. Bastard.

I keep strumming. I keep bleeding. But I don't really care.

At some point there's a knock again. Not having kept track, I have no idea which of my regular tormenters it is, not that it matters.

Knock. Knockity-knock. Knockity-knock-knock-knock. I strum quietly in time with the beat.

"Emily, I can hear you."

It's Him. I stop strumming. I stop myself from yelling at him to go away. He will. And he doesn't need to know how drunk I am.

"Please, *Cara Mia*. I should've come after you sooner. You must know I didn't do what you think I did. It wasn't me in there with her, I swear it."

I laugh out loud, then clap a hand over my mouth. It's silent for a moment.

"I know you don't believe me. It sounds so trite. But it's true." His sigh is audible through the door. Oh, he's good. Excellent performance.

"There's so much I want to tell you," he continues. I tip my head back and forth. Doesn't matter. Still can't. Won't. Whatever. "I almost wrote you a letter. But I knew you'd tear it up the instant I slipped it under your door."

I smile. He's not wrong.

"I wanted to leave you alone. To let you yell at me when you were ready." There's a soft thud on the door. His head? His hand? I'm almost curious. "But your brother, he told me not to let you do this. To make you listen. It almost made me laugh, *Cara Mia*. He of all people should know that nobody can make you do anything."

Make me. The words ring through my head. *Back off*, I say. *Make me*, he says. I shake my head, putting my hands over my ears. *No. You're not allowed in my head anymore.*

Through my fingers I can tell Alessandro is still talking. It's not until the talking stops that his words sink in. My brother told him. But that can't possibly be true. Bryce wouldn't tell Alessandro anything of the sort. Would he? More lies. Or are they?

Just like I knew it would, his voice goes away. But now I have something else to keep me awake tonight.

⁓

I WAKE UP COTTON-MOUTHED, WITH A POUNDING HEADACHE. GEEZ. I'M NEVER going to learn my limits with booze, am I? I get in the shower, hoping the hot water will do something for my aching head. But as soon as I'm in there, it wakes me up enough to remember that I had a visitor last night. And I remember enough of what he said to change my usual plans for the day of haplessly drinking and playing music.

Once I'm dried and dressed, I call Bryce.

"Oh, good, you're not dead," he greets me. "I take it the Italian must have paid you a visit then?"

I roll my eyes. Never one to mince words, my big brother. "Did you really send him here?"

"That I did. Now stop using me as an excuse. If you want to dump the bastard, step out of my shadow first. And while I'll deal if you decide not to, you know I'd be more than happy if you did."

"I don't know. You've got a pretty big shadow," I grumble. Seems like he's always up in my business anyway.

He laughs. "You're a big girl. Figure it out. But now that you've emerged, I expect you to be at brunch this Sunday. Mom's going out of her mind worrying about you. If you're not there and presentable I'm coming after you. For real this time."

"Fuck you," I grouse. No mercy, this one.

"Love you too, Em. See you Sunday." And he hangs up.

Guess my reign of solitude is at an end.

I find something presentable to wear and get ready to go out. I'm going to need food before I can deal with anything.

But when I open the door, I'm stopped short by an obscenely large vase full of purple hyacinths on my doorstep. I drag them inside, debating whether to throw them out. With a sigh, I pluck the card out. Might as well.

I never asked what your favorite flower is. I hope that you'll tell me someday. Forgive me, please, Cara Mia.

I make to tear up the card, but my gut protests. The rest of his words from last night come rushing back in a booze-stained swirl. And while I can't bring myself to get rid of his apology, I also can't bring myself to believe him. There's no point. It's over. Even if he's no longer my dirty secret, the fact remains that I never meant for it to turn into anything. Bryce is right. I'm going to have to dump him in a way that puts an end to things once and for all.

∾

A SOLID LUNCH AND A FEW TEXTS WITH SERA LATER, AND I'M HEADED TO Alessandro's place. While it's less than a ten-minute bus ride, I'm too impatient to wait, so I walk the twenty-five or so minutes into downtown from Capitol Hill. For October the weather's not bad. Fifty-eight degrees and partly cloudy, it's the perfect day for jeans, a light flannel, and some cute sneakers. Not that I'm trying to look cute for him. Though I'm not above rubbing it in either.

He lives in one of the monstrous skyscrapers near the library, and the elevator ride up to his floor is annoyingly long.

Finally, I arrive and head down the long hall to his door. I have to talk myself through every step, still not sure exactly what I'm going to say. And where I find the courage to knock, I'll never know.

The door swings open moments after I do, and Alessandro stands there looking ridiculously perfect in a black T-shirt and black sweats. Why, why does he have to be so good-looking?

I clear my throat and deliver the words every man fears the most. "We need to talk."

One of his eyebrows jumps, but he moves quickly to hide his shock, stepping back to let me in.

"I'm glad you're here," he replies evenly. "Come in."

I step inside and check out his bachelor pad while he closes the door behind me. It's pretty freaking nice, with richly dark leather furniture, and huge windows that let in as much light as is possible for fall in Seattle.

"Can I get you something to drink?" he asks politely from beside me.

I turn toward him and shake my head. "No, thank you."

With a small nod, he moves into the living room, taking a seat on the largest couch. I pointedly sit in the slightly smaller one across from him.

"You're looking well," he remarks. "I was worried."

I roll my eyes. "Thanks, but I'm fine." God, I'm such a liar.

He runs a finger under his chin. "Really?" he asks, clearly not buying it.

I press my lips together. "On second thought, do you have any vodka?"

He stares at me unemotionally before rising. A minute later, he returns with two tumblers, each containing an inch of cold, clear liquid. He hands me one, and I shoot it back and set the glass down on the coffee table between us.

Alessandro settles on his couch, cradling the glass in his hand, and takes a deep breath. "Is this the part where you tell me that you don't care what really happened? That it's over?"

I look at him, shocked. "How did you know that's what I was going to say?"

He takes a sip of his shot, grimacing against the sting of the alcohol. "Because it's what I would say in your shoes."

I narrow my eyes at him, unsure of whether this is him accepting the situation or not. "So you know where I'm coming from then."

He tosses back the rest of his drink and sets the glass down. "So you know I didn't fuck Valentina, then?" he parries, looking me dead in the eye.

I squirm uncomfortably. "Yes." As much of an ass as he was that night, I think even then I knew that wasn't something he would do. That I was looking for a reason to run.

He looks at me like he knows. "And you know your brother isn't going to stand in the way of whatever it is you want?"

I purposely still myself, though it kills me. I have got to keep cool. "I was a little surprised that he seemed so willing to let the fox into the henhouse, but yes, I know that too. But that's exactly it. I don't want you, Alessandro."

He laughs. "Is that so?"

I shrug. "Yes?"

Both of his thick, dark eyebrows jump at that. "Then why did that sound like a question?"

"Look, it was just a vacation thing. Anything we were feeling was just being out of our reality. That's not a relationship."

"Well, that's bullshit, but let's humor you for a moment. That doesn't mean you don't want me. That just means you think you only wanted me because of where we were."

His forthrightness makes me laugh. "Okay," I concede. "But that also assumes I want a relationship at all. Which I don't."

"Also bullshit," he insists.

I'm starting to get annoyed. "You think you know what I want better than I do?"

He sighs and rises, coming around the table to settle on the couch next to me.

"Yes. Because once again, you're simply fighting against what you really want, *Cara Mia*."

This close, I can see his long, dark lashes over his deep brown eyes. I can see his desire there. And his restraint.

"You're wrong this time," I assert. "I'm not looking for complicated. And you, sir, complicate things."

His eyes drop to my mouth, and I tighten inside. Ugh. He's right. I do still want him. But it's just physical. We're just too much alike, and I'm already exhausted by a short conversation with him.

"Then I'll make it simple," he replies, leaning in so I get a full whiff of his spicy scent. "Let me take you on a date. Here, in our reality. If you still feel like it's not what you want, then I'll have to accept that."

"You'll have to accept that now," I reply stubbornly.

He laughs. "You're afraid."

"Pfff. Am not." Even I realize I sound like a petulant child, so I work on softening my expression. "Exactly what do you think I'm afraid of? You? Hardly."

His full mouth pulls to the side in a smile. "That I'm right. That now that I'm not your dirty secret anymore, it's your own stubbornness holding you back from seeing how good we are together."

I don't even think about considering his words. He's just trouble. "Ugh, fine, whatever. If one date is what it will take to prove I'm right, then that's what we'll do." I stand up. "Coming?"

He stands up, looking down at his clothes. "I'm not exactly dressed for the occasion. And it's a weekday. I have to get back to work. Are you busy Saturday night?"

I frown, sticking my chin out. He's going to make me admit my only plans were with a bottle of booze.

I sigh heavily. "I guess I could make that work."

He smiles so widely it crinkles the corners of his eyes. "Then it's a date."

"Fine." I rise, heading to the door. I make to open it, but he puts a hand up to stop me. He's uncomfortably close.

His eyes search mine. "Do you have a black tie–appropriate dress?"

"Yes," I reply, hugging my arms around myself protectively.

His eyes settle on my lips, and I resist the urge to lick them. "Good. I'll pick you up at seven then."

I raise an eyebrow, but he says nothing more, simply opening the door. It takes everything I've got to tear my eyes from his and walk out the door.

Just before I cross the threshold, I turn to him. "Peonies." He looks at me questioningly. "They're my favorite flower." I don't wait for a response. I leave. Before he can see me blush.

EIGHT

EMILY

Two days. Two days of going back and forth between almost cancelling and asking myself if he's right. I want to sink back into a drunken stupor and avoid thinking too hard about it, but I've probably done enough of that lately.

So at seven on Saturday evening, here I sit, dressed in a deep blue lace and crystal gown, my chestnut waves tamed into a gentle cascade, nervous as I can ever remember being. Too nervous even to play anything to soothe myself.

When the knock on the door comes, I take a deep breath, rise, and smooth my dress. Opening the door is my first huge mistake. Because it gives me a full view of Alessandro, looking more devastatingly handsome than any man I've ever seen. And he's holding a huge bouquet of the most beautiful pink peonies I've ever seen.

He looks just as stunned, staring at me as I take him in, in his tailored black tux, with a black shirt, vest, and tie. He looks lean, and strong, and so hopeful I already feel guilty.

"You look…" he trails off, seemingly unable to form words.

I look down at the neckline that plunges to just above my belly button, the sheer sleeves and leg panels that show swaths of my pale skin under them. One of the perks of being skinny and flat-chested — I don't have to worry about falling out of the daring neckline. But maybe it was a bad choice.

"Too risqué?" I ask, blushing. "I can go change."

He closes his mouth and shakes his head, his eyes returning to mine. "No," he says hoarsely. "You're perfect." He extends the flowers. "These are for you. Though they're not half as beautiful as you are."

"Yeah, okay," I reply, rolling my eyes. I take the flowers anyway, quickly darting into the kitchen to put them in water. I purposely don't invite him in. But I'm back in a flash, only to find him uncomfortably standing on the doorstep. Good. He should be uncomfortable.

He gives me an uneasy smile, extending a hand. "Shall we?"

I slip my hand into his somewhat reluctantly and close the door behind me. "Where are we headed?" I try to sound casual, but I'm kind of dying to know what we're all dressed up for.

"I was thinking the café and wine bar a few blocks from here," he replies. "If you're not too hungry and don't mind walking?"

"That depends. Is it raining?"

He laughs. "For once, no. I wouldn't have asked if it were."

"Okay, then, that sounds perfect. Let's go."

We walk the few blocks in silence. I've been to the café a few times, but it's not a place I go often. It seems a bit laidback for our formal attire, but I can't argue that the wine is fantastic. We order a few appetizers as well, and the stare-off begins.

"So, this is awkward."

He chuckles. "There you go, saying what's on your mind again."

I shrug. "How's work? Everything okay with whatever made you cut your vacation short?"

"It will be fine," he replies with a note of annoyance in his voice. "Running your own business is not without its sacrifices. Though I had hoped for more of a break. Perhaps once things have died down a bit more. How is work for you?"

My eyes drop to my lap. "I quit."

"You quit?" His shocked tone is enough to make me look back up at him. "I thought you loved working there."

I chew on my upper lip and take a sip of wine. "Things change."

"In three weeks?" he asks.

I glare back at him defiantly. "Yes."

"Why did you quit, Emily?"

I jut my chin out. "It's not what I want to do for the rest of my life."

"Oh?" He raises an eyebrow. "And have you decided what you *do* want to do for the rest of your life, then?" A hint of a smile plays around his mouth.

I tug at my hair. "Not exactly."

"I see." He tilts his head and gives me an appraising look. "With your talent and your intelligence, *Cara Mia*, you could do whatever you want. I hope you know that."

This time I don't stop the eye roll. "You've barely heard me play."

He shrugs. "What can I say? I know talent when I see it."

"Are you always so blindly positive?" I grouse.

"I can be a negative asshole, if you'd prefer."

And I can't help it, it makes me laugh.

He smiles, clearly pleased to see me lightening up. I decide to at least try not to be such a sourpuss. But he just brings emotions out in me I can't control sometimes.

"Do you like classical music?" he asks as our appetizers are delivered.

"Of course," I reply.

"Good," he replies, digging in with a smile.

"Why?" I ask, suddenly suspicious.

"Because we're going to the symphony tonight."

My eyes go wide. "Seriously?"

He laughs. "Seriously. Is that okay?"

I blink hard, willing myself not to tear up. I've dated enough musicians to start a freaking orchestra, but not a single one has ever taken me to the symphony. Dingy little hole-in-the-wall clubs, sure. But never anything as overwhelmingly moving, or pricey, as the symphony. I've only been a handful of times with my parents.

I watch him as he continues eating, suddenly unsure that I can resist him if he's going to pull out all the stops like this.

The feeling only intensifies after we've finished and are headed into Benaroya Hall, just a couple blocks from the restaurant. The crowds of well-dressed patrons stream into the building, and I can't help feeling a bit like a princess. Alessandro leads me patiently by the hand, giving me plenty of time to ascend the steps in a way that doesn't snag the delicate material of my gown.

As I climb the last step, he squeezes my hand and shakes his head.

"What?" I ask.

"You'll just tell me to stop the charming shtick," he says with a smile.

I narrow my eyes at him. "You're probably right."

With a chuckle, he leads me inside and to our seats. My jaw drops when I see how close we'll be.

"How'd you get these seats? They're amazing," I breathe softly into his ear as he takes his seat next to me.

He turns a dazzling smile on me. "I told you. Music is one of my great loves. I've been a donor and subscriber for years. I'm not completely full of shit, you know."

I put my hand over my mouth, unwilling to burst into laughter in such a setting. As the lights dim, he turns from me to focus on the stage. I stare at him, remembering my thoughts the first night I met him. Wondering if he really was more than the man I thought him to be. But maybe it's because he is, and so much more, that I'm so unsure.

Before my emotions can completely carry me off, the music starts to swell, and it does the job for me. Mozart's Jupiter Symphony begins, and I'm carried into a world that only music can transport me to. My heart swells with the beauty of it, tears of joy leaking unbidden from my eyes. The few times I look over at Alessandro, he's, for once, not focused on me at all, seemingly similarly transported by the music.

And when it's over, I'm riding high on the excitement of the experience. "That was unbelievable," I sigh as I follow him out into the cool night. A little too cool. I shudder at the abrupt change of temperature. Seeing my discomfort, Alessandro removes his jacket and drapes it around my shoulders.

The lingering warmth and the scent of him settles over me. I look up at him, trying not to connect all the emotion that the music evoked to him. But he brings out his own response in me. And in this moment, that's pretty hard to deny.

I step up onto my toes and press my mouth to his. The familiar warmth makes me tighten inside. But he only returns the kiss for a moment before pressing back.

"Come, I'll walk you home," he says in a restrained tone.

I try not to be annoyed. Really, I do. But it's just the same as when we arrived in Italy. He's holding back, thinking too much. I can tell.

By the time we make it to my front door, I'm so over it all. I shrug out of his jacket, handing it back.

"I had fun. Thanks."

"You're welcome."

"Okay, well, take care then." I turn around, fishing my keys out of my bag.

But he has other ideas. He grabs me gently by the arms, turning me to face him.

"Tell me why."

"Why what?" I ask impatiently.

"Why do I scare you so?"

I feel the anger rise in me. But just as quickly, I realize he's right. He scares the shit out of me with his intensity. His insistence that we're perfect for each other. His expectations.

"You want things from me I can't give you."

"Bullshit." His dark eyes are filled with fire. "You're scared to give what you have."

"Yes," I admit with a tired laugh. To him. To myself. "I've been down this road before. It's never turned out well for me. Can't we just enjoy each other? Without giving ... more?"

"But you've given it to others." His mouth turns down, and the sorrow there is like a punch to the gut.

Again, he's not wrong. I've loved men before who could never give me back what I wanted to give them. But maybe the tables have turned.

Tears prick at the back of my eyes. "I'm sorry, I can't give you what you want," I repeat.

"You mean, you can't give me what you think I deserve."

"Is there a difference?"

He strokes a finger under his chin. "Yes. But perhaps you're not ready to see that yet."

"It doesn't matter. I don't belong with someone like you," I reply a little more angrily than I intended. I close my eyes, pushing back the tears, the rage. The truth is something I didn't expect. He cares about me in a way I struggle to even care for myself. He's way too good for me. He makes me wish I was more. Better. And I can't handle that kind of pressure. That's what's making me angry. I'm mad at myself for not being what he needs. I shove it all down deep, steel myself, and look up into his eyes.

He's strangely calm, watching my internal battle play out on my face. When I catch his eye, he gives me a hard look.

"Tell me honestly that you don't want me," he says in a low, even tone.

"It's not that simple," I hedge.

He steps closer, lifting my chin to force me to look in his eyes. "It never is, *Cara Mia*. But that doesn't mean it's not worth fighting for." He kisses me gently, completely in control this time as he ends it quickly. It leaves me wanting, brief as it was.

I shake my head, not knowing what to say. He's still watching me intently, with those dark, expressive eyes of his. He lifts his hand to my cheek, stroking it gently.

"I had an amazing night with you. Go, get some sleep. Think about things. I'll call you tomorrow."

I raise an eyebrow at him. "What, you're not even going to try to come in?"

He shakes his head and laughs. He looks down at me, with a dangerously sexy glint in his eye. "We're not going to fuck so you don't have to think, *Cara Mia*."

My eyes go wide. How did he know that that was exactly what I wanted?

"I see you," he says. "Just as you see me. Remember that."

With that, he turns and walks away. I go inside, dumbstruck as I undress and clean up for bed. And when I go to sleep, try though I might, all I see is his face.

∾

SUNDAY MORNING BRINGS NO REST. LITERALLY. I HAVE TO DRAG ASS OUT OF bed and get ready for brunch at Mom's. And prepare myself for the inquisition.

Not going would only be worse, because then Bryce would be pissed, *and* I'd still have to make an appearance.

I resign myself to the trip, and I'm about to call for a ride when Sera texts asking if I want to go with them. I accept, though I'm not as excited by the prospect as I normally would be. Though it does occur to me if I could get her on her own, she'd be the best person to talk to about this whole mess. After all, she knows me pretty well by now. And obviously she knows Alessandro in ways pretty much nobody else I could talk to would.

Ugh. I realize that means I *do* want to talk about it. He's getting under my skin, the persistent bastard.

When I get downstairs to meet Sera and Bryce, I'm actually pretty relieved to see them both. They're out of the car, and Sera gets to me first, wrapping me in a big hug.

"Hey," she greets me.

"Hey."

Bryce gives me a little wave. I let Sera go and throw myself bodily into him, hugging him tightly.

"Oof," he grunts. "Geez, Em."

I let him go and swing a fake punch toward his soft spot. He instinctively reaches out to stop me with a surprised look on his face. I stop my fist in midair, laughing. "Hey, bro."

He shakes his head and climbs in the back seat, and Sera gets in on the driver's side. "Hop in," she invites, gesturing to the front passenger door.

"Huh," I remark, climbing into the passenger seat. "I feel special."

Sera pulls out, giving Bryce a look in the rearview mirror. "Just pretend he's not here. You know, if you need to talk before we get to your mom's."

"Ugh," I remark. "She's pretty worried, huh?"

"We all are," she says quietly. "But you look good, Em. I missed you."

I shoot her a smile. "Missed you guys too. Did you have fun in Italy at least?" Sera turns bright red and Bryce chuckles. "Ew, never mind." We all burst out laughing.

"So, you and Alessandro, huh?" Sera asks pointedly.

I heave a sigh. "Sort of? I don't know."

"Well, for what it's worth, he's pretty into you," she remarks drily.

I snort. "Yeah, I got that much, funny enough." I look down into my hands.

"You can say what you want. Bryce has promised to keep his mouth shut. Right, babe?" Bryce says nothing and Sera smiles mischievously. "See?"

I shoot him a smile and he wrinkles his nose at me and sticks out his tongue. I can't help but laugh.

"It's fine. I've never exactly held back around him anyway," I tease.

"You have no idea," Bryce grumbles in Sera's direction. She shoots him a warning look and he pointedly shuts his mouth.

"Come on, Em. I'm here. Talk to me. I know Alessandro has his issues, but he's a good guy. And if you're really not interested in him, that's one thing. But if you think you're upsetting Bryce or I—"

"No," I cut her off. "I don't think that at all." I let out a frustrated sigh. "I know he's a good guy. And I know he's into me. And I'm into him. I just don't think I'm good for him."

Sera looks over at me, astonished, then quickly returns her eyes to the road. Bryce, to his credit, makes not a peep.

"That's the last thing I expected to be holding you back," she says bluntly. "I mean, I don't want to dismiss your feelings or anything, but you're pretty freaking amazing, Em. I mean, seriously. He'd be lucky to be with you."

I roll my eyes. "Thanks," I reply, unable to keep the sarcasm out of my voice.

"You think I'd lie to you?"

"No, I think you have love blinders on," I retort. "And I appreciate that. But honestly. I'm a freaking mess. What do I have to offer anyone right now? I've got no job, no prospects, and every long-term relationship I've had has blown up in my face. He's gorgeous, smart, successful, and has women tripping over themselves to be with him. What do I have to offer someone like that?"

Even voicing the doubts has me squirming. I've never lacked confidence like this. But something about my whole life right now is making me feel like I'm doomed to fail. At everything.

"He's not in love with those women; he's in love with you," Sera insists.

My eyebrows jump and I spin toward her, my jaw practically on the floor. "He's *what*?"

Bryce face-palms. "Way to scare her, babe."

I don't even look at Bryce. I'm glaring down Sera. And she looks pretty damn nervous. "Are you assuming or did he tell you that?"

She clears her throat. "I'm guessing he didn't tell you that, then."

"Um, that would be a big nope," I reply angrily. "I can't believe you guys even talked about all of this behind my back. Oh my god, I'm so humiliated." I put my hands over my face. This is just too much.

I'm silent the rest of the way to Mom's, and neither of them says another word.

When we get there, Bryce gets out first, then Sera. I lean forward and put my head on the dashboard, trying not to cry.

A minute later, Bryce climbs in the driver's seat, moving it back all the way to accommodate his long legs. I look up in surprise when he starts the car.

"What are you doing?" I ask, wiping at the tears that have mercilessly found their way out.

Bryce shakes his head and looks at me. "I'm taking you back," he explains quietly. "Unless you want to go in there?" His expression is apologetic and full of concern.

"I don't," I agree. "Please, just get me out of here."

We make the drive in silence. I stare out the window as we cross the bridge, wishing I was on one of the ships in the bay, headed far away from here. But when the car stops, it's not at my place. It takes me a minute to realize where we are. Before I can even react, Bryce speaks.

"I know you're scared, Em. And your life isn't what you expected." He turns to me and lays a hand over mine. "But I know you. You're falling for this guy. I've never seen that scare you, though, so I think that means this might be the kind of love that's exactly what you need. That will give you the strength and support to become the person you want to be." He pauses, letting his words sink in as the tears flow down my face. He gives my hand a squeeze. "And if it doesn't, and he breaks your heart, I'll break his fucking kneecaps. Deal?"

Through the tears, I laugh. My stupid big brother. Well, he's not so stupid. He knows me better than anyone. Or, almost anyone. Because I'm pretty sure Alessandro tried to tell me all of that, too. I was just too scared to listen.

"Deal."

Bryce grins. "Come on."

He gets out of the car and I follow, letting him lead me inside. "How do you even know where he lives?" I ask as I wipe the tears from my face.

Bryce shoots me a smirk. "Seriously?"

I roll my eyes. "Never mind." We get in the elevator. As we near Alessandro's floor, I look over at him. "Hey, Bryce?"

He looks at me furtively. "Yeah?"

"Thanks."

He shoots an arm out, wrapping it around my neck and bringing me in for a hug. "I've got you, Em."

We arrive, and Bryce gets out first. When he gets to Alessandro's door, he pulls me behind him so he's blocking me from view and hammers on it hard.

I hear the door open a moment later, and I realize I'd give anything to see the look on Alessandro's face. But I don't move, trusting whatever my big bro has planned.

"Ah. The giant. How nice. To what do I owe the pleasure?" If I didn't know him better, I'd say he sounded sincere, but I don't miss the undertone of his distaste.

"I'm only going to say this once. Hurt my sister and it'll be the last thing you ever do." His voice is low and menacing. I've heard him use the tone before. Never a good thing. I crack a smile behind his broad back.

I hear Alessandro heave a deep sigh. "Trust me, if she'd let me, I'd spend my life doing everything I could to keep her from ever hurting again."

"Huh. Well, cute words. Good luck with that." Bryce steps aside and gives me a look. "I'll make your excuses to Mom."

I nod and give him a small wave. He waves back as he heads to the elevator.

I turn, and Alessandro is leaning against his doorway, arms crossed over his black T-shirt.

"Hi," I say meekly.

His face is unreadable. "*Ciao.*"

"Did you mean that?" I ask. "What you said to my brother?"

"I don't think this is the best place to have this conversation," he hedges, stepping back. "Why don't you come in?"

I follow him in quietly. He sits by himself in the leather chair at the end of the two couches. My stomach sinks as I take a seat on the smaller couch. He's clearly distancing himself from me. So maybe he didn't mean what he said. Maybe he was just placating Bryce.

Alessandro scrubs his hands over his face. "Can you please tell me what is going on? Why your brother felt the need to threaten me?"

I take a deep breath, deciding to take the advice of my wise, if not annoyingly perfect, big brother.

"I've been scared shitless," I admit. "I've been adrift, for years really. As if my perfect brother getting married and taking over the family business wasn't bad enough, meeting you just made me feel completely inadequate." He starts to protest, but I hold up a hand. "You're amazing, Alessandro. I didn't get how someone like you could care about me. I feel like I've got nothing to offer. I'm such a mess. I don't know what I want to do. I'm like a balloon floating in the wind. But Bryce convinced me I could do with an anchor. Someone who makes me stronger. I don't know, I'm losing the metaphor. Am I making any sense?"

He leans back. "Yes." He pushes out a breath. "I feel like a failure."

"What? No," I object. "*I'm* the failure. I'm such a mess I can't even let someone care about me. And I'm so sorry."

Alessandro looks at me with a sad smile. "No, *Cara Mia*. I've failed you if I let you think for one moment that I wouldn't be the lucky one here. You are like nobody I've ever met. You're beautiful, honest, funny, talented, and so smart. You keep me on my toes."

"With my crazy," I grumble, starting to smile nonetheless.

He laughs. "Yes, exactly," he agrees. "My crazy, beautiful woman." He frowns. "So your brother convinced you to come here but then threatened me. Am I missing something?"

"You still don't get him at all, do you?" I ask, laughing. "That's his way of saying he approves."

He looks at me skeptically. "Are you sure?"

I rise, moving to settle on his lap. He reaches for me, pulling me into his embrace. "I'm sure," I reply. "And I'm sorry. I'm my own worst enemy. I do this. I tell myself I don't deserve things that make me happy and then I do everything I can to drive them away."

He holds my face in his hand, stroking my cheek. "We're going to have to work on that," he murmurs.

"We're going to have to work on a lot of things," I agree. "But you were right before. It may not be simple, but this is something worth fighting for."

"Hmmm. So I guess I'm not your dirty secret anymore," he says, fighting a smile.

"You can be my dirty something else instead," I murmur, covering his lips with mine, pulling at his clothes. Because I may have given him what he wants, but now I'm going to get what I want.

He doesn't resist, letting me pull his shirt off as he runs his hands over my breasts, my hips, my ass. I rise, stripping completely in seconds, then sink down and run my hands over his chest.

He slips his hand between my legs, stroking my core as he sucks on the tips of my breasts. He lifts me gently, then eases me onto the coffee table, kicking off his sweats. I twitch with anticipation as he bends over me, kissing his way from my mouth downward.

"*Leccamela tutta*," I plead. He laughs, but obliges, immediately disappearing between my legs and licking me into a frenzy. Before I can finish, he rises to kiss me, hovering just out of reach.

"Do you want to feel me?" he asks softly.

I bite down on my lip, glancing down at his full, hard, beautiful cock. "Yes," I agree. "Just you."

He wastes no time, burying himself in me. I throw my head back.

"You feel unbelievable, *Cara Mia*," he moans.

I nod in response, hitching my heels behind his backside, urging him on. He holds himself over me carefully as he rides me. And all I can do is hang on as he takes us both over the edge.

When we're done, and cleaned up, he stretches out on the sofa, still completely naked, gesturing for me to join him. Gladly, I stretch my body out next to his.

"Sera accidentally told me something," I confess.

He ceases stroking my arm and raises an eyebrow. "Do I want to know?"

I laugh. "It was about us," I reassure him. "She said you're in love with me."

"Ah."

"And you told Bryce you'd spend your life keeping me from being hurt."

He smiles and resumes stroking my arm. "I did."

I tilt my head back so I can look him full in the face.

"Does it scare you?" he asks softly.

I take a steadying breath. "Yes. But only because I'm falling for you too," I admit. "So maybe give me a little time to get used to it."

He presses his lips together and his eyes glitter fiercely. "*Amore mio*," he breathes. "Take all the time you need. I'm not going anywhere."

And I know enough Italian to translate that one. He loves me. I can't say it doesn't scare me. But at least now it's in a good way.

"I still don't understand why," I admit. "I think you might be a little crazy too."

He smiles so widely I can't help smiling back. "Yes, we're both a little crazy. It's what makes us so good together," he replies. "But as to why … why does anyone love someone? Some things are just meant to be." He thinks about it for a moment. "I realized it when you left me. But I think I might have loved you the moment you agreed to run away with me." He nuzzles his nose into my neck, lightly kissing its length. I stroke my fingers through his hair.

"Thank you for not giving up on me," I breathe into his ear.

"It's a good thing I'm more stubborn than you are," he teases, kissing me.

"Mmmm," I moan as he continues to stroke and kiss me. "You're going to need to be. I've got a lot of things to figure out. I'm going to need someone who is stubborn and patient enough to get through to me when I need a good talking to."

He laughs. "Yes, well, those are important qualities," he allows. "But I think there may be a better way to get your attention."

"Oh? How's that?" Though I think I know the answer, but damn do I want him to show me.

He presses his leg between mine, silently asking for entry. I open for him, and he slides between my legs, flipping me on my back under him. His semi-hard cock pushes between my thighs, and a moan bursts out of me.

"Something like this," he murmurs as he enters me.

As he fills me, it's like a switch flips inside me, and tears of joy fill my eyes as he makes love to me. He sees me. He gets me. He loves me. Really knowing it and accepting it, I feel free. Free to love him. Crazy, passionately, completely. He's the happiness I never thought I deserved.

NINE

ALESSANDRO

Ten years later…

"**D**ammit, Emily," I groan.

"Don't stop," she begs. "We've got time."

I lean around her to glance at the microwave clock. "We're already late," I reply.

She pouts, sliding her dress up. "You started it." She licks her lips, and I'm screwed.

With a growl, I pull her ass toward me and lay her down on the counter. I run my hand down her chest before sinking my fingers into her pussy while I undo my zipper with my other hand. I quickly replace my hand with my cock and bury it in her. I have to steady myself. The first thrust is always tight and sweet. Even after all this time, it nearly undoes me.

She writhes, grabbing at her breasts with one hand, working herself above where I'm thrusting with the other. So uninhibited, so sexy. I help her tease her nipples as I take her. I don't hold back, tilting into her exactly the way I know will have her screaming her orgasm in no time. Mere moments later, I'm not disappointed, and I follow her over as I explode inside her.

"See? That didn't take long," she teases, climbing down and heading to clean up.

"Sure, but now you're going to your niece's sixth birthday party with just-fucked hair," I joke. I follow her into the bathroom to see her smoothing her gorgeous chestnut waves back into place.

"Like it never happened," she murmurs, shooting me a fake dirty look in the mirror.

I grab her ass, slipping my hand under her skirt into the wetness still between her legs.

"The evidence suggests otherwise," I whisper in her ear.

"Mhm," she agrees, adjusting her makeup. "But you know you love it when I walk around with your cum dripping out of me."

I was just about to leave, but her words have me grabbing her from behind, running my hands all over her. "You're going to be the death of me," I say against the soft skin of her neck.

She smiles, finishes getting ready, and pulls me out of the house.

As we drive over the West Seattle Bridge, she rolls her window down and lets her arm drag through the warm summer air.

"You look happy," I tell her with a smile.

"What's not to be happy about? It's a beautiful day," she replies. "And we haven't seen Bryce, Sera, and the kids in weeks."

"And I imagine those three weeks in Paris didn't hurt, either," I reply drily.

She shoots me a huge smile. "Nope, definitely not."

I laugh, gunning the engine, and whipping around a bend. She giggles gleefully as I accelerate through a curve. "I love this car," she cries into the wind.

And like I have every day since she agreed to be mine, I think to myself, *Damn, I love this woman.*

We finally arrive, only half an hour late thanks to my crazy driving.

The kids rush out to greet their favorite aunt, and I hang back, taking the presents out of the back seat. Their father's distaste for me seems to have been passed down, as the children have never shown much interest in me. Still, I'm happy to let them crowd around Emily, knowing how much she enjoys these moments.

Serafina waddles out of the gate to the back yard, her hugely pregnant belly preceding her.

I go to her and wrap my arms around her carefully. "You look beautiful."

She smiles up at me. "Thanks. I feel like a whale."

Emily joins us, the children circling her. "Hey, Sera. How are you feeling?"

"She wants to get the darn thing out of her already," Hattie, their nine-year-old, proclaims. We all laugh.

Katherine, the birthday girl, pulls at Emily's hand. "Auntie Em, come see my princess party."

"Oooh, princesses are my favorite," Emily coos at her. "Which one are you, Kitty?"

The little girl, who looks so endearingly like her mother, rolls her eyes and points at her dress. "Duh, I'm the purple one."

We all share looks of barely suppressed laughter and let the children lead us into the backyard. True to her word, it's a princess paradise, with crowned little girls in dresses everywhere, piles of princess-wrapped presents, and a bouncy castle.

Emily leans down and scoops up the youngest, three-year-old Landon, named for Bryce and Emily's father. She carries him along as Kitty pulls her toward the food, wanting to show off her cake. I add Kitty's present to the pile, a little purple ukulele that Emily had made just for her.

I spot Bryce, the only man in a sea of tiny girls and a few mothers who have tagged along. Predictably, he's manning the barbecue. And he's dressed like a fucking prince. I roll my eyes, getting it out of my system before he notices me.

"Well, that's a little clichéd," I joke as I approach, gesturing at his outfit as I hand him the "present" I brought for him.

He gives me a tolerant smile, cracking open one of the ice-cold beers I just gave him. "Thanks." He passes me one. I open it and we drink in silence.

It gets to me after a bit. "Where's your brother-in-law?" I ask abruptly, noting Sera's brother's absence.

"He and his partner are traveling," he replies, flipping a burger. "They're taking an art tour of Europe."

"Ah. Well, that sounds like more fun than a kid's birthday party."

Bryce smirks at me. "How was your trip to Paris?" he asks.

"It was great. Just what we needed. Emily was reticent to leave the music shop to her assistant, but it all went fine."

Bryce shrugs. "I know, she wouldn't shut up about it. But I get it. She's worked hard to build that place. It's her baby."

I shoot him a look at his choice of words. I'd thought we were long over the "When are you guys getting married and having kids?" part of our lives. But I say nothing, and the big bastard just smirks back at me, letting the small needling stand. Thankfully, he says nothing further on the subject.

"When is baby number four supposed to make its appearance?" I ask, watching Sera struggle to take Landon from Emily so Emily can help Kitty open her present. Bryce and Emily's mother appears suddenly, wrestling the little guy away as the ukulele appears and they all fawn over the gift.

"A few weeks," he murmurs, watching his wife. "But damn if she doesn't look good pregnant."

I roll my eyes, knowing he's paying no attention to me.

"I saw that."

I laugh and shake my head. "I'm going to go help the women."

"With what?"

I shrug, smile, and walk away.

I approach Emily, now sitting next to Kitty on the ground as she teaches her how to play the tiny instrument. She looks radiant, her flowery sundress hugging her body, the sun shining on her face as she laughs at the little girl's clear enjoyment of her gift.

She looks up at me and smiles. It takes my damn breath away.

"I know that look," she says with a warning in her voice.

I wink at her. "You just look so good," I tease. "So happy."

She rises to her feet and tucks herself against me, wrapping her arms around my back and looking up into my face. "I am."

I look down at Kitty. "Not getting any ideas, are you?"

She laughs. "You ask me that every time. No." She puts her mouth to my ear. "I like being able to fuck you as often and loudly as I like with no tiny interruptions." She kisses my earlobe and it sends shivers down my spine. She pulls back a little. "I'm starting to think you might want me to get ideas."

I huff a laugh. "You know I love you, no matter what life brings us," I hedge. I lean in, also to whisper in her ear. "But you're not going to get me to fuck you at a children's birthday party, no matter how sexy you are or what dirty things you whisper in my ear."

She pulls away, laughing gleefully. "We'll see about that."

"We'll see about what?" Sera asks, appearing from the back door to the house with a lighter in one hand and a stack of paper plates in the other. I quickly move to take them from her, for which she shoots me a grateful look. "Thanks. Even small chores are tough right now. I can't wait for this to be over. For good, this time."

"Oh? This is the last then?" I ask, a teasing note in my voice.

She settles herself onto the padded swing next to the house. "Damn straight. This was a surprise baby, anyway. And I'm forty. Four seems like a good number of kids, anyway, doesn't it?" she muses.

I shrug. "I'm surprised you have time for it all. You both run your own companies, after all."

Sera snorts. "Don't kid yourself. There's no such thing as 'time for it all.' We run ourselves ragged every damned day and we're lucky if we even cover the basics."

I frown, laying a hand over hers. "Serafina, I'm so sorry. We should help more—"

"No," she interrupts, squeezing my hand. "I wasn't complaining. We have plenty of help. Rebecca lives here, for crying out loud." She gestures at Bryce and Emily's mother, who is now studiously tidying discarded wrapping material. "I even tolerate my mother's occasional whim to drop by, because every little bit helps, and the kids love her." She presses her lips together. I know how hot and cold their relationship has been over the years, so I say nothing. "We are ridiculously blessed, and I love my life." She looks up at her husband who is staring at us across the yard. She waves and smiles at him as Landon finds us and starts to crawl in what little lap she has left. She lifts him up, cradling him to her chest. "Really, I wouldn't have it any other way."

"I'm glad you're happy," I tell her sincerely. "It's all I ever wanted for you."

She tilts her head. "What about you and Emily?"

I look up at Emily, who is leading the children loudly in a song now, her beautiful voice carrying on the wind. "We are happier than I ever thought possible. I'm a very lucky man."

"Good," Sera concedes, letting her son down and struggling to her feet. "See that you keep it that way. Because Bryce is still ready to tear you limb from limb if you hurt her." She pats me consolingly on the back. "Time for cake."

I watch her walk away, meeting Bryce to ready the cake. When all the kids crowd around them, Bryce lifts Kitty to blow out her candles and everyone cheers. Kitty gives her father a big kiss before he sets her down to descend upon the giant, icing-slathered confection. I watch Emily too, helping Sera cut the cake. They all look so happy.

But as the throng of tiny princesses brim over with the excitement of dessert being served, madness returns, and Emily extracts herself with a roll of her eyes to join me on the sidelines. I fold her into my embrace, and we wait until things have died down to rejoin the crowd. Sera, Bryce, and the girls happily greet us as we do, and we allow ourselves to sink into this little slice of familial bliss.

Enjoyable though it was, when we get back home, I breathe a sigh of relief.

"It's so quiet," I remark happily.

"What, was a dozen little girls screaming all afternoon wearing on you?" Emily teases, heading into our bathroom to undress.

"A little," I admit, kicking off my shoes and following her. I lay on the big, soft bed, quietly watching her. When she removes her sundress, I realize she wasn't wearing any underwear. "*Cara Mia*, you're a naughty girl."

"What? The dress covered enough so nobody could tell. Besides, I was hoping you'd figure it out much, much sooner," she says with an affected pout, coming to the edge of the bed. She crawls next to me, snuggling against me. "But I had a good time anyway. Everyone seemed to be doing so well."

I stroke her hair, drifting a little after the heat and exertion of the day. "Mmmm, yes they did. They have a different kind of crazy going on there," I murmur sleepily.

"Do you still like our crazy?" she asks, a note of concern in her voice.

My eyes snap open, and I turn her head so I can look into her eyes. "Love. I love our crazy." I press my lips to hers, easing my tongue into her beautiful mouth. She responds, rubbing against me. Alas, it doesn't stir me in the way I'd like it to. "I think I'm getting too old to take you three times a day."

"And I never thought I'd still want you three times a day after so long. But I'm happy just being here with you," she assures me with a gentle kiss.

"You're amazing," I murmur. But I can't let it rest. I roll on top of her, rubbing into her center. "Say it."

She looks at me, confused for a moment before realizing what I want her to say. What I want her to ask.

"*Leccamela tutta,*" she whispers.

With a devilish smile, I waste no time pleasuring her. Claiming her with my mouth and hands, body and soul. Because she touches mine more every day. And there's nothing I won't do to make her happy for as long as she'll let me. And as I taste her, as she gives herself to me so completely and with abandon, I know if I have my way, it'll be forever.

BONUS NOVELETTE

BONUS NOVELETTE

Another twelve years later…

"For the degrees of Bachelor of Arts in business and Bachelor of Arts in criminal justice, Harriet Hoyt."

I hear my cheering section go nuts, but I don't look. I'm having a hard enough time focusing on not passing out. I take a deep breath, climb the stairs, and approach the dean, turning my back to her and dipping down so she can place the royal blue stole over my head.

I can't help taking a quick look at the crowd, but I still can't find Mom and Dad. I probably should have looked when they were making that godawful, horribly embarrassing racket. But as mortifying as it was, I can't help smiling about it anyway. Embarrassing enthusiasm is just how Hoyts say, "I love you."

Mrs. Angeles' hands gently steer me toward my next stop. I can barely breathe as I accept the dummy certificate from the chancellor, reaching for his hand with my right carefully as I accept the rolled-up document with my left. I can practically feel all the pictures being taken by my parents.

As I descend the opposite set of stairs, I wish I could say I was relieved to have survived walking across that stage in front of thousands of people without making an ass of myself, but unfortunately there's something even worse I'm going to have to do next. Something that most graduating seniors are looking forward to, but I dread. That's right: the time-honored graduation party.

I know, I know, I'm crazy. I'm a healthy twenty-one-year-old. I should want to party it up … right? Except, I really, really don't. In fact, I'd be happy just having dinner with Mom and Dad and my brother and sisters. And then going to bed early with a good book. That's my jam. Not so much a full-on house party with all of our relatives, friends, neighbors, and pretty much anyone else Dad has ever known. He's so damn proud. And Bryce Hoyt isn't easily impressed. So I'll get through it, for him.

I slink back into my assigned seat to wait for the ceremony to finish. I'm in no hurry, especially since the sun is shining, not a cloud in sight. For Seattle in June that's pretty damn good. Usually, the gloom doesn't let up until after the Fourth of July. At least there's that.

～

"God, your dad is a total DILF," Kimmie mutters as she stares googly-eyed at my father from our position at the picnic table across the yard while he mans the grill.

I wrinkle my nose. "I don't care if you've been my best friend since we were five, if you say that one more time …"

Kimmie flips her long, blond hair over her shoulder, her brown eyes sparkling mischievously. She's such a horn-dog. "Oh please, it's not like I'm going to do anything about it. He and your mom are obviously still totally smitten." She gestures over at them as my mom sidles up to him and kisses him. Gag. They've always been way too touchy-feely for my tastes. Kimmie observes my obvious look of disdain. "Come on, they're cute! You really need to loosen up."

I shoot her a deeply impatient look. "Like I need a gratuitous cranial aperture," I scoff.

"You're lucky I love you even though you're a total nerd," she scoffs. "So when do you and your aunt leave for your trip?"

"Day after tomorrow," I mutter.

"Don't sound so excited." The sarcasm is heavy, as usual.

I shrug in response. "It's just the San Juans."

"Why are you going? You're obviously not excited about it."

"I dunno. I like hanging out with Aunt Em. Besides, what else is there to do?"

"Well, if you don't want to go, *I* will. Your uncle is fucking gorgeous, too."

"And here I didn't think you could get any more disgusting. He's like sixty. And he's in Italy visiting family anyway."

"Sixty or sixteen, Italian men are *hot*," she insists, causing me to pull another disgusted face. "Whatever, I —"

"Oh, look, there's Aunt Emily, I should go talk to her about the trip," I interrupt as I spot my aunt coming out of the house. I slide off the bench and leave Kimmie to her own devices, knowing she'll be fine without me.

"It's the graduate!" Aunt Emily screams as I approach. She throws her hands out to catch me in a huge hug. "And if it's possible, you're even more beautiful than the last time I saw you."

I roll my eyes and laugh. "You say that *every* time you see me. And then you say —"

"But then, you look just like your Auntie Em, so why wouldn't you?" she cracks back with a grin.

It's infectious, and I grin back. I am pretty thankful I look like her — and Dad — with my long chestnut brown hair, blue eyes, and naturally slim build. It's certainly never hurt in the guy department ... not that I bother with most of them. Most boys are a distraction I don't care much for.

"I hope you've come to save me from socializing with," I drop my voice, *"normal people."*

Aunt Em wraps an arm around my shoulder. "Surely all the cash they must be slipping you is worth it?" she teases.

I scoff. "You didn't even look at your invitation, did you?" I accuse her. "It said *no cash.* Donations only to —"

"Yeah, yeah, yeah, I saw it, kid," she teases. "You really need to lighten up."

My pursed lips are the only sign of my deep annoyance. I'm so sick of people telling me to loosen up, lighten up, cut loose, or any of the other euphemisms for "I think you're really serious and boring."

"Aunt Em!" Two squeals at once can only mean one thing.

"Kitty! Thea!" Aunt Emily greets my sisters, drawing them in for a group hug. I'm not sure who, but someone pulls me in, too. I swear by the time this party is over I'll have been hugged enough to last the rest of my life.

I extricate myself as surreptitiously as possible as they banter, but Aunt Em grabs me before I get too far.

"I forgot to tell you," she says. "Alessandro is back tomorrow, early, and he brought his nephew with him. They'll be joining us on the trip, okay?"

My jaw tightens as I bite back what I really want to say. My sisters love "Uncle" Alessandro, and obviously so does my best friend, but I'm afraid I've inherited my father's natural bullshit detector. And I really can't stand the guy. Nor can I imagine any family of his being anything less than equally obnoxious. Besides, Aunt Em is pretty much my favorite person, so there goes any actual bonding time we might have had.

"Hey," she says softly, stepping away from my sisters. "We'll still do all kinds of stuff together. I promise, okay? But trust me, you know he's far more organized than I am, so we'll end up seeing a lot more, doing a lot more, and probably eating a whole lot better."

I laugh. "Fair enough," I agree, knowing what a disaster she can be when left to her own devices. "I'm going to go talk to Dad."

It takes me a while to pick my way through the not-inconsiderable crowd to get to him. I have to stop to talk to Uncle Hunter and his partner, Tristan; Grandma Becky; my mom's best friend, Allie; and a good half-dozen other people before I make it to my parents.

Mom pulls me into a hug as soon as she sees me, her hazel eyes sparkling with tears. Dad beams next to her.

"We're so proud of you, honey," she says for the thousandth time.

"Thanks, Mom."

"Seriously," Dad echoes. "And we're going to miss you next week."

I smile dimly as Mom releases me. "Yeah, about that …"

"You're still going, right?" Mom asks, clearly worried. I suppress the eye roll, which is a major feat for me.

"I'm still going. But I wanted to talk to you guys about something. I think I'm going to apply to the FBI after all, and I want to focus on that when I get back."

Mom's hands find her hips. "Hattie, you're not going to *study* while you're supposed to be on vacation, are you?"

Color me unsurprised. She's been on my case to, as she puts it, "have some fun before I launch into adulthood." Unfortunately, we have very different definitions of "fun."

"Of course she's not," Dad says firmly. "Because we already talked about this. I know being an intelligence analyst sounds glamorous, but there's a lot more to working for the FBI than you realize, Hattie." Dad glowers down at me, uncharacteristically stern. I jut my chin out defiantly, unsure why he's still so against it.

"Come on, Dad, I've been working with you every summer for five years. I think it's time for me to try something different."

Dad frowns and rolls his shoulders, looking extra glowery, and for an instant I find him intimidating. He's sure huge. But while I may have inherited his looks, I've got my mother's stubbornness, so I steel myself and glare back at him.

An unexpected smile splits his face and he laughs. "That's the exact same look you gave me when you were three and I wouldn't let you stay up late to watch *PJ Masks* as much as you wanted."

I roll my eyes and cross my arms over my chest as he and Mom have a laugh at my expense.

"Seriously, Dad," I insist. "I want to give this a shot."

Dad sets his spatula down and removes the apron he's wearing. "Hattie, you're already an important part of the company, and I thought we agreed you'd be coming on full time once you were back from your trip."

A sigh escapes me, and I deflate at the hurt under his tone. "I did. You're right, I'm sorry."

Dad slips a finger under my chin, titling my face up. "Hey, everything's going to be okay, kiddo," he assures me. "There are lots of positions in the company where you can do similar types of work. You'll see."

"I know," I grumble, not sounding particularly excited or convincing.

"And you can always try something else later if you decide Hoyt Corporate Services isn't for you," he says. Now he's the one who doesn't sound convincing. Ever since I started studying business, Dad's hopes have been high for me running the company someday. And it's not that I don't enjoy working there, I'm just not convinced it's where I belong. But he sure is. He considers me for a moment with a frown. "Just ... maybe not the FBI?"

And there it is. Despite repeated attempts at discussing it, Dad is dead set against me working for the FBI. Something about Great-Grandpa leaving because of some serious issues with the way they operated. But that was *ages* ago, and Dad is off-the-charts overprotective. It makes me want to heed him and defy him in equal measure. But we all know where I always land. I'm a born and bred daddy's girl.

Mom lays a hand on my shoulder and I look up at her.

"I have something that might make you feel better," she says softly.

Dad looks down at her lovingly and wraps an arm around her waist. The gesture makes me ache because I know he'd do anything for Mom ... just not for me, apparently.

"Yeah? What's that?" I ask, admittedly a little curious.

"Just a little gift," she says with a twinkle in her eye.

Now I'm really curious. They already got me a car when I went to college. It doesn't exactly need replacing. And I'm not really a gifts kind of person. Well, unless it's books.

"I'm listening," I tease, folding my arms over my chest with a smirk.

Mom looks up at Dad and he nods. With a grin, she pulls something out of her pocket. She keeps her fist closed around it as she extends her arm toward me.

"I know you've been saving for your own place, but the lease on my first apartment downtown just ended ..." She opens her hand to reveal a key.

"Really?" I ask, aghast, looking down at the key, then up at her and Dad. "That's ... are you sure?"

Mom laughs. "We're sure, honey. You've always worked so hard, it's the least we can do."

I snatch the key happily and dive into them, wrapping my arms around them.

"Thank you, thank you, thank you," I sing. "I promise I'll take really good care of it, pay rent on time, and all that."

Mom presses me away and gives me a funny look. "Hattie, we're *giving* you the apartment. It's already in your name, sweetheart. You just need to take care of insurance and taxes." My jaw drops, and they both laugh. "Did you think we were really going to make you pay us rent?"

My eyes fill with tears. "I can't even … I just … *thank you*." I sniff loudly and wipe the tears away as fast as I can. I'm not a particularly emotional person, but this is beyond anything I'd ever expect.

"You're welcome, sweetheart," Mom says. "Now use all that money you've saved to buy yourself some clothes or something."

We all laugh, knowing that's something I'd never do in a million years. "Yeah, sure, okay, Mom. But … are you guys sure, really? I mean, will you be okay with that?"

Mom rolls her eyes. "You won't be in Timbuktu, Harriet."

"Just checking. Since Kitty will be going to school out of state and all, I didn't know…" I shrug self-consciously.

"Yes, well, Thea and Landon are more than enough to keep us busy between school, her violin and swimming lessons, his football and basketball practices, not to mention that your Dad and I do run our own companies …"

"Okay, okay, I get the point," I grumble with a smile. "I guess maybe it'll be weirder for me than you." I shrug.

Dad throws me a wink as he tends the grill. "Well, I'll still see you every day at work, so no skin off my back."

I press my lips together and don't say anything. Mom shoots me a knowing look that I'm pretty sure Dad misses.

"I'm going to go take these to the table," Dad says, finishing plating up the burgers and hot dogs he'd been working on. "Be back."

As he walks away, Mom touches my elbow gently. "I'll work on him on the FBI thing while you're gone, okay?" Her expression is filled with love and concern.

I smile widely, grabbing her hand and squeezing. "Thanks, Mom."

"He loves you, Hattie. You've just always been a little too good at pleasing him, and he's used to getting his way. But I want you to know that I support you no matter what. And so will he, when it comes down to it."

I nod, blinking back tears. "Thanks, Mom," I say again, and this time my is voice thick with emotion. As much as I hate the vulnerability, this day turned out pretty good after all.

～

ON MONDAY MORNING, DAD DROPS ME OFF AT AUNT EM'S ON HIS WAY INTO work. Before I can get out of the car, he lays a hand on my arm.

"If the Italians give you shit, just call me."

I turn back to him with a grin. "Come on, Dad, give me some credit."

He laughs. "You're right. They'll never know what hit them," he replies with his own grin. "Love you, kiddo."

"Love you, too, Dad." I lean over and give him a peck on the cheek, and he blushes. It's something I haven't done since I was much younger, but then I can't remember the last time I've been away from him and Mom for a full week in … gosh, probably since they went on vacation alone together the summer before I started college. And while I lived at home during school, the prospect of being away from them, then coming back and living on my own … well, I guess I'm a little more sentimental than usual.

I duck out of the car quickly to hide my blush and retrieve my suitcase from the trunk. Aunt Em pops out and says hi to Dad before helping me put my bag directly into Alessandro's car that's sitting in the driveway.

"So hey," I say as we walk into the house, trying to contain my glee. "Mom and Dad gave me an *apartment*."

Aunt Em laughs. "I heard."

"You heard what?" a lilting voice calls as we enter the kitchen. It's the Italian, as Dad likes to call him.

"About Hattie's new apartment."

"Ah, yes. Do you want to tell her, or shall I?" Alessandro asks with his stupid sideways smile, running a hand through his graying hair. I find it annoying, as usual, that he's aged so gracefully. Damn Italian genes. Not that Aunt Em hasn't. They're both still attractive, even if older with some wrinkles. Mom and Dad are too, actually, so I guess it bodes well for me.

"Tell me what?" I ask.

"Alessandro had one of his interior designers furnish it for you," Aunt Em replies with a grin. "As a graduation present."

Alessandro looks down and blushes. I suddenly feel bad for all the years I've been cold to him. Well, a little. It was a nice thing for him to do, anyway. Definitely unexpectedly generous. But then, that seems to be the theme these days.

"Thank you," I say sincerely, wrapping Aunt Em in a hug. When I'm done I look at him hesitantly and he smiles, opening his arms to me. I keep it brief and hold my breath. "You guys really didn't have to do that, but I appreciate it."

"You're most welcome," he says, then clears his throat. "Shall we get on with our trip?"

"We'd best if we want to make the ten-twenty ferry," Aunt Em agrees. "Or we'll have to have lunch in Anacortes and we'll lose out on the whole afternoon."

"I'll go get Matteo," he replies lightly, then heads upstairs.

"Matteo, huh? How *Italian*," I remark drily.

"Play nice," Aunt Em warns me. "He's a good kid."

Kid. Great. I'm going to have to put up with some snot-nosed brat for the next seven days. Awesome.

Two sets of footsteps come pounding down the stairs. Alessandro appears at the door of the kitchen. "*Andiamo*," he says with a wink at Aunt Em.

When Matteo appears behind him, I'm shocked into silence. He's not a kid. Definitely not a kid, as he looks a few years older than me and, at a couple of inches taller than my five-foot-nine, he's a shade shorter than Alessandro. His hair is a darker brown, though, almost black, and he has startlingly blue eyes. He's even a bit lighter in complexion. Really, he doesn't look much like Alessandro at all. Except the sideways smile, but on Matteo it looks … ugh, I don't want to even think about how good it looks. Not to mention the broad shoulders and well-developed arms. Bad news. This guy is bad news.

I tear my eyes away to find Aunt Em giving me a knowing look. I shoot her a glare to tell her to stop thinking whatever it is she's thinking. She chuckles under her breath and gestures toward Matteo.

"Hattie, this is Matteo," her eyes flick to him. "Matteo, this is my niece, Hattie."

"*Piacere*," he says quietly with that damn sideways smile.

"Nice to meet you, too," I murmur, looking away quickly. I can feel the heat rising in my cheeks. I've never been comfortable using foreign languages. I sure hope he knows English or we're not going to have much to say to each other. On second thought, maybe it would be better if he didn't.

Thankfully, Aunt Em and Alessandro lead us to the car, saving me from further conversation. Even better, Matteo joins Alessandro in the front seat, and Aunt Em and I sit in the back. The whole drive to the ferry the men talk to each other lowly in Italian, and Aunt Em and I catch up. Between finals and her work at the music shop, we haven't seen each other much in a while.

The ferry ride from Anacortes to San Juan Island gives us more than enough time to talk, and we even wander out of the car to get drinks and sit on the glassed-in main deck, watching the gorgeous scenery around us. Matteo doesn't speak much to me, sticking to talking to Alessandro or simply quietly staring at the view.

When we get off the ferry, Alessandro drives us to their vacation house just north of Friday Harbor. As we pull onto their street, I chuckle to myself. It always cracks me up that they own a house on Hoyt Lane. It's no actual connection to our family, and I know they bought the sprawling estate because both the house and the views are beyond beautiful, but I imagine the street name made it feel even more like kismet.

We all unpack the car and head in, each going to our own rooms with instructions to be in the kitchen in half an hour for lunch. I take the time to freshen up by freeing my long hair from its ponytail, brushing it out, and changing into a pair of blue corduroy pants with a white, long-sleeved T-shirt.

It's sunny enough outside but still in the upper fifties this early in summer. Thankfully, it rains less out here in the islands this time of year than it does in Seattle. Go figure.

I spend the rest of my half hour reading until it's time for lunch. When I hit a chapter break, I put a bookmark in and bring it with me back to the main area, where something smells fantastic. I find Aunt Em and Alessandro at the kitchen bar munching on some roasted chicken sandwiches. Matteo sits in the living room eating his own while reading a book, causing me to do a double take. It reads. Damn.

"Ah, there she is," Aunt Em calls, rising and handing me a plate from the warmer. "Arugula and rosemary chicken panini with garlic aioli. There are chips in the cupboard if you want some." She gestures behind me, but I'm already drooling too much to bother with chips. I put my book down at the bar, sit, and dive into my sandwich.

"We're going to go on an art walk this afternoon if you'd like to join us," Alessandro offers as he puts his plate in the dishwasher.

"Mmm," I hedge as I swallow the bite I was working on. "I'm not much for art, but I'll go and hang out in the bookstore while you guys do that, if that's okay?"

"It's closed today." Aunt Em smiles apologetically.

"Damn. Okay, well, then I'll pass, thanks though."

Alessandro nods and presumably goes to ask Matteo the same thing.

"So does he speak English?" I ask Aunt Em quietly, shooting a furtive look toward the men.

She winks. "Why don't you go find out for yourself?"

"I'm good," I say shortly, taking another huge bite of my sandwich.

Aunt Em cackles. "He won't bite. Well, not unless you want him to, I'm sure."

My eyes go wide and she laughs even harder. Thankfully, she doesn't tell me to lighten up again, she just finishes putting away the dishes and goes into the living room.

I watch the three of them have a short conversation before Aunt Em comes back.

"Matteo's staying here, too. You know where the bicycles are if you want to go somewhere. Just lock up if you both go."

I roll my eyes and wave my book. "Thanks, but I think I'll just go back to my room and read."

"Hattie," Aunt Em says in an exasperated tone. "Look. I know Alessandro isn't your favorite person for whatever reason, but don't take it out on his nephew. It'd be rude if you just ignored him. Please. He's only visiting for a few months. Try to make him feel welcome."

"Fine," I sigh.

Aunt Em pats me on the hand. "Good. We'll be back in a few hours, then we'll all go out to dinner, okay?"

"Friday Harbor House?" I ask hopefully.

She laughs. "Sure, we can do that. Just *play nice*," she reiterates.

"Yeah, yeah, yeah," I reply with a smile. "Have fun, see you guys later."

I watch them head out the side door to the garage and take a deep breath. Best to get this over with. I walk over to the couch and wait until he sees me before settling on the other end. His blue eyes watch me curiously as he closes the book he's reading.

"Hi," I say awkwardly. "What are you reading?"

He turns the book around so I can see the cover.

"*Atlas Shrugged*?" I ask in surprise. "Wow. I'd never have guessed."

Matteo, ironically, shrugs, and I laugh.

"Why?" he asks simply.

My turn to shrug, and we both laugh. "Isn't Italy kind of on the socialistic side? That book is pretty 'yay capitalism' and 'boo socialism.' I'd think that'd be kind of off-putting to someone from a socialist-leaning country."

He taps the cover of the book now resting in his lap thoughtfully. "Italy is a blend of many things. Tradition. Modernity. And many different political views, much like your United States," he replies carefully, never breaking eye contact. His speech is much less accented than I expected, and his deep voice so pleasant, I'm mesmerized as I listen. "Our monarchy was abolished quite recently, really, and we are a democratic republic. And though there is a strong push for socialism, make no mistake, there is plenty of capitalism in my country. It's what I studied, actually."

"Capitalism?" I ask, surprised.

He laughs, and it's like sex and warm bread and a cozy sweater all at once. I swallow hard, ignoring the butterflies in my stomach.

"Not as such," he amends. "Business. I just finished my MBA."

My eyebrows shoot up. No. He cannot be sexy *and* smart. No. Fuck.

"Is that why you're here? To work for your uncle?"

He tips his head back and forth. "Mostly. But this is my first time to the States. I was hoping it would be more than just work," he says, the sideways smile settling on his lips as he looks at me.

It makes me blush hard, and I have to look away.

"I hear you just graduated," he presses on. "What did you study?"

I tug at the hem of my shirt, looking into my lap as I respond. "Business also, but criminal justice, too."

"Interesting combination," he muses. "What do you hope to do?"

I look back up at him. His stare is so direct and open, I can't respond with the answer I know I'm supposed to.

"I want to be an intelligence analyst for the FBI," I admit. "But my dad wants me to work for his corporate security company."

"Ah," he says thoughtfully, tossing his book on the coffee table and sitting upright. "So what will you do?"

I shake my head. "I have no idea."

"It's a hard thing, balancing your obligation to the family who supported you, who loves you, and the desires of your heart."

I close my eyes. "Yes," I breathe. "Exactly. That's exactly it." I feel a swell of emotion at the simple and powerful summary of the crossroads that is my life right now.

"You seem smart, and strong. I'm sure you'll figure it out."

I open my eyes and give him a funny look. "You just met me." But I don't say it harshly. He doesn't set off my bullshit detector like Alessandro does. On the contrary, everything he says seems so straightforward and without agenda.

"Yes, but I listen. I listened to you all the way here, talking to your aunt. And I'm a good judge of character," he says matter-of-factly.

"And very modest," I tease.

He frowns. "Not really. I … *non ho i capelli sulla lingua*. I don't know how you'd say it in English."

I pull out my phone and type it into a translator. "You don't have hair on your tongue?" I ask, confused.

Matteo laughs. "That's not what it really means," he explains. "I am too … honest?"

"Oh, you're *direct*. You don't mince words."

"Mince?" he asks, miming cutting.

I chuckle and shake my head. "Same spelling, but it means that you don't bother making your words sound nice."

"Ah, yes, exactly, that is what I meant. I apologize if it sounds … conceited."

"It doesn't. I'm the same way. It hasn't made me many friends," I say drily. "Nor me."

"Well, I'll be your first American friend," I offer. "Do you know what you want to do this week?"

"You mean besides read my book?" he teases. "I'm not sure. What is there to do?"

I blush at the thought that flits through my brain: *You.* Yeesh. I don't normally respond to guys this way, but between his being ridiculously gorgeous, smart, and up-front, I'm going to have a tough time not swooning over this guy all week. But that's all it can be. Looking. No touching. I can't date a Giordano. And I'm not the fling type. Tried it, hated it as much as I thought I would. No, Matteo Giordano is strictly off-limits for anything but a casual friendship.

In attempt to keep to neutral topics, I retrieve my laptop and show him all the things to do on the island. He seems pretty interested in Lime Kiln State Park and whale watching, but we have plenty of time to do pretty much everything, and even head over to Orcas Island or Victoria if we want.

When Aunt Emily and Alessandro return, we sit down and pick out a few must-schedule activities and sprinkle them throughout the week.

∽

BEFORE I KNOW IT, THE WEEK HAS FLOWN BY AND WE'RE PACKING UP TO MAKE the trek home. As expected, I spent the whole week trying not to ogle him, and probably failing miserably. But he was friendly and kind, and we all actually had a lot of fun together.

"So will you show me around Seattle once we're back?" Matteo asks curiously as we put our luggage in the trunk of Alessandro's car.

I shift feet. "I mean, sure, if you want me to," I reply.

A frown tugs at his full lips. "I didn't mean to presume. You don't have to if you don't want to."

"No, I do," I respond quickly. "I just figured you'd have your hands full with work and stuff, I guess."

Matteo graces me with a smile. "As I mentioned before, I'm hoping to do more than work while I'm here." We stare at each other for a moment, and for the first time I think he might actually be *interested* in me as more than friends.

"Everybody ready?" Alessandro calls, coming toward us and breaking the tension or whatever it was that was hovering between Matteo and me.

I shake myself as I climb in the back with Aunt Em. Just friends. Just because we had fun this week, just because I get along with him better than just about anyone besides Kimmie, it doesn't mean anything. And even if it does, well, it can't. Just. Friends.

But once we're on the ferry, Aunt Em drags me to get coffee, then away from the men to a cozy corner booth on the main deck.

"Matteo likes you," she declares in a whisper.

"We're just friends," I whisper back.

"I can tell he does," she insists in a slightly-less-quiet tone. "And you like him, too, don't you?"

I push my lips together and scrunch my nose. "He's all right."

She levels a skeptical look at me. "Hattie. I've known you your whole life. You can lie to yourself, but you can't fool me. What's the problem?"

I roll my eyes to the ceiling. "He's a *Giordano*."

Aunt Em's eyebrows jump. "And?" she asks archly.

Yeesh. Time to step lightly. I opt for the "blame it on Dad" tactic.

"You know Dad would kill me if I dated Alessandro's nephew."

And much to my surprise, Aunt Em laughs. So hard that tears start leaking out of her eyes. And then she laughs harder, until I'm a self-conscious ball curled up across the booth from her.

Finally, she calms down and wipes her eyes. "I'm sorry, it's just too funny," she gasps.

"I don't understand."

She takes a few deep breaths. "We are so much more alike than you know. Well, except I was a lot sluttier at your age." I go to respond, but she puts a hand up. "When Alessandro and I first got together, I refused to admit it was more than a fling. Because I was scared of really letting someone in. And I totally blamed it on your dad. Because he'd hated Alessandro long before he and I got together."

I gasp. "Really?"

"Really. There's a lot we haven't told you about that time in all our lives. Not because we don't trust you, but because it didn't matter anymore. But want to know what happened when your dad realized we were in love?"

I shake my head in disbelief. "I can't believe Alessandro is still alive," I muse. "What happened?"

"He gave his blessing," she replies simply. "Because he knew it's what I wanted."

I lean back in the booth in shock. "Wow. I don't even know what to say about that." I pause, thinking through what she's told me. "Is there a reason beyond the obvious why Dad hates him so much?"

Aunt Em shoots me a dirty look. "I'm going to ignore the part of that that's insulting," she gripes. "But yes, there is. And I think it's probably time you knew why. Hopefully Sera doesn't kill me."

"What's Mom got to do with this?"

Aunt Em folds her hand over mine. "Oh, Hattie," she sighs. And then she tells me everything.

When she's done, I sit there saying "wow" over and over. She patiently waits for the effect of the multiple bombshells she just dropped to subside.

"So what does this have to do with Matteo and me?" I finally ask.

"I told you so you'd know that I understand what it feels like to be in your place. To be scared of taking a risk for the effect it will have on the people you care about and, more importantly, on you. But it's worth it. Trust me, Hattie, you'll regret it if you don't go for it. I see how well you two get along. The way he looks at you when he thinks you're not looking. The way you look at him when you think he's not looking. Do you really care that much what your dad thinks, or are you just scared?"

I don't answer. I can't. Because the answers are *yes* and *yes*. And saying it out loud would breathe even more life into my inner torment. But Aunt Em, as usual, can read the answers on my face without my having to say a word.

"Do you want me to talk to your dad? Get him to chill a little?" she asks.

I laugh, and as I do a few tears I didn't know were there slip out and onto my cheeks. I wipe them away quickly.

"No, but thanks," I reply, my voice thick with emotion. "I couldn't bear to disappoint him."

"What about disappointing yourself?"

The question hits a little too close to home, and I rise from the booth. "Thanks for the pep talk, Aunt Em, but I think I need some time to absorb all of this."

Her blue eyes watch me for a moment before she nods and stands up. "Okay. Fair enough. I'll back off … for now. But if he asks you out, at least consider it, okay?"

"I'll consider it," I promise. *For about two seconds before I say no.*

∽

THE NEXT SATURDAY, I'VE MANAGED TO MOVE ALL OF MY THINGS AND I'M unpacking in my new apartment. My. New. Apartment. Since the family has gone back home to West Seattle, I'm alone, so I do a happy dance through the whole place until it's stopped abruptly by the doorbell.

I open the door to Aunt Emily, Alessandro, and Matteo. My heart does a little jump.

"Hey guys, I wasn't expecting you," I say nervously, stepping back to let them in.

Matteo comes in last, pulling a bunch of flowers from behind his back.

"Beautiful flowers for a beautiful woman," he pronounces with a small smile. "Congratulations on your new apartment."

I take them, inhaling deeply of their scent as my heart flutters in my chest. I haven't seen or spoken to Matteo since we got back last Sunday, despite having exchanged numbers.

"Thank you," I say. I set them on the kitchen counter, then return to the group as they look around. "I'll give you the tour?"

Aunt Em nods enthusiastically. "Sera had already moved out of here when we met, but Alessandro has been here."

"Not for a long time," he says quietly. His eyes land on the island in the kitchen. "Not much has changed, though."

Matteo gives me a questioning look, and I return it with a confused shrug. I give them all the tour, which doesn't take long. We make small talk about how it's going working full time for my dad now, and how Matteo is doing in his first week working for Alessandro. Rather, Alessandro does most of the talking, and it makes me wonder what Matteo really thinks. His face is a mask as we talk, and it makes me nervous.

I find myself wondering if he's met more people this week, maybe even some women his age. The idea doesn't sit well, despite myself.

When Aunt Em finally rises, declaring that they need to be off to get ready for an evening function, disappointment settles deep in my gut.

That is, until Matteo pipes up. "I'll stay, if that's okay?"

Alessandro looks at him in surprise, but Aunt Em looks anything but.

"Yes, of course," Alessandro replies. "I'm sure you young people would rather hang out with each other than with us old farts."

And the expression is so American I have to laugh hearing it come out in his still-distinctive Italian accent. I thank them again for coming, and soon the door closes behind them, leaving me and Matteo alone.

I turn back to him sitting on the couch.

"So how's work going, really?" I tease as I settle onto the opposite end.

He smiles and runs a hand through his dark hair, letting out a deep breath. "It's fine. Not nearly as exciting as my uncle made it sound, but that's okay."

"Well, I'm glad it isn't awful at least," I offer. "Have you gotten out to see any of Seattle yet?"

"Not much," he replies, tilting his head. "I was waiting for my favorite tour guide to be available. I missed talking to you this week."

I blush deeply. "You have my number, you could've texted or called."

He looks pleasantly surprised at the encouragement. "Then I'm sorry I didn't," he replies carefully. "But I'm here now. Are you busy tomorrow? Perhaps you could show me around."

"I'm free right now if you are," I say, and the words surprise even me.

Matteo looks equally surprised. "Don't you want to finish unpacking?" he asks skeptically.

"I can do that anytime. You look pretty bored. I say we go hit up Pioneer Square and do the Underground tour."

His brows furrow together. "What's underground?"

I laugh. "You'll see. Trust me. Just let me go get cleaned up and we can head out."

⌘

"HOLY SHIT, THAT WAS CRAZY," MATTEO LAUGHS AS WE ARRIVE BACK AT MY apartment that night. He follows me in, having been in the middle of a conversation. "I can't believe they still have all that down there. It's so creepy!"

"You should do that tour around Halloween. They make it extra spooky," I inform him as we settle back onto the couch. "I'm a big baby, though, so you'd have to go without me."

The smile that was on his face melts away. "Unfortunately, I have to leave in September," he reminds me stoically.

I chew at my bottom lip, internally kicking myself in the ass. "Sorry," I say softly. Then, considering his forlorn expression, I have to ask, "Are you really that attached to Seattle already?"

"Is it weird to say I'd miss you?" he asks plainly, looking deeply into my eyes.

My throat constricts. "No. I think I'd miss you, too," I reply honestly. I can't remember ever being so at ease with a guy before, much less one as good-looking as Matteo. And certainly not after knowing them only a couple of weeks.

His hand rises to cup my face, his thumb coming to rest on my cheek.

"I'm glad to hear you say that," he murmurs.

I want to protest, but I'm frozen in place by his touch and the electricity coursing through my body. In this moment, I can honestly say I've never wanted someone before like I want him. I mean, I've been attracted to guys before, but never on this level. And I realize Aunt Em is right. I can't ignore this. Though I don't think I could even if I wanted to with him this close to me.

He leans in, his lips hovering just a fraction of an inch away from mine. I can only register his amazing smell and that he's waiting for me to allow the kiss before my brain shuts off and my body takes over, pushing my lips into his.

When he feels me respond, he reacts like a man starved. His mouth becomes insistent upon mine, his teeth pulling at my bottom lip, begging me to open to him as his hands pull me roughly to him. On a gasp, my mouth opens, and his tongue greedily searches for mine. It's passion like I've never known, and within moments my whole body is humming under his touch, my hands grasping at his strong arms. When he finally pulls back, we're both flushed and gasping for breath.

"I'm sorry, I didn't mean to be so ..." He trails off, unsure.

"Don't be," I beg, grabbing his shirt and pulling him back to me.

I can feel his smile against my mouth for an instant before he opens to me again, this time hauling me into his lap as he kisses me feverishly, then roaming with his hands over my back, my hips, my thighs. I slide my hands down to his firm chest and push gently to break the kiss.

As I struggle to regain composure, I realize I'm balancing on the edge of something here. I can jump back to safety, or I can take a risk. I place my hands on either side of his face, looking seriously into his eyes.

"This can't go anywhere," I whisper, tears gathering in my eyes.

Matteo runs a finger along my jaw. "But it already has."

I smile dimly. "My dad hates your uncle. If he knew ..."

One dark brow rises. "You care so much about what your parents want. What about what you want?"

I ease farther back onto his lap, pulling his hand away from my face. But I absentmindedly hold it in mine, tracing his palm with the tip of my finger.

"What I want doesn't matter. Besides, you're leaving in two-and-a-half months anyway. I can't shake up my whole world for something that won't last."

"How will you find something that will last if you don't stop making excuses?" he poses with a small, knowing smile. I don't answer. But then, I don't think he expects me to. He grasps my hand in his, raising it to his lips. "I should go."

I nod, sliding off his lap and walking him to the door. He stops at the threshold, looking down at me seriously.

"The things I feel around you I haven't experienced for a long time," he admits. "Give me a chance. If you feel it, too, give us a chance."

Remembering my promise to Aunt Em, my next words become simple. "I'll consider it."

His sideways smile appears, and my insides tighten. Before I can stop myself, I pull his face to mine, grazing my lips gently over his. "Goodbye, Matteo."

"*Buona sera*, Hattie." His lips meet mine one last time, softly, and then he's gone.

⌒〜

"You look different," Mom remarks as we clean up from brunch. "If I didn't know better, I'd say … giddy? It's a boy, isn't it?"

I shoot her a skeptical look. "You talked to Aunt Em." It's not a question.

Mom laughs. "Guilty," she admits. "So, Matteo Giordano, huh?"

"So, Alessandro Giordano, huh?" I counter.

"Yeah, Em mentioned she filled you in on that little bit of ancient history," Mom grouses.

"Good. Now you can tell me why he was so fascinated by the island in my new kitchen."

Mom goes bright red and it takes me about two seconds to deduce why.

"Oh, god," I choke out. "I'm replacing that thing tomorrow."

"If it makes you feel any better, the counters have been redone since then," she replies, still flushed.

I shoot her a dirty look. "I guess it does. Anything else that I should consider replacing?"

Mom presses her lips together and looks up at the ceiling. "This is so not a conversation I ever thought I'd be having with my daughter." She heaves a deep sigh and looks back at me. "No, everything has been redone since I lived there *decades ago*. Happy?"

I wrinkle my nose at her. "I guess. But seriously Mom, ew. It's bad enough having to deal with you and Dad still being all up in each other's business, but now I have to think about it with you and Alessandro? In my new-to-me place? Ugh."

Mom throws her hands up in the air. "Fine, we'll sell the apartment and get you a brand-new place. The good lord knows I might as well use all this money for something," she snaps.

I give her some serious side-eye as I finish loading the dishwasher.

"Don't worry about it. I'm sure I'll get over it. Eventually."

"Are you done deflecting?" she asks testily.

"Never," I say with a suppressed smile. "But continue if you must."

"Look, I know your dad isn't fond of Alessandro—" I scoff and she shoots me a look, "—but even after we weren't together anymore, Alessandro and I were still friends. Because he's a good guy. Your dad just has a very hard time forgiving people of their shortcomings."

"Unless it's you," I point out.

She opens her mouth to protest but seems to think better of it. "Okay, except for me," she allows. "Anyway. My *point* is, just because Matteo is Alessandro's nephew and there's bad blood between him and your father doesn't mean you should let that stop you if you want to be with Matteo."

"It's not the only thing. He's going back to Italy in September."

"Oh, and nobody ever came back from Italy or got an extended visa, or any of the other countless ways he could stay here if he decides to," she chides. "Seriously, Hattie, you're reaching." Her expression softens and she leans back against the sink. "Look, honey, I know you're just as cautious as your father. But even your dad knows when to go after what he really wants. You don't want to regret not doing something you really wanted to do."

I arch my eyebrows at my mother talking about me "doing" Matteo. She waves her hand impatiently.

"You know what I mean," Mom says.

And I want to be snarky, but I do know. Still, I don't know what to say.

"Look. Normally, I stay out of your love life. But your aunt saw something, and I trust that she knows you well enough to know when to push and when to stay out of it."

"So you're saying you're both going to keep bugging me about this?"

Mom beams. "Yup. But it's for your own good, I promise."

"How about using a little of that on Dad about the FBI job?" I ask sweetly.

Mom stands up and pats me on the shoulder. "Trust me, I'm working on it. And while I do, you should work on letting yourself open up to someone. It wasn't easy for me, either, it never is. But it's—"

"Worth it, yes, Aunt Em said that, too. Don't you two have anything better to do?"

"Nope," she replies with a smile.

❧

WHEN I GET HOME THAT AFTERNOON, I STARE AT MY PHONE FOR A GOOD HALF hour before finally sending Matteo a message.

I'm home. Still looking for a tour guide?

His response comes swiftly. *Be there in ten.*

I swallow hard. Ready or not, here he comes.

I bolt into the bedroom to change, even though there's nothing wrong with my outfit. Still, I switch from regular jeans to skinny jeans, and from a plain T-shirt to a cute yellow lacy top. I brush out my long chestnut waves and apply as much makeup as I ever do — a bit of mascara and tinted lip gloss.

As I'm just putting on the last touches, the doorbell rings. Damn, he's fast. Before I open the door, I take a deep breath, realizing this is kind of our first official date. I force back the butterflies beating against my rib cage and open the door.

Standing there in dark jeans and a tan henley that fits tight against his muscled arms and shoulders, he looks positively yummy.

"*Ciao*," he greets me. "You look beautiful, as always."

I wrap my purse around my torso. "You don't look so bad yourself," I reply with a small smile. "Shall we?"

He shakes his head lightly and wraps an arm around my waist, pulling me into him. Since he's only a couple of inches taller than me, his mouth hovers just above mine as he looks into my eyes.

"First," he says, then places a tentative kiss on my lips.

I can't help melting under the warmth of his mouth. He takes the encouragement and slides his tongue across the seam of my lips. I want to allow it, but I also don't want to be tempted to have our first sexual encounter on my doorstep. So I let him in briefly, then gently pull back, pulse racing.

"Okay, now we can go," he teases, taking my hand as I pull the door closed behind me.

We spend hours walking downtown, through Pike's Place Market, then Seattle Center. He opts not to go to the observation deck of the Space Needle, being afraid of heights, and I can't say I mind — I'm not a huge fan, either. We tour the kooky Science Fiction Museum and the Experience Music Project before grabbing dinner at a fondue place down the road, chatting easily the whole time. But as we walk back to my apartment late that evening, I start to get nervous about how this night will end.

I both want him to stay with me, and I don't. When we get to my door, I'm still waffling.

"Thank you for the tour," he murmurs, eyeing my lips.

705

"You're welcome," I reply softly.

He squeezes my hand. "When can I see you again?"

I give a small laugh. "I guess that depends on what part of the city you'd like to see next?"

He gathers me in his arms, pressing his forehead to mine, and I'm hyper-aware of every inch of our bodies touching.

"Is 'your bedroom' too forward an answer?" he asks. Without waiting for an answer, his mouth closes over mine, and our tongues meld together in a dance I'm coming to enjoy a bit too much.

Just when I think he can't drive me any crazier, he pushes me up against the door, grinding his hips into mine. My mouth breaks from his as a moan escapes me.

"Another night, *bella*," he whispers in my ear. "I don't want to rush anything."

I nod as he pulls away, giving me time to catch my breath.

"How about we get dinner on Tuesday? I should be home by six."

"It's a date," he promises, raising my hand to his lips and sealing it with a kiss.

∽

I MAKE MATTEO MEET ME AT A RESTAURANT ON TUESDAY. THEN AGAIN ON Wednesday. Being in public keeps the lust-fest at bay long enough for us to keep getting to know each other. But I'd be lying if I said I didn't want him to take me to bed. Because everything I learn about him makes me want him more.

He's smart, and driven, but utterly bored working for Alessandro. I can tell he needs more of a challenge, and a dangerous thought starts to form in my mind. We can't see each other on Thursday, so I have to wait until Friday night to see what Matteo thinks.

In the meantime, we text each other constantly. Everything from idle chitchat to what I can only call pre-sexting, since we haven't actually had sex yet. But with the more than occasional racy messages bouncing between us, by the time he shows up at my place on Friday night, I'm wound up so tightly with anticipation I can barely stand it.

When I open the door, it's to him holding a dozen long-stemmed red roses, and his sweetness melts a good amount of my tension.

"Oh, Matteo, they're beautiful," I breathe. "But you just brought me flowers last weekend."

His blue eyes sparkle mischievously. "I couldn't help it. I see beauty and it reminds me of you. I had to get them."

I shoot him a look. That sounded an awful lot like something his uncle would say, and the thought occurs to me that Alessandro's cheesiness may simply be a product of his affection for my aunt. There's a thought.

"Well, thank you," I reply. "Come in and I'll put them in water."

Matteo enters but removes the flowers from my hand, putting them on the kitchen counter. "Later," he says, looking earnestly into my eyes.

I take his intent a moment before his hot mouth covers mine and his hands wind into my hair. I sink into him, lost to the force that's been pulling us together these last few weeks.

His mouth breaks from mine briefly. "I feel like I can't kiss you properly with others around. I'm glad we're here, now." His eyes bore into mine, one hand stroking my cheek, the other wrapped around my waist, holding me against him.

"Me, too," I agree. "So don't stop." My lips curl into a smile.

"Be careful, I only have so much control," he growls, sliding his hand to the nape of my neck and gripping my hair so my mouth tilts up to him.

A frantic moan escapes me and it spurs him into action. As his mouth works with mine, he half pushes me toward my bedroom. The other half is me pulling him there, my body and mind overcome by days of teasing.

We collapse onto my bed, a flurry of hands pulling at clothes. I'm stilled as one of his finds my breast and he squeezes into the tip. I grab him through his pants in revenge and he growls into my neck.

"Are you sure this is what you want?" he asks huskily into my ear.

I press against his chest until our eyes meet. "I want you so bad it hurts," I admit. I try not to think about everyone it *could* hurt. Instead, I focus on the way his lips make me feel as they trace down my neck. I close my eyes as his hands tug my shirt over my head, letting his mouth explore my chest with abandon.

My hands find the fabric of his shirt and I pull. He rears back, tearing the shirt off and throwing it to the floor. I'm dumbstruck by the toned muscles of his chest and abs, the sharp "V" shaping his lower abdomen to the top of his pants where dark, curly hair disappears in a line below his waistband. I lick my lips eagerly and divest myself of my own jeans and panties. He follows suit, and we're suddenly completely naked, eye-fucking each other in anticipation.

"I'm going to try very hard to stick to English," he promises, "because I want you to understand every word I say about your beautiful body."

Any self-conscious feelings I had at being naked in front of this gorgeous man evaporate.

"Touch me, Matteo," I beg, scooting back to the head of the bed.

He prowls onto the end of the bed, making his way up to me. I run my fingers through his hair as he gets close, sliding them down his neck and chest as he settles over me.

"Are you ..." I can't tell if he's searching for the word or is afraid to say it, and I realize quickly what could make him so hesitant right now.

"A virgin?" I guess. He nods, blushing a little. "Not even close. Are you?" Looking the way he does, I highly doubt it, so I ask more to get back at him. I'm a twenty-one-year-old introvert, not a fucking nun.

He looks relieved. "Decidedly not. Just making sure I wasn't about to do something that scared you."

I shake my head, grabbing his hand and moving it between my legs so he can feel how turned on I am.

"I'm definitely not scared," I say breathily.

His fingers slip into my folds until they're slick with my arousal. Matteo moans his approval, then runs a finger up to my clit and down to my entrance, sliding into me gently. I nod, arching into his hand, pushing him in deeper. He fucks me with his hand and, while it feels good, he just misses the spot inside.

"Palm up," I say, showing him my palm. "Then this." I flex my fingers like I'm inviting him in, which I'm also doing. But he takes the instruction immediately, and I feel his fingertip slide over my G-spot. I arch up every time it does until he starts to understand, then presses harder.

"That's a new one," he admits with a smile.

"Do both," I beg. He looks at me quizzically. "Keep fingering me while you use your tongue on my clit."

He gives one sexy jump of his left eyebrow before descending between my legs. His continued strokes inside me are roiling the fire in my core, so when his tongue hits my clitoris I ignite into an inferno of pleasure.

"Oh, fuck, yes," I scream. "More. Harder."

He pumps harder, faster with his fingers, pressing in with his tongue like he at least already knew what to do there. It takes a hot minute before I'm coming. As I descend, I sit up so his hand slips out, since I'm bordering on over-stimulated.

"I enjoyed doing that to you," he whispers, kissing me lightly.

I run my hands down his chest, over his abs, to his hips. I pull so he has to rise as his pelvis moves forward. He's uncut and hugely engorged, his shaft curling toward his abdomen. I grab it at the base, pulling the skin down so I can fully lick the sensitive tip. I swirl the salty bead of moisture there around with my tongue and he moans, his hands gathering my hair up so I can suck at him unimpeded.

And I happily oblige, as he makes the most erotic noises I've ever heard each time I suck him or slide my hand up his length. As I alternate between the two, his moans merge to one lengthy and continuous sound of pleasure. When he starts to shudder, I pull back.

"Not yet," I breathe, rising to meet his mouth with mine.

He pushes me over so I'm prone beneath him while he puts a condom on.

Just watching him has me biting my lip in anticipation. It's been far too long, and I'm halfway to another orgasm just having listened to him enjoy my blow job.

So when he teases at my entrance, running the head of his cock up and down, I squirm, greedily trying to pull him into me.

"Shhhh," he says with a grin before inching into me at a glacial pace.

The slow filling almost makes me lose my mind with need, my walls twitching with anticipation as he slides in. I grab desperately at my breasts, needing the stimulation to increase again, instead of enduring this slow torture. Then all at once he pushes hard until he's fully inside me. I deflate with a sigh. Until he pulls back out and does it all over again. And again, over and over. Until I'm practically weeping with every slow, deliberate inward thrust, and building up with every final, hard push.

When I think I can take no more, and I'm grabbing the sheets in frustration and desire, he looks down at me with his sexy-as-sin sideways smile.

"Hold on."

I bite my lip, bracing myself. Suddenly, he speeds up until he's thrusting in and out rapidly, just like I'd wanted. But now I'm so turned on that it's a whole other level of amazing as my body sprints toward orgasm. The peak is higher than any I've ever experienced, and my eyes slam shut as my body contracts inward before exploding outward in a blaze of heat that keeps going until I hear Matteo cry out his own release. Finally, he slows down, then stops. He lays over me, his chest heaving with exertion, his gorgeous body slick with sweat. But I couldn't care less, and I wrap my arms around him.

We eventually untangle ourselves, clean up, and have some dinner, but wind up going at round two not much later. As we lay naked in bed, surrendering the rest of the evening to enjoying each other, I remember my idea.

"This may seem out of the blue," I hedge, "but you're not happy working for Alessandro, are you?"

Matteo props himself up on one arm. "Not really," he admits. "But it's not so bad."

"What if I knew of somewhere else you might want to work more?"

"Go on," he says with a curious glint in his eye.

I tell him about my dad's company, and all the various departments and business opportunities. And that we take interns, albeit usually college students, but he's only twenty-four, so it's not like he'd be that much older than them.

"I'm intrigued," he admits. "But do you really want me to work at the same company as you and your father?"

"I'm not sure how much longer I'll work there anyway," I reply. "But I think it would be a good fit for you. Would Alessandro be upset?"

"I barely see him anyway, so I doubt it," he replies drily. "So are you thinking of going after your dream job, finally?" His knowing smile annoys me.

"Finally?"

He grins. "I've been wondering how long it would take. You don't seem all that happy working for your dad, either."

I mull that over while he traces light circles on my hip.

"I guess I'm not," I finally admit with a sigh. "I guess I've told myself that I could be, so I keep pretending like I am and hoping that I'll get there."

Matteo's fingers slip to my cheek, turning my face so I have to look into his eyes. "I have known you for only a short time, but even I can see that you aren't. I refuse to believe he doesn't know, deep down, that it isn't right for you."

I close my hand over his, removing it and shaking my head. "One thing at a time. First, we get you in. Then I'll figure out how to get myself out."

"Because you're not ready? Or because you're still putting your father's feelings before your own?" he asks shrewdly.

I narrow my eyes at him. "I think it's time we stopped talking again for a while." My free hand roams down his abs, lands on his cock, and pretty much ends the discussion.

⌒

Before I approach Dad, I know it's best to run my idea by Mom. So once Matteo and I manage to break apart, which pretty much takes until Sunday morning when I have to leave for our regular family brunch, I get Mom on her own after we're all done eating. Together, we come up with a strategy that just might work.

But when I walk into the staff meeting on Monday morning ready to put our plan into action, I struggle to keep myself from shaking with nerves.

Fortunately, an opportunity comes that I never expected. Stephanie Lefever, the organizational structure department lead, is giving her weekly rundown when I hear her say, "And I know we didn't ask for an intern this summer, but with Amanda out on maternity leave, we're really struggling to keep up."

Dad frowns into his lap for a moment, so I take his pause to leap in.

"I know someone who just got his MBA and is looking to switch jobs," I pipe up.

Dad and Steph both look at me. Steph's eyebrows jump in happy surprise. Dad quirks an eyebrow, as if he senses I'm up to something he isn't going to like.

"He'd be willing to intern?" Steph asks.

"Yes, he's here for only three months anyway. And before you ask, he's not being asked to leave his current job, it's just not exactly in his wheelhouse, and it was more a job of convenience. They don't really need him and he needs more of a challenge," I offer.

"You're talking about the Giordano boy," Dad says, finally finding his voice. His hands are folded seemingly casually in front of him, and he's leaned back in his chair. Anyone else would think it was a pose of relaxed indifference. But I know better.

"I am," I confirm, looking him in the eye. "We've talked about our jobs and aptitudes, and corporate structuring was one of his main interests. He's a serious and intelligent individual. I think he's worth giving a chance." I continue holding his gaze as I can see the wheels in his head turning, his hackles rising at the mention of a Giordano in his sacred place of business. And I know if I don't keep staring him down, I'm going to roll my eyes.

Dad runs his thumb over his bottom lip. Steph looks between us, clearly sensing there's something unspoken happening here but wisely keeping her mouth shut.

"Have him send his résumé to me," Dad finally responds. "I'll give it a look."

Steph looks a little confused but shrugs and nods. Usually, she'd do the hiring for her own department but clearly doesn't want to ask about my dad's unusual reaction to my suggestion.

The meeting moves on, and I sit tensely waiting to be able to show my relief in private. But when we adjourn, Dad holds me back, gesturing for me to move to the chair to his right. I don't miss the symbolism.

"I'm surprised," he says simply as I settle.

I shrug. "Me, too. I figured I'd hate him. But I don't. He's actually really smart, and surprisingly easy to get along with." The words tumble out, and I turn red, feeling like I've already said way too much. The last thing I want is for my dad to get wind of exactly how much I like this guy.

Dad taps his pen against his pad as he considers that.

"Well, I trust your judgment. Have his résumé to me today, please." With that he stands, indicating we're done, and I follow him out. As we part to our respective desks, I know without a doubt that Dad is off to dig up every piece of dirt he can on Matteo. I try to not think too hard about what he'll find.

∼

BY THE END OF THE DAY, NOT ONLY HAS MATTEO SENT IN HIS RÉSUMÉ, BUT HE texts to tell me my dad actually called him and did a phone interview. All he says is that my dad asked him a million questions. But thankfully none about me, so he obviously doesn't suspect that our relationship extends beyond a casual acquaintance formed from sharing that week of vacation.

Before I leave, Dad calls me into his office. I scurry in, slowing my steps as I enter to find him tapping away at his laptop. He stops, tossing his reading glasses onto the desk in front of him and gesturing for me to sit. I silently wait for him to speak.

"I didn't think I'd be both surprised and impressed when it came to this kid," he finally admits. "But you were right. He's very sharp and his record is clean."

I fight the smile that wants to break over my face, instead nodding as apathetically as I can. "I call it like I see it."

Dad grins. "That you do, kiddo," he murmurs, eyeing me appraisingly. Probably thinking about what a great CEO I'll be someday. I swear one day my eyeballs are going to fall out from the strain of not rolling them while I'm at work. "I'm going to hire him."

"Okay," I say casually, but internally high-fiving myself for pulling it off.

"And I want you to keep an eye on him."

I can't help it, my mouth drops open in shock. "*Me*? Why?" I demand.

"Your suggestion, your responsibility," Dad responds, a teasing note in his voice.

I can't help this eye roll, and it makes Dad chuckle. "He's not actually a kid, and I'm not actually a babysitter. I'm busy enough."

"I'll talk to your supervisor."

I stay perfectly still, unwilling to give any tells. "Fine," I concede tightly. "Though I'm not even sure what 'keep an eye on him' means."

Dad laughs. "I'm sure you'll figure it out. You busy for dinner? Mom's making lasagna."

"As it happens, I am."

Dad raises an eyebrow, not knowing I haven't really changed the subject, as Matteo is coming over after work. We might even get around to eating dinner, too.

⌒

As the weeks pass and Matteo settles happily into his new job, I'm absolutely shocked to see a relationship forming between him and my dad. Dad takes to him in a way I completely didn't expect. Don't get me wrong, obviously I get the appeal, but Dad has hated his uncle for so long that I'm stunned he's able to get past it and embrace Alessandro's nephew into his business. Almost literally, too, as I see lots of back-clapping from my dad to Matteo.

What I'm not able to do is work up the courage to quit. But then, with Matteo around me at work all day, and then at my place almost every night, albeit in a *very* different capacity, I find I'm not terribly inclined to.

Then one Saturday night, after grabbing dinner and a movie, we're laying in bed kissing when shit gets serious.

"When are you going to tell your father about us?"

I freeze, pulling away. "You did not just ask me that question before you hoped to get me naked."

Matteo smirks. "Maybe I'm interested in more than just getting you naked."

My heart stops in my chest. Sure, we've been dating for a while now. And sure, I'm crazy about him, but I've purposely tried not to think too hard about it. Or about how I'll be losing him in just over a month.

"There's no point in telling my dad anything he doesn't need to know. Do you really want to take your chances like that?"

Matteo frowns, and I can see him internally trying to translate that one to understand it, as he often does. It softens me a little, and I snuggle into him.

"My father really likes you," I murmur into his chest. "You've never had to see how scary he can be. Besides, it's not like you'll be here much longer anyway. No reason to rock the boat."

"Is that what you think? That I'm just going to leave and that's it?"

I look up at him and all trace of humor has vanished from his face. "What other option is there?"

"Your father has mentioned taking out a visa for me to keep working for Hoyt Corporate Services."

A gasp escapes me. "*No.*"

My reaction doesn't sit well with Matteo, and he pulls away, sitting up.

"Well, now I know how you feel about it."

I climb to my knees, positioning myself in front of him, gathering his face in my hands.

"I'm just surprised, that's all. Do you really like working there that much?"

"I *love* working there," Matteo admits for the first time, to me at least. I knew he'd found it interesting and challenging, but for the first time I can really see the passion in his eyes.

"Then ... that's great," I reply, letting his face go and sitting cross-legged in front of him.

"But that's not the only reason I want to stay," he says softly, touching a finger to my knee. "I love you more."

I look up at him in shock. He stares at me plainly, clearly knowing it would be scary for me. Because despite having had several boyfriends, I can't say I've honestly ever been in love. And certainly no boy, or man, has said that to me before who wasn't a relative.

"I just wanted you to know. I don't expect you to say it back."

The shock turns to numbness, and I can't feel anything under the dull blanket of detachment that settles over me. It's unnerving. My silence stretches on so long, Matteo finally starts to fidget.

"Please, say something. What do you want me to do? I can leave, if you'd like?" The tenderness in his tone finally breaks the shield that had settled around me, and I look up at him with tears in my eyes. "Oh, *amore.*" He pulls me into his lap, wrapping me in his strong arms as the tears quietly trail down my face.

"I love you, too," I finally weep into his chest.

His hands lift my face to his, his lips searching for mine. And when we connect, all the passion that was in his eyes … I realize it was for me. The understanding breaks something inside of me. The thing that was holding me back. And I give myself to him, body and soul.

◦◦◦

THE FOLLOWING WEEK, THE VISA PAPERWORK BEGINS. SO THAT FRIDAY WE GO out to celebrate, ending up back at my place, making love into the wee hours of the night. I fall asleep in Matteo's arms, feeling freer than I've ever felt. And I decide that Monday morning, I'm putting in my application to the FBI. I fall asleep on that thought, happier than I've ever felt.

◦◦◦

THE NEXT MORNING WE'RE WOKEN BY THE DOORBELL. I ROLL OVER SLEEPILY TO check the time on my phone. It's not even seven a.m.

"What the fuck?" I groan as the doorbell rings again insistently.

Matteo throws an arm over his face and moans as I turn on the light to find my clothes. "You go stop that awful noise. I'll get dressed, then make the espresso."

I nod, stumbling out into the living room. I open the door to my dad looking ridiculously peppy and holding two cups of coffee. But his appearance wakes me up far more than any cup of joe ever could.

"Dad!" I croak. "What are you doing here?"

"What do you mean, what am I doing here? It's the first Saturday of the month," he scoffs, pushing past me.

Fuck. Fuck, fuck, fuck, fuck. How could I have forgotten? Dad and I have gone shooting the first Saturday morning of every month for years. We had to skip last month because Dad had to work, so between being out of our routine and, well, Matteo …

I close the door in a hurry, remembering Matteo's plan to come out to make coffee.

"Um, yeah, sorry," I say, rushing across the living room. "I'll just go get dressed …"

But I'm too late. My eyes meet Matteo's as he stands in the living room entranceway. I can see on his face the moment my dad notices him. Sheer panic. I turn slowly on the spot. And my dad looks *terrifying*. I've seen him angry. I've seen him upset. But I've never seen him look like a homicidal rage monster.

Still, he's quietly seething in place as his eyes flick between us.

"How long?" he finally asks tightly. When I don't answer immediately, his hands curl into fists. "How long have you been lying to me, Harriet?" His voice is pure venom, and tears well in my eyes hearing my father speak to me with such hatred. My only choice is to answer.

"Two months," I whisper.

Dad looks up at the ceiling, a vein in his neck twitching. I shoot a worried glance back at Matteo, who seems frozen in place.

"I didn't mean for you to find out like this," I try to explain. "I'm sorry, Dad."

And he *laughs*. It's the coldest, cruelest sound I've ever heard him make.

"You say that like you planned to tell me," he barks. His gaze slides to Matteo. "And you —"

"Sir, please, I wanted to tell you, but I was waiting for Hattie to be ready —"

"You don't get to speak *my daughter's name*."

I can see his anger starting to boil over but feel helpless to stop it, to even know how to begin to defuse this situation.

"Daddy, please —"

"God, Harriet. In the apartment your mother and I gave you, no less," he spits at me. "And with a fucking *Giordano*." The word is a curse from his lips. "You're no better than your uncle, Matteo. I bring you into my company, I give you the benefit of the doubt, and this whole time you've been fucking my daughter. But then, I guess you've been fucking us both over."

"*Dad!*" I gasp.

"I've never purposely lied to you," Matteo objects hotly. "And it's not like that between me and your daughter. I love her."

And if my dad was mad before, it's nothing on how he reacts to Matteo's proclamation. My dad advances as if on instinct, and I press into his chest, yelling at Matteo to go. In all the years my dad has carried a gun, I've never known him to misuse it. But based on his maniacal lunge toward Matteo, I'm taking no chances that he will. Though he could just as easily tear him limb from limb with his bare hands, being the towering mass of muscle that he is.

"Get out of the way, Hattie," Dad growls as Matteo wisely circles the couch to bolt to the front door. As I continue to cling to my father, he yells after Matteo. "You're going back to Italy, I'll see to that! And you're never coming near my daughter again!"

As soon as Matteo is clear, I let go. But I don't stop. Tears in my eyes, I slap my father with everything I've got.

The look of shock on his face makes me recoil in horror, and we stare at each other for a minute. As the heaving of Dad's chest slows, I feel the tears start to fall.

Without another word, I turn on my heel and flee into the bedroom. I grab my suitcase from the closet, stuffing it full of anything and everything within reach.

"What are you doing?" Dad asks from the doorway.

I brush a fresh wave of tears out of my eyes. "I'm giving you back *your* apartment. Then I'm going to make sure Matteo is okay."

"You're not going to shack up with that, that —"

I whirl on the spot. "*Stop!*" I screech, covering my ears. "You don't get to say anything bad about him. What you just did is *unforgivable*. He's done nothing to you. *Nothing*. He's worked hard for you. And he loves me. But because of his last name you'll ruin us both?"

"He's ruined himself by using you. And I would *never* hurt you, Hattie."

I shake my head violently. "But you have. Because he's not using me. I love him, too. And the way you treated him ..." I stare up at my father, unable to recognize the haggard face as belonging to the man who raised me. "But then, it's always about you. I've always done everything you asked of me. But you can't tell me who to love any more than you can tell me where to work." As the words tumble out, I feel the chains of my father's expectations falling from me. "I can't work for you anymore. I quit."

"Hattie, *no...*"

But I can't. I whirl around, slamming the lid of my suitcase shut and stuffing my emergency pile of cash into my purse. I deliberately dump my cellphone and credit card onto the bed so he can see that I'm not about to let him track me anywhere. Then I hand him my keys.

"You can have your car back, too," I spit at him. And then I leave.

∽

Aunt Emily and Mom are waiting for me on the porch when I get to Aunt Em's house. My mother takes one look at my tear-stained face and opens her arms to me. I gladly fall into them, and she holds me until I'm able to beat back the sobs. She presses me away, looking into my eyes.

"Tell me everything that happened after Matteo left."

Aunt Em presses her lips together behind Mom. I sink onto the porch step and tell her everything. When I'm done, Mom looks at Aunt Em.

"I know," Aunt Em says, apropos of seemingly nothing. Mom nods.

"Alessandro and Matteo are inside. They'll take care of you. We're going to take care of your father." Mom's tone is just as terrifying as Dad's tantrum.

"You don't have to do that," I say quietly, just wanting the drama to be over.

Mom closes her eyes for a moment and takes a deep breath before reopening them. "Yes, I do. You have to understand, Hattie, this isn't about you."

I'm sure my confusion shows on my face, because Aunt Em places a hand on my shoulder. "It's about Alessandro. And me. And your mother. He's taking it out on you and Matteo. There's nothing you could have done to change that, no matter how he found out. He would always have taken his anger at Alessandro out on Matteo just for his being with you."

Mom nods. "Yes. This has been twenty-three years in the making. And I'm so sorry he did this to you two, honey."

"Not as sorry as I am," a voice comes from behind us. Alessandro walks tiredly down the steps, stopping in front of me. "Truly, Hattie, you've done nothing wrong. You're both paying for my mistakes." He looks at my mother. "I'm coming with you."

Mom snorts. "Like hell you are. That will just make things worse."

Aunt Em lays a hand on Alesssandro's arm. "She's right."

He looks down into her eyes, and I can see him backing down. He opens his arms to them both and embraces them, laying a kiss on each of their heads. "My strong, brave, beautiful women. I'm so sorry to you both, I hope you know that." When he pulls away, tears shine in all of their eyes.

Mom gives him a look of longing and love that nearly breaks my heart, and in that glance I can see what they once meant to each other. "We know," she whispers. "We knew this day would come, though."

"Yes, I suppose we did. *In bocca al lupo*, Serafina."

Mom laughs. "*Grazie.*" She gives his hand a squeeze and heads down the walkway.

Aunt Em gives him a gentle kiss, then follows after her. Alessandro and I stand next to one another, watching them go. He wraps an arm around me and steers me toward the house.

"I'm sure you've noticed that my nephew and I are very different people. Your father will figure that out, too, don't worry," he assures me.

I give a short, derisive laugh. "By the looks on their faces, I don't think he's going to have much of a choice." And after a pause, I look up at him. "But I don't think you're so bad."

Alessandro gives me his sideways smile. I can see the family resemblance more than ever, and I can't help opening myself to him a little.

"Matteo loves you deeply," he continues as we walk inside. "No matter what happens, don't ever doubt that."

I look up as the man himself appears at the end of the hall, worry creasing his beautiful face.

"I don't." Because I feel exactly the same way.

BONUS EPILOGUE

Another five years later …

"I never thought this day would come," I murmur, looking at myself in the full-length mirror.

"You mean the day your father gave you away to a *Giordano*?" my mother teases, smoothing creases out of the white silk gown.

I huff a laugh. "The day I'd *marry* a Giordano," I add. Mom steps back so I can take in the full effect of my dress. It's simple and stunning, and I feel more beautiful than I ever have before.

"Well, be prepared for your dad to cry when he sees you. You look …" Mom chokes up a little, "just perfect, honey."

I turn and she's clasping her hands, tears in her eyes. I step off the small stool and embrace her.

"Thanks, Mom."

We both sniff, daintily patting the moisture from our eyes. When Mom opens the door, Dad is there, nervously pacing. He looks up and his face breaks into a grin, tears welling in his eyes.

"Oh, Hattie."

"You two really need to stop crying, or I'm going to ruin my makeup before I ever get out there," I caution.

He laughs and blinks back his tears, then signals to an usher. Moments later, the music starts.

"They're playing your tune," he teases, offering his arm.

Mom places the bouquet in my hand as I slip my other hand into his elbow, then she darts around us to take her seat in the church. Dad walks me to the double doors at the end of the aisle, then turns to me, looking down at me seriously.

"Five years ago, I almost lost you by making a huge mistake. Today, in a way, I'm losing you, but for the best possible reason. I'm so proud of the woman you've become, Hattie. Never forget how much I love you."

My breath catches in my throat at hearing the words that are etched onto Mom's rings. That he says to her all the time. I think I always knew he loved me just as much. But hearing it today of all days ... well, it's the best wedding present ever.

∼

"Mrs. Giordano," Matteo purrs in my ear as I slip into his arms for our first dance.

"Mr. Giordano," I look up into his eyes. "Have I told you yet today how incredibly handsome you look?" I run my hands over the lapels of his navy tuxedo.

"Thank you," he murmurs, his blue eyes dancing with lust. "And you look stunning. But I still can't wait to get you out of that dress."

I shoot him a feline grin as he spins me on the dance floor like we're the only two people here. "Then you might need to help me change out of it before our flight. Because after that, it'll be a long trip to Italy."

He leans forward, his lips at my ear. "*Special Agent Giordano*," he whispers teasingly, "are you trying to *seduce* me?"

"Hmmm. I'm pretty sure it's still 'Special Agent Hoyt.'" He shoots me a mock impatient look, and I laugh. "But yes, pretty sure I am. Is it working?"

The song ends, and he kisses me gently for our audience before whispering in my ear, "Always."

Dad steps forward to claim me for the next dance, and I'm already regretting the beautiful, delicate silver heels I'm wearing.

"Congratulations, sweetheart," Dad says, his voice thick with emotion. "I'll give him the 'if you ever hurt her, they'll never find your body' speech again a little later. You know, just in case he missed it the first time." Dad winks to show he's kidding.

"That's cute, but we both know you can't make good on that threat. Who'll run Hoyt Corporate Services when you retire?" I tease back.

"You've got me there."

I grin up at him. "I bet you never thought you'd not only have a Giordano as a son-in-law but also be on the verge of handing over your company to one, did you?"

I was teasing, but Dad seriously thinks about that for a minute.

"You know, it feels really good to have let go of all that. With Kitty off on her own working as an engineer, Landon off at college playing ball, and Thea about to start at Juilliard … well, I think your mom and I have earned some peace. And I'm happy to welcome Matteo to the family, in every way. I think it'll be good for all of us."

"I think so, too," I say softly. "I love you, Dad."

He smiles down at me. "Love you, too, sweetheart."

I lay my head on his chest, enjoying my last dance as his little girl before returning to my now-husband and dancing the night away.

But when it's time to change into my traveling outfit, I can't find Matteo anywhere, so I slip back into my changing room alone. Only to find him already lounging on the couch there.

"Took you long enough to get here," he teases, rising to pin me against the closed door.

"How long have you been in here?" I ask as his mouth travels down my neck, igniting goosebumps over my whole body.

"Just a few minutes. I needed a break."

"Mmmm," I murmur as his hands caress my back. "And I need you."

He pulls back and looks into my eyes.

"Promise?"

I look up at him coyly from under my eyelashes. "Always."

RECIPES FROM THE HEART: A COMPANION TO THE SAFEGUARDED HEART SERIES

INTRODUCTION

I f you've read The Safeguarded Heart and its sequels, you've probably figured out that I love food, Italian especially. It started with my family, having grown up with an Italian grandmother, amongst other family members, that instilled that love of food in me. My mother is a good cook, too, but once I was out on my own I really fell in love with cooking for myself.

When I finished graduate school I treated myself to a trip to Italy. Part of that trip included a one-week cooking class in Tuscany through the Tuscan Women Cook program, which I highly recommend. For one week, I stayed in a small hotel in the gorgeous hilltop town of Montefollonico. Every morning we would receive a cooking lesson from a local restaurateur or the little old ladies that lived in the village and cooked at the hotel. We would eat what we made for lunch, then the afternoons would be filled with sightseeing, shopping, or cheese/wine tasting. Dinners were spent in restaurants scattered across Tuscany where we would spend the entire evening eating, drinking, and chatting. In one word, it was heaven. I learned to make pasta the Italian way. That their zucchini produced gorgeous, edible, delectable flowers. That nothing is better than the heavy fragrance of basil wafting through the air on a hot, sunbaked Tuscan summer afternoon.

In all, on that first visit I spent nearly a month exploring the country, often eating gelato twice a day, in additional to the bevy of other succulent dishes I sampled. Somehow, I still lost weight on that trip, though it might've been the ten or so miles I'd walk each day once I got to Rome. In any case, I was changed forever. I now knew what *real* Italian food tasted like.

That's not to diminish other Italian cuisines. Born and partially raised in

New York, their Italian-American dishes are a powerhouse in their own right. And having also lived in California for many years, it also has its own spin on Italian favorites, which capture the best of the west-coast with the decadence of Italy. My own cooking style has been vastly influenced by all three, and almost everything I cook ends up with Italian flavors.

While I'm no professional chef, I did hear from a number of readers that they drooled over the Italian dinner scene in the first book, so I figured I'd share those recipes. Because they're dishes I've actually made. And while I'm at it, I'll be sharing a few other dishes I love. Some are family dishes, some from Italian chefs I've picked up. Every single recipe is one I've tested and modified to my tastes over the years.

I'm also no professional cookbook writer but I'll do my best to lay everything out as best I can. In most cases these are simple, delicious meals that don't take all day to prepare. Because as much as I like to cook, I like to eat more, and I'm too impatient to wait that long. Either way, I hope you enjoy these recipes. From my kitchen, my heart, to yours.

"Recipes don't work unless you use your heart! "
—Dylan Jones

APPETIZERS

"All sorrows are less with bread."
—Miguel de Cervantes, Don Quixote

FOCACCIA

This deliciously dense and chewy bread is as versatile as it is tasty. It can be snacked on by dipping it in olive oil mixed with herbs or balsamic vinegar, it can be served with *antipasti*, it can be used as bread for paninis, or it can simply be served alongside a meal.

And while this is a basic recipe, it can also be dressed up to taste before baking by adding a light sprinkle of olives, onions, peppers, tomatoes, parmesan, or herbs such as thyme, rosemary, or sage. And though it has two rise cycles, it's exceedingly simple to make.

INGREDIENTS
    1-1/3 cups warm water
    1 envelope active dry yeast
    3 tablespoons extra-virgin olive oil
    3 1/2 cups all-purpose flour
    2 teaspoons salt

DIRECTIONS
    Combine water, yeast, and oil in a large bowl. Stir in flour and salt (can be done by hand or mixer). Once the dough comes together in a ball, knead it until it's smooth and elastic, about five minutes.

Put the dough into a lightly oiled bowl and cover with a damp cloth. Let rise until doubled, about an hour and a half.

Lightly oil a 9" x 13" pan. Press the dough into the pan until it's an even, flat layer. Cover with a damp cloth and let rise until doubled, about an hour and a half.

Preheat the oven to 425 degrees F. Dimple the dough with your finger every couple of inches, drizzle with olive oil, and sprinkle with salt.

Bake until golden brown, about 25 minutes. Number of servings varies by purpose, but generally makes about six servings.

BRUSCHETTA

Another simple recipe, this one actually does better with day-old bread, though the tomatoes should be top-notch for best flavor.

INGREDIENTS
    1 baguette
    2 lbs. tomatoes
    4 garlic cloves
    Extra-virgin olive oil to taste
    Salt and pepper to taste

DIRECTIONS
Slice bread and lightly grill on one side. Peel garlic and slice off one end. Rub garlic over the surface of the bread. Dice tomatoes and drizzle with olive oil. Sprinkle with salt and pepper. Toss to coat. Top the bread with the tomato when ready to eat. Serves 6-8.

INSALATA CAPRESE

S alad of Capri, in *tricolore* - the three colors of Italy. Served in the Italian dinner scene in *The Safeguarded Heart*, it's usually an *antipasto*. The ingredients are simple, but because of that the better quality the ingredients, the better the taste.

INGREDIENTS

4 large vine-ripened tomatoes
1 lb. fresh mozzarella loaf, drained
1/4 cup fresh basil leaves
Extra-virgin olive oil to taste
Salt and pepper to taste

DIRECTIONS

Slice the tomatoes and mozzarella in 1/4" thick slices. Arrange the tomato, mozzarella, and basil on a plate alternating and overlapping. Drizzle with olive oil and sprinkle with salt and pepper. Makes 4-6 servings.

STUFFED ZUCCHINI FLOWERS

I n *The Safeguarded Heart* I had these served as a first course, but these are more traditionally an appetizer (*antipasto*). I'd never had anything like it in the United States. I honestly didn't even know zucchini produced flowers, much less that they were edible and oh-so-delicious. I've ordered seeds from a U.S.-based Italian company so I can grow my own and dine on this delicious dish whenever I want!

INGREDIENTS

    15 oz can San Marzano tomatoes, crushed

    3 tablespoons olive oil

    1 tablespoons sugar

    1/4 cup water

    8 zucchini blossoms

    15 oz ricotta, drained

    1 egg

    3 tablespoons Parmesan cheese, grated

    1 tablespoon flat-leaf parsley, chopped

    Pinch of nutmeg

    Salt and pepper to taste

DIRECTIONS

Heat olive oil in a large skillet over medium heat and add the tomatoes.

Cook for half an hour. While the tomatoes stew, prepare the zucchini flowers by removing the centers then rinsing in cold water and patting dry. In a bowl, mix together the ricotta, egg, Parmesan, parsley, nutmeg, salt, and pepper. Use a small spoon or pastry bag to fill the flowers, cinching them closed with your fingers once nearly full (do not overfill).

Add sugar and water to tomatoes and stir. Add filled blossoms. Cook for 20 minutes on each side. Plate two blossoms, cover with tomato sauce. Serves 4.

SIDE DISHES

"You don't have to cook fancy or complicated masterpieces – just good food from fresh ingredients"
—Julia Child

BAKED ZUCCHINI

T his dish is pure, cheesy, creamy, vegetable-y decadence. So much so that I usually serve it alongside a lighter entree, like a simple chicken dish.

INGREDIENTS

2 lb. zucchini
1 cup heavy whipping cream
1 cup mozzarella cheese, grated
1 cup fontina cheese, grated
1/2 cup Pecorino Romano cheese, grated
1 cup Italian breadcrumbs
Salt and pepper to taste
Extra-virgin olive oil to taste

DIRECTIONS

Preheat the oven to 400 deg F. Grease a 9" x 12" baking dish. Slice the zucchini to finger-width. Line the pan with half of the zucchini. Sprinkle with salt and pepper. Drizzle half of the cream over the zucchini. Sprinkle with 1/2 cup each of mozzarella and fontina, 1/4 cup Pecorino Romano, then 1/2 cup of Italian breadcrumbs. Repeat with another layer. Drizzle or mist extra virgin olive oil lightly over the top. Bake until golden brown, about 30-35 minutes. Serves 4-6.

GRANDMA D'ANDREANO'S STUFFING

My great grandparents immigrated to New York after World War I from Pisciotta, Italy. I remember spending time with my feisty great grandfather, Daniel (Aniello) before he passed in 1989, but unfortunately my great grandmother, Teresa, passed away while my mother was pregnant with me, so I never had a chance to know her personally. But her legacy has lived on in the women of my family in many ways. Not least of which is through one of my most treasured holiday traditions — her stuffing recipe. In fact, it may be the only recipe I have that I know for sure came from her. I find that a bit odd since it's not strictly Italian, but it is amazing.

INGREDIENTS

    1 bag seasoned stuffing mix
    1 large onion
    1/2 cup celery, diced
    1/2 cup butter, melted
    1 cup cheddar cheese, shredded
    1 cup salami, diced
    1 egg
    1/2 cup Parmesan cheese, grated
    Garlic salt to taste
    Salt and pepper to taste
    1 cup warm water

· · ·

DIRECTIONS

Melt the butter in a saucepan over medium heat. Add the onion and celery and cook until soft, about ten minutes.

Mix all ingredients in a large bowl and toss until well mixed. If using in a turkey, stuff loosely. Bake (extra or all) stuffing in a 9" x 12" pan, with giblets on top if you choose. Drizzle 1 cup of warm water over and bake uncovered in a 350 deg F oven until brown, about 20-25 minutes.

MAIN DISHES

"Cooking is like love, it should be entered into with abandon or not at all."
—Harriet Van Horne

GNOCCHI

Gnocchi ... or as we sell them to our four-year-old who is, for some reason obsessed with Chinese dumplings ... Italian dumplings. Which they are, actually. Little plump pillows of potato-ey goodness covered in a delicious butter-thyme sauce.

INGREDIENTS

- 1/2 cup butter
- 1 tablespoon fresh thyme
- 1 lb. russet potato
- 1/2 teaspoon salt
- 1/4 teaspoon pepper
- 1 egg, beaten
- 1/4 cup all-purpose flour
- 1/4 cup Pecorino Romano cheese, grated

DIRECTIONS

In a medium skillet, brown the butter over medium high heat for two minutes. Add the thyme leaves and remove from heat.

Poke the potato with a fork all over and microwave on high for six minutes. Turn over and microwave for another six minutes. Cut the potato open and remove the flesh with a spoon. Add salt, pepper, and egg and mix together. Add flour and mix together. Roll out chunks of dough into a finger-width rope and cut into 1/2"-1" pieces (depending on what size you like). You can lightly roll them under fork tines to give them a fancier look if you'd like.

Bring a large pot of water to a boil and cook the pieces until they float, then cook for another four minutes. Use a slotted spoon and transfer the gnocchi to the butter sauce and toss gently to coat. Serve topped with Pecorino Romano. Makes 4 servings.

FETTUCINE ALFREDO

One of my favorite indulgences. I pair it with sliced, roasted chicken and oven-roasted broccoli to balance out the insanely creamy, luscious sauce.

Ingredients

    2 cups heavy whipping cream
1 lemon, juiced
8 tablespoons butter
2 teaspoons grated lemon zest
Pinch of nutmeg
1 lb. fettucine
1 cup Parmesan cheese, grated
Salt to taste

Directions

Put the heavy cream, lemon juice, and butter in a saucepan and heat over medium, stirring until the butter melts completely. Stir in the lemon zest and nutmeg and set aside.

Cook pasta per directions on packaging (or 3-4 minutes for fresh pasta). Drain and return to pot. Add cream sauce and parmesan and mix over low heat until blended and pasta is fully coated with sauce. Season to taste and serve. Serves 8.

LIGHT CHICKEN PARMESAN

C hicken Parmesan is an Italian-American classic, but the breaded and fried version is too heavy for me, so I love this lighter take.

Ingredients

4 slices of chicken breast, 1/4" thick
2 tablespoons extra-virgin olive oil
1 tablespoon fresh thyme leaves
1 tablespoon fresh rosemary, chopped
1 tablespoon fresh flat-leaf parsley, chopped
Salt and pepper to taste
1 cup tomato sauce
1/2 cup mozzarella, shredded
1/4 cup Parmesan, shredded

Directions

Season the chicken on both sides with salt and pepper. Mix the oil and herbs together and brush onto both sides of the chicken. Heat an ovenproof skillet on medium-high heat and brown each chicken slice on both sides, just a minute or two per side. Turn off the heat and cover each chicken cutlet with tomato sauce. Sprinkle each with 1/4 of the mozzarella and parmesan. Put the pan in a 500 deg F oven and bake for 5-10 minutes until the chicken is cooked through. Serves 4.

CHICKEN PICCATA

I love the lemony-buttery sauce in this dish. The breading isn't overly heavy, and the pan frying keeps it on the lighter side as well. The lemon and parsley garnish makes this a very presentable — and delicious — dish.

INGREDIENTS

    4 slices of chicken breast, 1/4" thick
    1/2 cup all-purpose flour
    2 eggs, beaten
    3/4 cup breadcrumbs
    2 tablespoon extra-virgin olive oil
    2 tablespoon butter
    2 lemons, juiced
    1 lemon, sliced into thin half-moons
    2 tablespoons flat-leaf parsley, chopped
    Salt and pepper to taste

DIRECTIONS

Salt and pepper both sides of the chicken breast slices. Prepare three plates, one each of flour, egg, and breadcrumbs. Heat the olive oil in a large skillet over medium heat. Coat the chicken on both sides in the flour, then the egg, then the breadcrumbs. Cook two minutes per side, then place on a large, lined sheet pan. Once all chicken slices are pan-cooked, place the sheet pan in a 425 deg F oven for 5-10 minutes.

Wipe out the pan you used to brown the chicken. Melt the butter over medium heat. Add the lemon juice, and salt and pepper to taste. Boil for a few minutes until the mix has reduced by half.

Top each chicken breast with a lemon slice, a sprinkling of flat leaf parsley, and a generous pour of sauce. Serves 4.

PAPPARDELLE WITH MEAT SAUCE

Another dish from the Italian dinner scene in the *The Safeguarded Heart*, the first time I had this was actually with boar meat (and fresh pasta, of course). I was trepidatious to say the least. Much to my surprise, it was delicious.

Pappardelle is less common here, but this wide, flat noodle holds sauce like a champ. My favorite is De Cecco. The sauce recipe takes some time, but it's totally worth it, and also multiplies nicely.

INGREDIENTS

    1 lb. Pappardelle pasta

    2 tablespoons extra-virgin olive oil

    1 onion, diced

    2 carrots, diced

    2 stalks celery, diced

    2 cloves garlic, minced

    1/2 cup flat-leaf parsley, chopped

    1 lb. ground beef and/or pork

    28 oz can San Marzano tomatoes, crushed

    1 cup tomato sauce

    1/2 cup red wine

    2 tablespoons tomato paste

. . .

Directions

Heat the olive oil in a large pot over medium heat and add onion, carrot, and celery, sautéing until translucent, about 10 minutes. Add garlic and parsley and cook another three minutes.

Add meat and red wine. Break up meat and cook through, about 10 minutes.

Add crushed tomatoes and tomato paste. Mix well and cook until bubbling. Lower heat to medium-low and cook for two to three hours, until the sauce is a rich, dark color.

Cook pasta according to package directions. Portion and ladle sauce over pasta. Serves 6-8.

LASAGNA

This Italian-American staple appears briefly in *All of Me* (*The Safeguarded Heart Series Book 2*). But even if it hadn't, I can't imagine putting together a list of my favorite recipes without including lasagna. I even served it at my own wedding. It's always a crowd pleaser!

INGREDIENTS

    2 lb. ground beef or pork
    1 onion, diced
    2 cloves garlic, chopped
    2-15 oz cans diced tomatoes
    2-15 oz cans tomato sauce
    1 tablespoon Italian seasonings
    1 box lasagna noodles
    2 eggs, beaten
    32 oz ricotta
    1 cup Parmesan cheese, grated
    1-1/2 cup mozzarella, shredded

DIRECTIONS

Heat a large pot over medium-high heat. Cook the meat, onion, and garlic until browned. Stir in undrained tomatoes, tomato sauce, and seasoning. Boil and simmer, covered, for 15 minutes, stirring regularly.

Cook lasagna noodles per the directions on the box while the sauce simmers, drain, and set aside.

In a large bowl, mix ricotta, egg, and 1/2 cup Parmesan cheese.

Using a large lasagna pan (~10" x 16") layer sauce on the bottom, then line with slightly overlapped noodles. Top with half of the cheese filling, smoothing into an even layer. Top with half of the meat sauce, smoothing into an even layer. Top with half of the mozzarella. Repeat. Sprinkle the top with the remaining 1/2 cup of parmesan.

Bake at 375 degrees F for 45-50 minutes, until heated through. Easily serves 10-12.

DESSERTS

"Life is uncertain. Eat dessert first."
—Ernestine Ulmer

PANNA COTTA

The Italian dinner in *The Safeguarded Heart* featured a *Panna Cotta* with berries for dessert. I'll be honest. No matter how hard I try, I can't get this dessert to have the exact smooth, firm, and wobbly texture of the one I had my first night in Italy. But you know what? It's pretty close, and still freaking delicious. Creamy, sweet, and rich, it really does need the balance of fresh berries, so top with your favorite and enjoy!

Ingredients

 1 cup whole milk
 1 envelope unflavored gelatin
 3 cups heavy whipping cream
 1/3 cup sugar
 1/2 teaspoon vanilla extract
 2 cups fresh berries

Directions

Put the milk in a pan, then sprinkle the gelatin on top and let sit for five minutes. Stir constantly over medium heat for five minutes until the gelatin dissolves, but the milk does not boil. Add the remaining ingredients and stir for a few minutes, until the sugar dissolves. Remove from the heat and whisk until its lukewarm (you can do this over an ice bath to speed it up). Then divide into eight 1/2 cup ramekins or glasses. Refrigerate overnight to let the dessert set. Top each with 1/4 cup fresh berries immediately before serving. Serves 8.

TIRAMISU

L iterally "lift me up" in Italian, this dessert is one of the most quintessential of Italian confections. And this variant is my hands-down favorite. It uses a rather non-traditional biscuit (or cookie as we Americans call it) that I order from Amazon.com. You plate it in large scoops, so this is not so much the "pretty" kind that you'll take pictures of, but it is out-of-this-world delicious.

INGREDIENTS

    4 eggs, separated
    5 tablespoons sugar
    12 oz mascarpone
    2.5 oz espresso
    3/4 cup Vin Santo or other dry, white dessert wine
    1 package Pavesini biscuits (or ladyfingers)
    4 oz dark chocolate, chopped into small chunks

DIRECTIONS

Mix the egg yolks and sugar in a mixer until pale and fluffy, about 5-7 minutes. In a separate bowl, whisk the mascarpone until it's light and fluffy. In a third bowl, whisk the egg whites until they form soft peaks. Fold the mascarpone into the egg whites, then fold that mixture into the yolk/sugar mix.

Mix the Vin Santo and espresso together. Dip the Pavesini in the mixture, lining a large bowl or dish with half of the biscuits. Cover with half of the filling. Place another layer of dipped biscuits on top, then cover with the remaining filling. Note, depending on the shape of the bowl/dish you may need to modify to more layers. Cover with the chocolate chunks, then chill in the refrigerator for 2-4 hours for the dessert to set. Makes 6-8 servings.

NEW YORK STYLE CHEESECAKE

I love this recipe because it's the easiest I've found, with no water bath required. I actually danced around my apartment with happiness the first time I tasted this cheesecake. I also had an at-home baking business for a few years and this was my absolute best-seller. You can top it with berries, chocolate, whipped cream, or just eat it plain. Any way you slice it (see what I did there?), it's ah-mazing.

INGREDIENTS

Crust:

2 cups graham cracker crumbs

4 tablespoons sugar

6 tablespoons unsalted butter, melted

FILLING:

2 lb. cream cheese

1-1/4 cup sugar

4 eggs

1/2 cup sour cream

1 teaspoon vanilla extract

DIRECTIONS

Adjust the oven rack to the middle and preheat the oven to 450 degrees F.

Mix the crust ingredients well until the graham cracker crumbs are uniformly moist, then press them into the bottom and sides of a 9-inch spring-form pan.

Beat the cream cheese with an electric mixer until light and fluffy (it gets there faster if you let the cream cheese come to room temperature first). Beat in the sugar completely. Beat in the eggs one at a time. Beat in the sour cream and vanilla. Scrape the sides and continue beating until everything is thoroughly mixed, then pour the mixture into the crust.

Bake for 15 minutes, then lower the temperature to 200 degrees F and open the oven door completely for a few minutes before closing it back up and baking until the edges are set, but the middle still wiggles, which will take around an hour.

Cool on a rack to room temperature, then refrigerate for at least four hours, preferably overnight, before topping and serving. Makes 10-12 servings.

Want more? Check out Melanie A. Smith's latest release *Finding His Redemption: An Enemies to Lovers Rock Star Romance* at https://melanieasmithauthor.com/books-finding-his-redemption.html

∾

Sign up for Melanie A. Smith's newsletter to get all the latest news and more https://mailchi.mp/melanieasmithauthor.com/nlsignup

A NOTE FROM THE AUTHOR

Thank you so much for reading! Now ... I need your help! Will you please take a minute to leave a review? It doesn't have to be long — just a couple sentences saying what you thought of the book on any retailer, goodreads, and/or BookBub. Your opinion is important to me, and for potential readers. Thank you!

ACKNOWLEDGMENTS

This is the end of an era for me, and there are so many people who helped along the way. My husband for not just allowing me time to write, but encouraging me and acting as my sounding board on so many levels. Jenny, for not just being a kick-ass copy editor, but for being an amazing friend these past twenty-one years. Lindsey, for being my romance-partner-in-crime. Katie for always giving it to me straight between the eyes. Carol, for your advice, friendship, and keeping it real. The writing and bookstagram communities on Instagram, without whom my road would've been much rockier and vastly lonelier. The support, wisdom, and availability of such a resource is without measure. And, of course, each and every person who has read my books — I'm immensely thankful that I'm not only able to share my work, but that people actually enjoy it.

I also want to acknowledge the people who inspired many of the characters and events in my stories. While it's largely fictionalized, much of what I write is based on my experiences, or at the very least, imbued with the emotions and struggles I've gone through.

It was only noticed by a few (who mentioned it, anyway), but Sera's romantic journey in these pages started with Alessandro and ended with Bryce, which was a parallel to a truth I've learned — that all the romantic partners before The One are merely preparation. That some guys are fun for the moment, or come with baggage that's a deal-breaker, or are simply just not the right fit for you. But they're part of the journey to realizing what you really need in a partner. So to all of my Alessandros, thank you. I couldn't have found my Bryce without you.

ABOUT THE AUTHOR

Melanie A. Smith is an award-winning and international best-selling author of steamy contemporary romance fiction. A voracious reader and lifelong writer, Melanie's writing began at a young age with short stories and poetry. After college and a career as an aircraft engineer, she shifted to domestic engineering and property management and eventually found a balance where she was able to return to writing fiction. Melanie is also a Mensan and enjoys spending time with her family, cooking, and driving with the windows down and the stereo cranked up loud.

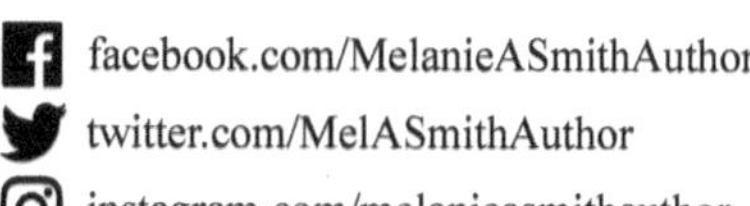

www.ingramcontent.com/pod-product-compliance
Lightning Source LLC
Chambersburg PA
CBHW030654190726
48286CB00001B/13